CIAPHAS CAIN
HERO OF THE IMPERIUM

For the Emperor • Caves of Ice
The Traitor's Hand

CIAPHAS CAIN, COMMISSAR in the Imperial Guard, only ever wanted a quiet life. But it seems the will of the Emperor is against this reluctant hero as he is thrown, time and again, into the hellish warzones of the 41st Millennium where he must fight for his survival and the glory of the Guard. With the enemies of the Imperium – the forces of Chaos, aliens and traitors – always turning up to cause trouble, will the commissar ever get a moment's peace?

More tales of the Astra Militarum from Black Library

• CIAPHAS CAIN •
by Sandy Mitchell

CIAPHAS CAIN: HERO OF THE IMPERIUM
(Contains books 1-3 in the series: *For the Emperor,*
Caves of Ice and *The Traitor's Hand*)

CIAPHAS CAIN: DEFENDER OF THE IMPERIUM
(Contains books 4-6 in the series: *Death or Glory,*
Duty Calls and *Cain's Last Stand*)

CIAPHAS CAIN: SAVIOUR OF THE IMPERIUM
(Contains books 7-9 in the series: *The Emperor's Finest,*
The Last Ditch and *The Greater Good*)

Book 10: CHOOSE YOUR ENEMIES

THE MACHARIAN CRUSADE OMNIBUS
by William King
(Contains the novels *Angel of Fire, Fist of Demetrius*
and *Fall of Macharius*)

HONOUR IMPERIALIS
by Aaron Dembski-Bowden, Rob Sanders and Steve Lyons
(Contains the novels *Cadian Blood, Redemption Corps*
and *Dead Men Walking*)

YARRICK: THE OMNIBUS
by David Annandale
(Contains the novels *Imperial Creed, Pyres of Armageddon*
and the novella *Chains of Golgotha*)

CADIA STANDS
A novel by Justin D Hill

HONOURBOUND
A novel by Rachel Harrison

THE LAST CHANCERS: ARMAGEDDON SAINT
A novel by Gav Thorpe

CIAPHAS CAIN

HERO OF THE IMPERIUM

Sandy Mitchell

BLACK LIBRARY

A BLACK LIBRARY PUBLICATION

For the Emperor first published in 2003.
Caves of Ice first published in 2004.
The Traitor's Hand first published in 2005.
Flight or Flight first published in *Inferno!* magazine, in 2002.
The Beguiling first published in *Inferno!* magazine, in 2003.
Echoes of the Tomb first published in *Inferno!* magazine, in 2004.
This edition published in Great Britain in 2023 by
Black Library, Games Workshop Ltd., Willow Road,
Nottingham, NG7 2WS, UK.

Represented by: Games Workshop Limited – Irish branch,
Unit 3, Lower Liffey Street, Dublin 1,
D01 K199, Ireland.

27

Produced by Games Workshop in Nottingham.
Cover illustration by Clint Langley.

See Black Library on the internet at

blacklibrary.com

Find out more about Games Workshop
and the worlds of Warhammer at

games-workshop.com

Printed and bound in the UK.

For Judith and the children.

For more than a hundred centuries the Emperor has sat
immobile on the Golden Throne of Earth. He is the
Master of Mankind. By the might of His inexhaustible
armies a million worlds stand against the dark.

Yet, He is a rotting carcass, the Carrion Lord of the
Imperium held in life by marvels from the Dark Age of
Technology and the thousand souls sacrificed each day so
that His may continue to burn.

To be a man in such times is to be one amongst untold
billions. It is to live in the cruellest and most bloody
regime imaginable. It is to suffer an eternity of carnage
and slaughter. It is to have cries of anguish and sorrow
drowned by the thirsting laughter of dark gods.

This is a dark and terrible era where you will find little
comfort or hope. Forget the power of technology and
science. Forget the promise of progress and advancement.
Forget any notion of common humanity or compassion.

There is no peace amongst the stars, for in the grim
darkness of the far future,
there is only war.

CONTENTS

INTRODUCTION

You QUITE FREQUENTLY come across the phrase 'this book changed my life,' usually on the cover of some dubious American self-help manual with a title like *I Was A Pathetic Loser Like You Until I Got Rich Preying On People's Insecurities*. I have to admit, though, that the experience of writing *For the Emperor*, the first Ciaphas Cain novel, had a pretty big impact on mine. I learned an enormous amount about the craft of authorship in the process, and have continued to do so as the series goes on; it's no exaggeration to say that without Cain I wouldn't be the writer I am today. (Whether or not that's a good thing I leave to your judgement.) Certainly, an awful lot of people seem to enjoy his adventures, something which continues to astonish me, as, like so many authors, I write purely to amuse myself. The fact that so many readers also find these tales entertaining, and the amount of enthusiasm for them they express at signing sessions, still surprises and delights me.

Ironically, when I wrote the first short story featuring Cain, I assumed that the idea of a self-obsessed commissar was a one-joke concept, and having told it I'd be turning my attention elsewhere. But Cain had other ideas, hanging around in the back of my head, and refusing to go away. Luckily, it seemed, he'd struck a chord with the readers too; almost as soon as his first adventure, *Fight or Flight*, had appeared in the pages of *Inferno!* I was asked if I'd like to follow it up with a sequel, and no sooner had I written that than I was asked if I'd like to feature him in a novel for the Black Library.

The answer to that, of course, was 'Yes!' Since then, the redoubtable commissar has gone from strength to strength, with the fifth volume of his adventures appearing at the same time as this collected edition of the first three (plus some odd bits). Which is not to say that I'm getting in the least bit tired of the series; on the contrary, I already have another one planned (possibly even underway by the time you read this), and hope to continue chronicling his activities for years to come. Or at least until my long-suffering editors' patience finally gives out.

One of the questions I'm often asked is how I manage to get away with being humorous in a universe as relentlessly grim as the one of the 41st millennium. Part of the answer is that it's a natural human trait to take refuge from horror in humour, and Cain's dry and ironic narrative voice seems to me to be a perfectly reasonable one in which to be recounting his memoirs. One of the pleasures of writing stories set in the Warhammer 40,000 universe is that it's so rich and textured that it can be used to tell pretty much any kind of tale. In fact it's only because the background is so solidly developed that the books succeed at all; I doubt that Cain would have worked half so well as a character in any other environment. Occasionally, I must admit, I get carried away and cross the line into out-and-out comedy, but when this happens I'm lucky enough to have supportive and vigilant editors (hi Lindsey, hi Nick!) looking over my shoulder and pointing out tactfully that this is, perhaps, a joke too far. Another member of the team who deserves a public pat on the back is Clint Langley, whose wonderful covers do so much to enliven these books; his illustrations capture Cain's sardonic personality perfectly, and his rendition of Jurgen instantly became the image I see in my mind whenever he wanders into the story.

The other thing the Cain novels have which, much to the relief of the typesetters, none of the other Black Library titles do, is the notorious footnotes. Almost as soon as I began the first novel I realised that the narrative needed opening out in order to take in a much bigger picture than Cain would be able to experience personally: something of a problem with a hero who tells his story entirely in the first person! The solution was to add an editorial voice, which would interpolate additional material and explanatory footnotes; a

FIGHT OR FLIGHT

'Like any newly-commissioned young commissar I faced my first assignment with an eagerness mixed with trepidation. I was, after all, the visible embodiment of the will of the Emperor Himself; and I could scarce suppress the tiny voice which bade me wonder if, when tested, I would truly prove worthy of the trust bestowed upon me. When the test came at last, in the blood and glory of the battlefield, I had my answer; and my life changed forever.'

— Ciaphas Cain, 'To Serve the Emperor:
A Commissar's Life', 104. M42

IF THERE'S A single piece of truth among all the pious humbug and retrospective arse-covering that passes for my autobiography, it's the last four words of that paragraph. When I look back over the past hundred years of cowardice, truth-bending, bowel-loosening terror, and sheer dumb luck that somehow propelled me to the dizzy heights of Hero of the Imperium, I can truthfully point to that grubby little skirmish on a forgotten mining world as the incident which made me what I am.

I'd been a fully-fledged commissar for almost eight weeks when I arrived on Desolatia IV, seven of them spent travelling in the warp, and I could tell right away that my new unit wasn't happy to receive me. There was a single Salamander waiting at the edge of the landing field as I stepped off the shuttle, its sand-scoured desert camo bearing the markings of the Valhallan 12th Field Artillery. But there was no sign of the senior officers that protocol demanded should meet a newly-arrived commissar. Just a single, bored-looking trooper, stripped down to the bare minimum of what might pass for a uniform, making the best of what little shade the parked vehicle offered. He glanced up from his slate of 'artistic engravings' as I appeared, and shambled in my general direction, his boots kicking up little puffs of the baking yellow dust.

'Carry your bag, sir?' He didn't even attempt a salute.

'That's fine,' I said hastily. 'It's not heavy.' His body odour preceded him like a personal force bubble. The briefing slate I'd glanced at before making the joyous discovery that the transport ship was stuffed with crewmen still under the fond illusion that games of chance had something to do with luck had mentioned that the Valhallans were from an ice world, so it was no surprise to me that the baking heat of Desolatia was making him sweat heavily, but I'd hardly expected to be met by a walking bioweapon.

I overrode the gag reflex and adopted an expression of amiable good humour that had got me out of trouble innumerable times during my years at the schola, as well as into it as often as I could contrive.

'Commissar Cain,' I said. 'And you are...?'

'Gunner Jurgen. Colonel sends his apologies, but he's busy.'

'No doubt,' I said. The ground crew were starting to unload the cargo, anonymous crates and pieces of mining machinery larger than I was floated past on lift pallets. The mines were the reason we were here; to ensure the un-interrupted supply of something or other to the forge-worlds of the Imperium despite the presence of an ork raiding party, which had been unpleasantly surprised to find an Imperial Guard troopship in orbit waiting for a minor warpstorm to subside when they arrived. Precisely what we were defending from our rapidly dwindling foes would be somewhere in the briefing slate, I supposed.

The mine habs loomed above us, clinging like lichen to the sides of the mountain their inhabitants had all but hollowed out. To a hive boy such as myself they looked comfortably nostalgic, albeit a little on the cramped side. The total population of the colony was just a few hundred thousand, including elders and kids; just a village really by Imperial standards.

I followed Jurgen back to the Salamander, weaving through the thickening scrum of workers; he walked straight towards it, unimpeded, the miasma from his unwashed socks clearing a path as effectively as a chainsword. As I swung my kitbag aboard I found myself wondering if coming here had been a mistake after all.

* * *

THE JOURNEY WAS uneventful; nothing so assertive as a landmark interrupted the monotony of the desert road once the mountains had diminished behind us to a low smudge against the horizon. The only thing even approaching scenery was the occasional burned-out hulk of an ork battlewagon.

'You must be looking forward to getting out of here,' I remarked, enjoying the sensation of the wind through my hair and revelling in the fact that perched up behind the gunner's shield, I was mercifully insulated from Jurgen's odour. He shrugged.

'As the Emperor wills.' He said that a lot. I was beginning to realise that where his intellect should have been was a literally-minded adherence to Imperial doctrine which would have had my old tutors at the schola dancing with glee. If they'd ever deigned to do anything so undignified, of course.

Gradually the outline of the artillery park began to resolve itself through the heat haze. It had been sited in the lee of a low bluff, which rose out of the parching sand like an island in a sea of grit; the Valhallans having adapted their instinctive appreciation of blizzard conditions to the sandstorms prevailing here without too much difficulty. Bulldozed berms extended out from the rockface, extending the defensive perimeter into a rough semi-circle blistered with sandbagged emplacements and subsidiary earthworks.

The first thing I made out with any clarity were the Earthshakers; even at this distance they were impressive, dwarfing the inflatable habdomes that clustered around the compound like camouflaged mushrooms. As we got closer I made out batteries of Hydras too, carefully emplaced along the perimeter to maximise cover against air attack.

Despite myself, I was favourably impressed; Colonel Mostrue obviously knew his business, and wasn't about to let the lack of a visible enemy lull him into a false sense of security. I began to look forward to meeting him.

'SO YOU'RE THE new commissar?' He glanced up from his desk, looking at me like something he'd found on the sole of his boot. I nodded, picking an expression of polite neutrality. I'd met his sort before, and my preferred option of breezy charm wouldn't cut it with him. Imperial Guard commanders tended to distrust the political officers assigned to them, often with good reason. Most of the time, about all you could hope for was to develop a tolerable working relationship and try not to tread on one another's toes too much. That worked for me; even back then I realised commissars who threw their weight around tended to end up dying heroically for the Emperor, even if the enemy was a suspiciously long way away at the time.

'Ciaphas Cain.' I introduced myself with a formal nod of the head, and tried not to shiver. The air in the habdome was freezing, despite the furnace heat outside, and I found myself unexpectedly grateful for the greatcoat that went with my uniform. I should have anticipated Valhallan tastes would run to air conditioning which left your breath vapourising when you spoke. Mostrue was still in his shirtsleeves while I was trying my best not to shiver.

'I know who you are, commissar.' His voice was dry. 'What I want to know is what you're doing here?'

'I go where I'm sent, colonel.' Which was true enough, so far as it went. What I didn't mention was that I'd gone to considerable trouble finding an Administratum functionary with a weakness for cards and an inability to spot a stacked deck that almost amounted to a gift from the Emperor; who, after a few pleasant social evenings, had left me in a position to pick practically any unit in the entire Guard to attach myself to.

'We've never had a commissar assigned to us before.'

I tried on an expression of bemused puzzlement.

'Probably because you don't seem to need one. Your unit records are exemplary. I can only assume...' I hesitated just long enough to pique his interest.

'Assume what?'

I feigned ill-concealed embarrassment.

'If I could be frank for a moment, colonel?' He nodded. 'I was hardly the most diligent student at the schola. Too much time on the scrumball pitch, and not enough in the library, to be honest.' He nodded again. I thought it best not to mention the other activities which had consumed most of the time I should have spent studying. 'My final assessment was marginal. I suspect this assignment was intended to... ease me into service without too many challenges.'

Worked like a charm, of course. Mostrue was flattered by the implication that his unit was sufficiently well-run to have attracted the favourable notice of the Commissariat, and, if not exactly pleased to have me aboard, was at least no longer radiating ill-concealed suspicion and resentment. It was also almost true; one of the reasons I'd settled on the 12th Field Artillery was that there didn't seem much for me to do there. The main one, though, was that artillery units fought from behind the lines. A long way behind. No skulking through jungles or city blocks waiting for a laser bolt in the back, no standing on the barricades face to face with a screaming ork horde, just the satisfaction of pulverising the enemy at a safe distance and a quick cup of recaff before doing it all over again. Suited me fine.

'We'll do our best to keep you underemployed.' Mostrue smiled thinly, a faint air of tolerant smugness washing across his features. I smiled too. If you let people feel superior to you, they're childishly easy to manipulate.

'GUNNER ERHLSEN. OUT of uniform on sentry duty.' Toren Divas, Mostrue's subaltern, glared at the latest miscreant, who had the grace to blush and glance at me nervously. Divas was the closest thing to a friend I'd made since I arrived; an amiable man, he'd been only too happy to hand over the chore of maintaining discipline among the troops to a proper commissar now one was available.

'Who isn't in this heat?' I made a show of reading the formal report, and glanced up. 'Nevertheless, despite the obvious extenuating circumstances, we have to retain some standards. Five days' kitchen duty. And put some trousers on.'

Erhlsen saluted, visibly relieved to have escaped the flogging normally prescribed for such an infraction, and marched out between his escorts, showing far too much of his inadequately patched undershorts.

'I must say, Cai, you're not quite what I'd expected.' Erhlsen had been the last defaulter of the day, and Divas began to collect his documentation together. 'When they told us we were getting a commissar...'

'Everyone panicked. The card games broke up, the moonshine stills were dismantled, and the stores tallied with inventory for the first time in living memory.' I laughed, slipping easily into the affable persona I use to put people at their ease. 'We're not all Emperor-bothering killjoys, you know.'

The habdome rocked as the Earthshakers outside lived up to their name. After a month here, I barely noticed.

'You know your job better than I do, of course.' Divas hesitated. 'But don't you think you might be a little... well...'

'Too lenient?' I shrugged. 'Possibly. But everyone's finding the heat hard to cope with. They deserve a bit of slack. It's good for morale.'

The truth was, of course, that despite what you've seen in the holos, charismatic commissars loved and respected by the men they lead are about as common as ork ballerinas; and being thought of as a soft touch who's infinitely preferable to any possible replacement is almost as good when it comes to making sure someone's watching your back in a firefight.

We stepped outside, the heat punching the breath from my lungs as usual, and were halfway to the officer's mess before a nagging sense of disquiet at the back of my mind resolved itself into a sudden realisation: the guns had stopped firing.

'I thought we were supposed to lay down a barrage for the rest of the day?' I said.

'We were.' Divas turned, looking at the Earthshakers. Sweat-streaked gun crews, stripped to the waist, were securing equipment, evidently more than happy to cease fire. 'Something's–'

'Sir! Commissar!' There was no need to look to identify the messenger; Jurgen's unique body odour heralded his arrival as surely as a shellscream presaged an explosion. He was running towards us from the direction of the battery offices. 'Colonel wants to see you right away!'

'What's wrong?' I asked.

'Nothing, sir.' He sketched a perfunctory salute, more for Divas's benefit than mine, a huge grin all but bisecting his face. 'They're pulling us out!'

'YES, IT'S TRUE.' Mostrue seemed as pleased at the news as everyone else. He pointed at the hololithic display. 'The 6th Armoured overran the last pocket of resistance this morning. They should have completed cleansing the entire world by nightfall.'

I studied it with interest, seeing the full dispersion of our units for the first time. The bulk of our forces in this hemisphere were well to the east, leaving a small, isolated blip between them and the mines. Us. The orks had fallen back further and faster than I'd expected, and I began to realise just how merited the Valhallans' reputation as elite shock troopers was. Even fighting in conditions about as hostile to them as they were ever likely to encounter, they had ground a stubborn and vicious enemy to paste in a matter of weeks.

'So, where next?' I asked, regretting it instantly. Mostrue turned his pale eyes on me in the same way my old tutor domus used to do at the schola, when he was sure I was guilty of something but couldn't prove it. Which was most of the time, incidentally, but I digress.

'Initially, the landing field.' He turned to Divas. 'We'll need to get the Earthshakers limbered up for transport.'

'I'll see to it.' Divas hurried out.

'After that,' the colonel continued, changing the display, 'we're to join the Keffia task force.' A fleet of starships, over a thousand strong, was curving in towards the Desolatia system. I was impressed. News of the uprising on the remote agriworld was only just beginning to filter back to the Commissariat when I'd been dispatched here; the Navy had evidently been busy in the last three months.

'Seems a bit excessive for a handful of rebels,' one of the officers remarked.

'Let's hope so,' I said, seeing the chance of regaining the initiative. Mostrue looked at me again, in evident surprise; he'd obviously thought he'd put me in my place the first time for having the temerity to interrupt.

'Do you know something we don't, commissar?' He still pronounced my title as though it were a species of fungus, but at least he was pretending to acknowledge it. That was a start.

'Nothing concrete,' I said. 'But I have seen indications...'

'Other than the size of the fleet?' Mostrue's sarcasm got a toadying laugh from some of the officers as he turned away, convinced he'd called my bluff.

'It was only gossip really,' I began, letting him savour his phantom triumph for a moment longer, 'but according to a friend on the Warmaster's staff...'

The sudden silence was truly satisfying. That the 'friend' was a minor clerical functionary with a weakness for handsome young men in uniform, when she wasn't sorting files and making recaff, was a detail I kept to myself. I went on as though I hadn't noticed the sudden collective intake of breath.

'Keffia might have been infested by genestealers,' I finished.

The silence lengthened while they digested the implications. Everyone knew what that meant. A long, bloody campaign to cleanse the world metre by metre. Virus bombing from orbit was the option of last resort on an agriworld, which would cease to be of any value to the Imperium if its ecosystem was destroyed.

In other words, years of rear echelon campaigning in a temperate climate, chucking high explosive death at an enemy without any means to retaliate in kind. I could hardly wait.

'If this is true,' Mostrue said, looking more shaken than I'd ever seen him, 'we've no time to lose.' He began to issue orders to his subordinates.

'I agree,' I said. 'How close is the fleet?'

'A day, maybe two.' The colonel shrugged. 'The astropaths at regimental HQ lost contact with them last night.'

'With the entire fleet?' I was getting an uncomfortable tingling sensation in the palms of my hands. I've felt it a great many times over the years since, and it never meant anything good. No reason why an Imperial Guard officer should find the lack of contact ominous, of course. To them the warp and anything to do with it is simply something best not thought about, but commissars are supposed to know a great deal more than we'd like to about the primal stuff of Chaos. There's very little which can cast a shadow in the warp so powerful that it can cut off communication with an entire battle fleet, and none of them are any-thing I want to be within a dozen sub-sectors of. 'Colonel, I recommend very strongly that you rescind the orders you've just given.' He looked at me as if I'd gone mad.

'This is no time for humour, commissar.'

'I wish I was joking,' I said. Some of my unease must have been show-ing on my face, because he actually started listening to me. 'Put the whole battery on full alert. Especially the Hydras. Call regimental head-quarters and tell them to do the same. Don't take no for an answer. And get every air defence auspex you can on line.'

'Anything else?' he asked, still visibly unsure whether to take me seri-ously or not.

'Yes,' I said. 'Pray to the Emperor I'm wrong.'

UNFORTUNATELY, I WASN'T. I was in the command post, talking to the captain of an ore barge which had made orbit that morning, when my worst fears were realised. He was a florid man, running slightly to fat, and visibly uncomfortable communicating with an Imperial official, even one as minor as me.

'We're the only thing in orbit, commissar,' he said, clearly unsure why I'd asked. I flipped through the shipping schedules I'd requisitioned from an equally bemused mine manager.

'You weren't due for another week,' I said. The captain shrugged.

'We were lucky. The warp currents were stronger than usual.'

'Or something very big is disturbing them,' I suggested, then cursed myself for saying it. The captain wasn't stupid.

'Commissar?' he queried, clearly considering most of the possibilities I already had, and probably wondering if there was time to make a run for it.

'There's a large Navy task force inbound to pick us up,' I reassured him, half truthfully.

'I see.' He obviously didn't trust me further than he could throw a cargo shuttle, sensible man. He was about to say something else, when his navigator interrupted.

'We're detecting warp portals. Dozens of them!'

'The fleet?' Divas asked hopefully at my elbow. Mostrue shook his head doubtfully.

'The auspex signatures are all wrong. Not like ships at all...'

'Bioships,' I said. 'No metal in the hulls.'

'Tyranids?' Mostrue's face was grey. Mine was too, probably, although I'd had longer to get used to the idea. Like I said, there wasn't much that could cast a shadow in the warp that big, and with genestealers running rampant a couple of systems away it didn't need Inquisitor Kryptmann to join the dots. I turned my attention back to the freighter captain before he could cut the link.

'Captain,' I said hastily, 'your ship is now requisitioned by the Commissariat. You will not break orbit without explicit instructions. Do you understand?'

He nodded, somberly, and turned to shout orders at his crew.

'What do you want an ore scow for?' Mostrue looked at me narrowly. 'Planning to leave us, commissar?' That was precisely what I had in mind, of course, but I smiled thinly, pretending to take his remark for gallows humour.

'Don't think I'm not tempted,' I said. 'But I'm afraid we're stuck here.'

I called up the tactical display. Outside, the staccato drumbeats of the Hydras opened up, seeking the first mycetic spores to breach the atmosphere. Red dots began to blossom on the hololith, marking the first beachheads. To my relief and as I'd expected, the 'nids had homed in on the largest concentration of visible biomass: the main strength of the regiment. That would buy me a little time.

'Where did they come from?' Divas asked, an edge of panic entering his voice. I found myself slipping into my role of calm authority. All my training was beginning to pay off.

'One of the splinter fleets from Macragge.' The segmentum was full of them, fallout from the Ultramarines' heroic victory over Hive Fleet Behemoth almost a decade before. Scattered remnants, a tiny fraction of the threat they'd once presented, but still enough to overwhelm a lightly defended world. Like this one. 'Small. Weak. Easy pickings.' I slapped him encouragingly on the back, radiating an easy confidence I didn't feel, and indicated the data coming in from the ore barge's navigational auspex. 'Less than a hundred ships.' Each one of which probably held enough bioconstructs to devour everyone on the planet, but I couldn't afford to think about that just now.

Mostrue was studying the display, nodding thoughtfully.

'That's why you wanted the barge. To see what's going on up there.' Most of the regimental sensor net had been directed downwards, towards the planet's surface. 'Good thinking.'

'Partially,' I said. I indicated the surface readouts. Our air defence assets were doing sterling work, but the sheer number of spores was unstoppable. Red contact icons on the surface were beginning to make the hemisphere look like a case of Uhlren's pox. 'But we'll need it for an evacuation too.'

'Evacuate who?' The suspicious look was back on Mostrue's face again. I pointed to the mining colony.

'I'm sure you haven't forgotten we have a quarter of a million civilians sitting right next to the landing field,' I pointed out mildly. 'The 'nids haven't noticed them yet; thank the Emperor for underground hab zones.' Divas dipped his head at the mention of the Holy Name, pulling himself together with a visible effort. 'But when they do they'll think it's an all you can eat smorgasbord.'

'Will one barge be enough?' Divas asked.

'Have to be,' I said. 'It'll be cramped and uncomfortable for sure, but it beats ending up as Hormagaunt munchies. Can you get things started?'

'Right away.' Now he had something to do, Divas's confidence was returning. I clapped him on the back again as he turned to leave.

'Thanks, Toren. I know I can rely on you.' That should do it. The poor sap would take on a carnifex with a broken chair leg now rather than feel he'd let me down. Which just left Mostrue.

'We'll need to buy time,' I said, once the young subaltern was out of the way. The colonel looked at me, surprised by the change in my demeanour. But I knew my man; plain speaking would work better with him.

'The situation's worse than you were letting on, isn't it?' he asked. I nodded.

'I didn't want to discuss it in front of Divas. He's got enough to cope with at the moment. But yes.' I turned to the tactical display again. 'Even with every shuttle they can lay their hands on, it's going to take at least a day to get everyone aboard.' I indicated the main tyranid advance. 'At the moment the 'nids are here, engaging our main force. When they notice the colony...'

'Or overrun the regiment.' Mostrue could read a hololith as well as I could. I nodded.

'They'll head west. And when they do we'll have to hold them for as long as we can.' Until we're all dead, in other words. I didn't need to spell it out. Mostrue nodded, gravely. Small crystals of ice drifted down from the ceiling as the Earthshakers got back to work, abrading the odds against us by the most miniscule of fractions. To my surprise he held out his hand, grasping mine and shaking it firmly.

'You're a good man, commissar,' he said. Which just goes to show what an appalling judge of character he was.

Now I'D SET everything in motion there was nothing to do but wait. I hung around the command post for a while longer, watching the red dots blossom in the desert to the east of us, and marvelled at the tenacity of our main force. I'd expected them to be annihilated within a matter of hours, but they held their positions doggedly, even gaining ground in a few places. Even so, with the steady rain of mycetic spores delivering an endless tide of reinforcements, they were only delaying the inevitable. Mostrue watched tensely, stepping aside to afford me a better view as he noticed my presence. Under other circumstances I'd have gloated quietly over my sudden popularity, but I was too busy trying to suppress the urge to run for the latrines.

'We've you to thank for this,' he said. 'Without your warning they'd have been all over us.'

'I'm sure you'd have coped,' I said, and turned to Divas. 'How's the evacuation coming?'

'Slowly,' he admitted. I made a show of studying the data, and smiled encouragingly.

'Faster than I'd expected,' I lied. But fast enough. If I was going to join them I couldn't wait too much longer. Divas looked pleased.

'Nothing more I can do here,' I said, turning back to Mostrue. 'This is a job for a real soldier.' I gave him a moment to savour the compliment. 'I'll go and spend some time with the men. Try and boost morale.'

'It's what you're here for,' he said, meaning 'frak off and let me get on with it, then.' So I did.

Night had fallen some hours before, the temperature plummeting to levels the Valhallans were almost comfortable with, and the guardsmen seemed happier, despite the prospect of imminent combat. I wandered from group to group, cracking a few jokes, easing tension, instilling them with a confidence I was far from feeling myself. Despite my personal shortcomings, and I'd be the first to admit that they're many, I'm very good at that side of things. Which is why I was selected for the Commissariat in the first place.

Gradually, without seeming to have any specific destination in mind, I was heading for the vehicle park. I'd almost reached it when I ran out of time.

'They're here!' someone shrieked, opening up with a lasgun. I whirled at the distinctive crack of ionising air, in time to see a trooper I didn't recognise going down beneath a dark, nightmare shape which plummeted from the sky like a bird of prey. I didn't recognise him because his face was gone, eaten away by the fleshborer the thing carried.

'Gargoyles!' I shouted, although the warning could barely be heard above the unearthly shrieking which presaged a bioplasma attack. I leapt aside just quickly enough to avoid a seething bolt of primal matter vomited up by a winged horror swooping in my direction. I felt the heat on my face as it went past, detonating a few yards away and setting fire to a tent. Without thinking I drew my chainsword, thumbed the selector to full speed, and waved it over my head as I ducked. Luck was with me, because I was rewarded by a torrent of stinking filth which poured down the neck of my shirt.

'Look out, commissar!'

I whirled, seeing it swooping back towards me in the light from the fire, screaming in rage, ragged entrails streaming behind it like a banner. Erhlsen was kneeling, tracking it with the barrel of his lasgun, leisurely, as if he was at a recreational target shoot. I threw myself flat, just as he squeezed the trigger, and the thing's head exploded.

'Thanks, Erhlsen!' I waved, rolled to my feet, and drew my laspistol left-handed. He grinned, and turned to track another target.

Time to be somewhere else, I thought, and ran as hard as I could towards the vehicle park. On the way I shot frequently, and swung my humming chainsword in every defensive pattern I could recall, but whether I hit anything only the Emperor knows. Apparently I struck a heroic figure, though, shrieking what was taken for a stirring battle cry rather than an incoherent howl of terror, which encouraged the men no end.

The Hydras were firing continuously now, stitching the air over the compound with tracer fire which looked dense enough to walk on, but the gargoyles were small and fast-moving, evading most of it with ease. Craning my neck around for potential threats, I saw most of the guardsmen taking whatever cover they could find; anyone left out in the open was in no condition to move by this time as the fleshborer fire and bio-plasma bolts rained down furiously. My attention thus diverted, I tripped, going down hard on something which swore at me, and tried to brain me with the butt of a lasgun.

'Jurgen! It's me!' I said, blocking frantically with my forearm before he could stave my skull in. Even over the smell of the gargoyle guts I could tell who it was without looking. He'd dug in between the tracks of a Salamander, protected from the blizzard of falling death by the armour plating above him.

'Commissar.' He looked relieved. 'What should we do?'

'Get this thing started,' I said. Anyone else might have argued, but Jurgen's dogged deference to authority sent him out into the open without hesitation. I half expected to hear a scream and the wet slap of a fleshborer impact, but after a moment the engine rumbled to life. I took a deep breath, and then another. Relinquishing the safety of overshadowing armour plate for the exposed deck of the open-topped scout car seemed almost suicidal, but staying here for the main assault would be worse.

With more willpower than I believed I possessed, I holstered the pistol, tightened my grip on the chainsword, and rolled out into the open.

'Up here, sir.' Jurgen reached down a grubby hand, which I seized gratefully, and swung myself up behind the autocannon. Something crunched under my bootsoles: tiny beetle-like things, thousands of them, discharged by the gargoyles' fleshborers. I shuddered reflexively, but they were dead, not having found living flesh to consume in their brief spasm of existence.

'Drive!' I shouted, and was almost thrown off my feet as Jurgen accelerated. I ducked below the gunner's shield, dropped the melee weapon, and opened fire. It had little effect, of course, but it would look good, and anyone seeing us would assume that the extra firepower was the reason I'd commandeered the vehicle.

Within moments we were beyond the camp perimeter, and Jurgen began to slow.

'Keep going!' I said. He looked puzzled, but opened the throttle again.

'Where to, sir?'

'West. The mines. As fast as you can.' Again, I was expecting questions, doubts, and from any other trooper I might have had them. But Jurgen, Emperor bless his memory, simply complied without demur. Then again, in his position I'd have done the same, relieved to have been ordered away from the battle. Gradually the noise and fireglow began to fade behind us in the night. I was just beginning to relax, estimating the time remaining until we reached safety, when the Salamander shook violently.

'Jurgen!' I yelled. 'What's happening?'

'They're firing at us, sir.' He sounded no more concerned about it than he did about making his regular report as latrine orderly. It took me a moment to realise that he trusted me to deal with whatever we were facing. I pulled myself up to look over the gunner's shield, and my bowels spasmed.

'Turn!' I screamed, as a second venom cannon blast scored the armour plating centimetres from my face. 'Back to the compound!'

Even now, after more than a century, I still wake sweating from dreams of that moment. In the pre-dawn glow the plain before us seemed to move like a vast grey ocean, undulating gently; but instead of water it was a sea of chitin, flecked with claw and fang rather than foam, rolling inexorably on towards the fragile defensive island of the artillery park. I would have wept with disappointment if I wasn't already too terrified for any other emotion. The 'nids had outsmarted me, sweeping round to cut us off and block our escape.

I bounced off the hull plating, falling heavily back into the crew compartment, as Jurgen threw one of the tracks into reverse and swung us around, practically on a coin. My head cracked painfully against something hard. I blinked my swimming eyes clear, and recognised it as a voxcaster. Something like hope flared again, and I grabbed the microphone.

'Cain to command! Come in!' I screamed, voice raw with panic. Static hissed for a moment.

'Commissar? Where are you?' Mostrue's voice, calm and confident. 'We've been looking for you since we drove off the attack...'

'It was a diversion!' I yelled. 'The main force is coming from the west! If you don't redeploy the guns we're all dead!'

'Are you sure?' The colonel sounded doubtful.

'I'm out here now! I've got half the hive fleet on my arse! How sure do you want me to be?' I never found out, as the aerial melted under the impact of a bioplasma blast. The Salamander shook again, and the engine howled, as Jurgen pushed it up past speeds it had never been designed to cope with. Despite my trepidation I couldn't resist peering cautiously over the lip of the armour plate.

Merciful Emperor, we were opening the distance! The incoming fire was becoming less accurate as the scuttling swarm receded slowly behind us. Emboldened, I swung the pintel-mounted bolter around and fired into the densely packed mass of seething obscenity; there was no need to aim, as I could hardly miss hitting something, but I pointed it in the general direction of the largest creature I saw. As a rule, the larger the creature the higher it was in the hive hierarchy, and the more vital it was to co-ordinating the swarm. And seeding swarms, I vaguely recalled from some long-forgotten xenobiology lecture, tended to be thinly supplied with them. I missed the tyrant I'd spotted but one of its guard warriors went down, mashed instantly to goo by the weight of the swarm scuttling on and over it.

The compound was in sight now, ant-like troopers lining the fortifications, and, Emperor be praised, the Hydras rumbling into position to defend them, their quad-barrelled autocannon turrets depressing to face the oncoming tide of death. I was just beginning to think we might make it–

When, with a loud crack and a shriek of tortured metal, our howling engine fell silent. Jurgen had pushed it too far and we were about to pay for that with our lives. The Salamander lurched, slipping sideways, and slewed to a halt in a spray of sand.

'What do we do now, sir?' Jurgen asked, hauling himself up out of the driver's compartment. I grabbed my chainsword, suppressing the urge to use it on him; he could still be useful.

'Run like frak!' I said, demonstrating the point. I didn't have to be faster than the 'nids, just faster than Jurgen. I could hear his boots scuffing in the sand behind me, but didn't turn, that would have slowed me momentarily, and I really didn't want to see how close the swarm was getting.

The Hydras opened up, shooting past us, gouging holes in the onrushing wall of chittering death, but barely slowing it. Lasgun bolts began following suit; although the small arms fire would only be marginally effective at this range, every little helped. Return fire from the warriors was sporadic, and directed at the defenders behind the barricades rather than us, the hive mind apparently deciding we weren't worth the bother of singling out. Suited me fine.

I was almost at the berms, encouraging shouts from the men in the emplacements ringing in my ears, when I heard a cry from behind me. Jurgen had fallen.

'Commissar! Help!'

Not a chance, I thought, intent on reaching the safety of the barricades, then my heart froze. Ahead of me, angling in to cut us off, was the huge, unmistakable bulk of the hive tyrant, accompanied by its attendant bodyguards. It hissed, opening its jaws, and I dived to one side expecting the familiar blast of bioplasma, but instead a ravening blast of pure energy detonated where I'd stood seconds before, throwing me to the ground. I rolled upright, moving as far away from it as I could, and found myself running back towards Jurgen. He was on the ground, a hormagaunt about to disembowel him with its scything claws, and its brood mates lining up to dice what was left. Caught between the 'gaunts and the hive tyrant the choice was clear; I had an outside chance of fighting my way through the swarm of smaller creatures, but going back would mean certain death.

'Back off!' I screamed, and swung my chainsword at the 'gaunt attacking Jurgen. It just had time to look up in surprise before its head came off, spraying ichor which smelled nearly as bad as Jurgen did. He rolled to his feet, snapping off a shot from his lasgun that exploded the thorax of another, which I'd barely had time to register was about to eviscerate me. Looked like we were even. I glanced around. The rest of the brood were hemming us in, and the tyrant was getting closer, looming huge against a sky reddened by the rising sun.

Then suddenly the tyrant wasn't there, replaced by shreds of steaming flesh which fell almost leisurely to the sand, its attendant warriors exploding around it. One of the Hydras had rolled around the edge of its emplacement to get a clear shot, the hail of autocannon rounds taking the entire group apart at almost point blank range.

I swung the chainsword to block a sweeping scythe from the closest 'gaunt, and missed as it abruptly pulled away. The whole swarm was hesitating, milling uncertainly, deprived of its guiding intelligence.

'Fire! Keep firing!' Mostrue's voice rang out, clear and confident from the barricades. The gunners complied enthusiastically. I swung the chainsword again, fear and desperation lending me superhuman strength, carving my way through the 'gaunts like so many sides of grox.

Abruptly the swarm broke, scattering, scuttling away like frightened rodents. I dropped the chainsword, trembling with reaction, and felt my knees give way.

'We did it! We did it!' Jurgen let his lasgun fall, his voice tinged with wonder. 'Emperor be praised.' I felt a supporting arm go round my shoulders.

'Well done, Cain. Bravest thing I've ever seen.' Divas was holding me up, his face alight with something approaching hero worship. 'When you went back for Jurgen I thought you were dead for sure.'

'You'd have done the same,' I said, realising the smart way to play it was modest and unassuming. 'Is he–?'

'He's fine.' Colonel Mostrue joined us, and looked at me with the old tutor domus expression. 'I'd like to know what you were doing out there, though.'

'Something didn't feel right about the gargoyle assault,' I improvised hastily. 'And I remembered tyranids tend to use flanking attacks against dug-in defenders. So I thought I'd better go out and take a look.'

'Thank the Emperor you did,' Divas put in, swallowing every word.

'You could have assigned someone,' Mostrue pointed out.

'It was dangerous,' I said, knowing we'd be overheard. 'And, let's be honest, colonel, I'm the most expendable officer in the battery.'

'No one in my battery's expendable, commissar. Not even you.' For a moment I saw a flicker of amusement in those ice-blue eyes and shivered. 'But I'll remember your eagerness to volunteer for dangerous assignments in future.'

I'll just bet you will, I thought. And he was as good as his word, too, once we got to Keffia. But in the meantime he had one more favour to do me.

'I've been thinking, commissar.' Mostrue glanced up from the hololith, where the image of our newly-arrived fleet was enjoying a rare turkey shoot against the vastly outnumbered bioships. 'Perhaps I should assign you an aide?'

'That's hardly necessary, colonel,' I said, flattered in spite of myself. 'My workload's far from excessive.' That wasn't the point, though, and we both knew it. My status as a hero of the regiment demanded some recognition, and assigning a trooper as my personal flunkey would be a public sign that I was fully accepted by the senior officers.

'Nevertheless.' Mostrue smiled thinly. 'There was no shortage of volunteers, as you can imagine.' That went without saying. The official version of my heroism, and my self-sacrificing rescue of Jurgen, was all over the compound.

'I'm sure you'll make the right choice,' I said.

'I already have.' Suspicion flared, and I felt the pit of my stomach drop. He wouldn't, surely...

My nose told me that he had, even before I turned, forcing a smile to my face.

'Gunner Jurgen,' I said. 'What a pleasant surprise.'

FOR THE EMPEROR

Editorial Note:

What, for want of a better phrase, I will henceforth be referring to as the 'Cain Archive' is, in truth, barely deserving of so grandiloquent a title. It consists merely of a single dataslate, stuffed full of files arranged with a cavalier disregard for chronology, and to no scheme of indexing that I've been able to determine despite prolonged examination of the contents. What can be stated with absolute certainty, however, is that the author was none other than the celebrated Commissar Ciaphas Cain, and that the archive was written by him during his retirement while serving as a tutor at the Schola Progenium.

This would pin the date of composition to some time after his appointment to the faculty in 993.M41; from occasional references to his published memoirs (*To Serve the Emperor: A Commissar's Life*), which first saw the light of day in 005.M42, we can safely conclude that he was inspired by the process of writing them to embark on a fuller account of his experiences, and that the bulk of the archive was composed no earlier than this.

His motives for so doing we can only guess at, since publication would have been impossible; indeed, I placed them under Inquisitorial seal the moment they came to light, for reasons which should be immediately apparent to any attentive reader.

31

Nevertheless, I believe they are worthy of further study. Some of my fellow inquisitors may be shocked to discover that one of the Imperium's most venerated heroes was, by his own admission, a scoundrel and self-seeking rogue; a fact of which, due to our sporadic personal association, I have long been aware. Indeed, I would go so far as to contend that it was this very combination of character flaws which made him one of the most effective servants the Imperium has ever had, despite his strenuous efforts to the contrary. For, in his century or more of active service to the Commissariat, and occasional less visible activities at my behest, he faced and bested almost every enemy of humanity: necrons, tau, tyranids and orks, eldar, both free of taint and corrupted by the ruinous powers, and the daemonic agents of those powers themselves. Reluctantly, it must be admitted, but in many cases repeatedly, and always with success; a record few, if any, more noble men can equal.

In fairness, it should also be pointed out here that Cain is his own harshest critic, often going out of his way to deny that the many instances in which he appears, despite his professed baser motives, to have acted primarily out of loyalty or altruism were any such thing. It would be ironic, indeed, if his awareness of his shortcomings should have blinded him to his own (admittedly often well-hidden) virtues.

It is also worth reflecting that if, as is often asserted, courage consists not of the absence of fear but the overcoming of it, Cain does indeed richly deserve his heroic reputation, even if he always steadfastly denied the fact!

However much we may deplore his professed moral shortcomings, his successes are undeniable, and we can be thankful that Cain's own account of his chequered career has at last been discovered. To say the least, these memoirs shed new light on many of the odder corners of recent Imperial history, and his eyewitness accounts of our enemies contain many valuable, if idiosyncratic, insights into understanding and confounding their dark designs.

It is for this reason that I preserved the archive and have spent a considerable amount of leisure time in the years since its discovery editing and annotating it, in an attempt to make it more accessible to those of my fellow inquisitors who may wish to peruse it for themselves. Cain appears to have had no overall structure in mind, simply recording incidents from his past as they occurred to him, and, as a result, many of the anecdotes are devoid of context; he has a disconcerting habit of beginning in media res, and many of the shorter fragments end abruptly as his own part in the events he is describing comes to a conclusion.

I have therefore chosen to begin the process of dissemination with his account of the Gravalax campaign, which is reasonably coherent, and with which the members of our ordo will be at least passingly familiar as a result of my own involvement in the affair. Indeed, it contains an account of our first meeting from Cain's perspective, which I must admit I found rather amusing when I first stumbled across it.

For the most part, the archive speaks for itself, although I have taken the liberty of breaking up the long and unstructured account into relatively self-contained chapters to facilitate reading. The quotations preceding them are something of an indulgence on my part, having been culled from a collection of such sayings compiled by Cain himself for the apparent amusement and edification of the cadets in his charge, but I justify this as perhaps providing an additional insight into the workings of his mind. Apart from this, I have confined myself to occasional editorial interpolations where I considered it necessary to place Cain's somewhat self-centred narrative into a wider context; unless otherwise attributed, all such annotations are my own, and I have been otherwise content to let his own words do the work.

Amberley Vail, Ordo Xenos

ONE

'I don't know what effect they have on the enemy,
but by the Emperor, they frighten me.'

– General Karis, of the Valhallans
under his command

ONE OF THE first things you learn as a commissar is that people are never pleased to see you; something that's no longer the case where I'm concerned, of course, now that my glorious and undeserved reputation precedes me wherever I go. A good rule of thumb in my younger days, but I'd never found myself staring down death in the eyes of the troopers I was supposed to be inspiring with loyalty to the Emperor before. In my early years as an occasionally loyal minion of his Glorious Majesty, I'd faced, or to be more accurate, ran away screaming from, orks, necrons, tyranids, and a severely hacked off daemonhost, just to pick out some of the highlights of my ignominious career. But standing in that mess room, a heartbeat away from being ripped apart by mutinous Guardsmen, was a unique experience, and one that I have no wish to repeat.

I should have realised how bad the situation was when the commanding officer of my new regiment actually smiled at me as I stepped off the shuttle. I already had every reason to fear the worst, of course, but by that time I was out of options. Paradoxical as it might seem, taking this miserable assignment had looked uncomfortably like the best chance I had of keeping my precious skin in one piece.

The problem, of course, was my undeserved reputation for heroism, which by that time had grown to such ludicrous proportions that the Commissariat had finally noticed me and decided that my talents were being wasted in the artillery unit I'd picked as the safest place to sit out my lifetime of service to the Emperor, a long way away from the sharp end of combat. Accordingly, I'd found myself plucked from a position of relative obscurity and attached directly to Brigade headquarters.

That hadn't seemed too bad at first, as I'd had little to do except shuffle datafiles and organise the occasional firing squad, which had suited me fine, but the trouble with everybody thinking you're a hero is that they tend to assume you like being in mortal danger and go out of their way to provide some. In the half-dozen years since my arrival, I'd been temporarily seconded to units assigned, among other things, to assault fixed positions, clear out a space hulk, and run recon deep behind enemy lines. And every time I'd made it back alive, due in no small part to my natural talent for diving for cover and waiting for the noise to stop, the general staff had patted me on the head, given me another commendation, and tried to find an even more inventive way of getting me killed.

Something obviously had to be done, and done fast, before my luck ran out altogether. So, as I often had before, I let my reputation do the work for me and put in a request for a transfer back to a regiment. Any regiment. By that time I just didn't care. Long experience had taught me that the opportunities for taking care of my own neck were much higher when I could pull rank on every officer around me.

'I just don't think I'm cut out for data shuffling,' I said apologetically to the weasel-faced little runt from the lord general's office. He nodded judiciously, and made a show of paging through my file.

'I can't say I'm surprised,' he said, in a slightly nasal whine. Although he tried to look cool and composed, his body language betrayed his excitement at being in the presence of a living legend; at least that's what some damn fool pictcast commentator had called me after the Siege of Perlia, and the appellation stuck. The next thing I know my own face is grinning at me from recruiting posters all over the sector, and I couldn't even grab a mug of recaf without having a piece of paper shoved under my nose with a request to autograph it. 'It doesn't suit everybody.'

'It's a shame we can't all have your dedication to the smooth running of the Imperium,' I said. He looked sharply at me for a moment, wondering if I was taking the frak, which of course I was, then decided I was simply being civil. I decided to ladle it on a bit. 'But I'm afraid I've been a soldier too long to start changing my habits now.'

That was the sort of thing Cain the Hero was supposed to say, of course, and weasel-face lapped it up. He took my transfer request from me as though it was a relic from one of the blessed saints.

'I'll handle it personally,' he said, practically bowing as he showed me out.

AND SO IT was, a month or so later, I found myself in a shuttle approaching the hangar bay of the *Righteous Wrath*, a battered old troopship identical to thousands in Imperial service, almost all of which I sometimes think I've travelled on over the years. The familiar smell of shipboard air, stale, recycled, inextricably intertwined with rancid sweat, machine oil and boiled cabbage, hissed into the passenger compartment as the hatch seals opened. I inhaled it gratefully, as it displaced the no less familiar odour of Gunner Jurgen, my aide almost since the outset of my commissarial career nearly twenty years before.

Short for a Valhallan, Jurgen somehow managed to look awkward and out of place wherever he was, and in all our time together, I couldn't recall a single occasion on which he'd ever worn anything that appeared to fit properly. Though amiable enough in temperament, he seemed ill at ease with people, and, in turn, most preferred to avoid his company; a tendency no doubt exacerbated by the perpetual psoriasis that afflicted him, as well as his body odour, which, in all honesty, took quite a bit of getting used to.

Nevertheless he'd proven an able and valued aide, due in no small part to his peculiar mentality. Not overly bright, but eager to please and doggedly literal in his approach to following orders, he'd become a useful buffer between me and some of the more onerous aspects of my job. He never questioned anything I said or did, apparently convinced that it must be for the good of the Imperium in some way, which, given the occasionally discreditable activities I'd been known to indulge in, was a great deal more than I could have hoped for from any other trooper. Even after all this time I still find myself missing him on occasion.

So he was right there at my side, half-hidden by our combined luggage, which he'd somehow contrived to gather up and hold despite the weight, as my boot heels first rang on the deck plating beneath the shuttle. I didn't object; experience had taught me that it was a good idea for people meeting him for the first time to get the full picture in increments.

I paused fractionally for dramatic effect before striding forward to meet the small knot of Guard officers drawn up to greet me by the main cargo doors, the clang of my footsteps on the metal sounding as crisp and authoritative as I could contrive; an effect undercut slightly by the pops and clangs from the scorched area under the shuttle engines as it cooled, and Jurgen's tottering gait behind me.

'Welcome, commissar. This is a great honour.' A surprisingly young woman with red hair and blue eyes stepped forward and snapped a crisp salute with parade ground efficiency. I thought for a moment that I was being subtly snubbed with only the junior officers present, before I reconciled her face with the file picture in the briefing slate. I returned the salute.

'Colonel Kasteen.' I nodded an acknowledgement. Despite having no objection to being fawned over by young women in the normal course of events, I found such a transparent attempt at ingratiation a little nauseating. Then I got a good look at her hopeful expression and felt as though I'd stepped on a non-existent final stair. She was absolutely sincere. Emperor help me, they really were pleased to see me. Things must be even worse here than I'd imagined.

Just how bad they actually were I had yet to discover, but I already had some presentiment. For one thing, the palms of my hands were tingling, which always means there's trouble hanging in the air like the static before a storm, and for another, I'd broken with the habit of a lifetime and actually read the briefing slate carefully on the tedious voyage out here to meet the ship.

To cut a long story short, morale in the Valhallan 296th/301st was at rock bottom, and the root cause of it all was obvious from the regiment's title. Combining below-strength regiments was standard practice among the Imperial Guard, a sensible way of consolidating after combat losses to keep units up to strength and of further use in the field. What hadn't been sensible was combining what was left of the 301st, a crack planetary assault unit with fifteen hundred years of traditional belief in their innate superiority over every other unit in the Guard, particularly the other Valhallan ones, with the 296th; a rear echelon garrison command, which, just to throw promethium on the flames, was one of the few all-women regiments raised and maintained by that desolate iceball. And just to put the cherry on it, Kasteen had been given overall command by virtue of three days' seniority over her new immediate subordinate, a man with far more combat experience.

Not that any of them truly lacked that now, after the battle for Corania. The tyranids had attacked without warning, and every Guard regiment on the planet had been forced to resist ferociously for nearly a year before the navy and a couple of Astartes Chapters[1] had arrived to turn the tide. By that time, every surviving unit had sustained at least

---

1. *A common mistake. It is, of course, virtually unheard of for an entire Astartes Chapter to take the field at once, let alone two; what Cain obviously means here is that elements from two different Chapters were involved. (A couple of companies apiece from the Reclaimers and the Swords of the Emperor.)*

fifty per cent casualties, many of them a great deal more, and the bureaucrats of the Munitorium had begun the process of consolidating the battered survivors into useful units once again.

On paper, at least. No one with any practical military experience would have been so half-witted as to ignore the morale effects of their decisions. But that's bureaucrats for you. Maybe if a few more Administratum drones were given lasguns and told to soldier alongside the troopers for a month or two it would shake their ideas up a bit. Assuming by some miracle they weren't shot in the back on the first day, of course.

But I'm digressing. I returned Kasteen's salute, noting as I did so the faint discolouration of the fabric beneath her rank insignia where her captain's studs had been before her recent unanticipated elevation to colonel. There had been few officers left in either regiment by the time the 'nids had got through with them, and they'd been lucky at that. At least one of the newly consolidated units was being led by a former corporal, or so I'd heard.[1] Unfortunately, neither of their commissars had survived so, thanks to my fortuitously timed transfer request, I'd been handed the job of sorting out the mess. Lucky me.

'Major Broklaw, my second-in-command.' Kasteen introduced the man next to her, his own insignia equally new. His face flushed almost imperceptibly, but he stepped forward to shake my hand with a firm grip. His eyes were flint grey beneath his dark fringe of hair, and he closed his hand a little too tightly, trying to gauge my strength. Two could play at that game, of course, and I had the advantage of a couple of augmetic fingers, so I returned the favour, smiling blandly as the colour drained from his face.

'Major.' I let him go before anything was damaged except his pride, and turned to the next officer in line. Kasteen had rounded up pretty much her entire senior command staff, as protocol demanded, but it was clear most of them weren't too sure about having me around. Only a few met my eyes, but the legend of Cain the Hero had arrived here before me, and the ones that did were obviously hoping I'd be able to turn round a situation they all patently felt had gone way beyond their own ability to deal with.

I don't know what the rest were thinking; they were probably just relieved I wasn't talking about shooting the lot of them and bringing in

---

1. *He'd heard wrong, or is possibly exaggerating for effect. The newly appointed colonel of the 112th Rough Riders was a former sergeant, true, but had already received a battlefield promotion to lieutenant during the defence of Corania. None of the senior command staff in any of the recently consolidated units had made the promotional jump directly from non-commissioned officer.*

somebody competent. Of course, if that had been a realistic option I might have considered it, but I had an unwanted reputation for honesty and fairness to live up to, so that was that.

The introductions over I turned back to Kasteen, and indicated the tottering pile of kitbags behind me. Her eyes widened fractionally as she caught a glimpse of Jurgen's face behind the barricade, but I suppose anyone who'd gone hand to hand with tyranids would have found the experience relatively unperturbing, and she masked it quickly. Most of the assembled officers, I noted with well-concealed amusement, were now breathing shallowly through their mouths.

'My aide, Gunner First Class Ferik Jurgen,' I said. In truth there was only one grade of gunner, but I didn't expect they'd know that, and the small unofficial promotion would add to whatever kudos he got from being the aide of a commissar. Which in turn would reflect well on me. 'Perhaps you could assign him some quarters?'

'Of course.' She turned to one of the youngest lieutenants, a blonde girl of vaguely equine appearance who looked as if she'd be more at home on a farm somewhere than in uniform, and nodded. 'Sulla. Get the quartermaster to sort it out.'

'I'll do it myself,' she replied, slightly overdoing the eager young officer routine. 'Magil's doing his best, but he's not quite on top of the system yet.' Kasteen nodded blandly, unaware of any problem, but I could see Broklaw's jaw tighten, and noticed that most of the men present failed to mask their displeasure.

'Sulla was our quartermaster sergeant until the last round of promotions,' Kasteen explained. 'She knows the ship's resources better than anyone.'

'I'm sure she does,' I said diplomatically. 'And I'm sure she has far more pressing duties to perform than finding a bunk for Jurgen. We'll liaise with your Sergeant Magil ourselves, if you have no objection.'

'None at all.' Kasteen looked slightly puzzled for a moment, then dismissed it. Broklaw, I noticed from the corner of my eye, was looking at me with something approaching respect now. Well, that was something at least. But it was pretty clear I was going to have my work cut out to turn this divided and demoralised rabble into anything resembling a fighting unit.

Well, up to a point anyway. If they were a long way from being ready to fight the enemies of the Emperor, they were certainly in good enough shape to fight among themselves, as I was shortly to discover.

I haven't reached my second century by ignoring the little presentiments of trouble which sometimes appear out of nowhere, like those itching palms of mine, or the little voice in the back of my head which tells me something seems too good to be true. But in my first few days aboard the *Righteous Wrath* I had no need of such subtle promptings from my sub-conscious. Tension hung in the air of the corridors assigned to us like ozone around a daemonhost, all but striking sparks from the bulkheads. And I wasn't the only one to feel it. None of the other regiments on board would venture into our part of the ship, either for social interaction or the time-honoured tradition of perpetrating practical jokes against the members of another unit. The naval provosts patrolled in tense, wary groups. Desperate for some kind of respite, I even made courtesy calls on the other commissars aboard, but these were far from convivial; humourless Emperor-botherers to a man, the younger ones were too overwhelmed by respect for my reputation to be good company, and most of the older ones were quietly resentful of what they saw as a glory-hogging young upstart. Tedious as these interludes were, though, I was to be grateful for them sooner than I thought.

The one bright spot was Captain Parjita, who'd commanded the vessel for the past thirty years, and with whom I hit it off from our first dinner together. I'm sure he only invited me the first time because protocol demanded it, and perhaps out of curiosity to see what a Hero of the Imperium actually looked like in the flesh, but by the time we were halfway through the first course we were chatting away like old friends. I told a few outrageous lies about my past adventures, and he reciprocated with some anecdotes of his own, and by the time we'd got onto the amasec I felt more relaxed than I had in months. For one thing, he really appreci-ated the problems I was facing with Kasteen and her rabble.

'You need to reassert some discipline,' he told me unnecessarily. 'Before the rot spreads any further. Shoot a few, that'll buck their ideas up.'

Easy to say, of course, but not so easy in practice. That's what most commissars would have done, admittedly, but getting a regiment united because they're terrified of you and hate your guts has its own drawbacks, particularly as you're going to find yourself in the middle of a battlefield with these people before very long, and they'll all have guns. And, as I've already said, I had a reputation to maintain, and a good part of that was keeping up the pretence that I actually gave a damn about the troopers under my command. So, not an option, unfortunately.

It was while I was on my way back to my quarters from one such pleasant evening that my hand was forced, and in a way I could well have done without.

* * *

IT WAS THE noise that alerted me at first, a gradually swelling babble of voices from the corridors leading to our section of the ship. My pleasantly reflective mood, enhanced by Parjita's amasec and a comfortable win over the regicide board, evaporated in an instant. I knew that sound all too well, and the clatter of boots on the deck behind me as a squad of provosts double-timed towards the disturbance with shock batons drawn was enough to confirm it. I picked up my pace to join them, falling in beside the section leader.

'Sounds like a riot,' I said. The blank-visored head nodded.

'Quite right, sir.'

'Any idea what sparked it?' Not that it mattered. The simmering resentment among the Valhallans was almost cause enough on its own. Any excuse would have done. If he did have a clue, I never got to hear it; as we arrived at the door of the mess hall a ceramic cup bearing the regimental crest of the 296th shattered against his helmet.

'Emperor's blood!' I ducked reflexively, taking cover behind the nearest piece of furniture to assess the situation while the provosts waded in ahead of me, striking out with their shock batons at any target that presented itself. The room was a heaving mass of angry men and women punching, kicking and flailing at one another, all semblance of discipline shot to hell. Several were down already, bleeding, screaming, being trampled on by the still active combatants, and the casualties were rising all the time.

The fiercest fighting was going on in the centre of the room, a small knot of brawlers clearly intent on actual murder unless someone intervened. Fine by me, that's what the provosts were for. I hunkered down behind an overturned table, scanning the room as I voxed a situation report to Kasteen, and watched them battle their way forward. The two fighters at the centre of the mêlée seemed evenly matched to me; a shaven-headed man, muscled like a Catachan, who towered over a wiry young woman with short-cropped raven black hair. Whatever advantage he had in strength she could match in agility, striking hard and leaping back out of range, reducing most of his strikes to glancing blows, which is just as well, as a clean hit from those ham-like fists would likely have stove her ribcage in. As I watched he spun, launching a lethal roundhouse kick to her temple; she ducked just a fraction slow, and went sprawling as his foot grazed the top of her head, but twisted upright again with a knife from one of the tables in her hand. The blow came up towards his sternum, but he blocked it, opening up a livid red gash along his right arm.

It was about then that things really started to go wrong. The provosts had made it almost halfway to the brawl I was watching when the two sides finally realised they had an enemy in common. A young woman, blood pouring from a broken nose, was unceremoniously yanked away from the man whose groin she'd been aiming a kick at, and rounded on the provost attempting to restrain her. Her elbow strike bounced harmlessly off his torso armour, but her erstwhile opponent leapt to her defence, swinging a broken plate in a short, clinical arc which impacted precisely on the neck joint where helmet met flak; a bright crimson spurt of arterial blood sprayed the surrounding bystanders as the stricken provost dropped to his knees, trying to stem the bleeding.

'Emperor's bowels!' I began to edge my way back towards the door, to wait for the reinforcements Kasteen had promised; if they hadn't been before, the mob was in a killing mood now, and anyone who looked like a symbol of authority would become an obvious target. Even as I watched, both factions turned on the provosts in their midst, who disappeared under a swarm of bodies. The troopers barely seemed human any more. I'd seen tyranids move like that in response to a perceived threat, but this was even worse. Your average 'nid swarm has purpose and intelligence behind everything it does, even though it's hard to remember that when a tidal wave of chitin is bearing down on you with every intention of reducing you to mincemeat, but it was clear that there was no intelligence working here, just sheer brute bloodlust. Emperor damn it, I've seen Khornate cults with more self-restraint than those supposedly disciplined Guard troopers displayed in that mess hall.

At least while they were ripping the provosts apart they weren't likely to notice me, so I made what progress I could towards the door, ready to take command of the reinforcements as soon as they arrived. And I would have made it too, if the squad leader hadn't surfaced long enough to scream, 'Commissar! Help!'

Oh great. Every pair of eyes in the room suddenly swung in my direction. I thought I could see my reflection in every pupil, tracking me like an auspex.

If you take one more step towards that door, I told myself, you're a dead man. They'd be on me in seconds. The only way to survive was to take them by surprise. So I stepped forward instead, as though I'd just entered the room.

'You.' I pointed at a random trooper. 'Get a broom.'

Whatever they'd been expecting me to say or do, this definitely wasn't it. The room hung suspended in confused anticipation, the silence stretching for an infinite second. No one moved.

'That was not a request,' I said, raising my voice a little, and taking another step forward. 'This mess hall is an absolute disgrace. And no one is leaving until it's been tidied up.' My boot skidded in a slowly congealing pool of blood. 'You, you, and you, go with him. Buckets and mops. Make sure you get enough to go round.'

Confusion and uncertainty began to spread, troopers flicking nervous glances at one other, as it gradually began to dawn on them that the situation had got well out of hand and that consequences had to be faced. The Guardsmen I'd pointed out, two of them women, began to edge nervously towards the door.

'At the double!' I barked suddenly, with my best parade-ground snap; the designated troopers scurried out, ingrained patterns of discipline reasserting themselves.

And that was enough. The thunderstorm crackle of violence dissipated from the room as though suddenly earthed.

After that it was easy; now that I'd asserted my authority the rest fell into line as meek as you please, and by the time Kasteen arrived with another squad of provosts in tow I'd already detailed a few more to escort the wounded and worse to the infirmary. A surprising number were able to walk, but there were still far too many stretcher cases for my liking.

'You did well, I hear.' Kasteen was at my elbow, her face pale as she surveyed the damage. I shrugged, knowing from long experience that credit snowballs all the faster the less you seem to want it.

'Not well enough for some of these poor souls,' I said.

'Bravest thing I ever saw,' I heard from behind me, as one of the injured provosts was helped away by a couple of his shipmates. 'He just stood there and faced them down, the whole damn lot...' His voice faded, adding another small increment to my heroic reputation, which I knew would be all round the ship by this time tomorrow.

'There'll have to be an investigation.' Kasteen looked stunned, still not quite capable of taking in the full enormity of what had happened. 'We need to know who started it, what happened...'

'Who's to blame?' Broklaw cut in from the door. It was obvious from the direction of his gaze where he thought the responsibility should lie. Kasteen flushed.

'I've no doubt we'll discover the men responsible,' she said, a faint but perceptible stress on the pronoun. Broklaw refused to rise to the bait.

'We can all thank the Emperor we have an impartial adjudicator in the commissar here,' he said smoothly. 'I'm sure we can rely on him to sort it out.'

Thanks a lot, I thought. But he was right. And how I handled it was to determine the rest of my future with the regiment. Not to mention leaving me running for my life yet again, beginning a long and unwelcome association with the Emperor's pet psychopaths,[1] and an encounter with the most fascinating woman I've ever met.

---

1. *Not the most flattering or accurate description of His Divine Majesty's most holy Inquisition, it must be admitted.*

TWO

*'You get more with a kind word and
an excruciator than with just a kind word.'*

– Inquisitor Malden

'So WHAT YOU'RE trying to tell me,' I said, turning the piece of crockery over in my hand, 'is that three people are dead, fourteen still in the infirmary, and a perfectly serviceable mess hall reduced to kindling because your men didn't like the plates they were served their meal on?' Broklaw squirmed visibly on one of the chairs I'd had Jurgen bring into my office for the conference – I'd told him to fetch the most uncomfortable ones he could find, as every little bit helps when you're trying to exert your authority – but the major's discomfiture wasn't due to just that alone. Kasteen was still visibly suppressing a smirk, which I was planning to wipe away in a moment.

'Well, that may be overstating it a little...' he began.

'That's precisely what happened,' Kasteen cut in acidly. I hefted the plate. It was good quality porcelain, delicate but strong, and one of the few pieces remaining intact after the mess hall riot. The regimental crest of the 296th was prominent in the centre of it. I turned to the dataslate on my desk, and made a show of paging through the reports and witness statements I'd spent the past week collecting.

'According to this witness statement, the first punch was swung by a Corporal Bella Trebek. A member of the 296th prior to the amalgamation.' I raised an inquisitive eyebrow in Kasteen's direction. 'Would the colonel care to comment?'

'She was clearly provoked,' Kasteen said, losing the smirk, which seemed to hover in the air for a moment before jumping across to Broklaw.

'Just so.' I nodded judiciously. 'By a Sergeant Tobias Kelp. Who, it says here, threw his plate down declaring that he would be damned if he ate off some...' I made a show of getting the quotation scrupulously correct. '"Mincing tart's front parlour tea service." Does that strike you as a reasonable comment, major?'

The smirk disappeared again.

'Not particularly, no,' he said, clearly wondering where this line of questioning was going. 'But we still don't know the full circumstances.'

'I think the circumstances are perfectly clear,' I said. 'The former troopers of the 296th and the 301st have cordially detested one another since the regiments were amalgamated. Under the circumstances the use of the 296th's regimental dinner service was bound to be regarded as an insult by the stupider elements of the former 301st.' Broklaw flushed at that. Good, let him get angry. The only way to salvage the situation was to make radical changes, and that wouldn't work unless I could get the senior officers to feel passionately that they were necessary.

'Which begs another question,' I went on smoothly. 'Just who was stupid enough to order the use of the dinner service in the first place?' I aimed my second-best intimidating commissarial glare at Kasteen for a fraction of a second, before snapping it round to nail the junior officer sitting at her right. 'Lieutenant Sulla. That would be you, would it not?'

'It was founding day!' she retorted. That did take me by surprise. I didn't often get people bouncing back from a number two glare, but I concealed it with the ease of long practice. 'We always use the regimental ceramics on founding day. It's one of our proudest traditions.'

'It was.' Broklaw broke in with sardonic amusement. 'But unless you've got some traditional adhesive...'

Both women bristled. For a moment I thought I was going to have to put down a brawl in my own office.

'Major,' I said, reasserting my authority. 'I'm sure the 301st had their own founding day traditions.' That was a pretty safe bet, as practically every regiment celebrated the anniversary of its First Founding in some way. He began to nod, before my use of the past tense registered with him, and then an expression curiously close to apprehension flickered across his face. I leaned back in my chair, which, unlike theirs, I'd made sure was comfortably padded, and looked approving. It's always good to keep people off-balance. 'I'm glad to hear it. Such traditions are important. A vital part of the *esprit de corps* we all rely on to win the Emperor his victories.' Kasteen and Broklaw nodded cautiously, almost together. Good. That was one thing at least they could agree on. But Sulla just flushed angrily.

'Then perhaps you could explain that to Kelp and his knuckle-draggers,' she said. I sighed, tolerantly, and placed my laspistol on the desk. The officers' eyes widened slightly. Broklaw's took on a wary expression, Kasteen's one of barely suppressed alarm, and Sulla's jaw dropped open.

'Please don't interrupt, lieutenant,' I said mildly. 'You can all have your say in a moment.' There was a definite edge in the room now. I had no intention of shooting anyone, of course, but they weren't going to like what I was about to say next and you can't be too careful. I smiled, to show I was harmless, and they relaxed a fraction.

'Nevertheless, you've just illustrated my point perfectly. While the two halves of this regiment still think of themselves as separate units, morale is never going to recover. That means you're sod-all use to the Emperor, and a pain in the arse to me.' I paused just long enough to let them assimilate what I'd just said. 'Are we in agreement on that, at least?' Kasteen nodded, meeting Broklaw's eyes for the first time since the meeting began.

'I think so,' she said. 'The question is, what do we do about it?'

'Good question.' I passed a slate across the desk. She took it, and Broklaw leaned in to scan it over her shoulder as she read. 'We can start by integrating the units at squad level. As of this morning, every squad will consist of roughly equal numbers of troopers from each of the former regiments.'

'That's ridiculous!' Broklaw snapped, a fraction behind Kasteen's far from ladylike exclamation. 'The men won't stand for it.'

'Neither will my women.' Kasteen nodded in agreement with him. So far so good. Making them feel they had common cause against me was the first step to getting them to co-operate properly.

'They're going to have to,' I said. 'This ship is *en route* to a potential warzone. We could be in combat within hours of our arrival, and when that happens they'll have to rely on the trooper next to them, whoever it is. I don't want my people getting killed because they don't trust their own comrades. So they're going to train together and work together until they start behaving like an Imperial Guard regiment instead of a bunch of pre-schola juvies. And then they're going to fight the Emperor's enemies together, and I expect them to win. Is that clear?'

'Perfectly, commissar.' Kasteen's jaw was tight. 'I'll start reviewing the SO&E.'[1]

'Perhaps it would be best if you did so with the major's help,' I suggested. 'Between you, you should be able to select fire-teams which at least have a reasonable chance of turning their lasguns on the enemy instead of one another.'

'Of course.' Broklaw nodded. 'I'll be pleased to help.' The tone of his voice said otherwise, but at least the words were conciliatory. That was a start. But they really weren't going to like what was coming next.

'Which brings me on to the new regimental designation.' I'd been expecting some outburst at this, but the trio of officers in front of me just stared in stupefied silence. I guess they were trying to convince themselves they hadn't heard what I'd just said. 'The current one just emphasises the divisions between what used to be the 301st and the 296th. We need a new one, ladies and gentleman, a single identity under which we can march into battle united and resolute as true servants of the Emperor.' All good stirring stuff, and for a moment, I actually thought they were going to buy it without any further argument. But of course it was that daft mare Sulla who burst the bubble.

'You can't just abolish the 296th!' she almost shouted. 'Our battle honours go back centuries!'

'If you count slapping down stroppy colonists as battles.' Broklaw rose to the bait. 'The 301st has fought orks, eldar, tyranids–'

'Oh. Were there tyranids on Corania? I guess I was just too busy with my needlepoint to notice!' Sulla's voice rose another octave.

'Shut up! Both of you!' Kasteen's voice was quiet, but firm, and stunned both her subordinates into silence. I nodded gratefully at her, forestalled from having to do the job myself, and pleasantly surprised. It was beginning to look as though she had the makings of an effective commander after all. 'Let's hear what the commissar has to say before we start inventing objections to it.'

'Thank you, colonel,' I said, before resuming. 'What I propose is to treat the date of amalgamation as a new First Founding. I've had the ship's astropath contact the Munitorium, and they've agreed in principle. There

---

1. *Slate of Organisation and Equipment. Not actually a physical dataslate, but an archaic term for the details of the disposition of troopers and equipment within an Imperial Guard unit. Still in use among many regiments with more than a thousand years of unbroken tradition.*

is currently no regiment designated the Valhallan 597th, so I've proposed adopting that as our new identity.'

'Two hundred and ninety-six plus three hundred and one. I see.' Kasteen nodded. 'Very clever.'

Broklaw nodded too.

'A very neat way of preserving the identities of the old regiments,' he said. 'But combined into something new.'

'As was always the intention,' I agreed.

'But that's outrageous!' Sulla said. 'You can't just redesignate an entire regiment out of existence!'

'The Commissariat gives its servants wide discretionary powers,' I said mildly. 'How we interpret them is a matter of judgment, and sometimes temperament. Not every commissar would have resisted the temptation to discourage further dissension in the ranks by decimation, for instance.' Quite true, of course. There were damn few who'd go quite so far as to randomly execute one in ten of the troopers under their command to encourage the others, but they did exist, and if ever a regiment was so undisciplined that such a drastic measure might have been justified, it was this one, and they knew it. They were just lucky they'd got Cain the Hero instead of some gung-ho psychopath. I've met one or two in my time, and the best thing you can say for them is that they don't tend to be around long, particularly once the shooting starts. I smiled to show I didn't mean it.

'If the new designation is unacceptable,' I added, 'the 48th Penal Legion is also available, I'm told.' Sulla blenched. Kasteen smiled tightly, unsure of how serious I was.

'The 597th sounds good to me,' she said. 'Major Broklaw?'

'An excellent compromise.' He nodded slowly, letting the idea percolate. 'There'll be some grumbling in the ranks. But if ever a regiment needed a new beginning, it's this one.'

'Amen to that,' Kasteen agreed. The two senior officers looked at one another with renewed respect. That was a good sign too.

Only Sulla still looked unhappy. Broklaw noticed, and caught her eye.

'Cheer up, lieutenant,' he said. 'That would make our next Founding Day...' He paused fractionally, glancing at me for confirmation as he worked it out. '258.' I nodded. 'You'll have nearly eight months to come up with some brand new traditions.'

OF COURSE, THE changes I'd imposed didn't go down too well with the rank and file, at least to begin with, and I got most of the blame. But then I've never expected to be popular; ever since I got selected for commissarial training I've known I could expect very little from the troopers around me apart from resentment and suspicion. As my undeserved reputation has snowballed, of course, that's got to be the case less and less of the time, but back then I was still taking it more or less for granted.

Gradually, though, the reorganisation I'd insisted on began to work and the training exercises we put the troopers through were beginning to make them think like soldiers again. I instituted a weekly prize of an afternoon's downtime for the most efficient platoon in the regiment, and a doubling of the ale rations for the members of the most disciplined squad within it, and that helped remarkably. I felt we'd really turned a corner the morning I overheard one of the new mixed squads chatting together in the freshly repainted mess hall instead of splitting into two separate groups as they'd tended to do in the beginning, and exulting over their higher place in the rankings than a rival platoon. These days, I'm told, 'Cain's round' is a cherished tradition in the 597th, and the competition for the extra ration of ale still hotly contested. All in all, I suppose there are worse things to be remembered for.

The one problem we still had to resolve, of course, was the matter of those responsible for the riots in the first place. Kelp and Trebek were for it, there was no doubt about that, along with a handful of others who had been positively identified as responsible for the worst of the deaths and injuries. But for the time being, I'd put off the question of punishment. The wholesale reforms I'd instigated, and the subsequent improvement in morale, were still fragile, and I didn't dare risk it by ordering executions.

So I did what any sensible man in my position would have done; dragged my feet under the pretext of carrying out a thorough investigation, kept the defaulters locked away where, with any luck, most of their comrades would forget about them in the general upheaval, and hoped something would turn up. It was a good plan, and it would have worked too, at least until we arrived in a warzone somewhere and I could quietly return them to a unit or have them transferred away with no one any the wiser, if it hadn't been for my good friend Captain Parjita.

Technically, of course, he was well within his rights to demand copies of all the reports I'd been compiling, and I hadn't thought there was any harm in letting him have them. What I'd been forgetting was that the *Righteous Wrath* wasn't just a collection of corridors, bunkrooms, and training bays; it was his ship, and that he was the ultimate authority aboard. Two of the dead had been his provosts, after all, and he wasn't about to sit back and let the perpetrators get away with it. He wanted a full court-martial of the guilty troopers while we were still on board, and he could make sure they were punished to his satisfaction.

'I know you want to be thorough,' he said one evening, as we set up the regicide board in his quarters. 'But frankly, Ciaphas, I think you're overdoing it. You already know who the guilty parties are. Just shoot them and have done with it.'

I shook my head regretfully. 'But what would that solve?' I asked. 'Would it bring your men back to life?'

'That's not the point.' He held out both fists, concealing playing pieces. I picked the left, and found I was playing blue. A minor tactical disadvantage, but one I was sure I could overcome. Regicide isn't really my game, to be honest – give me a tarot deck and a table full of suckers with more money than sense any day – but it passed the time pleasantly enough. 'There really can't be any other verdict. And every day you delay just leaves the cowardly scum cluttering up my brig, eating my food, breathing my air...' He was getting quite emotional. I began to suspect that there had been more than a simple line of command relationship between him and one of the dead provosts[1].

'Believe me,' I said. 'There's nothing I'd like better than to draw a line under this whole sorry affair. But the situation's complicated. If I have them shot the whole regiment could unravel again. Morale's just starting to recover.'

'I appreciate that.' Parjita nodded. 'But that's not my problem. I've got a crew to think about, and they want to see their comrades avenged.' He made his opening move.

'I see.' I moved one of my own pieces, playing for time in more senses than one. 'Then it's clearly long past time that justice was served.'

'Are you insane?' Kasteen asked, looking at me across the desk, and trying to ignore the hovering presence of Jurgen, who was shuffling some routine reports I couldn't be bothered to deal with. 'If you condemn the defaulters now, we'll be right back where we started. Trebek's very popular with the...' she shot a quick glance at Broklaw, seated next to her, and overrode the remark she'd been about to make. 'With some of the troopers.'

'The same goes for Kelp.' Broklaw moved quickly to back her up. Exactly the reaction I'd been hoping for; now the regiment was beginning to function properly, Kasteen and Broklaw had begun to slip into their roles of commander and executive officer as smoothly as if the bad feeling between them had never existed. Well, up to a point, anyway; there was still an air of strained politeness between them

---

1. *Cain is correct in this assumption. Strictly against regulations, of course, but boys will be boys...*

occasionally, which betrayed the effort, but they were well on the way. And to be honest it was far more than I could have hoped for when I stepped off the shuttle.

'I agree,' I said. 'Thank you, Jurgen.' My aide had appeared at my shoulder with a pot of tanna leaf tea, as was his habit whenever I was in my office at this time of the morning. 'Could you get another couple of bowls?'

'Of course, commissar.' He shuffled away as I poured my own drink, and pushed the tray to the side of my desk. The warm, aromatic steam relaxed me as it always did.

'Not for me, thank you,' Broklaw said hastily as Jurgen returned, a fresh pair of teabowls pinched together by a grubby finger and thumb on the inside of the rims. Kasteen blenched slightly but accepted a drink anyway. She kept it on the desk in front of her, picking it up from time to time to punctuate her side of the conversation, but never quite getting round to taking the first sip. I was quietly impressed. She'd have made a good diplomat if she hadn't been so honest.

'The problem is,' I went on, 'that Captain Parjita is the ultimate authority aboard this ship, and he's well within his rights to insist on a court martial. If we don't let him have one he'll just invoke his command privilege and have Kelp and the others shot anyway. And we simply can't let that happen.'

'So what do you suggest?' Kasteen asked, replacing the teabowl after another almost-sip. 'Regimental discipline is supposed to be your responsibility, after all.'

'Precisely.' I took a sip of my own tea, savouring the bitter aftertaste, and nodded judiciously. 'And I've been able to convince him that I can't have that authority undermined if we're to become a viable fighting unit.'

'You've got him to agree to some kind of compromise?' Broklaw asked, grasping the point at once.

'I have.' I tried not to sound too smug. 'He can have his court martial, and run it himself under naval regulations. But once they're found guilty, they'll be turned over to the Commissariat for sentencing.'

'But that takes us right back to where we were before,' Kasteen said, clearly puzzled. 'You have them shot, and discipline goes to the warp. Again.'

'Maybe not,' I said, taking another sip of tea. 'Not if we're careful.'

I'VE SEEN MORE than my fair share of tribunals over the years, even been in front of them on occasion, and if there's one thing I've learned it's this; it's easy to get the result you want out of them. The trick is simply to state your case as clearly and concisely as possible. That, and making damn sure the members of it are on your side to begin with.

There are a number of ways of ensuring that this is the case. Bribery and threats are always popular, but generally to be avoided, especially if you're likely to attract inquisitorial attention as they're better at both and tend to resent other people resorting to their methods.[1] Besides, that sort of thing tends to leave a residue of bad feeling which can come back to haunt you later on. In my experience it's far more effective to make sure that the other members of the panel are honest, unimaginative idiots with a strong sense of duty and a stronger set of prejudices you can rely on to deliver the result that you want. If they think you're a hero, and hang on your every word, so much the better.

So when Parjita announced his verdict of guilty on all charges, and turned to me with a self-satisfied smirk, I had my strategy worked out well in advance. The courtroom – a hastily converted wardroom generally used by the ship's most junior officers – went silent.

There were five troopers in the dock by the time the trial had begun; far fewer than Parjita had wanted, but in the interests of fairness and damage limitation I had managed to persuade him to let me deal summarily with most of the outstanding cases. Those guilty of more minor offences had been demoted, flogged, or assigned to latrine duty for the foreseeable future and safely returned to their units, where, in the unfathomable processes of the trooper's mindset, I had somehow become the embodiment of justice and mercy. This had been helped along by a little judicious myth-making among the senior officers, who had let it be known that Parjita was hellbent on mass executions and that I had spent the past few weeks exerting every iota of my commissarial authority in urging clemency for the vast majority, finally succeeding against almost impossible odds. The net result, aided no end by my fictitious reputation, was that a couple of dozen potential troublemakers had been quietly integrated back into the roster, practically grateful for the punishments they'd received, and morale had remained steady among the rank and file.

The problem now facing me was that of the hardcore recidivists, who were undoubtedly guilty of murder or its attempt. There were five of them facing the courtroom now, wary and resentful.

Three of them I recognised at once, from the mêlée in the mess hall. Kelp was the huge, over-muscled man I'd seen being stabbed, and Trebek, to my complete lack of surprise, was the petite woman who had

---

1. *This is, of course, entirely untrue. As His Divine Majesty's most faithful servants, we're most definitely above such petty emotions as resentment.*

almost disembowelled him. They stood at opposite ends of the row of prisoners, glaring at one another almost as much as at Parjita and myself, and if it hadn't been for their manacles, I had no doubt they'd be at one another's throats again in a heartbeat. In the centre was the young trooper I'd seen stab the provost with a broken plate; his datafile told me his name was Tomas Holenbi, and I'd had to look twice to make sure it was the same man. He was short and skinny, with untidy red hair and a face full of freckles, and he'd spent most of the trial looking bewildered and on the verge of tears. If I hadn't seen his fit of homicidal rage for myself I would hardly have believed him capable of such insensate violence. The real irony was that he was a medical orderly, not a front line soldier at all.

Between him and Trebek was another female trooper, one Griselda Velade. She was stocky, brunette, and clearly out of her depth as well. The only one of the group to have killed a fellow trooper, she had claimed throughout that she'd only intended to fend him off; it was an unlucky blow that had crushed the fellow's larynx and left him to suffocate on the mess room floor. Parjita, needless to say, hadn't bought it, or cared whether she intended murder or not; he just wanted as many Valhallans in front of a firing squad as he could manage.

On Holenbi's other side was Maxim Sorel, a tall, rangy man with short blond hair and the cold eyes of a killer. Sorel was a sharpshooter, a long-las specialist, who snuffed out lives from a distance as dispassionately as I might swat an insect. Of all of them, he was the one who most threw a scare into me. The others had been carried away by the bloodlust of a mob, and hadn't really been responsible for their actions past a certain point, but Sorel had slid a knife through the joints of a provost's body armour simply because he hadn't seen any reason not to. The last time I'd looked into eyes like those they'd belonged to an eldar haemonculus.

'If it was up to me,' Parjita said, continuing, 'I would have the lot of you shot at once.'

I glanced down the line of prisoners again, and noted their reactions. Kelp and Trebek glared defiantly back at him, daring him to make good on the threat. Holenbi blinked, and swallowed rapidly. Velade gasped audibly, biting her lower lip, and began to hyperventilate. To my surprise I saw Holenbi reach across and give her hand a reassuring squeeze. Then again, they'd been in adjoining cells for weeks now, so I suppose they'd had time to get to know each other. Sorel simply blinked, a complete lack of emotional response that sent shivers down my spine.

'Nevertheless,' the captain went on, 'Commissar Cain has been able to persuade me that the Commissariat is better suited to maintaining discipline among the Imperial Guard, and has requested that they be permitted to pass sentence according to military rather than naval regulations.' He nodded cordially to me. 'Commissar. They're all yours.'

Five pairs of eyes swivelled in my direction. I stood slowly, glancing down at the dataslate on the table in front of me.

'Thank you, captain.' I turned to the trio of black-uniformed figures sitting at my side. 'And thank you, commissars. Your advice in this case has been invaluable to me.' Three solemn heads nodded in my direction.

This was the trick, you see. My earlier contact with the other commissars on board had unexpectedly paid off, showing me who would be the most easily swayed by my arguments. A couple of eager young pups just past cadet, and a jaded old campaigner who had lived most of his life on the battlefield. And all of them flattered from here to Terra to be taken into the confidence of the celebrated Ciaphas Cain. I turned back to the prisoners.

'A commissar's duty is often harsh,' I said. 'Regulations are there to be obeyed, and discipline to be enforced. And those regulations do indeed prescribe the ultimate penalty for murder, unless there are extenuating circumstances – circumstances, I have to admit, I have striven to find in this case to the best of my abilities.' I had them all on the hook by now. The fans in the ceiling ducts sounded almost as loud as a Chimera engine. 'And to my great disappointment, I have been unsuccessful.'

There was an audible intake of breath from practically every pair of lungs present. Parjita grinned triumphantly, sure he'd got the blood vengeance he lusted after.

'However,' I went on after a fractional pause. A faint frown appeared on the captain's face, and a flicker of hope on Velade's. 'As my esteemed colleagues will undoubtedly agree, one of the heaviest burdens a commissar must carry is the responsibility to ensure that the regulations are obeyed not only in the letter, but the spirit. And it was with that in mind that I took the liberty of consulting with them about a possible interpretation of those regulations which I felt might offer a solution to my dilemma.' I turned dramatically to the little group of commissars, taking the opportunity to underline that it wasn't just me cheating Parjita out of his firing squad, it was the Commissariat itself. 'Again, gentlemen, I thank you. Not only on my behalf, but on behalf of the regiment I have the honour to serve with.'

I turned to Kasteen and Broklaw, who were observing proceedings from the side of the courtroom, and inclined my head to them too. I was laying it on with a trowel, I don't mind admitting it, but I've always enjoyed being the centre of attention when that doesn't involve incoming fire.

'A commissar's primary concern must always be the efficiency of the unit to which he is attached,' I said, 'and, by extension, the battlefield effectiveness of the entire Imperial Guard. It's a heavy responsibility, but one we are proud to bear in the Emperor's name.' The other commissars nodded in sycophantic self-congratulation. 'And that means that I'm always loath to sacrifice the life of a trained soldier, whatever the circumstances, unless it's the only way to win His Glorious Majesty the victories He requires.'

'I assume that you're eventually going to come to a point of some kind?' Parjita interrupted. I nodded, as though he'd done me a favour instead of disrupting the flow of an oration I'd been practising in front of the mirror in my stateroom for most of the morning.

'Indeed I am,' I said. 'And the point is this. My colleagues and I,' – no harm in reminding everyone again that this was a carefully contrived consensus, not just me – 'see no point in simply executing these troopers. Their deaths will win us no victories.'

'But the regulations...' Parjita began. This time it was my turn to cut him off in full flow.

'Specify death as the punishment for these offences. It just doesn't specify immediate death.' I turned to the line of confused and apprehensive prisoners. 'It's the judgement of the commissariat that you all be confined until it becomes expedient to transfer you to a penal legion, where an honourable death on the battlefield will almost certainly befall you in the fullness of time. In the interim, should a particularly hazardous assignment become available, you will have the honour of volunteering. In either case you can expect the opportunity to redeem yourselves in the eyes of the Emperor.' I raked my eyes along the shabby little group again. Kelp and Trebek, their truculence mitigated by surprise, Holenbi still bewildered by the sudden turn of events, Velade almost sobbing with relief, and Sorel... Still that blank expression, as though none of this mattered at all. 'Dismissed.'

I waited until they'd shuffled out, assisted by the shock batons of the escorting provosts, and turned back to Parjita.

'Will that satisfy you, captain?'

'I suppose it'll have to,' he said sourly.

'CONGRATULATIONS, COMMISSAR.' Kasteen raised a glass of amasec, toasting my victory, and the mess hall erupted around me. I smiled modestly, walking towards the table occupied by the senior officers, while men and women clapped and cheered and chanted my name, and generally carried on as though I was the Emperor Himself dropping in for a visit. I half expected some of them to try patting me on the back, but respect for my position, or an understandable reluctance to get too close to Jurgen, who was dogging my heels as usual, or both, held them in check. I held up my hands for silence as I reached my seat, between Kasteen and Broklaw, and the room gradually fell quiet.

'Thank you all,' I said, injecting just the right level of barely perceptible quaver into my voice to suggest powerful emotion held narrowly in check. 'You do me too much honour for just doing my job.' A chorus of denial and adulation followed, as I'd known it would. I waved them to silence again. 'Well, if you insist...' I waited for the gale of laughter to die down. 'While I have everyone's attention; and that's a refreshing novelty for a political officer...' More laughter; I had them in the palm of my hand now.

I waved them to silence again, adopting a slightly more serious mien. 'I would just like to offer some congratulations of my own. In the short time I've had the privilege of serving with this regiment you have all far exceeded my most optimistic expectations. The past few weeks have been difficult for all of us, but I can state with confidence that I have never served with a body of troops more ready for combat, and more capable of seizing victory when that time comes.' With confidence, certainly. Truthfully? That was another matter entirely. But it had the desired effect. I picked up a glass from the table, and toasted the room. 'To the 597th. A glorious beginning!'

'The 597th!' they all shouted, men and women alike, swept along with cheap emotion and cheaper rhetoric.

'Nicely done, commmissar,' Broklaw murmured as I sat. The cheers were still deafening. 'I believe you've turned us into a proper regiment at last.'

I'd done something a lot more important than that, of course. I'd established myself as a popular figure among the common troopers, which meant they'd watch my back if I was ever careless enough to find myself anywhere near the actual combat zone. Pulling them together into an effective fighting force was just a useful bonus.

'Just doing my job,' I said as modestly as I could, which is what they all expected, of course. And they lapped it up.

'And not before time,' Kasteen added. I kept my features carefully composed, but felt my good mood begin to evaporate.

'We've had our orders?' Broklaw asked. The colonel nodded, picking at her adeven salad.

'Some backwater dirtball called Gravalax.'

'Never heard of it,' I said.

Editorial Note:

Given Cain's complete, and typical, lack of interest in anything that doesn't concern him directly, the following extract may prove useful in placing the rest of his narrative in a wider context. It must be said that the book from which it comes isn't the most reliable of guides to the campaign as a whole, but it does, unlike most studies of the Gravalax incident, at least attempt to sketch in the historical background to the conflict. Despite the author's obvious limitations as a chronicler of events, his summing up of the causus belli is substantially correct.

From *Purge the Guilty! An impartial account of the liberation of Gravalax*, by Stententious Logar. 085.M42

THE SEEDS OF the Gravalax incident were sown many years before the full magnitude of the crisis was realised, and in retrospect, it may well be easy to discern the slow unfolding of an abhuman conspiracy over the span of several generations. A historian, however, has the perspective of hindsight, which, alas, cannot be said of the actual participants. So, rather than pointing an accusatory finger, with righteous cries of 'how could they have been so stupid?' it behooves us more to shake our heads in pity as we contemplate our forebears' blind stumbling into the very brink of destruction.

It goes without saying that no blame can be attached to the servants of the Emperor, particularly those concerned with the ordering of His Divine Majesty's fighting forces and the diligent adepts of the Administratum; the Ultima Segmentum is vast, and the Damocles Gulf an obscure frontier sector. After the heathen tau were put in their place by the heroic crusader fleet in the early seven-forties, attention rightly shifted to more immediate threats; the incursion of hive fleet Leviathan, the awakening of the accursed necrons, and the ever-present danger from the traitor legions not least among them.

Nevertheless, the tau presence remained on the fringes of Imperial space, and, all but unnoticed, they began once again to encroach on His Divine Majesty's blessed dominions.

Up until this point Gravalax had been an obscure outpost of civilisation, barely noticed by the wider galaxy. Enough of its landmasses were fertile to keep its relatively sparse population tolerably well fed, and it possessed adequate mineral reserves for such industry as it supported. In short, it had nothing to attract any trade, and an insufficient population base to be worth tithing for the Imperial Guard. It was, to be blunt, a backwater, devoid of anything of interest.

If Gravalax thought it was to remain undisturbed indefinitely, however, it was sadly mistaken. Within a century of their drubbing at the righteous hands of the servants of the Imperium, the black-hearted tau were back, spreading their poisonous heresies through the Gulf once more. When they first chanced upon Gravalax no one knows,[1] but by the turn of the last century of the millennium they were well established there.

It will come as no surprise to my readers, aware as we must be of the innate treachery of all aliens, that they had arrived at this pass by an insidious process of infiltration. And, shocking though it is to record it, with the willing assistance of those whose greed and thoughtlessness made them the perfect dupes of this monstrous conspiracy. I refer, as you have no doubt already guessed, to the so-called rogue traders. Rogues indeed, who would place their own interests above those of the Imperium, humanity, and the divine Emperor Himself!

---

1. *837.M41, according to surviving records. Like many amateur historians, Logar is long on rhetoric and short on actual scholarship.*

[Several paragraphs of inflammatory but non-specific denunciation of rogue traders, omitted. Logar seems to have had something of an obsession about their untrustworthiness. Perhaps one owed him money.]

How and why these pariahs of profit first began trafficking with the tau, history does not record.[1] What is certain is that Gravalax, with its isolated position on the fringes of Imperial space, and close to the expanding sphere of influence of these malign aliens, became the perfect meeting place for such clandestine exchanges.

Inevitably, the corruption spread. As trade increased, it became more open, with tau vessels becoming a common sight at the new and expanding starports. Tau themselves began to be seen on the streets of the Gravalaxian cities, mingling with the populace, tainting their human purity with their soulless, alien ways. Heresy began to run rife, even ordinary citizens daring to use blasphemous devices unblessed by the techpriests, supplied by their insidious offworld allies.

Something had to be done! And at last it was. The rising stench of corruption eventually attracted the ceaseless vigilance of the Inquisition, which lost no time in demanding the dispatch of a task force of the Imperium's finest warriors to purge this festering boil in the body of His Holiness's blessed demesne.

And that's precisely what they got. For in the vanguard of this glorious endeavour was none other than Ciaphas Cain, the martial hero at whose very name the enemies of humanity trembled in terror...

---

1. *Or Logar couldn't be bothered to do the research.*

THREE

'Old friends are like debt collectors; they have a
tendency to turn up when you least expect them.'

– Gilbran Quail, Collected Essays

As I'VE RATTLED around the galaxy I've seen a great many cities, from the
soaring spires of Holy Terra itself to the blood-choked gutters of some
eldar reiver charnel pit,[1] but I've seldom seen anything stranger than
the broad thoroughfares of Mayoh, the planetary capital of Gravalax.
We'd disembarked in good order, the freshly sewn banner of the 597th
snapping proudly in the breeze that blew in gently across the rockcrete
hectares of the starport as the Valhallans formed up by company, and I
resisted the temptation to lean across and compliment Sulla on her
needlepoint. I doubt that she'd had anything to do with procuring it,
but it wasn't that which dissuaded me. She just wasn't the kind to take
a joke, and was still harbouring a germ of resentment at the organisa-
tional changes I'd instituted. We were a fine sight to behold, I have to

---

1. Cain was part of the invasion force which cleansed Sanguia. His account of this action is
also recorded in the archive.

admit, the other regiments glancing at us sidelong as they marched away; although that may just have been surprise when they realised we were a mixed unit.[1]

'All present and accounted for, colonel.' Broklaw snapped a drill manual salute, and fell into place beside Kasteen. She nodded, inflated her chest, and then hesitated on the verge of giving the command.

'Commissar,' she said. 'I think the honour should be yours. This regiment wouldn't even exist if it wasn't for you.'

I don't mind admitting I was touched. Although I have overall authority in whatever unit I'm attached to, commissars are always outside the regular chain of command; which means I don't really fit in anywhere. By letting me give the order to move out, she was demonstrating in the most practical form imaginable that I was as much a part of the 597th as herself, or Broklaw, or the humblest latrine orderly. The unaccustomed sense of belonging choked me for a moment, before the more rational part of my mind started gloating about how much that would mean in facilitating my own survival. I nodded, making sure I looked suitably moved.

'Thank you, colonel,' I said simply. 'But I believe the honour belongs to us all.' Then I filled my chest, and bellowed: 'Move out!'

So we did. And if you think that sounds like a simple proposition, you haven't thought it through.

To put it into some kind of perspective, a regiment consists of anything up to half a dozen companies – five in our case, most of which had four or five platoons. The exception was Third Company, which was our logistical support arm, and consisted mainly of transport vehicles, engineering units, and anything else we couldn't find a sensible place for on the SO&E. All told, that came to much the same thing in a headcount. Factor in five squads a platoon, at ten troopers each, plus a command element to keep them all in line, and you're looking at nearly a thousand people by the time you've added in the various specialists and the different layers of the overall command structure.

Just to add to the confusion, Kasteen had decided to split the squads into five-man fire-teams, anticipating that any open conflict was likely to take place in and around the urban areas. Beating off the tyranids on

---

1. *It was hardly unprecedented for men and women to serve together in the Imperial Guard. Notable units in which this was the norm included the Omicron Rangers, Tanith First, and Calderon Rifles. However, with women making up fewer than ten per cent of the total number under arms, and the vast majority of those serving in single-sex regiments, it wouldn't be that surprising if the 597th excited a certain amount of curiosity among the onlookers present.*

Corania had convinced her that smaller formations were easier to coordinate in a city fight than full-strength squads.[1]

All this made for a fine martial display as we moved out, you can be sure, with banners flying, and the band thumping and parping away at *If I Should Forget Thee, O Terra*, as though they had a grudge against the composer. There hadn't really been time for rehearsals, what with all the excitement aboard the *Righteous Wrath*, but they were making up in enthusiasm for whatever they lacked in proficiency, and a high old time was being had by all. It was a fine fresh day, with a faint taste of salt in the breeze from the nearby ocean; at least until our chimeras and transport trucks started up and began farting promethium fumes into the air.

We intended to make an impression with our arrival, and by the Emperor, we surely did, setting out to march the ten kloms[2] or so into the city. Most of the troopers were glad of the exercise, revelling in the fresh air and sunshine after so long between decks, and swung along the highway, lasguns at the slope. Being an old hive boy myself, it was all one to me, but I was affected by the general holiday atmosphere I think, and I don't mind admitting to a general diffuse glow of well-being as we got underway.

Kasteen and Broklaw couldn't march, of course, having to look grander than the common ground-pounders, and so trundled along at the front of the regiment in a Salamander, and I seized the excuse to do the same.

'Can't have the regiment's most vital officers plotting behind my back,' I'd said at the briefing, smiling to show I didn't mean it, and pouring everyone a fresh cup of recaf to show I was part of the team. So I lounged back in the open compartment at the rear of a scout variant, which Jurgen kept half a track's length behind theirs in the interest of protocol and reinforcing the impression of my generally assumed modesty, and took the opportunity to feel rather pleased with myself. The synchronised slapping of two thousand boot soles on the surface of the highway and the squarking of the band almost drowned out the throb of our engine, and we must have looked a splendid sight as we left the

---

1. *A widespread, though unofficial practice among units experienced in urban warfare. So much so that it's now become part of the standard operating procedure in many regiments, the ad hoc arrangement persisting to become a permanent feature of their organisation.*

2. *A Valhallan slang abbreviation for 'kilometre.' Cain served with Valhallan units for most of his life, and almost inevitably his speech became peppered with colloquialisms acquired from them.*

main cargo gate of the starport behind us and began to approach the city.

It was then that my palms began to itch again. There was nothing I could put my finger on initially to explain my gradually intensifying sense of disquiet, but something was definitely tapping my subconscious on the shoulder and whispering 'That's not right...'

As we entered the city itself my disquiet grew. I wasn't surprised to find the streets free of traffic, the local authorities having cleared the way for us; a thousand troopers and their ancillary equipment take up a lot of room, and we were far from the first regiment to have disembarked. Indeed, the occasional muffled curse from behind me which cut through the din made it all too clear that the front few ranks would have preferred it if the Rough Riders could have been held back for a while longer instead of being sent through immediately ahead of us. Come to that, I don't suppose Kasteen was too thrilled about having to gaze at a street's width of horse arses for the duration of our march either. But the broad thoroughfares were a little too quiet for my liking, and a little too open as well. I'm not agoraphobic by any means, not like some hivers who never feel comfortable under an open sky, but there was something about those wide streets that made me think of snipers and ambush.

That made me scan the buildings as we passed, and my unease grew the more I saw of them. There was nothing wrong with them as such, not like the bizarre architectural forms of a Chaos incursion which seem to twist reality and which hurt to look upon, or the brutal slap-dash functionalism of orkish habitations, but there was something in their sweeping forms which seemed vaguely inhuman. I was put in mind of some eldar architecture by their elegant simplicity, and then it finally hit me: there were no right angles anywhere, even the corners having been rounded and smoothed. But beneath this strange styling, the shapes were clearly those of warehouses, apartment blocks, and manufactoria, as though the whole city had been left out in the sun for too long and had started to melt.

That alone should have been enough warning of an insidious alien influence at work here, but before we reached our destination, I was to see far more than that.

'There's something seriously wrong here,' I said to Jurgen, who looked up briefly from the road ahead to nod in agreement with me.

'Something doesn't smell right,' he agreed, without a trace of irony. 'Have you seen the civilians?'

Now that he came to mention it, there were remarkably few of them lining the route. Normally a big military parade would have brought them out in droves, waving their aquila flags and their icons of the Divine One, cheering themselves hoarse to see so many of the Emperor's finest ready to see off the foe so they could scuttle back to their meaningless lives without the fear of having to fight for themselves. But the pavements were half empty, and for every shopkeeper or habwife or juvie who cheered and waved, or smiled wanly at us with sidelong glances at their neighbours, there were just as many who scowled or glared at us. That put a shiver down my spine, awakening uncomfortable and all-too-recent memories of the mess hall riot, and the blood-maddened troopers a hair from turning on me.

At least no one was shouting, or throwing things. Yet. But I reached down unobtrusively, and loosened my laspistol and my trusty chainsword ready to be drawn in a hurry if I needed them.

And right on cue I noticed the first of the banners. 'MURDERERS GO HOME!' it said, in shaky capitals, hand lettered on what looked like an old bedsheet. Someone had strung it from a luminator pole so that it hung out across the street, comfortably above head height, but low enough to brush irritatingly over the head and shoulders of anyone riding in a vehicle.

Or on a horse, for that matter. As I watched, one of the Rough Rider officers reached up irritably and tore it down.

Bad move, I said to myself, expecting some trouble from the crowd, but beyond a little catcalling from a small knot of juvies nothing happened. But I was getting a distinctly uncomfortable feeling about all this. There was a perceptible undercurrent of tension in the air now, like a fainter echo of the incipient violence I'd felt aboard the *Righteous Wrath*.

'Go back to your Emperor and leave us alone!' a pretty girl shouted, her head shaven, apart from a single shoulder-length braid, and I felt as though I'd been doused with cold water. *Your* Emperor. The words had been unmistakable.

'Heretics!' Jurgen said with loathing. I nodded, still unable to credit it. Could the Great Enemy have a foothold here, as well as the tau? But common sense argued against it. If that were the case we'd have bombarded the place from orbit, surely, and the Astartes would have been sent in to cut out the cancer before it could spread.

Things weren't as far gone as I'd feared, however, as I turned back to look, a squad of Arbites forced their way through the crowd and began laying into the juvies with shock batons. Good order was still being maintained here, by the Emperor's grace, but for how much longer?

That, I very much feared, depended on us.

* * *

WE REACHED OUR staging area without further incident, fanning out
through a complex of warehouses and manufactoria which had been
set aside for our use. We weren't the only regiment quartered there, I
recall, as the Imperium had been fortifying against an expected incursion by the tau for some time, and I gathered that the *Righteous Wrath's*
complement (three full regiments apart from our own) brought the
total up to around thirty thousand all told. That should have been
more than enough to keep a backwater planet, even spread out across
the whole globe, but rumour had it we could expect still more reinforcement, which worried me more than I wanted to show. With that
amount of build-up it seemed the aliens wanted this place quite badly,
and we'd more than likely be expected to hold it the hard way.

We were quartered next to one of the Valhallan armoured regiments
– the 14th I think – but I couldn't tell you who most of the others were.
There was definite evidence that the Rough Riders were still somewhere
in the vicinity though, so you had to watch your feet, but apart from
that I hadn't a clue. Except for one other unit I already knew well, of
course, which I'll come to in a moment.

I was still feeling spooked from our journey through town, so I was
relieved to come across Broklaw posting sentries around our corner of
the compound as I left Jurgen to sort out my quarters and went for a
wander around to get my bearings. I haven't reached my second century by not knowing where the best boltholes and lines of retreat are,
and finding them was always a high priority for me whenever I found
myself somewhere new.

'Good thinking, major,' I complimented him, and he gave me a wry grin.

'We should be safe enough here,' he said. 'But it never hurts to be careful.'

'I know what you mean,' I agreed. 'There's something about this place
which really gets under my skin.' The warehouses around us all had that
peculiar rounded-off look I'd noticed before, and the subtle sense of
wrongness left a vague apprehension hovering around me like Jurgen's
body odour. The major knew his business, though, setting up lascannon
in sandbagged emplacements to cover the gaps between the buildings
around us, and sharpshooters on the roof. I was just admiring his thoroughness when the ground began to shake, and a couple of our sentinels
appeared, clanking and humming and swivelling their heavy multilasers as
they took up position in front of the main loading doors which gave access
to the ground floor where our vehicles were parked.

Somewhat reassured by this, I made my way across the compound,
passing into areas controlled by other units, watching the familiar bustle of troopers coming and going, and finding the familiar air of
controlled chaos and the constant background hum of vehicle engines

and profanity curiously soothing. I wasn't sure quite how far I'd gone when an engine note both louder and deeper than the others cut through the babble of sound around me.

For a moment, I was assailed by that formless sense of recognition that you get when something you once knew so well it never registered consciously comes back to your notice after a passage of years, and then I turned my head with a nostalgic smile. A Trojan heavy hauler, with an Earthshaker howitzer in tow, was growling its way across a vast open area which had probably once been used to park the private vehicles of the workers who toiled here in happier times, but which was now choked with equipment and supplies. I hadn't seen one of those up close in a long time, but I recognised it at once, having started my long and inglorious career in an obscure artillery unit. The flood of memories the sight brought back, a few of them even pleasant, was so overwhelming that for a moment I was unaware of the voice calling my name.

'Cai! Over here!'

Now, I've never been what you'd call oversupplied with friends, it goes with the job I suppose, but of the few I've acquired over the years only one has ever had the presumption to use the familiar form of my given name. So, despite the changes that the years since I'd seen him last had wrought, there was no mistaking the officer who was running across the compound towards me, grinning like an idiot.

'Toren!' I called back, as he sidestepped another Trojan just in time to avoid being squashed into the tarmac like a bug. 'When did they make you a major?' The last time I'd seen Toren Divas he'd just made captain, and was nursing a hangover as he saw me off from the 12th Field Artillery. I remember thinking at the time he was probably the only man in the battery who was sorry to see me go. 'And what in the name of the Emperor's arse are you doing here?'

'The same as you, I suppose.' He came panting up to me, the familiar lopsided grin on his face. 'Keeping order, purging the heretics, same old thing.' There were streaks of grey at his temples now, I noticed, and his belt was out another notch, but the same air of boyish enthusiasm still hung around him as on the day we'd first met. 'But I'm surprised to find you in a backwater like this.'

'Same here,' I said. I turned my head, taking in the bustle surrounding us. 'This seems like an awful lot of firepower to put the frighteners on a bunch of stroppy provincials.'

'If the tau mobilise, we'll need every bit of it,' Divas said. 'Some of their wargear has to be seen to be believed. They've got these things like dreadnoughts, but they're fast, like Astartes infantry but twice the size, and their tanks make the eldar stuff look like they were built by orks...'

As usual, he seemed to be relishing the prospect of combat, which is easy to do when you're kilometres behind the front line chucking shells into the distance, but not so much fun when you're facing an enemy close enough to spit at you. And if that's all they've got in mind think yourself lucky, unless they're one of those Emperor-forsaken xenos that come equipped with venom sacs.

'But it won't come to that, surely,' I said. 'Now we're here they'd be mad to attempt a landing.' To my astonishment, Divas laughed.

'They won't have to. They're here already.' This was new and unwelcome information, and I goggled at him in surprise.

'Since when?' I gasped. Now I'd be the first to admit that I'm seldom that diligent when it comes to reading the briefing slates, but I was sure I'd have noticed something that crucial to my well-being in my cursory glance through it. Divas shrugged.

'About six months, apparently. They were already deployed on the planet when the *Cleansing Flame* dropped us off here three weeks ago.'

This was seriously bad news. I'd been looking forward to a nice brisk round of target practice on civilian rioters, or, at worst, a turkey shoot against the odd renegade PDF unit. But now we were facing a foe that could give us a real run for our money. Emperor's bowels! If half of what I'd heard about the tau and their technosorcery was true, we could be the ones getting our arses kicked. Divas grinned at my expression, misinterpreting it entirely.

'So you could see some fun after all,' he said, clapping me on the back. I could have killed him.

I DIDN'T, OF course. For one thing, as I've said, I don't have so many friends that I can afford to waste them, and for another, Divas had been here long enough to pick up some vital information which I currently lacked. Namely, the location of the nearest bar we could get to without attracting too much attention to ourselves.

So we set out through the streets of Mayoh together, my commissar's uniform getting us through the guard on the compound gate without any argument, although he did give us a word of caution.

'Be careful, sir. There's been disturbances up in the Heights,[1] they say.' That meant nothing to me, so I smiled, and nodded, and said we'd be

---

1. *The most affluent area of the city, where it began to rise up into the surrounding hills. Though tau influence on the local architecture was widespread, as Cain notes elsewhere, it was more overt here than anywhere else in Mayoh. As a result, it was popular with the most radical of the pro-tau citizens, and a natural focus of protest for the Imperial loyalists. As the political situation continued to deteriorate, clashes between the two factions became commonplace here.*

careful, and checked with Divas that we'd be going nowhere near there as soon as we were out of earshot.

'Good Emperor, no,' he said, frowning. 'It's crawling with heretics. The only way you'd catch me up there is with a squadron of Hellhounds to cleanse the place.' Needless to say, he'd never seen what incendiary weapons can do to a man, or he wouldn't have been half so keen on the idea. I have, and I wouldn't wish it on my worst enemy. Actually, there are one or two I would wish it on, come to think of it, and sit there happily toasting caba nuts while they screamed, but they're all dead now anyway, so it's beside the point.

'So where did they all come from?' I asked, as we made our way through the streets. Dusk was falling now, the luminators and the cafe signs flickering to life, and the swirl of bodies around us growing thicker as the night descended. Small knots of passers-by stood aside to let us pass, intimidated no doubt by our Imperial uniforms and the visible sidearms we carried – some with respect, and others resentful. Several of the latter had the curious tonsure the heretic juvie had sported, their heads shaved except for a long scalplock. The significance of it wasn't to dawn on me until some time later, but even then, I realised it was a badge of allegiance of some kind, and that those who bore it were liable to turn traitor if the shooting started. For now, though, they were content merely to mutter insults under their breath.

'They're local,' Divas said, not deigning to notice them, which was fine by me. Of all the ways I could have ended up dead over the years, getting sucked into a pointless street brawl would have been among the most embarrassing. 'The whole planet's infested with xeno-lovers.'

A bit of an exaggeration, that, but he was more or less right, as I was later to discover. To cut a long story short, the locals had been trading with the tau for several generations by now, which wasn't terribly sensible, but what can you expect from a bunch of backwater peasants? The end result was that most of them were quite used to seeing xenos around the place, and despite the sterling efforts of the local ecclesiarchy to warn them that no good would come of it, a lot of them had started to absorb unhealthy ideas from them. Which was where we came in, ready to guide them back into the Imperial fold before they came to too much harm, and all very noble of us too I'm sure you'll agree.

'The trouble is,' Divas concluded, downing the rest of his third amasec in one, 'the hard core are so far gone they don't see it like that. They think the tau are the best thing to hit the galaxy since the Emperor was in nappies, and we're the big bad bullies here to take their shiny new toys away.'

'Well, that might be a little more difficult now the tau are digging in,' I said. 'But I'm surprised they're prepared to risk it.' I followed suit, feeling the smoky liquor warming its way down through my chest. 'They must know we'll never allow them to annex the place without a fight.'

'They claim they're just here to safeguard their trading interests,' Divas said. We both snorted with laughter at that one. We knew how often the Imperium had said exactly the same thing before launching an all-out invasion of some luckless ball of dirt. Of course when we did it, it was true, and it was my job to shoot anyone who thought otherwise.

'One for the diplomats, then,' I said, signalling for another round. A nicely rounded waitress bustled over, full of patriotic fervour, and replenished our glasses.

One thing I can say for Divas, he knew how to find a good bar. This one, the Eagle's Wing, was definitely in the loyalist camp. The wide, smoky cellar full of Planetary Defence Force regulars were delighted to see some real soldiers at last, and fulminating at the governor for not letting them loose on the aliens years ago. The owner was a corporal in the PDF reserves, recently retired after twenty years' service, and he couldn't seem to get over the honour of having a couple of real Guard officers in the place. And once Divas had introduced me, and I'd been appropriately modest about my earlier adventures in the Emperor's name, there was no question of us having to pay the bill either. After signing autographs for some of the civilian customers – all of whom urged us to pot a few of the 'little blue bastards' on their behalf – and charming the waitress had begun to pall, we'd retreated to a quiet side booth where we could talk uninterrupted.

'I think the diplomats could be getting a little help on this one,' Divas said, tapping the side of his nose conspiratorially as he lifted the glass. I drank a little more slowly, acutely aware that we'd have to start making our way back through a potentially hostile city soon, and wanting to keep a reasonably clear head.

'Help from who?' I asked.

'Who do you think?' Divas dipped his finger in the glass, and sketched a stylised letter I with a pair of crossbars bisecting it on the surface of the table, before erasing it with a sweep of his hand. I laughed.

'Oh yeah, them. Right.' I've yet to arrive any place where the political situation's fluid without hearing rumours of Inquisition agents beavering away behind the scenes, and unless I happen to be the errand boy in question, I never believe a word of it. On the other hand, if there aren't any rumours, then they probably are up to some mischief and no mistake about it.[1]

'You can laugh.' Divas finished his drink, and replaced the glass on the table. 'But I heard it from one of the Administratum adepts, who swore he'd got it from... somewhere or other.' An expression of faint bewilderment drifted across his face. 'I think I need some fresh air.'

'I think you do, too,' I said. Leaving aside what I thought then were his ridiculous fantasies about the Inquisition, he'd still given me a lot to think about. The situation here was undoubtedly far more complex than I'd been led to believe, and I needed to consider things carefully.

So we took our leave of our kindly hosts, the waitress in particular looking sorry to see me go, and staggered up the stairway and into the street.

The cold night air hit me like a refreshing shower, snapping me back to alertness, and I glanced around while Divas communed loudly with the Emperor in a convenient gutter. Fortunately, the bar he'd steered us to was down a quiet side alley, so no one saw the dignity of the Imperial uniform being sullied. Once I was sure there were no more eruptions to come, I helped him to his feet.

'You used to be able to hold it better than that,' I chided, and he shook his head mournfully.

'Local rotgut. Not like the stuff we used to drink. And I should have eaten something...'

'It would just have been a wasted effort,' I consoled him, and glanced around, trying to get our bearings. 'Where the frak are we, anyway?'

'Dock zone,' he said confidently, hardly swaying on his feet at all now. 'This way.' He strode off towards the nearest luminated thoroughfare. I shrugged, and followed him. After all, he'd had three weeks to get his bearings.

As we made our way through the well-lit street, however, I began to feel a little apprehensive. True, we'd been deep in conversation on our way to the bar, but none of the landmarks looked familiar to me, and I began to wonder if his confidence had been misplaced.

'Toren,' I said after a while, noticing a gradual increase in the number of scalplocks and murderous glances among the passers-by, 'are you sure this is the way back to our staging area?'

'Not ours,' he said, the grin back on his face. 'Theirs. Thought you'd like to get a look at the enemy.'

---

1. *A reasonable assumption on both accounts. Details of Cain's subsequent activities as my 'errand boy,' as he puts it, can be found in the Ordo's libram if any readers care to check the official accounts; his own version of these events can be found elsewhere in the archive, but need not concern us at the moment.*

'You thought what?' I yelped, amazed at his stupidity. Then I remembered. Divas bought the myth of my purported heroism completely and without question, and had done ever since he'd seen me take on an entire tyranid swarm with just a chainsword when we were callow youths together. Purely by accident, as it happened, I'd had no idea the damn bugs were even there until I'd blundered into them, and if I hadn't ended up inadvertently leading them into the beaten zone of our heavy ordnance and saving the day, they'd have torn me to pieces. Waltzing up to the enemy encampment and thumbing our noses at them probably struck him as the kind of thing I did for fun. 'Are you out of your mind?'

'It's perfectly safe,' he said. 'We're not officially at war with them yet.' Well, that was true, but I still wasn't keen on jumping the gun.

'And until we are, we're not going to provoke them,' I said, all commissarial duty. Divas's face fell, like a child denied a sweet, and I thought I'd better put a gloss on it that would match his expectations of me. 'We can't put our own amusement ahead of our responsibilities to the Emperor, however tempting it is.'

'I suppose you're right,' he said reluctantly, and I began to breathe a little more easily. Now all I had to do was manoeuvre him back to the barracks before he got any more stupid ideas. So I took him by the arm, and turned him around. 'Now how do we get back to our compound?'

'How about in a body bag?' somebody asked. I turned, feeling my stomach drop. About a dozen locals stood behind us, the street light striking highlights from their shaven heads, a variety of improvised weapons hanging purposefully from their hands. They looked tough, at least in their own minds, but when you've been face to face with orks and eldar reiver slavers you don't intimidate that easily. Well, all right. I do, but I don't show it, which is the main thing.

Besides, I had a laspistol and a chainsword, which in my experience trumps a crowbar every time. So I laid a restraining hand on Divas's shoulder, as he was still intoxicated enough to rise to the bait, and smiled lazily.

'Believe me,' I said, 'you don't want to start anything.'

'You don't tell me what I want.' The group's spokesman stepped forward into the light. Fine, I thought, keep them talking. 'But that's what you Imperials do, isn't it?'

'I don't quite follow,' I said, affecting mild curiosity. Movement out of the corner of my eye told me that our retreat had been cut off. A second group emerged from the alley mouth behind us. I started calculating the odds. If I made a move to draw the laspistol, they'd rush me, but I'd probably manage to get a shot off. If I took out the leader with it, and ran forward at the same time, I stood a good chance of breaking through the line and making a run for it. That assumed they'd be surprised or intimidated enough to hesitate, of course, and I was able to open up a decent lead. With any luck they'd turn on Divas, buying me enough time to get away, but I couldn't be sure of that, so I continued to play for time and look for a better chance.

'You're here to take our world!' the leader shouted. As he came forward fully into the light I could see that his face was painted blue, a delicate pastel shade. It should have made him look ridiculous, but the overall effect was somehow charismatic. 'But you'll never take our freedom!'

'Your freedom is what we're here to give you, you xeno-hugging moron!' Divas broke free of my restraining arm, and lunged forward. 'But you're too brainwashed to see it!'

Great. So much for diplomacy. Still, while he was set on re-enacting Gannack's Charge,[1] I might be able to make a run for it.

No such luck, of course – the surrounding heretics drove in on us as a concerted wedge. I just managed to draw my laspistol and snap off a shot, taking out half the face of one of the group, which, I'm bound to say, didn't make much of a difference to his overall personal charm, before an iron bar came down hard on my wrist. I've been in enough mêlées to have seen the blow coming, and to have ridden it, which saved me from a fracture or worse, but that didn't help the pain, which exploded along my arm, deadening it. My fingers flew open, and I ducked, scrabbling after the precious weapon, but it was futile. A knee drove up into my ribs, slamming the breath from my lungs, and I was down, cold, hard rockcrete scraping the skin from my knuckles (the real ones anyway), and knowing I was a dead man unless I could get away somehow.

'Toren!' I screamed, but Divas had problems of his own by now, and I wasn't going to get any help from that quarter. I curled up, trying to protect my vital organs, and tried frantically to get at my chainsword. Of course, I should have gone for that first, holding the mob at bay with it, but hindsight's about as much use as a heretic's oath, and now the bloody thing was trapped under my own bodyweight. I scrabbled frantically, feeling fists and boots thudding against my ribs. Luckily there were so many of them that they were getting in each others way,

---

1. *A famous military blunder in the Spiron campaign, which took place on 438.926.M41. Captain Gannack's sentinel troop, from the 3rd Kalaman Hussars, misinterpreted their orders and charged an ork redoubt containing an artillery battery. No one survived.*

and my uniform greatcoat was thick enough to absorb some of the impact, or I'd have been in even worse shape than I was.

'Greechaah!' something shrieked, an inhuman scream that raised the hairs on the back of my neck, even under those conditions. My assailants hesitated, and I rolled clear, in time to see the largest of them yanked back by sheer brute force.

For a moment I thought I was hallucinating, but the pain in my ribs was all too real. A face dominated by a large hooked beak was gazing down at me, surmounted by a crest of quills that had been dyed or painted in some elaborate pattern, and hot, charnel breath washed across my face, making me gag.

'You are comparatively uninjured?' the thing asked, in curiously accented Gothic. It's hard to convey in writing, but its voice was glottal, most of the consonants reduced to hard clicking sounds. It was perfectly understandable, mind you. My stupefaction was due entirely to the fact that something that looked like that was able to talk in the first place.

'Yes, thank you,' I croaked after a moment. Whenever you don't have a clue what's going on, I've always found, it never hurts to be polite.

'That is gratifying,' the thing said, and threw the heretic in its left hand casually away. The others were standing around aimlessly now, like sulky schola students when the tutor turns up to spoil the fun. Then it extended the same thin, scaly hand equipped with dagger-like claws towards me. After a heartstopping moment, I divined its intention, and accepted the proffered assistance in gaining my feet. As I did so, it turned to the sullen group of heretics.

'This does not advance the greater good,' it said. 'Disperse now, and avoid conflict.' Well, that was a challenge if ever I'd heard one. But to my surprise, and, I must admit, my intense relief, the little knot of troublemakers slunk away into the shadows. I eyed my rescuer a little apprehensively. He (or she – with kroot it's impossible to tell, and only another kroot would care anyway) was slightly taller than I was, and still looked pretty intimidating. They're tough enough to take on an ork in hand-to-hand combat, and I, for one, wouldn't be betting on the greenskin, but if it wanted me dead, it would only have had to wait a few moments. I retrieved my fallen laspistol anyway, and tried to get my breath back.

'I'm obliged to you,' I said. 'I must admit I don't understand, but I'm grateful.' I fumbled the weapon back into its holster with some difficulty. My arm was swelling up now, and my fingers felt thick and unresponsive. My rescuer made a curious clicking sound, which I assumed to be its equivalent of laughter.

'Imperial officers murdered by tau supporters. Not a desirable outcome when the political situation is tense.'

'Not a desirable outcome at any time when one of them is me,' I said, and the xeno made the clicking noise again. That reminded me of Divas, and I staggered across to check on him. He was still breathing, but unconscious, a deep gash across his forehead. I'd picked up enough battlefield medicine to know he'd recover soon enough, but have the Emperor's own headache when he woke, and that was fine with me – serve the idiot right for nearly getting me killed.

'I have the honour to be Gorok, of the Clan T'cha,' the creature said. 'I am kroot.'

'I know what you are,' I said. 'Kroot killed my parents.' And thereby got me dumped in the Schola Progenium, and thence into the Commissariat, instead of following my undoubted true destiny of running some discreet little house of ill repute for slumming spirers and guilders up from the sump with more money than sense to splash around. I vaguely resented that, far more than the loss of my progenitors, who hadn't been all that much to have around while they were alive, to be honest. But it never hurts to grab the moral high ground. My new acquaintance didn't seem terribly concerned, though.

'I trust they fought well,' he said. I doubted it. They'd only joined the Guard to get out of the hive ahead of the Arbites, and would certainly have deserted the first chance they got, so there must be something in genetics after all.

'Not well enough,' I said, and Gorok clicked his amusement again. It was a slightly unnerving experience, feeling that something so unhuman was able to read me more readily than my own people.

'Go carefully, commissar,' he said. 'And feed on your enemies. May we have no cause for conflict.'

Well, thank the Emperor for that. But somehow I doubted that it was going to happen, and of course, I was right. I was surprised, though, by how quickly the crisis came upon us.

Editorial Note:

It is perhaps worth pointing out at this juncture that the account of his background that Cain gives during his conversation with the kroot, although superficially plausible, doesn't quite hold together on further examination. For one thing, admittance to the Schola Progenium is a privilege usually reserved for the offspring of officers. If he was indeed the son of common troopers his parents must have acquitted themselves with singular valour in the action which resulted in their demise, which, to say the least, seems remarkably at odds with his characterisation of them. Moreover, he implies that they enlisted and served together. Although mixed units are, as pointed out elsewhere, not unheard of in the Imperial Guard, it would have been extremely unusual for this to have been the case.

Cain makes frequent references throughout the archive to having spent his early years on a hive world, but never specifies which one; which, in turn, makes the verification of any such claims virtually impossible. However, no hive world of which I'm aware raised a mixed Guard regiment in the time frame consistent with his narrative.

We should also bear in mind that, by his own admission, the man was a pathological liar; given to saying anything he judged would be effective in manipulating his listeners.

FOUR

*'It's often remarked that diplomacy is just warfare by other means.
Our battles are no less desperate for being bloodless,
but at least we get wine and finger food.'*

– Tollen Ferlang, Imperial Envoy to the Realm
of Ultramar, 564-603 M41

'ARE YOU SURE you're fit enough?' Kasteen asked, a faint frown of concern appearing between her eyebrows. I nodded, and adjusted the sling I'd adopted for dramatic effect. It was black silk, matching the ebony hues of my dress uniform, and made me look tolerably dashing, I thought.

'I'm fine,' I said, smiling bravely. 'The other fellows got the worst of it, thank the Emperor.' In the day or two since the brawl with the heretics, my arm had more or less healed, the medicae assuring me that I'd suffered nothing worse than severe bruising. It was still stiff, and ached a little, but all in all I thought I'd come off lightly. Far better than Divas had, anyway. He'd spent the night in the infirmary, and still walked with a stick. For all that, though, he was as irritatingly cheerful as ever, and I'd been finding as many duties as I could to keep me out of the way whenever he suggested socialising again.

Luckily for me, he'd lost consciousness before the kroot turned up, so my reputation had received another unmerited embellishment. He assumed I'd seen off our assailants single-handed, and I saw no good reason to disabuse him. Besides, the conversation I'd had with the creature had been curiously unsettling, and I found myself reluctant to think about it too hard. I noticed Divas's account had tactfully glossed over the reason why we were in the thick of the tau sympathizers' heartland, so maybe they'd finally knocked a little common sense into him. Knowing Divas, though, I doubted it.

'Well, that's what they get for picking on the Imperium's finest,' Kasteen said, eager to buy the generally accepted version of events, as the latest evidence of my exceptional martial abilities reflected well on the regiment she led. She adjusted her own dress uniform, tugging the ochre greatcoat into place with every sign of discomfort. Like most Valhallans, she had an iceworlder's tolerance for cold, and found even the mildest of temperate climates a little uncomfortable. Having spent most of my service with Valhallan regiments, I'd long become inured to their habit of air conditioning their quarters to temperatures which left the breath smoking, and tended to wear my commissarial greatcoat at all times, but they were still adjusting to the local conditions here with some difficulty.

'If I might suggest, colonel,' I said, 'tropical order would be perfectly acceptable.'

'Would it?' She hovered indecisively, reminding me again how young she was to be in such an elevated position, and I felt an unaccustomed pang of sympathy. The prestige of the regiment was in her hands, and it was easy to forget how heavily the responsibility weighed on her.

'It would,' I assured her. She discarded the heavy fur cap, disordering her hair, and began to unfasten the coat. Then she hesitated.

'I don't know,' she said. 'If they think I'm too informal it'll reflect badly on all of us.'

'For the Emperor's sake, Regina,' Broklaw said, his voice amused. 'What sort of impression do you think you'll make if you're sweating like an ork all evening?' I noted his use of her given name, the first time I'd heard him do so, with quiet satisfaction. Another milestone on the 597th's march towards full integration. The real test would come with their first taste of combat, of course, and all too soon at that, but it was a good omen. 'The commissar's right.'

'The commissar's always right,' I said, smiling. 'It says so in the regulations.'

'Well, I can't argue with that.' Kasteen pulled off the coat with evident relief, and smoothed the jacket beneath it. It was severely cut, emphasising her figure in ways that I was sure would attract the attention of most of the men in the room. Broklaw nodded approvingly.

'I don't think you need to worry about making an impression,' he said, proffering a comb.

'So long as it's a good one.' She smoothed her hair into place, and began buckling her weapon belt. Like mine it held a chainsword, but hers was ornately gilded, and worked with devotional scenes that decorated scabbard and hilt alike. The contrast with my own functional model, chipped and battered with far too much use for my liking, was striking. The holster at her other hip was immaculate too, the glossy black leather holding a bolt pistol which also gleamed from every highly polished surface and which was intricately engraved with icons of the saints.

'No doubt about that,' I assured her.

Her nervousness was quite understandable, as we'd been invited to a diplomatic reception at the governor's palace. At least I had, and in the interests of protocol, the colonel of my regiment and an appropriate honour guard would also be expected. This sort of soirée was quite beyond her experience, and she was all too acutely aware that she was out of her depth.

I, on the other hand, was well within mine. One of the many benefits of being a Hero of the Imperium is that you're regarded as a prime catch by a certain type of society hostess, which meant that I'd had plenty of opportunity to enjoy the homes, wine cellars, and daughters of the idle rich over the years, and had developed an easy familiarity with the world in which they moved. The main thing to remember, as I confided to Kasteen, was that they had their own idea of what soldiers were like, which had very little to do with the reality.

'The best thing you can do,' I said, 'is not to get sucked in to all that protocol nonsense in the first place. They'll expect us to get it wrong anyway, so to the warp with them.' She smiled in spite of herself, and settled a little more comfortably into the upholstery of the staff car Jurgen had found somewhere. Armed with my commissarial authority, which let him requisition practically anything short of a battleship without argument, he'd developed quite a talent for acquiring anything I considered necessary for my comfort or convenience over the years. I never asked too many questions about where they'd come from, as I suspected some of the answers might have complicated my life.

'That's easy for you to say,' she said. 'You're a hero. I'm just–'

'One of the youngest regimental commanders in the entire Guard,' I said. 'A position that, in my opinion, you hold entirely on merit.' I smiled. 'And my confidence is not lightly earned.' It was what she needed to hear, of course; I've always been good at manipulating people. That's one of the reasons I'm so good at my job. She began to look a little happier.

'So what do you suggest?' she said. I shrugged.

'They might be rich and powerful, but they're only civilians. However hard they try to hide it, they'll be in awe of you. I've always found it best at these things just to be a plain, simple military man, with no interest in politics. The Emperor points, and we obey...'

'Through the warp and far away.' She finished the old song line with a smile. 'So we shouldn't offer any opinions, or answer questions about policy.'

'Exactly,' I said. 'If they want to talk, tell them a few stories about your old campaigns. That's all they're interested in anyway.' That was certainly true in my case. I was sure I'd only been invited as patriotic window-dressing, to impress the tau with the calibre of the opposition they'd be facing if they were foolish enough to try and make a fight of it with us. Of course, in my case, that meant they could pretty much run their flag up the pole of the governor's palace any time they felt like it, but that was beside the point.

'Thank you, Ciaphas.' Kasteen put her chin on her hand, and watched the street lights flicker past outside the window. That was the first time anyone in the regiment had addressed me in personal terms since I joined it. It felt strange, but curiously pleasant.

'You're welcome... Regina,' I said, and she smiled.

(I know what you're thinking, and you're wrong. I did come to think of her as a friend in the end, and Broklaw too, but that's as far as it went. Anything else would have made both our positions untenable. Sometimes, looking back, I think that's a shame, but there it is.)

THE GOVERNOR'S PALACE was in what the locals called the Old Quarter, where the fad for tau-influenced architecture which had infected the rest of the city had failed to take hold, so the vague sense of unease which had oppressed me since we arrived began to lift at last. The villas and mansions slipping past outside the car had taken on the familiar blocky contours of the Imperial architecture with which I'd been familiar all my life, and I felt my spirits begin to rise to the point where I almost began to anticipate enjoying the evening ahead of us.

Jurgen swung the vehicle through an elaborate pair of wrought-iron gates decorated with the Imperial aquila, and our tyres hissed over raked gravel as we progressed down a long, curving drive lit by flickering flambeaux. Behind us the truck with our honour guard followed, no doubt making a terrible mess of things with its heavy duty tyres, the soldiers making the most of the grandstand view afforded by its open rear decking to point and chatter at the sights. Beyond the flickering firelight, we could make out a rolling landscaped lawn, dotted with shrubs and ornamental fountains – automatically, some part of my mind was assessing the best way of using them for cover.

An audible gasp from Kasteen signalled that the palace itself had come into view from her side window, and a moment later, the curve of the drive brought it into my field of vision.

'Not a bad little billet,' I said, with elaborate casualness. Kasteen composed herself, wiping the bumpkin gawp off her face.

'Reminds me of a bordello we used to visit when I was an officer cadet,' she replied, determined to match my blasé exterior. I grinned.

'Good,' I said. 'Remember we're soldiers. We're not impressed by this sort of thing.'

'Absolutely not,' she agreed, straightening her jacket unnecessarily.

There was a lot of the building not to be impressed by. It must have covered over a kilometre from end to end, although of course much of that area would be given over to courtyards and interior gardens currently hidden behind the outer wall. Buttresses and crenellations protruded like acne from every surface, encrusted with statuary commemorating previous governors and other local notables no one could now remember the names of, and vast areas had been gilded, reflecting the firelight from outside in a manner which was to prove eerily prophetic had we but known. At the time, though, it simply struck me as one of the most stridently vulgar piles of masonry I'd ever encountered.

Jurgen pulled up outside the main entrance, halting at the end of a red carpet as skilfully as a shuttle pilot entering a docking port. After a moment the truck pulled up behind us and our honour guard piled out, deploying on either side of it a full squad, five pairs of troopers facing each other across the crimson weave, lasguns at the port.

'Shall we?' I extended an arm to Kasteen as a flunkey dressed as a wedding cake bustled up to open the door for us.

'Thank you, commissar.' She took it as we emerged, and I stopped for a moment to have a word with Jurgen.

'Any further orders, sir?' I shook my head.

'Just find somewhere to park, and get yourself something to eat,' I said. Strictly speaking I could have had my aide accompany us, but the thought of Jurgen mingling with the cream of the Gravalaxian aristocracy was almost too hideous to contemplate. I turned to the noncom in charge of the honour guard, a Sergeant Lustig, and tapped the combead I'd slipped into my ear. 'You too,' I added. 'You might as well be comfortable while you wait for us. I'll contact you when we're ready to leave.'

'Yes sir.' A faint smile tried to form on his broad face before discipline reasserted itself, and he inhaled.

'Squad... Atten... Shun!' he bellowed, and they snapped to it with nanosecond precision. No surprise that they'd won the extra drink ration this week, I thought. The crash of synchronised heels caused heads to turn all around us, minor local nobles looking mightily impressed, and their chauffeurs even more so.

'I think we've made an impression,' Kasteen murmured as we gained the elaborately carved entrance doors.

'That was the idea,' I agreed.

Inside, it was exactly as I'd anticipated, the kind of vulgar ostentation too many of the wealthy mistake for good taste, with crystal and gilt and garish tapestries of historic battles and smug-looking primarchs strewn around the place like a pirate's warehouse. The high arched ceiling was supported by pillars artfully carved to mimic the bark of some species of local tree, and my feet sank into the carpet as though it were a swamp. It took me a moment to realise that the weave would form a vast portrait, presumably of the governor himself, if viewed from the upper landing, and I noted with faint amusement that someone had trodden on a dropped canapé making it look as though his nose was running. Whether it was a genuine accident, or the act of a disgruntled servant, who could say? Kasteen's lips quirked as she absorbed the full opulence of our surroundings.

'I take it back,' she said quietly. 'A bordello would have been done out in far better taste.' I suppressed a smile of my own as another flunkey ushered us forward.

'Commissar Ciaphas Cain,' he announced. 'And Colonel Regina Kasteen.' Which at least established who we were. It was pretty obvious who the unhealthy-looking individual sitting on a raised dais at the end of the room was. I've met a good few planetary governors in my day, and they all tend towards inbred imbecility,[1] but this specimen looked like he should take the prize. He somehow contrived to look both undernourished and flabby at the same time, and his skin was the

---

1. *Like many of Cain's sweeping generalisations, this does contain an element of truth. The majority of planetary governorships are hereditary positions, and many of the incumbents aren't up to the challenge of the job. However, the truly incompetent tend to be weeded out by the ceaseless round of dynastic power struggles and coups d'état which keep the aristocracy amused, and in cases where Imperial interests are directly threatened, we can always turn to the Officio Assassinorum.*

pallor of a dead fish. Watery eyes of no particular colour goggled at us from under a fringe of thinning grey hair.

'Governor Grice,' I said, bowing formally. 'A pleasure.'

'On the contrary,' he said, his voice quivering a little. 'The pleasure's entirely mine.' Well, he wasn't wrong on that account, but he was ignoring me entirely. He stood, and bowed to Kasteen. 'You honour us all with your presence, colonel.'

Well, that was a new experience, being ignored in favour of a slip of a girl, but I suppose if you'd ever met her you'd understand it. She was pretty striking, if redheads were your thing, and I supposed the old fool didn't get out much. Anyway, it enabled me to fade out of the picture and go looking for some amusement of my own, which I did with all due dispatch.

As was my habit I circulated widely, keeping my eyes and ears open as you never know what useful little snippets of information will come in handy, although the main thing that caught my attention was the entertainment. A young woman was standing on a podium at the end of the room, surrounded by musicians who sounded almost as well rehearsed as our regimental band, but they could have been playing ork wardrums for all I cared because her voice was extraordinary. She was singing old sentimental favourites, like *The Night Before You Left* and *The Love We Share*, and even an old cynic like me could appreciate the emotion she put into them, and feel that, just this once, the trite words were ringing true. Snatches of her husky contralto carried through the room wherever I was, cutting through the backbiting and the small talk, and I felt my eyes drifting in her direction every time the crowd parted enough to afford me a view.

And the view was well worth it. She was tall and slim, with shoulder-length hair of a shade of blonde I've never seen on anyone else before or since, hanging loose to frame a face which nearly stopped my heart. Her eyes were the hazy blue of a far horizon, and seemed to transfix me whenever I looked in her direction. Her dress was the same colour, almost exactly, and clung to her figure like mist.

Now, I've never believed in sentimental nonsense like love at first sight, but I can say without a word of a lie that, even now, after almost a century, I can close my eyes and picture her as she was then, and hear those songs as though she's still in the same room.

But I wasn't there to listen to cabaret singers, however enchanting, so I tried my best to mingle and pick up whatever gossip I could that would help us fight the tau if we had to, and keep me out of it, if at all possible.

'So you're the famous Commissar Cain,' someone said, passing me a fresh drink. I took it automatically, turning a little to use my right hand

and emphasize the sling, and found myself looking at a narrow-faced fellow in an expensive but understated robe which positively screamed diplomat. He glanced at the sling. 'I hear you nearly started the war early.'

'Not from choice, I can assure you,' I said. 'Just defending an officer who lacked the self-restraint to ignore a blatant piece of sedition.'

'I see.' He eyed me narrowly, trying to size me up. I kept my expression neutral. 'I take it your self-restraint is a little stronger.'

'At the moment,' I said, choosing my words with care, 'we're still at peace with the tau. The internal situation here is, I'll admit, a little disturbing, but unless the Guard is ordered to intervene, that's purely a matter for the Arbites, the PDF, and His Excellency.' I nodded at Grice, who was listening to Kasteen explain the best way of disembowelling a termagant with every sign of interest, although his retinue of sycophants was beginning to look a little green around the gills. 'I'm not averse to fighting if I have to, but that's a decision for wiser heads than mine to take.'

'I see.' He nodded, and stuck out a hand for me to shake. After a moment's juggling, more to put him off balance than anything, I transferred the glass to my other hand and took it. 'Erasmus Donali, Imperial Envoy.'

'I thought as much.' I smiled in return. 'You have the look of a diplomat about you.'

'Whereas you seem quite exceptional for a soldier.' Donali sipped his drink, and I followed suit, finding it a very pleasant vintage. 'Most of them can't wait for the shooting to start.'

'They're Imperial Guard,' I said. 'They live to fight for the Emperor. I'm a commissar; I'm supposed to consider the bigger picture.'

'Which includes avoiding combat? You surprise me.'

'As I said before,' I told him, 'that's not my decision to make. But if people like you can solve the conflict by negotiation, and keep troopers who would have died here alive to fight another enemy another day, and maybe tip the balance in a more important battle, then it seems to me that you're serving the best interests of the Imperium.' And keeping my skin whole into the bargain, of course, which was far more important to me. Donali looked surprised, and a little gratified.

'I can see your reputation is far from exaggerated,' he said. 'And I hope I can oblige you. But it may not be easy.'

That wasn't what I wanted to hear, you can be sure. But I shrugged, and sipped my drink.

'As the Emperor wills,' I said, a phrase I'd picked up from Jurgen over the course of our long association. Of course when he says it he means every word; from me it's just the verbal equivalent of a shrug. I've never really bought the idea that His Divine Majesty can spare some attention from the job of preventing the entire galaxy from sliding into damnation to look out for my interests, too, or anyone else's for that matter, which is why I'm so diligent about doing it for myself. 'The difficulty, I take it, being the public support for the tau in certain quarters.'

'Exactly.' My new friend nodded gloomily. 'For which you can thank the imbecile over there talking to your colonel.' He indicated Grice with a tilt of his head. 'He got so carried away counting his bribes from the likes of him...' another tilt of the head to the far corner of the room, 'that he hardly even noticed his planet slipping out from under him.'

I turned in the direction he'd indicated. A cadaverous, hawk-nosed individual dressed in unwise scarlet hose and a burgundy tabard was holding forth to a knot of the local aristocracy. Flanking him were a couple of servants in livery, who looked about as comfortable as an ork in evening dress; hired guns if I'd ever seen them. A scribe hovered next to him, making notes.

'One of the rogue traders we've heard so much about,' I said. Donali shrugged.

'So he says. But no one here is entirely what they seem, commissar. You can certainly depend on that.'

Well he was right on the money so far as I was concerned. So I exchanged a few more inconsequential words and resumed circulating.

After a few more conversations with local dignitaries whose names I never quite caught, my glass was in need of replenishment, and I headed towards the table at the far end of the room where an enticing display of delicacies had been laid out. On the way, I noticed Kasteen had managed to extricate herself from the governor's presence, and was working the room as though she'd been a habitué of high society since she could walk. The air of confidence she now radiated was remarkable, especially set against her earlier nervousness, but the ability to seem calm and in control whatever the circumstances is a vital quality in a leader, and for all I knew, she was shamming it as shamelessly as I was. It certainly looked as though she was enjoying herself, though, and I gave her a light-hearted salute as our eyes briefly met. She responded with a flashing grin, and whirled away towards the dance floor with a couple of aristocratic fops in tow.

'It looks like you've lost your date,' a voice said behind me. I turned, and found myself falling into the wide blue eyes of the singer I'd been watching before. Uncharacteristically for me, I was momentarily at a loss for words. She was smiling, a plate of finger food in her hand.

'She's, ah, just a colleague,' I said. 'A fellow officer. Nothing like that between us. Strictly against regulations, for one thing. And anyway, we're not–'

She laughed, a warm, smoky chuckle which warmed me like amasec, and I realised she was pulling my leg.

'I know,' she said. 'No time for romance in the Imperial Guard. It must be grim for you.'

'We have our duty to the Emperor,' I said. 'For a soldier, that's enough.' It's the sort of thing I usually say, and most civilians lap it up, but my beautiful singer was looking at me quizzically, the ghost of a smile quirking at the corner of her mouth, and I suddenly got the feeling that she could see right through me to the core of deceit and self-interest I normally keep concealed from the world. It was an unnerving sensation.

'For some, maybe. But I think there's more to you than meets the eye.' She picked up a bottle from the nearby table with her free hand, and topped up my glass.

'There's more to everyone than meets the eye,' I said, more to deflect the conversation than anything else. She smiled again.

'That's very astute, commissar.' She extended a hand, slim and cool to the touch, the middle finger ornamented with a large and finely wrought ring of unusual workmanship. Evidently she was extremely successful in her profession, or had at least one wealthy admirer; I would have laid money on both. I kissed it formally, as etiquette demanded, and to my astonishment she giggled.

'A gentleman as well as an officer. You are full of surprises.' Then she surprised me by dropping a curtsey, in imitation of the bovine debutantes surrounding us, the light of mischief in her dazzling eyes. 'I'm Amberley Vail, by the way. I sing a bit.'

'I know,' I said. 'And very well too.' She acknowledged the compliment with a tilt of her head. I bowed formally, entering into the game. 'Ciaphas Cain,' I said, 'at your service. Currently attached to the Valhallan 597th.' Her eyes widened a little as I introduced myself.

'I've heard of you,' she said, a little breathlessly. 'Didn't you fight the genestealers on Keffia?' Well I had, if you count hanging around drinking recaf while the artillery unit I was with dropped shells on the biggest concentrations of stealers we could find from kloms away as fighting. I'd been in at the death, so to speak, and emerged with a great deal of the credit, more by luck than good judgement. It was one of the early incidents that had laid the foundations of my undeserved reputation for heroism, but my misadventures since had tended to overshadow what most of the galaxy still regarded as a minor incident on a backwater agriworld.

'Not entirely alone,' I said, slipping easily into the modest hero demeanour I could adopt without thinking. 'There was an Imperial battlefleet in orbit at the time.'

'And two full divisions of Imperial Guard on planet.' She laughed again at my astonished expression. 'I have relatives in Skandaburg.[1] You're still talked about back there.'

'I can't think why,' I said. 'I was just doing my job.'

'Of course.' Amberley nodded, and again I got the feeling that she wasn't fooled for a moment. 'You're an Imperial commissar. Duty before everything, right?'

'Absolutely,' I said. 'And right now, I think it's my duty to ask you to dance.' It was a transparent attempt to change the subject, which I hoped she'd put down to modest embarrassment, and I half expected her to refuse. But she smiled, discarding her plate of half-eaten delicacies, and took my uninjured arm.

'I'd love to,' she said. 'I've a few minutes before my second set.'

So we drifted across to the dance floor, and I spent a very pleasant few minutes with her head on my shoulder as we spun around to an old waltz I never learned the name of. Kasteen galloped past a couple of times, a different swain in tow on each occasion, raising an eyebrow in a way which forewarned me of some relentless leg-pulling on our drive back to the compound, but just at that moment I couldn't have cared less.

Eventually, Amberley pulled away, with what seemed like reluctance unless I was succumbing to wishful thinking, and began to return to the stage. I walked with her, chatting to no purpose, intent simply on prolonging a pleasant interlude in what otherwise promised to be a dull evening, and it was thus that I noticed a quiet, vehement altercation between Grice and the hawk-faced rogue trader.

'Do you know who that is?' I asked, not really expecting an answer, but it seemed my companion was well-versed in the intricacies of Gravalaxian politics. It came with performing for the aristocracy, I supposed. She nodded, looking surprised.

'His name's Orelius. A rogue trader here to deal with the tau. So he says.' The qualification was delivered in precisely the same tone of scepticism as Donali's had been, and for some reason I found myself remembering Divas's cloak-and-dagger fantasies from our night in the Eagle's Wing.

'Why do you say that?' I asked. Amberley shrugged.

'The tau have been dealing with the same traders for more than a century. Orelius arrived from nowhere a month or two ago, and tried

---

1. *The provincial capital of the smaller of the Northern continents. Most of the action in the cleansing of Keffia took place on the southern continent, where the genestealer cult was most deeply entrenched; so Skandaburg and its population would have been relatively untouched by the fighting.*

opening negotiations with them, through Grice. It may just be a coincidence, but...' She shrugged, her dress slipping across her slim shoulders.

'Why now, with the political situation destabilising?' I asked. She nodded.

'It does seem a little unusual.'

'Perhaps he's hoping to take advantage of the confusion to strike a better deal,' I said. Orelius turned on his heel as I watched, and marched away trailed by his bodyguards. Grice was pale and sweating, even more than usual, and reached out to pluck a drink from a nearby servitor with a trembling hand. 'He's thrown a scare into our illustrious governor, at any event.'

'Has he?' Amberley watched him go. 'That seems a little presumptuous, even for a rogue trader.'

'If that's what he really is,' I said, without thinking. Those depthless blue eyes turned on me again.

'What else would he be?'

'An inquisitor,' I said, the idea taking firmer root in my head even as I said it. Amberley's eyes widened.

'An inquisitor? Here?' Her voice became a little tremulous, as though the enormity of the idea were too huge to grasp. 'What makes you think that?'

The urge to impress her was almost irresistible, I have to confess; and if you could only know how bewitching she was, I know you'd have felt the same. So I looked my most commissarial.

'All I can say,' I told her, lowering my voice for dramatic effect, 'is that I've heard from a reliable military source' – which sounded a lot better than 'from a drunken idiot,' I'm sure you'll agree – 'that there are Inquisition agents active on Gravalax.'

'Surely not.' She shook her head, blonde tresses flying in confusion. 'And even if there were, why would you suspect Orelius?'

'Well, just look at him,' I said. 'Everyone knows that undercover inquisitors disguise themselves as rogue traders most of the time.[1] It's by far the easiest way of travelling incognito with the rabble of hangers-on they all seem to attract.'

'You could be right,' she said, with a delicate shiver. 'But it's no concern of ours.'

---

1. *It is indeed regrettable that this predilection has become so widely known. Personally, I blame popular fiction for perpetuating the stereotype, although it has to be said that some inquisitors are simply woefully lacking in imagination when required to adopt a disguise.*

Well, I couldn't agree more, of course, but that's not what my heroic reputation leads people to expect of me, so I put on my best dutiful expression and said 'The security of the Imperium is the concern of all of His Majesty's loyal servants.' Well, that's true too, and it lets me out, but no one needs to know that. Amberley nodded, sombrely, and trotted back to the stage, and I watched her go, cursing myself for an idiot for puncturing the mood.

As you'll no doubt appreciate, the rest of the evening promised to be anticlimactic, so I drifted back to the food and drink. Our rations back at the compound were adequate enough, but I wasn't going to pass up the opportunity to savour a few delicacies while they were there for the taking, and it was as good a vantage point as any to enjoy Amberley's performance from. It was also, as I'd learned from uncountable similar affairs, the best spot from which to cull gossip, since everyone gravitated there sooner or later.

Thus it was that I made the acquaintance of Orelius, without the faintest presentiment of the trouble that innocent conversation would lead to.

If anything, I suppose, it was the sling that was to blame. It had seemed a good idea at the time, but now I came to fill a plate the damn thing got in the way, preventing me from reaching out for the palovine pastries perched on the opposite side of the table. If I transferred the plate to my left hand I was turned awkwardly, my centre of mass shifted, so I still couldn't reach. I was trying to work out a way of getting to them when a thin arm reached across to pick up the dish.

'Allow me.' The voice was dry and cultured. I transferred a couple of the delicacies to my plate, and found myself addressing the man I'd almost convinced myself was an inquisitorial agent. It was ridiculous, of course, but still...

'Thank you, sieur Orelius,' I said. 'You're most kind.'

'Have we met?' His eyes were shadowed, the irises were almost black, and had an unnerving piercing quality that increased his resemblance to a bird of prey.

'Your reputation precedes you,' I said blandly, letting him make of that what he would. I don't mind admitting I was less relaxed than I tried to look. If he really was an inquisitor, there was a good chance he was a psyker, too, and might know me for what I was, but I'd encountered mindreaders before and knew that they weren't as formidable as most people thought. Most of them can only read surface thoughts, and I was so long practiced at dissembling that I did so without any conscious awareness of the fact.

'I'm sure it does.' He was an old hand at this game too, I realised, an essential skill whether his profession was as it appeared or as I had surmised.

'You seem to have the ear of His Excellency,' I said, and the first momentary flicker of emotion appeared on his face. I'd got in under his guard, it seemed.

'I have both. Unfortunately, His Excellency appears to lack anything between them.' He took one of the pastries for himself. 'He's paralysed with indecision.'

'Indecision about what?' I asked ingenuously.

'Where his best interests lie. And those of his people, of course.' Orelius bit into the delicacy as though it were Grice's neck. 'Unless he starts showing some leadership, this world will go down in blood and burning. But he sits and vacillates, and hopes it will all go away.'

'Then let's hope he comes to his senses soon,' I said. The keen eyes impaled me again.

'Indeed.' His voice was level. 'For all our sakes.' He smiled then, without warmth. 'The Emperor be with you, Commissar Cain.' My surprise must have shown on my face, because the smile widened a fraction. 'Your reputation precedes you too.'

And then he was gone, leaving me curiously troubled. I didn't have long to dwell on my unease, though, because the flunkey who'd announced our arrival was back, looking a little flustered. He'd called out a number of names since Kasteen and I had made our entrance, but it was clear that this time he expected to be listened to. He pounded a staff on the polished wooden floor, and the babble of voices gradually diminished; Amberley's trailed away in mid-chorus, which was a real shame. The flunkey's chest inflated with self-importance.

'Your Excellency. My lords, ladies, and gentlemen. O'ran Shui'sassai, Ambassador of the tau.'

And for the first time since arriving on Gravalax, I was face to face with the enemy.

FIVE

'Treachery is its own reward.'

Callidus Temple proverb

ONE THING I'LL say for the tau, they certainly know how to make an impressive entrance. Shui'sassai was draped in a simple white robe, which made all the Imperial dignitaries look ridiculously overdressed, and was surrounded by others of his kind similarly attired. There was no mistaking who in charge, though, as his charisma filled the room, his entourage bobbing in his wake as he strode confidently across the polished wooden floor towards Grice like seabirds around a fishing boat. I didn't realise at the time how apt the mental image was, of course.[1]

What I did notice almost at once was the bluish cast of his skin, and that of his compatriots, which I'd been led to expect from Divas's gossip and the various reports I'd read. What I hadn't expected was the single braid that grew from his otherwise hairless skull, plaited and ornamented with ribbons in a variety of colours which contrasted vividly with the plain simplicity of his garment. The meaning of the bizarre hairstyle sported by their human dupes, which I'd noted many

---

1. *The ambassador, like all tau diplomats, would be one of the Water caste.*

times since our landing, thus became clear to me, along with the face paint the leader of the street gang had worn, and I found myself suppressing a shiver of unease. If so many citizens had been influenced so openly by these alien interlopers, the situation was dire indeed, and my chances of keeping well away from trouble, problematic at best.

It reminded me of something else, too, and after a moment I recalled the decoration Gorok the kroot had applied to the quills on his head. Clearly the races of the tau empire saw nothing wrong in absorbing the mores and fashions of one another's cultures, eroding their very identities in the name of their union, a notion any loyal Imperial citizen would have regarded with as much horror as I did. I'd seen at first hand what happened when traitors and heretics abandoned their humanity to follow the twisted teachings of Chaos, and the thought of how fertile a soil the warp-spawned abominations would find the Imperium if it were ever to become as unwittingly open to alien influence as the tau and their dupes chilled my very soul.

Shui'sassai's flunkies also had their single tail of hair ornamented, though slightly less flamboyantly, and I found myself wondering if the pattern denoted some subtle graduations of status among them, or were merely intended to be decorative.

'Smug little grox-fondler.' Donali was at my elbow again, the words delivered through almost motionless lips as he made brief eye contact with the xeno and raised his wineglass in greeting. 'He thinks he's got the whole planet sewn up.'

'And does he?' I asked, more out of politeness than actually expecting an answer.

'Not yet.' Donali watched as the xeno delegation made its ritual greeting to Grice. 'But he's certainly got the governor in his pocket.'

'Are you sure about that?' I asked. Donali must have detected something in my intonation because his attention switched to me at once, a sensation I found mildly disconcerting.

'You suspect he might be under... other influences?' he suggested, watching my face for a flicker of reaction. Well, good luck to him – a lifetime of dissembling had left me virtually impossible to read in that way. I indicated Orelius with a tilt of my head; he was watching the exchange between Grice and the tau diplomat warily, trying not to look as though he was paying it any attention.

'Our rogue trader friend had quite a conversation with His Excellency earlier this evening,' I said. 'And neither of them seem terribly happy about it.'

'You've spoken to Orelius?' Once again, I found myself in the middle of a verbal fencing match. Emperor's bowels, I thought irritably, doesn't anyone around here ever say what they mean?

'We exchanged a few words,' I said, shrugging. 'He seems to think the shooting's about to start–'

The bark of a bolt pistol going off echoed around the ballroom, and I dived for cover behind an overstuffed sofa even before the rational part of my mind had identified the source of the sound. I may not be a paragon of virtue, but I like to think my survival instincts more than makes up for any moral shortcomings I might possess.

Donali stood, gaping, as the room erupted in panic and screams. Half the guests started running in no particular direction, while the others stared around themselves in half-witted stupefaction. Priceless crystal goblets shattered underfoot as drinks were dropped and swords were unsheathed, and every kind of sidearm imaginable suddenly appeared in hands on every side.

'Treachery!' one of the tau shrieked, glaring around itself and drawing some kind of handgun from the recesses of its robes. Shui'sassai was down, thick purple blood everywhere, and I knew from experience that he wouldn't be getting up again.

The bolter round had exploded inside his chest cavity, redecorating the immediate vicinity with tau viscera, which I was mildly intrigued to note was darker in colour than the human equivalent; something to do with the colour of their skin, I assumed.[1]

'Kasteen!' I activated the combead in my ear. 'Where are you?'

'Over by the stage.' I lifted my head, scanning the room, and located her as she scrambled up next to Amberley, who was gazing at the crowd as though mesmerised.

'Did you see where the shot came from?'

'No.' She hesitated a fraction of a second. 'My attention was elsewhere. Sorry, commissar.'

'No need to be,' I said. 'You weren't to know this was going to turn into a warzone.' In truth, that looked uncomfortably like what was happening. Practically everyone with a ceremonial sidearm had drawn it in a panic-stricken reflex, except for Kasteen and myself, and was looking for someone to use it on. Which meant identifying the assassin would be virtually impossible by now.

'Gue'la animals! Is this how you respond to proposals of peace?' The gun-waving tau was getting hysterical, swinging the weapon wildly. It was only a matter of seconds, I thought, before he pulled the trigger, or, more likely, someone else shot him before he had the chance. Either

---

1. *The tau equivalent to haemoglobin contains cobalt, rather than iron, so their blood and viscera vary from dark blue to purple, depending on the degree of oxygenation. Don't even get me started about the smell.*

way, it was going to start a massacre, and I had no intention of getting caught in the middle of it.

'Lustig,' I voxed. 'Jurgen. We're leaving now. There may be resistance.'

'Sir.' Jurgen's voice was as phlegmatic as ever.

'Commissar?' Lustig's was inflected with the query he was too well-trained to ask. But I wasn't about to let the honour guard blunder into a firefight without warning. I was going to need them if I expected to get out of here.

'The tau ambassador has just been assassinated,' I said. Then I cursed my own stupidity. The channel wasn't secured, which meant every listening post on both sides had probably picked up my transmission. Oh well, too late to worry about that now. My main priority was getting the hell out of here in one piece. Unfortunately that meant getting past the tau delegation, which looked like it was becoming a fire magnet for every Imperial hothead in the room.

There was only one thing for it. With a curious sense of déjà vu, I strode forwards, my hands held out from my sides, away from my weapons.

Please bear in mind that barely a minute had passed by this time, and the room, was far from silent. Practically everyone was shouting at everyone else, and no one was listening. The rest of the tau were babbling away in their own language. It sounded like frying grox steaks to me, but the gist of it was obviously 'put that bloody thing away before you get us all shot,' and the other guests were screaming 'drop it!' at him and each other. I realised that with the tangle of competing factions and interests in the room there would be a complete bloodbath the moment anyone pulled a trigger. Which was probably what the assassin was counting on to cover his tracks.

'Colonel. With me.' Kasteen could cover my back, at least. I saw her slip off the stage and start towards me through the milling mob; Amberley had already disappeared, sensible girl.

'You! You did this!' The tau stuck the muzzle of his curiously featureless pistol under Grice's chin. The governor seemed to lose even more colour, if that were possible, and spluttered incoherently.

'That's ridiculous! What would I have to gain–'

'More lies!' The tau shrugged off the restraining hands of his colleagues. 'The truth, or you die!'

'This does not advance the greater good,' I said, echoing the words of the kroot. I wasn't quite sure what they meant, but I hoped they had more resonance for the tau than yet another variation on 'put it down before I shoot you,' which didn't seem to be having much effect.

It worked better than I'd dared to hope. Every tau in the group, including the maniac with the gun, stared at me with something I took to be astonishment. Their faces are harder to read than human or eldar, but it gets easier the more practice you have, and these days I can usually catch even the most carefully concealed half-truth.

'What the frak's that supposed to mean?' Kasteen subvocalised into my combead, breaking through the crowd to stand beside me. I noticed with a flicker of relief that she still hadn't drawn her weapons either, which was going to make things a lot easier.

'Warped if I know,' I responded, before stepping forward to where the xenos could get a better look at me.

'What do you know of the greater good?' the tau asked, lowering his weapon a fraction, but keeping Grice covered nevertheless. His companions hesitated, clearly wondering if it was safe to disarm him yet. Grice obviously thought otherwise, sweating more profusely than Jurgen reading a porno slate.

'Not much,' I admitted. 'But adding more deaths to tonight's piece of treachery won't help anyone, surely.'

'Your words have merit, Imperial officer.' One of the other tau spoke up cautiously, an eye on his gun-toting friend.

'My name is Cain,' I said, and a whisper of voices around me echoed it. 'That's him, that's Ciaphas Cain...' The reaction seemed to bemuse my new friend.

'You are well-known to these people?'

'I seem to have acquired something of a reputation,' I admitted.

'Commissar Cain is well-known as a man of integrity,' a new voice cut in. Orelius was edging his way through the crowd, flanked by his bodyguards. At a gesture from him, they holstered their bolt pistols.

'That's right.' Donali backed him up, taking the initiative back into official hands. 'You can trust his word.' Which didn't say much for his skills as a diplomat when you come to think of it, but then he didn't know me as well as I do.

'I am El'sorath,' the conversational tau said, extending a hand in human fashion. I took it, finding it slightly warmer than I'd expected; something to do with the blue skin, probably.

'Did your friend...?' I indicated the tau with the gun.

'El'hassai,' El'sorath supplied helpfully.

'Did anyone actually see who fired the shot?' I asked, directing the question to El'hassai personally, as though we were simply having a normal conversation. A flicker of doubt passed across his features for the first time.

'We were talking to this one.' The gun came up to point at Grice again. 'I heard Shui'sassai say "What–" and then the sound of the shot. When I turned back there was no one else there. It must have been him!'

'But you didn't actually see the murder,' I persisted. El'hassai shook his head, a gesture I assumed he'd learned from his long association with humans.

'It could have been no one else,' he insisted.

'Did you see the governor with a gun?'

'He must have concealed it.' True, Grice's overly ornamented robes might have concealed almost anything in their voluminous folds, but I tried to picture this indolent lump of lard drawing a pistol, killing the ambassador, and palming it again within a matter of seconds and fought to keep a smile off my face.

'There are hundreds of people in this room,' I said calmly. 'Isn't it more likely that one of them is responsible? Maybe a servant you simply didn't notice?'

'Vastly more likely,' El'sorath agreed, holding out a hand for the pistol. After a moment, El'hassai capitulated, and handed it to him. A collective sigh of relief echoed round the room behind us.

'This will be investigated,' Donali said, 'and the murderer brought to account. You have my word.'

'We are aware of the value of Imperial promises,' El'sorath said, with the barest trace of sarcasm. 'But we will make our own enquiries.'

'Of course.' Grice wiped his face with the sleeve of his robe, quivering like a plasmoid, and failing to recover a shred of dignity. 'Our Arbites will keep you apprised of everything we're able to uncover.'

'I would expect nothing less,' El'sorath said.

'We're in position, commissar,' Lustig said in my ear. Kasteen and I exchanged glances.

'What's it like out there?' she subvocalised.

'Panic and confusion, ma'am. And there seems to be something going on in the city.'

'Perhaps you'd better return to your compound,' Donali suggested to El'-sorath, unaware of the ominous messages we'd been getting. 'My driver–'

'Wouldn't get fifty metres from the gate,' Kasteen put in. I switched frequencies to the tactical net, as I was sure she had, and heard a confused babble of voices in my ear. PDF units were mobilising in support of Arbites riot squads, and unrest was spreading across the city like jam across toast.

'What do you mean?' Grice quivered, looking around for a flunkey to blame. Palace security troops were finally beginning to deploy, guarding the exits, although I didn't expect much help from them if they actually had to defend the place. Lots of ceremonial gold armour which wouldn't stop a thrown rock, and old-fashioned lasguns with the ridiculously long barrels I'd only seen before in museums, and which probably hadn't been fired in the last couple of millennia.

'There are riots breaking out all over the city, Your Excellency.' Kasteen almost sounded as though she was enjoying breaking the bad news to him. 'Mobs are attacking the Arbites sector houses and the PDF barracks, denouncing the Imperium for the ambassador's murder.'

'How could they know?' Grice blustered. 'The news hasn't had time to spread...'

For a moment I wondered if my ill-timed transmission to Lustig had been the cause of all this, then common sense reasserted itself. There hadn't been time to disseminate the information even if someone had been listening. There was only one possible explanation.

'A conspiracy,' I said. 'The murderer had confederates who were spreading the rumour even before he struck. This wasn't just meant to disrupt the negotiations, it was supposed to signal a full-scale revolt.'

'More lies!' El'hassai had been quiet for the last few minutes, staring at the ambassador's corpse as though he expected it to sit up and start giving us the answers. 'You think we'd sacrifice one of our own to seize control here?'

'I think nothing,' I said carefully. 'I'm just a soldier. But someone's orchestrating this, Emperor knows why. If it's not your people, then maybe it's some Imperial faction trying to smoke out your supporters here.'

'But who would consider such a thing?' Grice burbled. I glanced at Orelius, my suspicions about him flooding back. The Inquisition was certainly ruthless enough, and had the resources to do it.

'That's for wiser heads than mine to determine,' I said, and for a moment, the rogue trader's gimlet eyes were on me.

'Our prime concern must be the welfare of your delegation,' Donali insisted. 'Can we get a skimmer into the grounds?'

'We can try.' El'sorath was keeping it together, at least. He produced some sort of voxcaster from the recesses of his robe, and hissed and sighed a message into it. Whatever the response was, it seemed to satisfy him, and calm the others, even El'hassai seemed a little less jumpy.

'An aircar has been dispatched,' he said, tucking the vox away. 'It will be with us shortly.'

'And in the meantime, my guards will ensure your personal safety,' Grice said, beckoning a few forward. The tau looked dubious at this.

'They were signally unable to do so in the case of O'ran Shui'sassai,' El'sorath pointed out mildly. Grice flushed a darker shade of grey.

'If anyone has a better suggestion, I'd be delighted to hear it,' he snapped, grabbing a large glass of amasec from one of the servitors which continued to circle the room, oblivious to all the commotion.

'I believe the commissar arrived with an honour guard,' Orelius said. 'Surely a man of his reputation can be trusted with so delicate a task.'

Thanks a lot, I thought. But with that reputation at stake, all I could do was mutter something about it being an honour I didn't deserve. Which was perfectly true, of course.

Donali and the tau were all for it, once the idea had sunk in, so I found myself leading a small gaggle of xenos and diplomats out of the hall, and into the open air. Lustig and the others came pounding up as we emerged, lasguns primed, and took up station around us.

'Be on your guard,' Kasteen warned them. 'The assassin's still at large. So trust no one, apart from us.'

'Especially the diplomats,' I added. Donali shot me a sharp look, and I smiled to pretend I was joking.

'I don't like it here,' I said quietly to Kasteen. 'It's too exposed.' She nodded agreement.

'What do you suggest?'

'There's a shrubbery over that way.' I pointed, blessing the instinctive paranoia that had had me looking out for boltholes on our drive in. 'It'll give us some cover at least.' It was also out of the pool of light surrounding the house, less exposed to prying eyes and sensor equipment.

So we scurried over to it, the troopers double-timing, and the tau keeping up with remarkable ease. Donali kept up with difficulty, but managed to converse with El'sorath the whole way, slipping between platitudes in Imperial Gothic and the sibilant tau tongue for what I assumed to be remarks too sensitive for the likes of us.

Not that I had the time to eavesdrop on their conversation, even if I'd had the inclination. Vox traffic on the tactical band was getting more urgent, the situation deteriorating rapidly.

'The governor's declared a state of martial law,' I relayed to Donali, who took the news remarkably well, only kicking two ornamental bushes to pieces before calming down enough to respond verbally.

'He would. Cretin.'

'I take it you don't think that will be helpful,' I commented dryly.

'It's about as helpful as putting a fire out with promethium,' he said. Even I understood the logic of that. The riots on their own were bad enough, but putting several thousand PDF troopers like the ones I'd encountered in the Eagle's Wing on to the streets, itching for an excuse to bust heads, was just asking for trouble. And that was assuming none of them were secretly xenoist sympathisers.

'So long as none of the PDF trolls take it into their heads to attack the tau...' I began, then trailed off, unwilling to complete the thought. The notion of the aliens being forced to defend themselves, unleashing the wargear Divas had enthusiastically described to me, was truly horrifying; because if that happened it was credits to carrots we'd be mobilised to stop them. And, aside from my natural desire to keep as far away from the killing zone as possible, I was by no means sure that we could.

'Our enclave is surrounded by agitated citizens,' El'sorath announced after another brief and incomprehensible conversation on his own vox. 'But overt hostilities have not yet occurred.'

Well, thank the Emperor for small mercies, I thought, and stepped aside to talk to Kasteen, who was still monitoring the tactical net.

'There's a mob of rioters heading this way,' she said. 'And a PDF platoon with orders to secure the palace grounds. When they get here it'll be bloody.'

I listened to the traffic myself for a few moments, overlaying the sitreps with my still somewhat hazy mental map of the city. If I was right, we had barely ten minutes before the slaughter began.

'Then let's make sure we're somewhere else,' I said. 'As soon as our little blue friends are airborne, we're leaving.'

'Commissar?' Kasteen was looking at me, a little curiously. 'Shouldn't we stay to help?'

Help a bunch of gold-plated nancy boys hold a virtually indefensible fixed position against a mob of blood-maddened lunatics? Not if I had anything to do with it. But I needed to put it a little more tactfully than that, of course.

'I appreciate the sentiment, colonel,' I said. 'But I suspect it would be very unwise politically.' I turned to Donali for support, unexpectedly pleased that the diplomat had hung around. 'Unless I'm misreading the situation, of course.'

'I don't think you are,' he said, clearly reluctant to agree with me. In his position, I wouldn't be too happy to see the only competent soldiers in the vicinity moving rapidly away, either. 'At the moment this is still an internal Gravalaxian matter.'

'Whereas if we get involved, we run the risk of bringing the rest of the Guard in behind us,' I finished. 'Which would be just as destabilising as a tau incursion.'

'I see.' Kasteen's face fell, and I suddenly realised that she'd been hoping for a chance to prove herself and her regiment. I smiled at her, encouragingly.

'Cheer up, colonel,' I said. 'The Emperor has a galaxy full of enemies. I'm sure we can find one more worthy of us than a rock-throwing rabble.'

'I'm sure you're right,' she said, though still with a faint air of disappointment.

Well, she'd just have to get over it. I switched channels again.

'Jurgen. Get over here now,' I voxed. 'We're going to have to leave in a hurry.'

'On my way, sir.' The growl of an engine preceded him, the large military truck ploughing parallel gouges in the immaculate lawn that would take generations of gardeners to completely erase; he swung it to a halt beside us with his usual disdain for the conventional use of brakes and gears.

'Good man.' I waved to my malodorous aide, who popped the cab doors, but kept the engine running. Time began to drag now. Lustig had fanned the troopers out into a textbook defensive pattern, making good use of the available cover, and I could see that the two fire-teams had set up in mutually supporting positions as Kasteen had intended. They looked tight and disciplined, their minds on the job, and with no trace of the old rancour I'd half feared would surface the first time any of our troopers found themselves in combat together.

Of course, they still had to face that ultimate test, but this was far more than an exercise, and they were still responding well. I began to feel reasonably confident about getting back to our staging area in one piece with them to hide behind.

'Listen.' Kasteen tilted her head. I strained to hear over the thrum of our truck's idling engine, but failed to hear anything else for a moment; then I could distinguish it, the faint susurration of a nulgrav flyer approaching at speed, the humming of its ducted fans quite different from the powerful roar of an Astartes speeder or an eldar jetbike. It was the first time I'd ever encountered tau technosorcery at first hand, and its quiet efficiency was subtly unnerving.

'There.' Donali pointed, his outstretched finger tracking the curved metal hull as it swept over us and swung around to align itself on the headlights of our truck. I breathed a quiet word of thanks to the Emperor, even though I was sure he wouldn't be listening, and turned to El'sorath.

'Bring them in,' I said, and watched while Lustig's troopers moved quickly and smoothly to cover the area of lawn next to us. 'It looks safe enough.'

One day, I'm going to learn not to say things like that. No sooner had the words left my lips, and the tau diplomat raised his vox to contact the pilot, than a streak of light rose from the streets beyond the perimeter wall.

'Holy Emperor!' Kasteen breathed, and I spat out something considerably less polite. I snatched the smooth plastic box from an astonished El'sorath.

'Evade!' I screamed, not even sure if the pilot spoke Gothic. Within seconds it was academic anyway. The missile impacted on the underside of the vehicle, punching through the thin metal plating, and exploded in a vivid orange fireball. Flaming debris began to patter down around us, but the burning wreck of the fuselage carried on moving, trailing down to impact harmlessly on one of the wings of the palace. As it struck, tearing through the walls, it set off a secondary explosion, probably the fuel or the powercells. The noise was incredible, making us flinch almost as though it were a physical thing, and I was blinking the afterimages clear of my retina for some moments to follow.

'What happened?' Donali stared in bewilderment, as screaming figures erupted from what was left of the palace.

'More gue'la treachery!' El'hassai screamed, glaring around as though he expected us to turn on him any second now. To tell the truth, it was getting more and more tempting every time he opened his mouth, but that wasn't going to get my skin out of here intact. My best chance of doing that depended on keeping Donali and the xenos sweet.

'I'm inclined to agree,' I said, shutting him up through sheer astonishment. 'It seems our assassin has confederates in the PDF.'

'How can you be sure?' Donali asked, clearly not wanting to believe it.

'That was a krak missile,' Kasteen explained. 'We're the only Guard unit in the city, and we didn't fire it. Who else does that leave?'

Well, too many possibilities for my liking, but there wasn't time to go into that now. I cut into the tactical net, using my commissarial override code.

'Krak missile fired in the vicinity of the governor's palace,' I snapped. 'Who's responsible?'

'I'm sorry, commissar, that information isn't available.'

'Then find out, and have the brainless frakker shot!' I was suddenly aware that my voice had risen. Kasteen, Donali, and the little group of tau were staring at me, their faces flickering yellow in the light of the burning palace. I hesitated, more considered courses of action beginning to suggest themselves. 'No, wait,' I corrected myself, to the evident relief of the unseen vox operator. 'Have everyone in that squad arrested and held for interrogation.' I bounced off Donali's questioning look.

'We don't know yet if it was someone panicking, a deliberate attack on the surviving tau, or just sheer stupidity,' I explained. 'But if it was an attempt to finish what the assassin started, it might lead us to the conspirators.'

'If you are able to identify the assailants.' El'sorath nodded, the human gesture strangely unsettling.

'If it is a conspiracy they'll have covered their tracks,' Donali predicted gloomily. 'But I suppose it's worth a try.'

'What I don't understand,' Kasteen said, frowning, 'is why they didn't wait until the aircar took off again. Surely if they wanted to kill the other tau, downing it on the run in was pointless.'

'No, colonel. It was exactly the point.' Sudden realisation hit me like a punch to the gut. One thing to be said for being paranoid is that sometimes you begin to see patterns no one else can. 'Killing the ambassador was meant to make them run. The mobs in the streets were meant to leave them with nowhere to go. They're supposed to have only one option now.'

'Call in their military to extract them.' She nodded, following my chain of reasoning. Donali put the last link in place.

'Bringing them into direct conflict with Imperial forces. The one thing we can't allow to happen if we're to have any hope of avoiding a full-scale war over this miserable mudball.'

'Then we must die.' El'sorath said, as though he'd been suggesting a stroll through the park. 'The greater good demands it.' His companions looked sober, but none of them argued.

'No.' Donali did, though; he wasn't about to have any little blue martyrs offing themselves on his watch. 'It demands that you live, to continue the negotiations in good faith.'

'That would be preferable,' El'sorath said. I was beginning to suspect that the tau had a sense of humour. 'But I see no way to effect so desirable an outcome.'

'Colonel. Commissar.' Donali looked at Kasteen and me a moment after a sudden sinking feeling in my gut warned me that this was about to happen. 'You have a vehicle, and a squad of soldiers. Will you try and get these people home?' For a moment, I struggled with the idea of the xenos as people. I suppose Donali's diplomatic training made him think a little differently from the rest of us[1], but I couldn't think of an excuse to refuse, try as I might. 'Not just for the good of the planet. For the Emperor Himself.'

Well, I'd pulled that one on enough people in my time to be aware of the irony, but it was an appeal I couldn't turn my back on without sacrificing my hard-won reputation, and even though I'd be the first to admit it's completely undeserved, it's proven its worth to me far too often to be casually discarded.

Besides, however unhealthy trying to smuggle a truck full of xenos through a city in flames was likely to be, staying here to be caught in the crossfire between rioters and the PDF looked like being a whole lot worse. So I smiled my best heroic smile, and nodded.

'Of course,' I said. 'You can count on us.'

---

1. *'Going xeno,' as it's colloquially known, is an occupational hazard among diplomats who spend a lot of time in contact with an alien culture. The prolonged immersion in a foreign mindset sometimes leads them to identify closely with the beings they're negotiating with. In this case, however, it seems clear that Donali was just being polite.*

Editorial Note:

Once again, as we might expect, Cain's account of this crucial night's events is completely self-centred and lacking in any wider perspective. I've therefore taken the liberty of inserting another extract from Logar's history of the Gravalax incident, which, like the one quoted earlier, provides a moderately accurate summary of the overall situation despite his manifest shortcomings as a historian in almost every other respect. Hopefully it may prove useful in placing Cain's narrative into some kind of context.

From *Purge the Guilty! An impartial account of the liberation of Gravalax,* by Stententious Logar. 085.M42

With the advantage of hindsight, we can see how the conspirators had prepared the ground carefully for their coup d'etat, spreading rumours of the assassination so far in advance of its execution that few, if any, thought to demand proof of these claims when the deed was actually accomplished. Tension between the loyal subjects of His Divine Majesty and the turncoat dupes of the alien interlopers had by now become so pervasive that only the tiniest spark was needed to ignite an inferno of lawlessness which threw the entire city into disarray.

The greatest bloodshed of the night was to occur around the governor's residence, as the heroic palace guard held off a rampaging mob of turncoats with the aid of the most loyal cadre of PDF volunteers. Despite the appalling losses they endured, which were exacerbated by the treacherous defection of those perfidious PDF units who turned their weapons against their erstwhile comrades, these brave souls were able to hold out until daybreak brought relief in the shape of a loyalist armoured unit.

By the cruellest stroke of irony, it was later to transpire that one of the guests at the governor's reception earlier that evening had been none other than Commissar Cain, the paladin of martial virtues against whom no enemy could possibly have prevailed, but he had left shortly before the fighting broke out. This was a tragedy indeed, since his inspiring leadership would surely have turned the tide of battle, routing the unrighteous in short order! But alas, it was not to be, and those gallant warriors were left to their own, far from inconsiderable, resources.

Elsewhere, the situation proved equally grave. Widespread rioting choked the city centre, overwhelming the Arbites units posted there, until they had no option but to call in PDF units for support. Some responded loyally, while others, perfidious as their fellow traitors in the Old Quarter, revealed their true colours, turning against all that they had professed to hold dear, the insidious influence of the alien corrupting them utterly. Small wonder, then, that ordinary citizens took to the streets in their thousands, incensed at the sheer magnitude of this betrayal, armed only with their faith in the Emperor and such makeshift weapons as they could lay their hands on to wreak bloody revenge on the traitors in their midst.

The worst of the fighting took place in the Old Quarter, as we have previously noted, and, predictably, in the Heights, the most poisonous nest of pro-alien sentiment in the city, but in truth, no street was safe.

As the unrest continued, one question was paramount. Where were the Guard? Why did the Emperor's finest continue to sit in their barracks and staging areas while his loyal subjects bled and died in his name?

It was, and still is, clear that some hidden cabal was directing events, hindering the decisive action the situation manifestly called for, in pursuit of their own selfish agenda. In the years since, many theories have been put forward as to the true identities of those responsible, the vast majority of them laughably paranoid, but a careful sifting of the evidence can lead to only one conclusion; the unseen hand behind so much mayhem and treachery is unquestionably that of the rogue traders.

[At this point the narrative diverges, albeit quite amusingly, from anything resembling scholarship, or, indeed, historical accuracy.]

SIX

WELL, I'VE SEEN my share of city fighting over the years, and given my choice of battlefield, an urban area's about the last one I'd pick. The streets channel you into firelanes, every window or doorway can conceal a sniper, and the buildings around you frak up your tactical awareness – if they're not blocking your line of sight they're distorting sounds, the overlapping echoes making it virtually impossible to pinpoint where the enemy fire is coming from. In most cases the best thing you can say for it is that at least there aren't any civilians around to get caught in the crossfire, as by the time the Guard gets sent in they're either dead or have fled from the airstrikes and the artillery bombardments.

Mayoh that night was different. Instead of the piles of rubble I'd nor-mally expect to find in an urban warzone, the buildings were, for the time being at least, intact. (Although the ominous orange glow in the distance suggested that wasn't going to be true for much longer.[1]) And the streets were full. Not bustling, exactly, but by no means deserted either. As the truck gathered pace, we caught sight of civilians running for cover, to join or avoid the swelling groups of shouting rioters who seemed to be congregating at every corner. Some wore the xenoist braids, others symbols of Imperial loyalty. Aquilae were common, of course, and several of the loudest and most militant sported scarlet sashes, like the one which marked my own commissarial authority. Regardless of their nominal allegiance, however, most of the groups we passed were energetically engaged in breaking open the nearest storefronts and looting the contents.

'Not much of an advertisement for the Imperial cause,' Kasteen muttered acidly in my ear. She was crammed in the cab with me, jammed up against the passenger door, as far from Jurgen as she could get. The wind of our passage ruffled her hair, the window wide open. Well, why not? The glass wasn't going to stop a las-bolt anyway, and I was even closer to our pungent driver than she was, so I wasn't about to object.

'Or theirs.' I indicated a mob of scalplocked xenoists running from a burning pawnbroker's, their pockets bulging with currency.

'Must be something to do with the greater greed,' she joked grimly.

As we approached, the xenoists recognised our truck as an Imperial military model and began to shout abuse. A few bottles and other makeshift missiles flew in our direction.

'Over their heads, Lustig,' I ordered. The squad of troopers in the cargo space behind us fired, just low enough to make the troublemakers flinch away from the crackling las-bolts, and they scattered as Jurgen put his foot down.

'Very restrained,' Kasteen commented. I shrugged. I couldn't have given a damn if the troopers had killed the lot of them, to be honest, but I was trying to make a good impression on our little blue guests, and there was always that reputation to consider.

We'd left the governor's palace as soon as we could get the tau aboard the truck, scrambling over the tailgate in the flickering light from the burning building. Lustig's squad split into teams again, five on each side, leaving the xeno diplomats in the middle. It wasn't exactly high security, but it was the best we could do under the circumstances, and I hoped it would be enough.

---

1. *Since Cain was already aware of the fire at the governor's palace, which eventually rased approximately two-thirds of the structure, he must have noticed one of the many smaller fires which broke out across the city that night. Despite his apprehension, few of them spread very far, and much of the urban infrastructure remained intact, for a short while, at any rate.*

'Good luck, commissar.' Donali's sober tone told me he thought we'd need it as he grasped my hand. I shook it firmly, thankful for the augmetics that prevented the tremors in my bowels from transmitting themselves as far as my fingers, and nodded gravely.

'The Emperor protects,' I intoned with pious hypocrisy, and climbed into the cab. At least with a box of metal and glass around me I was afforded some degree of shelter, and with Kasteen and Jurgen on either side to absorb any incoming fire, I'd be safer there than anywhere else. The Emperor, as I'd noted on more than one occasion, tends to extend his protection more readily to those who take as many precautions as possible for themselves.

Donali stood and watched us leave, silhouetted in the flickering light from the flames, and turned back towards the burning building as he passed out of sight. To my vague surprise, I found myself hoping he survived the night. I don't normally have much time for diplomats, but he struck me as a decent sort, and he seemed to be going to a lot of trouble to keep me from getting shot.

At least in the abstract; preventing a war wasn't going to do me a damn bit of good if some xenoist rioter stove my skull in with a paving slab this evening, so I was alert for any potential threat as we made our way through the troubled city.

'Left here.' Kasteen was guiding Jurgen with the aid of the tactical net, hoping to avoid the worst of the trouble. We passed a couple of street brawls, but the worst of the rioting appeared to be happening elsewhere.

'So far so good,' I said, tempting fate once more, and, typically, fate obliged. As we turned out of the alleyway into one of those broad thoroughfares which had so excited my unease on the journey into the city from the starport, I could see figures up ahead through the windscreen. Metal barrels had been pushed into the roadway, forming the spine of a makeshift barricade, and fires had been set inside a couple of them.

'Roadblock,' Jurgen said unnecessarily, and glanced at me for orders.

'Ease off,' I said, considering the situation. 'No point drawing their fire unless we have to.' Figures were moving slowly towards us, lasguns levelled, silhouetted against the firelight. I squinted, trying to identify them. They wore plain fatigues, of a colour I couldn't quite identify in the yellowish glow, but which looked grey or blue, and light flak armour of an even darker shade[1].

---

1. *Cain's memory might be playing him false here, as the standard uniform colour of the Gravalaxian PDF was actually magenta, with terracotta body armour. On the other hand, he might just have been confused by the firelight affecting his colour perception.*

'PDF,' Kasteen confirmed after a moment listening to the tactical net. 'Loyalist, supporting the Arbites.'

'Thank the Emperor for that,' I said, and voxed Lustig. 'They're friendlies. Apparently.'

'Understood.' The sergeant's voice was calm, picking up on my qualification, and I was pretty sure the troopers would be ready if we turned out to be mistaken. Call me paranoid if you like, and I'll cheerfully admit to it, but I didn't get to an honourable retirement by having a trusting nature.

A single figure was stepping out in front of the truck now, a hand raised, and Jurgen coasted to a halt. I straightened my uniform cap, and tried to look as commissarial as I could manage.

'Who goes there?' He was young, I noticed, his face still pitted with acne scars, and his helmet looked too big for his head. A lieutenant's rank insignia had been painted in the centre of it, clearly visible; typical PDF sloppiness. The last thing you want in a firefight is an obvious sign saying, 'Shoot me, I'm an officer.' But then no one in the PDF ever really expects to go into combat, unless they make the grade the next time the Guard come recruiting, and that hadn't happened on Gravalax in generations.

'Colonel Kasteen, Valhallan 597th. And Commissar Cain.' Kasteen leaned out of the cab window to talk to him. 'Order your men aside.'

'I can't do that.' His jaw took on a stubborn set. 'I'm sorry.'

'Really?' Kasteen looked at him as though she'd just found him on the sole of her boot. 'I was under the impression that a colonel outranks a lieutenant. Isn't that so, commissar?'

'In my experience,' I agreed. I leaned past her to address the young pup directly. 'Or do you do things differently on Gravalax?' He paled visibly as I raked him with the number two glare.

'No, commissar. But I've been ordered not to let anyone past under any circumstances.'

'I think you'll find my authority supersedes any orders you may have been given,' I said confidently. His jaw worked convulsively.

'But the rebels are in control of the next sector,' he said. 'The tau are leaving their enclave–'

'Lies!' El'hassai jumped up on the flatbed behind us, now clearly visible to the young lieutenant and his PDF troopers. I was really beginning to suspect that the hotheaded tau had some sort of death wish, and one I'd be happy to grant if he carried on like this for much longer. 'They remain behind the boundaries we agreed!'

'Bluies!' The lieutenant swung his lasgun up to cover us. Behind the barricade his men did the same. To my intense relief Lustig and his troopers kept their cool, keeping their own weapons lowered, or there would have been blood spilt within a heartbeat. 'What's going on here?'

'You don't have the security clearance to know,' I said calmly, hiding my jangling nerves with the ease of years of practice. 'I'm ordering you in the name of the Commissariat to let us pass.'

'Traitors!' one of the PDF trolls shouted. 'They're xeno-lovers! Probably stole the truck!'

'Check with your superiors,' I said, calmly as before, loosening the laspistol in its holster below the level of the window. 'The Guard liaison office will confirm our identities.'

'Yes.' The young lieutenant nodded, trying to sound resolute, and wavered the barrel of his lasgun between Kasteen and me, unsure of which one of us to threaten. 'We'll do that. Right after you hand over the bluies.'

'String 'em up!' someone else yelled, probably the same idiot who'd shouted before. The tau began to look agitated.

'The xenos are under Imperial Guard protection,' I said levelly, taking heart from his obvious indecision. 'And that means mine. Stand aside in the Emperor's name, or face the consequences.'

I suppose I was to blame for what happened next. I'd got so used to being around Guardsmen, who accepted my authority without question, that it never even occurred to me that the young lieutenant wouldn't back down. But I'd reckoned without the PDF's relative lack of discipline, and the fact that to them a commissar was just another officer in a fancy hat. The fear and respect that normally goes with the uniform just wasn't there so far as they were concerned.

'Sergeant!' the lieutenant turned towards one of the troopers outlined by the firebarrels. 'Arrest these traitors!'

'Lustig,' I said. 'Fire.' Even as I spoke I was levelling the laspistol. The lieutenant's eyes widened for a fraction of a second as he began to turn back to us, the glint of vindictive triumph giving way to a momentary panic, and then half his face was gone as I squeezed the trigger.

I've killed a great many men over the years, so many that I lost count about a century back, and that's not even taking into account the innumerable xenos I've dispatched. And I've barely lost a night's sleep over any of them. It's usually been them or me, and I don't suppose they'd have been unduly troubled if things had gone the other way. But the lieutenant was different – not an enemy, or guilty of a capital crime – just stupid and overeager. Maybe that's why I can still picture his expression so vividly.

The troopers in the back of the truck raised their lasguns, snapping out a burst of rapid fire while the PDF were still in shock. Only a few had time to react, diving for cover as the bolts burst around them, and Jurgen floored the accelerator.

'Warp this!' Kasteen ducked as a lasbolt from the defenders scored the cab door beside her, and drew her bolt pistol.

'Take them all,' I ordered. If there were any survivors, they'd be on the vox net in moments, betraying our position to whoever might be listening, and marking us as a target to be hunted down by either side. I was within my rights, you understand, they'd refused a direct order, which was more than enough reason for any commissar to have done the same, but I couldn't help thinking of the lengths I'd gone to in order to avoid executing the five troopers aboard the *Righteous Wrath* who deserved it far more than these fools had.

No matter. Jurgen floored the accelerator and we burst through the barricade, a tardy PDF trooper falling beneath our wheels with a scream and an unpleasant crunching sound vaguely reminiscent of someone treading hard on a thin wooden box. The first line of barrels scattered like skittles, spinning away across the thoroughfare, clanging into the sides of buildings and inflicting severe dents in the bodywork of the groundcars parked nearby. By the time they stopped moving, most of the men opposing us were already dead. Whatever skills they'd acquired in basic training were pitifully inadequate in the face of veteran troopers who'd fought a hive fleet and survived. A few tried to stand their ground, snapping off hasty and badly aimed shots before the superior marksmanship of the Valhallans blew bloody, self-cauterising craters through heads and body armour. A muffled curse over the vox link told me that one of the troopers had been hit by the ragged return fire, but if she was able to swear like that it couldn't be all that serious.

'Hold on, commissar.' Jurgen gunned the engine, and a jolt bounced through the truck as he knocked one of the burning barrels in the second rank aside. It spilled, blazing promethium spreading across the road behind us, consuming the bodies of the dead.

'Runner.' Kasteen tracked her target with the bolt pistol and fired. A thin trail of smoke connected the barrel with the back of a fleeing PDF man, punching through his body armour, and exploding in a rain of blood and bowel.

'Nice shooting, colonel.' I tapped the combead. 'Lustig?'

'That was the last one, sir,' he said flatly. I could tell how he felt. Gunning down a virtually defenceless ally was hardly the blooding any of us would have chosen for our new regiment. But it had been necessary, I kept telling myself.

'Any casualties?'

'Trooper Penlan caught a ricochet. Just minor flash burns.'

'Glad to hear it,' I said. I hesitated. I needed to say something now, to maintain morale, but for once in my life my glib tongue had deserted me. 'Tell them... Tell them I appreciate what they just did.'

'Yes sir.' There was an unexpected note of sympathy in the sergeant's voice, and I realised that I'd said the right thing after all. They knew what was at stake here as much as I did.

We were silent for a long time after that. There was nothing to say, after all.

I'D HOPED THAT distressing incident would have been enough of a blood price to see our mission through, but of course, I'd reckoned without the insensate mentality of the mob. The divisions between the loyalist and xenoist factions had had generations to fester here, and the animosity ran deep. As we came closer to the tau enclave, we began to see signs of bloody faction fighting that would have looked less out of place in the underhive than the prosperous merchant city we were driving through. Bodies were lying in the streets, or, in a few cases, hung from luminator poles, loyalists and xenoists alike, but most of them were in no condition to determine allegiance, or, for that matter, very much else. Kasteen shook her head.

'Have you ever seen anything like this?' she asked, more in shock than because she expected an answer. To her visible surprise, I nodded.

'Not often.' And then only in the wake of a Chaos incursion or an ork attack. Never inflicted by ordinary citizens on their neighbours. I shuddered, reflecting on how close to the surface of the mundane world such savagery lurked, and how easily everything we fought to defend against it could be swept away if it wasn't for the ceaseless vigilance of the Emperor.

'Disturbance up ahead, commissar,' Jurgen said, easing up on the accelerator again. I peered through the windscreen. A baying mob filled the street, milling around a high wall with a huge bronze gate in the centre of it, blocking the thoroughfare. Even without the distinctive curving architecture I would have been sure we'd reached our destination.

'The perimeter of the tau trading enclave,' El'sorath confirmed when I retuned my combead to his portable vox. 'But gaining entry may prove problematic.'

'Problematic be warped,' I snapped undiplomatically. I hadn't come all this way and shed all that blood to be baulked this close to our goal. 'I'll get you in there if I have to throw you over the wall.'

'I doubt that gue'la muscles are sufficiently well developed,' the tau responded dryly. I'd been right, he did have a sense of humour. 'An alternative strategy would be preferable.'

'I have a plan,' Jurgen offered. I stared at him in surprise. Abstract thinking was never exactly his forte.

'A particularly devious one, no doubt,' I said. He nodded, immune to sarcasm.

'We could go through the gate,' he suggested. Kasteen made a peculiar noise, halfway between a snort and a hiccup.

'We could,' I agreed. 'Except that there's about a thousand rioters between us and it.'

'But they're all xenoists,' Jurgen said. 'So they'll just let us through, won't they?'

Well, they might have done, I thought, if we weren't wearing Imperial Guard uniforms and driving an Imperial Guard truck. But then again...

'Jurgen, you're a genius,' I said, with a little less sarcasm than before. 'Why frak around when the direct approach might work?' I voxed Lustig and El'sorath again. 'Can we get the tau somewhere visible?'

In a moment, the xenos were standing, flanked by the troopers, and El'sorath was hissing away on his vox again. Jurgen slowed the truck to a crawl, and blew the horn loudly to attract the crowd's attention.

A few heads turned in our direction, then more, as a sullen groundswell of hostility began to build. A couple of rockcrete chunks bounced from the windscreen, leaving small starred impact craters in the armourglass. Kasteen wound her side window up, clearly deciding that Jurgen's body odour was better than concussion, at least for a short while.

'Whenever you're ready,' I suggested, thankful I wasn't out in the open in the back of the truck. Maybe this wasn't such a brilliant idea after all, I found myself thinking.

'Please desist, for the greater good.' El'sorath must have had an amplivox function built into his 'caster, because his voice rang out across the crowd. To my amazement they complied, falling silent and parting in front of us. I contrasted it with the response of the crowd in Kasamar,[1] who'd charged our lines with berserk fury as soon as the Arbites commander had tried to address them, and wondered at the degree of influence the tau were able to wield over their supporters and one another.[2]

---

1. *A minor civil insurrection, at which Cain had been present a few years before.*

2. *Still a subject of great interest to the Ordo Xenos, although investigation of this phenomenon remains frustratingly difficult.*

Jurgen rolled the truck to a halt in front of the huge gates, ten metres high and wide as the thoroughfare they blocked, just as they began to swing open. Eerily, they were completely noiseless, or at least so quiet I could hear nothing over the murmur of the crowd and the throbbing of our engine, even after Kasteen and I had disembarked to see our guests safely home. I noticed she breathed deeply once her boot-heels hit the rockcrete.

'What's that?' Lustig's voice crackled in my ear. Something small and fast swooped down from over the wall, heading in our direction, then several more, wheeling and diving like birds.

'Hold your fire,' I said hastily, fighting the urge to draw my own weapon. 'They're still on their side of the line.'

Well, technically, at least. They were still above the slope of the wall, even though they'd passed the crest. I tried to focus on the nearest one, but it was small and fast-moving, and all I got was a vague impression of something resembling a large platter with a rifle slung underneath it.

'A courtesy,' El'sorath assured me, hopping down from the flatbed with remarkable dexterity. 'To ensure your departure goes smoothly.'

Well, there was more than one way to take that, of course, but I chose to interpret it as a guarantee that the crowd would continue to behave themselves.

'Much appreciated,' I assured him, as the rest of the xenos clambered down and began trooping into their enclave. Armed warriors in body armour came forward to meet them, their faces hidden inside blank-visaged helmets. I caught sight of something else moving behind the gate, and turned my head for a better look.

'Dreadnoughts,' Kasteen breathed. They were certainly large enough for that, but they moved with an easy grace far removed from the lumbering war machines I'd encountered before. Their lines were angular, topped off with headpieces which resembled the helmets of their line troopers, but the resemblance ended with their size, towering at least twice the height of an ordinary tau.

'Just battlesuits,' El'sorath said, with a faint trace of amusement. 'Nothing special.'

Kasteen and I glanced at one another. I couldn't make out much detail at this distance, but they were clearly heavily armed, and the idea of facing a foe that fielded such things as a matter of course wasn't exactly comforting. I began to suspect that this was precisely the impression we'd been meant to get.

'I'm sure they're not,' I said, radiating an easy confidence I didn't feel, and enjoying the momentary flicker of doubt in the xeno's eyes.

'Go with your Emperor, Commissar Cain. You have our gratitude,' he said at last, and followed his friends inside. The gates began to swing closed.

'Time we were gone,' I said, hoisting myself back into the cab. Kasteen decided to ride in the back this time. Can't say I blamed her after getting the full benefit of Jurgen, so I suggested the wounded trooper Penlan rode back in the cab with us instead.

'Better safe than sorry,' I said, 'until we get back to the medicae at least.' So, despite her understandable reluctance, I was able to replace my human shield and enhance my reputation for concern about the troopers under my command at the same time.

And we'd succeeded in doing our bit to prevent a full-scale war from breaking out, which was no mean feat, so all in all I could have been forgiven for feeling a little smug as we made our way back to our own staging area. So why, instead, did I keep thinking about the PDF troopers we'd been forced to kill, and wondering whose plans we'd derailed by their sacrifice?

SEVEN

'The gratitude of the powerful is a heavy weight to bear.'
– Gilbran Quail, Collected Essays

DAWN BROKE AT last across the wounded city, columns of smoke cracking the porcelain blue of the sky above the compound as the sun rose higher and ceased to echo the glow from the scattered fires, and my mood remained foul all morning. To my relief, we'd managed to make it back without having to shoot anyone else, apart from a couple of looters who'd been so high on some vicious local pharmaceutical they hadn't even realised the truck they were trying to hijack was full of armed soldiers until after they were dead, and all I wanted was a few hours' sleep. I'd been so pumped full of adrenaline since the assassin's gun went off that, when I finally got the chance to relax, I collapsed like a puppet with its strings cut, and even Jurgen's appearance with a fresh pot of tanna tea hadn't been enough to revive me. Nevertheless I made my report to brigade headquarters as quickly as I could, reasoning that the sooner the whole sorry mess was someone else's problem the better, and after an hour or so of paperwork, crawled away to my bunk with strict orders that I wasn't to be disturbed for anything short of a summons from the Emperor Himself.

In the event, I got about an hour's sleep before the next best thing.

'Frak off!' I shouted, after the knocking on my door had finally become loud and insistent enough to wake me, and had gone on for long enough to convince me that it wasn't going to stop unless I responded in some way.

'I'm sorry to disturb you, commissar.' Broklaw's head appeared round the doorframe, looking remarkably free of regret. 'But I'm afraid I can't. There are some people wanting to see you.'

Tired as I was, I knew there was no point in arguing. The mere fact that it was an officer of his rank rousting me out, instead of Jurgen or some other lowly trooper, told me that. I yawned, trying to force my sluggish brain into gear, and reluctantly rolled out of bed.

'I'll be right there,' I said.

In the event that turned out to be a bit of an optimistic forecast. By the time I'd thrown some clothes on, splashed some water on my face, (and for once, the Valhallan habit of washing in ice water didn't provoke a stream of blasphemy from me, which gives you some idea of how far gone I was) and got Jurgen to brew some double-strength recaf, nearly twenty minutes had passed. But I followed the directions I'd been given, picking my way carefully across the compound (the Rough Riders were still around somewhere) and entered a building I'd vaguely recalled being earmarked for the brigade-level communications specialists. That meant Intelligence, of course, and I assumed I was about to be debriefed about the events of last night by some high-level spook.

If I hadn't been so tired, I would probably have wondered about the number of high-ranking officers in the echoing marble corridors, and the increasing opulence of the furnishings in the succession of anterooms I was waved through by dress-uniformed troopers with gold-plated lasguns, but it all passed in a haze of irritation, and I never thought to question where I was and who had sent for me so peremptorily.

'Commissar. Please, come in.' The voice was familiar, but, dazed as I still was from lack of sleep, it took me a moment to recognise Donali. He smiled what looked like a genuine welcome, and motioned me towards a side table where a fresh pot of tanna tea steamed invitingly next to several large platters of food.

I smiled in return, equally pleased to see him, although his night's adventures had obviously been at least as traumatic as my own. His expensive attire was now crumpled and stained, smelling of smoke and blood, and a dressing patch was stuck to his forehead.

'This is an unexpected pleasure,' I said, spooning a large portion of salma kedgeree onto a plate, and pouring tea into the most capacious mug I could find. 'I must admit I was rather concerned for your safety.'

'You weren't the only one.' Donali fingered the dressing patch rue-fully. 'Things got a little hectic after you left.'

I took a seat at the conference table in the middle of the room. Several officers I didn't recognise were already there, along with other men and women in civilian dress. The latter I assumed to be Donali's colleagues, from the cut of their garments and their general air of bureaucratic prissiness. The only one who stuck out from the crowd was a woman slightly younger than the others, who wore an elegant green gown a couple of sizes too small for her, which showed rather too much décolletage for so early in the day, and who seemed curiously distracted, twitching and mumbling to herself from time to time before snapping upright and glaring round at the rest of us as though we'd somehow insulted her. I'd have taken her for an astropath, if it weren't for the fact that she still had her eyes, which seemed to swim in and out of focus. Probably a psyker, then – I resolved to keep my mental barriers up – but as I've remarked before, I've never had much trouble dissembling in front of them despite their curse.

'Sorry I missed all the fun,' I said, playing up to the audience's expectations of me, and started in on the food. I still had no idea why I was here, but I was a seasoned enough campaigner to make the most of the rations while they were on offer. While I plied my fork, I took the opportunity to study the officers' insignia, hoping for some clue as to their identities and why I was there, and found them a mixed bunch indeed.

My gaze swept across a couple of majors, a colonel, and as I got my first good look at the man seated at the head of the table, I almost dropped my cutlery. This could only be Lord General Zyvan himself, the supreme commander of our little expedition. I hadn't seen any pictures of him, but his rank and campaign medals were clearly visible, and I'd heard enough descriptions of his steely blue eyes (actually slightly watery) and neatly trimmed beard (concealing the beginnings of a double chin) to have no doubt as to his identity. He was half turned away from me, discussing the contents of a dataslate with an aide, and Donali was able to continue our conversation as he dropped into the seat beside me.

'Don't be,' he said. 'You did us a far greater service last night than you could possibly have done by staying.'

'I'm glad to hear it,' I said. 'But you seem to have managed all right. The palace guard must be better soldiers than they look.'

'Hardly.' He shook his head in disgust. 'Half of those antique weapons of theirs malfunctioned, and the ones who did shoot couldn't hit the side of a starship. We barely held out until the PDF platoon arrived. If it hadn't been for Orelius and his bodyguards picking off the ringleaders, the mob would have rolled right over us.'

'Orelius. Hm.' I took a welcome sip of the tea, and noticed that no one else seemed to be drinking it. Well, it's an acquired taste, I admit, I'm one of the few non-Valhallans I know who likes the stuff, but the implication was flattering; they'd clearly provided it for my personal benefit. Whatever I'd been called here for they wanted to keep me happy, which was fine by me. 'You were right about him, obviously.'

'I was?' Donali looked at me curiously, and again I felt he was playing some subtle diplomatic game. Trying to gauge how much I'd surmised of what was going on behind the scenes, I supposed. I nodded, clearing the plate, and wondered if I could get away with going back for another portion.

'You said there was more to him than met the eye,' I reminded him.

'So I did.' He might have been about to say more, but Zyvan turned back to the conference table and cleared his throat. Blast, I thought, there goes my chance at a second helping of kedgeree. There was still plenty of tea in the mug, though, so I sipped at it, regarding the room through a haze of pleasantly scented steam.

'Commissar.' Zyvan addressed me directly. 'Thank you for joining us so promptly.'

'My lord general.' I nodded a formal greeting. 'If I'd known your chef was so talented I would have been even less tardy,' I added, enjoying the sudden intake of breath from around half those present. A commissar, of course, is outside the normal chain of command, so technically I didn't have to show deference to him or to anyone else, but most of us do our best not to remind the officers around us of the fact. As I like to tell my cadets these days, treat them with respect and they'll do the same to you. All frak, of course, but it greases the wheels. My status as a widely acknowledged hero allows me a bit more latitude, though, and I knew Zyvan had a reputation for bluntness himself, so I felt a bit of the bluff old soldier routine would go down well with him. I was right, too. He warmed to me at once, and we got on like a downhive bar brawl after that.

'I'll pass on your compliments,' he said with a half-smile, and the sycophants around the table decided they ought to like me too. 'If you'd care to avail yourself further before we proceed?'

'Proceed with what, exactly?' I asked, moving to refill my plate. I'd forgotten to take my mug with me, so I took the teapot back to the table and topped it up there, keeping it beside me in case I wanted another refill. Partly, I admit, for the pleasure of upsetting some of the bootlickers again. 'Anyone else, while I'm up?'

'Thank you, no.' Zyvan waited until I'd sat down again before deciding he'd like some more recaf after all, and dispatching the most disapproving-looking of his aides to deal with it. As he did so his eye caught mine, and the gleam of mischief in it was unmistakable. I decided I liked the lord general.

'I've been reading your report,' he said, once his recaf had arrived. 'And I think I speak for everyone here when I say that I'm impressed.' A chorus of mumbled assent rippled around the table, not all of it grudging. Donali smiled warmly at me as he nodded, and I reflected that I seemed to have found a friend in the diplomatic corps, which could be very useful in future. The strange woman in green met my eyes for a moment.

'Choose your friends carefully,' she said suddenly, her voice harsh with flattened vowels. I almost choked on my tea.

'I beg your pardon?' I said. But her gaze was already unfocussed again.

'There's too many out there,' she said. 'I can't hear them all.' One of the bureaucrats handed her an ornate silver box, a little smaller than her palm, and she scrabbled a couple of tablets out of it, swallowing them whole. After a moment her attention seemed to sharpen again.

'You'll have to make allowances for Rakel,' Donali murmured. 'She's useful, but can be a little difficult.'

'Evidently,' I replied.

'Not quite the envoy I would have chosen to send to this little get-together,' the diplomat went on, 'but under the circumstances I suppose they needed her talents the least at the moment.'

'Who did?' I asked, but before he could reply Zyvan called the meeting to order.

'Most of you know why we're here,' he began, with a sip at his recaf. 'But for those of you who are new to these discussions,' and he acknowledged me with a conspiratorial quirk of his mouth, 'let me reiterate. Our orders were to reclaim Gravalax for the Imperium, by force of arms if necessary.' The military officers harrumphed approvingly. 'However, the sheer size of the tau military presence here changes the situation radically.'

'We can still throw them out, my lord general.' One of the officers cut in. 'It would take longer than we'd anticipated, but–'

'We would end up mired in a protracted campaign. Maybe for years.' Zyvan cut him off dismissively. 'And, to be blunt, I doubt the planet is worth it.'

'With respect, lord general, that isn't your decision to make,' the officer persisted. 'Our orders are–'

'For me to interpret,' Zyvan said. The officer shut up, and the general turned to Donali. 'You still believe a diplomatic solution is possible?'

'I do.' Donali nodded. 'Although, with the civil unrest persisting, it may prove more difficult. Not to mention the matter of the ambassador's assassination.'

'But the tau are still willing to negotiate?' Zyvan persisted.

'They are.' Donali nodded again. 'Thanks to Commissar Cain's resourcefulness last night, we still have a residue of good faith to draw on.'

Everyone but Rakel, who seemed more interested in the underside of her recaf cup, looked approvingly at me.

'Which brings me to the assassination itself.' Zyvan tried to attract the woman's attention. 'Rakel. Has the inquisitor made any progress in the investigation?'

I suppose I should have expected it, especially after my suspicions about Orelius the previous night, but I'd still been half inclined to dismiss them as the result of Divas and his drunken fantasies getting lodged somewhere in my brain. I stared at Donali.

'You knew about this?' I murmured.

'I suspected,' he replied, sotto voce. 'But I didn't know for sure until Rakel turned up this morning with a message bearing the inquisitorial seal.'

'What did it say?' I whispered, ignoring the young psyker's attempts to reply. Donali shrugged.

'How should I know? It was addressed to the lord general.'

'The investigation continues. Yes.' Rakel nodded eagerly, forcing herself to concentrate with a visible effort, her flat, nasal voice grating against my sleep-deprived nerves. 'You will be informed. When the conspiracy is exposed.' She paused, cocking her head as though listening to something, and stood abruptly. 'Have you got cake?' She wandered over to the food table to check.

'I see.' Zyvan tried to look as though she'd made some kind of sense.

'If I may, lord general.' I spoke up, trying to sound confident. 'I suspect that there may be a faction here with an interest in provoking conflict between us and the tau.'

'So messire Donali informs me.' Zyvan seized the opportunity to return the meeting to business with barely concealed relief. 'Which is the main reason I invited you to join us. Your reasoning appears sound.'

'No cake. No frakking cake!' Rakel muttered in the background, scuffling around the food table. 'I can't eat that, it's too green...'

'Thank you.' I acknowledged the compliment, and tried to ignore her.

'Does it extend as far as to who might be responsible?' Zyvan asked. I shook my head.

'I'm a soldier, sir. Plots and intrigue aren't really my specialties.' I shrugged. 'Perhaps the inquisitor can enlighten us when his enquiries are complete.'

'Perhaps.' Zyvan looked a little disappointed, no doubt hoping I could have helped him to second-guess the inquisition. Rakel returned to her seat, clutching a cyna bun, which she proceeded to nibble at for the rest of the meeting; at least with her mouth full she kept quiet.

'The other reason I wanted to consult you, commissar, is that you've met Governor Grice. What's your assessment of his understanding of military matters?' I shrugged.

'About as good as his understanding of anything else, if I'm any judge. The man's an imbecile.' More indrawn breaths around the table, but Zyvan and Donali nodded their agreement.

'I thought as much,' the lord general said. 'Although you'll no doubt be gratified to hear that he was very impressed with you.'

'He was?' I couldn't imagine why, until Donali spoke.

'After all, you did save his life last night.'

'I suppose I did,' I said. 'I hadn't really thought about it.' Which was perfectly true; I'd disarmed the tau to save my own skin, and so much had happened since then it had driven almost everything else out of my mind. Luckily, this was exactly the sort of thing everyone expected me to say, so I had the unexpected pleasure of receiving a warm smile of approval from one of the most powerful men in the Segmentum. Of course, that would come back to haunt me in time, which only goes to prove that no good deed ever goes unpunished.[1]

'Well, he's been thinking about you,' Donali said. 'He wants to give you some sort of medal.[2]'

'That may have to wait,' Zyvan said. 'We've a more urgent problem to deal with right now.' He touched a control stud on the arm of his chair, and the surface of the table lit up from within, proving to be a hololithic display of a size and resolution I'd seldom seen before. If I'd realised, I'd have been a bit more careful with the teapot. I wiped the ring of beverage away with my handkerchief as the image flickered drunkenly in the air before me, finally steadying into decipherability as Zyvan leaned forward and banged the tabletop hard with a clenched

---

1. *From this point on Zyvan took a personal interest in Cain's career, eventually appointing him to his personal staff. This in turn led to a number of life-threatening incidents which are recorded elsewhere in the archive.*

2. *The Order of Merit of Gravalax, second class. In later years Cain was to joke that if he'd let the tau shoot Grice after all, the grateful populace would probably have given him the first class decoration.*

fist. He must have spent considerable time with the techpriests, because it functioned perfectly after that, staying sharp and in focus more than half the time.

'That's the city,' I said, stating the obvious. Rakel nodded, spraying crumbs across the image like block-sized meteors.

'All the little people look like ants,' she said, resting her head on the tabletop. The scale was far too small to show individual people, of course, or vehicles, even ones the size of a Baneblade, but she was bonkers, after all. 'Scurry, scurry, scurry. Looking up when they should be looking down. You never know what's under your feet, but you should, 'cause you could trip up and fall.'

I ignored her, picking out the salient tactical information with the instinctive ease of years of practice.

'There's still fighting going on.' I could see a handful of hotspots across the city. 'Haven't the Arbites managed to restore order yet?'

'Up to a point.' Zyvan shrugged. 'Most of the civilian rioters have either been arrested, shot, or got bored and gone home. The big problem now is the rebel PDF units.'

'Can't the loyalists sort them out?' I asked. It seemed obvious from where we were sitting that the xenoists were outnumbered at least three to one in most cases. Zyvan looked disgusted.

'You'd think so. But they're bogging down. Half of them are refusing to fire on their own comrades, and the rest might just as well not be bothering for all the good they're doing.' He hesitated. 'So the governor has, in his infinite wisdom, petitioned the Guard to go in and clean up his mess for him.'

'But you can't!' Donali was aghast. 'If the guard mobilise in the city the tau will too! You'll spark the very war we're trying to prevent!'

'That hadn't escaped my notice,' Zyvan said dryly.

'The man's a cretin!' Donali was fuming. 'Can't he see the consequences of his actions?'

'He's panicking,' I said. 'All he can see now is the prospect of the rebellion spreading. If the xenoists in the general population join them–'

'We're frakked,' Donali said.

'Not quite.' Zyvan compressed his lips into a grim parody of a smile. 'I can still play for time. Briefly. Can you use it to convince the tau that any Guard deployment in the city is no threat to them?'

'I can try,' Donali said, without much enthusiasm. Zyvan nodded encouragingly.

'I can't ask for more than that.' He turned to me. 'Commissar. Would you say that the tau have reason to trust you?'

Well of course they didn't, but that wasn't what he wanted to hear, so I nodded judiciously.

'More than most other Imperial officers, I suppose. I did save them a bit of a walk last night.' As I'd expected, my modest joking at my own expense went down well, fitting these idiots' idea of a hero. Zyvan looked pleased.

'Good,' he said, and turned back to Donali. 'You can inform the tau that Commissar Cain will be overseeing the operation personally. That might allay their concerns.'

'It just might.' Donali looked a little happier at the prospect. Which is more than I was, you can be sure. After all I'd been through the night before, the prospect of being sent back to the firing line again was agonising.

But I was supposed to be a hero after all, so I sat there impassively sipping tea, and wondered how I was going to get out of this one.

EIGHT

'Inquisitors? They're sneaky bastards. Useful, yes, even necessary, but I wouldn't buy a used aircar from any of them.'

– Arbitrator General Bex van Sturm

IN THE END, of course, I had no choice but to go along with it. The lord general himself had picked me for this mission, so all I could do was hope for the best and prepare for the worst. Fortunately, Donali's negotiations with the tau gave me a bit of a breathing space, and I was able to devise a plan of action which gave everyone the impression of leading from the front while staying sufficiently far back from the firing line to appreciate the full tactical overview. Kasteen and Broklaw had been fired with enthusiasm as soon as I took them into my confidence, certain that the lord general's special interest in me boded well for the future of the regiment, so I was able to let them take the lead without really seeming to. Between us, we'd come up with a plan which actually looked like it might work, at least, if the bluies (as the troopers had begun to refer to the tau, picking up on the local slang) could be persuaded not to take our incursion into the city in bad faith. That, of course, was a question only the Emperor could answer, and he was otherwise engaged, so I just thumbed my palm[1] and got on with the things I could do something about.

Even then, I couldn't quite shake the suspicion that we were overlooking something important, that whatever shadowy cabal was trying to ignite a full-scale war on this worthless mudball wasn't about to give up that easily, but thinking about it only worried me, so I tried to forget it. For the life of me I couldn't see what anyone could hope to gain by forcing a confrontation, and unless you know what your enemies are after, you can't devise any countermeasures to their plans. I don't mind admitting that it irked me a little. I'm used to my innate paranoia keeping me a jump ahead of most things, but even Chaos cultists generally have an agenda of sorts (even if it's just 'kill everything on the planet') which makes itself obvious after a while. Still, that's what we have inquisitors for, so I wished Orelius the best of Imperial luck and gave up thinking about it in favour of the best way to give the rebellious PDF units a bloody nose. This was just as well, I suppose. If I'd had a clue as to what was really going on I'd have lost even more sleep, believe me.

'They couldn't be making it easier for us if they tried,' Broklaw said with some satisfaction as he looked at the hololith. I'd prevailed on the lord general to lend us the conference suite he'd summoned me to before, citing the need to co-ordinate the input of more than one regiment, and Broklaw was as pleased with the tabletop display unit as a juvie with his first set of toy soldiers. I half expected to find it smuggled aboard the troopship when we departed. He gestured at the disposition of the xenoist units. 'What's that phrase you artillerists use? Cluster-frag?'

'Close enough.' Colonel Mostrue of the 12th Field Artillery nodded curtly, his ice blue eyes, as always, regarding me with something akin to suspicion. Throughout my posting to his unit he'd always tried to give me the benefit of the doubt, but of all the battery officers I've come across, he'd come closest to guessing the truth about Desolatia, and never quite seemed to trust me after that. Which was extremely sensible of him when you think about it. Certainly, he'd responded with almost indecent haste on the few occasions I'd been forced to call in a barrage close to my own position, but, in turn, I'd preferred to think he was just doing his job as efficiently as possible. He hadn't changed a bit

---

1. *A gesture used on many worlds in the segmentum to bring good luck or ward off misfortune. The thumb is pressed into the palm of the hand, leaving the fingers to form a stylised aquila wing.*

in the years since I'd seen him last, unlike the visible marks the passing of time had left in Divas. The major was with him too, still limping slightly after our brawl with the xenoist supporters a week or so ago, and grinned at me with the same unrestrained enthusiasm he always displayed.

'It'll be like shooting fish in a barrel,' he declared confidently.

'For you, maybe,' Kasteen said. 'But we'll be where the fish can shoot back.' The xenoists were lightly armed, for the most part, with nothing much stronger in terms of firepower than missile launchers, so the artillery unit wouldn't have to worry about return fire, but unfortunately they'd had enough sense to dig in, for the most part in the area around the Heights. That meant winkling the survivors of the barrage out building by building, which would be hard, bloody work if things didn't go well. Fortunately, Kasteen and Broklaw's experience of urban fighting was just what was needed here, and I hoped the men and women of the 597th would find the PDF defectors easy meat after the tyranids they'd faced on Corania.

'We'll keep their heads down for you,' Divas promised. 'All you'll need to clean them up afterwards is a mop.' Kasteen and Broklaw exchanged glances, but let it go. Divas might have had only the vaguest idea of what city fighting entailed, but he did know his artillery, and I'd spent enough time with his unit to understand his confidence. The xenoist defectors had gradually linked up as they pulled back to the Heights, packing tighter and tighter into the network of boulevards and parkland around the mansions, until they might just as well have been standing there with a big target painted around their perimeter.

'It's all a little too neat for me,' I said. 'You'd think they'd have had the sense to disperse.'

'Amateurs.' Mostrue's contempt was obvious. Like most senior guard officers, he had a low opinion of the majority of PDF regiments, although I'd come across a few in my time who could have given a Guard unit a run for their money. In this case, though, his opinion seemed more than justified. A heavy barrage would take out the majority, I had no doubt. Of course, the survivors would be well dug in and hard to shift, especially with all that fresh rubble to burrow into, but I couldn't see there being too many of them. Certainly nothing the 597th couldn't handle in pretty short order.

Even allowing for the defectors' lack of experience, though, it seemed remarkably stupid of them to offer so tempting a target, and the tingling sensation was back in my palms. I tried to concentrate on the briefing, and not think about the undercurrents of conspiracy I was sure Orelius was tracking down even as we sat here. I had hoped to set my mind at rest by interrogating the PDF idiots who'd shot down the tau aircar, and determining once and for all whether it had been a simple act of stupidity or part of a more sinister agenda, but despite my order to arrest them, the perpetrators had simply vanished. Or joined the defectors, which raised even more questions I wasn't sure I wanted the answers to.

'What do you make of this?' Broklaw asked, studying the display more closely. I followed the line of his finger, to where a platoon of loyalist PDF troopers had cordoned off a couple of blocks of an industrial zone near the Old Quarter, and shrugged.

'The local boys afraid to get their fingers dirty.' The icon at the centre of the cordon marked a hostile contact, but they didn't seem to be in any hurry to close the noose. Presumably some stragglers, too late to join the exodus to the Heights, I thought. That was followed by the sudden realisation that I could use this little anomaly to my advantage.

'I'll swing by and see if I can buck their ideas up,' I said. 'It's not far out of our way.' And by the time I'd finished the extra piece of makework I'd just found for myself, Kasteen and Broklaw should have the xenoist survivors pretty much dealt with. If all went well, most of the dust would have settled before I got anywhere near the firing line. It seemed my luck hadn't deserted me after all.

'Are you sure, commissar?' Kasteen was looking at me curiously, and that old expression was back in Mostrue's eyes. 'It doesn't seem all that important. Surely it can wait until we've dealt with the main force?'

'It probably can.' I shrugged. 'But the lord general himself is trusting me to clean up this mess. I don't want a nucleus of rebellion left to deal with after we've broken the back of the conspiracy. I'd feel a lot happier if we knew for sure they weren't going to break out before we can get to them.'

'Good point.' She nodded. I decided it was time to lighten the mood, and smiled.

'Besides,' I said, 'It's not as though any of you need your hands held. I think you know one end of a lasgun from another by now.'

Kasteen, Broklaw and Divas laughed, and Mostrue essayed a wintery grin.

'I'd rather not divide our force, though,' Kasteen added. 'If we're going to mop up the bluie-lov... The xenoist sympathisers, I want to keep our net tight.'

'Agreed,' I said. 'We'll stick to the timetable. I'll just peel off, put the fear of the Emperor into the PDF drones guarding the perimeter to make sure none of the rebels inside escape while we're busy, and catch up. I should be back with you before the fun begins.'

'I'd put money on it.' Kasteen smiled. 'I've seen the way Jurgen drives.'

She would have lost the bet, of course. I was going to make damn sure I got delayed sorting out the PDF rabble until after the shooting stopped. That was the plan, anyway. If I'd known what I was letting myself in for as a result of that little diversion, I'd have led the charge into the Heights in a heartbeat.

DONALI FINALLY CONTACTED us about an hour after noon, saying the tau weren't exactly happy at the prospect of Imperial Guard units running rampant in the city, but so long as I was there to keep an eye on things and we stuck to the plan they'd been shown, they'd let us get on with it without interference. Of course, the language was a bit more diplomatic than that, but you get the gist. I was also aware of the subtext, even before Donali helpfully spelled it out for me, that if they got so much as a sniff of treachery they'd be on our backs with guns blazing before you could say 'fubar'.

So as you can imagine, I was feeling somewhat under pressure as the force of which I was titular head left our compound and entered the city, so much so that I wasn't even able to enjoy the unique position I found myself in.[1]

As I said before, I'd had the sense to let Kasteen and Broklaw make the tactical decisions, as their experience of city fighting was rather more practical than mine, so I was pretty confident we had the right mix of resources to achieve our goal. Reasoning that the ground would be pretty chewed up by the time the artillery had finished (which I could attest to from personal experience after my time with the 12th), they'd suggested going in on foot, with a troop of Sentinels for heavy fire support. That sounded good to me, as the walkers would have a devastating psychological effect on the shell-shocked survivors of the barrage, or, at least, I hoped so. Taking the Chimeras in close was right out, their tracks would be shredded in moments once they entered the rubble, but if they held back on the perimeter after debarking their troopers, their heavy bolters would certainly encourage any rebels still inclined to make a fight of it to keep their heads down.

---

1. *Cain is mistaken in his assumption that his position was unique. It was by no means unprecedented for a commissar to be given direct command of an ad hoc task force when circumstances demanded it, although it was, and is, an extremely rare occurrence. In fact, there is at least one instance on record of a commissar being given overall command of an entire regiment for a period of several years; albeit with the dual rank of colonel to facilitate the paperwork.*

We'd debated about bringing in an armoured unit too, but decided against it. A couple of Leman Russes would have made little difference against dug-in infantry, especially after Mostrue's Earthshakers had finished doing their stuff. And it would have meant bringing another regiment into the operation. Given the delicacy of the situation, I wanted to keep the opportunities for fouling things up to a minimum, and my paranoia was tingling again, warning me not to spread our plans any further than we needed to. Besides, tanks would have slowed us down, and the key to this operation was speed. Especially if I wanted it to be all but over by the time I arrived.

'The harder and faster you go in, the better,' I concluded my briefing speech, breaking off to glare at Sulla, who'd whispered something to her neighbour and giggled. 'Are there any questions?'

There weren't, which meant the plan was either brilliant or so fatally flawed no one could spot it, so I made one of the standard encouraging speeches I'd been trotting out by rote since the head of my old scholar had presented me with my scarlet sash and told me to get lost, and dismissed the sergeants and officers who started to trickle back to their squads. I caught Lustig's eye, and he grinned at me. I'd made sure his squad were assigned to the centre of the battle line, as I thought getting stuck into a proper stand-up fight would be good for their morale. Gunning down the PDF loyalists had left a sour taste in their mouths, I knew, although they were good enough soldiers to have appreciated the reasons for it. A couple had been to talk to the chaplain, but all in all, they'd held up remarkably well. I knew if they were left with time to brood on it, though, their morale might start to suffer, so it had seemed prudent to take steps quickly before the rot had a chance to spread.

'I take it you approve, sergeant,' I said. One of the most important things I'd found over the years, and which I try to instil in my cadets these days, is that you should always take the time to talk to the troopers as individuals. You'll never make friends of them, except possibly a couple of the officers if you're lucky, and you'll never get the job done if you try, but they'll follow you a damn sight more readily if they think you care about them. And what's far more important, at least to me, is that, if they start to think of you as one of their own, they'll watch your back when the shooting starts. I've lost count of the number of times one of the grunts around me has taken out a xeno or a traitor who would have put a round in my back before I even noticed them, and I've returned the favour, too, which is why I'm well into my second century while the graveyards are full of by-the-book commissars who relied on intimidation to get the job done.

'It's a good plan, sir.' Lustig nodded. 'My boys and girls won't let you down.'

'I'm sure of that,' I said. 'I wouldn't have asked for them otherwise.' A faint flush of pride worked its way up past his jaw line.

'I'll tell them you said that, sir.'

'Please do.' I returned his salute, and looked around for Jurgen as Lustig strode off, his shoulders set. There shouldn't be any morale problems with his squad now, I thought. My aide was nowhere to be seen, so I walked towards the door, past the row of chairs where more than a dozen officers and noncoms had been sitting a few moments before. If I knew Jurgen, he'd be in the vehicle park, conscientiously checking over our Salamander.

'Commissar.' I turned, momentarily startled by the voice at my elbow. Sulla was still seated, her face flushed with uncharacteristic nervousness. She juggled the briefing slate in her lap.

'You have a question, lieutenant?' I asked, keeping my voice neutral. She nodded rapidly, swallowing a couple of times.

'Not exactly. Sort of...' She stood, the top of her head level with my eyes, and tilted it back slightly to speak directly to me. 'I just wanted to say...' She hesitated again, then blurted it out in a rush. 'I know you haven't formed a very high opinion of me since you joined us, but I appreciate you giving me a chance. You won't regret it, I promise you.'

'I'm sure I won't.' I smiled, a warm expression calculated to boost her confidence. 'Your platoon was my first choice for this mission, because I know they can get the job done.' In truth, it was Lustig's squad I wanted, for the reasons I've already gone into, and the rest of the platoon just came along with them. But she didn't have to know that. 'Integrating the two old regiments into a new unit has been tough on everyone, especially those of you who were thrust into positions of responsibility you weren't prepared for. I think you've coped admirably.'

'Thank you, commissar.' She coloured visibly, and trotted out with a slightly uncoordinated salute.

Well, that was an unexpected bonus. If I was any judge, she'd be so keen to justify my non-existent confidence in her that she wouldn't be making any more trouble, at least for a while. Despite the prospect of imminent combat, there was a definite spring in my step as I went to find Jurgen.

THE FIRST PART of the plan went like clockwork. We formed up in the main vehicle park, two full platoons, which I thought would be enough for the job, plus the Sentinels, which hissed and clanked their way over the rockcrete to join us like vast robotic chickens. And if you think they look ungainly, try hitching a lift on one some time. I've been in boats in a storm and felt less motion sick. Mind you, when the alternative is being ripped apart by orks, I'll take an upset stomach any time. If you think that sounds a little on the puny side, remember the xenoists only numbered about a dozen squads themselves, so we had them pretty well outnumbered even so, and given the delicacy of the diplomatic situation, I didn't want to go in with any more troopers than we needed. Besides, I was counting on the artillery barrage to take most of them out, so the firepower we had seemed more than enough for mopping up with.

And before you ask, yes, I suppose dropping shells on a part of the city we'd been sent to protect did seem a little paradoxical to us at the time, but it was all a question of expediency. To my way of thinking, anyone still in the target area was there by choice, and any civilians who hadn't fled were either traitors themselves or so stupid we were doing future generations a favour by removing them from the gene pool.

I mounted the command Salamander Jurgen had procured and looked out over our expeditionary force, feeling a surge of pride in spite of my obvious trepidation. The infantry squads were mounted in Chimeras, the two platoon command ones standing out from the rest by virtue of the vox antennae that clustered their upper surfaces. Sulla's head and shoulders protruded from the top hatch of hers, a pair of earphones protecting her from the engine noise. Seeing me look in her direction, she raised the mic in her hand.

'Third Platoon ready,' she reported.

'Fifth Platoon ready.' Her opposite number, Lieutenant Faril, echoed her words. A dogged, somewhat unimaginative commander, he none-the-less had the respect and confidence of his troopers, largely due to a dry sense of humour and an earnest concern for their welfare, which meant he was unlikely to press too hard if they ran into stiff resistance. I'd selected him precisely because of this, knowing he'd wait for the Sentinels to back him up if things got sticky instead of throwing his troopers lives away taking stupid risks. Some casualties were inevitable, of course, but I wanted to keep them to a minimum. If the regiment's first clash of arms resulted in an easy victory, it would boost their confidence and consolidate morale, whereas a high body count could easily undo all the hard work we'd done getting them back into fighting trim.

'All squadrons ready.' That was Captain Shambas, head of the Sentinel troop; we had all three squadrons with us, which gave us a total of nine walkers. Considerable overkill, given the quality of the resistance we were expecting, but there's nothing like overwhelming fire superiority to give you a sense of self-confidence.

'Confirm.' Broklaw's voice joined the others in my combead. He was in another Salamander, which, like mine, had been fitted out as a command unit. I was more used to the lighter, faster scout variant, which was always my vehicle of choice (I prefer to be able to outrun trouble if I have to), but under the circumstances, I wanted to be able to keep a close eye on things. Besides, the command version had a heavy flamer fitted, which might come in handy in the brutal close-quarter fighting I expected through the rubble of the Heights.

Which reminded me...

'Artillery units commence firing,' I said. A moment later, the ground beneath our treads started to tremble as Mostrue's Earthshakers began living up to their name. I swept my gaze around, tallying the assembled task force. A dozen Chimeras, nine Sentinels, and two Salamanders. I drew my chainsword and gestured towards the gate.

'Move out!' I ordered. Jurgen gunned the engine, and we lurched into motion. Inured to his robust driving style by years of familiarity, I kept my balance with little difficulty. Broklaw's driver moved smoothly in behind us, and I could see his head and shoulders in the open rear compartment; he caught my eye and waved. Kasteen, I knew, would dearly have loved to take command herself, but had stepped down in favour of her subordinate. After all, he too deserved a chance to prove his mettle, and technically, the operation was too small to be overseen by someone of her rank anyway. I was pleased she'd given way without prompting, though, and I could tell Broklaw appreciated it. It was another example of the way the regiment was beginning to function as it was supposed to.

Kasteen was there to see us off, though, along with everyone else who didn't have pressing duties to attend to, or who thought they might get away with skiving off for a few minutes. A cheer went up from our comrades which, for a moment, managed to make itself heard above the roar of engines, the din of the Sentinels, and the rolling thunderclaps of the Earthshakers.

As we hit the streets, the city was in turmoil. We'd kept our plans secret, of course, so none of the natives had a clue what was going on; they scattered in front of us like frightened sump rats, and Jurgen gunned the engine as though it were capable of the speeds he usually drove at. Ahead of us, a plume of dust and smoke marked our destination.

I flipped vox channels to the tactical net. The loyalist PDF units were being told to stand down and let us through, which came as a relief, although ill-disciplined rabble that they were, many were arguing or demanding to know what was going on.

'Major.' I switched back. 'It's all yours for the moment. Try to save a couple for me, eh?'

'I'll do my best.' Broklaw waved as Jurgen peeled us away from the rest of the convoy, mowing down a couple of ornamental shrubs and a litter basket as we swung off the broad boulevard into a narrower cross street which would take us to the industrial area.

The muffled crump of the shells detonating was audible now, the shriek and whine of their passage presaging each explosion, and the noise cleared the street for us far more effectively than any Arbites siren could have done. After a few moments, and several lurching turns any driver but Jurgen would probably have flipped us over attempting to execute, the buildings around us were unmistakably industrial in nature. Still that Emperor-forsaken xenoist-style architecture, admittedly, but sufficiently grubby for their purpose to be obvious.

'Broklaw to command.' The major's voice was calm and competent. 'Cease barrage. We're in position.'

I was glad to hear it. I hadn't even begun my makework errand yet, and he was already on the verge of clearing the traitors out. Jurgen began to slow the Salamander, and, with a sense of *déjà vu*, I could see a PDF officer stepping out in front of us, his hand raised. Manufactoria rose all around us, tall enough to shadow the streets, but apart from the man in uniform, there was no sign of life. That struck me as strange, as the work shifts should still have been in full swing.

'Commissar,' Jurgen said, his voice uncertain. 'Can you hear firing?'

As the engine idled down, I realised he was right. For a moment, I found myself wondering at the acoustics, assuming that what I was hearing must be echoes of the firefight up in the Heights, which a series of crisp exchanges in my combead told me had already broken out. Then I realised it was coming from somewhere ahead of us, inside the line of the PDF cordon marked on the mapslate in front of me.

'What's going on?' I asked, glaring down at the officer. He looked a little panicky.

'I'm not sure, sir. We had orders to hold, but there's dozens of them. Have you brought reinforcements?'

'I'm afraid we're it,' I said, playing for time. 'Who are you holding against?'

'I don't know. We were pulled out of barracks last night, and told to cordon off the area.' He didn't seem any older than the officer I'd shot, I noticed with a sudden flare of apprehension, and the rapid tumble of his words told me he was on the verge of panic. Whatever I'd blundered into was heading for the sump, that much was obvious, and I cursed my luck; but it was too late to back out now. 'We were just told to secure the area until the inquisitor's party got back...'

Merciful Emperor, this was just getting better and better. Clearly, whatever stones Orelius had been turning over had revealed more than the shadowy conspirators he was chasing were happy with, and they were determined to make sure no one lived to pass on their secrets.

'Did he say what he was after down here?' I asked, and the officer shook his head.

'I didn't speak to any of them. Only the captain did, and he's dead now...' His voice began to rise, hysteria bubbling below the surface. I jumped down to stand beside him, feeling the rockcrete jar beneath my boot-heels, and tried to project all the reassurance and authority I could.

'Then I take it you're the officer in charge, lieutenant.' That got through to him. He nodded, a short, myoclonic twitch. 'So report. Where did they go? When? How many? What can you tell me?' His jaw worked for a moment, as though he were trying to force it to function. Gunfire and screams continued to echo between the buildings.

'There's a warehouse. Back there.' He pointed to one of the structures. A las-bolt cracked from one of the upper windows, passing between our heads, and struck the side of the Salamander. I ducked, pulling him down to safety, while Jurgen rotated the sturdy little vehicle on its tracks to bring the hull-mounted heavy bolter in line. It roared in response, gouging away part of the wall, and reducing the sniper to an unpleasant stain.

'Thank you, Jurgen.' I returned my attention to the young officer. 'And the inquisitor went in there?'

'They all did. Just before dawn. We were told to let no one in or out until they came back.' That would have been about ten-and-a-half hours ago, by my reckoning, and something told me Orelius wouldn't be returning any time soon.

'How many of them were there?' I asked. He thought for a moment. 'I saw six,' he said at last. 'Four men and two women. One of them seemed a bit peculiar.' That would be Rakel the psyker, I assumed.

'What about the hostiles?' I prompted him. He shook his head.

'They're everywhere, dozens of them...' His head twitched nervously from side to side as he tried to keep the entire street in view.

'Where? Inside the warehouse?'

'Mostly.' He stood up, about to flee, and another las-bolt caught him in the shoulder. He fell back, shrieking like a child.

'You'll be fine,' I told him after a cursory glance at the injury. One thing you can say for being shot by a las-bolt is that they cauterise the wound they cause, so at least you won't bleed to death from a glancing hit; a fact that has saved my own miserable life on a couple of occasions. I looked back down the street, trying to spot where the fire had come from, and caught sight of some movement behind a pile of shipping crates. I pointed. 'Ours or theirs?'

'I don't know! Emperor's blood, it hurts–'

'It'll hurt a damn sight more in a moment if you don't stop frakking me around!' I shouted suddenly. 'Your men are dying out there! If you can't start behaving like an officer and help me save them, I'll finish you off myself!' That was the last thing I was going to do, of course, the way he was yelling he'd draw the enemy fire off me like a champion when we moved, but it did the trick. I could see the coin drop behind his eyes as he suddenly remembered what had happened to the last PDF unit to get in the way of a commissar.

'They're all civilians,' he gasped out after a moment. 'Anyone in a uniform is one of ours.'

'Thank you.' I pulled him into the shadow of a dumpster. 'Keep your head down and you'll be fine.' I scrambled back aboard the Salamander, grateful for the armour plate surrounding me.

'Broklaw to Cain.' The major's voice rang in my combead. 'Are you all right? We're getting some odd feedback off your frequency.'

'So far.' I checked the flamer, finding it fully charged and ready to go. Emperor bless Jurgen and his streak of thoroughness, I thought. 'It seems our PDF boys weren't holding back after all.'

'Resistance is light here...' His voice was drowned out for a moment by the crack of ionising air I associated with one of the Sentinel multi-lasers. 'But we'll be a while yet.'

'Don't hurry on my account,' I said. The renegades could only have small arms, judging by the sounds I heard, and the Salamander's armour was thick enough to afford complete protection. I switched frequencies, searching for the PDF squad's internal tactical net, but found only static; I should have known better, of course,[1] but old habits are hard to break.

A few more las-bolts from behind the crates confirmed the identities of the rebels lurking there, making a mess of our paintwork in the process, so I triggered the flamer, sending a gout of burning promethium down the

---

1. *Unlike the Imperial Guard units Cain was used to fighting with, most Planetary Defence Force troopers on Gravalax weren't equipped with personal combeads. This lack of contact between individuals outside line of sight of one another partially accounts for the relative lack of co-ordination within a squad, which most Guard veterans disparagingly attributed to poor levels of training and discipline. Of course, most PDF units were inferior to them in this regard, in any case.*

alley. The results were impressive. The crates bursting into flame, and the rebels behind them got caught in the backwash. They burst into the open, their clothes and hair on fire, shrieking like the damned, and Jurgen cut them down with the bolter. Their bodies exploded under the impact, spraying the walls of the building with burning debris, and I was incongruously reminded of fireworks.

'Let's finish this,' I said, and my aide gunned the engine, rolling us forward over the pool of burning promethium which now carpeted the alleyway. As I glanced behind us, the PDF officer was gazing at the devastation we'd wrought, his eyes wide with shock.

The alley opened out into a cross street, the wall of the warehouse forming one side of it, stretching away in front of us in both directions. The distinctive crack of lasgun fire continued to echo through the roads around it, and as our field of vision widened, I could see the sparks of muzzle flashes inside the building, and the puff of vaporising rockcrete where other bolts were impacting around the upper windows. Shadowy figures were visible inside, snapping off shots before ducking back, and I could make out little of them; just that, as the wounded lieutenant had said, they were all in civilian clothes. They were a mixed bunch, too. I caught a glimpse of velvet and the crest of one of the merchants' guilds, and someone who looked like a pastry cook, before I swept the flamer over the whole façade. The results were spectacular; the firing stopped at once, the wood of the window frames igniting with a roar, and a few short-lived screams cut the air.

'That ought to keep their heads down,' Jurgen said with satisfaction, sending a burst of bolts after the promethium to make sure of the fact. Thick black smoke continued to pour from the building, and a ragged cheer mingled with the roar of the flames.

I turned to see a wary group of PDF troopers emerging from the buildings opposite the warehouse, or whatever cover they'd been able to find among the parked trucks and other detritus of the street. A few ragged shots continued to echo between the buildings, indicating that not all the traitors had been incinerated, but their sporadic nature spoke of a panic-stricken retreat which was running into the troopers on the other side of the cordon. The plume of thick black smoke must have been visible from where they were by now, and they were evidently taking heart from the sight. I jumped down from the Salamander.

'Sergeant Crassus, 49th Gravalaxian PDF.' A tall, grey-haired man snapped a salute, but kept his eyes on the street; the first PDF trooper I'd seen since I arrived on planet who actually seemed to know what he was doing. I returned it smartly.

'Commissar Cain, attached to the 597th Valhallan.' Once again, I had
the quiet satisfaction of noting that my name had been recognised, the
low murmur of voices among the troopers flattering my ego with its
awestruck tone.

'We're grateful for your assistance,' Crassus said. 'Did the inquisitor
send for you?' I shook my head.

'Just poking my nose in,' I admitted. 'I noticed your little sideshow on
the tactical display and wondered what was going on.' Crassus
shrugged.

'You'd have to ask one of the officers.'

'I did.' I pointed back up the alleyway, where the promethium pool
had burned itself out, leaving a scorched patch of blackened rockcrete.
'Back there. He needs a medic, by the way.'

'Ah.' Crassus didn't seem surprised. 'I thought he'd done a runner, to
be honest.' My lack of a reply seemed to confirm something for him,
but after a moment, he detailed one of the troopers to take a medkit
and see to the lieutenant.

'You seem to be standing up to combat better than most of the PDF,'
I said.

Crassus shrugged. 'I'm a fast learner. Besides, I'm used to looking
after myself.' Taking in his physique and his air of watchfulness, I didn't
doubt it. 'I was in the Arbites before I joined up.'

'That seems like an odd career move,' I said. His jaw tightened for a
moment.

'Office politics,' he said curtly. I nodded sympathetically.

'It's the same in the Commissariat,' I told him.[1] But before we
could exchange any more words, a loud crack from behind us presaged the collapse of one of the upper stories of the burning
warehouse. 'Better pull your men back,' I told him. 'That's going to
go any minute.'

'I think you're right.' He summoned the squad vox operator, relayed
the instruction, and led his men up the alley at a rapid trot. I turned to
look at the warehouse again. It was well ablaze by now, and pieces of
debris were starting to drop from the roof and outer walls. I scrambled
back aboard the Salamander while Jurgen gunned the engine, and
began to reverse us to safety.

---

1. *This is another prime example of Cain's manipulative streak, in which he invites confidence
by pretending to have shared the experiences of others. Though there are, of course, divisions
within the Commissariat over matters of doctrine and procedure, they can hardly be described
as anything so trivial as 'office politics.' They are also, let us note, considerably less fratricidal
than similar disagreements among fellow inquisitors.*

Abruptly, I became aware of the sound of small arms fire, echoing from inside the building, audible even over the pop and crackle of the flames.

'Crassus,' I voxed, chafing at the necessity of relaying messages through his squad vox operator. 'Are any of your men inside the building?' He had just begun to reply when the link went dead, overridden by a message on a higher priority command channel. I'd done the same thing enough times to recognise what was happening, but it had been a long time since I'd been the one cut out. Still, I supposed it showed Orelius was still alive, at any rate, and I'd heard enough of the reply to be reassured that I hadn't accidentally killed any more loyal subjects of the Emperor. That was a relief, as I was still slogging through the paperwork on the last lot of collateral damage I'd inflicted on the PDF.

I'd just decided that the firing I'd heard was overheated ammo cooking off, or xenoist traitors deciding they'd rather shoot themselves than be burned to death, when Crassus was back on my combead.

'Commissar. The inquisitor's team are pinned down inside the warehouse. They want immediate extraction.'

Well, what they want and what they'll get are two different things, I thought. Venturing into that inferno would be suicide. Let Crassus try if he wanted, but it looked to me as though Orelius and his cohorts were about to report to the Emperor in person, and there was damn-all any of us could do about it.

Then a truly horrifying thought struck me. I'd been the one who set fire to the building. If the Inquisition thought I'd been responsible for the death of one of their own, and had just stood by and let him burn without even trying to rescue him, I'd be a dead man – if I was lucky. I dithered for a fraction of a second, which seemed like eternity, and came to a decision.

'Stay back. We'll handle it,' I told Crassus, and leaned over the driver's compartment to call to Jurgen. 'Take us in!' I shouted.

As usual, where anyone else might have hesitated or argued, he simply followed orders without thinking. The Salamander lurched forwards, accelerating towards the blazing building as rapidly as it could.

'There! Those loading doors!' I pointed, but my faithful aide had already seen them, and a hail of bolter shells ripped them to shreds an instant before we hit. We bounced into the shadowy interior of the warehouse, billows of smoke shrouding everything, pieces of tattered door spraying from under our tracks. I coughed, tore off my sash, and tied it around my face. It didn't do a lot of good, to be honest, but my lungs felt a little less choked than before.

Las-bolts started striking the front armour of the vehicle, which at least gave us a clue as to where the enemy was, and Jurgen was about to reply with the heavy bolter again when I forestalled him.

'Wait,' I said, 'you might hit the inquisitor.' That would have been the crowning irony. Instead, he swung us over to one side, slamming into a pile of stacked crates, and bringing them crashing down. Sudden screams were abruptly cut off. I twisted my head frantically, trying to orientate us, and the whole vast space was suddenly lit in vivid orange as the roof whooshed into flame.

'Frak this!' I said, on the verge of ordering Jurgen to withdraw, then I caught sight of a small knot of figures hurrying towards us. I pointed, and Jurgen swung the Salamander round, stopping us almost dead. There were five of them, running for their lives, with an indeterminate number of shadowy figures in pursuit. Orelius I recognised at once, turning as he ran to loose off a volley from his bolt pistol. A couple of the pursuers fell, but las-bolts continued to impact around the inquisitor and his retinue. A heavily muscled man I recognised as one of his bodyguards from the governor's party was firing, too, but went down hard as one of the las-bolts caught the back of his head. Orelius hesitated for a moment, but even from where I was standing it was obvious the fellow had been dead before he hit the floor.

The rest of his party were in real trouble, so, despite my natural reservations about making myself a more obvious target, I clambered up to the pintle-mounted bolter I'd made sure was installed. Not every Salamander has them, but I've been grateful enough for their presence in the past to insist on having one available if at all possible, and I blessed that foresight now as I took advantage of the extra height the vehicle afforded me to fire over the heads of the inquisitorial party and strike home against their pursuers. A gratifying number went down, or scattered, but too many carried on firing. I'd expected them to start shooting at me, but to my relief they continued to concentrate their fire on the fleeing figures before them.

The scribe I'd seen with Orelius was out in front; long white beard flapping as he ran with surprising dexterity for a man of his age. It was only after I saw him take a las-bolt to the leg, which sparked but continued to function, that I realised his lower limbs were augmetic. Behind him were two women: Rakel, whose green dress was now heavily stained with blood, apparently from a chest wound, but who was still babbling nonsense without appearing to inhale, and another who held her up. She was swathed in a hooded cloak of the deepest black I'd ever seen, which seemed to swallow the light that fell on it, blurring her outline. I saw her flinch as a las-bolt scorched the material, but she kept coming, supporting the gibbering psyker with surprising strength.

I hosed down their pursuers again, hoping to throw off their aim at least, but for every one I felled, another seemed to replace it, moving with an eerie precision which seemed somehow familiar. There was no time to worry about it now, though. I reached down to grasp the fingers of the old scribe, which to my total lack of surprise were also augmetics, and haul him aboard.

'Much obliged,' he said, dropping into the crew compartment, and glancing around with evident interest. 'An Imperial Guard Salamander. Good solid piece of kit. Manufactured on Triplex Vall, unless I miss my guess...'

I left him to gather whatever wits he had, and turned to the others.

'Jurgen!' I shouted. 'Help the women!' Orelius took a las-bolt to the shoulder, dropping his handgun. I wasn't about to lose him now, not after going through all this, so I jumped down, drawing my laspistol, and went to help him up.

'Commissar Cain?' He looked slightly confused until I remembered my makeshift smoke mask and pulled it down; it wasn't doing a damn bit of good now anyway. The whole building around us was ablaze, the heat terrific, and I suddenly remembered the promethium tanks of the heavy flamer aboard the Salamander. Well, it was too late to worry about that now. 'What are you doing here?'

'I heard you needed a lift,' I said, hauling him to his feet, and aiming a couple of speculative shots in the vague direction of the enemy. I dragged him back to the vehicle, where Jurgen was doing his best to help the women, but Rakel wasn't exactly cooperating. She seemed terrified of him, struggling against her companion's grip in an effort to get away.

'He's nothing! Nothing!' she shrieked, which seemed a little harsh to me. All right, he wasn't the most prepossessing trooper in the guard, but once you got past the smell and the interesting collection of skin diseases, he had his good points. Then she convulsed suddenly and passed out, dribbling foam between her clenched teeth.

I hustled Orelius aboard, hefted Rakel's dead weight like a sack of tubers, and let the scribe take her. He lifted her easily with his augmetic limbs, and I climbed up myself beside the woman in black as Jurgen returned to the driver's compartment and gunned the engine.

'Jurgen! Get us out of here!' I yelled, and he opened the throttle fully.

'With pleasure, commissar.' The Salamander leapt forwards, breaking for the shattered loading door we'd come in by, and clipped the frame as we passed through, gouging a shower of sparks from it. As we gained the street, the furnace heat seemed to drop away, although it was still hot enough to raise blisters from our paintwork. I sagged with relief, trembling with the reaction, still trying to comprehend what an insanely risky thing I'd done. As if to underline how close we'd come, the building collapsed behind us with a roar of tumbling masonry.

Well, there's no point cheating death with an act of insane bravery if no one's in a position to praise you for it, so I voxed Crassus.

'Crassus,' I said. 'The inquisitor's safe.'

'So I am.' The woman in black dropped her hood, revealing a face I'd thought about often in the last few days. With blonde hair and blue eyes, she was even more beautiful than I'd remembered, and the voice I'd last heard singing sentimental ballards still had the faint edge of huskiness that had made my heart skip.

Amberley Vail gazed at me with what I took to be faint amusement as my jaw dropped open, an inquisitorial electoo flashing into visibility in the palm of her hand. 'Thank you, commissar,' she added, smiling sweetly.

Editorial Note:

Once again, it seems prudent to insert a little material from other sources here, as the Valhallans' expedition against the xenoist defectors was to have unexpected repercussions. Cain, as we might expect, has little to say on the matter himself as his attention was elsewhere.

The first is extracted from the after-action report of Major Ruput Broklaw, made on 593.931 M41, shortly after the engagement was successfully concluded.

AFTER THE PRELIMINARY bombardment ceased both infantry platoons disembarked from their Chimeras, which had been dispersed around the perimeter of the rebel-occupied zone in accordance with the previously determined deployments. Third Platoon was supported by First Sentinel Squadron on the left flank, Fifth Platoon by Second Squadron on the right, leaving Third Squadron with the company command element as a mobile reserve.

Resistance was light, as anticipated, and Fifth Platoon rolled up their flank with little difficulty apart from a couple of heavy exchanges of fire with dug-in survivors of the bombardment. Lieutenant Faril called in Sentinel support for the two squads thus engaged, which committed our reserve squadron. The flamer-equipped Sentinel in each group clear out the entrenchments with little difficulty after the other two laid down suppressive fire from their multi-lasers to allow them to approach.

On the left, things didn't run quite so smoothly. As Fourth Squad of Third Platoon came under crossfire from two enemy positions, pinning them in place. The flamer Sentinel sent to assist was struck and disabled by a krak missile, forcing its fellows into a defensive posture which severely attenuated the effectiveness of their suppressive fire.

At this point, Lieutenant Sulla broke the deadlock by leading her command squad in a flank attack against one of the enemy positions, while Second Squad under Sergeant Lustig hit the other. By luck or good judgment, both were able to carry the positions almost simultaneously, allowing the remaining Sentinels to close and Fourth Squad to advance.

I am still undecided as to whether Lieutenant Sulla's action was bold or reckless, but it was undeniably effective.

Extracted from *Like a Phoenix From the Flames: The Founding of the 597th*, by General Jenit Sulla (retired), 097.M42

Notwithstanding Commissar Cain's assurances that resistance would be light, as indeed was to prove the case, I felt more than a touch of apprehension as the barrage ceased and Major Broklaw gave the order to advance. Not at the prospect of combat itself – the pitiful handful of rebels we faced seeming little to fear after the tyranid hordes we'd bested on Corania scant months before – but at the realisation that my first real test as an officer was upon me, and the fact that one of the most renowned heroes in the Segmentum had reposed his trust in me was an added burden which I felt ill-equipped to bear.

All went well at first, however, with the squads in my platoon advancing swiftly to contact. My readers may well imagine the frustration I felt as I sat in my command Chimera, listening to the vox chatter, reliant on the reports from my subordinates for a full tactical analysis, for until my unlooked-for promotion, I would have been among them, facing the Emperor's enemies head-on, as a soldier should. My impatience increased as it became clear that one of my squads, women I'd served alongside and men I was beginning to know and respect, was pinned down, taking casualties and unable to advance. As the Sentinels which should have relieved them ran into trouble themselves, I could stand by no longer, regardless of the commissar's admonition to be cautious. Especially since, knowing his reputation, I was certain he would not have hesitated to put himself in danger for the good of his fellows were he to find himself in a similar position.

Calling on my troopers to follow me, and taking but a moment to switch the command channels to the combead in my ear, I jumped from the rear ramp, eager to join the fray.

The sight which met my eyes was to give me pause. The elegant buildings and thoroughfares through which we'd driven were no more, their places taken by heaps of rubble through which barely recognisable pieces of their original form could still, in places, be discerned. A thick pall of dust and smoke hung over everything, reducing the bright afternoon sun to a sullen grey, and for a moment, I couldn't still the flicker of regret which rose unbidden in my breast. Even tainted by the alien as it had been, the architecture had been undeniably elegant.

I had little time for reflection, however, as the crack of las-fire reminded me forcefully of the dire peril my soldiers were in, and with a cry of 'For the Emperor!' I led my doughty quartet to the rescue. A quick study of the tactical slate in the Chimera had shown me that I had an unengaged squad sufficiently close to the most distant of the enemy positions to flank it with a high probability of success, and after a few terse instructions to the sergeant leading it, this indeed was to prove to be the case. That left the nearest to us.

We took them completely by surprise, a couple of frag rounds from our grenade launcher bursting among them and causing great dismay, before charging home to dispatch the survivors with pistols and chainsword. Cowards all, as those who oppose the Emperor invariably are, they broke and ran, exposing themselves to the vengeful fire of the squad they'd been pinning down, who were only too keen to even the score. I'm proud to say that of the team under my direct command only one man was wounded, taking a las-bolt to the leg as we charged, while none of the traitors escaped alive.

[From which we may safely conclude that, whatever her martial abilities, Sulla was no literary stylist.]

NINE

*'Things are very seldom what they seem. In my
experience, they're usually a damn sight worse.'*

– Inquisitor Titus Drake

IT GOES WITHOUT saying that, given my profession, I've had more than
my fair share of unpleasant surprises. But to find that the woman I'd
spent a pleasant social evening trying to impress with my half-formed
speculations about events she was privy to, and, it must be admitted,
had been quite smitten by (insofar as I've ever been susceptible to such
things[1]), was really an undercover inquisitor came pretty close to the
top of the list. And if that wasn't bad enough, the expression of tolerant amusement on her face at my utter stupefaction increased my
discomfiture a thousandfold.

'But I thought... Orelius...' I said, barely making sense even to myself.
Amberley laughed as the Salamander hurtled through the streets back
to the fortified compound where Zyvan had established the headquarters of our expeditionary force. Through the vox bead in my ear, I could

---

1. *At the risk of appearing egotistical, I suspect he's protesting a little too strongly here...*

hear the firefight in the Heights continuing. Sulla had apparently done something stupid, but we were winning comfortably with few enough casualties for things to be fine without any further interference from me, so I felt justified in ordering Jurgen to take us back to the staging area as quickly as possible. Rakel and Orelius quite clearly needed medical attention, which gave me the perfect excuse, and I supposed it was my duty to see the inquisitor safely on her way as quickly as possible.

As it turned out, of course, I was to see a great deal more of her before we left Gravalax, and even that would be just the beginning of a long and eventful association which was to leave me in mortal peril on more occasions than I care to contemplate. Sometimes I wonder whether, if I'd had some premonition of who she really was the first time I saw her, I'd simply have left the room and avoided all the horrors to come in the ensuing decades; but I doubt it. Her company, on the rare occasions I was able simply to enjoy it for its own sake, more than made up for all the times I was left fleeing for my life or facing imminent painful death. Hard as that may be to understand, if you'd met her you'd think the same, I'm sure.[1]

'Orelius?' She braced herself as Jurgen swung us around a bend most other drivers would have thought too tight at half the speed. 'He helps me out on occasion.' She smiled again. 'He seemed very impressed with you at the governor's party, by the way.'

'Then he's an inquisitor too?' I asked, my head still spinning. Amberley laughed, like water over stones, and shook her head.

'Good Emperor, no. He's a rogue trader. What in the warp made you think he's an inquisitor?'

'Just something a friend said,' I said, thinking that would be the last time I took Divas's word for anything. But I suppose, to be fair, he hadn't been all that wrong as it turned out, and he hadn't been responsible for my own febrile imaginings.

'And the guy with the beard?' I indicated the scribe, who was leaning over the lip of the driver's compartment carrying on an enthusiastic conversation with Jurgen about the finer points of Salamander maintenance.

'Caractacus Mott, my savant.' She smiled fondly. 'A mine of information, some of it useful.'

'The others I've met,' I said. I indicated Orelius, who had taken out a medkit and was tending to Rakel as best he could with a damaged arm. 'What's wrong with her?'

---

1. Frankly, I doubt it. But we certainly seemed more at ease in one another's company than either of us were used to with anyone else. Make of that what you will.

'I'm not exactly sure,' she replied, a thoughtful frown appearing for a moment on her face. That, I was later to discover, wasn't entirely true; she had her suspicions, but the truth about Jurgen wouldn't be confirmed for some time yet.

To cut a long story short, we made it back to HQ without further incident, and dispersed to our various duties. Amberley went off with the medicae to ensure that her friends were properly patched up, although as I was to find out for myself on subsequent occasions, having an inquisitor hovering in the corner doesn't exactly help them to concentrate on stemming the bleeding or whatever. I went off for a shower and a change of clothes, but was still smelling faintly of smoke when Broklaw and the others returned in high spirits.

'You did well, I hear,' I congratulated him as he disembarked from his Chimera. He nodded, still a little high from the adrenaline.

'Cleared out the whole nest of them. Minimal casualties, too.' He broke off to return Sulla's salute; her face was shining as though she'd just been out on a heavy date. 'Well done, lieutenant. That was a tough call.'

'I just asked myself what the commissar would have done,' she said. At that point I still didn't have a clue what either of them were talking about, but I assumed she'd distinguished herself in some way, so I tried to look pleased. It turned out later she'd pulled some damn fool stunt that had almost got her killed, but the troopers thought she was the hero of the hour, so it had all turned out for the best. Besides, it was the sort of thing I was assumed to have done myself, so I could hardly chew her out for it when the reports came in, could I?

'And then did the opposite, I hope,' I said, then raised an eyebrow at her expression. 'That was a joke, lieutenant. I'm sure whatever decision you made was the correct one under the circumstances.'

'I hope so,' she said, saluting again, then trotting off to check on the wounded from her platoon. Broklaw watched her go with a thoughtful expression.

'Well, it worked, anyway. Probably saved us a heap of casualties too. But...' He shrugged. 'She'll probably do well in the end, if she doesn't get herself killed first.'

Well, he was right there, of course, although none of us could see at the time just quite how far she'd go. Like they say, it's always the ones you least expect.[1]

---

1. *For further details of Sulla's illustrious career see Dragen's biography* Valhallan Valkyrie, *a populist but accurate work, and* Like a Phoenix From the Flames, *if you can tolerate her prose style.*

After a few more words of little consequence, Brocklaw went off to report to Kasteen, and I went to look for a drink.

I FOUND IT in a quiet booth at the back of the Eagle's Wing. The place was almost deserted, in an eerie contrast to my visit here with Divas, but I supposed it was still a bit too early in the evening for things to be lively, and anyway the solitude fitted my mood. I'd noticed, on my short walk to the bar, that the streets were unusually quiet, too, and the few civilians I'd seen had seemed nervous, scuttling away from me as they caught sight of my uniform. Our show of strength against the rebels in the Heights had put everyone on edge, and if anything, anti-Imperial sentiment seemed to be gaining ground.

I can't say I blamed them entirely, either. If I'd been a Gravalaxian, I'd probably be thinking that the tau might be blue, bald, and barmy, but at least they hadn't blown up part of the city. My opinion of Grice would have fallen even further for ordering us to intervene, if that were possible.

As the amasec started to kick in, I found myself brooding over the events of the afternoon: a hair's-breadth escape from death does that to me, I start to contemplate my own mortality, and wonder what the hell I'm doing in a job where I'm liable to be killed pretty much all of the time. The answer, of course, is that I didn't have a choice – the assessors at the Schola Progenium decided I was commissarial material, and that was that.[1]

I was just working myself into a perversely comforting mood of gloom and despondency when a shadow fell across me and a mellifluous voice asked, 'Do you mind if I sit here?'

Normally, I'm never averse to feminine company, as you'll know if you've read much of these memoirs, but right then all I wanted was to be left alone to contemplate the unfairness of the universe in a self-pitying haze of alcohol. However, it never pays to be impolite to an inquisitor, so I gestured to the seat across the table and masked my surprise as best I could. She'd found the time to change and freshen up too, I noticed, into a mist-grey gown which showed off her colouring to the best advantage.

'Feel free.' I gestured to the waitress, who looked vaguely disappointed as she delivered our order. 'Two more, please.'

---

1. *A decision which, on the face of it, seems remarkably perverse, given Cain's manifest character flaws. However, it's a decision his subsequent career triumphantly vindicates. We can only speculate how he would have fared if directed into some other branch of Imperial service, such as the Navy, or, Emperor help us, the Arbites.*

'Thank you.' Amberley sipped delicately at the drink, a faint *moue* betraying her opinion of its quality, before replacing the glass on the tabletop and regarding me quizzically. I tried to pull away from her depthless blue eyes, then decided I didn't really want to after all. 'You're a remarkable man, commissar.'

'So I've been told.' I waited a heartbeat before smiling. 'Though I can't say I see it myself.' The corner of Amberley's mouth twitched, with what looked like genuine amusement.

'Oh yes, the modest hero routine. You've got that one off pat, no question.' She knocked back the rest of her drink in one, and signalled for another, leaving me gaping like an idiot. Her smile widened. 'What's next? "I'm just a humble soldier," or "Trust me, I'm a servant of the Emperor?"'

'I'm not quite sure what you're insinuating–' I began, but she cut me off with a chuckle.

'Ooh, honest indignation. I haven't seen that one in a while.' She picked at the bowl of nuts on the table, some local variety I didn't recognise, and flashed a grin of pure mischief at me. 'Lighten up, commissar, I'm only pulling your leg.'

Yes, right, I thought. And letting me know you can see right through every little manipulative trick in my repertoire in the process. Something of this must have shown on my face, because her eyes softened.

'You could just try being yourself, you know.'

The thought was terrifying. I'd spent so long hiding behind masks I was no longer sure there was a genuine Ciaphas underneath them any more, just a quivering little bundle of self-interest. Then an even more terrifying thought hit me; she could tell what I was thinking! Everything I'd tried to conceal about my fraudulent reputation would be open to her, and the inquisition... Emperor's bowels!

'Relax. I'm not a psyker. Just very good at reading people.' She watched me sag into my seat with relief, not even trying to conceal it, the faint amusement still dancing in the back of her eyes. 'Whatever you're afraid I'll find out is still safe. And it'll stay that way. Unless you give me a reason to start looking for it.'

'I'll do my best not to,' I promised, picking up my own drink with a shaky hand.

'I'm glad to hear it.' Her smile was warm again. 'Because I was hoping you could help me.'

'Help you with what?' I asked, already sure I wasn't going to like the answer.

* * *

THE CONFERENCE SUITE was less crowded this time, although since two of the others present were Lord General Zyvan and an inquisitor who was already making it perfectly clear that she was in charge here, it certainly seemed full enough to me. The only other person present was Mott, the elderly savant, who sat bright and alert, occasionally poking at the dent in his leg left by a hasty techpriest who hadn't quite finished patching him up when the summons to the meeting had arrived.

'Thank you for joining us, commissar.' Amberley flashed me a smile which looked genuinely warm, although as an experienced manipulator myself, I wasn't quite sure how far I could trust it. Zyvan nodded a greeting, also pleased to see me.

'Hello again.' Mott smiled, surprisingly clear brown eyes flickering behind his excess of beard. He evidently hadn't found the time to wash the smell of the fire out of his hair and robes, or simply didn't care. 'You've caused us a great deal of inconvenience, young man. Although I suppose you weren't to know.'

'Know what?' I asked, trying not to snap. I'd grabbed a couple of sandwiches to try and mop up the alcohol I'd drunk, and got Jurgen to find me some recaf, but between the amasec and the reaction from the day's adventures, my head was still buzzing.

'All in good time.' Amberley smiled indulgently at the wizened sage. 'Caractacus does tend to skip the dull bits given half a chance.'

'When you get to my age, you don't have the time to waste on them,' he responded, smiling in return. I realised that this was all part of an easy familiarity between them, which spoke volumes for the trust the inquisitor placed in him, and the length of their association. He turned back to me. 'Which reminds me, thank you for coming to our assistance. It was most timely.'

'My pleasure,' I said.

'Then you have an extremely perverse idea of what constitutes fun. You should get out more.'

Amberley shook her head, and raised an eyebrow at me, in an exaggerated mime of exasperation.

'You just can't get the help these days,' she said. I couldn't think of any adequate response to this, so I said nothing. I'd never had a really clear idea of what an inquisitor was supposed to be like, although like most people, I had a vague impression of some scary psychopath who slaughtered their way through the Emperor's enemies. Amberley, on the other hand, seemed to be the complete antithesis of this. She had her ruthless streak, of course, as I was to find out during our long association, but back then, the cheerful, slightly whimsical young woman with the strange sense of humour seemed about as far removed from the general preconception of her profession as it was possible to get.[1] Zyvan cleared his throat.

'Inquisitor. Perhaps we could get to the matter at hand?'

'Of course.' She activated the hololith, thumping it in just the right spot to bring the image into focus. 'It goes without saying that everything you see and hear is completely confidential, commissar.'

'Of course.' I nodded.

'Good. I'd hate to have to kill you.' She smiled again, and I wondered if she was joking or not. These days, of course, I know she meant every word of it.

'In case you haven't been paying attention,' she went on, 'I'm an agent of the Ordo Xenos. You know what that means?'

'You deal with aliens?' I hazarded. Back then, I had only the vaguest idea that the inquisition was divided into multiple ordos with specific areas of interest and responsibility, but it was a pretty easy deduction to make. Amberley nodded approval.

'Exactly,' she began.

'For the most part, anyway,' Mott chimed in helpfully. 'There was that Chaos cult on Arcadia Secundus, and the heretics of Ghore–'

'Thank you, Caractacus,' she said, meaning, 'shut the warp up,' so he did. As I was soon to discover, being a savant meant being obsessed with detail and trivia, and all the pedantry that went with it. Imagine the worst barroom know-it-all you ever met, who really does, and is cursed with a tourette-like compulsion to spill out everything relevant on any topic that comes up, and you're about halfway there. Although he could be incredibly annoying at times, I found him good company in his own way once I got to know him. Especially as his gifts included an uncanny intuitive grasp of probability which we put to good use in a number of gambling establishments over the years.

Amberley pulled up a star chart on the hololith, which I recognised without too much difficulty, as it had been reproduced in far less detail in the briefing slate I'd skimmed through before we made planetfall.

'The Damocles Gulf,' I said, and she nodded.

'We're here.' She pointed out the Gravalax system, seemingly alone and isolated on the fringes of Imperial space. 'Notice anything about the topography of the region?'

'We're close to the tau border,' I said, playing for time as I studied the images. She wouldn't be alluding to anything that obvious, I was sure. Several of the neighbouring systems were tagged with blue icons, marking them as tau-held worlds. In fact they almost engulfed our present

---

1. *Which was, of course, the whole point...*

Sandy Mitchell

position, with only a thin chain of friendly yellow beacons connecting us to the welcoming haven of Imperial space. 'Too close,' I concluded finally. 'If we had to fight a war here, our supply lines would be far too thin for comfort.'

'Precisely.' Zyvan nodded approval, and indicated a couple of choke points. 'They could cut us off here, and here with no trouble at all. We'd be blockaded and swallowed up in months. While they could reinforce at their leisure from at least four systems.'

'Which is why we're so desperate to avoid a full-scale war over this miserable mudball,' Amberley said. 'Keeping it would tie up our naval assets from at least three sectors just to secure our supply lines, and we'd be funnelling Guard and Astartes units in from all over the Segmentum. Putting it bluntly, it's not worth the effort.'

To say that I was astonished would be putting it mildly. It had been an article of faith for as long as I could remember that the sacred domains of His Majesty's Imperium should never be polluted by the alien no matter the cost. And here was an inquisitor no less, and the lord general himself, apparently quite happy to let the tau just walk in and have the place. Well that was fine with me, of course, especially if it kept me out of the firing line, so I nodded judiciously.

'I can sense a "but" coming,' I said.

'Quite right.' Zyvan nodded, clearly pleased by my astuteness. 'Just letting the little blue grox-lovers walk in and take the place isn't acceptable either. It would send entirely the wrong message to them. They're already popping up on worlds all over the sector and arming to keep them. If they take Gravalax without a fight, they'll think half the Segmentum is up for grabs.'

'But we could beat them in the long run,' I said, trying not to picture the decades of grinding attrition that would ensue as the overwhelming might of the Imperium met the technosorcery of the tau. It would be the biggest bloodbath since the Sabbat Worlds crusade.

'We could. Eventually.' Amberley nodded soberly. 'If they were the only threat we had to face.' She widened the view, systems falling into the centre of the hololith, new ones coalescing at the fringes of the projection field. Several systems were tagged in red. I recognised one of them as Corania, and then, a moment later, I picked out the Desolatia system where I'd first been blooded against a tyranid horde over a decade before.

'In the last few years, tyranid attacks have been increasing in this region of the galaxy,' Zyvan said. 'But you'd know all about that.'

'I've seen a few,' I admitted.

'There's a pattern,' Mott butted in. 'Still not clear, but definitely beginning to form.[1]

'Our greatest fear is that they could be the harbingers of a new hive fleet,' Amberley said soberly. I tried to envision such a thing, and shivered involuntarily. The hordes I'd encountered before had been weak, the scattered survivors of hive fleet Behemoth which had been shattered centuries before, but still dangerous shards of poison in the body of the Imperium. Even attenuated as they were, they could still overwhelm a lightly defended world, growing in strength with each one they consumed. The prospect of facing a fresh fleet with almost limitless resources was, quite simply, terrifying.

'Then let's pray you're wrong,' I said. Unfortunately, as we now know, she was right twice over, and the reality was far worse than even my craven imaginings.

'Exactly.' Zyvan made the sign of the aquila. 'But if she's not, those ships and men will be needed to defend the Imperium. And it's not just the 'nids...' He trailed off as Amberley shot him a venomous look. Clearly I wasn't supposed to be let in on everything.

'Necrons,' I said, jumping to the obvious conclusion. I pointed out the tomb world I'd been lucky to escape from a couple of years before. 'Not the friendliest of xenos. And cropping up more frequently of late, if these contact icons are anything to go by.' I indicated a couple of others in the same purple script.

'That would be pure speculation, commissar,' Amberley said, a clear warning tone entering her voice, but Mott nodded enthusiastically.

'A two hundred and seventy-three per cent increase in probable necron contact over the last century,' he said. 'Only twenty-eight per cent fully confirmed, however.' That would be because the majority of contacts left no survivors, of course.

'Be that as it may,' Amberley said, 'the fact remains that the resources we would expend fighting a war for Gravalax are likely to be needed elsewhere, and if we're forced to use them now, we would be fatally weakened.'

'Which still begs the question of who would be insane enough to try to provoke such a war, and what they could hope to gain by it,' I said, eager to show I was paying attention.

'Precisely what the inquisitor was sent here to find out,' Zyvan assured me.

'Not exactly.' Amberley killed the hololith display, probably to stop me from making any more uncomfortable guesses about what might

---

1. *In hindsight, these were clearly the precursors of Hive Fleets Kraken and Leviathan, the bulk of which had still to be detected at this time.*

be lurking in the outer darkness. 'Our attention was drawn to the increase in tau influence on Gravalax, and the activities of certain rogue traders who seemed to be profiting from it. I came to look into that, and assess the loyalties of the governor.'

'That's why you had Orelius pressuring him for trade concessions,' I said, the coin suddenly dropping. 'You wanted to see if he had any influence with the tau.'

'Quite right.' She smiled at me, like a schola tutor whose least promising pupil has just recited the entire catechism of abjuration. 'You're really quite astute for a soldier.'

'And your decision?' Zyvan asked, carefully not taking offence at the remark.

'I'm still considering it,' she admitted. 'He's certainly weak, probably corrupt, and undeniably stupid. He's let the alien influence take root here far too deeply to be dislodged without considerable effort. But he's no longer our primary concern.'

'You mean the conspirators?' I asked. 'Whoever's trying to provoke a war over this?'

'Precisely.' She nodded, favouring me with another smile, which, perhaps due to wishful thinking, looked remarkably like praise. 'Another astute deduction on your part.'

'Do you have any clue as to their identities?' Zyvan asked. Amberley shook her head.

'There's no shortage of enemies who would stand to gain from weakening the Imperial presence in this sector,' she said, with a warning glance at Mott, who seemed on the verge of listing them. 'Not least the tau themselves.' He subsided with visible disappointment. 'But whoever it is is undoubtedly working through the xenoist faction here, and the PDF units they control. Fortunately, the Guard seem to have drawn their teeth without dragging the tau into it, for which we can all be thankful.'

Zyvan and I took the implied compliment without comment.

'How is the investigation into the ambassador's murder going?' I asked. 'If you find the assassin, you find the conspirators, don't you?'

'Probably.' Amberley shook her head. 'But so far we don't have a suspect. The autopsy showed he was killed by an imperial bolt pistol at close range, but we already knew that, and half the guests at the party were carrying one. Our best lead is still the xenoist connection.'

'Or it was,' Mott chimed in with a censorial glare at me. 'Until this young man set fire to it.'

'I'm sorry?' I gazed at him in confusion.

'So you should be,' he said, without rancour. Amberley sighed.

'The local Arbites have been keeping tabs on the most vocal xenoist groups. One of them used to hold meetings at that warehouse, so we went to check it out.'

'And found a bit more than you bargained for,' I chipped in helpfully. She nodded.

'That we did. We found a way down to the undercity.'

'Definite surprise there,' Mott chipped in helpfully. 'Although given the amount of relatively new tau-influenced architecture in the city as a whole, finding one wasn't totally unexpected.'

I suppose I must seem naive, but up until this point it had never occurred to me that there wasn't an undercity – part and parcel of growing up in a hive, I suppose. You see, most imperial cities are millennia old, each generation building on the remains of the last, leaving a warren of service tunnels and abandoned rooms under the latest level of streets and buildings, often tens, or even hundreds, of metres thick. Mayoh, being so sparsely populated in imperial terms, didn't have anything like so thick a layer beneath it, but I'd just taken it for granted that it was bound to have the same labyrinth of sewers and walkways below its citizens' feet as any other urban area I was familiar with.

'Seems like a good place to plot sedition,' I conceded.

'Ideal,' Amberley agreed. 'As we found to our cost.'

'We were ambushed,' Mott said, 'though not before determining that the tunnel system is extremely extensive.'

'Ambushed by who?' Zyvan asked.

'Ah. Well, that's the question.' Amberley cocked her head quizzically. 'Whoever they were, they were well armed, and well trained. We barely got out alive.'

'Tomas and Jothan didn't,' Mott reminded her, and her brow darkened for a moment.

'Their sacrifice will be remembered,' she said, in the reflex way people do when they don't really mean it. 'They knew the risks.'

'More PDF defectors?' Zyvan asked. I shook my head.

'I don't think so. My aide and I got a good look at several of them. They were definitely civilians.'

'Or in civilian clothes,' Mott suggested. 'Not necessarily the same thing.'

'In either case,' Amberley said decisively, 'we need more information. And there's only one place we can get it.' I began to develop a familiar sinking feeling in the pit of my stomach.

'The undercity,' Zyvan said. The inquisitor nodded.

'Precisely. Which is why I require your assistance.'

'Anything at all, of course.' Zyvan spread his hands. 'Although I don't quite see–'

'My retinue is out of action, lord general. And I'm not stupid enough to undertake an expedition of this nature entirely alone.' Well, anyone could see that. 'I'd like to request the use of some of your Guard troopers.'

'Well, of course.' Zyvan nodded. 'You can hardly rely on the loyalty of the local PDF.'

'Exactly.' She nodded again.

'How many do you want?' Zyvan asked. 'A platoon, a company?' Amberley shook her head.

'No. We'll need to move fast, and light. One fire-team. And the commissar to lead them.' She turned those dazzling eyes on me again, and smiled. 'I'm sure a man of your formidable reputation will be up to the challenge.'

I wasn't, you can take my word for it, but I couldn't refuse a direct request from an inquisitor, could I? (Although if I'd known what I was getting into, I'd probably have given it a damn good try.) So I nodded, and tried to look confident.

'You can rely on me,' I said, with all the sincerity I could fake, and from the grin which quirked the corner of her mouth, I could tell she wasn't fooled for a second.

'I'm glad to hear it,' she said. 'I gather your regiment has had a great deal of experience in city fighting, so I'm sure they'll be ideal.'

'I'll ask for volunteers,' I said, but she shook her head.

'No need.' She skimmed a dataslate over the tabletop to me. I stopped it, a premonitory tingle beginning in the palms of my hands. 'You've already assigned some.'

I glanced at the list of names, already knowing, in the way you can see the avalanche start even before the rocks begin to slide, what I'd read there. Kelp, Trebek, Velade, Sorel and Holenbi. The five troopers on the planet I'd least trust to watch my back, unless it was to stick a bayonet in it. I lifted my head.

'Are you sure, inquisitor? These troopers are hardly the most reliable–'

'But they are the most expendable.' She grinned at me, the mischievous light back in her eyes. 'And I'm sure you can keep them in line for me.'

It was official, then. This was a suicide mission. I swallowed, my mouth suddenly dry.

'You can count on it,' I said, wondering how in the name of the Emperor I was going to get out of this one.

TEN

'Trust? Trust's got nothing to do with it.
I just don't want them out of my sight.'

      – General Karis, after promising full access
to his command bunker to the local PDF
commanders on Vortovan

'ARE YOU SURE about this, commissar?' Kasteen asked, clearly as troubled by the prospect as I was. She and Broklaw had joined me in my office at my request, and I'd filled them in on as much of the assignment I'd been handed as Amberley would permit. I sighed deeply.

'No, I'm not,' I admitted. 'But the inquisitor was quite insistent. These are the troopers she wants.'

'Well, we'd better give them to her,' Broklaw said. 'At least they'll be off our hands at last.' Kasteen nodded, clearly cheered by the prospect.

'That's true,' she conceded. Despite my best efforts to arrange their transfer to a penal legion, the Munitorium was proving as slow and obstructive as usual, and didn't seem the least bit inclined to send a ship all the way out here just to pick up a handful of cannon fodder. Normally, that wouldn't have been a problem, I'd simply have found space on the next outbound freighter or something, but Gravalax wasn't exactly the hub of the Segmentum, and even what little shipping there normally was had almost dried up as the political situation deteriorated. Even if the worst-case scenario I'd been shown on the hololith didn't come to pass, it looked as though we were going to be stuck with the five defaulters until we returned to Imperial space, which was going to be months away at this rate.

Which, in turn, had meant they were our responsibility for the foreseeable future, which wasn't exactly what I'd had in mind when I cheated Parjita out of his firing squad back aboard the *Righteous Wrath*.

'And on the plus side,' Broklaw went on cheerfully, 'at least we won't be losing anyone we'll miss.' He stopped suddenly, realised what he'd just said, and floundered in a way I would have found comical under any other circumstances. 'Not you, commissar, obviously. I mean, we would miss you, but I'm sure we won't. Have to, I mean. You'll be back.'

'I certainly intend to be,' I said, with more confidence than I felt. I still hadn't been able to think of a plausible reason to wriggle out of the assignment, so I'd bowed to the inevitable and started trying to find ways of ensuring my own survival instead. None of the troopers could be trusted, that much was certain, but Amberley seemed confident enough so my best bet was to stick close to her and hope she had a plan of some kind. On the other hand, chances were that Orelius's luckless bodyguards had thought the same thing. Like most hivers, I was comfortable enough in a tunnel complex unless someone was actually shooting at me, so maybe the most prudent thing would be to get conveniently lost at the earliest opportunity and make my way back to the compound after a reasonable interval had passed. Then again, if I did that and Amberley survived she wouldn't be terribly pleased with me to say the least, and the prospect of hacking off an inquisitor wasn't one to contemplate lightly.

The upshot of all this was that I'd spent a largely sleepless night vacillating about my non-existent choices until sheer exhaustion had tumbled me into old nightmares of fleeing from gleaming metal killers down endless corridors, heaving grey masses of tyranid chitin roaring in towards me like a tide of death, and a green-eyed seductress trying to suck the soul from my body in the name of the Chaos power she worshipped.[1] And probably others too, which I was glad not to recall on waking.

---

1. *These dreams would appear to refer obliquely to some of Cain's earlier experiences. The last one in particular can certainly be matched to a specific incident recorded elsewhere in the archive, although the others are a little more problematic. He had encountered both necrons and tyranids on more than one occasion prior to this date.*

Jurgen appeared at my elbow, presaged by his usual miasma, and poured me my habitual bowl of tanna leaf tea. Instead of withdrawing as he normally did, though, he hesitated next to my desk.

'Was there something else, Jurgen?' I asked, anticipating some routine query about paperwork I couldn't be bothered to deal with. If I was going to die today, I wasn't going to waste my final hours filling out forms in triplicate. And if I didn't, which I swore to the Emperor I was going to do my damnedest to achieve, he could sort it out for me while I was gone. That was supposed to be an aide's job, after all. He cleared his throat stickily, and a faint expression of nausea ghosted across Broklaw's face.

'I'd like to go with you, sir,' he said at last. 'I wouldn't trust any of those frakheads further than I could throw a Baneblade, if you don't mind me saying so, and I'd feel a lot better if you'd let me watch your back.'

I was touched and I don't mind admitting it. We'd been campaigning together for the best part of thirteen years by that point, and faced innumerable perils together, but his loyalty never ceased to amaze me. Probably because the nearest I've ever got to the concept myself is looking it up in a dictionary.

'Thank you, Jurgen,' I said. 'I'd be honoured.' A faint flush crept up from behind his shirt collar, which, as usual, was open at the neck and stained with something that probably used to be food. Kasteen and Broklaw looked suitably impressed, too.

'I'd best go and get ready then.' He sketched a salute, about turned with the closest I'd ever seen him get to precision, and marched out, his shoulders set.

'Remarkable,' Broklaw said.

'He has a strong sense of duty,' I said, feeling cautiously optimistic about my chances of survival for the first time since Amberley dropped her bombshell. We'd been in some pretty tight spots together over the years, and I knew I could rely on him completely, which is more than I could say for anyone else in the team.

'He's a brave man,' Kasteen said, seemingly surprised by the idea. Most people tended to avoid him, put off by his appearance and body odour, and the vague sense of wrongness he exuded, but I'd been close to him for so long I'd got used to seeing past that to his well-hidden virtues. Though I was the last person you'd normally expect to appreciate them.

'I suppose he is,' I said.

* * *

'WELL, THERE THEY are,' I said. 'They're all yours.' Amberley nodded, and walked along the line of troopers, meeting their eyes one by one. They were as sullen a bunch as I remembered, gazing back at us in silence.

I'd had them marched to one of the storage sheds in our sector of the compound at the double, and was pleased to note that none of them seemed particularly out of breath, so their weeks of confinement hadn't left them as out of condition as I'd feared; but then, I don't suppose they'd had much to do except exercise anyway. They'd looked vaguely surprised when I dismissed the guards, except for Sorel, whose expression never seemed to change whatever happened, and stared at me as I sat casually on a nearby crate.

'I promised you a chance to redeem yourselves,' I said. 'And that chance has now come.' That got their attention. Velade looked vaguely apprehensive, Holenbi baffled as always, and even Sorel seemed to take slightly more interest than usual. Kelp and Trebek just stared at me, but at least they didn't seem inclined to go for one another again. Perhaps it was my personal charisma, or my unmerited reputation, but it was most likely the laspistol in the holster at my hip which I'd visibly left unfastened for a quick draw. I gestured to Amberley, who stepped forward from the shadows, the black cloak she'd worn before rendering her almost invisible until she moved. 'This is Inquisitor Vail. She has a little job for us.'

Velade gasped audibly as Amberley raised her hand, and her electoo flashed into visibility. Dressed in black as she was, she fit the popular conception of an inquisitor far more closely than the sultry lounge singer that I'd first encountered, or the cheerful young woman I'd been getting to know, and I could tell that most of them, at least, were properly intimidated.

'What kind of a job?' Trebek asked. I waited for Amberley to reply, but after a moment I realised she was leaving the briefing to me. Not that I knew much more than the rest of us, of course, but I'd pass on everything I could. The longer they survived, the longer I could hide behind them from whatever was waiting for us in the tunnels below.

'Recon,' I said. 'Into the undercity. Resistance is expected.'

'Resistance from who?' Trebek asked. I shrugged.

'That's what we're supposed to find out.'

'I take it we aren't expected to survive,' Kelp cut in. Amberley met his eyes, staring him down.

'That rather depends on you,' she said. 'The commissar certainly intends to. I suggest you follow his lead.'

'It's not going to make any difference to us anyway, is it?' Velade asked, with surprising vehemence. 'Even if we get through this one alive, we've only got another suicide mission to look forward to.'

'I'd worry about that later if I were you,' I said. But Amberley was nodding slowly, as though she was being perfectly reasonable. I certainly wouldn't have mouthed off to an inquisitor in her boots, but I suppose she felt she had nothing to lose in any case.

'Good point, Griselda,' she said. Velade and the others looked a little taken aback at the use of her given name. I recognised the technique as a subtle piece of psychological manipulation, quietly enjoying the chance to watch an expert at work. Amberley smiled, suddenly, the full force of her capricious personality manifesting itself again. 'All right, you need an incentive. If you make it back in one piece, you have my word you won't be transferred to a penal legion. How's that?'

A total pain in the fundament so far as I was concerned. The paperwork alone would be a nightmare, not to mention the morale and disciplinary problems which would undoubtedly ensue from trying to integrate such an insubordinate rabble back into a line company. I wasn't about to undermine my own authority by having it verbally overridden by an inquisitor in front of them, though, so I stayed quiet. Maybe I could get them transferred to another command, or assigned somewhere relatively harmless after she'd gone. The local PDF could certainly use a professional training cadre to bring them up to scratch once this mess was sorted out, and we were hardly likely to be coming back to Gravalax...

'All of us?' Holenbi asked, clearly not quite believing his own ears. Amberley shrugged.

'Well, she did ask first. But I suppose so. Wouldn't be much of an incentive for the rest of you otherwise, would it?'

No one answered, so I resumed the briefing.

'An undetermined number of hostiles are holed up down there. Our job is to find out how many, their disposition, and what they're up to.'

'Do we have a map of the tunnels?' Kelp asked. For what it was worth, they seemed to be focussing on the mission at least. I turned to Amberley.

'Inquisitor?' I asked. She shook her head.

'No. We didn't penetrate very far the first time before we were forced to retreat. We have very little idea of their extent, or what's down there.'

'Who's we?' Trebek asked.

'My associates,' Amberley replied. Trebek glanced pointedly around the shed.

'I can only see you.'

'The others were injured. That's why I need you.' No mention of the dead ones, I noticed, which was probably just as well. It wouldn't fool the troopers anyway, they knew enough about firefights in confined spaces to realise that not everyone she'd gone down there with would have made it out.

'So, to recap,' Kelp said, 'you want us to go into an unmapped labyrinth, looking for something you think might be down there, but you don't know what, protected by an indeterminate number of heavily armed guards, and the last time you tried you were the only one who made it out in one piece.'

'That about sums it up, yes,' Amberley admitted cheerfully. 'But you are forgetting one thing.'

'Which is?' I asked, already sure I wouldn't like the answer.

'They know I'm on to them now.' She smiled, as though it were a tremendous joke. 'So this time they'll be expecting us.'

'Another question.' Sorel spoke up for the first time, puncturing the sombre silence. 'Your generous offer notwithstanding , you've obviously chosen us because we're expendable.' His voice was as flat and colourless as his eyes. 'I assume you're not expecting many survivors from this little excursion.'

'As I said before, that rather depends on you.' Amberley nailed him with her eyes. 'I certainly intend to come back. So does the commissar.' She'd got that right, at least. 'And your question is?'

'What's to stop any of us putting a las-round through your head and disappearing over the horizon the first chance we get?' His wintry gaze swept the other prisoners. 'Don't tell me you're not all thinking about it.'

'Good point.' Amberley smiled, the amused expression I'd seen before back on her face. If it disconcerted Sorel he gave no sign of the fact, but it certainly worried the others. She jerked a thumb in my direction. 'There's always the commissar to get past before you can reach me, of course.'

'And I'll execute any one of you who even looks like they're thinking of making a run for it,' I promised. I would, too, because they'd have to kill me as well if they were to have a hope of getting away with it, and that would be a highly undesirable outcome from my point of view.

'Even if you could take us both,' and the amusement was abruptly gone from her voice, 'and I sincerely doubt that, I've lost count of the number of people I've met who thought they could outrun the Inquisition. But you might as well give it a try if you really want to.' Then the undercurrent of mirth was back in her voice. 'After all, there's a first time for everything.'

I smiled too, to demonstrate my confidence in her, but none of the others did. Sorel nodded, slowly, like a debater conceding a point.

'Fair enough,' he said.

* * *

No one had anything constructive to add, so after a few more desultory questions about the mission parameters (the answers to which all boiled down to 'Emperor only knows' in any case), I led them outside to where Jurgen had a Chimera waiting, its engine running, and tried to look confident. I would have preferred my usual scout Salamander, given the choice, but there wouldn't have been room for the entire team aboard it, and besides, the fully enclosed passenger bay would discourage any last-minute attempts at desertion, or so I hoped.

'Your equipment's already aboard,' I told them, standing well back until they'd embarked, like an ovinehound shepherding a flock through a gate. (Although the canines tend not to use laspistols to emphasise the point, of course.) Five bundles of kit were waiting for them, each one wrapped in a carapace vest with a name stencilled on it, and they all picked out their own as they boarded.

'Check it carefully,' Amberley told them. 'If there's anything missing you won't get a chance to come back for it.'

'Discharge papers?' Trebek said, raising a tension-relieving laugh from Velade and Holenbi.

'Something's wrong here,' Kelp said, shrugging into the body armour. 'It fits. Quartermaster must be slipping.' It was an axiom among the Guard that kit only came in two sizes – too large and too small.

'I had a word with him,' Amberley said. 'He assured me that there wouldn't be any complaints.'

'I'll just bet he did,' Kelp muttered.

'Hellguns. Shady!' Velade hefted her new weapon, looking incongruously like a juvie on Emperor's day morning. As a regular line trooper, she was only used to handling a standard-issue lasgun, the more powerful variant normally being reserved for storm-troopers and other special forces. At least her evident enthusiasm for her new toy seemed to be keeping her apprehension in check.

'Nice,' Kelp agreed, snapping a powercell home with practiced precision.

'We thought the extra punch might come in handy,' I said. Amberley had suggested I replace my battered old laspistol with the handgun version of the heavier weapon, but after some hesitation, I'd demurred. I'd got so used to it over the years that it was more like an extension of my own arm than a weapon, and no amount of added stopping power would compensate for the different weight and feel of a replacement throwing off my instinctive aim. In a firefight, that could mean the difference between life and death.

I'd grabbed a set of the body armour, though, and wore it now, concealed beneath my uniform greatcoat. It felt a little heavy and uncomfortable, but a lot less so than taking a las-bolt to the chest.

'It just might,' Trebek agreed. She was busily hanging frag grenades from her body harness. Most of them had a couple, along with smoke canisters, luminators, spare power packs, and all the other odds and ends troopers carry into the field. The exception was Holenbi, who carried a medpack in place of the grenades, but his expertise in battlefield medicine made him more valuable patching the others up if the necessity arose. And if it came down to grenades in a confined space, we were pretty much fragged in any case, so a couple more or less wouldn't make any difference.

'You can take the brute force approach if you like.' Sorel sighted along the length of his long-las, and made a minute adjustment to the targeter. I'd taken the trouble to find the weapon that used to be assigned to him, knowing that a sniper gets as attached to his weapon as I was to my old pistol, and that he would have customised it in a dozen subtle ways to improve its accuracy. 'I've got all the edge I need right here.' He must have realised the strings I'd had to pull to obtain it for him, because he met my eyes at that point and nodded, a barely perceptible thanks. I was astonished. Up until then I'd been convinced he had no emotions at all.

'Just make sure you keep it pointed in the right direction,' I said, with enough of a smile to take most of the sting out of the warning. It was still there, though, and an expression I couldn't quite identify came close to surfacing on his habitually impassive face.

'I could use a few more pressure pads,' Holenbi said, inventorying the medkit with the speed of long practice. I gestured to the primary aid box bolted to the Chimera's inner bulkhead.

'Help yourself,' I invited. He burrowed rapidly through it, scavenging several items which made the bag on his belt bulge, and stowed a few more in other pouches and pockets, discarding a couple of ration bars to make room for them.

'Better eat that,' Velade advised, taking the seat next to him. 'You'll only get hungry later if you leave it.'

'Yeah, right,' he agreed, breaking one in half and offering the rest to her. She took it with a smile, their hands touching for a moment as her fingers closed around it, and Amberley grinned at me.

'Aww,' she mouthed, her back to them. 'How sweet.'

Maybe to her, I thought, but to me it was little more than another potential complication in a catastrophe just waiting to happen. I quelled my irritation, and picked the remaining bar off the bench.

'She's got a point.' I split the bar with Amberley. 'Better stock up with carbohydrates while you can. You'll be burning a lot of energy soon enough.'

'You're the expert,' she said, as though anyone else's opinions mattered a damn on this foolhardy expedition. She sniffed at the grey fibrous mass, and bit into it cautiously. 'You people actually eat this frak?'

'Not if we can help it,' Velade said.

'Then I'm definitely surviving this.' Amberley swallowed the remains of her ration bar with a grimace of distaste. 'No way that's going to be my last meal.' The troopers all laughed, even Sorel, and I marvelled again at her powers of manipulation.[1] By playing the civilian outsider, she'd reinforced their sense of identity as soldiers with great subtlety. I doubted whether it would be quite enough to weld them into a cohesive unit, but that wasn't really an issue on this assignment. All that was necessary was that they work well enough together to get Amberley the intelligence she required. And me out in one piece, of course.

There were still far too many weak links for my liking, though. Kelp and Trebek were professional enough to put their rivalries aside for long enough to get the job done, I hoped, especially with an inquisitorial pardon up for grabs, but the way they kept avoiding eye contact with each other was a far from encouraging sign. And whatever was going on between Velade and Holenbi might just be enough for them to put their concern for each other ahead of the mission objective, or the survival of anyone else. Like me. And as for Sorel; well, he flat out gave me the creeps, and I was determined not to let him get anywhere I couldn't keep an eye on him. I'd met psychopaths before, and he had all the hallmarks. He wouldn't hesitate to sacrifice the rest of us to save his own skin, of that I was sure.[2]

And then there was Amberley. Charming as I found her, she was still an inquisitor above all else, and that meant that all we were to her was a means to an end. A noble and important one, no doubt, but that would be of little comfort to me when the black bell tolled.[3]

So it was little wonder that my palms were tingling as I closed the tail ramp and activated my combead.

'All right, Jurgen,' I said. 'We're ready to go.'

* * *

1. *Coming from Cain, that's a real compliment.*

2. *An old expression about pots and kettles springs to mind at this point, as well as the saying about taking one to know one...*

3. *He is speaking figuratively here, the tolling of the Black Bell of Terra being a well-known soldier's euphemism for death in action. I hardly think he would have expected such an accolade in actual fact!*

THIS TIME, THERE were no waves and cheers as we left the compound, although I had no doubt that the rumour mill had spread the news of our departure just as far as before. I was quietly relieved by that, to be honest, as this was to be no easy victory for our newly forged regiment to take pride in and celebrate. This would be a desperate struggle for survival, I didn't need my itching palms to tell me that. Although how desperate, and against how terrible a foe, I still at that time had no inkling. (And that was a mercy, let me tell you. If I'd known then what awaited us in the undercity of Mayoh, I would probably have broken down in hysterics from sheer terror.)

As it was, I masked my concern with the ease of long practice, and kept a stern eye on the troopers, hoping any agitation I felt would be mistaken for vigilance. To my relief they seemed to be settling, focussing more on the mission now that it was underway, and if they weren't exactly on the same wavelength yet, at least they weren't jamming each other.

That reminded me I hadn't reported our departure to Kasteen yet, so I retuned my combead to the command frequency and exchanged a few words with her. As I'd expected, her mood was sombre, and she wished me luck as though she thought I might actually need it.

I was beginning to find the tense atmosphere inside the vehicle a little claustrophobic, not to mention being rattled around like a pea in a can by Jurgen's habitual driving style, so I popped the turret hatch and stuck my head out for some fresh air. The sudden rush was invigorating, almost taking my cap with it as I emerged, and I checked the heavy bolter so I'd have an excuse for staying out there for as long as I could. It was primed and ready, of course, Jurgen having done his usual thorough job, so I was able to settle back and enjoy the spectacle of the local civilian traffic swerving out of our way. There seemed to be a lot of it, I noticed, particularly in the main boulevards; but there was no obvious pattern to the movement. There was just as much going in each direction, and when I glanced down the crossways, they all seemed choked as well.

'Inquisitor,' I subvocalised, switching to the channel Amberley had given me earlier. I hadn't seen any sign of a bead in her ear, but that didn't surprise me. For all I knew, she'd disguised it in some way, or was stuffed with augmetics that did the same job. (And a great many others, as I was to discover over the course of our association.) 'There seems to be a lot of civilian activity. Anything we should be aware of?' There was actually a great deal we should have been aware of, of course, the conspiracy we tracked was far more extensive and dangerous than we had imagined, but at that point, I was still blissfully ignorant of how much trouble we were in.

'Probably lots of things.' Amberley sounded wary, though not particularly concerned. 'But we'll just have to make do with what we know, and proceed with caution.'

Easier said than done with Jurgen driving, I thought, but she was the expert. I watched as he swerved us around a slow-moving cargo lifter, its flatbed jammed with civilians carrying hastily assembled bundles of possessions. Probably just spooked by our raid on the Heights, but the implications troubled me. I began to look out for similar sights, and found several in the space of a handful of seconds. I voxed Amberley again.

'It's looking like refugee traffic up here,' I said.

'Intriguing,' she responded, a note of curiosity entering her voice. 'What would they be fleeing, I wonder?'

'Nothing good,' I said, speaking from bitter experience, although in truth it wouldn't be that unexpected for anyone who could to be leaving the city by now. The political and military situation was still balanced on a knife-edge, and it wouldn't need someone of Mott's intellect to deduce that things would be a lot healthier somewhere else if it all boiled over. No harm in checking everything, I thought, so I hopped through the tactical frequencies, finding a lot of garbled traffic on the PDF net. Very little of it seemed to be making sense, though.

'Commissar.' Kasteen's voice cut in suddenly. 'I think you should know. We've just had instructions to go to combat readiness.'

'Who from?' Amberley interrupted before I could respond. I suppose I might have resented her butting in, let alone monitoring my supposedly secure messages, but right then I was too busy swinging the bolter round and taking the safety off. A thick column of smoke was visible ahead of us, rising from a burning truck in the middle of the road, and the traffic was beginning to stall and gridlock as panicked drivers tried to find a way around it or turn back. Bright las-bolts were scoring the air, but who was shooting and what they were aiming at remained obscured behind the smoke.

'By order of the governor,' Kasteen said.

'Imbecile!' Amberley said, along with some qualifying adjectives which I'd last heard in an underhive drinking den when someone turned out to have more than the conventional number of emperors in their tarot deck. I began to suspect that Governor Grice's political future was going to be short and uncomfortable. 'We'll have the tau on our arses like flies round a corpse.'

'I think we already have,' I said. Something was moving inside the smoke, fast and agile, twice the height of a man. It wasn't alone, either. There were more of them moving back there, and the whole pack of them was surrounded by little darting dots. I suddenly remembered the flying platters we'd seen at the tau enclave, and that they were armed too.

Abruptly, unnervingly, the leading dreadnought (the same type El'-sorath had called battlesuits) swung its head in our direction, and turned, a pair of long-barrelled weapons mounted on its shoulders coming to bear. We were still a long way away from being an easy target, but I've always been cautious, so I hailed our driver.

'Jurgen!' I shouted, 'get us out of here!'

By way of reply, he swung us abruptly towards a narrow alleyway, crushing a raised bed of ornamental shrubs beneath our left-hand tread, and barging a small, sleek groundcar out of the way. The driver's volley of profanity was drowned out by a sudden thunderclap of displaced air as something hit the front of an omnibus right where we'd been a moment before, reducing its entire nose to metallic confetti before raking the length of it, blowing a tangled mass of wreckage, blood and bone out of the back. Before I could see anything more, we were behind the shelter of a building, our hurtling metallic shell gouging lumps out of the walls, our tracks leaving a trail of burst and flattened waste containers in our wake.

'Emperor's bowels!' I said, stunned by the narrowness of our escape.

'What was that?' Amberley asked, her voice almost drowned out by the complaints of the troopers around her. I tried to explain the best I could, still shaken by the range and accuracy of the weapon deployed against us. 'Sounds like a railgun,' she said, apparently unperturbed. 'Nasty things.'

'Could it have damaged us?' I asked, making sure the spare ammo boxes were in easy reach. There was nothing ahead of us now except more panicking civilians, but I wasn't planning on being taken by surprise twice, you can be sure.

'Easily,' she replied cheerfully. 'Even at that range it could have gutted us like a fish.'

'The Emperor protects,' Jurgen said piously. Well He hadn't done a hell of a lot for the bus passengers, I thought, but decided it wouldn't be tactful to say so. He'd only take it as a sign that we were important to His ineffable plan anyway.

'Who were the tau engaging?' I asked.

'The PDF,' Kasteen said. 'Who else? We're getting reports in that some of the loyalists have mutinied, and opened fire on the tau compound. The diplomats are trying to calm things, but the bluies are claiming they have a right to retaliate, and have entered the city. They're engaging every PDF unit they come across.'

'What about the Guard?' I asked, already sure I wouldn't like the answer.

'The governor's orders are to contain the situation by any means necessary. The lord general is asking for clarification.' Playing for time, in other words. If the Guard units entered the city, they'd be caught in the middle; with half the PDF unreliable, they'd become a target for both sides. My stomach lurched, and for once, it wasn't due to Jurgen's driving.

'Well, that's it then,' I said, the words like ashes in my mouth. 'We've run out of time.' The war so many people had sacrificed so much to avoid was upon us at last, and it seemed there wasn't a damn thing we could do about it.

Editorial Note:

It goes without saying that the unrest which Cain noticed breaking out across the city was being duplicated to a lesser extent across the whole of Gravalax; although with the bulk of both the Imperial and tau expeditionary forces based around the capital, the situation deteriorated further and faster in Mayoh than anywhere else on the planet. Minor clashes did take place around several of the starports, as both sides realised keeping them open or denying them to the enemy would be vital in either reinforcing or evacuating their forces. For the most part, the warfare was internecine, pro- and anti-xenoist factions within the PDF turning on one another with the terrible ferocity unique to civil war.

The following extract may prove useful in appreciating the wider picture.

From *Purge the Guilty! An impartial account of the liberation of Gravalax,* by Stententious Logar. 085.M42

Thus it was, spurred by the workings of a vast, malign conspiracy, the entire world was rent asunder in an orgy of fratricide which shames the survivors and their descendants even to the present day. If anything at all can be said to have been learned from these terrible events, it must surely be this; that however benign they may appear, the alien is not to be trusted, and that turning aside from the word of the Emperor in even the smallest respect is the most certain route to damnation for us all.

It must have been the belated realisation of this which spurred the loyal cadre of Planetary Defence Force regulars into turning on the traitors in their midst, taking heart from the salutary way in which the Imperial Guard had dealt with the alien-lovers who had dared to desecrate the streets of an Imperial city with open rebellion. Their patriotic fervour at last aroused, His Divine Majesty's most loyal servants began to cleanse the hideous stain on their honour in the only way possible; by shedding the blood of those whose craven panderings to the aliens in their midst had led the whole planet to the very brink of the abyss.

At first, the renewal of martial spirit was sporadic, beginning with the arrest of those unit commanders whose loyalties were, for one reason or another, suspect. Inevitably, however, faced with the threat of exposure, those whose souls were stained with the guilt of collaboration resisted, proving their black-heartedness by opening fire on the heroic defenders of Imperial virtue. The rot spread exponentially after that, until almost every PDF unit was engaged on one side or the other; indeed, such was the confusion that many were unable to tell friend from foe and simply engaged every other unit they encountered indiscriminately.

Under these circumstances, it was hardly surprising that the most fervent of the loyalists lost no time in placing the blame squarely on the shoulders of those ultimately responsible, the xenos themselves, and resolved to rid our world of the taint of their presence without further delay. These heroes of legendary proportions, whose names would undoubtedly ring down the ages of Gravalax forever more if enough of their bodies had remained intact to identify, turned on the corruption at its source and threw themselves against the very citadel of the invader.

Alas, faced with the overwhelming firepower of this redoubt of the unholy, they were cut to pieces, but the damage had been done. Aware for the first time of their own vulnerability, the tau advanced into the city to slaughter the righteous, and the very future of Gravalax hung in the balance.

Throughout these events, one question remains unanswered. Why did the Imperial Guard take so long to respond? Accusations of cowardice are clearly ridiculous, if not treasonous, the lord general's reputation alone being sufficient to belie them without a moment's thought. Once again, the only credible explanation is that of conspiracy, some dark machination hindering their deployment for reasons we can only guess at. As to the hand behind that conspiracy, a careful sifting of the evidence once again points us firmly to the shadowy presence of the rogue traders...

[*And after a reasonably concise summary of events up to that point, he veers off on his personal obsession once more. Perhaps it's just as well, though; if anyone were to deduce the real enemy we were facing, we would have to take steps to obscure the truth.*]

ELEVEN

'Whatever happens, we have got The Emperor's
blessing. They have not.'
— From *'The Guardsman's Duty,'*
a popular ballad (trad.)

THE WAREHOUSE WAS just as we'd left it, which is to say it was a tangled mess of collapsed rubble and gently smoking debris. As we disembarked from the Chimera, the scent of old burning caught at the back of my throat, making me cough. We hadn't seen any more of the supernaturally fast tau dreadnoughts before we reached our destination, but I remained cautious nevertheless, ordering the troopers to consider the area enemy territory as we left the relative safety of the armoured carrier. What little I'd been able to glean from the vox traffic was less than encouraging, and my attempts to get through to someone more senior at divisional HQ for clarification were futile; no one there seemed to have a clue what was going on either. Besides, this was the inquisitor's little expedition, and she showed no sign of calling it off, so I gave up after a while and just let her get on with it.

'It seems clear enough,' Amberley said, consulting an auspex she'd produced from somewhere, and for a moment, I wondered what else the dark cape concealed. Nevertheless, the troopers debarked with commendable precision, covering each other as they moved. Kelp on point, while the others remained protected by the vehicle's armour plate until he'd reached the cover of a nearby heap of rubble, then Trebek, who headed for a tumbled wall on the opposite flank. Once they were established, Velade followed, taking up a position behind them, then Holenbi, who, I noticed, picked a spot where he could cover her as effectively as possible despite leaving a small blind spot in his coverage of Trebek. After a moment's hesitation, I decided to let it go just this once. After all, they weren't the most cohesive team I might have wished for, and it could have been an honest mistake. Sorel swept the area with the targeter of his long-las, and raised a hand.

'It's clear, commissar,' he said. 'You can move.'

'After you,' I said. He shrugged, almost imperceptibly, and was gone, crouching low, hurrying over the uneven ground to a point about fifty metres ahead of Kelp, where a fallen structural beam lay across a tumbled internal wall. He scrambled up it, worming his way into a gap between the chunks of masonry, and froze, scanning the rubble around us through his magnifying sight. If I hadn't been keeping an eye on him the whole way, I would barely have known he was there.

Amberley raised a quizzical eyebrow at me.

'Wouldn't it have been more prudent to have moved out while he kept you covered?' she asked.

'Any other sharpshooter, yes,' I said. 'But after what he said at the briefing–'

'Better safe than sorry,' she finished for me. I nodded, and indicated the open ramp.

'Whenever you're ready, inquisitor.'

'After you,' she said, and I almost missed the grin that accompanied her echo of my own words. I wouldn't have been all that surprised if she didn't trust me, mind you; I wouldn't have trusted me either, but then I suppose I know myself better than most.

So I smiled in return, to let her think I thought she was joking, and dropped to the ground, my boots crunching on the scattered ash. Jurgen had left the driver's compartment by now and I was joined by his odour, followed an instant later by the man himself. In spite of myself, my eyebrows rose.

'Are you sure you're not a little lightly armed for this?' I asked, and a momentary frown of concern flashed across his face before he realised I was joking.

Like the rest of us, except for Amberley (for all I knew, she might just have concealed hers the way I had), he was wearing a carapace jacket, but in a reassuring nod to the Guard I knew, his was definitely one of the standard sizes – too big – although most of his kit looked like that at the best of times. He had a hellgun like the others, but it was slung across his shoulders. In his hands was the unmistakable bulk of a meltagun, a heavy thermal weapon normally used to give tanks a hard time in close terrain, which was about the only time you stood a chance of getting near enough to use one without being spread across the landscape. Emperor alone knew where he'd got it from, but it was a reassuring sight nonetheless. He shrugged.

'I thought if we were tunnel fighting we might want to clear a path quickly,' he said. Well, it would certainly do that, I thought, whether our path was blocked by rubble or enemy troopers.

'Good idea,' I said. On this kind of mission there was no such thing as overkill.

'Did you remember the marshmallows?' Amberley asked, appearing at my elbow. Jurgen looked a little worried.

'I don't think so...' he began.

'She's joking, Jurgen,' I reassured him. A slow grin spread across his face.

'Oh, I get it. It's a thermal weapon, and you toast–'

'Quite.' I turned to see Sorel signal the all-clear, and Kelp begin the next step in the complex game of leapfrog which would get us to our objective.

I'D HALF EXPECTED us not to find it, what with the building having collapsed and all, but Amberley's auspex pointed us in the right direction, and after a few moments of alternately dashing forward, ducking for cover, and trying to keep an eye on five former mutineers I didn't trust for a second, we assembled again in the shadow of a wall. Or what was left of one, at least.

'It should be around here,' Amberley said, sweeping the little instrument around so its guiding spirit could get a better view. Something on the readout seemed to satisfy her, and it vanished into the recesses of her cloak as deftly as it had appeared in the first place. She indicated a small heap of rubble, and smiled. 'Under that, if I'm not mistaken.'

'Kelp, Sorel,' I said, indicating the debris, and the two men stepped forward, Kelp with a scowl and the sniper with his usual lack of expression. They slung their weapons and began the onerous task of shifting the rubble. 'The rest of you keep watching our perimeter,' I ordered, diverting their attention from the work. Somewhat shamefaced, Trebek, Velade, and Holenbi stopped gawping at the rapidly growing hole and resumed their guard duties.

'Not good,' I muttered to Jurgen. They shouldn't have let themselves get distracted that easily, even if the inquisitor's little gadget had assured them there were no hostiles in the area. He nodded.

'Sloppy,' he agreed, unconscious of the irony.

'Is that what you're looking for?' Kelp asked, after a few more moments of heavy lifting. What looked like a maintenance hatch of some kind had been revealed, bent and twisted by the heat and the pounding it had received from the falling rubble. He wiped a grimy hand across his sweating face, leaving a streak of soot and masonry dust. Sorel, more fastidious, wiped his hands against the knees of his trousers.

'I think so,' Amberley said. Kelp nodded, grasped the handle, and pulled, every one of his overdeveloped muscles standing out as he strained against it. After a moment he gasped and let go.

'We'll need a demo charge to shift that.'

'Maybe if I...' Jurgen took a step forward, and aimed the melta at it. Kelp and Sorel scrambled back with almost indecent haste, and even Amberley looked a little disconcerted as she raised a hand to forestall him.

'We just want the hatch open, not the whole building down.'

'Right idea, though,' I added, seeing his crestfallen expression. 'Velade, Holenbi, front and centre. Five rounds rapid.' The twisted metal flashed into vapour under the combined power of the hellgun volley, and I clapped Jurgen on the back encouragingly. 'Good thinking.' Which, by his standards, it had been.

'Or that might do it,' Kelp conceded, staring down into the darkened hole which had opened up at our feet. I aimed my trusty pistol at it, but it was a pointless precaution; anyone waiting in ambush would have been vaporised along with the inspection panel, and anyone outside the hellguns' area of effect would have been shooting back by now.

'Good.' Amberley looked satisfied. 'I was hoping they'd think this way down had been blocked off.'

I wasn't about to take anything for granted, though, so I assembled the squad quickly.

'Kelp,' I said, 'you're on point.' He nodded, but didn't look happy. 'Then Sorel, Velade, Jurgen, me, the inquisitor, Holenbi. Trebek has the rear.' That ought to keep the biggest potential troublemakers as far apart as possible, and separate the two lovebirds just enough to keep their minds on the job instead of each other. I hoped. Amberley caught my eye and nodded. Good, she wasn't going to undermine my authority by contradicting me.

'Whatever happened to "ladies first"?' Kelp grumbled, and dropped into the dank-smelling darkness below.

WELL, IT MIGHT have been a consequence of my upbringing, but the labyrinth of service ducts we found ourselves in felt almost reassuring. I was careful not to let myself get too comfortable, though, as in my experience complacency is just a shortcut to a body bag. No one was shooting at us, and the auspex, now back in Amberley's hand, remained reassuringly free of hostile contacts.

Or, indeed, contacts of any kind. Our footsteps echoed back at us, despite every attempt at stealth, and the beams of our luminators picked out nothing more threatening than the occasional rodent.

After a while, I noticed that the dust in the corridor ahead of us was undisturbed, a thick layer which puffed up under our footfalls before settling slowly back down again. I felt the residue tickling my eyes and the back of my throat, and fought the impulse to sneeze.

'This isn't the way you came before, is it?' I asked, and Amberley shook her head.

'No,' she admitted. 'I thought a detour might be prudent, given the welcome we got the last time.'

'But you do know where we're going, right?' I persisted. She repeated the gesture.

'Haven't a clue,' she said cheerfully. Something of what I felt must have shown on my face, because she smiled then, and qualified the remark. 'I mean we should be heading roughly south-west, but all these corridors look alike to me.'

'Then we need to bear off more in that direction,' I said, indicating a side corridor that intersected the one we were in about thirty metres ahead.[1] Kelp flattened himself against the wall next to it, and signalled the all clear.

I was beginning to pick up a clearer idea of Amberley's destination, which, despite her claims of uncertainty, she manifestly had. If I still had my bearings we were heading in the general direction of the old quarter, which made some kind of sense. The tunnels would be closer to the surface there, making them more accessible to whoever else was

---

1. *Cain's sense of direction underground was indeed remarkably good, as I had the opportunity to observe a number of times, a fact which adds some plausibility to his claim to have been native to a hive world. Although it should be noted that he could become as lost as anyone else on occasion, particularly when under fire or attempting to move closer to the enemy, a minor discrepancy over which I have tended to give him the benefit of the doubt.*

down here. Who they might be, and what they might be hoping to achieve was still a mystery to me, however.

We proceeded in silence for some time, until Sorel held up a hand, warning us to stop. Amberley and I padded over to join him.

'What is it?' I asked. Kelp's face, a pale disc in the gloom, stared back at us, waiting for the signal to proceed.

'Movement,' he said, pointing away into the darkness ahead of us. Amberley checked the screen of her auspex.

'Nothing on this,' she said. I didn't care what the box said. Techpriests might have complete faith in their machines, but I'd been let down by them too often in the past. Sorel had a sniper's instincts, and was as much a survivor as me, and if he was feeling spooked, then so was I.

'Kelp?' I asked. The point man made a negative gesture. No contact.

'I didn't see anything,' he added verbally.

'OK. Proceed,' I said. Then quietly I added to Sorel, 'Keep your eyes open.' He nodded an acknowledgement and moved out, his gun at the ready. The others followed, a little more nervous now, and I waited until they'd all passed before dropping into line behind Trebek.

'Taking the rearguard now?' Amberley asked, falling into step beside me. 'Isn't that dangerous?'

It was, of course, the second most dangerous spot in the column, vulnerable to being picked off by an ambusher or a pursuer. But if Sorel was right, the enemy was definitely ahead of us now. I shrugged.

'As opposed to the position of perfect safety that you're in at the moment?' I asked, and was rewarded with another throaty chuckle, which lifted my spirits in spite of myself. The mood didn't last long, though; as we passed the mouth of a service duct, I noticed the dust around it had been disturbed, and not long ago, either. I pointed it out to Amberley, my voice low so as not to alarm the others. 'What do you make of that?'

The duct was a good two metres above the floor, but the dust beneath it showed only the marks of our own boots. My palms tingled, and I swept the beam of my luminator across the tangle of pipework that hung from the ceiling over our heads. It was possible someone had lurked there, but why had they moved just as we approached? And how had they got up there in the first place?

'Remind you of anything?' Amberley asked quietly. Now that she asked, it did – a maddening sense of familiarity that refused to gel. The only thing I was certain of was that it had been something bad, but with all the horrors I'd faced up to that point, it didn't help much in narrowing it down. I was about to say something sarcastic to Amberley about another clue helping when my attention was firmly distracted.

'Commissar.' Kasteen's voice hissed in my ear, hazed with static. 'Can you hear me?'

'Barely,' I said. The metres of masonry and rockcrete over our heads were attenuating the signal, and if we went much further, we would be out of contact entirely. 'What's happening?'

'The governor has ordered the arrest of Lord General Zyvan!' Even through the static the outrage in her voice was palpable. 'And he's demanding the Guard move into the city right away!'

'On what charge?' Amberley said. Whatever vox gear she had was evidently a little stronger than mine, because Kasteen recognised her voice.

'Cowardice!' Kasteen sounded even more outraged than before. 'How he has the nerve–'

'Will be determined by the proper authorities.' Amberley's voice was crisp and commanding now. 'Until such time as that can be arranged the armies of the Imperium will remain under the command of the lord general, and if the governor objects to that, he is more than welcome to take the matter up with the Inquisition.'

'I'll relay that message,' Kasteen said, evidently relishing the prospect of the governor's reaction.

'Colonel,' I added, before she could cut the link. 'What's the situation with the tau?'

'Grim,' Kasteen admitted. 'They're still engaging PDF units all over the city. Civilian casualties are already up in the thousands, and we have rioters choking the streets. But so far they've held off from attacking us. If the lord general and the diplomats can buy us a little more time–'

'They'll have to,' Amberley cut in. 'Whatever happens, the Guard must not get sucked into an open war with the tau.'

'Understood,' Kasteen said. It must have been galling for her, though, and the strain was clear in her voice. Being forced to stand by and do nothing while an imperial city burned, and xenos massacred the citizens with impunity was probably the hardest thing she ever had to do.

'Well, that's something,' Amberley said, as the vox link went dead. 'At least there's still hope.'

'Hope for who?' I asked, trying not to think of the civilians who, even as we stood here, were losing their homes and their lives. I'd be the first one to admit that I'm a self-centred hedonist, but even I felt a surge of sympathy for their plight.

'For half the segmentum,' Amberley replied, sounding suddenly weary, and for the first time, I had an inkling of the terrible weight of responsibility her calling imposed. 'You need to focus on the big picture, Ciaphas. Emperor knows, sometimes that's hard.' Moved by an impulse I couldn't explain, I took her hand for a moment, imparting what moral support I could through simple human contact.

'I know,' I said. 'But someone has to do it. And today that someone is us.'

Amberley laughed, only slightly forced, and squeezed my palm for a moment before letting go.

'That was completely ungrammatical, you realise.'

'Never my strong point,' I admitted. It was strange, now I come to recall it, but her use of my given name seemed so natural I never thought to be surprised.

SHORTLY AFTER THAT, we lost contact with the surface entirely. Or at least I did, and if Amberley was still able to get a signal through she wasn't saying. Even though we were beyond all realistic hope of reinforcement in any case, I found the sensation profoundly dispiriting, and tried to concentrate on the job at hand. It was in one of these moments of distraction that I collided with Trebek, who had stopped suddenly in the tunnel ahead of me.

'What is it?' I asked, knowing that she wouldn't just freeze like that for no reason.

'I thought I heard something,' she said. I cocked my head, listening hard, but couldn't make out anything over the scuff of our footfalls and our breathing. We were moving stealthily enough – these troopers had been hunting tyranids less than six months before in conditions not dissimilar to this, don't forget, and if there's anything in the galaxy more calculated to teach you caution than that, I've yet to come across it – but the multiplicity of hard surfaces around us magnified every sound we made, however slight, with dozens of overlapping echoes. And, paradoxically, the quieter we moved the louder we sounded to our own ears, straining all the harder to hear over it.

So I issued the order to halt, and we waited tensely for the echoes to die away.

'There,' Trebek breathed after a moment. 'Hear that?'

I could. It was the sharp crack of lasguns, and a similar, deeper note which sounded both familiar and slightly wrong. At the time I put it down to the echoes, but we were to discover the real reason soon enough.

'Gunfire,' I confirmed. 'About half a klom that way.' I indicated the direction without thinking, before realising it lay almost dead on to Amberley's preferred route. Just great. Trebek looked a little puzzled.

'Are you sure, sir?'

'Absolutely,' I said, before realising that no one else here would be quite so at home in these tunnels as me.[1] Valhalla has its cavern cities, of course, but they're quite different to the average hive, with wide open spaces under well-lit roofs of rock and ice. It was perishingly cold too, the way the locals like it, but it takes all sorts to make a galaxy, and you can always turn up the heat in your hotel suite. (Not too much, though, as I discovered once, or you can end up with bits of the wall dripping onto your belongings.) Amberley took another look at her auspex, which was as quietly unhelpful as before.

'If you say so,' she said. After a moment, the firing stopped, and a deeper, more unnerving silence descended. We listened for a little while longer, but it soon became apparent that we would learn nothing more by remaining where we were, and Amberley urged us to proceed. Not having a plausible reason to go back, I agreed, and we moved on as before, though not without a considerable amount of trepidation on my part.

It was about five minutes later that Kelp, who was still on point, held up his hand and halted.

'What is it?' I asked.

'Bodies. Lots of them.' Well, that was a bit of an exaggeration, but there were at least half a dozen spread out across the large open space which the corridor had eventually led us into. It seemed to be a junction point of some kind because a number of other tunnel mouths led away from it, to all points of the compass, and by my estimation it had been used for storage or something quite recently. About a dozen stacking units had been broken open, though what they had contained was now a mystery, and the smashed remains of a glow globe showed that someone had been working here not too long ago.

'Recognise this?' I asked Amberley, who was looking around with obvious signs of familiarity. She nodded.

'This was as far as we got before,' she said. 'We came in through that corridor there.' She pointed to one of the other entrances. 'We took them by surprise, but there were more of them than we'd anticipated, and then the reinforcements showed up.' I spotlighted the nearest corpse with my luminator, a stocky fellow in work overalls with most of his chest missing.

'Was he among them?'

'I wasn't waiting around to be introduced,' she said. 'But I don't think so.' Her eyes glazed over for a second with the effort of recall. 'Rakel was

---

1. *Again, I can vouch from personal experience that Cain did have an almost uncanny ability to disentangle sounds from echoes in a confined space, his estimates of their sources being remarkably accurate in most cases.*

having some kind of seizure, and then she took a las-bolt to the stomach. After that it got a little confusing.'

The troopers were acting like proper soldiers, I noted absently, spreading out to secure our perimeter as best they could without waiting for orders, which was something at least, so I returned my attention to what the inquisitor was saying. This was the most she'd let slip about her previous excursion into these tunnels since we started, and I hoped to find out a little more.

'What kind of a seizure?' I asked. 'Like the one she had when she saw Jurgen?' Amberley shook her head.

'No,' she said slowly, 'that was something quite different. I'm still not sure what it means.' But she had her suspicions, I could tell, even if she wasn't about to share them with me. She moved on rapidly, in a transparent attempt to change the subject, which vaguely surprised me, as I'd come to expect more subtlety from her than that. 'We were standing over there.' She pointed. 'Rakel had been getting more agitated the deeper we came, sensing something, but not really able to tell me what it was. Then as we got closer to the people here, it got worse.'

'They were psykers too?' I asked, feeling even more uneasy, if that were possible. I'd encountered those before, and it had never ended well. Amberley shrugged, a delicate ripple of her shoulders.

'Possibly.' Whether she was uncertain, or just being non-committal, I couldn't tell.

'Sir. Inquisitor.' Holenbi gestured diffidently from the side of one of the corpses. 'I think you should see this.'

'What?' I moved to join him, Amberley at my side.

'This one was killed by something else.' He indicated the body, a young woman with a shaved head and a xenoist braid, who had apparently been eviscerated by a close combat weapon of some kind. I'd seen a lot of people killed the same way over the years, but the wounds the weapon had left were unfamiliar. That didn't necessarily mean much, of course; there are plenty of ways of mounting a blade, but there's usually a fair degree of consistency within a culture, and I hadn't seen anything here which looked that unusual.

'I'm still trying to work out what killed the others,' I said. The wounds were too heavy for lasguns, even the hellguns we carried. I'd heard them being fired though, I was sure about that. By the insurgents, then; there were several lying around close to the corpses, so it didn't need an inquisitor to join those dots.

'It looks like plasma rounds to me,' Jurgen volunteered. The doubt in his voice told me how unlikely he thought it, though; plasma weapons were big, bulky, and unreliable, and took an age to recharge between shots. You'd have to be mad to arm an entire squad with them. Not to mention being rarer than an ork with a sense of humour. 'Plasma pistols, maybe?'

'Maybe,' I conceded. Those were even rarer, but suppose someone had found a whole cache of them from the fabled Dark Age of Technology? That would be worth going to almost any lengths to protect, wouldn't it?

'There's... something else,' Holenbi said, redirecting our attention to the dead woman. He looked a little green for a medic, I thought, then I noticed it myself. A large chunk of flesh had been ripped from her torso, as though by teeth.

'Merciful Emperor!' I made the sign of the aquila almost without thinking. I hadn't seen wounds like that since my last encounter with the tyranids. Even then, though, a small dispassionate part of my mind recognised that this was different, something I'd never seen before. 'What in the galaxy could do that?'

'Whatever it was, it didn't like the taste,' Amberley said, directing her luminator beam to a detached chunk of bloody flesh lying a few feet from the corpse. Holenbi turned greener, and eating his discarded ration bar earlier turned out to have been a bit of a waste of time for him.

'I've got movement!' Sorel called from the entrance to one of the tunnels.

'Are you sure?' Amberley was looking at that bloody auspex again, and the screen was still blank. 'I'm getting no human lifesigns at all.'

'What about abhuman ones?' I asked, and she shrugged.

'It's only calibrated for–'

A ball of light, eye-achingly bright, shot from the mouth of the tunnel Sorel was guarding, and exploded against an empty crate. Whoever the enemy was, they were upon us.

Editorial Note:

With the situation in the city deteriorating by the moment, Lord General Zyvan and the troops under his command were growing increasingly impatient to do something, notwithstanding the explicit instructions I had given to the contrary. Governor Grice's heavy-handed attempt to seize control of the imperial expeditionary force had tried their patience to the limit, and, as a man of honour, Zyvan clearly felt the slight of the accusations levelled against him. His subsequent actions may therefore be understood, if not entirely condoned.

What follows is a summarised partial transcript of the meeting he held with the senior officers of the expeditionary force, taken from the hololithic recording made by the equipment in the conference room, supplemented by a few personal observations subsequently gleaned from some of those present: most notably savant Mott, who represented the Inquisition in my absence, Colonel Kasteen of the 597th Valhallan, and Erasmus Donali of the Imperial Diplomatic Service.

The lord general is clearly irritated at this point, but keeping his temper by focussing on the issue at hand. He begins by asking Colonel Kasteen to confirm the instructions I gave her over the vox link regarding the governor's demands.

'That is correct, sir,' Kasteen replies, seeming cool and efficient despite being the youngest regimental commander present. Only someone very skilled at the interpretation of body language could detect her nervousness. 'You have complete command of this army by the express order of the Inquisition.'

'Good.' Zyvan's voice is clipped and decisive. 'Then I propose to calm the situation by removing the primary cause of the problem.'

'The inquisitor was also quite explicit that we cannot engage the tau under any circumstances.' Kasteen is clearly nervous here about appearing to contradict her commander, but her sense of duty out-weighs the prospect of any personal consequences – a commendable trait which stood her in good stead throughout her career. Zyvan concedes the point.

'I wasn't referring to the tau,' he reassures her, and everyone else at the table. 'I meant that cretinous excuse for a governor.'

There is general approval of this proposal. Several of the officers present suggest courses of action ranging from arrest to assassination. Eventually, the mood calms as Mott outlines the Inquisition's position on the matter.

'It does indeed appear that Govenor Grice is ultimately responsible for this situation,' he agrees. 'But there is still some ambiguity as to the degree of his culpability.' He begins to quote legal precedent at length, until Donali, who is familiar with the savant's peculiar mental processes, is able to steer him back to the topic at hand. 'In short,' he eventually concludes, 'we would rather have him available to account for his actions.'

'If the Inquisition wants him, they can have him,' Zyvan says. 'But in my opinion, his removal is a necessary prerequisite to restoring the situation to any kind of stability,' Donali agrees.

'The tau are also in agreement with this proposition,' Donali adds, which throws the meeting into turmoil for a few moments until Zyvan is able to restore order.

'You've discussed it with them?' he asks.

'Informally,' Donali admits. 'We still have a residue of goodwill, thanks to the actions of Commissar Cain, and I've been attempting to build on this. If we send troops to remove the governor, I believe they won't interfere.'

'Tell that to the PDF!' someone shouts. 'Or the civilians they're butchering!' Donali stares him down.

'They recognise the distinction between us and the local militia,' he says. 'By their logic, the PDF attacked them first, so they're fair game, and the civilians merely collateral damage. They can be persuaded that it's in everyone's interests to back off, I'm sure.'

'I'd like to see how,' Colonel Mostrue of the 12th Field Artillery cuts in. Mott begins to explain.

'Tau psychology is very peculiar by human standards. They crave stability, and are terrified at the prospect of any loss of order. In fact, it would be no exaggeration to say that, for them, it's as disturbing as we would find an eruption of Chaos.' This casual reference to the Great Enemy creates considerable consternation. Zyvan restores order with some difficulty.

'So you're saying that the situation in the city right now is essentially their worst nightmare come true?' he asks. Mott agrees.

'Anarchy, rioting, civil war between rival imperial factions, nothing fixed or reliable. If someone wanted to goad them into reckless behaviour, they could arrange nothing better.' A few of the more astute officers, Kasteen among them, pick up on the unspoken assumption behind those words.

'If they're so panicked and disorientated,' Zyvan asks, 'what makes you think they'd give us the benefit of the doubt?'

'They have this dogma they call the Greater Good,' Donali explains. 'If we can promise them that the governor's removal will improve the situation, they're as bound to let us try as we would be to accept an oath sworn in the Emperor's name.' The audio recording is swamped for a few seconds by sharp intakes of breath, and mutterings about heathen heresies. Zyvan brings the meeting back to order.

'Very well,' he concludes. 'Make overtures to them, and see if they'll swallow it.' Donali bows and leaves, making the sign of the aquila. Zyvan turns to Kasteen.

'Colonel,' he says. 'The 597th have been more deeply involved in these events than any other regiment, and your commissar seems to have the confidence of the inquisition as well as the xenos. If we can cut a deal with the tau, you'll supply the troops to carry the operation out.'

Kasteen salutes, looking stunned, and manages to respond in the affirmative.

TWELVE

'My enemy's enemy is a problem for later.
In the meantime, they might be useful.'
– Inquisitor Quixos (attributed)

I'M PROUD TO say that, despite the suddenness of the attack, my intellectual faculties remained undimmed. Which isn't to say that I didn't dive for the nearest piece of cover the instant I realised we were under fire, of course. A level head is a fine asset on the battlefield, but not when it's been shaped like that by a fragment of shrapnel. As I drew my faithful laspistol, the analytical part of my mind was already assessing the positions of the troopers, and the nearest lines of retreat, but my chances of making it to one of the tunnel mouths without being blown halfway to golden throne seemed on the slim side of pitiful, so I decided to stay put behind the nice solid piece of piping I'd found. More enemy fire was pouring in on us by now, and to my horror, I realised that Jurgen was right. These were plasma weapons we were facing, and even the heavy body armour we were wearing would be all but useless against it. I'd doused the luminator at once, of course, the others following suit, but the sun-bright flashes of the enemy weapons lit the space around us in a dazzling strobe that made my eyes ache.

A bolt of incandescent energy burst against the metal piping close to my head, just missing my face with a spray of molten metal. If profanity was a weapon our assailants would all have been dead in seconds at that point, believe me. Stray pieces of debris ignited from similar accidents, suffusing the chamber with a flickering orange glow that only intensified my sense of disorientation.

'Jurgen!' I shouted. 'Can you get a shot?'

'Not yet, commissar!' He was tucked in behind a barricade of crates, the melta gun rested across it, covering the tunnel entrance. When they burst through he'd be able to catch them, but they didn't seem in any hurry to assault us, probably anticipating just such a contingency.

'I have movement,' Sorel said calmly, sighting carefully down the barrel of his long-las. I noticed with some distaste that he'd concealed himself behind one of the corpses, lying prone and resting the barrel of the weapon across its chest as though it were a sandbag.

'What are they waiting for?' Amberley asked. 'Last time they were on us like a rash by now.' She'd taken cover behind an upturned table a few metres away. My palms tingled. In my experience, people didn't change their strategies that radically, that quickly. Especially if they'd seemed to work the last time...

'Kelp, Velade,' I ordered. 'Watch the cross corridors. They're trying to flank us!' Both troopers waved an acknowledgement, and began scanning the dark openings around us. I was suddenly uncomfortably aware of just how many there were to keep track of. Trebek and Holenbi kept their hellguns aimed at the entrance the enemy were firing from, sending an occasional las-bolt back in the vague hope of keeping their heads down.

'I have a shot,' Sorel said, his voice as emotionless as ever, and pulled the trigger. This one was undoubtedly effective, resulting in a screech of pain from deep in the tunnels that raised the hairs on the back of my neck.

'What the hell was that?' Velade asked, her face ashen. I was equally shocked, I have to admit, but for a very different reason; even despite the echoes and the gunfire, I'd recognised it.

'That was a kroot!' I said, in stunned amazement. Now it was Amberley's turn to look taken aback.

'Are you sure?' she asked. I nodded.

'I've spoken to one.' I expected her to query it, but instead she stood.

'Cease fire!' she yelled, with more volume than I would have thought her capable of. Although, come to think of it, her voice wasn't as loud as all that. It was the authority behind it which made it cut through the noise, and the troopers responded at once, even though every instinct they possessed probably told them to keep fighting. Of course, our assailants were under no such inhibition, and the volume of fire continued to pour into our makeshift barricades with undiminished vigour. Despite having made herself the most obvious target in the vicinity, however, Amberley seemed quite unperturbed. (At the time, I wasn't sure whether I was more impressed with her coolness or amazed at her recklessness, although, as I was to find out later, she had less reason to fear the plasma bolts than the rest of us. She could still have been hurt or killed, though, don't get me wrong – they're a tough-minded breed, inquisitors, make no mistake.)

She shouted again, her voice magnified by some amplivox device she produced from inside the robe, but this time, to my amazement, it was the hissing speech of the tau that came from her lips.[1]

I clearly wasn't the only one to be astonished by this, as the incoming fire ceased immediately. After a tense pause, she was answered in the same tongue, and gestured to me.

'Stand down and show yourselves,' she said. 'They want to talk.'

'Or shoot us more easily,' Kelp said, keeping his hellgun aimed.

'They can do that anyway,' I said. I gestured to the corpses surrounding us as I stood, flinching involuntarily from the anticipation of a plasma round impacting on my chest. Nothing happened, of course, and if I'd seriously expected it to I would have stayed huddled behind my nice, cosy pipes, and to the warp with the Inquisition. 'These heretics were pinned down in exactly the same position as us, and they tried to make a fight of it.'

'Can't argue with that.' Sorel stood, holding his sniper rifle by the barrel, arm outstretched from his body, making it obvious that he wasn't going to use it. One by one, the others revealed themselves, stepping out from behind whatever concealment they'd been able to find. Kelp was the last to move, complying at last with ill grace.

'Stay where you are.' Amberley moved forward, taking up a station in the middle of the largest open space she could find, and reactivated her luminator. She'd been visible before, of course,

---

1. *To understand an enemy, you have to understand how they think; and language, according to the magos of the Ordo Diologus, shapes perception. Accordingly, many inquisitors of the Ordo Xenos take the time to learn the languages of the species they expect to encounter in the course of their duties. Without wishing to appear immodest, I can claim reasonable fluency in the most common forms of the tau and eldar tongues, and communicate quite effectively in orkish (which is not that impressive an accomplishment, to be honest, as this particular 'language' consists largely of gestures and blows to the head.)*

silhouetted in the flickering firelight, but now, if the xenos intended treachery, she might just as well be holding up a sign saying, 'Shoot me, I'm here!' Once again, I found myself marvelling at her courage, and having to remind myself that this attractive young woman was actually an inquisitor with far more resources at her command than I could begin to imagine.

'Something's moving,' Sorel said. Thanks to his sharpshooter training, he'd kept his eye on the tau position ever since he'd first spotted them, even despite the order to disengage. As I strained my eyes through the murk, and the drifting smoke which was beginning to make them itch and to catch at my chest, I could see vaguely humanoid figures begin to take form.

At first, there were only the tau, their distinctive fatigues and hardshell body armour dulled with black and grey camouflage patterns ideally suited to blending into the shadows of this dusty labyrinth. Their faces were obscured by visored helmets – ocular lenses where the features should have been – which gave them a blank, robotic look. That brought back uncomfortable memories,[1] and I shuddered involuntarily. Usually, even xenos have expressions you can read, but those impassive visages gave nothing away about either their mood or their intentions.

Behind them padded a trio of kroot, three faces I would have been quite happy to have had obscured. As they entered the cavern, one of them sniffed the air, its head turning in my direction, then to my distinct unease, walked directly towards me.

Amberley continued to hiss and aspirate at the tau, one of whom had stepped out at the head of the half-dozen troopers. I conjectured, rightly, as it later turned out, that this was the leader of the group. I knew nothing of the language, of course, but I'd heard enough of it spoken to realise that things weren't going well.

'Inquisitor?' I asked, raising my voice slightly and trying to sound calm as the kroot padded closer, 'is there a problem?'

'They seem reluctant to trust us,' Amberley said shortly, and returned to the negotiations.

'Anything I can do to help?' I persisted. The kroot was almost on top of me now, and I couldn't help noticing the combat blades attached to its peculiar long-barrelled weapon were stained with blood. A vivid mental picture of the eviscerated woman we'd discovered, and how those wounds had been caused, rose up in my mind.

'None of them speak Gothic,' Amberley snapped, not needing to add, 'so shut up and let me get on with it,' because her tone did it for her.

---

1. *Presumably of his past encounters with the necrons.*

'Then how were they expecting to interrogate any prisoners?' Velade asked, before reaching the obvious conclusion, and trailing off with a sudden 'Oh!' of realisation.

'That would be my function, should the situation require it,' the kroot said, in the familiar combination of clicks and whistles I'd heard before. 'I'm pleased to find you in good health, Commissar Cain.'

Well, you're probably thinking I'm pretty dense not to have recognised Gorok straight away, but you should bear all the circumstances in mind. It was dark, we'd just been in the middle of a firefight, and why in the galaxy should I have expected him to be there in the first place? Besides, unless you're very close to them, kroot look remarkably alike. At least with orks you've got the scars to help tell them apart, in the unlikely event that you'd ever have to.

His use of my name had an immediate, and somewhat gratifying, effect on the tau, whose heads snapped round to stare at me. Then the leader turned back to Amberley, and asked something. Gorok made the peculiar clicking laughter-equivalent I'd heard before.

'The shas'ui is asking if it is really you,' he translated with evident amusement. I gathered that 'shas'ui' was some sort of rank, roughly equivalent to a sergeant or officer, and he meant the tau in charge.

'I was the last time I looked,' I said. Gorok clicked again, and translated the remark into tau, which he seemed to have mastered as thoroughly as Gothic. (I found it curious that so feral a creature should appear to be so educated, and questioned him about it later. He claimed to have learned both during his career as a mercenary in order to facilitate negotiations with his employers. Needless to say, I found the notion that he'd served alongside imperial troops somewhat hard to believe.[1])

Amberley said something, apparently confirming my identity, and the shas'ui looked in our direction. His next words were clearly addressed to me. I bowed formally to him.

'At your service,' I said.

'He states that your service to the greater good is remembered with gratitude,' Gorok translated helpfully. 'El'sorath remains in good health.'

---

1. *Difficult, but not impossible. Although kroot mercenaries are generally associated with the tau, and their homeworld appears to be a tau fiefdom, there have been sufficient reports of kroot fighting alongside other races to raise the possibility that they may not be quite so faithful servants as their patrons appear to believe. It's not entirely beyond the bounds of possibility that this particular one found employment on a backwater human world somewhere, or, more likely, had been part of a temporary alliance with Imperial forces against a mutual foe.*

'Pleased to hear it,' I said, tactfully refraining from hoping out loud that El'hassai wasn't. Amberley seized on the opening, and began speaking rapidly again. After a few more exchanges, the tau fire-team, or 'shas'la'[1] as they called themselves, withdrew to confer together in muttered undertones. Quite pointless really, as only Amberley had a clue what they were saying and she'd already heard it, but it was an oddly human gesture which I found vaguely reassuring.

'That was a lucky break,' she said. 'They weren't inclined to believe me at first. But apparently they think they can trust you.'

Well, more fool them, I thought, but of course I had more sense than to say it out loud. I just nodded judiciously.

'That's all well and good,' I said. 'But can we trust them?' Amberley nodded slowly.

'That's a good question,' she said. 'But right now I don't think we've got the option.'

'Begging your pardon, miss,' Jurgen coughed deferentially to attract her attention. 'But did they happen to mention what they're doing down here?'

'The same as us,' Amberley said. 'Following a lead.' My paranoia started twitching at that one, you can be sure.

'What kind of a lead?' I asked. But it was Gorok who answered.

'The intelligence reports provided by Governor Grice, as he agreed after the assassination of Ambassador Shui'sassai, made mention of a violent pro-Imperial group meeting in these tunnels. It was felt that further investigation was merited.'

'Did they indeed?' Amberley looked thoughtful, and in a way which boded ill for the governor.

'I take it that this is the first you've heard of it,' I said. She nodded.

'You take it correctly. But it's not entirely out of the question that such a group exists.' Her eyes went back to the dead woman with the xenoist braid, and clouded thoughtfully.

'I don't understand,' Jurgen said, frowning with the effort of concentration. 'If the governor knew about something like that, why tell the tau and not the Inquisition?'

'Because the tau could eliminate them for him without having to admit to his own weakness in allowing such a group to get established,' I suggested. Amberley nodded.

---

1. *Generally rendered into Gothic as 'pathfinders,' these are reconnaissance specialists roughly equivalent to Imperial Guard storm-troopers or the forward observers normally attached to an artillery battery. Cain would no doubt have had some pertinent observations on the topic had he been able to speak to them.*

'Or to consolidate his position with the xenos if he really was planning to hand the planet over to them.' She shrugged. 'Doesn't really matter. Incompetence or treachery, he's dead meat now whatever his motives.' The casual way she said it dripped ice water down my spine.

While we were talking, the tau had concluded their own deliberations, and came over to join us, the other two kroot in tow. The shas'ui said something, and Gorok translated it.

'Your proposal is acceptable,' he said. 'It would appear to serve the greater good.'

'What proposal?' Kelp asked, an edge in his voice. Amberley stared at him for a moment until he subsided.

'It appears our objectives are the same,' she said. 'So we're joining forces. At least until we know what we're up against down here.'

'Makes sense,' I agreed. 'I'd rather have those plasma guns on our side than shooting at us.' Now I came to look at one close up they were surprisingly compact, no larger than a lasgun, but the amount of firepower they could put out wasn't to be sniffed at.

'Team up with the bluies?' Kelp was outraged. 'You can't be serious! That's... That's blasphemy!'

'That's what the inquisitor wants. Live with it.' Trebek exchanged glares with him for a moment, until Amberley intervened.

'Thank you, Bella. As you so helpfully point out, my decisions are not requests.' She raised her voice a little, so all the troopers could hear. 'We're moving out. Anyone who objects is welcome to stay behind. Of course, the commissar will have to execute them before we leave to maintain operational security.' She smiled at me. 'I think it's very motivating for people to feel they have a choice, don't you?'

'Absolutely,' I said, wondering just how many more ways she'd find to surprise me before the day was over.

So we formed up, the tau leading, which was fine by me – let them soak up any fire from the ambushers I was sure would be lurking in the dark ahead of us – then our motley group of troopers. Jurgen took the whole business as phlegmatically as he did everything else, but I could see Kelp wasn't the only one with reservations about our new alliance. Warp only knows, I had my share too, but then I'm paranoid about everything (which in my job is the only prudent state of mind.) Velade and Holenbi kept a wary eye on the xenos, particularly the kroot, which really spooked them. Hidden under their armour, and their faces concealed by helmets, the tau might almost have passed for human if it hadn't been for the finger missing from each hand, but the kroot just looked like bad luck waiting for someone to happen to. Trebek professed to be entirely comfortable with the inquisitor's decision, but I suspected that was more to bait Kelp than from any sense of conviction. Only Sorel seemed completely at ease.

I turned to Kelp as we began to file out of the chamber.

'Coming?' I asked, my hand resting lightly on the butt of my laspistol. After a moment he fell in with the others, his eyes burning, but I've been glared at by experts, so I just returned the favour and waited for him to blink.

To my surprise, Gorok joined me at the rear of the column, but then I don't suppose there would have been much point in the interpreter being out of earshot of the monoglots. His companions were at the front, loping along next to the shas'ui, and as I watched their easy gait something struck me.

'I can't see a wound,' I said. 'Which kroot did Sorel shoot?'

'Kakkut,' he said, 'of the Dorapt clan. A fine tracker. Died quickly.' He seemed remarkably matter-of-fact about it. 'Your marksman is commendably skilled.'

Sorel, overhearing, looked quietly pleased at the compliment.

WE PROCEEDED ONWARDS and downwards in an uneasy silence, weapons at the ready, although truth to tell, I suspect both parties would have been just as happy to use them on each other than on the mysterious enemy we still seemed no closer to identifying. We were making better time now, though, the tau appearing to have some way of seeing in the dark. They certainly had no visible luminators, so I assumed the lenses on the front of their helmets enabled them to see in some way I couldn't quite comprehend. The kroot had no need of visual aids of any kind, slinking through the dark as though they were born to it. Maybe they were, who knows.

A muffled whisper from the lead tau brought everyone else to a halt – or to be more accurate, the tau stopped, and the rest of us ran into the back of them.

'What is it?' I asked. Amberley listened for a moment.

'Turn off your luminators,' she ordered. I complied, but not without some misgivings. I didn't trust our own troopers where I could see them, let alone in the dark, and as for the xenos... But she was an inquisitor after all, and I assumed she knew what she was doing.

I'd closed my eyes before dousing the light, so I knew they'd adjust quickly when I opened them again, but even so, the few moments it took were unnerving. I waited in the shrouding darkness, listening to the rapid beat of my heart, and tried to distinguish the other sounds around me: the scrape of boot soles against the floor, the muffled clinking of weapons and equipment, and the susurrus of a dozen pairs of lungs. The air felt warm and thick against my face, and I remember being obscurely grateful for Jurgen's distinctive odour, which was no more pleasant than usual but at least felt reassuringly familiar.

Gradually, I began to distinguish shapes in the gloom around me, and became aware of a faint background glow in the distance ahead of us.

'Lights,' Jurgen whispered. 'Someone's down here.' One of the tau said something in an urgent undertone.

'There are sentries,' Amberley translated quietly. 'The kroot will deal with them.'

'But how can they see?' Velade asked, confusion obvious even in the undertone.

'We don't have to,' Gorok assured her, and a swirl of displaced air at my elbow told me he was gone. With my eyes now adjusted to the darkness, I could see three faint shadows against the faint light in the distance, and abruptly, they vanished.

A moment later there were a few muffled cries abruptly cut off, the sounds of a scuffle, and the unmistakable crack of snapping bone. Then the silence descended again, to be broken by a muffled whisper from the tau sergeant.

'All clear,' Amberley assured us, and we scurried forward towards the light, which now seemed cosy and welcoming despite the potential threat it represented. It wasn't all that bright really, just the first in a chain of low-powered glowglobes embedded in the ceiling with long stretches of shadow between them, but after the darkness it seemed positively effulgent.

Just beyond the first of them, a makeshift barricade had been erected across the corridor, which gave on to a slightly wider chamber beyond, narrowing the way to the width of a single man.

'It looks like a checkpoint,' Trebek said, and Kelp snorted loudly.

'What was your first clue?' he asked.

She was right, though, the obstruction was clearly meant more to regulate traffic than to keep intruders out; presumably that had been the job of the contingent further back, until the tau had relieved them of the responsibility. Otherwise it would have been sited with a great deal more care, and I mentioned as much to Amberley.

'What do you mean?' she asked, which told me that whatever else they know, inquisitors tend not to think like soldiers.[1]

'It's in the illuminated area,' I pointed out. 'If they were seriously expecting intruders, they would have placed their pickets forward, in the dark,

---

1. *And why should we, when we can call on our own Astartes chapters for that kind of thing?*

where their eyes would adjust and they'd be able to see down the corridor. As it is, they can't see anything from here outside the pool of light.'

'Which greatly assisted us in gaining the element of surprise,' Gorok added helpfully. Reminded of his presence, I turned just in time to see him bend down and take a large bite out of the human corpse lying at his feet. Bile rose in my throat, and the troopers muttered anxiously, or vented expletives of disgust. Kelp started to bring his hellgun to bear, then thought better of it.

The tau, I noticed, all seemed to be looking somewhere else as their allies began their obscene meal, as though they were equally disgusted but too polite to mention it. Then, to my even greater surprise, Gorok spat the gobbet of meat out, and I was reminded of the similar thing we'd seen before. He rattled off something in his native tongue, and the other kroot dropped their potential snacks too.

'What in the Emperor's name was all that about?' I whispered to Amberley, but she just shrugged.

'Sorry, I don't speak kroot.' Gorok's hearing must have been preternaturally acute, though, at least by human standards, because he answered me.

'Tainted, like the others.' He made a sound I took to be indicative of disgust.

'Tainted, how?' Amberley asked. Gorok spread his hands, a curiously human gesture for an alien, which I assumed he'd picked up from whoever had taught him Gothic.

'It is the...' He lapsed into kroot for a few whistles and clicks. 'There's no exact equivalent in your tongue which I know. The twisted molecules which replicate...'

'The genes? DNA?' Amberley asked. Gorok cocked his head on one side, apparently considering it, and asked one of the tau a question in that language. 'Something similar,' he said at last. 'The tau know of it too, but not as we do.'

'You're trying to tell me you can taste their DNA?' I asked incredulously. Gorok cocked his head again.

'Not exactly. As you lack the ability, it would be like describing colour to a blind man. But I am a shaper, and I can perceive such things.'

'And their genes are tainted.' Amberley nodded to herself, as though it confirmed something she suspected, and a terrible realisation hit me. The nagging memories of some previous campaign, our conversation at the palace the first time we met; suddenly I knew what she expected to find down here, and it was all I could do not to turn on my heels and run, screaming, for the surface.

Extracted from *Like a Phoenix From the Flames: The Founding of the 597th*, by General Jenit Sulla (retired), 097.M42

Imagine, if you can, the awful sense of futility which hung over us in those darkest of days. As the city we were here to protect burned around us, the flames of our impatience blazed no less furiously in our breasts. For here we were, sworn warriors of the Blessed Emperor, enjoined we knew not why to step back from the fray which every woman and man of us yearned to enter. Yet we stayed our hand, grim duty no less inflexible for being unwelcome, for had we not sworn to obey? And obey we did, despite the anguish we all felt at our enforced inaction, until at last the lord general gave the order to mobilise.

I think I can truly speak for all when I say that at the news that our
regiment, newly born, all but untried, was to take the lead in this mag-
nificent endeavour, our hearts swelled within us, borne aloft on the
wings of pride, and a determination to show that the lord general's
confidence had not been bestowed upon us in vain.

As I led my platoon to our Chimeras, I could see the whole regiment
lined up and battle-ready for the first time, and a sight to stir the
blood it truly was. Dozens of engines rumbled, and our sentinels
formed up alongside us. I noticed that Captain Shambas was smiling
broadly as he checked the heavy flamer mounted on his doughty steed,
and I paused to exchange a few words with him.

'I love the smell of promethium in the morning,' he said, and I nodded, understanding the urge he felt to unleash the cleansing fire of
retribution against the Emperor's enemies.

As I mounted my command Chimera and took my accustomed place in
the top turret, I kept turning my head hoping for a glimpse of the legendary Commissar Cain, the man whose courage and martial zeal was an
inspiration to us all, and whose dedication and selflessness had turned us
from an ill-disciplined rabble into a crack fighting unit that even the lord
general deemed worthy of notice; but he was nowhere to be seen, no
doubt even then bestowing the benefit of his wisdom on those entrusted
with ensuring our final victory. Indeed, as the Emperor willed it, I wasn't
to set eyes on him until that final climactic confrontation which lives on in
the annals of honour to this day. At length, Colonel Kasteen took to her
own Chimera, and gave the eagerly awaited order to advance.

A stirring sight we must have been as we moved out, to the cheers
and envious glances of less fortunate regiments. Beyond the perimeter,
however, I must admit that my spirits were somewhat dampened by
the devastation which met our eyes. Hollow-eyed civilians gazed at us
from the ruins of their homes, and curses and lumps of masonry were
frequently thrown in our direction. Fruitless to protest that this
wilderness of desolation was none of our doing, for they had every
right to expect protection from the tau invaders, and we had left them
bereft. Everywhere wreckage burned, and the bodies ere scattered in
profusion – many in the uniform of the PDF, some modified with
strips of blue cloth to proclaim their allegiance to the alien despoilers.
Naught had it benefited them though, and they had reaped the just
reward of all turncoats; but whether at the hands of their more loyal
fellows or the interlopers they had sought to appease, His Divine
Majesty alone knew.

Of the tau themselves we saw little sign, save, on occasion, a rounded tank hull hovering ominously at the end of a street, or a swiftly darting dreadnought keeping pace with us for a block or two. For the most part, however, they seemed content to watch us through the eyes of their aerial pictcasters, which floated like flying plates above the rooftops or flitted around our vehicles like flies around grox. Had it not been for our orders, I'm certain that many would have been downed by our sharpshooters; but however intolerable they found this provocation, not one of our stout-hearted cohort broke faith by opening fire.

It was only as we approached the precincts of the governor's palace that the resistance we'd expected truly began, and it was of a kind we were ill-prepared to face, and had no reason to expect.

THIRTEEN

'Taking the long view is all well and prudent, but take care that you don't become so preoccupied with it that you miss what's right under your nose.'

– Precepts of Saint Emelia,
Chapter XXXIV, Verse XII

WE PRESSED ON, even more warily now if that were possible, because it was obvious from the presence and layout of the checkpoint that we were somewhere deep inside the perimeter of the enemy encampment. The tau took the lead again, which was fine by me, as whatever sensor gear they had inside those odd-shaped helmets of theirs seemed a good deal more reliable than Amberley's auspex. She'd consulted it a few more times since it had failed to detect our alien companions, but after Gorok's announcement and my panic-stricken deduction of what we truly faced, I wasn't expecting anything more from it. Of course, some of the enemy down here might still be sufficiently human to register on the thing, but I'd be a damn sight more worried about the ones that weren't. So I relied on my eyes and ears, and dropped back far enough to voice my fears to Amberley where the others were unlikely to overhear us.

'This isn't what you were expecting to find, is it?' I asked, trying desperately to keep my voice calm. Even so, it seemed to be rising in pitch to an alarming degree. Amberley looked at me with her usual appearance of cheery good humour, which I was beginning to suspect was as much a mask as my own attempt at professional detachment.

'To be honest, no,' she admitted. 'I thought we were just after some run-of-the-mill insurrectionists when we came down here. If we're right, this changes things a bit.'

A damn sight more than a bit so far as I was concerned, but I wasn't about to be out-cooled by anyone, so I just nodded agreement as though I was considering our options carefully.

'I can't get a message back to command,' I said. 'We've come too deep.' All I'd been able to raise on my combead for some time was static. I looked at her hopefully. 'Unless you've got something more powerful?'

'Fraid not.' She shook her head, apparently only mildly put out by the inconvenience. 'So I guess we're on our own.'

'I could take Jurgen and backtrack a bit,' I suggested. 'Try to get a message through at least. The lord general should be informed of our suspicions right away. If we're right, we need a couple of regiments down here, not half a squad and a handful of xenos.'

'I appreciate the offer, Ciaphas.' She looked at me with those wide blue eyes, a twinkle of amusement in the back of them, and I felt suddenly sure that she could read my true intentions with ease. 'But at the moment, suspicion is all we have. If we're wrong,' and I hoped to the Emperor we were, 'mobilising that number of troops would only undermine our truce with the tau.'

'And if we're right, chances are none of us will survive to warn him,' I said. 'I've done this before, remember?'

'I've had a little experience with aliens too,' she reminded me, and I suddenly realised I was all but arguing with an inquisitor. That was a sobering thought, and I shut up fast. Amberley smiled at me again. 'But you do have a point. As soon as we have confirmation one way or the other, we'll pull back.' That was something at least. I nodded my agreement.

'I think that would be prudent. Even with the xenos' firepower we wouldn't stand much of a chance otherwise.'

'Oh, I don't know.' She smiled again, to herself this time, as though she knew something I didn't. (Which she did, of course, but she was an inquisitor after all, so I guess she was supposed to.) 'We might have a bit of an edge ourselves.' She was glancing at Jurgen as she said it, and I remember thinking one melta gun wasn't going to make all that much of a difference. But of course, it did in the end, and that wasn't the edge she'd been thinking of in any case.

* * *

WE'D GONE ON for maybe another three kilometres when the shas'ui held up his curious malformed hand for silence. Over the last couple of hours we'd become quite adept at reading the non-verbal signals of our alien companions, although none of us were really at ease with them. Kelp at least looked as though he was just waiting for an excuse to open fire, and much as I disliked the man, I had to admit that he probably had a point. Xenos were xenos after all, and even though we were supposed to be on the same side at the moment, I knew from bitter experience that any such alliances could only be temporary, and were liable to be bloodily severed without warning at any time.

'He says he's picking up life forms ahead, in large quantities,' Gorok said quietly, translating the flickering finger signs. The tau all had voxcasters and Emperor knew what else built into their helmets, but their kroot allies had no such aids to communication, and, I was beginning to suspect, would have spurned them if they'd been offered anyway. So they used this peculiar semaphore to pass orders and information silently, in much the same way that Guard units did when the troopers didn't have individual combeads, or the enemy was so close they might have overheard a verbal transmission.

'How large?' Amberley whispered, taking a final look at the screen of the auspex, which, for once, actually seemed to be displaying some life signs that weren't ours or the six troopers with us. The answer seemed to perturb her slightly, as I could see far fewer blips than the number Gorok translated, but then that worried me too as it seemed to confirm our worst fears.

'We're going to have to confirm this visually, aren't we?' I asked, not because I expected an answer, but because asking the question gave me the comforting illusion of some measure of control over my destiny. Which, at that point, I thought was all too likely to be short, bloody, and messily terminated. Amberley nodded, looking grimmer than I would have thought possible, and it suddenly struck me that even an inquisitor could feel fear under the right circumstances (and if ever the circumstances were right to be terrified, these were the ones).

'I'm afraid so,' she said, sounding as though she actually meant it.

I've often wondered since if things would have worked out any differently if we'd warned the troopers in advance what we were getting into. After all, they were all veterans, and had fought a tyranid invasion to a standstill, so they weren't likely to have flown into a panic at the news. But on the other hand, I didn't trust them, and that was the plain, honest truth. For all I knew, if I told them what we'd surmised, they'd simply desert, killing Amberley to cover their tracks as Sorel had suggested. And me too, of course, which was the really important issue so far as I was concerned.

So, rightly or wrongly, I kept my mouth shut, and let them go on thinking we were simply after an insurrectionist cell; and if that left their blood on my hands I can live with it. It's not like I haven't done far worse, to far less-deserving people over the years, and I haven't lost any sleep over them either.[1]

After a few more moments of consultation, which Amberley and Gorok helpfully translated, we moved on, more cautious than before. A few metres ahead, the corridor seemed to open out into a wider chamber, as we'd seen several times already on our journey through the undercity, and I expected this one to be little different – like the one we'd discovered the checkpoint in, or the larger one where the tau had slaughtered the outer guards. So as I reached the opening, and peered cautiously round it, my breath left my body in an involuntary gasp.

The chamber was huge, vaulted tens of metres over our heads, like the schola chapel where I'd spent many dull and draughty hours as a juvie listening to old Chaplain Desones droning on about duty and loyalty to the Emperor, and furtively swapping salacious holopicts with the other cadets. The atmosphere here was about as far from musty piety as it was possible to get; however, palpable danger seeped from every corner.

We'd come out on a mezzanine gallery some twenty metres above the floor, and, Emperor be praised, there was a waist-high balustrade around it which afforded us a measure of concealment. We crouched behind it, humans and aliens alike, equally appalled at the sight which met our eyes.

The space below us was vast, receding into the distance like a forge-world manufactoria. I'd seen a Titan maintenance bay once, where Warhounds were rearmed and readied for battle, and the huge echoing space had bustled with the same sense of martial purpose. Instead of towering metal giants, however, this space held only people, scurrying to and fro in their hundreds, tending to vast machines of great antiquity whose purpose I could only guess at.[2] Of rather more immediate interest to me, though, were the ones carrying, drilling with, and maintaining with a meticulousness which would have done credit to a

---

1. *I suspect this isn't entirely true; I've certainly known him to be woken by nightmares on several occasions.*

2. *Subsequent study of the city records leads me to believe we were in one of the primary distribution centres of the water purification system. Like many examples of technology from the early days of settlement on human worlds, it had apparently been functioning undisturbed for several millennia, and would no doubt have continued to do so indefinitely if we hadn't started blowing holes in it shortly thereafter.*

member of the Imperial Guard, more small arms than I was happy to see in the hands of anyone other than His Majesty's most loyal servants.

'Emperor's bones!' Trebek muttered. 'There's an entire army of them down here!' A few short, sibilant exclamations from among the tau were enough to confirm that they were as unpleasantly surprised as we were.

'It's worse than that,' Kelp muttered. Amberley and I exchanged concerned glances, already aware of what he'd noticed, but then we'd been expecting it, and had known what to look for.

'How do you mean?' Holenbi whispered, his habitual frown of puzzlement back on his face.

'They're mutants,' Sorel told him, scanning the chamber through the magnifying optics of his sniper scope. 'Some of them, anyway.' A ripple of unease stirred the troopers, an atavistic loathing of the unclean rising to the surface despite their training and discipline. Now that someone had pointed it out, the contamination was obvious: though many of the cultists below us were human, or could pass for it, others were unmistakably something else. In some cases, it was as subtle as a wrongness of posture, a peculiar hunching of the back, or an elongation of the face, but in others it was far more pronounced. In these individuals the taint of the alien was obvious, their skin hardened almost to armour, their jaws wide and filled with fangs; a few sprouted extra limbs, tipped with razor-sharp claws.

'No they're not,' Jurgen chipped in helpfully, blissfully unaware of my frantic 'shut up!' hand gestures as he shaded his eyes for a closer look. 'They're genestealer hybrids. We saw plenty just like them on Keffia, and...' His voice trailed off lamely as he finally turned his head in my direction, and saw the expression on my face.

'And we wiped them all out,' I finished, trying to sound decisive and confident. Kelp's jaw clenched.

'You knew.' It was a flat statement, an accusation, and the others all hung on his words. 'You knew what was waiting down here all along, and you led us right into it to get slaughtered!'

'No one's getting slaughtered unless I do it,' I snapped back, realising that if I lost the initiative now I'd never regain it, and that would mean the end of everything – the mission, me, Amberley, and probably Gravalax too, although the welfare of the planet wasn't exactly at the top of my priority list. 'This is a recon mission, nothing more. Our objective was to identify the enemy, which we've done, and get back to report that information. We're pulling back to the surface now, to call in reinforcements, and we'll only engage in self-defence. Satisfied?'

He nodded, slowly, but the truculence remained on his face.

'Works for me,' Sorel said. Velade, Trebek, and Holenbi nodded, following his lead.

'Not for me.' Kelp raised his hellgun, aiming squarely at Amberley. Sibilant whispers of consternation rippled through the tau, but the shas'ui gestured the ones who'd begun to raise their weapons to stand down, and to my relief, they complied. The last thing we needed now was to start killing each other; there were plenty of 'stealers around to do that job, and attracting their attention was right up there with challenging an ork to an arm-wrestling contest so far as really bad ideas went. 'I'm out of here. And I'll kill her if you try to stop me.' I reached for my pistol, but she shook her head.

'No, commissar. He's not going to shoot, are you, Tobias?' She tilted her head towards the bustling throng of half-human monsters below. 'The noise would bring them all running, and you wouldn't get a hundred metres before they ripped you to pieces.'

The same thing would apply to my sidearm, I realised, as I let it slip back securely into its holster.

'You'll never get away with this,' I said levelly, absurdly conscious of sounding like a character in a holodrama. A sneer of derision crossed his face.

'Like I've never heard that before.'

'Get out of here.' Amberley's voice was stiff with contempt. 'I've no use for cowards. You had a second chance, and you pissed it away.' For the first time, a flicker of unease moved across his face, and he took a step backwards.

'You'd better hope the 'stealers find you first,' I added, with all the bravado which comes from issuing an empty threat you know you'll never have to back up. 'Because if I ever catch up with you, you're in for a world of hurt.'

'Dream on, commissar. I've taken my last order from you.' He looked at the others, hoping for some show of support, but they just stared back, their faces set. I was surprised, I don't mind admitting it, but when you came down to it, they were still soldiers of the Emperor before anything else. After a moment, Kelp stepped back into the shadows and turned, and we heard the sound of running feet receding down the tunnel.

'I reckon I've still got a shot,' Sorel offered, raising the long-las and sighting carefully in the direction of the sound. 'And this thing's silenced.' I shook my head.

'Let him go,' I said. 'At least he's still good for drawing their fire.' The sniper nodded, and lowered his weapon.

'Your call,' he said.

Amberley was still engaged in earnest conversation with the tau, though how she was hoping to retain their confidence after this was beyond me, so I did my best to rally the troops with a few quiet words of praise for their loyalty.

'The shas'ui is saying it would be most prudent to divide our forces again,' Gorok translated helpfully. Big surprise there, I thought. If I was the shas'ui and I'd just seen one of our allies pull a gun on his commander, I'd be having second thoughts about our little arrangement now too.

'We both need to report this to our own forces,' Amberley said, breaking off just long enough to meet my eye, then returning to her sibilant dialogue.

'No question of that,' I agreed. 'So what's taking so long?'

'The tau were unaware of this ability of the creatures you call genestealers,' Gorok said. 'They knew them only as a warrior form of the tyranid overmind. Your inquisitor is attempting to enlighten them as to their true nature.'

'They're infiltrators,' I explained. 'They worm their way into a planet's society, and weaken it from within before the hive fleets arrive. Wherever they go they sow disorder and anarchy.'

'Then they are indeed a potent threat,' the kroot agreed.

'Sir,' Velade whispered urgently, trying to attract my attention. I turned towards her, and she gestured down towards the chamber floor. 'Something's happening down there.'

'Time to leave,' I said, tapping Amberley on the shoulder. She glanced up at me and nodded.

'I think you're right.' One of the hybrids, an ugly fellow who might have passed for human in a bad light if it wasn't for a complexion which looked as though he'd recently showered in acid, was running into the chamber. He was carrying something under his arm, and after a moment I realised it was the head of the kroot Sorel had shot.

'Oh frak,' I said. They were on to us now, and no mistake. As he moved further into the cavern, more and more of the cultists stopped what they were doing and crowded around him. The most eerie thing about it was that none of them said anything, just clustered together in silence and stared at the grisly trophy.

'What are they doing?' Trebek asked quietly.

'Communicating,' Amberley responded, turning to lead us back up the corridor we'd entered by.

'They've all got this hive mind thing, remember?' Velade was tense but determined. 'You just have to shoot the big ones.'

'It's not like the tyranid overmind,' Amberley said. 'They're all individuals. They're just linked to each other telepathically, at least up close.'

'Like psykers,' Jurgen added helpfully.

'I hope so,' Amberley said, though what she meant by that I still didn't know at the time.

'Pull back slowly,' I ordered. 'They haven't noticed us yet. We've still got time to make it back to the surface before they realise where we are.' And we probably would have done too, if it hadn't been for the bloody kroot.

'They taint the flesh,' Gorok said. 'And they must not taste ours.' Before I had a chance to react, or even realise what the hell he was on about, he shouted something in his own tongue to his compatriots.

My bowels froze. As that avian screech echoed round the chamber, every head turned in our direction as though tugged by the same string. I was uncomfortably reminded of a Hydra battery coming to bear. Uncounted eyes stared at us for a moment, then they broke and ran, as Gorok and the other kroot aimed their long-barrelled weapons at the centre of the group and opened fire.

'What the hell do they think they're doing?' Holenbi asked.

'Who cares? Run!' I ordered. Looking back I could see they'd felled the hybrid carrying the kroot head, and another volley pulped the trophy to mush.

I'm still not sure why that was so important to them. All I can assume is that they'd grasped some of what Amberley had been saying about the genestealers' peculiar ability to overwrite the genetic code of their victims and had thought possession of the severed head would have let them infect other kroot in some way. Palpable nonsense of course. Genestealers need live victims to infect so that when they have children of their own, they unwittingly spread the taint, but I suppose it got mixed up in some way with their religion, or whatever else it is that makes them go around chewing lumps out of corpses. At the end of the day a xeno's a xeno, and who knows why they do anything?[1]

One thing I was sure about, though, was that the tau were as surprised as we were. The shas'ui was shouting something I could make a pretty good guess at the gist of without an interpreter, but the kroot weren't listening, and he gave up in favour of trying to organise his own squad. Not a moment too soon either, because the amount of noise from the corridor we'd entered by told me we were about to have company.

A volley of plasma fire from the tau guns ripped down the corridor, almost blinding me with its brightness, and I turned away. We wouldn't

---

1. *For a rather more accurate and informed analysis of kroot psychology, see Zigmund's* War-riors of Pech: The Savage Sophisticates, *which is readily available from the restricted stacks of any Ordo Xenos libram.*

get back out the way we'd come in, that was for sure, and our only hope was to move off along the gallery and hope to find a clear route through one of the other tunnel mouths.

Incredibly, the enemy kept coming, although I half expected that after my adventures on Keffia, where they'd just kept leapfrogging the pile of their own dead in their eagerness to close. A ragged volley of las-bolts and autogun fire thundered in reply, and one of the tau went down, his armour shredded by multiple impacts.

'Tell them to pull back before they're slaughtered,' I said to Amberley, and she nodded before shouting something in tau. Not that I cared, of course, but the longer the xenos kept firing the further away we'd get. I hoped.

'There's another tunnel up ahead,' Velade called excitedly, then turned back to face us, raising her hellgun. I flinched, anticipating treachery after all, but the high-powered las-bolt went wide of us, impacting on the thorax of the first of the enemy to emerge from the tunnel behind us.

'Emperor's bowels!' Trebek said, following suit. My heart froze with terror. I'd seen too many, on Keffia, and as part of the screeching mass of a tyranid army, to mistake it for anything else.

A purestrain genestealer. One of the deadliest creatures in creation. And it wasn't alone.

FOURTEEN

'Never take a gamble you're not prepared to lose.'

– Abdul Goldberg, rogue trader

MY ORDER TO pull back had bought us a little time, at least. The horde of mutant crossbreeds vomited out of the tunnel between us and the tau, forcing the two parties apart, taking punishing casualties, but still laying down a withering volley of fire as they came. I recognised the tactic from the cleansing of Keffia, and Jurgen evidently, did too, as he raised the melta before falling back. The blast of superheated air roared against my face, vaporising the oncoming stealer and chewing a chunk out of the front few ranks.

The firing continued, with las-bolts and bullets chewing up the masonry around us, and I felt a sudden blow against my chest. I glanced down; a las-bolt had impacted against the borrowed armour beneath my greatcoat, and I blessed the foresight that had impelled me to requisition it. We were all shooting continuously now, the troopers retreating in good order by fire and movement, much to my relief. Amberley had produced a bolt pistol from the depths of her cloak, and wielded it with a skill no less greater than my own, bringing down two more of the bounding monstrosities with carefully placed shots. The explosive bolts detonated inside their chitinous shells, blowing their thoraxes to bloody mist.

'Keep your distance!' I shouted. The hybrids were hoping to pin us, allowing the purestrains to close, and if that happened it would all be over. They bounded forward eagerly, claws scything, and if you think that's not intimidating to a man with a gun, then all I can say is count yourself lucky you've never been close to one. I was there when the Reclaimers boarded the *Spawn of Damnation*,[1] and saw the purestrains which infested it tearing open their Terminator armour as though it were cardboard to get at the Astartes within. After that you can be sure I never wanted to be within arm's length of those killing machines again. And since they have four of the damn things, that can be harder than it sounds.

'You don't have to tell me twice!' Trebek placed a couple of accurate shots, downing a purestrain and a hybrid with a flamer. Thank the Emperor she'd spotted that, I thought, or it would have been the end of us for sure. Sorel followed up, putting a round through the promethium tank, and the width of the gallery erupted in flame.

'Good shooting,' I said. He acknowledged the compliment with a nod, and turned to retreat.

He'd bought us some time, I noted with gratitude, the inferno blocking us off from our assailants, and consigning many of them to an agonising death. The most terrifying thing, though, was that they burned in silence, trying to walk towards us through the flames until their musculature gave out and they collapsed, consumed by the imperative to kill the swarm's enemies no matter what the cost.

On the other side of the blazing barrier, the kroot were overwhelmed in seconds, despite their phenomenal skill in close-quarter combat, swinging the blades of their curious polearm/rifle hybrids to tremendous effect. But for every eviscerated cultist that fell, another stepped forward, and then the purestrains tore into them, and it was all over in less than a second. Gorok was the last to fall, standing alone and defiant on a pile of the dead, until a frenzied flurry of blows shredded his body in a shower of blood.

What happened to the tau I couldn't see, but they'd stopped firing, so they'd either managed to disengage or they were all dead by now. My money was on the latter, but even if I was wrong we'd never be able to rejoin them now so the question was merely academic in any case.

---

1. *A space hulk which drifted into the Corolian Gap in 928; Cain was liaising with the Astartes Chapter in question at the time, as a member of the Brigade command staff, and went in with the Imperial Guard unit detailed to mop up after the initial Astartes assault.*

I swear I'd only glanced back for a second, but when I looked round I was alone; the others had retreated as I'd ordered, but which of the half-dozen tunnel mouths they'd disappeared down was anybody's guess. The terror of isolation gripped me for a moment, then I pulled myself together. The pool of promethium wouldn't burn forever, and the cultists presumably knew this labyrinth well enough to circumvent it without too much difficulty in any case, so if I stayed where I was any longer, I was a dead man.

'Jurgen!' I shouted. 'Inquisitor!' There was no answer, so I picked the nearest tunnel, and started to run.

As I entered the welcoming darkness, the panic I'd tried to force down resurfaced, stronger than before, and try as I could to make myself slow down and get my bearings, fear had control of my limbs now. I ran as hard and as fast as I could, heedless of the dangers that might be lurking in the darkness around me, or the hidden obstacles which were likely to be lying in wait for an unwary shin or an ankle to turn, and didn't stop until my breath was rasping my lungs like sandpaper and my legs had begun to tremble from the exertion.

Panting hard, I sat on a convenient heap of rubble, and tried to take stock of my situation, which was undoubtedly grim whichever angle I looked at it from. For one thing, I was still deep underground, in a labyrinth I didn't know how to get out of, infested with slavering monsters. For another, the only allies I had down here probably thought I was dead, and even if they didn't, they weren't likely to waste any time searching for me. The information we'd gathered about the true nature of the threat gnawing away beneath our feet was too important to risk, and Amberley would insist on returning to the surface as quickly as possible to warn the lord general. At least, if our positions were reversed, that's what I would have done.

On the plus side, however, I was quietly confident of finding my way back to the surface given enough time, provided I didn't run into any more company on the way, and my solitude was a positive advantage in that regard, as a man moving alone will always be more stealthy than a group. Corridors like these had been my playground as a child, and I'd never quite lost the knack of finding my way around them; despite my panic-stricken flight, I still had a vague idea of which direction our compound lay and how far we'd come. In fact, if my guess about us being somewhere under the old quarter was accurate, I might even be closer to the surface than I realised. And once I'd made it back to the open air, returning to the compound shouldn't prove at all difficult. (And in case you were wondering, the irony of genuinely experiencing what I'd briefly considered feigning the previous night wasn't lost on me.)

Fleeing in terror, I'd just like to note in passing for those of you who have so far been lucky enough to avoid the experience, generally leaves you both hungry and thirsty. At least that's been the case with me on most occasions, and I've done it frequently enough to qualify as something of an expert on the topic, so I hope you'll take my word for it.

Anyhow, I decided to take advantage of this relatively peaceful interlude to replenish my energy, so I sat for a while longer sipping water from my canteen and chewing a ration bar, the flavour of which, as usual, hovered just outside the range of identification. The impromptu picnic raised my spirits somewhat, and I took advantage of the quiet moment to still the thudding of my heart and try to distinguish the sounds in the darkness around me. I briefly considered turning the luminator back on, but decided against it, as it would give my position away, besides which, my eyes had adjusted to the gloom as well as they were going to by now, and I could quite readily distinguish vague shapes of lighter or darker shadow. My other tunnel-rat senses had come into play too: I could tell by the echoes how close I was to a wall, for instance. I've often tried to explain it, but the only way you could really understand is if you'd spent a large part of your early life in the lower levels of a hive somewhere.

It was while I was gradually recovering my wits that I first heard the faint scrape of something moving in the dark. Now, I daresay most people's reaction under those circumstances would have been to call out, or snap the luminator on, neither of which was a particularly attractive option given my current situation, as I'm sure you'll appreciate. Besides, I wasn't particularly concerned as to what it might be. As I've said before, the environment was one I knew well, and I'd be happy to match my experience of blind fighting in tunnels against almost any foe. I was also pretty confident that any 'stealers or hybrids in the vicinity wouldn't have bothered lurking either, just charged straight in, so I simply waited, and was rewarded a moment later by the faint skittering sound of a small piece of rubble falling away.

That was a sound I could identify with some confidence, and I concluded that I was sharing my refuge with some kind of vermin. (An accurate assessment, as I was soon to discover, but not quite in the way I'd imagined.) Before I could consider the matter further, however, I was distracted by a faint tinnitus in my ear, which gradually rose in volume until I was able to distinguish an almost inaudible wash of static. My combead was active, and that could mean only one thing – someone was transmitting on the command frequency reasonably close by. Moreover, there was only one person it could possibly be, a conclusion confirmed by the faint voice, unmistakably feminine, which ebbed in and out of audibility.

'… can you hear… commissar… respond…'

The breath sighed from my lungs as relief punched me in the gut. They might have moved out, as the mission demanded, but it seemed they hadn't given up on me entirely after all.

'Inquisitor?' I asked cautiously.

'You wish.' The voice was close and harsh, and if Kelp had been able to resist the taunt, the rifle butt which followed it would probably have stove my skull in. As it was, he'd been considerate enough to warn me, so I ducked it easily, and drove my fist into the pit of his stomach – which was still protected by his hardshell body armour, of course, so much good it did me apart from bruising my knuckles. (The real ones anyway, the augmetics were rather more robust than that.) He was still off balance, though, so I drove my hip in and tried to throw him, but he twisted out of the way just in time. For a big man he was a pretty fast mover, I'll give him that.

A vivid memory of the brawl in the mess hall flashed across my mind, so I ducked again, and sure enough, he'd tried the same spinning kick he'd almost managed to bring Trebek down with. Advantage to me, I thought, that'll teach you to play tag with a hiver in a tunnel, and I began to draw my chainsword to finish this quickly.

Consequently, I was completely unprepared for the low-level sweeping kick that followed, cracking into the back of my knee, and pitching me to the floor.

'You were almost right,' he sneered. 'I am in a world of hurt. But it's not mine, is it?' He kept trying to kick me while I was down, but the armour under my greatcoat protected me for the second time that day, and the impacts against my ribs were merely annoying rather than crippling. Then again, I suppose he might have done a better job if he'd concentrated on what he was doing instead of talking about it. I stayed silent, masking all but my general position in the darkness, and rolled aside, drawing the chainsword at last.

'If you're going to fight, fight,' I said, using the sound of my voice to draw him in, and mask the whine of the blade as it powered up. 'Don't make speeches.' He must have thought he had me, because he charged in with a roar of triumph, striking down with the rifle butt at where he must have thought my head was, but I'd already moved by then, rolling aside and slashing at his legs with the weapon. I'd hoped to take the treacherous mongrel off at the knees to be honest, but the keening of the blade must have warned him, and he turned aside at the last second, so all I got was a good cut across one of his calves.

'Emperor's guts!' It must have done the job though, because he was backing off, and the chamber was suddenly bright with half a dozen luminators, bobbing in hands or utility-taped to the barrels of hell-guns.

'Commissar.' Amberley nodded to me, a casual greeting, as though we'd just met in the street.

'Inquisitor.' I rolled to my feet, advancing on Kelp, who limped backwards, his expression panicky. A trail of blood followed him. 'Excuse me a moment. I'll be right with you as soon as I've finished this.'

'Stay back.' He raised the hellgun, aiming it at my chest. Incredibly, he still didn't seem to realise that I'd concealed armour there, or he'd have gone for a head shot I'm sure. 'One more step and I'll kill you.' I stopped, still a couple of metres too far to finish him off with the chainsword, and he smiled maliciously. 'Or do you still think you can do something from there?' I shrugged.

'Jurgen, kill him,' I said. The expression on Kelp's face was almost comical for the half-second or so that he still had one, then he exploded into a small pile of gently steaming offal. I turned to my aide, who was lowering the melta, and nodded an acknowledgement. 'Thank you,' I added.

'You're welcome, sir,' he replied, as though he'd rendered me no greater service than pouring my tea, and I turned back to Amberley.

'This is a pleasant surprise,' I added, playing the unflappable hero for all it was worth. 'I didn't think I'd see you again until I got back to the barracks.'

'Neither did I,' she admitted, with a slight smile. 'But I picked up the carrier wave from your combead, and we just headed in the direction the signal was strongest in.'

'I'm glad you did.' I glanced across to where Trebek was scraping a gooey piece of Kelp residue from her boot. Amberley's smile broadened.

'You seemed to have the situation well in hand.' I shrugged.

'I've faced worse odds.'

'No doubt. But he did you a favour, in a way.' I must have looked puzzled at that point, because she explained as though pointing out something obvious. 'He made you a lot easier to find. Once we got close enough we just had to follow the noise.'

Her words hit me like a bucket of ice water. (Or a Valhallan shower, which I don't recommend to the unwary, by the way.)

'Form up,' I said to the troopers. 'We're moving out.'

'Just a moment, sir.' Holenbi was rummaging in his medkit. 'I'd like to get you patched up first.' I swear that was the first time I realised I'd taken any damage from the scuffle, or possibly the firefight in the big chamber, my knuckles were smeared with blood. My first thought was that it served me right for punching a suit of carapace armour, but they hadn't been skinned all that badly (and the augmetic ones not at all); most of it had come from the large graze on my forehead, which, now that I'd finally noticed it, had begun to sting abominably. I fended the young medic off as he sprayed it with something.

'We don't have time for that,' I said. 'If you heard something, you might not have been the only ones.'

That got them moving, let me tell you. The thought of facing another horde of hybrids and purestrains was enough to motivate anyone. We moved out in good order, though, I was pleased to note the surviving members of the team actually seemed to mesh together as soldiers should. Now Kelp was gone, the friction which had marred the mission since it started had dissipated, seemingly along with his molecules, and Trebek took point without needing to be ordered to. If she kept this up, I found myself thinking, I might even consider letting her have her corporal's stripes back.

'We were lucky back there,' I said, falling in beside Amberley again. She raised an eyebrow.

'How so?'

'When they attacked before. Most of them went for the tau rather than us.'

'And you found that curious?' I nodded.

'When I fought 'stealers before, on Keffia, they didn't prioritise. Just went for the nearest targets.'

'Intriguing,' she said. 'Mind you, after that promethium tank went up they could only get to the xenos anyway.'

'It was before then,' I said. 'Right at the start. They only seemed to come after us once we'd started to retreat.'

'And you say this isn't typical genestealer behaviour,' she prompted.

'Not in my experience,' I confirmed.

'I see. Thank you, commissar.' She looked thoughtful, and, once again, her eyes were fixed on Jurgen.

WE PUSHED ON quickly, following a run of piping which seemed to be tending upwards, but I couldn't shake the sense of unease that settled over me as we trotted through the dark. I'd suggested dousing the luminators again, but Amberley overruled me, insisting we make the best time we could, so I left my own off and hurried along at the rear of the group; that way I got the benefit of the others' lights without making myself quite so obvious a target. I didn't like it, though, my palms were tingling again, and my scalp crawled with the anticipation of a sudden shot from the shadows, or an eruption of purestrains from the darkness. One thing I'd learned from my previous encounters with the creatures, they were remarkably stealthy and preferred to strike from the shadows, as the Astartes I'd boarded the space hulk with had learned the hard way. The hybrids weren't so worrying, their human genes making them both more conspicuous and easier to kill, even if they were able to use ranged weapons against us.

'So far so good,' Amberley muttered, which was tempting fate if ever I heard it. We'd been remarkably lucky so far, but I knew that couldn't be expected to last.

'They won't be too far behind,' I reminded her. In fact, given the speed at which they moved, I was vaguely surprised that they hadn't caught up with us yet...

Sudden understanding hit me like a blow to the stomach. They didn't have to comb an entire labyrinth to try and find us – they had sentries posted on the main routes in and out. All they had to do was wait, and reinforce their perimeter guards, and we'd walk right into them in our own good time.

'Wait,' I said. 'We could be running into an ambush.' I thought rapidly, calculating our most probable position, and the distance we'd penetrated after finding the cavern full of the tau's victims. We were still comfortably short, but–

The sudden detonation of a las-bolt ahead, blowing shards of rockcrete from the wall beside Trebek, derailed my chain of thought at once. I'd missed a trick; they were combing the corridors from their outer perimeter, tightening the noose around us–

'Pull back! Consolidate!' I yelled, as Trebek crouched low to return the fire. Running figures could be seen beyond her, picked out by the beam of the luminator taped to the barrel of her gun, and she squeezed the trigger, felling a young man in the uniform of the PDF. For a moment, I wondered if we'd made a horrible mistake, and were opening fire once more on our own allies, but some of the other figures beside him were unmistakably hybrids. One young woman, who might have been attractive if it wasn't for the third arm growing from her right shoulder blade, tipped with a genestealer's razor-sharp claws, flicked the tip of a xenoist braid from her eyes with the monstrous appendage (a surprisingly delicate gesture, I remember thinking at the time), and levelled the heavy stubber cradled in her other two hands. Before I could cry a warning, Sorel punched a hole through her head with his usual unerring accuracy. A second PDF trooper, his uniform embellished with a blue towel tied round his upper arm for some reason, cried out in anguish, dropping his lasgun, and cradled the body.

'I don't think we can, commissar.' Jurgen was his usual phlegmatic self, seemingly as unconcerned as if he was asking me to approve a routine piece of paperwork. 'They're behind us as well.' He was right, too, the sounds of scurrying feet echoing down the tunnel in the direction from which we'd come.

'We have to punch through,' Amberley said decisively. Velade and Holenbi nodded grimly to one another, and opened fire on the cultists in support of Trebek, hugging the walls to present the lowest target profile.

'Better do it fast!' I shouted. I'd shone my luminator back down the corridor, and my heart nearly stopped – instead of more ragged cultists, the narrow passage was choked with purestrains, jaws gaping, their teeth dripping slobber, as they charged forward at what looked like the pace of a landspeeder. I drew my laspistol and fired a futile volley at them. The lead one fell, and was instantly trampled to goo by the weight of the others as they ran right over it, the snapping of chitin and the squish of its bodily fluids turning my stomach. (And you really don't want to know about the smell.) 'We're running out of time!'

Jurgen sent a melta blast down the corridor, but it barely slowed them; for every one that fell there seemed to be an army in reserve.

'We're doing our best,' Trebek called, aiming and firing in one smooth motion. Every time she squeezed the trigger, another cultist died, and her torso armour was scored with las-bolt impacts. Whatever crimes she'd committed aboard the *Righteous Wrath*, she'd more than atoned for, and the flush of satisfaction I felt at this vindication of my decision to prevent her execution almost managed to drive out the rising terror I felt at the onrushing tide of chitinous death which by now was almost upon us.

Abruptly Trebeck took a bolt to the chest, the explosive tip bursting through her ribcage, spattering the wall next to her with viscera. She just had enough time to look surprised before the light faded from her eyes.

'Bella!' Holenbi lowered his hellgun, and scrabbled for his medkit. I grabbed his shoulder.

'Keep firing!' I shouted. 'She's beyond help!' And so would we be in a few more seconds, if we couldn't punch a way out of here. He nodded, and brought the weapon back on aim, squeezing the trigger reflexively. Amberley's bolt pistol barked in my ear, and another former PDF trooper died as messily as Trebek had done.

'This could be it,' I said, feeling the peculiar light-headed fatalism that often kicks in when death looks inevitable. The tight knot of fear dissolved, replaced by the calm certainty that nothing I did now would make any difference, but I was damn well taking as many of the bastards with me as I could. The inquisitor turned to answer me, but before she could say anything a las-bolt burst against the side of her head.

'Amberley!' I yelled, but to my astonishment she was suddenly gone, vanishing without a trace apart from the sudden thunderclap of displaced air rushing in to fill the sudden vacuum in the space which she'd occupied. 'What the hell–'

'Commissar.' Her voice was suddenly in my combead. 'Tell Jurgen to shoot the wall, about three metres back from his current position. Hurry!' Sudden hope flared, and I did as I was bid, though as you'll appreciate, I wasn't in any position to understand what had happened to her or why she would issue so strange an instruction.

To his credit, Jurgen complied as quickly and efficiently as he obeyed any order, and to my astonishment, a large hole appeared instantly, about a metre across. The wall there was barely the width of my forearm, and I dived through before the sides had even had a chance to cool.

'This way!' I shouted. Velade and Holenbi started to fall back, while Sorel took a final shot at the onrushing purestrains. Jurgen turned to do the same, unleashing another blast of ravening energy, and then the masonry over the gap started to crumble. 'Hurry!' I yelled, but it was too late; with a grinding roar the wall collapsed behind me, raising a cloud of choking dust, and sealing my companions in with the creatures, which would surely kill them all.

Now, under any normal circumstances, the idea that I was safely sealed away from a genestealer horde behind tons of fallen masonry would just leave me feeling intensely relieved. I can only assume I got hit on the head or something, because without a second's thought I started scrabbling at the rubble, trying to clear the way back to the corridor which, by now, would undoubtedly be decorated with the internal organs of the others. I only desisted when I felt a hand on my shoulder.

'Leave it, Ciaphas.' Amberley shook her head regretfully. 'They're past helping now.' I stood, slowly, brushing the dust from my clothes, and wondered how I was ever going to manage without Jurgen. Thirteen years was a long time to serve together after all, and I was going to miss him. 'What happened?' I asked, blinking dust from my eyes. It felt as though my brain was full of it too. 'Where did you go?'

'Here, apparently.' Amberley looked around at the chamber we were in. It wasn't very prepossessing, but at least it was free of genestealers. 'The displacer field dumped me here when I got shot.'

'The what?' I shook my head, dazedly. My hair was full of dust too, and I couldn't find my cap. For some reason that seemed very important, and I kept looking round for it, even though it was almost certainly buried under piles of debris.[1]

'Displacer field. If I take a strong enough hit, it teleports me out of the way.' She shrugged. 'Most of the time, anyway.'

'Useful toy,' I said.

'When it works.' She glanced around the chamber. 'Shall we go?'

'Go where?' I asked, still trying to take it all in.

'Away. Fast.' She swung her luminator beam over a darker shadow in the corner of the room. 'This looks like a way out.' I nodded.

'I can feel an air current.'

'Good.' She looked at me curiously, and I realised that she couldn't. What is it they say? You can take the boy out of the hive... 'Let's go then.'

Well, I didn't have any better ideas, so I trailed along after her. Although if I'd known what we were heading into, I might just have decided to stay put after all.

---

1. *A common symptom of shock. Hardly surprising under the circumstances...*

Editorial Note:

Once again, I must apologise for this, but it really is the only eyewitness account I've been able to find.

(Actually, there are the official after-action reports, too, which might yield a more coherent picture if someone were to go through them and collate the various view-points of a dozen different officers, but to be honest, I haven't the time or the patience.)

Extracted from *Like a Phoenix From the Flames: The Founding of the 597th*, by General Jenit Sulla (retired), 097.M42

By the time we had reached the old quarter, we had almost grown used to the shadowy presence of the tau, flitting about us like malign ghosts, and it is greatly to the credit of the troopers I was honoured to serve with that not one of them gave way to the temptation to exact retribution for the destruction of the city, despite the presence of an obvious target on more than one occasion. However strong this urge might become, and strong it was, we remained mindful of the injunction placed upon us, and focused our minds on the delicate mission with which we had been entrusted. Truly, there can be no foe more despicable than an imperial servant who has betrayed the trust of the Emperor, and we were, if anything, even more eager to call the wretched governor to account for his perfidy than we were to wreak deserved vengeance on the alien interlopers whose presence he had tolerated for so long, with such dire consequences.

We had anticipated little difficulty in achieving this end, for what forces could he possibly have had at his disposal to defy His Divine Majesty's most loyal servants? A handful of palace guards, if that, whose martial abilities had been found sorely wanting when they were called upon to defend his residence from no more than a street-brawling mob. So it was with ever-rising confidence that we swept through the desolated streets on our errand of vengeance; a confidence which was soon to seem gravely misplaced.

My first warning that all was not well was the sound of an explosion, as a krak missile detonated against the hull of one of the Chimeras ahead of us. From my position in the turret of my command vehicle, I could see the bright blossoming of the explosion, an unfolding red rose of destruction that scored the armour plating on one side. It evidently failed to penetrate, however, as the dauntless gunner swung the turret round, unleashing a hail of heavy bolts at the importunate enemy. My sense of satisfaction at seeing the building from which the attack came scoured with the Emperor's retribution was short-lived, however, as a number of other missiles followed it, hissing from positions concealed in the rubble around us.

Inevitably, some found their mark, penetrating armour and shattering tracks, bringing several of our Chimeras to a halt; and the chatter on the vox channels told me that our company was not alone in being so treacherously defied. The other elements of our regiment, strung out along many of the adjacent roads in an effort to surround the palace, were under similar attack, and a glance at my tactical slate was enough to tell me that this was a well-planned operation, executed with a meticulous precision greatly at odds with the bedraggled and dispirited force we had expected to meet. Without further thought I dropped back inside the Chimera, where the specialised sensoria and vox equipment would let me direct my subordinates to greater effect, and began to plan our response.

'Halt and dismount!' I ordered, realising that our advance would be stalled indefinitely unless we closed with the enemy on foot, our lumbering vehicles being easy targets for the dug-in missile teams, and our drivers made haste to obey.

It was then that I took to my feet myself, for the whole vehicle rang with a sudden impact, and we slowed to a halt, thick smoke billowing through the crew compartment. Swift enquiry made it obvious that our driver was dead, so I lost no time in forming up my command team and bailing out of our now crippled Chimera.

A scene of sheer pandemonium met my appalled gaze as we pounded down the ramp. Two of the armoured carriers were on fire, and a handful of others immobilized; the rest were manoeuvring into what cover they could find. I followed suit smartly as a flurry of las-bolts erupted from the enemy positions, impacting around us as we took whatever shelter presented itself.

'Third Platoon, report.' Major Broklaw's voice was strong in my combead, his calm demeanour reassuring despite the confusion surrounding us. I responded as crisply as I could, as befitted a warrior of the Emperor.

'We're immobilised, and taking fire,' I reported. 'The enemy seems well dug in.'

'They were waiting for us,' he said. That was my opinion, too; the positions they occupied had to have been prepared some time in advance. The implications of this were staggering. The governor had obviously realised the game was up, but where had he found the troops we were facing? I levelled my optical enhancers, and inhaled sharply.

'The enemy are PDF elements,' I reported. A couple of the lurking figures still had blue rags tied around an arm, but the squad leader, confusingly, bore the makeshift insignia of the imperial faction in the recent civil disturbances.

'Loyalist or xenoist?' Colonel Kasteen cut in. For a moment I was at a loss as to how to answer.

'Both,' I said at last. 'Both factions seem to be working together now—'

'That doesn't make sense!' Broklaw said, an edge of frustration beginning to enter his voice. But Kasteen remained unruffled, fine commander that she was.

'Nothing about this Emperor-forsaken rathole makes any sense,' she pointed out reasonably. But the major was right about one thing.

'There are no loyalists any more,' he said. 'Take them all.'

That was an order we could obey with enthusiasm, and we went to it with a will, of that you may be sure. All the frustration we had endured since our arrival on Gravalax came boiling to the surface, transmuted into true martial zeal, and I vowed that the blood of the traitor would surely be shed this day.

As I urged my troopers forward, and watched the sentinels move up to suppress the first line of resistance, a flash of motion in the corner of my eye drew my attention skyward. Sure enough, it was one of the tau's aerial pictcasters, and a momentary shiver of apprehension passed through me as my mind became crowded with questions. What were the enigmatic aliens making of all this? And, more to the point, what, if anything, were they intending to do about it?

FIFTEEN

'It's never too late to panic.

– Popular Valhallan folk saying

I DON'T MIND admitting that the aftermath of the fight in the corridor had left me completely drained, both mentally and physically. I washed the worst of the dust from my throat with a couple of swallows from my canteen, but I couldn't shake the gritty feel of it from my skin, or my hair, or the inside of my clothes, and I wouldn't be able to, either, until about the third shower. As it turned out, by the time I got the opportunity for that, the dust would be the least of my worries.

And Jurgen was dead. I still couldn't quite believe it, after so many years and so many dangers faced and bested together. The sense of loss was numbing, and quite unexpected. Somehow I'd always assumed we'd meet our ends together, when fate finally pitched me into something my luck and finely-honed survival instinct couldn't get me out of.

So, for an indeterminate time, I said nothing, and trailed after Amberley, who at least seemed to have some kind of plan. All this time, I remember, I kept my pistol in my hand, a curious thing to do as we were in no apparent danger, but I'd somehow kept hold of it when the wall collapsed and felt strangely reluctant to return it to its holster. Later, I found bruising on my palm where I'd been grasping it, so tight was my grip.[1]

We'd gone some distance in silence before Amberley spoke again, the pressure in my ears telling me that the tunnel we were in had begun to descend gradually, but there didn't seem to be any obvious route back to the surface, so I guessed this was as good a direction as any. I suppose I should have mentioned it, but it never occurred to me that she wouldn't have noticed. If I'd realised that she hadn't, and thought we were still moving on the level, I certainly would have mentioned it, believe me, especially if I'd known what was waiting down there on the lowest tier.

'Well, I guess that answers the main question anyway,' she said.

'Which question?' I asked. By now, the whole situation had become so bizarre that none of it seemed to make any sense. I was beginning to feel that the only thing I could truly rely on was the prospect of more treachery and confusion to come, and in that I was far from disappointed. Amberley looked momentarily surprised, and then pleased that I'd responded.

'The main one,' she repeated. 'Who would have something to gain by provoking a war with the tau?'

'The hive fleet,' I said, and shuddered despite the clammy warmth of the tunnel. If the 'stealers were indeed the harbingers of a fresh tyranid onslaught, then they were working to a more grandiose strategy than any I'd heard of before, and the implications of that were far from comforting. She nodded, clearly pleased with my response, and intent on prolonging the conversation. I assume she was trying to keep me centred on the mission,[2] and prevent me from dwelling too much on what had happened to our companions .

'The 'stealer cult has obviously been active here for several generations already. Lucky it's such a backwater, or the contagion might have spread halfway across the sector by now.'

'That's something,' I agreed. I know from my subsequent contacts with her that she followed up the possibility anyway, and managed to eradicate a couple of small subcults which had made the hop to

---

1. *As I said before, he seemed to be suffering from shock for some time after we lost our companions. He was, however, remarkably robust, and recovered far more quickly than I would have believed possible; no doubt the many perils he'd faced and escaped before had inured him to some extent to psychological traumas most men would have found incapacitating.*

2. *He assumes correctly; right then I needed a warrior with me, not a basket case.*

neighbouring systems before they got properly established, but the danger did indeed seem to have been contained; at least, until the hive fleets showed up in person, and we realised we were facing a war on two fronts. I thought for a moment, then added, 'They've obviously been here long enough to infiltrate the PDF pretty thoroughly.'

'Among other things,' the inquisitor agreed. I nodded too, beginning to be drawn into the conversation in spite of myself.

'It looks like they managed to get involved in the local political groups too. The xenoist faction...'

'And the loyalist.' She smiled grimly. 'Raising the tension between the two, splitting the PDF. It's currency to cabbages it was cultists in both factions who started them shooting at each other, and got the loyalists to attack the tau.'

'Hoping to draw us into a war, so we'd chew each other to pieces, and let the hive fleet walk into the sector practically unopposed.' I shuddered again. 'It's diabolical. And it came so close to succeeding...'

'It still might.' Amberley's voice was grim. 'We're the only two left who know about this. If we can't tell the lord general...'

'They might still succeed,' I finished for her. The prospect of that was almost too grim to be contemplated, and we walked on together in silence for some time.

Perhaps it was just as well that we did, for, after a while, I began to detect a faint murmur up ahead over the scuff of our boot soles through the thick dust which carpeted the corridor ahead of us. I had found that reassuring, since it would muffle our footfalls, and indicated quite clearly that no one else had been this way in decades; which meant we were unlikely to be running into any more ambushes. The presence of other sounds down here, though, might be a cause for concern. I held up my hand and doused my luminator, waiting again for my eyes to adjust, the last remnants of my torpor dropping away like a blanket at reveille, replaced by a sudden surge of adrenaline.

'What is it?' Amberley asked, following suit and plunging us into even deeper darkness.

'I'm not sure,' I admitted. 'But I think I can hear something.' To my pleased surprise, she didn't ask for more details, evidently trusting me to provide them if I had them, so I concentrated my energies on listening. It wasn't even a sound, as such, more of a vibration in the air, The nearest I can come to explaining it is by saying that it was akin to the way I could tell roughly how close I was to a wall in the dark by the way the echoes changed. Bottom line is you either know what I'm talking about, in which case you probably grew up in the underhive, too, or you'll just have to take my word for it.

In any event, there was nothing to be gained by staying here, so we moved on at last, trusting my dark-attuned senses rather than activating the luminators again. My palms were tingling in that old familiar way, and Amberley seemed to trust my instincts, at least in this environment. The corridor continued to be relatively open ahead of us, so moving in the dark was less taxing than you might think, and I gradually became aware of a faint luminescence ahead of us in the gloom.

'Is that light ahead?' Amberley murmured, confirming my thought, and I whispered an agreement. The sounds were getting louder too, but still too faint to discern. There was an organic quality about them, though, which raised the hairs on the back of my neck.

'About half a klom,' I added, still keeping my voice low, and hefting the pistol in my hand.

'Maybe it's a way up to the surface,' she whispered hopefully. I shook my head, not sure whether she would be able to see the movement yet against the gradually intensifying glow.

'We've come too deep for that. We must have gone down at least three levels in the last couple of hours—'

'And you didn't think to say anything?' Her voice was a furious hiss, and for the first time I realised she hadn't noticed the change in depth. 'We were supposed to be looking for a way out, in case you'd forgotten!'

'I thought you knew,' I snapped back, feeling oddly defensive. 'You're the one in charge of this expedition, remember?'

'Am I? Oh yes, now you come to mention it, I suppose I am!' There was a petulant edge to her voice which I found incongruously at odds with her rank and power, and all at once, I felt an overwhelming urge to laugh. It was probably just the tension, but the full absurdity of the situation suddenly hit me. Here we were, the only two people left alive to warn the Imperium of a terrifying threat, lost, alone, outnumbered, surrounded by an army of monsters, bickering like a couple of juvies on a disappointing date. I bit my lower lip, but the harder I tried to suppress it the more the laughter effervesced inside my chest, until it finally escaped with an audible snort.

That did it. She lost her temper completely.

'You think that's funny?' she snapped, all thoughts of concealment now completely forgotten. I should have been terrified, of course, the wrath of inquisitors not being something to be lightly invoked, but hysteria had me now, and I simply howled with glorious, tension-relieving laughter.

'Of... Of course not,' I managed to get out between rib-shaking paroxysms. 'But... This whole thing... It's just... So ridiculous...'

'I'm glad you think so,' she said frostily. 'But if you think I'm just going to forget...' a brief hiccup interrupted her flow of invective. 'Forget this... Oh Emperor damn it all...' and it infected her too, the throaty chuckle I'd found so appealing before erupting from her chest like magma. After that, there was no stopping either of us, and we simply held each other up until we could finally force the air to remain inside our aching ribs.[1]

Afterwards, we both felt more like ourselves again, and were able to press on with renewed vigour. We'd resumed moving stealthily, though, as the mere fact that more cultists and 'stealers had failed to boil out of the walls at us probably meant we were alone down here, but we'd made enough noise between us to attract any search parties in the vicinity. Having nothing else to aim for, we kept moving towards the mysterious glow in the distance, and the closer we got, the brighter it became.

'That's definitely artificial,' Amberley said, the yellowish tinge of electrolumination unmistakable from this distance. By the backwash of light it gave, I was able to make out more of our immediate surroundings, and was surprised to note that the stonework surrounding us was now carefully dressed, the vaulted roof being supported by well-crafted columns.

'I think we're in a cellar of some kind,' I hazarded in an undertone. Amberley nodded.

'I think you're right.' She had the auspex out again, and was studying the display. 'And there are people down here. Not many according to this, but...'

She didn't have to finish the sentence. Hybrid cultists might not register on it, and any purestrains in the vicinity certainly wouldn't. Advancing would be a terrible risk, but turning back, trying to find another route to the surface through a tunnel complex swarming with 'stealers and their dupes would be almost as bad. And there was the time factor too. The longer we took to report back, the longer the conspirators would have to provoke their war; assuming it hadn't broken out already.

'Only one way to find out,' I agreed, and we started cautiously forward again.

The light was coming from a huge chamber, a high vaulted ceiling supported by columns similar to the ones I'd noticed in the corridor,

---

1. *I would just like to point out here that this is a perfectly normal reaction to severe stress, which can in no way be interpreted as irresponsible behaviour under the circumstances.*

but far higher and thicker. Like the chamber we'd seen before, where the cultists had attacked us, there was a wide gallery running around the edge of the room, with a number of smaller tunnel mouths opening onto it, but to my relief I couldn't see anyone or anything up there.

This time, however, there was no humming machinery filling the space. It was light and airy, with braziers burning incense on marble plinths, and littered with antique statuary. Dusty boxes were everywhere, and I surmised we'd stumbled across some long-forgotten depository which the cultists had appropriated for their own purposes. We slunk into it like thieves, and took shelter behind one of the pillars holding the roof up. It was as thick as a cathedral column and almost as wide as I am tall, and concealed the pair of us with ease.

'Stairs.' Amberley nudged me, and pointed. Off to one side, a wide stone staircase rose to the gallery, from where another flight rose, cut into the stonework, rising out of sight.

'Great,' I whispered back. But getting to them would be another problem entirely. I could see figures moving around in the distance, some of them armed. There was the usual mixture of civilian clothing and PDF uniforms I'd grown used to seeing among the cultists, and something else; a bright flash of crimson and gold. I nudged Amberley and pointed. 'Palace guard.' She nodded in response.

That was a real surprise. From what Donali had said, I'd assumed they were all dead by now, but the cultists, as I'd seen on Keffia, would always try to look after their own. I began to suspect that their defence of the governor hadn't been quite as inept as they'd wanted us to think, forcing the situation to escalate by bringing the PDF onto the streets where their brood brothers could begin to work their insidious mischief. Instead of the antique longarm he'd been issued with, he was carrying a modern lasgun, looted, I assumed, from the PDF armoury.

'We'll have to get past them,' she whispered. I nodded. Not an appealing prospect, by any means, but one we would have to attempt. If we kept to the cover of the pillars and the other detritus, we might just make it, at least most of the way, before we were spotted. When that happened we'd just have to make a run for the stairs as best we could.

As we moved off, I glanced around again, more by reflex than anything, trying to fix a sense of the space in my mind – disorientation can be a killer in a firefight. And then it struck me.

'This is a shrine,' I murmured. Amberley didn't seem in the least surprised, but then I suppose she'd realised that the moment we'd walked in here.

There were tapestries on the walls, which, now I came to look at them, I found myself recoiling from in horror. Blasphemous things they were, holy images of the Emperor profaned and debased, the Father of All depicted as a hunched hybrid with too many arms, or a monstrous purestrain 'stealer which seemed to tower over its adoring acolytes. I resolved to send a squad down here with flamers the moment we reported back. It seemed almost intolerable to me that such things should be allowed to exist.

'Ready?' Amberley asked at my shoulder, and I nodded, making the sign of the aquila for luck. My pistol was already in my hand, as I've said, and I drew my chainsword quietly with the other, thumb poised over the activator. Amberley drew her bolt pistol, checked that the first round was chambered, and nodded grimly. 'Right. Go.' We scuttled as far as the next pillar and went to ground again, my heart pounding in my ears. I was acutely aware of the background noise now, the sound I'd noticed in the corridor; the hum of activity as the cultists moved to and fro, but in eerie silence, as they had done in the chamber full of machinery.

Praise the Emperor, none of them had spotted us. We moved again, making it to the shelter of the next column, and then on to the one after that. I was just beginning to hope that we would make it all the way to the stairs, and whatever lay beyond, when the crack of a las-bolt against the stonework close to my head told me we'd been spotted.

I turned, in time to see the palace guard levelling his lasgun for another shot, and brought up my pistol, but Amberley was faster and her bolt pistol spat first. His chest exploded in a rain of red entrails and shredded gold armour, and before you know it we were in the middle of a serious firefight. Two more armed cultists appeared, attempting to catch us in a crossfire, and we took one each; another chest shot for Amberley, and a head shot for me, blowing the fellow's brains out through the back of his skull.

'Showoff!' Amberley grinned at me, and I didn't have the heart to tell her it had been a fluke. I'd aimed for the chest as well, and he'd ducked at just the right moment. More shots were being aimed at us from behind other pillars, but they were as well protected as we were, and our return fire had little effect beyond persuading them to keep their heads down. 'Looks like a standoff. What'll they do now?'

'Rush us,' I said, not relishing the prospect. Sure enough, a moment later we could discern a scuttling in the shadows, and my heart fell. 'Merciful Emperor, it's purestrains!' A swarm of them, about a dozen strong, was hurrying towards us across the stone floor of the vault. A couple went down to our bolts and las-shots, more by luck than judgment, I suspect, and in another moment I knew they'd be on us. I gripped my chainsword, determined to fend them off for as long as I could, clinging to the last desperate hope that I could somehow cut my way through to the stairwell, which right then looked about half the segmentum away.

Suddenly, an explosion rocked their ranks, then a couple more. Dazed and uncomprehending I glanced upwards, expecting I knew not what, perhaps the Emperor himself since only divine intervention looked like saving us now. What I saw was almost as unexpected; the familiar shambling form of Jurgen, even grubbier than usual, lobbing frag grenades over the balustrade of the gallery. A small explosion of joy and relief shook my chest, and I grabbed Amberley's arm.

'Look!' She glanced up and nodded, as though she'd half expected something of the sort, and stood.

'Time to run,' she said, cool as you please. She headed for the stairs, and I followed, waving an acknowledgement to Jurgen. He waved back, grinning, and chucked another grenade into the milling mass of 'stealers for luck. Most of them were down by now, leaking foul-smelling ichor, but one was up and running, inhumanly fast, heading straight for Amberley.

'Amberley!' I shouted, and she half turned towards it, but I could see the warning had come too late. Her bolt pistol would never come up to aim in time, and I was too far away to intervene. The claws I'd seen tear open Terminator armour as though it were a crusty meat pie were already slicing at her cape when its head exploded, showering her with an unpleasant organic residue, and leaving the body to topple to the floor. I looked up at the gallery again and saw Sorel already seeking a fresh target for his long-las.

'Emperor be praised!' I breathed, my head still reeling with incomprehension, but grateful for this apparent miracle. I should have known better, of course; that moment of distraction almost cost me my life, and surely would have done if Jurgen hadn't shouted a warning.

'Commissar! Behind you!'

I turned, expecting another foe to be charging in, and swung the chainsword in a reflexive defensive pattern. That surely saved my life, for instead of a cultist or a purestrain, which would have been bad enough, I came face to face with a creature from the worst of nightmares. (Or, to be more accurate, face to belly, as it was at least twice the height of a man.) It was a twisted, grotesque, vast, bloated parody of a genestealer, and the whining blade bit deep into the arm which would surely have ripped my head off if it hadn't been for Jurgen's shouted warning. It howled then, in anger and pain, and I was fighting desperately for my life.

'It's the patriarch!' Amberley yelled, as though I didn't know; from the corner of my eye, I could see her levelling the bolt pistol, waiting for an opening, but I was blocking her shot. I tried to twist out of the way, leaving room for her to aim, but the flailing multiple limbs of my bloated antagonist had me boxed in, and it was all I could do to keep parrying frantically with the chainsword as it swung one talon-tipped arm after another at me. This, then, was the source of the cancer which had infected Gravalax, the centre of the brood mind which the cultists shared, the instrument of the will of the tyranid overmind which had sought to devour the sector unopposed by playing us off against the tau.

'Die, damn you!' I tried to bring my pistol to bear, but couldn't spare the concentration from the more urgent requirement to stay alive for the next few seconds, my entire attention on ducking, blocking, searching for an opening–

Amberley's bolt pistol barked at last, and for an instant I thought I was saved, but the patriarch fought on unharmed, and I realised she was keeping the cultists off my back. They were swarming out of the shadows now, desperate to help their sire, and closing fast. The only mercy was that the ones with guns couldn't use them, for fear of hitting the monster I battled.

Sorel had no such inhibitions, however; a chunk of chitin on the creature's head suddenly burst into bloody fragments, and it roared again, but barely staggered, its natural armour proof against a conventional las-bolt. It was momentarily distracted, though, and I was able to get a good cut across its belly at last. It staggered, thick, foul-smelling ichor beginning to leak from the wound, then came at me again with renewed fury. Seeing that the creature was invulnerable Sorel switched his aim, and began taking down the cultists who were trying to get to me, while Amberley continued to do the same.

'Hold on, commissar!' Jurgen was running down the stairs, his melta readied, and I prayed to the Emperor that he wasn't going to try a shot from there as I'd never survive it. But he had more sense than that, at least.

'Sorel!' Amberley called. 'Clear a path for Jurgen!' The two of them began to concentrate their fire on the cultists between my aide and the desperate battle I still fought. I sprang back a fraction too late and felt talons scrape my ribs, ripping through the armour beneath my coat and burning like fire. I swore, and struck back at the thing, taking the hand which had wounded me off at the wrist. Ichor pumped from it like a fire hose, spraying me and everything else in the vicinity, and if anything, it redoubled its efforts.

I turned my head reflexively, trying to keep my eyes clear, and thus got a clear view of Jurgen as he raced across the floor towards me. For a heart stopping instant, I thought a couple of purestrains were about to eviscerate him, but for some reason they hesitated for a fraction of a second as they were about to close, and Sorel and Amberley dropped them both with well-aimed shots in the nick of time.

I turned back to the patriarch, encouraged by my success in wounding it, and swung the chainsword again. It never even flinched, batting the humming blade aside, and I ducked a wild swing of its lower left arm.

'What does it take to kill you, you bastard?' I snarled, carried away by my own anger and disgust.

'How about this?' Jurgen asked, appearing at my elbow. As he approached the creature, it staggered back, like the purestrains had done, momentarily disorientated, and he jammed the barrel of the melta into the wound I'd cut into its belly. As he pulled the trigger, its entire midsection flashed into steam and foul-smelling offal; it staggered back, its eyes glazing, and swung its head in confusion. Then, slowly, it toppled over, vibrating the stone floor with the violent impact of its fall.

'Thank you, Jurgen,' I said. 'Much obliged.'

'Don't mention it, sir,' he said, turning the weapon to seek other targets, but the cultists were scattering back into the shadows. For the first time, some of them gave voice, a keening wail that sent shivers down my spine. We sent a few shots after them, but I, for one, had had my fill of combat for the time being, and was more than happy to leave them for the follow-up teams. Without the patriarch to focus and direct them, they would be easy enough to pick off, but they would have to be eradicated eventually; otherwise one of the surviving purestrains would grow to take its place, and the whole vile cancer would start to take root again.

'I thought you were dead,' I said. Jurgen nodded.

'So did I, to be honest,' he said. 'They were almost on us when the wall collapsed. Then I thought it might be just as thin on the other side, so I took a shot at it on the off chance.'

'I take it you were right,' I said. He nodded again.

'Lucky, that,' he said.

'What about the others?' Amberley asked, as we began to climb the stairs. Jurgen looked sombre.

'Sorel made it through with me. We didn't see what happened to anyone else.' But then, he didn't have to. They would have been overwhelmed in seconds.

'Lucky you found us when you did,' I said.

'Not really.' Sorel had come to join us as we reached the level of the gallery. 'We found your tracks in the dust, and just followed along.'

'How did you know it was us?' Amberley asked. The marksman shrugged.

'One pair of Imperial Guard boots, one pair of lady's shoes. Didn't need an inquisitor to work that one out.'

'I suppose not.' She looked at him with something like respect.

'Once we heard shooting, we just moved to flank the position,' Jurgen added. 'Standard operating procedure.'

'I see.' She nodded, and pointed to the solid wooden door we'd reached at the top of the staircase. 'Jurgen, if you'd be so kind?'

'My pleasure, miss.' He grinned, like a schola student picked out to answer a question he knows the answer to, and vaporised it with a single blast from the melta, along with a generous section of wall.

'Emperor's teeth,' I breathed, as we entered the passageway beyond. It was paneled in burnished wood, a thick carpet on the floor, and delicate porcelain stood on occasional tables of unmistakable antiquity.

Bright afternoon sun stabbed our eyes through mullioned windows, and a dreadful suspicion began to form in my mind.

'I think I know where we are,' I said. Amberley nodded, her jaw set.

'Me too,' she said grimly.

The silence was shattered by the bark of a bolt pistol and Sorel fell, chunks of his brain spattering an expensive-looking tapestry and staining it beyond repair.

'Commissar Cain. And the charming Miss Vail.' Governor Grice was standing at the end of the corridor, gun held firmly in his hand, the air of vapid imbecility now totally dispelled. 'You really are most annoyingly persistent.'

Editorial Note:

My apologies for this, once again – if it's any consolation it really is the last time...

Extracted from *Like a Phoenix From the Flames: The Founding of the 597th,* by General Jenit Sulla (retired), 097.M42

The renegades resisted doggedly, with a determination I could scarcely credit, and despite the faith I had in the women and men under my command, I must confess I began to doubt that our eventual inevitable victory could be won other than at a terrible cost in the blood of these noble warriors. The traitors had prepared their positions well, and we could make little progress other than by fire and movement, scurrying from one piece of cover to the next. I gathered from the transmissions I could overhear that I was far from the only officer who found these delays unconscionable. Colonel Kasteen had already requested support from one of the armoured regiments among the expeditionary force, and some vigorous debate ensued as to whether the tau would regard this as a provocation. Why anyone would care about the aliens' feelings was beyond me, I must confess, but much of what had transpired since our landing had left me in a state of some confusion, and I comforted myself with the knowledge that my understanding was not a requirement in any case. Duty and obedience was enough, as it should be for anyone privileged to wear the uniform of the Emperor. In the event the lord general had acceded to her request, and the knowledge that a troop of Leman Russes from the 8th Armoured was on their way had bolstered the spirits of our heroic forces to no little degree.

In the meantime, we were still pinned here, and the certainty that our reinforcements, however formidable, were still half an hour away was, I must confess, taking a tithe of the exhilaration we might otherwise have felt. I had no doubt that we could hold on until relieved, but even with the spirit of the Emperor burning within us, it could prove to be a close-run thing if fate had any more surprises to throw at us.

It was while I was reflecting thus that fate did indeed surprise me, and in a fashion I could never have anticipated. My first presentiment was a vox message from Sergeant Lustig, the doughty leader of Second Squad, who broke into my command frequency with some degree of urgency.

'We have movement on our flank,' he informed me. 'Tau units, closing fast. Requesting instructions.' To his great credit, it must be said that, despite the trepidation he no doubt felt, his report was never anything less than wholly professional. A few more exchanges, equally crisp, flew between us, during which time we established the presence of a handful of battlesuits and at least one of the grav tanks our intelligence analysts had tagged 'Hammerheads.'

'Hold position,' I ordered, despite the doubts which rose unbidden to my mind. Our rules of engagement had been clear, and despite the treachery we could no doubt expect from the inhuman, they had done nothing overt so far to break our incomprehensible truce. Lustig acknowledged, and we both waited tensely to see if the gamble we were taking with our soldiers' lives would be won or lost.

I must confess that, for a brief moment as that sinister hull rose over the crest of the hillock of rubble my command squad had concealed itself behind, I had cause to curse myself for an overcautious fool; for as they came into sight, the cannon mounted atop it spoke, a thunderclap of sound which rolled over us like a physical wave, and I apprehended treachery afoot at last. But the ensuing explosion erupted in the centre of the insurrectionist fortifications, silencing their guns in a single display of sorcerous fury that left us all momentarily breathless.

The tank moved on, humming quietly with the energies keeping it aloft, and the battlesuits bounded after it, spraying the enemy positions with a prodigious amount of firepower. Rapid-fire plasma rounds burst and scorched among them, and salvos of missiles from the bulbous pods over the leader's shoulders poured into them in rippling waves, bursting in gouts of flame and shrapnel, shredding and pulping the bodies of those who defied retribution. Bewildered as I was at this sudden turn of events, for I could conceive of no reason for the xenos to turn against their erstwhile allies, I still had no doubt of my duty.

'Follow up!' I ordered. 'After the tau!' Bounding to my feet I led the troopers under my command forward, towards the hole they'd punched for us through the enemy defences. 'For justice! For vengeance! For the Emperor!'

SIXTEEN

'Life's so much easier when you've got someone to blame.'
– Gilbran Quail, Collected Essays

'TRAITOR!' JURGEN RAISED the melta and took a determined pace forward, placing himself between Amberley and myself and the turncoat governor. Grice winced visibly as my aide moved closer to him, although his ever-present bouquet was no stronger than usual so far as I could tell, then squeezed the trigger again. The bolt exploded against the oversized helmet protecting Jurgen's head, flinging him backwards in a shower of shattered carapace; but thanks to the Emperor, or sheer good fortune, it hadn't penetrated this time, the sturdy armour protecting him from Sorel's grisly fate. He staggered back into us, and we both moved instinctively to catch him, dropping our weapons as we did so. My pistol and Amberley's miniature bolter thudded into the spongy carpet, and my chainsword, still activated, spun into a corner where it began chewing energetically through the skirting board.

'He's still alive,' I told Amberley, feeling for the pulse at Jurgen's neck, and taking his weight fully into my arms. After all, I thought, if Grice fired again I should be all right behind that amount of protection.

'Not for long, if you don't keep him away from me,' Grice threatened.

'You're one of them,' Amberley stated flatly, as though this merely confirmed her suspicions. She took another step towards him, and Grice shifted his aim to cover her. I watched, with some trepidation, for although she was still protected by the miraculous displacer field, she had told me herself that it was not to be wholly relied upon, and even if it worked its magic again, her sudden absence would leave me wide open to a follow-up shot.

I sagged a little, as though Jurgen's weight was greater than it was, and tried to work my hand towards the hellgun still slung across his shoulder. The governor grimaced, his mouth working in a manner not entirely human now I came to study it closely, and I berated myself for not having seen the truth sooner. The excessive bulk beneath his robes had not, as I'd assumed on our first meeting, resulted from over-indulgence and the commonplace inbreeding of most noble families,[1] but from a far more sinister source.

'The brood will survive,' he said. 'A new patriarch will arise–'

'But not in your lifetime,' I said, swivelling the hellgun under Jurgen's pungently damp armpit and squeezing the trigger. The supercharged lasblast screamed through the air between us, blasting a smoking crater through the left side of the governor's chest, and for a moment I felt the exultation of victory. It was short-lived, however, because to my horrified astonishment he didn't drop, just twisted aside with inhuman speed, and switched the aim of the bolt pistol back to me. Thick plates of chitin were visible beneath the ruin of his robes now, and a third deformed arm emerged from the rent in the garment. Through my nausea a sudden shaft of understanding lit up my synapses. 'You were the assassin!' I gasped.

A vivid mental picture of the events of that fateful night reeled through my brain. With a weapon concealed in that hidden extra hand, he could have shot the tau ambassador before anyone had even the faintest suspicion of his murderous intent, and whatever disarray withdrawing it might have left in his clothing would be put down to the turmoil of the moment. Certainly all I'd seen was two empty hands, and a hysterical El'hassai who, I must reluctantly concede, had been right all along.

'What was your first clue?' Amberley snapped, diving for her discarded weapon. I tried to take aim with the hellgun again, but the strap was tangled in Jurgen's armour, and the dead weight of my unconscious aide was hindering me. As Grice's bolt pistol came up I already knew I wasn't going to make it.

---

1. *Something of an exaggeration, but widely believed nevertheless.*

Then, for a blessed second he hesitated, still moving with preternatural speed, and pointed the gun back at Amberley. I suppose he realised that she would get to her bolt pistol and drop him if he didn't take her down first. I tried to shout a warning, but the first syllable of her name had barely made it through my horror-constricted throat before he fired.

The bolt detonated against the floor, twisting the gun her fingertips had almost reached into scrap and sending splinters of wood flying into the air, but once again, she was suddenly somewhere else. Some highly unladylike language and the crash of falling china a few metres further up the corridor told me that she'd collided with one of the little tables and its display of porcelain.[1]

Grice looked astonished just long enough for me to tug the recalcitrant hellgun around far enough to take another shot at him, which made a terrible mess of that tasteful wood panelling but unfortunately did nothing worse to the tainted governor. He turned, following the sound of Amberley's landing, just in time to see her roll to her feet with the dextrousness of an accomplished martial artist.

'Consider yourself relieved of your position,' she said, pointing an accusing finger at him like a schola tutor admonishing an unsatisfactory student. He actually started to laugh, bringing the weapon round to bear on her again, when a bright flash erupted from the ornate ring I'd noticed at our first meeting. Grice staggered, falling back, and two hands went to his throat. The third continued to clutch his bolt pistol, which discharged again randomly as he sank to his knees. His face worked, as though gasping for air, and darkened with clotting blood. Pale yellow foam frothed over his engorging lips.

'Digital needler,' Amberley explained, stepping delicately over the now spasming corpse. 'The toxin's excruciatingly painful, I'm told.'

'Good,' I said, aiming a bad-tempered kick at the erstwhile governor, and hoping he was still conscious enough to feel it before he expired.

'How's Jurgen?' She took the weight of his other shoulder, and helped me to get him laid out on the floor. I began to remove the remains of his helmet carefully.

'Not good,' I said, a surprising amount of concern entering my voice. There was a lot of blood, but most of it seemed to be from superficial

---

1. *The displacer field, as those of you who've used one can no doubt attest, will readily teleport you out of immediate danger. Unfortunately, you rematerialise moving at the same speed and in the same direction as when the field activates, and, as Cain points out, I was diving for a gun on the floor at the time. And it was a stupid place to put a table in any case.*

wounds caused by the shattered armour. Rather more worrying was the
clear fluid mixed in with it. 'I think his skull's fractured.'

'I think you're right.' She began administering first aid with a speed
and competence I found astonishing. 'Better call for a medicae unit.'

Cursing myself for my own stupidity, I activated my combead, realising belatedly that I'd be able to get a message through to Kasteen now
we'd returned to the surface. To my astonishment, however, the command channels were choked with traffic, and I turned back to Amberley
with the bitter taste of failure burning in the back of my throat.

'We're too late,' I said. 'It sounds as though the war's already started.'

'Then we'll just have to stop it,' she said, matter-of-factly, her attention still on Jurgen. At the time, still not realising his significance, I was
simply grateful for her concern for his welfare, even as I found the time
to marvel at her indefatigable spirit. If ever a woman seemed capable
of stopping an all-out war single-handedly, it was her. I was just on the
verge of replying when the wall blew in, throwing me to the floor yet
again, and showering what was left of the elegant decor with rubble.

'What the frak...' I began, scrabbling for my fallen laspistol. I'd just
managed to grab it when human figures in flak armour burst through
the new gap, lasguns levelled. Behind them, I noted absently, someone
was making a hell of a mess of the garden. I just managed to prevent
myself from squeezing the trigger in the nick of time as I recognised the
armour as Imperial Guard issue.

'Stand up! Slowly!' a familiar voice barked, then took on a tinge of
astonishment. 'Commissar! Is that you?'

'Right now I'm not entirely sure,' I said. Kasteen looked at me, for a
long, searching moment, before taking in the dishevelled state of the
inquisitor; then her gaze moved on and down to the prostrate figures
of Jurgen and the governor. I indicated my aide. 'He needs a medic,' I
said, then for some reason my legs gave way beneath me.

'THERE'S NO DOUBT at all, then?' Kasteen had listened to our story in
silence, or at least to as much of it as Amberley felt like telling her, and
I'd spent the last half hour or so alternately nodding, saying 'yes, really,'
and similar helpful remarks, and scrounging the largest mug of tanna
leaf tea I could find. It was not the most obvious thing to find on a battlefield, you might think, but these were Valhallans after all, and it
didn't take me long to discover a fire-team brewing up once the immediate danger was past.

Broklaw was running around like the good second-in-command he
was, detailing troopers to secure the perimeter and clear out the tunnels
beneath what was left of the palace, and once I'd seen Jurgen safely on

his way back to the aid station, I relished the chance to simply enjoy the feeling of sun on my face and the astonished realisation that, against all the odds, I'd survived again.

'None,' Amberley said. 'The body's all the proof we need. Grice was a 'stealer hybrid, and killed the ambassador to try to provoke a war. All the death and destruction in the city was just part of the same agenda.'

'Merciful Emperor,' Kasteen breathed, appalled at the thought. 'His own people, sacrificed in their thousands... The bastard.'

'His own people were the genestealers,' I said. 'The rest of us, humans, tau, even the kroot, were never anything more to him than fodder for the hive fleets.'

'Exactly.' Amberley looked sober for a moment, before the familiar carefree smile was suddenly back on her face; but it was there with an effort, I found myself thinking. 'And if we hadn't kept our heads, things might have turned out very differently.'

'They still might,' I said, indicating the hulking figures of the tau dreadnoughts around the perimeter, and the curiously rounded vehicles hovering over the surface of the grass. Tau troopers were beginning to deploy from some of them, eyeing our own soldiers suspiciously, but so far, at least, the two forces were keeping well apart. 'Can we trust them now we don't have an enemy in common?'

'For the time being, at least,' Amberley said. She might have said more, but we were interrupted by a sudden shout from the direction of the ruins.

'They've found some survivors!' Kasteen hurried off, to where a small knot of figures was emerging from the wreckage of the palace. Amberley and I exchanged glances, an unspoken presentiment sparking between us, and trotted after her as best we could. Now we were safe the exhaustion of our exertions had crashed in on us like a landslide, and I felt my calf muscles cramping as I tried to keep up.

Even before we reached them I caught a glimpse of red hair, so it was little surprise to me when the search team (one of the squads from Sulla's platoon, I seem to recall, but I couldn't tell you which one) parted to reveal Velade and Holenbi, each supported by a trooper with an arm around the shoulders, holding hands like a pair of courting teeners. It's no exaggeration to say they both looked like hell, but that's precisely what you'd expect I suppose, their uniforms ragged, and bandages leaking blood where the squad medic had applied field dressings to the worst of their wounds. Holenbi stared at me in numb confusion, but that was nothing new.

'Where did you find them?' I asked the sergeant in charge, and he saluted me smartly.

'Down in the tunnels, sir. Lieutenant Sulla told us to spread out and secure the perimeter below ground, and they were about half a klom in. They must've been in a hell of a fight, sir.'

'Velade?' I asked gently. She turned her head towards me, her eyes unfocussed. 'What happened?'

'Sir?' Her brow furrowed. 'We were fighting. Tomas and me.'

'They were everywhere,' Holenbi cut in, his voice distant.

'Then the roof came in, and we lost the others. So we fought our way out.'

'I see,' I said, nodding slowly, and glanced across at Amberley. The same doubt was clouding her eyes, I could see. I turned back to the bedraggled troopers, then brought up my laspistol and shot them both through the head before either of them had a chance to react.

'What the hell...?' Kasteen shouted, her hand moving instinctively towards the bolt pistol on her hip until common sense reasserted itself and aborted the gesture. She glared at me, her jaw tight, and the troopers around us froze in shock, anger and confusion in their eyes. I had a sudden flash of *déjà vu*, an unbidden memory of the mess room aboard the *Righteous Wrath*. For a moment, I was horribly unsure of myself, afraid I'd made a terrible mistake, then I glanced again at Amberley for reassurance. She nodded, a barely noticeable acknowledgement, and I felt a little better. At least if I was wrong, an inquisitor was, too, which wouldn't help much with rebuilding morale in the regiment, but at least I wouldn't be the only one left feeling embarrassed.

'I've seen this before,' I said, addressing Kasteen directly, but keeping my voice loud and clear enough to be heard by everyone. 'On Keffia.' I took the combat knife from the sergeant's harness and knelt beside Holenbi's body, ripping one of the dressings away to reveal a small deep wound slanting up under the ribcage. I sliced it open, ignoring the horrified gasps from those around me, and felt around with blood-slick fingers. After a moment I found what I'd expected to be there, and yanked out a small fibrous bundle of organic material.

'What the hell's that?' Kasteen asked, over the sound of Sulla being violently sick.

'A genestealer implant,' Amberley explained. 'Once it takes root in a host, it gradually subverts their own genetic identity, turning any offspring into hybrids. A generation or two after that you start to get purestrains showing up, along with hybrids almost indistinguishable from humans, and the taint continues to spread.' She indicated an identical wound on Velade's torso. 'They were both infected when the 'stealers overran them.'

'The disorientation was the real giveaway,' I added. 'The implant messes with the brain chemistry, so the host remains unaware of being infected. All they recall is a confused impression of fighting, and assume they've escaped.'

'It's often mistaken for combat fatigue,' Amberley finished. 'Luckily, the commissar could tell the difference, or your regiment would have been leaving hidden stealer cults behind wherever you were deployed.'

'I see.' Kasteen nodded once, crisply, and turned to the sergeant. 'Burn the bodies.'

'A wise precaution,' Amberley said as the three of us turned away, and the sergeant went looking for a flamer.

'Colonel! Commissar!' Broklaw was waving from the ramp of a command Chimera. 'One of our patrols found some tau down there too. They're on their way back to the surface now!'

Amberley and I looked at one another, and went to meet the survivors of the shas'la we'd met in the tunnels. Trepidation churned in my gut as the little group, reduced to three now, staggered into the sunlight. One had lost his helmet, and squinted at the sudden brightness. I shivered, finding myself plunged into shadow as a Devilfish troop carrier swept overhead and grounded to receive them. They looked disorientated, it was true, but they would have been as exhausted as we were, and I just couldn't be sure what the cause might be. These were xenos, after all, and I just couldn't read them the way I could my own kind.

So I stood there, paralysed with indecision, while they staggered up the ramp and into the transport, aided by their fellows, and by then it was too late anyway. As I turned away, sick with apprehension, I found Amberley watching me with what I can only describe as a smile of satisfaction.

For some reason, that failed to raise my spirits. If anything it had quite the opposite effect.

Editorial Note:

Once again we need to turn to other sources for a wider perspective on the aftermath of the affair than Cain's typically self-centred account gives us.

From *Purge the Guilty! An impartial account of the liberation of Gravalax,* by Stententious Logar. 085.M42

And thus it was that the world we so dearly love was saved from the depredations of the alien by the heroism of the warriors of His Divine Majesty and the martial fortitude of heroes whose names live on in the glory of their deeds. Even those of the calibre of the celebrated Commissar Cain, who, though his own contribution to this campaign was never more than peripheral, was no doubt proud to have been associated with so noble an endeavour. It is indeed a pity that, like most of the Imperial Guardsmen deployed in this most glorious of enterprises, he was able to do no more than remain on the sidelines, but he was at least in at the death, so to speak, having been present when the treacherous Governor Grice at last met deserved retribution at the hands of the Inquisition. Indeed, some even assert that he witnessed the celebrated duel to the death between the wretched traitor and the inquisitor herself, although like most conscientious historians I must reluctantly concede that this is, in all probability, nothing more than a charming myth. After a thorough examination of the evidence, it seems far more likely that an officer of his calibre would have been in the thick of the battle for control of the palace, especially once the perfidious tau had moved in to try to protect the puppet their insidious rogue trader accomplices had installed on the throne there.

Be that as it may, the Battle of the Palace was undoubtedly the true turning point in the history of our fair globe, when the grip of the xenoist interloper was finally broken, and the relieved and grateful populace brought back at last under the protection of the Divine Emperor and his tireless servants. Broken and dispirited, the tau departed, slinking away like the vagabond thieves they were, having failed to seize the fair world of Gravalax for their own. Within hours of their defeat at the hands of the Imperial Guard, they withdrew, not only from the city, but from the planet itself. One by one they fled aboard their starships, retreating back into the hinterland of space from whence they'd come, never to trouble us again.

For you can be sure that we, the generations that followed, have been careful not to make the mistakes of our ancestors, and remain ever vigilant against the hour of their return. Even now, our PDF units stand ready, at a moments' notice, to defend the sacred soil of His Majesty's most holy dominions to the uttermost drop of their blood, and it is our most fervent hope that one day the cream of these doughty warriors may be found worthy to take their place in the blessed ranks of the Imperial Guard itself.

As to the rogue traders, we must be equally on our guard, for they remain among us, spreading their insidious web of treachery...

[And so on, and so on...

From which you might fairly deduce that the genestealer infestation remains a secret known only to a few; and since those few are either servants of the Inquisition or members of an Imperial Guard unit never likely to return to the wretched place, it's a secret which will remain secure. As to why this should be so important...]

EPILOGUE

*'Stories are much tidier than real life. Stories
have neat, happy endings, but all you ever
really get is unfinished business.'*

– Janni Vakonz, holo director

I'D SEEN LITTLE of Amberley in the week that followed our adventures in
the undercity, but we both had plenty to keep us occupied over those
few days, so I hardly found her absence surprising. Jurgen was still
recovering slowly, so I'd lost my principle buttress against most of the
tedious minutiae of my job, and found my workload drastically
increased as a result. Add to that the fatigue and minor injuries I'd sustained, and I did little else apart from eat, sleep, and shuffle datafiles.
Divas dropped round one evening with a bottle of amasec, which provided a pleasant enough diversion, and filled me in on the latest gossip
(which, after the last time, you can be sure I did my utmost to ignore;
no point in taking any chances).

'No one can understand it,' he said at one point. 'The tau are just
pulling out.' I'd heard as much from other sources, most of them a
good deal more reliable thanks to my connections in the lord general's
office, but I nodded nonetheless as I poured us both refills.

'Well, that's xenos for you,' I said helpfully. 'Who knows why they do
anything?' It still didn't make much sense when Donali explained it to

me, but he seemed to know what he was talking about, and Amberley confirmed it later, so it's the best I can do.

You see, peculiar little devils that they are, they don't seem to value the objective of the fighting purely for itself, the way we do. As best as I can understand it, they reckoned that if we were that determined to pitch into a meat grinder war to hang on to this worthless mudball, we might as well have it. They'd go off and do something more productive until we got bored or complacent or distracted, and come back for it later when we couldn't put up a decent fight for the place.[1] And in the meantime, there was the hive fleet to worry about, assuming it was actually out there. (Which, as we were subsequently to discover, it most certainly was.)

So, as you can appreciate, I was pleasantly surprised when a message arrived from Amberley inviting me to dinner at a discreet waterfront restaurant in a quarter of the city which seemed to have escaped the worst of the fighting; even more so, given that I'd never expected to see her again. (Just how far off the mark that assumption was you'll find ample evidence of elsewhere in this memoir, as I've already mentioned.)

'How's Jurgen?' she asked, over a mouthwatering smoked vyl crêpe. Touched by her solicitude, I filled her in on his recovery, and asked how her associates were getting on in return. (Reasonably well, as it turned out: Rakel was up and about and as bonkers as ever, and Orelius had already returned to his ship.)

She nodded at the news. 'I'm glad to hear it. He's a remarkable man.'

'He's certainly unusual,' I agreed, savouring the local vintage she'd obtained from somewhere – light and piquant, it complimented the food wonderfully. She smiled at that.

'More so than you realise.' Something about the way her tone changed alerted me, and I began to pay more attention to her words. This was more than mere small talk. 'I don't think we'd have made it out of the tunnels without him.' I thought back to my desperate duel with the patriarch.

'If he hadn't scrounged that melta from somewhere–' I agreed, but she cut me off before I could finish.

'That isn't what I meant. Do you know what a blank is?' I must have looked baffled, because she went on to explain. 'They're incredibly rare; about as rare among psykers as psykers are compared to the rest of us.'

---

1. *A little vague, but substantially accurate. Tau tacticians tend to take the long view, with-drawing to regroup whenever they meet stronger resistance than they were expecting, or, as in this case, the situation proves to be more complex than anticipated.*

'You think Jurgen's a psyker?' I asked, laughing in spite of myself, and inclining my body slightly to the left to give the waiter room to remove my plate. The idea was so ridiculous I just couldn't help it. But Amberley shook her head.

'No. Quite the reverse. He's a blank, I'm sure of it.' I echoed the gesture.

'You've lost me,' I admitted.

'Blanks are like anti-psykers,' she explained. 'They can't be affected by psykers or warp entities. They block telepathic communication. You saw how the patriarch reacted to him...'

'It seemed to get disoriented when he got close to it,' I said, remembering. 'And Grice was desperate to keep him away.' Amberley nodded.

'Exactly. His presence disrupted the brood telepathy.'

'That explains a lot,' I said, recalling a number of incidents over the years which had seemed no more than mildly puzzling at the time, but which I now realised formed a pattern, confirming my aide's resistance to psychic attack. 'How long have you known?'

'Since the first time I saw him,' she admitted. 'When Rakel had a seizure while he was trying to help her into the Salamander.' A terrible suspicion began to form.

'You're going to recruit him, aren't you?' I said. 'If he can face down daemons and sorcerers you're not going to leave him buried in an obscure Imperial Guard unit.' She was smiling again, as though something amused her.

'The Inquisition is an odd organisation, Ciaphas,' she said. 'Not like the Guard, where everyone's united against a common foe, and you can rely on your comrades and your command structure.' I wasn't sure what she was driving at then, but I've had rather more dealings with the Inquisition since than I'm comfortable with, and believe me, it makes sense. Just take my word for it, and hope you never have cause to find out. 'We're not very big on sharing our sources and resources, because we never really know who else in the ordos we can trust.' As you'll appreciate, astonishment barely begins to cover what I felt listening to those words. 'So, no, I think for the time being I'd rather leave him where he is. It's safer that way.'

'Safe? In a front line Guard unit?' I thought she was joking at first, until I got a good look at her eyes. Blue and guileless, they shone with a sincerity that would have been impossible to fake. (Believe me, I'm an expert at that.) She nodded again.

'I'll be able to find you again if I need you. Either of you.' And I was so caught up in the moment that the full implication of those words never struck me at the time. 'But if I take him on as one of my staff he'll attract attention. The sort I'd rather avoid.'[1]

'I see.' I didn't really, but the main point seemed to be that I wouldn't have to worry about losing my aide after all, at least in the short term. And it also hadn't escaped my notice that while he was around I wouldn't have to worry about any passing psykers ferreting out secrets I'd rather leave buried. I started in on my toffee cream dessert with well-deserved enthusiasm.

'Good.' Amberley grinned again, the mischievous expression I found so appealing back on her face. 'Besides, Rakel's hard enough to deal with at the best of times, without passing out on me every five minutes.'

'I'm sure,' I said. The silence stretched awkwardly for a moment, so I made an attempt to change the subject. 'You've heard about the tau withdrawal?' She nodded.

'El'sorath still insists that the world is theirs by right, but they're agreeing to respect the status quo for the time being. I guess they blinked first.' She shrugged. 'Besides, they're spooked by the idea of a hive fleet moving in, even if they don't want to admit it. They've had a few skirmishes with splinter fleets in the last couple of centuries, and they're under no illusions about what a full-scale invasion would mean.' Neither was I, and I shuddered at the thought. 'Hanging on to one small planet doesn't mean much in the face of that, especially if it would weaken their response to the greater threat.'

'Speaking of which...' I coughed delicately. 'I'm still not entirely sure those pathfinders... You know...'

'Who cares?' Amberley sipped at her wine appreciatively. 'If they were, then at least it'll draw the hive fleets down on them instead of us a few generations down the line. And in the meantime, we can exploit the chaos in the tau empire for our own ends.'

'Good for us, then,' I said. I raised my own glass. 'Confusion to our enemies.'

'And kudos to our friends.' Our glasses clinked together, and Amberley grinned at me again. 'Here's to the beginning of a beautiful friendship.'

Not to mention half a lifetime of running, shooting, and bowel-clenching terror, of course. But looking back, I have to say she made it well worth the effort.

[*And on that somewhat ego-boosting note, this extract from the Cain Archive comes to a natural conclusion*].

---

1. *Like Radicals with an agenda, or Ordo Malleus fanatics looking for daemon-fodder for their next crusade. Not my department, thank the Emperor.*

ECHOES OF THE TOMB

IF THERE'S ONE basic principle I've learned in over a century of rattling around the galaxy fighting the Emperor's enemies (whenever I couldn't avoid it), it's 'leave well alone'. Three simple words which have stood me in good stead over the years; judiciously applied they've made my commissarial duties a great deal easier than they might have been. Unfortunately it's a phrase the Adeptus Mechanicus seems incapable of grasping, a failing which almost cost me my life.

I suppose I'd better explain. By the end of 928 my undeserved reputation for heroism had grown to such a ridiculous level that I'd finally attracted the attention of the upper echelons of the commissariat, who had decided that a man of my obvious talents was wasted in the posting to an obscure artillery unit I had so carefully aranged for myself in the hope of being able to sit out my lifetime of service to the Emperor a long way away from any actual fighting. As it turned out, by sheer bad luck I'd managed to put myself in harm's way an inordinate number of times, emerging on every occasion trailing clouds of undeserved glory, so that to the sector at large I seemed to be the very epitome of the swashbuckling hero that commissars are generally considered not to be. (Most regiments regard us as something akin to the engineseers in the transport pool; sometimes necessary, occasionally useful, generally best avoided.)

Accordingly I found myself transferred to a desk job at brigade headquarters, which at first seemed like a gift from the Emperor himself. I had a nice comfortable office, with an anteroom in which Jurgen, my aide, was able to lurk, deterring all but the most determined of visitors with his single-minded devotion to following orders as literally as possible and his paint-blistering body odour. For a while it seemed that my days of fleeing in terror from genestealers, chaos cultists, and blood-maddened orks were over. But of course it was all too good to be true. The staff officers were delighted to discover that they had a bona fide hero among them (at least, so they believed), which meant every time they needed an independent commissar to accompany some particularly dangerous or foolhardy mission, they sent for me.

Thanks to my finely-honed instinct for self-preservation I managed to make it back every time, though this which only encouraged them to think I was the greatest thing since Macharius, and just the man to send out on an even more dangerous assignment just as soon as they could think of something sufficiently lethal.

Enough was enough, I decided, and hearing that someone was needed to liaise with an Astartes company which was campaigning alongside the Guard in a routine action to clear some heretics off an agriworld on the spinward fringes of our sector decided to volunteer for the job. After my last little jaunt, rescuing some hostages from an eldar pirate base, I thought a bit of quiet diplomacy would be just the change of pace I needed.

'You don't think you'll find this sort of thing a little... tame?' General Lokris, a genial old buffer I'd probably quite like if he didn't keep trying to get me killed, asked, raising a shaggy white eyebrow in my direction. We were dining together in his private chambers, the skill of his chef more than making up for the tedium of his company, and I had a shrewd suspicion that this demonstration of his regard was intended to sway me into changing my mind. I took another mouthful of the salma, which was poached to perfection, to give myself time to formulate an acceptable answer.

'Well it's got to be more interesting than shuffling datafiles,' I said, smiling ruefully. That fitted his mental image of Cain the Man of Action quite nicely, and he nodded sympathetically. 'Besides,' I went on, seeing no harm in laying it on with a trowel, 'how often am I going to get the chance to go into battle alongside the Astartes?' Never, if I had anything to do with it, but Lokris didn't need to know that. He nodded eagerly at the prospect, quite enthused on my behalf, and took an extravagant pull at his wineglass to restore his composure.

'Quite right, my boy. What an experience that would be.' He sipped at his drink again, growing quietly contemplative. 'By the Emperor, if I were a hundred years younger I'd volunteer myself.'

'It's not as though there's anything urgent I need to do here,' I went on. 'Jurgen can take care of the routine stuff while I'm gone.' I would have preferred to take him with me, of course, but I was uncomfortably aware of the impression he was bound to make on the genetically-enhanced supermen of the Astartes, and had no wish to undermine my credibility before the assignment had even begun. Besides, while he was here he could watch my back, making sure I wasn't earmarked for any more suicide missions. I knew something was in the wind, which was why I'd seized on this diplomatic assignment so eagerly. For once, whatever Lokris and his cronies were planning they could leave me out of it.

'You should reach the Viridian system in about a month,' the general said. 'I don't suppose the heretics will be able to hold out for much longer than that, but even if they do you ought to be back here by around two hundred next year at the latest.'

'Emperor willing,' I said, making a mental note to spin the assignment out for longer than that if I could. He might not have a specific reason for wanting me back by then, but you never know.

MY FIRST SURPRISE was the transport ship I'd been assigned to. Instead of a troopship or a supply vessel, both of which I was intimately acquainted with after all my years of shuffling from one warzone to the next, I found my shuttle docking at a light freighter bearing the unmistakable sigil of the Adeptus Mechanicus. They seemed to be expecting me. There was an honour guard of their augmetically enhanced troopers lining the walls of the hanger bay, and a tech-priest with a wide smile and a couple of mechadendrites waving lazily over his shoulders was waiting at the bottom of the shuttle's exit ramp. He stuck out a hand for me to shake as I descended, and on taking it I was surprised to find it was still unaugmented flesh.

'Commissar Cain,' he said. 'Welcome aboard. I'm Magos Killian, leader of the expedition, and this really is a tremendous honour. We've heard all about you, of course, and I must say we're thrilled to have you travelling with us.'

'Expedition?' I said, trying to ignore the sudden lurching sensation in the pit of my stomach. 'I was under the impression I've been assigned to liaise between the guard units and the Reclaimers task force in the Viridia system.'

'Didn't they tell you?' Confusion, exasperation and amusement chased themselves across Killian's face. 'Well, that's the munitorium for you, I suppose. We're making a rendezvous with a Reclaimers battle barge in the Interitus system, so some clerical drone obviously thought it would save you a bit of time to hitch a lift with us and transfer across when we meet them.' He fished a data-slate from some recess of his immaculate white robes, and fiddled with it for a moment. 'The next scheduled departure for Viridia is in another three weeks. Allowing for the wait before the barge arrives in orbit around Interitus Prime, you should be there about...' he consulted the slate again, making a couple of quick calculations as he did so, 'about thirty-six hours ahead of them. If the warp currents are favourable, of course.'

'Of course,' I said. I wasn't sure whether to be relieved or angry. On the one hand I'd be spending an extra three weeks on a roundabout voyage to Emperor-knew-where, but on the other that was three weeks I wouldn't have to worry about Lokris and his friends trying to find some new and inventive way of getting me killed. On balance that was an acceptable trade-off, I felt. I smiled, and nodded with every appearance of polite interest I could summon up. 'I'm looking forward to hearing all about this expedition of yours.'

A servitor scuttled past me and up the ramp of the shuttle to retrieve my kitbag, which from habit I'd left lying where it was on the subconscious assumption that Jurgen would deal with it. Killian nodded with every indication of eagerness as we strolled past the line of tech-guards, every one of them immaculate, hellguns at the port. They looked formidable enough on parade, I found myself thinking, but I was by no means sure their fighting prowess would be a match for real guardsmen.

As it turned out I was to see for myself how effective they were before very long, and if I'd realised that at the time, and against how terrible a foe, I would certainly have thanked the tech-priest politely for his offer and bolted for the shuttle without a second thought. But of course I didn't, so I simply strolled along beside him, blithely unaware that we were all on a voyage to perdition.

DESPITE MY FOREBODINGS the trip itself turned out to be remarkably pleasant. In striking contrast to the basic conditions aboard the troopships I was used to, the *Omnissiah's Blessing* felt more like a luxury liner. I had a well-appointed stateroom assigned to me, with a couple of hovering cyber-skulls humming quietly in the corner with nothing better to do than scoot off to find anything I required, and the cuisine was first rate. A real surprise this, as in my experience tech-priests tend not to worry about that sort of thing, looking on the necessity of taking in regular nourishment as a distasteful reminder of their fleshly origins or some such nonsense. I'd been steeling myself to face a plateful of soylens viridiens or something equally unappetising the first time I wandered down to the mess hall, only to find a pleasantly appointed dining room which wouldn't have looked out of place in a smart hotel, and was immediately assailed by the mouth-watering odour of sauteed grox.

I was still enjoying my first meal aboard when Killian ambled over, a plate of grox and fresh vegetables in one hand, a large bowl of ackenberry sorbet in the other, and a steaming mug of recaf waving precariously from a mechadendrite. I gestured for him to join me, and after a few preliminary pleasantries he began to chat about their voyage.

'No reason you shouldn't at least know where we're going,' he said cheerfully, the unoccupied mechadendrite diving into the recesses of his robe for the dataslate. He placed it on the table and continued to manipulate the controls with the mechanical limb, while his real ones plied knife and fork with evident enthusiasm. A star chart appeared, the Viridian system just at the fringes of the display, and a small, sullen stellar revenant centred in the screen.

'Looks inviting,' I said, with heavy irony. To my surprise Killian chuckled.

'Does rather, doesn't it?' he said, zooming the display so that the target system filled the screen. A handful of dark and airless worlds orbited the decaying star, seared to cinders when it went nova millions of years before, taking whatever life had existed there into oblivion before sinking back into the sullen, cooling ember about which the few surviving rocks still drifted.

'This is the Interitus system,' he said. 'Well named, I'm sure you'll agree.' I nodded.

'I can't for the life of me see what you'd want there,' I admitted. 'Let alone why an Astartes chapter would divert a battle barge from a war-zone to meet you.'

Killian positively beamed, and pointed to the largest chunk of rock in the system.

'This is Interitus Prime. The whole system was surveyed by explorers back in the twenty-eighth millennium. In the most cursory fashion I may add, if the surviving records are anything to go by.'

'Your records go back that far?' I couldn't keep an edge of incredulity from my voice. That was the all but unimaginable golden age when the Emperor still walked among men and the Imperium was young and vigourous, its domination of the galaxy uncontested, instead of being riven by heresy and threatened on all sides by malevolent powers. Killian nodded.

'Only in the most fragmentary form, of course. But there are still tantilising hints for those prepared to meditate for long enough upon them, and put their trust in the benevolence of the Omnissiah.'

'And you think there's something there worth going after,' I said. There wasn't much which would drag a ship full of cogboys halfway across the sector, and it wasn't hard to guess which item on that very short list was the attraction here. 'Some significant stash of archeotech perhaps?'

'Perhaps,' Killian nodded, evidently pleased at my perspicacity. 'We won't know for sure until we get there, will we?'

'I suppose not,' I conceded, turning my attention to the desserts.

THE REST OF the voyage passed pleasantly enough, although apart from Killian I had little to do with the tech-priests on board. For company I gravitated naturally to the tech-guards, with whom I had a little more in common, finding that despite their augmetic enhancements and a devotion to the cult of the machine which I found a trifle disconcerting (I've little enough patience with Emperor-botherers at the best of times, let alone ones who seem to think he runs on clockwork), they were as disciplined and professional in their way as any of the warriors I'd served with. Moreover they'd heard of me, and believed every word of my reputation. Their only drawback from my point of view was that they didn't seem to have any currency, being some sort of vassals of the adeptus, so there wasn't much point in getting my tarot deck out. Their commanding officer, a Lieutenant Tarkus, was a keen regicide player however, and a hard opponent to beat, so I was able to keep my brain ticking over while the ship scuttled nervously through the warp towards whatever might be lurking at our destination.

It was Tarkus who finally put my mind at rest about the battle barge; it seemed that, despite my obvious concerns, its formidable firepower wasn't to be deployed in our defence.

'Omnissiah no!' he said, casually dispatching one of my lancers with a sudden flanking movement I should have seen coming. 'It's on its way to clean out the rebel base on Viridia Secundus.' I nodded gravely, pretending I'd read the briefing slate about the tactical situation in the Viridia system. It seemed the heretics had taken control of more than just the main world, then. 'They're only hooking up with us long enough to transfer a squad of Space Marines over. And to pick you up, of course.'

Well that was something, although a potential threat potent enough to require an Astartes squad to contain wasn't to be taken all that lightly. I consoled myself with the reflection that it wasn't my problem anyway, I'd be safe aboard one of the most powerful vessels in space and a long way away from Interitus Prime before anyone started to meddle with whatever chunk of archeotech the cogboys were after. I nodded judiciously, playing for time, and made a feint with a trooper hoping to draw his ecclesiarch out of position.

'I'm sure you'll feel safer having them around,' I said blandly. 'Can't be too careful, after all.' As I'd hoped, the half of his face which wasn't made of metal coloured visibly as he considered the implied slur on his command, and he moved a little too hastily, creating an opening I should be able to exploit a couple of moves further on in the game.

'I don't see why that'd make a difference,' he said, a little too levelly. 'My boys can cope with anything the galaxy might throw at us.'

'I don't doubt it,' I said. 'From what I've seen we could do with a few more like them in the Guard.' Tarkus nodded as I moved my portside citadel, setting up what I hoped would be a chance to win in another three turns. I waited until he was considering his response before adding: 'But Magos Killian obviously doesn't share my confidence.'

Tarkus almost knocked his ecclesiarch over as he picked it up and moved it, blowing his only chance of blocking my next attack. His jaw clenched.

'It's not a question of confidence,' he said. 'There are... longstanding obligations.'

I perked up at that, as you can imagine, although what sort of pact there might be between an Astartes chapter and the Adeptus Mechanicus I was at a loss to understand. I don't doubt that I would have been able to worm a little more out of Tarkus given time, but I decided not to press him any further that evening (having just set myself up for a comfortable win despite his superior skill at the game, and wanting to savour it), and by the time we'd agreed on for our next joust across the board he was already dead.

WELL, THERE IT is.' Killian waved an expansive hand at the armourcrys window which dominated the far end of the ship's lounge. Beyond it the dying star guttered fitfully, casting a dim blue glow over us which reminded me of autumn twilight. A slice of darkness distorted the glowing sphere, the bulk of the planet we'd come so far to reach rising up to take a bite out of it.

The landscape below us was in darkness, but enough of the wan glow of the system's primary leaked across the horizon for me to make out a blasted wasteland, cracked by heat almost impossible to imagine, and riven with impact craters. That alone was a testament to how old this place was, as it must have been left almost smooth by its fiery transformation;

the pockmarking of its face would have been the work of aeons. Despite the awful bleakness of the prospect I couldn't deny that it had a desolate grandeur to it, and a faint chill akin to awe touched my soul as I took it all in.

'It's certainly... impressive,' I agreed. Nonetheless a vague sense of unease took hold of me, and I found myself grateful for the thought that I'd be transferring to the Reclaimers' battle barge and leaving this system forever within a day or two.

'We've already begun to establish our base camp,' Killian continued. I strained my eyes in the direction he'd pointed, failing to see anything for a moment, then picked out a faint flash of light as one of our shuttles ignited its engine many kilometres below. 'I think you'd be impressed.'

'No doubt I would,' I agreed, grateful for the secrecy he'd displayed up to now, which almost certainly meant I wouldn't have to leave the security of the ship. 'But I'm sure you don't want me getting underfoot.'

'Well...' Killian hesitated, clearly torn between conflicting impulses, and not entirely sure whether he was doing the right thing. 'Obviously we're on a mission from the Omnissiah. Normally we wouldn't dream of involving an outsider...' Here it comes, I thought, with an ominous sinking feeling in the pit of my stomach. That reputation for heroism is about to hit me over the back of the head again. The techpriest cleared his throat. 'But given your extensive experience as a military man, do you think Lieutenant Tarkus would listen to your opinions at all?'

'Lieutenant Tarkus strikes me as a man who doesn't need much advice from anyone,' I said smoothly, cursing myself for undermining his confidence the previous evening. 'And if he does, I'm sure the Astartes contingent will have far more pertinent comments to make when they get here than anything I might have to say.'

'Well, that's the thing.' Killian coughed delicately again. 'Technically, they'll be led by a sergeant, won't they?'

Of course. And Tarkus would be too stubborn to ask the opinion of a lower ranking squad leader now his pride had been hurt. Notwithstanding the fact that the marine sergeant would probably have decades of combat experience, and refuse to take orders from anyone outside his chapter in any case. I had a sudden premonition of the administrative problems which would be awaiting me on Viridia, and wondered for a moment if I'd done the right thing in volunteering.

Oh well. I might as well get a little practice in now. I had nothing better to do until the barge arrived after all.

'I'll do my best to help, of course,' I said. 'Perhaps if I had a little chat with him?'

'Would you?' Killian snagged a plate of canapes from a passing servitor, and offered me one. 'We'd be very grateful. He's an admirable young man, of course, but rather headstrong.'

'Where is he?' I asked, biting into the delicacy. 'Still in his quarters?'

'Omnissiah no.' Killian smiled, and gestured towards the planet below. 'He's down there.'

As it happened that was a stroke of luck which was to save my life, but I had no idea of that at the time, so spent the shuttle ride down to the surface of Interitus Prime feeling resentful at being dragged off on a pointless errand. Technically I had no authority over Tarkus in any case, since he wasn't a member of the Imperial Guard, but Killian didn't seem to think that would matter, sure that the young officer would be sufficiently impressed with my fraudulent reputation to listen to whatever advice I might have to offer. He was also very grateful for my assistance, as he kept telling me from the adjacent seat as we descended, and in the end I found myself feigning interest in the desolate landscape below just to shut him up for a minute or two.

Truth to tell, after a while my interest was becoming genuine, even if it remained somewhat muted. The closer we got to landing, the more forbidding that airless landscape became, smaller craters becoming visible as we got closer to them, and faint spiderwebs of shadow swelling into chasms deep beyond measure and wide enough to swallow a hive block. The shuttle continued to descend, and I began to wonder whether the pilot was paying attention to the altitude, despite knowing it to be a servitor which could by its very nature be nothing but vigilant. There was still the faint possibility of malfunction, of course, and I began to tense subconsciously, waiting for the retros to kick in, but they never did.

'Aren't we getting a little close to the ground now?' I ventured after a while, and Killian smiled lazily.

'I suppose we are,' he said, showing no sign of concern. Well I wasn't going to make a fool of myself in front of the magos, so I simply shrugged with the best expression of casual indifference I could summon up.

'Thought so,' I said. A few moments later the reason for his lack of concern became evident even to me. A grey haze in the distance, which I'd taken for the horizon, began to close in on us, looming over the slowly descending shuttle like a thunderhead, and I nodded in sudden understanding. We were sinking gently into one of those titanic rifts in the planet's surface, already at least a couple of hundred metres below ground level. 'How far down does this go?'

'About eight hundred kilometres,' Killian said casually. 'It's the deepest chasm on the planet.' He produced a flask of something from the depths of his robe with his right hand, the mechadendrites pulling out a cup apiece. 'So we've got time for a recaf before we land if you like.' I did like; under the circumstances I thought I deserved one.

The dim illumination of the dying star above had dwindled to nothing by now, but the running lights of the shuttle were enough to let me pick out a few of the details of that incredible fissure. Layer after layer of different strata slipped past the porthole, subtle graduations of hue marking the ticks of some long wound-down geological clock, and a couple of times I thought I caught a glimpse of something white, fossils perhaps, of creatures already extinct for millions of years before their planet died in its turn. The thought was a morbid one, and I tried to turn my mind away from the contemplation of death and eternity with casual conversation.

'I can see why you think this place is so special,' I ventured after a while. 'It's quite...' I tried in vain to think of a suitable adjective, before concluding somewhat lamely with 'impressive.' Killian chuckled throatily. I have to say that of all the tech-priests I've ever met he was by far the most likable, as well as the most untypical of his kind. Factors which were probably not unconnected, come to think of it.

'I think we can still surprise you, commissar.' At that point I rather doubted it, to be honest, although I have to concede that he was right.

My first presentiment that there was even more to this chasm than at first met the eye was a faint glow from below us, which soon resolved itself into the actinic glare of several gigantic luminators set on pylons around a makeshift landing pad. Our shuttle settled gently in what seemed to be the exact centre of the flattened area, and Killian bounced from his seat with every sign of eagerness to get outside; it was only as he hit the rune to lower the exit ramp that I remembered the world was airless.

'Wait a minute!' I called, struggling up from the deeply-padded seat which suddenly seemed a lot less comfortable now that I needed to stand in a hurry. He might have some augmetic enhancements that let him manage without air, but I most certainly didn't. Killian smiled at me.

'I told you you'd be surprised,' he said as the seals broke with an audible hiss. But it was the sound of equalising pressure, I realised with a sudden surge of relief, having become all too familiar with the sound of explosive decompression when the *Hand of Vengeance* took a torpedo volley amidships at the seige of Perlia. Thin, cold air began to seep into the shuttle, leeching the warmth away with tendrils of mist. Having

spent most of my career with Valhallan units, who like their air conditioning turned up to the maximum, I found the chill bearable, but
oddly dispiriting.

'I am,' I admitted. 'I didn't think you'd been here long enough to create an atmosphere.' I followed him down the ramp, my boots
crunching gently on the gravel beneath, which had something of the
texture of ash.

'We haven't.' Killian was rubbing his hands together, although
whether for warmth or from enthusiasm I couldn't tell. Probably both.
'So the survey reports were right about that at least.'

'So why haven't the gasses frozen?' I asked. Even if the feeble sun
were warm enough to prevent them turning to ice it never penetrated
this deep below the surface, and the world was too long dead to have
any residual heat left in its core. My breath puffed the words into little
clouds as I spoke, although Killian's, I noticed absently, did not.

'Exactly!' Killian said, as though I were his favourite pupil, and led
the way between the two nearest luminator gantries, following a
clearly-defined trail in the brittle ground. Once we were beyond the
glare my eyes adjusted, and I could make out a cluster of dimmer lights
on the walls of the chasm. 'There has to be something else down here
emitting energy. It's the only explanation.'

I was intrigued in spite of myself, I don't mind admitting it. As we
approached the lights I could see they were suspended in the mouth of
a vast cavern, with servitors scuttling about reinforcing the makeshift
ramp of broken shale leading up to it. I'll never know if Killian's enthusiasm would have led him to expound further on what he was after, or
if he would have realised he was revealing adeptus secrets to an outsider and clammed up again, because at that point a young tech-priest
appeared in the cave mouth gesticulating wildly.

'Magos!' he called, practically jigging up and down on the spot with
excitement. 'We've found something!' Without even pausing to ask
what it was, Killian picked up the pace and practically ran inside the
gaping hole in the cliff face, which was large enough to have taken our
shuttle with room to spare. Not wanting to lose my guide I trotted after
him, more than a little intrigued.

Killian barely slowed at any of this, hurrying on into the darkness
which surrounded that scene of activity. Red-uniformed tech guards
were hovering deferentially at the fringes of the illuminated area, and I
made a mental note to suggest to Tarkus that they be redeployed a little further out, where their eyes would be adjusted to the surrounding
gloom and better able to distinguish any infllitrators moving in on the
bustling researchers. Of course there didn't seem the remotest chance

of anyone else being here, and for all I knew they had augmetic eyes which could see perfectly well in the dark anyway, but by that stage in my career I was already beginning to acquire the healthy sense of paranoia which has probably done more than anything else to ensure my survival long enough to reach an honourable retirement.

Plunging into the gloom after him I found the way easy enough to negotiate despite the lack of illumination, as he was making more noise than an ork in a distillery. Another patch of light was visible in the distance and I hastened towards it, picking out a cluster of white robes and red uniforms without difficulty. More of the peculiar circle-and-stick markings were embossed on the far wall, and as I moved closer it became obvious that the surface here was worked to a glossy smoothness which somehow seemed to swallow the light falling on it.

'These sigils are undoubtedly of necrontyr origin,' a tall, cadaverous techpriest was saying as I entered the circle of brightness. He broke off to glare at me, until Killian gestured to him to continue. The name meant nothing to me at the time, of course, although when I finally reported back to Lokris he showed me some highly classified files which did nothing at all to make me feel better. I suppose he thought if something was going to try that hard to kill me without him instigating it, the least he could do was let me know what it was.

'This is all very interesting, Brother Stadler,' Killian said, with every sign of impatience. 'But what about the artifact?'

'It's over here,' Stadler said after a moment, during which I'd made it abundantly clear that I wasn't moving. The circle of light surrounding us shifted a little, moved by some technosorcery I wasn't privy to, revealing the mouth of a tunnel. Like the wall it penetrated the archway was perfectly smooth, composed of stone blocks of an eerie glossy blackness which only served to intensify the darkness beyond. 'We started down the tunnel hoping to find more hieroglyphs, and stumbled over this.' He permitted himself a wintery smile. 'Quite literally, in the case of our escort.'

A couple of red-uniformed figures emerged from the gloom, the scowl on Tarkus's face enough to tell me who the techpriest was referring to. The trooper with him was walking backwards, his hellgun aimed at something still in the darkness beyond, and a moment later a couple of techpriests appeared leading something metallic between them. It was big, I could tell that even before it came into the light, supported by a dozen cyber skulls which had managed to wedge themselves into the interstices of its body. A small, detatched part of my mind noted that the cogboys at least must be able to see in the dark, as there was no sign of illumination further back.

'Remarkable!' Killian looked like a juvie on Emperor's Day morning who's just seen the toy soldiers he always wanted at the top of his bowl. I could have thought of a number of other adjectives to describe the thing, starting with 'hideous' and growing steadily more pejorative.

It resembled nothing so much as a metallic sump spider, although even one of those would have seemed cuddly by comparison. Mechanisms protruded from its head, and six limbs dangled from its bloated body. Even inert it exuded a palpable malevolence which wrapped itself around me like a suffocating blanket.

'What have we here?' Killian bent over it, probing with the mechadendrites. 'Looks like a power core. Completely inert, of course.' He shrugged. 'Pity, but there you go. It would have been interesting to see what it does.' *Interesting* wasn't quite the word I would have used, needless to say. The other techpriest nodded in agreement.

'I dare say we could rig something up. Possibly a fusion bottle...' He seemed to remember my presence all of a sudden, and subsided, glaring at me again.

'Are you sure that's wise?' I asked. Everyone looked at me, and I shrugged, determined not to seem too concerned at their evident hostility. 'I'm no expert, but –'

'Quite right, you're not,' Stadler snapped. 'So kindly leave theological matters to those who are.'

'Fine.' I tried to look as reasonable as I could. 'But might I suggest you at least delay the attempt until the Astartes arrive?' And I was a long way away from any potential danger, of course. 'That should at least minimise any risk to the security of the expedition.'

'The expedition is perfectly secure,' Tarkus cut in, his voice tight, and I cursed myself for wounding his pride all over again. 'I see no reason to delay the furtherance of the Omnissiah's work.'

At that point it all became academic anyway. Killian muttered something under his breath, and a faint click came from somewhere in the bowels of the machine.

'Ah,' he said. 'That looks like a power coupling...'

Without any warning at all, a thin metal probe shot from the depths of the arachnoid automaton and buried itself in one of the hovering cyber skulls. A blue arc of energy sparked between them and the servitor fell lifeless to the ground, bouncing off into a corner somewhere.

'Remarkable!' Killian said again, and stepped forward for a closer look. I did exactly the opposite, you can be sure, retreating just far enough to ensure that Tarkus and his trooper stood between me and the sinister device.

'Stay back!' I warned, drawing my las-pistol. Tarkus seemed to remember my reputation at that point, and clearly reasoning that if I was concerned he ought to be too, began to follow suit. The trooper raised his hellgun again.

'Put those down!' Killian was outraged. 'Have you any idea of the importance of this artifact?' Tarkus and the trooper began to obey, although I wasn't about to holster my weapon under any circumstances. Before we could debate the point, however, a loud crack echoed through the cavern. The spider thing had teleported away, leaving air to rush into the void it had occupied like a miniature thunderclap.

We stared at one another in mutual incomprehension for a moment.

'Where did it go?' the trooper asked, an expression of bafflement on his face which was almost comic. I shook my head.

'Emperor alone knows,' I said.

'It must be somewhere nearby,' Killian said. 'How far do these tunnels extend?' Stadler shrugged.

'Kilometres. We've barely begun to map them.' Killian began to look as though his new soldiers had been trodden on by an adult before he got the chance to play with them.

'We'll establish a search pattern,' he said. 'We're bound to find it eventually.'

'If it doesn't find you first,' I added, before I could prevent the words from slipping out. Tarkus, to his credit, took my meaning at once.

'You think it's a guardian of some kind?'

'I don't know,' I admitted. 'But it's a reasonable guess. Whatever it's for it was built to last.'

'I'll double the sentries around the base camp,' Tarkus said. But I already had an uncomfortable feeling that wasn't going to be enough.

MY FIRST INSTINCT, I might as well admit it, was to find some excuse to get back on the shuttle and return to the safety of the orbiting starship. This wasn't as easy as it sounds, though; despite the fact that I was clearly unwelcome so far as the majority of the techpriests were concerned, and Tarkus remained as prickly as ever, he was sensible enough to realise that someone who'd survived as many clashes with the enemy as I had was someone whose advice he should listen to. So despite my impatience I spent most of the day reviewing his plans for the defence of the camp (which were pretty sound, I'm bound to admit, although I was able to plug a couple of holes that would only have been obvious to someone with field experience), and it was several hours before I had the chance to contact the *Omnissiah's Blessing* and let them know I was on my way back.

I'd just finished talking to the officer of the watch, whose image was floating in the hololith display, when his expression changed.

'Just a moment, commissar.' He turned to confer with someone out of the hololith's field of vision. When he turned back his expression was one of mild surprise. 'We're picking up a discharge of warp energy. It looks like the Astartes are here already.' That was the best news I'd heard since boarding the freighter. I had no doubt they'd make short work of the metal spider, and anything else that might be lurking down here with us.

'Good,' I said. 'If you can arrange to transfer my kit I'll report aboard the barge directly from here.' No point in taking any chances, after all, and I'd certainly be safer scrounging a ride in a Thunderhawk than an unarmed shuttle. The officer just had time to look mildly surprised before his expression turned to one of alarm.

'Unknown contact, closing fast. They're making an attack run!'

'Download your sensor data!' Killian ordered at my elbow. Someone on the bridge must have complied because the image in the hololith changed suddenly, showing us the pin-sharp starfield you only ever see from above an atmosphere. Something was moving across it, a crescent of darkness visible against the blackness of space only because of the flickering of the stars it briefly occulted.

'What the hell...' I began, then found myself stunned into silence. A burst of light blazed from somewhere within that sinister silhouette, branching and spreading as it came, until an instant later it enveloped our point of view. The hololith went blank.

'They've gone!' Stadler was standing at a nearby lectern, his face lined with shock.

'They can't be,' I said, already feeling the truth of his words in the pit of my stomach. Killian nodded in confirmation.

'I'm afraid he's right. All we're picking up is a cloud of debris.'

'Then we're just going to have to sit tight,' I said, fighting to keep my voice calm. 'The Astartes ship will be here soon, and it ought to be more than a match for these raiders.' I wished I was as confident as I sounded. 'So long as nobody panics we'll be fine.'

But of course we weren't.

THE FIRST ATTACK came an hour or so later, while I was talking to Tarkus about the possibility of barricading the tunnel mouth we'd found. It would only have been a token gesture, of course, but one of the first things they teach you at the schola is that anything you can do to make the troops feel they're taking the initiative is good for morale. And, needless to say, after the casual destruction of our ship, morale was pretty low. We'd been reviewing the available supplies, hoping to find something we could use, when Tarkus broke off in mid-conversation.

'Can you hear that?' he asked. I nodded. A faint scuttling sound had been tickling my eardrums for the last few moments, but until he mentioned it my subconscious had been editing it out. It was a sound I was so familiar with I could identify it without thinking.

'It's just vermin,' I said. In my extensive experience of underground passageways it had been a constant background noise. Then I remembered how desolate this world was, and that we'd seen no sign of life since we got here. I drew my las-pistol slowly. Tarkus followed suit, picking up a nearby luminator with his other hand and pointing it into the surrounding darkness.

My first impression was that the floor was moving, the beam shining back from a rippling surface which reminded me of sunlight on ocean waves, and then with a cry of revulsion I began shooting. The metallic carpet which surged towards us was composed of miniature duplicates of the spider machine, thousands of them, and the las-bolts detonated in the middle of the swarm with about as much effect as if I'd been throwing stones. True, every shot was rewarded with a satisfying impact and a spray of metal, but there were so many that even with Tarkus's help I couldn't even hope to slow them down.

'First squad to me!' the lieutenant ordered, and within seconds we'd been joined by half a score of his redshirts, who directed a withering volley of hellgun fire at the scuttling swarm. They began to break, to my momentary relief, but only to part like the tide around a rock before rushing on towards the main bulk of the camp.

They hit it like a tsunami, swarming over the precious equipment and ripping it to pieces with their metallic mandibles. Guards and techpriests alike scattered in panic, but many were too slow, being pulled down and engulfed by that hideous carpet of scuttling death. Within seconds a few muffled screams, quickly silenced, were the only traces of their presence left.

'Pull back!' I ordered, taking command by reflex as I'd been trained to do. A few scattered survivors regrouped around us, Killian and Stadler among them. The cadaverous techpriest's eyes were wide as he watched the swarm of automata demolishing the camp.

'Merciful Omnissiah!' he gasped. 'What are those things?'

'Beats me,' I said. 'I'm not qualified to comment on theological matters.' It was a cheap shot, and I suppose I ought to be ashamed of myself, but I must admit to taking some quiet satisfaction in his venomous expression. I began edging the ragged group back towards the wall, hoping that with our backs to it at least the machines couldn't get behind us.

'Good thinking,' Tarkus agreed, fanning his remaining subordinates out to form a skirmishing screen between us and the scuttling horrors. Stadler reached that obsidian surface first, and pressed his back against it as though hoping he could squeeze an extra couple of millimetres of space out of the cavern.

All at once his expression changed to one of astonishment, blood and lubricants fountaining from his augmented body as something invisible slashed him to pieces from behind. I whirled, seeking a target, and suddenly saw it looming over his shattered corpse. A ghastly skeletal visage hovered in the air on gently humming grav units, the razor-edged blades of its fingers stained crimson, its torso ending in a long, curved tail which looked like vertebrae. To add to the horror the apparition was constructed of the same gleaming metal as the spider and its miniature offspring.

'It came through the wall!' One of the troopers was gibbering in shock, his face white, at least the parts of it which were still composed of flesh. 'It came through the wall!' He raised his hellgun and ripped off a burst on full auto. The entity drifted forwards unhurriedly, the flurry of las-bolts detonating against the wall behind it, defacing the enigmatic symbols etched there. With a deepening sense of horror I realised that the volley had been on target, but the las-bolts had simply passed through the apparition, whatever it was. The trooper was still firing, his finger clamped on the trigger in a rictus of panic, as the drifting horror reached out casually and tore his face off. The man's screams were abruptly terminated as the thing's tail lashed up to transfix him; his spasming corpse hung there for a moment before dropping to the floor again.

The group disintegrated immediately, troopers and techpriests alike fleeing in panic whichever way their feet took them. I laid a restraining hand on Killian's arm as the metallic ghoul accelerated after them, casually slashing down a couple of victims as it passed.

'Stay put!' I snapped. 'These things are trying to panic you!' The strategy was obvious: split everyone up and hunt us down one by one. If we stayed together we could watch one another's backs, and greatly increase our chances of survival.

Tarkus had clearly realised this too.

'Regroup!' he was bellowing, despite the obvious disinclination of any of his men to follow orders. Hellguns spat almost at random, a few of the las bolts actually managing to hit the hovering ghoul as it solidified for long enough to eviscerate another unfortunate cogboy, but the vast majority of shots passed through it or missed altogether. 'Reform at once, you sons of–'

His voice broke off abruptly, rising to a suddenly terminated scream, as a bolt of vivid green light enveloped him. For a moment I could see a bloody mess of internal organs as he seemed to fade away from the outside in, dwindling like candle wax, and then he was gone as though he'd never existed.

'Emperor on Earth!' I turned to see what fresh horrors this place had disgorged, and a sudden rush of terror hit me in the gut. Thin, skeletal automata were advancing across the cavern, casually blasting everything that still lived with those hideous beams. Wherever those messengers of death walked people died, dwindled to nothing by their hellish guns, or sliced apart by the combat blades attached to the barrels.

To give them their due the tech guards gave a good account of themselves in the main, their hellguns felling two or three of their assailants, but it seemed to take a lot of fire to down one. I even saw one with its chest blown open stir and rise to its feet again, the eldritch metal of which it was composed flowing like liquid to heal its wounds.

'Frak this!' I said, dragging the magos towards the mouth of the tunnel. If we stayed where we were we'd be killed with the others, but there was a remote chance that we might find some kind of refuge if we slipped away while these ghastly automata were slaughtering our companions. All we had to do, I kept telling myself, was hold on until the Astartes arrived. How we'd know they were here, or let them know we'd survived, was a problem for later which I resolutely refused to consider right now.

To my astonishment we made it to the tunnels without further mishap, and I hurried Killian along as rapidly as I could, the sounds of carnage diminishing in our ears. The slick black stone seemed to absorb sound as well as light, silence descending around us like a shroud. My old hive boy's senses were sufficently acute for me to be able to tell from the subtle change in the echoes around us when we passed the openings of cross corridors, but on several occasions I was grateful for my companion's apparent ability to see in the dark.

At least the metallic warriors were easy to evade, their hellish weapons giving off an eerie green glow which forewarned us of their presence in plenty of time to dive for cover.

It was after we'd been wandering for some time that I noticed the darkness around me was beginning to attenuate, a diffuse green refulgence becoming visible from up ahead. At first I thought it was merely another patrol but after lurking cautiously for a moment and finding that it remained unchanged in its intensity, we pressed on. Killian was curious to discover the source, still hoping to bag a piece of archeotech probably, and if I was going to have to fight again I preferred to do it where I could see what was trying to kill me.

As the glow grew brighter I began to hear something too, a faint buzzing sound which resonated in my skull and set my teeth on edge.

The palms of my hands began to tingle as we reached a chamber bathed in that sick, green glow, and a faint sense of nausea rose within me.

Killian, on the other hand, seemed enraptured. The cavern was vast, even larger, if that were possible, than the one we'd first discovered, but rather than being empty was stuffed with strange devices beyond my ability to comprehend. Most were emitting that strange, necrotic light, however, and I began to apprehend that it was somehow connected to their power source.

'Fascinating.' The techpriest wandered into the centre of the room, his eyes darting everywhere, trying to take in every detail of his surroundings. Mine, on the other hand, were concerned only with making sure we were alone. At least we appeared to be safe in that assumption...

Abruptly the light flared, and a sudden thundercrack of displaced air echoed across that unholy room. A dozen of the skeletal warriors were suddenly standing on a raised dais before a curtain of rippling green light, and turning their expressionless heads towards us.

'A warp portal!' Killian seemed transfixed. 'We've known it's a theoretical possibility of course, but...'

'Fight now, talk later!' I screamed, certain we were staring death in the face and determined to defy it for as long as possible. As I unleashed a flurry of las-bolts at the nearest figure I could see that its torso was already damaged, a couple of holes punched through it by what looked like armour piercing rounds. I hadn't noticed any bolters among the tech guards' armoury, but I was glad of somebody's foresight as one of my rounds entered the gap and blew the automaton apart from the inside. The others all lifted their greenly-glowing weapons as one, and aimed them at me; for an instant the conviction of my own immanent death left me paralysed.

'Get down!' Killian cannoned into me the instant they fired, knocking me to one side, and taking the full force of the barrage himself. He flashed into vapour in an instant, leaving me rolling across the floor towards those murderous statues. I raised my right hand to aim the laspistol and found it was gone, along with two of my fingers, but there was no time to worry about that now. My survival instinct had kicked in like never before and I lunged desperately past the dreadful automata, a direction they never expected me to take, diving headfirst into the curtain of energy behind them.

You might be wondering how anyone could be so foolish, but consider: remaining where I was would be certain death, there was absolutely no doubt about that, whereas taking my chances with the portal meant death was only virtually assured. And it was that narrow difference which preserved me for long enough to record this account.

The actual passage was a timeless instant: one moment I was in the chamber below the bowels of Interitus Prime, the next I found myself surrounded by the noise of combat. The light, wherever I was, was the same bilious hue, but the chamber I was now in was far smaller, and, as I was subsequently to discover, my immediate guess that I was aboard the starship which had attacked our freighter was an accurate one.

Staccato explosions echoed from the sloping walls surrounding me and I rolled to my feet, dazed, as another of the metal warriors came at me. I tried to draw my chainsword, but stumbled, weak from the loss of blood, and would surely have fallen had not a vast forearm encased in ceramite swung out of nowhere to bear me up. A storm bolter barked about a metre away, deafening me for a moment, and tearing the gleaming assassin to shreds.

'Brother-captain. I've found a survivor,' a voice louder than any I'd previously heard boomed, and I turned to find myself in the grasp of a giant, encased in a suit of terminator armour.

'Bring him,' a second giant said, looming into view from behind another of the incomprehensible alien devices. 'The demolition charges are set.'

Despite everything, I found a smile beginning to force its way onto my face.

CAVES OF ICE

Editorial Note:

This, the second extract from the Cain archive which I have prepared and annotated for those of my fellow inquisitors who may care to peruse it, is in much the same format as the first. The astute among you will realise that it follows my previous selection, Cain's account of the Gravalax incident, quite closely chronologically although with his usual disregard for such niceties it was actually recorded at an earlier point in the archive itself. I have chosen this section of his memoirs not only because it is relatively self-contained, requiring little background knowledge of his earlier exploits to appreciate, but also because the records of the Ordo Xenos contain quite a bit of detail about events on Simia Orichalcae that year and anyone with cause to consult them is certain to find the only complete eyewitness account of considerable interest. (Not least because it confirms the suspicions many of us have long harboured about the part played by certain members of the Adeptus Mechanicus in the affair, which may be useful in future dealings with them.)

It may be argued that Cain is not the most reliable chronicler of events, but I am inclined to accept his version of events as absolutely true. Here, as throughout the whole archive, he rarely gives himself credit for what, to any unbiased observer, appear to be acts of genuine courage and resourcefulness (however few and far between).

293

As before I have been largely content to let Cain tell his story in his own words, confining myself to annotating the original text to clarify occasional points and expand upon the wider background to the events he describes since typically he tends to concentrate almost exclusively on things that affected him personally without much regard for the bigger picture. I have also, as before, taken the liberty of breaking his account down into chapters to facilitate reading, although Cain himself didn't seem particularly bothered by such stylistic niceties. Where I've drawn on other sources they are credited appropriately; all other footnotes and interpolations are mine alone.

Amberley Vail, Ordo Xenos

ONE

WARP KNOWS I'VE seen more than my fair share of Emperor-forsaken hell-holes in more than a century of occasionally faithful and dedicated service to the Imperium, but the iceworld of Simia Orichalcae[1] stands out in my memory as one of exceptional unpleasantness. And when you bear in mind that over the years I've seen the inside of an eldar reaver citadel and a necron tomb world, just to pick out a couple of the highlights (so to speak), you can be sure that my experiences there rank among the most terrifying and life-threatening in a career positively littered with hairs'-breadth escapes from almost certain death.

Not that it seemed that way when our regiment got its orders to deploy. I'd been serving with the Valhallan 597th for a little over a year by that point, and had managed to settle into a fairly comfortable routine. I got on well with both Colonel Kasteen and her second-in-command Major Broklaw; they appeared to consider me

---

1. *Despite my best efforts to track it down, the origin of this name remains obscure. It seems fairly safe to conjecture that the world in question was famed for the presence of some statue or effigy in a past epoch, but why anyone should have chosen to commemorate this particular animal in such a way remains a mystery.*

as much of a friend as it was possible to be with the regimental commissar, and the kudos I'd earned as a result of our adventures on
Gravalax stood me in good stead with the men and women of the
lower ranks as well. Indeed most of them seemed to credit me, not
entirely wrongly, with having provided the inspirational leadership
which had allowed them to prevail against the vile conspiracy that
had unleashed so much bloodshed on that unhappy world and provided them with an initial battle honour to which they could all
point with pride.

At the risk of seeming a little full of myself, I did have some cause
for satisfaction on that score at least; I'd inherited responsibility for
a divided, not to say mutually hostile, regiment, cobbled together
from the combat-depleted remnants of two previously single-sex
units who had disliked and distrusted one another from the beginning. Now, if anything, I was faced with the opposite problem: I was
charged with maintaining discipline as they became comfortable
working together and the new personnel assignments started bedding in. (Quite literally in some cases, which only made matters
worse of course, particularly when acceptable fraternisation spilled
over into lovers' tiffs, acrimonious partings, or the jealousy of others. I was beginning to see why the vast majority of regiments in the
Imperial Guard were segregated by gender.) Fortunately, there were
very few occasions when anything harsher than a stiff talking-to, a
quick rotation of the protagonists to different squads, and a rapid
palming off of the problem to the chaplain were called for, so I was
able to maintain my carefully-constructed facade of concern for the
troopers without undue difficulty.

Being iceworlders themselves, of course, the Valhallans were over-
joyed to hear we were being sent to Simia Orichalcae. Even before we
made orbit the viewing ports were crowded with off-duty troopers
eager for a first sight of our new home for the next few months and a
chatter of excited voices had followed Kasteen, Broklaw and myself
through the corridors towards the bridge. My enthusiasm, needless to
say, was rather more muted.

'Beautiful, isn't it?' Broklaw said, his grey eyes fixed on the main
hololith display. The flickering image of the planet appeared to be suspended in the middle of the cavernous chamber full of shadows and
arcane mechanisms, surrounded by officers, deckhands and servitors
doing the incomprehensible things starship crewmen usually did.
There must have been a dozen at least of them buzzing about, waving
data-slates at one another, or manipulating the switches inlaid into the
age-darkened wood of the control lecterns which littered the main deck

below us. Captain Durant, the officer in charge of the old freighter that had been hastily pressed into service to transport us from our staging area on Coronus Prime,[1] shook his head.

'If you like planets I suppose it's allright,' he said dismissively, his optical implants not even flickering in that direction. Of indeterminate age, he was so patched with augmetics that if it hadn't been for his uniform and the deference with which his crew treated him I might have mistaken him for a servitor. It had been courteous of him to invite the three of us to the bridge though, so I was prepared to overlook his lack of social graces. It wasn't until some time later that I realised that doing so was probably the only way he would ever meet his passengers, as he showed every sign of being as much a part of the ship's internal systems as the helm controls or the Navigator (whose quarters were presumably behind the heavily shielded bulkhead which loomed ominously over where we stood.)

Cynical as I was about such things, I had to concede that Broklaw had a point. From this altitude, as we slipped into orbit, the world below us shone like an exotic pearl, rippled with a thousand subtle shades of grey, blue and white. Thin veils of cloud drifted across it, obscuring the outlines of mountain ranges and deep shadowed valleys which could have swallowed a fair sized city. Despite the poor resolution, I couldn't help searching for some sign of the impact crater where a crudely hollowed-out fragment of asteroid had ploughed into the surface of this pristine world, vomiting its cargo of orks out to sully it.

'Breathtaking,' Kasteen murmured, oblivious to the exchange. Her eyes were wide like a child's, the blue of the iris reflecting the projected snowscape in front of us. The clear light struck vivid highlights in her red hair, and like her subordinate she seemed lost in a haze of nostalgia. I could readily understand why: the Guard sent its regiments wherever they were needed, and the Valhallans rarely got the chance to fight in an environment where they felt completely at home. Simia Orichalcae was probably the closest thing to their homeworld either officer had seen since they joined up, and I could sense their impatience to get down there and feel the permafrost beneath their boot soles. I was rather less eager, as you can imagine. I've never been agoraphobic like some hivers, and quite enjoy being outdoors in a

---

1. *Coronus Prime was a major Imperial base on the fringes of the Damocles Gulf where the Imperial forces withdrawn from Gravalax were sent for reassignment. Presumably the Munitorium decided it wasn't worth diverting a fully-fitted troopship to deploy just a single regiment, and commandeered a suitable civilian vessel for the job.*

comfortable climate, but where iceworlds are concerned I've never seen
the point of having weather, as we used to say back home.[1]

'We'll get you down as soon as possible,' Durant said, barely able to
hide his enthusiasm for getting nearly a thousand Guardsmen and
women off his ship. I can't say I altogether blame him; the *Pure of Heart*
wasn't exactly a luxury liner, and the opportunities for recreational
activities had been few and far between. The crew clearly resented their
facilities being swamped by bored and boisterous soldiers, and the
training drills we'd devised to keep our people busy in the few cargo
holds that weren't stuffed with vehicles, stores, and hastily-installed
bunks hadn't been enough to let them blow off steam completely and
there had been some friction.

Luckily the few brawls which had broken out had been swiftly dealt
with, Kasteen being in no mood for a repeat of our experiences aboard
the *Righteous Wrath*,[2] so I'd had relatively little to do beyond telling the
freshly-separated combatants that they were a disgrace to the Emperor's
uniform and dish out the appropriate penalties. And of course when
you have several hundred healthy young men and women cooped up
in a confined space for weeks on end many of them will find their own
ways of amusing themselves which raised the whole range of other
problems I've already alluded to.

Despite the constant irritation of dealing with a host of minor infractions, I wasn't particularly eager for our voyage to end. I'd fought orks
before – many times – and despite their brutishness and stupidity I
knew they weren't to be underestimated. With numbers on their side,
and the orks always had superior numbers in my experience, they could
be formidably difficult to dislodge once they'd gained a foothold anywhere. And by luck or base cunning they had found a prize on Simia
Orichalcae worth fighting for.

'Can we see the refinery from here?' Kasteen asked, reluctantly tearing her eyes from the hololith. Broklaw followed her lead, his dark hair
flicking against the collar of his greatcoat as he turned. Durant nodded,
and apparently obedient to his will a section of the gently-flickering

---

1. *Despite his frequent references throughout the archive to his being native to a hive world,*
Cain never specifies which one; and most of the (few) details he gives about his origins are
inconsistent. The folk saying he quotes here isn't recorded in any of the anthropological data-
bases, but that doesn't necessarily mean much; it could easily have been common in one small
section of his home hive, such as a particular hab level or underhive settlement.

2. *A serious disturbance broke out on board this troopship shortly after Cain joined the regi-*
ment, and several troopers and Naval provosts died. For further details see his account of the
Gravalax incident.

planet in front of us expanded vertiginously as though we were plummeting down towards it in a ballistic re-entry.

Despite knowing that it was only a projection my stomach lurched instinctively for a second before habit and discipline reasserted themselves and I found myself assessing the tactical situation before us. The slightly narrowed eyes of my companions told me that they were doing the same, no doubt bringing their intimate knowledge of the environment below us into play in a fashion that I never could. Within seconds we were presented with an aerial view of the installation we'd been sent to protect.

'That valley looks reasonably defensible,' Broklaw mused aloud, nodding in satisfaction. The sprawling collection of buildings and storage tanks was nestled at one end of a narrow defile, which would be a natural choke point to an enemy advance. Kasteen evidently concurred.

'Place a few dugouts along the ridgeline there and we can hold it until hell thaws out,' she agreed. I was a little less sanguine, but felt it best to appear supportive.

'What about the mountain approaches?' I asked, nodding in apparent agreement. The two officers looked mildly incredulous.

'The terrain's far too broken,' Broklaw said. 'You'd have to be insane to try coming over the peaks.'

'Or very tough and determined,' I pointed out. Orks weren't the most subtle tacticians the forces of the Emperor ever faced, but their straightforward approach to problem solving was often surprisingly effective. Kasteen nodded.

'Good point,' she said. 'We'll set up a few surprises for them just in case.'

'A minefield or two ought to do it,' Broklaw nodded thoughtfully. 'Cover the obvious approaches, and lay one here, on the most difficult route. If they meet that they'll assume we've fortified everywhere.'

They might not care, of course. Orks are like that. Casualties simply don't matter to them. They'll just press on regardless, especially if there are enough of them surviving to boost each other's confidence. But it was a good point, and worth trying.

'How far have they got?' I asked. Durant swept the hololith display round to the west, skimming us across the surface of the barren world with breathtaking speed. The broken landscape of the mountain range swept past, the higher peaks dotted with scrub, lichen, and a few insanely tenacious trees – apparently the only vegetation which could survive here. Just as well too, or there wouldn't be an atmosphere you could breathe. Beyond the foothills was a broad plain, crisp with snow, and for a moment I could understand the affection my colleagues had for this desolate but majestic landscape.

Abruptly the purity of the scene changed, revealing a wide swathe of churned-up, blackened snow, befouled with the detritus and leavings of the savage horde which had surged across it. A couple of kloms[1] wide at least, it resembled a filthy dagger-thrust into the heart of this strangely peaceful world. The resolution of the hololith wasn't good enough to make out the individual members of this barbaric warband, but we could see clumps of movement within the main mass, like bacteria under a microscope. The analogy was an apt one, I thought. Simia Orichalcae was infected by a disease, and we were the cure.

'Seems like we got here just in time,' Kasteen said, putting all our thoughts into words. I extrapolated the speed of the ork advance, and nodded thoughtfully; we should have the regiment down and deployed roughly a day before they reached the valley where the precious promethium plant lay open and defenceless. It was cutting it fine, but I was just thankful we'd get there ahead of them at all. Fortunately they'd crashed in the opposite hemisphere, and that had given us just enough time to make the journey through the warp to oppose them.

'I'll get everyone moving,' Broklaw offered. 'If we get the first wave embarked now we can launch the shuttles as soon as we make orbit.'

'Please yourselves.' Durant somehow managed to make his immobile shoulders convey the impression of a shrug. 'We'll be at station-keeping in about an hour.'

'Are the datafeeds set up?' I asked, while I still had some measure of his attention. He repeated the gesture.

'Not my department.' He inflated his lungs, or whatever he used instead of them. 'Mazarin! Get up here!'

The top half of a woman almost as encrusted with augmetics as the captain rose on a humming suspensor field to join us on the command dias. The cogwheel icon of a tech-priest hung from a chain around her neck. As we spoke she hovering roughly at my head height, the tunic she wore stirring unnervingly in the faint current from the air recirculators at what would have been level with her knees if she'd had any. 'The one in the fancy hat wants to know if you've wired up his gadgets.'

'The Omnissiah has blessed their activation,' she confirmed, in a mellifluous voice. Her hard stare at the captain told me his irreverence was an old and minor annoyance. 'They are all functioning within acceptable parameters.'

'Good.' Kasteen, to my mild surprise, was looking distinctly uneasy, her eyes flickering away from the tech-priest whenever she thought she

---

1. *Kilometres: a Valhallan colloquialism Cain acquired from his long association with the natives of that world.*

could politely do so. 'We'll have full sensor coverage of the planet's surface then.'

'As long as this old blasphemer remembers how to keep his collection of scrap in orbit,' she agreed. Once again the two of them exchanged a look that confirmed my initial suspicion that their bickering was a sign of an easy familiarity rather than any genuine friction. A waving mechadendrite reached forward across Mazarin's shoulder, clutching a data-slate, which she thrust towards the colonel. Kasteen took it with every sign of reluctance, all but shying away from the mechanical limb. 'The appropriate rituals of data retrieval are on this.'

'Thank you.' She handed the slate to Broklaw as though it were contaminated. The major took it without comment, and began scanning the files.

'Waste of a perfectly good starship if you ask me,' Durant grumbled. 'But the money's good.'

'We're most grateful for your co-operation,' I assured him. A troopship would have been equipped to deploy a proper orbital sensor net, which would have been infinitely preferable, but the battered old freighter's navigational array would just have to do. Our deployment was a hurried one, made in response to a frantic astropathic message from the staff of the installation below us, so we had to make do with what we could grab instead of waiting around for the right equipment.

'You've got the easy job,' Broklaw assured him. This much was true: the *Pure of Heart* only had to stay in orbit over the refinery, feeding her sensor data into our tactical net, so we could keep an eye on our enemies from above. Given the size of the horde we'd seen, that was a comfort. It looked even larger and more formidable than my most pessimistic imaginings, outnumbering us by at least three to one. On the other hand we'd be on the defensive, which would be to our advantage. And they'd want to take the place intact, so we wouldn't have to worry too much about incoming artillery fire. The extra intelligence our orbital eye would give us would help immeasurably in deploying our defences to frustrate their attacks.

'You call this easy?' Durant asked rhetorically. A sweep of his arm took in the humming activity of the bridge. 'Having half my systems rewired, trying to hold it all together...' His voice trailed off as Mazarin floated away with a faint *tchah!* of disapproval, and something a little softer entered his body language.

'Your tech-priest seems efficient enough,' I said, trying to sound encouraging. He nodded.

'Oh, she is. Far too good to waste her time on a tub like this really, but you know. Family ties.' He sighed, some old regrets surfacing in spite of himself, and shook his head. 'Would have made a good deck officer if she hadn't got religion. Too much of her mother in her, I suppose.' Startled, I tried to make out traces of a family resemblance, but the main feature they had in common seemed to be an abundance of augmetics rather than anything genetic.

I TOOK THE first shuttle down, of course, as befitted my entirely unwarranted reputation for preferring to lead from the front. I'd be well under cover before the orks arrived and should have my pick of the quarters planet-side; I wasn't expecting much in the way of comfort in an industrial facility, but whatever there was I meant to find it. In this I had a valuable ally, my aide Jurgen who had an almost preternatural talent for scrounging, which had made my life (and no doubt his own, although I was careful not to enquire about that) considerably more comfortable than it might otherwise have been in our decade and a half together. He dropped into the seat next to me, preceded as always by his spectacular body odour, and fastened his restraint harness.

'Everything's in order, sir,' he assured me, raising his voice a little so that it carried over the chatter of the troopers surrounding us, meaning that our personal effects had been stowed in the cargo bay to the rear with his usual efficiency. Despite his unprepossessing exterior, and his apparent conviction that personal hygiene was something that only happened to other people, he possessed a number of positive qualities which few people apart from me were ever able to appreciate.

From my point of view, the most important was his complete lack of imagination, which he more than made up for with his dogged deference to authority and an unquestioning acceptance of whatever orders he was given. As you can imagine, having someone like this as a buffer between me and some of the more onerous aspects of my job pretty much amounted to a gift from the Emperor. Add to that the innumerable perils we'd faced and bested together, and I can honestly say that he was the only person I ever fully trusted – apart from myself.

The familiar kick of the shuttle engine igniting cut our conversation short. It went without saying that rather than military dropships, the *Pure of Heart* was equipped with heavy-duty cargo haulers which had been hurriedly converted to meet our needs as far as possible. The end result was better than I could have reasonably expected, but was far from ideal. The front third of the cargo space had been partitioned off with a hastily welded bulkhead, and then subdivided into half a dozen decks with metal mesh flooring. Somehow Mazarin and her acolytes had managed to cram some five score seats with their associated crash webbing into this space so that we were able to disembark a couple of platoons at a time. The rest of the hold had been left open, to take our Chimeras, Sentinels, and other vehicles, along with a small mountain of ammo packs, rations, medicae supplies, and all the other stuff necessary to keep an Imperial Guard regiment running at peak efficiency.

Looking around I could see men and women hugging their kitbags, holding lasrifles across their knees, their faces half hidden by the thick fur caps worn in anticipation of the bone-biting cold on the planet's surface. Most had fastened their uniform greatcoats too. These were mottled with the blues and whites of iceworld camouflage, and I was suddenly acutely aware of what an obvious target my dark uniform and scarlet sash would make me out in that icy waste. No point worrying about it now though, so I gritted my teeth and forced a relaxed smile as the first faint tremors of the hull announced that we'd started to enter the upper atmosphere.

'Pilot's making the most of it,' I said, half joking, and raising a few grins from the troopers around me. 'Must have been watching *Attack Run*[1] in the mess hall.' Jurgen grunted something. He too was swathed in a greatcoat, but, like everything else he ever wore, it contrived to look as though it were intended for someone of a slightly different shape. He suffered from motion sickness on almost every combat drop, but that never seemed to affect his fighting ability once he was back on terra firma. I suspected he was so relieved to be back on solid ground he'd take on the enemy with a sharpened stick rather than have to face the possibility of retreat and being airborne again.

This time though, he wasn't the only one. The overloaded shuttle was being buffeted by the thickening atmosphere, bouncing around like a stone on a lake, and pale, sweating faces were everywhere I looked. Even my own stomach revolted on a couple of occasions, threatening to spray the narrow compartment with the remains of my lunch. I swallowed convulsively; I wasn't going to compromise the dignity of my office, not to mention become a laughing stock among the troopers, by throwing up. Not where anyone could see, at any rate.

'What the hell does he think he's playing at?' Lieutenant Sulla, commander of third platoon, and a sight too over-eager for my liking, scowled, which made her look even more like a petulant pony than

---

1. *A popular holodrama of the time, about a squadron of Lightning pilots who shoot down an unfeasible number of enemy fighters during the Gothic War. I quite enjoyed it, although Mott, my savant, claims to have counted four hundred and thirty-seven historical and technical inaccuracies in the first episode alone.*

usual.[1] Nevertheless the distraction from my somersaulting stomach was a welcome one, so I invoked my commissarial privileges and retuned the comm-bead in my ear to the frequency of the cockpit communicator to find out.

'Say again, shuttle one.' The voice was calm and methodical, undoubtedly the ground controller at the refinery landing field. The answering voice was anything but: a civilian suddenly in the middle of a war zone without a clue as to how to survive, and clearly not expecting to. Our pilot, without a doubt.

'We're taking ground fire!' The edge of hysteria in his voice was unmistakable. Any moment now he was going to panic, and if he did we were all likely to die. I doubted that our overloaded engines had any tolerance left for evasive manoeuvres, and if he tried, the chances were that he'd lose control completely. As if to emphasise the point we hit another air pocket, and dropped vertiginously for a handful of metres.

There was nothing else for it: I unbuckled my seat restraints and lurched to my feet, conscious of Sulla's eyes on me. I grabbed the nearest stanchion for support. It was embossed with an Imperial aquila, which I found reassuring, and with its support I was able to take a couple of halting steps towards the cockpit.

'Is that wise, commissar?' she asked, a faint puzzled frown appearing on her face.

'No,' I snapped, not having time to waste on courtesy. 'But it's necessary.' Before I could say any more another lurch slammed my body weight into the narrow door to the flight deck, propelling it open, and I staggered inside. My overriding impression was one of flashing lights and control lecterns, uncannily like miniature versions of the ones on the starship bridge, and the bleak white snowscape passing below us at an alarming speed. The pilot stared up at me, his knuckles white on the control yoke, while his navigational servitor continued regulating the routine functions of the ship with single-minded fixity of purpose. 'What's the problem?' I asked, trying to project an air of calm.

'We're under attack!' the man shouted, raw panic edging into his voice. 'We have to pull back to orbit!'

---

1. *This is the celebrated General Jenit Sulla, at a very early stage in her career. Despite the illustrious reputation she was later to achieve, Cain tends to regard her with, at best, mild antipathy throughout the archive; we can only speculate as to why. My own feeling is that he considered her tendency to decisive action unnecessarily reckless, since it put the lives of the troopers under her command (and by extension Cain's) at risk. Ironically it's clear from her own (almost unreadable) memoirs that she regarded Cain very highly, and as something of a mentor.*

'That wouldn't be wise,' I said, keeping my voice level, and grabbing the servitor's shoulder to steady myself as the shuttle lurched again. It just kept on adjusting controls with a complete lack of concern. Beyond the thick vision port the bleak and frozen landscape hurtled past as serenely as before. I could see no sign of enemy activity anywhere. 'We'd take hours to rendezvous with the ship if we abort on this trajectory, and we only have limited life support. You'd probably suffocate along with everyone else.'

'We have a safety margin,' the pilot urged. I shook my head.

'The rest of us do. You don't.' I let my right hand brush the butt of my laspistol, and he turned even paler. 'And I don't see any immediate danger, do you?'

'What do you call that?' He pointed off to starboard, where a single puff of smoke burst briefly. A moment later a small constellation of bright flashes sparkled for an instant some distance below and to the left. Bolter shells detonating against the ground, after some trigger-happy greenskin took a hopeless potshot in our direction.

'Nothing to worry about,' I said, almost amused. 'That's small arms fire.' The analytical part of my mind noted that the main bulk of the ork advance was still some distance away, which meant we ought to be on alert for a small scout force attempting to infiltrate the refinery (which was now looming reassuringly in the viewport), or reconnoitre our lines. 'The chances of anything actually hitting us at this range are astronomical.'

One day I'm going to learn to stop saying things like that. No sooner had the words left my mouth than the shuttle shuddered even more violently than before, and pitched sharply to port. Red icons began to appear on the data-slates, and the servitor began punching controls with greater speed and abhuman dexterity.

'Pressure loss in number two engine,' it chanted. 'Combustion efficiency dropping by sixteen per cent.'

'Astronomical, eh?' Strangely the pilot seemed calmer now his fears had been realised. 'Better strap in, commissar. It's going to be a rough landing.'

'Can you make it to the pad?' I asked. He looked tense, his lips tight.

'I'm going to try. Now get the hell off my flight deck and let me do my job.'

'I've no doubt you will,' I said, boosting his confidence as best I could, and staggered back to my seat.

'What's going on?' Sulla asked as I buckled in and tensed for the impact.

'The greenskins put a dent in us. There's going to be a bump,' I said. I felt strangely calm; there was nothing I could do now except trust in the Emperor and hope the pilot was as competent as he sounded. I considered saying something to reassure the troopers, but I'd never be heard over the noise of the crash alarms anyway, so I decided to save my breath.

The waiting seemed to take forever, but could only have lasted a minute or two. I listened to the chatter in my comm-bead while the pilot read off a number of datum points which meant nothing to me but sounded pretty ominous, fighting down the growing conviction that we weren't going to make it as far as the pad. In fact, the traffic controller seemed pretty insistent that we avoid the installation altogether, which I could well understand, as dropping an unguided shuttle into the middle of the promethium tanks would end our mission pretty effectively before it had even begun. The pilot responded with a couple of terse phrases which managed to impress me even after fifteen years of exposure to the most imaginative profanity of the barrack room, and I began to think we were in safe hands after all, and might just make it.

This impression lasted all of a dozen seconds. Then a violent impact jarred my spine up into the roof of my skull, driving the breath from my lungs. A sound uncannily reminiscent of an ammunition dump exploding echoed through the hull. I gasped some air back into my aching lungs, and tried to clear my blurring vision as the screech of tortured metal set my rattling teeth on edge. I became gradually aware, through the ringing in my ears, that Jurgen was trying to say something.

'Well, that wasn't so...' he began, before the whole ghastly cycle repeated itself another couple of times.

At last the noise and vibration ceased, and I gradually became aware of the fact that we'd stopped moving and I was still alive. I struggled free of the seat restraints, and wobbled to my feet.

'Everybody out!' I bawled. 'By squads. Carry the wounded with you!' In the back of my mind a lurid picture of overheated engines exploding into flame tried to ignite a little beacon of panic, but I fought it down. I turned to Sulla, who was trying to stem a nosebleed. For that matter I suppose we all looked a bit the worse for wear, except possibly Jurgen, as with him it was hard to tell. 'I want casualty figures ASAP.'

'Yes, sir.' She turned to the nearest NCO, Sergeant Lustig, a solid and competent soldier I had a lot of time for, and started snapping out orders in her usual brisk fashion.

The door to the cockpit burst open, and the pilot staggered out, looking as bad as I felt.

'Told you we'd make it,' he said, and threw up on my boots.

TWO

THE FREEZING AIR outside was worse than even my most pessimistic anticipation, and I'd been on enough iceworlds before to have had a pretty good idea of what to expect. In truth, I suppose, it was no colder than Valhalla or Nusquam Fundumentibus, but it had been some time since I'd trodden the snows of either, and my memory had obviously skipped over the worst of those experiences. The bone-numbing wind seemed to flay me alive the moment I set foot on the ramp, despite the extra layers of insulation I'd put on before leaving my quarters aboard the *Pure of Heart*.

As I staggered down the metal incline, already treacherously slippery from the thin coating of snow which had settled on it, needles of ice seemed to penetrate my temples, replacing the residual headache from the crash with one a thousand times worse. I buried my face in the muffler at my throat, being careful to breathe through it in case my lungs froze, but even so the air rasped in my chest like acid fumes.

A broad plain of ice spread out before me, hazed with wind-driven snowflakes which reduced visibility to a few tens of metres, although the flurries cleared occasionally to reveal the low, grey ramparts of the encircling mountains. They stood out clearly against the lighter grey of the sky, and a moment later I realised that what I'd at first taken for some unusually regular outcrops were the towers and storage tanks of the refinery, still too distant to make out any detail.

'Seventeen injured, fourteen of them walking.' Sulla bounced up to me, the trickle of blood from her nose now frozen to her face, and saluted eagerly. 'Eight of those are ours.' The others would be from first platoon then. I nodded, not trusting myself to talk yet. It would have been a wasted effort anyway, as behind us an engine roared into life and the first of our Chimeras rumbled down the exit ramp, filling the air with the noise of its passage and the rank smell of burned promethium. Thank the Emperor for that, I thought, at least I wouldn't have to slog all the way to the refinery on foot. Sulla noticed the direction of my gaze. 'Lieutenant Voss is assessing the condition of the vehicles now.'

Her opposite number glanced up from a huddle of troopers near the ramp, a data-slate in his hand, and waved a cheery acknowledgement. That came as little surprise, as Voss tended to be cheerful about everything. He was clearly in his element now, grinning widely as the churning tracks bit into the snow, and, dear Emperor, his greatcoat was still unfastened. I immediately felt another ten degrees colder just looking at him.

'We got off lightly,' he told us, his voice crackling over the commbeads. 'Minor damage only. Nothing we can't get fixed.'

'Should be easy enough,' Sulla agreed. 'A place like this must be crawling with tech-priests.'

'Maybe they can do something with this heap of junk too,' I said sourly, kicking a lump of snow at our downed transportation and deciding to risk talking despite the rush of razor blade air to my lungs. If they couldn't, the loss of one of our shuttles would be a major blow, severely delaying the deployment of our forces, perhaps to the point where we wouldn't be fully prepared by the time the orks arrived.

'We're in the right place at least.' Jurgen had materialised at my elbow. I was mildly disconcerted not to have noticed his approach, feeling that something was inexplicably wrong, before I realised the cold had effectively neutralised his body odour. Either that, or my nose had frozen off.

He was right about that at any rate. The pilot, who I was beginning to forgive for having soiled my footwear, had been as good as his word, bringing us down on the main landing pad after all. Not being entirely reckless he'd aimed for the outer edge though, leaving us with a kilometre or so of packed snow and ice to trudge across before reaching the shelter of the storage tanks I'd noticed before. The faint scar of melted and refrozen ice that marked where we had bounced and skidded our way to a stop was already beginning to disappear under the drifting snow.

'It looks more like a starport than a landing pad,' Sulla observed. I nodded, quite impressed by the scale of things myself, but determined not to show it.

'The shuttles from the tankers are over five hundred metres long,' I said, dredging up a half-digested fact from the largely ignored briefing slate.[1] 'And they land up to twelve at a time.' Sulla looked suitably impressed. Certainly the thought of a swarm of shuttles almost half the size of the starship we'd arrived in filling the air above where we stood was an awe-inspiring one – or it would have been if I hadn't been freezing my gonads off at the time.

Any further thoughts I might have had on the subject were quickly driven from my head at that point, however, by the rather more urgent matter of a bolter shell exploding against the ceramite hull less than a metre from where we were standing.

'Orks!' Sulla shouted, rather unnecessarily under the circumstances I thought. I whirled around to look in the direction she was pointing. At least she had the common sense to do it with her lasgun, though, and opened fire on a small knot of greenskins that was closing fast, slogging through the snow with implacable ferocity.

'Are they mad?' Voss's voice crackled in my ear. 'We must have them outnumbered about ten to one!'

That did strike me as pretty stupid behaviour, even for orks, and I was just casting about desperately for the main force which must surely be flanking us when the explanation suddenly hit me. I was the only human they could see; the Valhallans' camouflage uniforms were blending them into the snowscape, as they were supposed to, and with my commissar's black and scarlet making me stand out like an ogryn in a beauty pageant, they hadn't bothered looking for anyone else. I breathed silent thanks to the Emperor for the flakes of drifting snow which obscured the others from their sight.

'Cease fire!' I snapped, seeing the opportunity for the perfect ambush. A quick glance around me made out at least three squads fully disembarked. They were lying flat in the snow which they'd scraped out

---

1. *A quirk of behaviour Cain repeatedly alludes to in the archive. His habit of neglecting to read the background information provided to senior officers prior to deployment on a new planet is rather odd, given his caution in most other respects. (Although given the density and dryness of most munitorium documentation, it's probable that he'd developed the ability to extricate anything relevant with a quick skim of the contents, and felt little would be served by wading through it page by page.)*

into small hollows. A tactic, I vaguely recalled, which had worked well for their forefathers when an ork horde had had the temerity to attack their homeworld. 'Let's draw them in.' Far better to cut them down at short range than engage at a distance, where we would run the risk of a survivor or two escaping to report our arrival back to the warboss.

'Good plan,' Sulla said, as though it were up for debate, and I suddenly realised that it left me the only one in immediate danger. Ork marksmanship wasn't much to worry about most of the time but even greenskins got lucky occasionally, as the downing of our shuttle had proved, so I dropped suddenly with a dramatically out flung arm and a theatrical scream. It was a performance which wouldn't have fooled a five-year-old, but I heard a whoop of triumph from the leading ork, who was carrying what looked like a crudely-fashioned bolter. The others began remonstrating in harsh gutturals, and I was able to hear enough to gather that they were arguing about who should get the credit for killing me.[1] But then if I had a coin for every time that's happened...

'Hold your fire,' I broadcast over the comm-net. Hardly necessary of course, these troopers knew what to do, but I didn't want any mistakes. The orks came on regardless, running apparently tirelessly despite the treacherous footing and the biting wind which would have sapped the strength from an unprotected man in seconds. I began mentally counting off the distance. Two hundred metres, one hundred and fifty...

The closer they got, the more detail I could make out, and the less I wished I could see. There were ten of them in all, about half carrying the bolters I'd noticed before. The others held heavy close combat blades and pistols which looked as deceptively ramshackle as the bolters. I'd seen enough examples in previous encounters not to be fooled, though. Crude as they appeared, the firearms were perfectly functional, and quite lethal if they should happen to hit anything. The same went for the axes, which, with the power of an ork's muscles behind them, were capable of shearing through even Astartes armour.

On they came, snarling and bickering, crude icons decorating their sleeveless vests, which alone spoke volumes for their inhuman robustness in this killing climate. Oddly, I noticed, they were all dressed alike, in dark grey, which blended better into the winter landscape than the more vivid hues I generally associated with greenskins. Then I realised the last ork in the group wasn't armed like the others. A huge calibre barrel was slung across his shoulder, the bulk of the weapon hidden

---

1. *Cain wasn't exactly fluent in orkish, but had managed to pick up a few phrases in the course of his adventures. Mostly insults and obscenities, of course, but it could be argued that they make up the whole language.*

behind his body. What it was I had no idea, but I was pretty sure I wouldn't like the answer.

The mystery was solved a few seconds later as they caught sight of the idling Chimera, which had been hidden from them by the bulk of the downed shuttle. Evidently intent on looting it, and arrogantly sure they could slaughter any surviving defenders, the sudden appearance of a military vehicle threw them into momentary disarray. After a quick exchange of snarls, during which the leader, who I was able to identify with a fair degree of certainty thanks to his habit of emphasising instructions with blows to the head (not unlike one of the less popular tutors during my time at the schola progenium) pointed to the Chimera. The ork with the bulky weapon swung it round to reveal a crude rocket launcher. This at least explained how they'd managed to damage the shuttle, albeit with an incredibly lucky shot. Before I could vox a warning the ork fired, a streak of smoke marking the vector of the warhead, which detonated a few metres to the left of the Chimera.

No point expecting the crew to delay their retaliation, I realised, as the next shot might get them. And sure enough the heavy bolter in the turret swung round to bracket the orks. Puffs of snow and ice were thrown up around them as the explosive projectiles detonated thunderously, tearing a couple of them apart. One of them, to my intense relief, was the rocketeer.

It was then that we saw what makes these creatures so dangerous on the battlefield. Where other, more sensible foes would have taken cover or retreated to regroup, these savages felt no urge stronger than to close quickly and neutralise the threat. With a bone-shaking cry of '*Waaaaarghhhh!*' they ran forward as one, charging headlong into a hail of withering fire.

Well, there was no point hesitating after that, particularly as one foul-smelling foot missed my head by centimetres as it passed, so I rolled to my feet and issued a general order to fire at will.

I don't suppose they even knew what hit them: suddenly struck by the concentrated fire of a couple of score lasguns, not to mention the unrelenting hail of heavy bolter fire, there was nothing much left of them apart from some unpleasant stains on the snow within seconds. Sulla ambled over to inspect the mess, and spat a small gobbet of ice into it.

'So those were orks,' she said. 'They don't look so tough.' I bit down on the sharp rejoinder that rose to my lips, suppressing it. She might as well feel confident for as long as possible. I knew from bitter experience that when the main force got here the next day it would be a different story.

* * *

'FIRST BLOOD TO you, then, commissar.' Kasteen grinned at me, her red curls falling free as she took off her heavy fur cap, and glanced around the conference room in the heart of the refinery. The smile faltered a bit as her eyes flickered past the little group of tech-priests at one end of the heavy wooden table, but re-established itself as she took in the other people present: a mixed bunch of Administratum functionaries seated in strict order of precedence, and a group of men and women whose hard hands and lined faces indicated that they did most of the actual work around here.

'Luck rather than judgement, I can assure you,' I said. Kasteen had come down on the second shuttle, about twenty minutes after our advance party had made it to the shelter of the refinery hab units, and I was still feeling like a freezy stick.[1] I tightened my fingers around the mug of recaf Jurgen had found for me, feeling the warmth spread through the real ones (the augmetics felt the same as they always did, of course.) I could have done without the transparent wall at the end of the conference suite, beyond which the snow was falling steadily – a visual reminder of the chill which still had me in its grip. Nevertheless the view of the processing plant with its huge structures and belching flames was undeniably spectacular. The sheer size of it struck me for the first time, and I began to understand why it took hundreds of people to extract the raw materials from the ice beneath our feet and process it into the precious fuel.

'You call that luck?' Mazarin hummed into the room behind us, making Kasteen start. 'Bending a perfectly good shuttle?'

Perhaps there was a family resemblance to her father after all, I thought. She'd come down on the same drop as Kasteen to assess the damage, and had just returned from the landing field, thick flakes of snow beginning to melt across her head and shoulders. 'Nothing I can't fix though, praise the Omnissiah.' That was a relief, at least our deployment wouldn't be as delayed as I'd feared. She levitated across to the little group of tech-priests we'd noticed before, and began to converse with them in a weird twittering language that set my teeth on edge.

'She's asking for the use of their facilities to repair the shuttle,' one of the Administratum adepts said, evidently noticing our confusion. He was a youngish man, with thinning blond hair and the pasty complexion of someone who spends too much time with a data-slate.

'You understand that gibberish?' I asked, impressed in spite of myself. He grinned.

---

1. *A popular snack on many worlds with a temperate or tropical climate, particularly among juves; fruit juices are frozen solid, with a stick embedded in it to facilitate eating. It sounds bizarre, I know, but is really very refreshing.*

'Dear Emperor, no. If I did they'd have to kill me.' He smiled as he said it, although for all I knew he wasn't joking.[1] 'She's just filed a request with the main depository for the spare parts.' He stuck out a hand, and Kasteen shook it formally. 'I'm Scrivener Quintus, by the way. If you need anything, come to me. If I can't get my hands on it, I'll know who can.'

'Thank you.' Kasteen smiled warmly. 'Colonel Kasteen, Valhallan 597th. This is our regimental commissar, Ciaphas Cain.'

'An honour.' His handshake was firm and direct. 'I've seen your statue in Liberation Square on Talethorn. I must say it doesn't really do you justice.'

'That'll be the pigeon droppings,' I said dryly. 'Tends to erode my natural dignity.' He laughed, with every sign of good humour, and I decided I liked him.

'Let me introduce you to a few people,' he said. He waved at the group of tech-priests, singling out a man of about his own age who was talking to Mazarin with every sign of rapt attention. 'That's Cogitator Logash. My opposite number, so to speak.' His voice dropped slightly. 'You'll get more done if you go to him first instead of wasting your time with anyone higher up in the Mechanicus, if you get my drift.'

'Not unlike you and the Administratum,' I suggested, and he smiled.

'I didn't say that,' he pointed out. 'But Logash and I aren't quite so rigid in our thinking as some of the higher ranks in our respective orders.'

'You can say that again.' The man I took to be the leader of the workers joined our conversation. 'How many more of us are going to have to die down there before they sit up and take notice?' He had the hard eyes of a man used to physical toil, and his hair was grey; nonetheless he burned with a passion which seemed at odds with the coldness that permeated everything else around here.

'Technically, no one has died,' Quintus said.

The man snorted.

'Disappeared, then. Five people in as many weeks.' Quintus shrugged.

'I've done my best to get them to investigate, you know that.' The man nodded reluctantly. 'But they just argue that accidents happen. Icefalls, gas pockets...'

'I've been working here for over twenty years,' the man said. 'I know all about icefalls, and a dozen other hazards you quill-pushers haven't even heard of. And they all leave bodies.'

---

1. *Almost certainly not. 'Binary,' as the tech-priests refer to their secret language, is one of their most sacred mysteries. Cracking it has long been a priority of the Inquisition, but so far even the most rudimentary syntax has yet to be established.*

'But officially, without a body there's nothing to investigate.'

'That's insane,' Kasteen said. The man smiled for the first time.

'That's what I keep telling them. But the lad here's the only one with a functioning brain, apparently.' He stuck out a hand. 'I'm Artur Morel, by the way. Guild of miners.' His grip was firm.

I have to admit, all this talk of death and mysterious disappearances had me spooked. If we were going to fight a battle I didn't want to be looking over my shoulder the whole time, and I resolved to have a longer talk with him at the earliest opportunity. We'd already encountered one ork scouting party after all, and if there was another one already lurking in the mine we'd have to clear them out as a matter of priority.

But first things first: we had a war to plan. Mazarin left the room with Logash trotting along behind her, evidently detailed to sort out her requirements, and the highest ranking Administratum adept, a white-haired woman called Pryke, called the meeting to order with every sign of enthusiasm.

Needless to say, it turned out to be interminable. The facility seemed to be equally dependent on the three factions present to keep functioning, or at least that's what Pryke fondly imagined, although I'd have laid a small wager that putting the Administratum drones out in the snow to keep the orks amused while we prepared our defences would have had a negligible effect on the promethium output. Every point she raised was politely challenged by Magos Ernulph, the senior tech-priest, who would remind everyone that without his people to perform the appropriate rituals the plant would simply grind to a halt. Of course without Morel's miners to provide the raw materials it would do so anyway, but the guildsman was tactful enough not to drag things out even further by pointing this out, for which I was extremely grateful, especially since my stomach had started to realise how empty it was.

Fortunately Kasteen had a much lower level of tolerance for idiots than I did, so it was with some relief that I saw her stand to interrupt the ageing bureaucrat in mid flow.

'Thank you all for your input,' she said crisply. 'It's clear that you all have particular insights to offer, which we will be calling upon as and when we see the need.'

'I think my colleagues will require a little more than that,' Pryke rejoined. 'May I suggest you provide us with daily progress reports?' Ernulph nodded in agreement, his blank metal eyes turning on the colonel. She ignored him, with an effort only I knew well enough to discern.

'You may not. We're here to fight a war, not push files around.' There was an edge to Kasteen's voice now which every officer in the regiment had learned to be wary of. Pryke bristled.

'That's just not good enough. There are procedures to be followed...'

'Then let me relieve you of them,' Kasteen snapped. 'This facility is now under martial law.' The result was hugely enjoyable, I have to admit. Pryke went scarlet, then white, then scarlet again. Ernulph probably would have done too, if he'd had enough organic bits left to manage it. Both stood at once, shouting excitably.

'You can't do that!' Ernulph boomed, his voice apparently magnified by some implanted amplivox unit. It was a cheap trick, and one which remained resolutely un-terrifying to anyone who'd been shouted at by a daemon as I had.

'Yes she can,' I confirmed quietly, my voice carrying all the more effectively for not being raised like all the others. 'A field commander has the right to declare martial law at any time with the approval of the highest ranking member of the Commissariat present. Which is me. And I do.' I stood, and gestured to the plant outside, and the barren snowscape beyond. 'By this time tomorrow all you'll see out there is orks. We're your only hope of not ending up dead or worse. So shut up, keep out of our way, and let us do our job.' Morel and Quintus, I noticed, were openly enjoying their colleagues' discomfiture.

'This is unacceptable,' Pryke said, her voice tight with outrage.

'Live with it,' Kasteen said. 'Unless you prefer the alternative.'

'I most certainly do.' Pryke glared at both of us.

'Fine.' I drew my laspistol, and dropped it on the table from just the right height to produce a nicely resonant thud. 'Under the powers bestowed upon me by the commissariat in the name of His Divine Majesty, I serve notice that any civilian obstructing His forces in the defence of His realm will be subject to summary execution under article seventeen of the rules of military justice.' I raised an interrogative eyebrow at Pryke and the tech-priest. 'You were saying?'

'I withdraw my objections,' she said tightly. Ernulph nodded too.

'On reflection, the colonel's assumption of authority seems entirely the best course of action,' he conceded.

'Good,' I said, leaving the gun where it was – no harm in concentrating their minds a little further. 'Colonel. You have the floor.'

Editorial Note:

There can be very few readers who will be unaware of the enormous importance of the promethium production facility which Cain describes, both strategically and economically. Since its retention or seizure was so vital an objective for the contending armies, I felt a little extra information on this amazing substance wouldn't come amiss. Unfortunately I haven't been able to lay my hands on very much, as such things remain the jealously-guarded province of the Adeptus Mechanicus, so this is the best I could do.

From *Our Friend Promethium*, Imperial Educational Press, 238th edition, 897 M41

FROM THE EMPEROR-BLESSED fighting machines of the Astartes to the most humble spaceport cargo-hauler, it can truly be said that the Imperium runs on promethium. This might seem amazing enough on its own, but this miraculous substance gives us so much more than just the power to feed the animating spirits of our vehicles. The alchemical by-products of its production provide the raw materials to create a vast array of everyday necessities, from dyes, plastics and pharmacopoeia to the synthetic protein bars which make up the bulk of the proletarian diet on some of the drearier forge worlds.

But it's the combustibility of promethium which allows its most holy use. From the flamers which scourge the unholy with the purifying fire of the righteous to the alchemical constituents of the explosives which blast them into oblivion, it's this most blessed of substances which keeps us safe and preserves our homes from the depredations of the alien, the mutant, and the heretic.

Promethium itself can be produced in a variety of ways, and from an astonishing number of sources. Among the most common are the atmospheres of gas giant planets, subterranean deposits of ancient organic materials, and certain kinds of rare ices found only on the coldest of worlds...

[Of course it's the illustrations which are the real charm of this little book, particularly those of its narrator, Pyrus the Flame. Even now I can't help smiling at the expressions on the faces of the heretics he's burning on page twenty-eight, just as I did as a child all those years ago.]

THREE

'Sieur Morel. I'd like a quick word with you if you can spare the time.' I judged my movement precisely, so that to the casual observer it would look as though we'd reached the door of the conference room together purely by chance. The grizzled miner turned in my direction, assessed the situation with keen intelligence, and nodded, dismissing his staff with a casual wave. They filed out along with the tech-priests and the quill-pushers, Ernulph and Pryke, still simmering nicely leaving us alone with Kasteen and Broklaw.

The major had joined the conference shortly after Kasteen dropped her little bombshell, taking over the tactical debriefing of the refinery staff. Now the two of them were huddled over data-slates refining their strategy for the defence of the plant. Ernulph, Pryke, and their respective hangers-on had turned out to be quite helpful after the sight of my sidearm had cleared the air, no doubt reflecting that the orks might very well get them if they didn't do all they could to help, and if the greenies didn't I most certainly would.

A handful of troopers were bustling in and out of the conference suite, setting up map boards and a large urn of tanna leaf tea. It looked as though this was going to be our command post, at least for the time being. (Kasteen claimed it was an excellent vantage point from which to direct the troops, but I suspected she just liked the view from the window.) I found the gradual transformation from civilian decadence to the purposeful military atmosphere quietly reassuring; how the miner viewed it I had no idea, or interest, come to that.

'Of course. How can I help?' Morel asked. I poured myself a bowl of tanna tea, and offered him one. After a moment he took it, sipped cautiously, and appeared to approve, although the Valhallan brew isn't to everyone's taste.

'Earlier you mentioned some of your miners had disappeared in mysterious circumstances. Would you care to elaborate?' An expression of mild surprise crossed his grizzled features. I suppose after being stonewalled by the other factions here for so long our interest was unexpected.

'Five people, in just over a month. It might not sound much out of a workforce of six hundred, but believe me it matters to us.' He shrugged. 'Of course the Administratum and the Mechanicus don't give a damn. Just trot out the same old line about the losses being within acceptable statistical parameters.'

'What's your opinion?' I asked. Morel sipped his tea, formulating a response, and I forestalled him. 'I want your gut reaction. Don't feel you have to be polite.' He laughed, and looked at me with renewed respect.

'Just as well. Diplomacy isn't exactly my strong point.' He sipped again. 'Something's definitely wrong down there. Don't ask me what, though.'

'Then we need to find out,' I said. Kasteen broke off from her conversation with Broklaw long enough to nod.

'Quite,' she said. Broklaw nodded too.

'Absolutely. No point in fortifying the place if the trouble's already inside with us.'

'You think we've got orks in the tunnels?' Morel paled at the thought. Whatever he'd thought the problem might be, this clearly wasn't it. I shook my head doubtfully.

'It's possible. Although sneaking around picking people off one at a time isn't exactly their style.'

'And I don't see how they could have got here that soon,' Kasteen added, with a glance at the hemisphere map pinned to the wall close to her seat. 'It's taken them over six weeks to get here from the crash site. If an advance party was taking your miners they'd have had to have got halfway round the planet within a few days of their arrival, and we've seen no sign of any rapid deployment capability.'

'Unless they teleported,' I suggested. 'It has been known.'[1]

---

1. Ork units were deployed by teleporter on several occasions during the Armageddon campaign, for instance.

'We're not jumping to conclusions are we?' Broklaw mused. 'Could it just be an unfortunate series of accidents after all?'

'That hardly seems likely.' Morel stared at the plan on the opposite wall. The straggling and meandering lines looked like nothing so much as a detailed diagram of a plate full of noodles. A map of the tunnels beneath us, I realised, where the precious veins of ice which could be transmuted into promethium had been hauled out for countless generations.[1]

'Can you show us where the missing miners vanished from?' I asked. That might give us some kind of clue. Morel nodded, picking up a stylus from the desk, and marked the points in rapidly; I realised he must have done this before, no doubt hoping to find some connection himself. I stared at the rumpled sheet of paper, translating the lines in my mind into a three dimensional image, and trying to get a feel for the space.[2] If there was a pattern to be discerned, however, it eluded me.

'Have you spotted something?' Kasteen asked hopefully, aware of my tunnel rat's instincts from my reports on the Gravalax incident. I shook my head.

'There's no obvious connection between these points,' I said. I tapped one with a fingernail. 'This gallery's a dead end, for instance. An assailant would have to get past an entire shift of workers unobserved.'

'And that's just not possible,' Morel confirmed. Which begged another question that Broklaw was obliging enough to ask.

'Unless one of the refinery staff is responsible...' he began, but trailed off as Morel's face darkened.

'If you're planning to accuse any of my people of murder, you'd better have some damn good evidence.'

'No one's accusing anyone of anything,' I soothed, biting back the unspoken *yet*. 'You've brought a potentially serious security breach to our attention, and we're trying to get to the bottom of it, that's all.'

'If it saves any more of my people I'm glad to help,' the miner said, somewhat mollified.

'I'm glad to hear it.' I gazed at the map of the mine workings again, as though deep in thought. 'But I don't think we'll solve the problem talking about it over a bowl of tea.'

'Then what do you suggest?' Kasteen asked. I sighed with every appearance of reluctance and shook my head.

---

1. *Only about half a dozen, in actual fact. The processing plant on Simia Orichalcae was relatively new.*

2. *As I've noted elsewhere, Cain had an uncanny affinity for the layout of underground passageways, probably as a result of his early upbringing on a hive world.*

'I'll just have to go down there and take a look around,' I said.

Now if you've been reading my memoirs with any degree of attention it's probably struck you that this apparent willingness to put myself in harm's way is somewhat uncharacteristic, to say the least. But try to see things from my point of view. For one thing, if I hung around here while the defences were being prepared there was a pretty good chance I'd end up in that bone-chilling cold again, and I was most reluctant to do so. Not to mention the fact that there was a horde of greenskins on the way. True, they weren't expected to arrive in force for another twenty-four hours or so, but that hadn't held back the advance party we'd encountered already, and who knew how many more of them might be lurking out there waiting for an unwary target to show itself?

Tunnels, on the other hand, were an environment I felt right at home in, and I could match my fighting skills in a dark confined space with anything we might find down there. And it wasn't as if I was going in alone either; anything used to taking on solitary unarmed civilians was in for a big surprise if it tried jumping a squad of troopers with lasguns. So all in all I was pretty confident that whatever might be lurking in the dark lower levels, it wouldn't pose nearly as much of a threat to my continued well-being as hanging around outside like a chunk of deep-frozen ork bait. (In this assumption I was, as it turned out, both quite correct and catastrophically wrong. Of course I had no reason to suspect at that point what our investigation would ultimately lead to.)

I'VE SEEN SOME sights in my time, and it takes a lot to impress me, but I have to admit that even today, after more than a century, the ice caves of Simia Orichalcae stand out in my memory as a sight to behold. I don't know what the troopers made of them, but to a born and bred tunnel rat like me they were quite spectacular. Though broad mining galleries ran off into the distance beyond the reach of our luminators, it was never quite dark, as the ice surrounding us reflected the light back so that it rippled away in a faint blue sheen as far as the eye could see.

And the walls glittered, every single irregularity in the surface reflecting and refracting the beams, so we moved through an ever-scintillating constellation of ephemeral stars. Our boots crunched gently on frost-packed floor, and our breath puffed visibly with every exhalation, but down here, away from the flensing wind, I found the temperatures tolerable enough. They were certainly no worse than those in the average Valhallan billet when they could get the air conditioning to work, and I was used to that. It was even warm enough for Jurgen's characteristic odour to have returned, albeit in a slightly muted fashion, for which we were all grateful. I'd requested Lustig's squad for backup, as after our adventures on Gravalax I was confident in their abilities, and I found the familiar faces and the sergeant's taciturn presence a welcome boost to my spirits. I'd declined the offer of a guide from among the miners as I was confident in my own tunnel sense, and if there really were orks down here the last thing I wanted was some hysterical civilian getting in the way in the middle of a fire fight.

The early stages of our descent had been through the bustle of the upper workings, where miners and servitors hurried through broad, well-lit thoroughfares reminiscent of the streets of a Valhallan cavern city, and mobile ore bins full of shimmering ice shoved everything else unceremoniously out of the way. But as we penetrated further into the complex, into the lesser-used passages, they grew narrower and less well lit, until the only illumination was what we carried with us. From time to time we heard sounds of activity from the main galleries, where Morel's colleagues were still hacking the precious ice away with the aid of tools which looked alarmingly like the meltas we used as weapons, but after an hour or so of steady descent even this had faded away.

'What are we looking for, exactly, sir?' Sergeant Lustig asked. I shrugged.

'Emperor knows,' I said. 'Just something unusual.' His squad was spread out in a standard search pattern, with everyone in visual range of at least two other troopers. I wasn't going to have any more mysterious disappearances if I could help it, particularly if one of them was likely to be me. The sergeant's broad face creased in a grin.

'Well that narrows it down,' he said, glancing round at our surroundings. Coming from an iceworld as he did, I suppose he found them bordering on the mundane. In a way, that's what I was counting on; between the Valhallans' feeling for ice and my hive boy's affinity for enclosed spaces, whatever was down here was bound to have left some traces which would strike one or another of us as odd.

'Penlan here.' The voice of one of the troopers hissed in my commbead, followed a moment later by the attenuated sound of her actual speech overlapping the transmission like a distorted echo. She could only be a hundred metres or so away. 'I've got something. Looks like tracks.'

'Hold your position,' I ordered, and worked my way towards her silhouette. She was backlit by the luminator she'd taped to the barrel of her lasgun. Jurgen trotted at my heels, his own weapon levelled and ready for use. Experience had taught both of us you could never be too cautious in circumstances like this.

'What do you make of it, sir?' Penlan asked, turning towards us. As she did so, she brought the patch of discoloured skin on her left cheek where she'd taken a glancing las hit on Gravalax into the beam of Jurgen's luminator. Her expression was as puzzled as her voice, brown hair falling into her grey eyes from around the rim of her hat.

'Damned if I know,' I said, not relishing the doubt. She shone her light directly on the marks she'd found, deep gouges in the frozen floor, which indeed looked uncomfortably like claw marks. After more than a decade and a half in Imperial service, during which time I thought I'd encountered pretty much every malevolent life form in the galaxy, I should have been able to recognise them. The fact that I couldn't was deeply disconcerting. Even the mark of ork boots, which I'd been half expecting, would have been preferable.

'They look a bit like genestealer tracks,' Jurgen said uncertainly. He was partially right: they'd been gouged out by what looked like powerful talons, but the spacing was all wrong to be the work of a 'stealer. 'Or 'nids, maybe?'

'I don't think so,' I said. 'The weight distribution's all wrong.' Which given the hive fleets' ability to conjure new and unpleasant creatures out of thin air wasn't exactly a certainty, but if there was a bio-ship or two in the sector the chances of them getting this far into Imperial space undetected were negligible. I pointed that out too, and pretended I hadn't seen the momentary flicker of visible relief on Penlan's face. The two original regiments which now made up the 597th had fought the tyranids shortly before I joined them, and both had been all but annihilated. Come to that, I'd seen more than enough of the 'nids to last me more than a lifetime by this point too.

'We'd best press on,' I decided after a few moments' reflection. Somehow the confirmation that there was something down there made it easier to do that than go back, however strong the impulse to retreat I now felt. I knew from experience that an unknown enemy is always a bigger threat than one you've identified, and, in truth, nothing much had changed. I still had a crack squad of veteran troopers between me and anything malevolent lurking up ahead. Not to mention Jurgen, whose peculiar gifts had saved my hide on more than one occasion, even though neither of us had been aware of their existence until our encounter with Amberley and her entourage on Gravalax.[1] Lustig nodded, and gave the order to move on.

The mood was, if anything, even more sombre after that. The occasional outbreaks of joking and banter between the troopers sounded

---

1. *Very early on in my association with Cain and his aide, it became obvious that Jurgen was a blank: a staggeringly rare attribute which made him immune to daemonic possession or psychic attack.*

hollow now, uncomfortable, and soon petered out into silence punctuated only by the terse monosyllables of report and response. The trooper on point, Penlan still I think, began communicating by hand signals wherever possible, and resorted to the comm-net only when absolutely necessary. Almost without thought we'd slipped into the assumption that we were now in hostile territory.

I found that comforting. A healthy dose of paranoia goes with my job, of course, but it was nice to know that everyone else was as jumpy as me for once, with the possible exception of Jurgen, who never seemed particularly put out by anything which didn't involve aerodynamics. Almost without thought my hands went to my weapons, loosening the chainsword in its scabbard and drawing the laspistol. No point in not being prepared, I thought.

'If there's anything down here we must be right on top of it,' Lustig muttered. I nodded. We were only a few dozen metres from the end of the gallery by now, and the dead end I'd spotted on the map. The chances of whatever had left those tracks staying behind to be bottled up by our advance were remote in the extreme, I knew, but still my mouth went dry, my stomach cramping with the anticipation of combat, my imagination running wild with images of rampant Chaos spawn.

'That's it. Dead end.' Penlan's voice had an unmistakable edge of relief, which rippled around the rest of the squad like a breeze through summer grass. I exhaled, feeling my muscles relax, unaware until then of how tense I'd become.

'Take a look round,' I said, starting forward to join her. Jurgen stayed at my shoulder as always, and behind me I heard Lustig issuing orders with his usual calm efficiency. He was deploying the rest of the squad to secure our perimeter. Good. That meant no unpleasant surprises while we were poking around.

'Frak all that I can see.' Penlan moved carefully, sweeping her luminator ahead of her. The beam picked out a blank wall, where the tunnel had simply been abandoned when the seam of refinable material had run out. Then it swept on to pick out a jumble of ice boulders over to the right. The palms of my hands started to tingle as they always did when my subconscious alerted me to something untoward. Penlan started towards the heap of rubble.

'Be careful,' I started to say, as the realisation began to seep through to my forebrain. The tumbled pattern of ice blocks looked familiar, scattered like the debris from an underhive roof fall. I swept my own luminator beam towards the ceiling, where a crack began, no thicker than a hair, before widening to the width of my fist as it reached the wall. From there the fissure grew exponentially, terminating in the pile of frozen rubble.

It still didn't feel right to me. For the debris to have fallen in that pattern, the wall itself must have been undermined. A faint, but ominous cracking sound echoed through the chamber.

'Penlan!' I shouted. 'Get back!' But I was too late. She was half-turning towards me, an expression of puzzlement on her face, when the floor gave way beneath her and she vanished from sight with a single startled shriek.

'Penlan!' Lustig started forward, until I restrained him with an arm across the chest; there was no knowing how far the treacherous deadfall extended. 'Penlan, report!' Static hissed in our comm-beads.

'Watch that first step, sarge.' Her voice sounded winded, but if she could crack jokes she couldn't be that badly hurt. 'It's steeper than it looks.'

'Better move carefully,' I counselled the sergeant. 'No telling how unstable the rest of the floor is.' I inched forward cautiously, Jurgen at my side, just enough to shine the beam from our luminators down into the hole. It seemed sufficiently solid. From here I could see that a thin crust of ice had formed across the gap where the roof fall had breached the ceiling of a chamber below us. A chamber, I suddenly realised, which didn't appear anywhere on the map.

'That froze over recently,' Jurgen said, with the certainty of an ice-worlder. I edged a little closer to the hole, from where I could see Penlan. She'd fallen about five or six metres, but most of that, thank the Emperor, had been down a steep slope rather than a sheer drop. A friction-gouged channel in the ice showed where she'd slid most of the way. Seeing my face appear in the gap, she waved.

'Sorry about that, sir,' she said. 'My foot slipped.'

'So I see.' I got Jurgen to direct his luminator around the chamber she was in. It was roughly circular, no more than a few metres wide, and I began to suspect that it might have been a natural ice pocket. It was easy to imagine a solitary miner falling the way Penlan had, and being less lucky about landing. The gap they'd left behind them could have frozen over before the search party arrived. Perhaps Morel's mysterious disappearances had been accidents after all. 'Does that hollow look natural to you?'

'Maybe.' Penlan shone her own beam around, then stiffened, aiming the lasgun. 'There's another tunnel here. I can't tell how far it goes.'

'Sit tight.' Lustig appeared at my elbow, a coil of climbing rope in his hands. He began looping it round himself, and threw the end down to Penlan. She grabbed it, slung her lasgun, and began to swarm up the rope. After a second she hesitated.

'Sarge. There's something down here. I can hear movement.' After a second or so I heard it too. The scrape of claw against ice, moving fast, and the loud panting of a predator which has caught a fresh scent. I joined Lustig, grabbing the rope, and hauled until the muscles in my back cracked.

'Get her up!' I shouted. Jurgen ran to help too, and between us we dragged Penlan a good three metres up the ice face. From there her boot soles caught some purchase, and she was able to scramble her way up the wall. I dropped to my knees, feeling the cold bite through the fabric of my trousers, and extended a hand down into the darkness. 'Grab it!'

Penlan did so, a firm grip clamping round my wrist, and I tightened my grip on hers. We'd nearly made it, when something seized the dangling rope below her and jerked it hard.

'Frak!' Lustig and Jurgen dropped suddenly, pulled off balance, and Penlan's weight dragged me down. For a moment I thought we'd make it, but the ice beneath me had too little traction, and for a long, agonised moment I felt myself slipping. My hand tightened reflexively around her wrist, instead of letting go which would have been far more sensible, and before I knew it I was plunging forwards into the shadowy pit.

I landed hard, the breath driven from my lungs, a dozen small pains flaring across my body where I'd bounced on the way down. Penlan groaned beside me, face down and winded. Just as well, a small analytical part of my mind told me, or the slung lasgun might have broken her back.

'Commissar!' Bright light shone down on us, the luminator taped to Jurgen's lasgun, and I heard the distant echo of running feet as the rest of the squad responded to our plight. They wouldn't be quick enough, I thought, as the creature – whatever it was – rushed out of the darkness. I had a brief, panic-stricken image of claws and jaws too large and terrifying to be real, and as I scrabbled frantically backwards. My hand fell against the lasgun on Penlan's back. Without thinking I twisted it round, finding just enough play in the sling, and fired without even aiming properly.

Either luck or the Emperor was with me, because she'd left it on full auto. As my panic-spasmed hand locked on the trigger a hail of las bolts sprayed the chamber, blowing chunks of ice from the walls and deafening us with the roar of ionising air and ice flashing into steam. The creature screamed and fled, even more terrified than I was, and as the power cell died and relative silence descended on our ringing ears, Penlan stirred.

'I've got to stop doing that...'

'I'd appreciate it,' I agreed. A degree of understanding returned to her eyes.

'What happened?'

'The commissar saved your hide,' Lustig said. I was suddenly aware of the ring of faces around the hole over our heads. No point mentioning that it was purely by accident, of course, so I made a show of mild embarrassment, and patted the frost from my greatcoat.

'Better get the medic to check you over,' I said, just to reinforce my caring image.

I took a glance around the chamber. It looked bigger from down here, and the hail of las bolts had melted a number of small pits into the walls. Something seemed to be embedded in one, and I tried to focus on it, to stop my head spinning. Then my brain finally interpreted what I was seeing, and I regretted my curiosity at once.

'Looks like we found our missing miner,' Penlan said, with what I felt was rather unseemly relish.

'Almost,' I agreed. It was a human hand, severed at the wrist, the stump scored with vicious bite marks.

'What was that thing?' Jurgen asked, his habitual phlegmatic tone a welcome calming influence.

'I haven't a clue,' I admitted, scooping my laspistol up from the floor where it had fallen. As I did so I noticed a thick smear of ichor on the ice. The sight cheered me remarkably, not least because if I'd managed to wound the creature it was unlikely to come back for a while. 'But it bleeds.' I thrust the sidearm back into the holster on my belt with a sense of grim satisfaction. 'And if it bleeds, we can kill it.'

FOUR

'AND YOU DON'T have a clue what it was?' Broklaw asked. I shook my head. In the three or four hours since we'd returned from the depths of the mine I'd been asked that question often.

'None. But you wouldn't want one as a house pet, believe me.' A few of those present in the command centre chuckled dutifully. Besides myself and the major, Kasteen was the only other person seated on what I couldn't help thinking of as the military side of the conference table. Facing us was Morel, whose interest in the situation was undeniable and whose reaction had fallen somewhere between shock at the news that his worst fears were founded and grim satisfaction that his forebodings had been vindicated. Alongside him sat representatives from the Administratum and the Adeptus Mechanicus. Around us the rest of our senior officers continued to monitor troop positions and intelligence reports, ignoring the little knot of civilians in our midst as best they could as they bustled in and out with data-slates and mugs of tanna.

Remembering Quintus's advice I'd requested that he and Logash be our liaisons with their respective orders, and was pleased that this decision had proven to be wise. The young scrivener was as affable as I remembered, and Logash had turned out to have a quick wit and a courteous manner at marked odds with the defensiveness of his superior. To Kasteen's evident relief he had few visible marks of augmentation as well, beyond a pair of faceted metal eyes, which caught the light as his head moved, and although the Emperor alone knew what his robes concealed, she was able to keep her revulsion in check. (When I asked her why she found the tech-priests so disturbing she just shrugged, and said, 'They're weird, that's all.' She never reacted that way towards me, or anyone else in the regiment with augmetic replacements, so I guess it was just the sense she got from them of having voluntarily, if not eagerly, surrended part of their humanity.)[1]

'I've taken a look through the Codex Ferae,' Logash volunteered, 'based on the commissar's description of the beast. I'm pretty sure whatever it is, it isn't native to Simia Orichalcae.'

'Then how the hell did it get here?' Morel asked. Logash shrugged.

'Maybe the orks brought it with them.'

'That's highly unlikely,' Kasteen said, taking a little too much satisfaction in contradicting the tech-priest. But he took it in his stride and gave way to her greater expertise.

'You'd be a better judge of that than me.' He shrugged again. 'Maybe it stowed away on one of the tanker shuttles then.' Quintus nodded in agreement.

'They're certainly big enough for something to hide in undetected. I remember a couple of years back a few of the miners thought it would be funny to smuggle in some...'

'Who cares how it got here?' Morel broke in. 'The question is, what are we going to do about it?'

'Go back down there and kill it,' I said. Morel nodded with grim satisfaction, but Quintus's eyes narrowed a little.

'I don't want to sound as though I'm doubting your sense of priorities, but surely the orks are the real threat. Can't this thing wait until you've seen them off?'

'It's not the creature we're worried about,' Kasteen said. 'It's the unmarked tunnels the commissar found down there.'

'Probably burrowed by the beast,' Logash said. He pulled a data-slate from the recesses of his robes, and started scribbling notes with a lux-pen embedded in the tip of a finger. 'That might account for the size of the claws the commissar saw...'

---

1. *A common reaction to members of the Adeptus Mechanicus. Personally it's their air of smugness I find most off-putting. And isn't it about time the Ordo Hereticus started asking some pointed questions about this Omnissiah cult of theirs?*

'It doesn't matter who dug them,' I pointed out. 'What matters is that they're a potential hole in our defences.' As if to underline my words a bright flash cut through the flurrying snow outside the window, followed almost at once by the concussive thud of explosive detonation. The orks had obligingly arrived on schedule and were busily throwing themselves (or more probably their gretchin cannon fodder) against our outer defensive line with a gratifying lack of success so far. Luckily, Mazarin and her acolytes had managed to get the damaged shuttle flying again in a matter of hours, and the rest of our deployment had gone without a hitch, so we'd been more than ready to meet them despite my fears.

'I take your point,' Quintus said. 'What do you suggest?'

'I'm going back down there,' I said. 'With a squad of troopers. We'll map the tunnels as we go, and kill the creature when we find it.'

'You're leading the group personally?' Logash asked. I nodded.

'Commissar Cain is by far the best man for the job,' Kasteen explained. 'He has more experience of tunnel fighting than anyone else in the regiment.' Not from choice, I might add, but if it kept me out of the cold and away from the orks, I wasn't about to object.

'I'd like to come too, if I may,' Logash said. I think I'm hardly exaggerating when I say the rest of us simply stared at him in blank astonishment. 'Xenology's a bit of a hobby of mine. I might be able to identify what we're looking for.'

'This is a search and destroy mission, not a stroll around the zoo,' Kasteen said irritably. Logash looked a little crestfallen, I thought she was being unnecessarily hard on the boy. At least he was trying to help, which was more than his superiors were willing to do, and it didn't seem too good an idea to squash that enthusiasm. Besides, I had no objection to presenting the beast with another potential meal, to stand between me and it. (Of course if I'd known just how much trouble he was going to turn out to be I'd have left him behind, or even shot him on the spot, but regrets are a waste of good drinking time, as my old friend Divas used to say.)

'It would be at your own risk,' I told him. 'And you'd be under military authority. That means you do what you're told at all times. All right?'

'Fine.' He nodded eagerly. 'Do I get a gun?'

'Absolutely not,' Kasteen and I said simultaneously.

AFTER SEEING THE civilians out, Kasteen, Broklaw and I returned to the business of fighting the war. Our strategy seemed to be working, at least for now, keeping the main line of the ork advance bottled up in the neck of the valley quite nicely. The peculiar nature of an iceworld, and the Valhallans' understanding of how to exploit it, were paying handsome dividends, as the latest sensor downloads from the *Pure of Heart* were making abundantly clear. I gazed at the blurry image in the tactical hololith. It looked like someone had dropped it on the journey up here from the landing pad, as the three-dimensional representation of the battlefield would occasionally jump a few centimetres to the left, blank out, and reset itself. I reflected ruefully that perhaps we shouldn't have been quite so eager to get rid of Logash. (Who had practically skipped out of there, eager to be off, and prattling about various unpleasant life forms our intruder probably wasn't.)

'Never a tech-priest around when you need one,' Broklaw murmured, obviously thinking the same thing. He cast a sidelong glance at the colonel who pretended not to have heard.

Thanks to the frozen landscape we'd been able to fortify in depth with an ease which would have been impossible practically anywhere else. I was looking (when the blasted hololith would let me) at an extensive network of trenches and firing pits which would have taken weeks to dig in more normal terrain, but which had been hollowed out in mere hours by adroit use of our heavy flamers and multilasers. Of course half the troops manning them would have frozen to death by now if they'd been anyone else, but these were Valhallans, and the bone-chilling temperatures outside were just like a holiday resort so far as they were concerned. I'd even had to break up a couple of snowball fights before the orks turned up to spoil the party.[1]

'So far so good,' I said, quietly satisfied with the conduct of our troopers. The line was holding nicely, and the view from orbit showed that the ork advance had pretty much ground to a halt in the face of this unexpected resistance. So far as I could tell, the topography of the valley was working to our advantage as well as we'd hoped, with the broad front of the ork advance funnelling into the mouth of it and running right into our killing zone. Of course being orks this didn't diminish their enthusiasm, quite the reverse. Some flashes of gunfire on the outer fringes of the mob indicated that fratricidal firefights had broken out as the groups farthest from the fighting had run out of patience and had started blasting their way through their own comrades to get to us. Well that was fine with me, the more of them who killed each other the better I liked it, but there were still plenty left where they'd come from.

---

1. *From which we can infer that, despite his reluctance to step outside, Cain had visited the front line at least once by this point, probably after his return to the surface.*

'What's that?' Broklaw asked, pointing at a blip some way behind the bulk of the ork army. Whatever it was it was massive, and moving slowly but inexorably towards us. A heavy sense of foreboding sank into my stomach as I stared at it. I had a horrible suspicion as to what it might be, but prayed fervently to the Emperor that I was wrong. (Not that I thought for a moment that He might actually be listening, but you never know, and it relieved the stress.)

'According to this, it's huge,' Kasteen said, a hint of confusion in her voice. Rather than verbalise my fears, which would somehow make them more concrete, I voxed Mazarin aboard the orbiting starship to request a more detailed analysis. That way I could continue to cling to the hope that I might be wrong for a few more precious minutes.

'Single contact, about two hundred kloms... kilometres to the west,' I said. 'Can you give us a little more detail?'

'If the Omnissiah wills it,' the tech-priest said cheerfully, and busied herself for a few moments with the appropriate rituals. After a short pause her voice returned, with a slightly harder edge to it. 'It's a single artefact, approximately eighty metres in height. Self-propelled, with a high thermal signature which indicates combustion processes of some kind. Metallic shell, mainly ferric in composition.' Her voice faltered. 'I'm sorry, commissar, I don't have a clue what it is. I can meditate on it, but...'

'There's no need, thank you,' I said. 'You've just confirmed what I suspected. It's a gargant.' Kasteen and Broklaw stared at one another in horror. The orkish equivalent of a battle titan, the approaching construct might be crude but it would certainly have enough firepower aboard to punch through our defensive lines without even so much as slowing down. 'Any suggestions you might have about vulnerabilities we can exploit would be gratefully received.'

'I'll analyse the data and see what I can find,' she promised.

'We can't ask for more,' I said, and turned back to the other officers. We studied the hololith together, brows furrowed. 'I reckon we've got less than a day before it gets here...' I began, then Mazarin's voice interrupted me again.

'Sorry to break in, commissar, but the captain would like a word.'

'This isn't exactly a good time,' I said, then changed my mind. If things went horribly wrong, which they looked very like doing at the moment, the *Pure of Heart* was my best chance of getting out of the system with my hide intact. And annoying Durant would be a seriously bad idea. 'No, put him on.'

'Why's my ship crawling with groundlings?' the captain asked, his voice tinged with an asperity which didn't seem entirely affected. 'I've just got rid of your troopers and now you're shuttling up half the population of this miserable iceball.'

'We're sending up rather more than half,' I said, trying to sound reasonable. 'I thought the Administratum here had cleared it with you.'

'You mean Pryke?' A phlegmy sound of disgust rattled the speakers of the vox unit. 'Impossible woman, doesn't listen to a word you say. How in the Emperor's name did you manage to get her to co-operate with you?'

'It was surprisingly easy after the commissar threatened to shoot her,' Kasteen said, with a hint of a smile. Durant seemed speechless for a moment.

'Harrumph. Worth a try I suppose.' A faint tinge of amusement entered his tone. 'But that still doesn't answer my question.'

'We're evacuating as many of the civilians as we can,' Broklaw explained. 'Especially the workers' families. They'll be a lot safer with you than they are down here.'

'And we can fight more effectively if we're sure they won't be getting underfoot,' Kasteen added, a little more candidly.

'Under your feet, you mean.' The captain sounded mollified. 'I suppose we can stick them in a couple of the cargo holds now they're not cluttered up with your military junk.'

'That would be appreciated,' I said.

'No problem. I'm sure the Administratum can afford their fares.' He broke the connection abruptly.

Of course there was another, unspoken reason for evacuating the workers from the plant, although none of us wanted to think about it. If we were unable to hold the place, and I was a lot less sanguine about that now than I had been twenty minutes ago, the orks would want to make use of it. No point in leaving them a pool of highly skilled slave labour which would maintain promethium output at the current high levels. Their own meks would figure out the process eventually, of course, but they wouldn't be nearly so efficient. And with any luck we'd have had time to launch a counter attack or call the Astartes in to sterilise the place before they got the plant up and running again.

I stared at the hololith, and the almost imperceptibly moving blip of the gargant. We had nothing in our inventory capable of fighting something like that: no tanks, no artillery, and most especially no titans of our own. Broklaw noticed the direction of my gaze.

'Cheer up,' he said. 'We'll think of something.'

'Better make it quick,' Kasteen said.

Editorial Note:

It is with profound apologies that I append the following excerpt, but feel that some wider perspective on the tactical situation than Cain's typically self-centred one may prove of interest. I just wish I'd been able to find something a little more readable. If you find the prose style (or more accurately, lack of one) as painful as I do, feel free to skip it.

Extracted from *Like a Phoenix From the Flames: The Founding of the 597th,* by General Jenit Sulla (retired), 097.M42

THE GREEN TIDE broke against the bulwark of our defences as surely as an ocean wave against a harbour wall. For such we were, protecting the little islet of civilisation at our backs from the monstrous sea of barbarity which threatened to wash it clean. To the pride of all, it was us, Third Platoon, Second Company, which had been given the all-important task of holding a hastily-constructed redoubt at the very centre of our forward line, and not a woman or man of us shirked that responsibility. Crouched below the parapet of a rampart of ice I scanned my tactical data-slate, heedless of the bolter shells bursting against it to shower me with a refreshing powdering of frozen dust, noting with satisfaction the disposition of the squads under my command. As I'd come to expect, all were positioned with perfect precision, and I permitted myself a moment of pride in the level of battle-readiness they showed.

'Here they come!' someone shouted, a voice shaded, to my great satisfaction, by exultation rather than fear, and a quick glance over the frozen rampart confirmed it. A horde of orks was running towards us, yelling in their barbarous tongue, and I gave the order to hold fire. On they came, trampling the corpses of the dead we'd already left strewn across the virginal icefields, kicking up powdered snow as they came, so that it seemed as if the front ranks were wading waist-deep in mist. Like the wave that had assaulted us before they seemed scrawny specimens, quite unlike the heavily-muscled monstrosities which Commissar Cain had so resourcefully defeated after our shuttle was grounded,[1] but they died no less easily as I divined when they came within close range of our lasguns. 'Fire!' I ordered, and a devastating wave of las-bolts tore into the front ranks. Dozens fell, and more behind them as the casualties tripped those who followed after: forthwith the emplaced lascannons and multi-lasers we'd carefully sited finished the job, putting out a withering crossfire which ripped them to pieces. After a moment of indecision the survivors broke and fled in all directions, leaving a few more normal-sized specimens who seemed to have been directing them cruelly exposed to our sight and firepower; and this was to prove their death warrant, as they were summarily cut down by a second barrage.

'Like shooting rats in a box,' the young corporal next to me remarked. I reproved her, but could scarce keep the satisfaction from my own voice.

'I doubt they'll give up that easily,' I said, and of course I was right. The frontal attack, as I had half suspected, was a diversion, and the roar of engines heralded a flank attack by a squadron of curious vehicles which resembled motorcycles with tracks replacing the rear wheels. Heavy weapons, bolters I assumed, were slung from them on outriggers, and opened up with a roar which almost drowned the noise of their engines.

'Fire at will,' I ordered, and the snow around them erupted with the concentrated firepower of our doughty host. 'Death to the enemies of the Emperor!'

I must confess my heart swelled at the answering cheers of the heroes under my command, and the conviction of our inevitable victory buoyed my spirits to such an extent that, despite our peril, a smile forced its way onto my face.

---

1. *Almost certainly the weaker subspecies known as 'gretchin,' a distinction Cain was well aware of, as his earlier remark makes clear.*

FIVE

OF ALL THE experiences which have befallen me in a century or more of service to the Golden Throne, creeping through a network of darkened tunnels in search of a foe which could be lurking almost anywhere is one I could very well have done without becoming so familiar with. I don't know why, but show me an enemy of the Emperor and chances are I can point to the nearest hole in the ground with the near certainty of finding their lair festering away down there. Chaos cults, genestealer swarms, mutants, you name it, they all seem to scurry for the darkest corners they can find; and then, of course, someone has to go in after them and winkle them out.[1]

And, far more frequently than I'd like, that someone turns out to be me. Partly, I suppose, that's due to my inflated reputation (when something dangerous needs doing who better than a hero of the Imperium to get stuck with it?), but in truth I suspect that, as Kasteen told Logash, in most cases I really am the best man for the job. (In theory at any rate,

---

1. *Cain is exaggerating a little here, but it's certainly the case that a significant proportion of the heretical and unclean gravitate naturally to undercities and similar habitats. Then again, given the hostile nature of many worlds, both Imperial and xeno, the population may have had little option but to burrow underground to survive, which at least partially explains the prevalence of such labyrinths throughout inhabited space.*

my old hiver's tunnel sense brings a definite advantage, but in practice
enthusiasm for the job is most definitely absent, you may take my word
for that.)

In this case, though, while not exactly pleased to be back in the network of tunnels, it was rather more attractive than the alternative. True,
there was our mysterious beast to worry about, but I'd already wounded
it once and didn't anticipate it putting up much of a fight, not with a full
squad of troopers to back me up, and the indispensable Jurgen, who'd
managed to scrounge a melta from somewhere. He'd done the same on
Gravalax, and we'd both found cause to be thankful for his foresight.
Indeed, after that little incident he'd become quite partial to that particular item of equipment, and tended to bring it along whenever we might
meet heavier resistance than we anticipated. As it turned out I was to
have occasion to be even more grateful than usual for this little habit of
his. But in all honesty if I'd known what we were going to find down
there I would have charged the orks, even the gargant, with a broken
chair leg rather than set foot in those caverns again.

As it was though, I remained in blissful ignorance, and even felt
relaxed enough to joke with my aide as he fell in at my shoulder, preceded as always by his distinctive bouquet.

'Did you remember the marshmallows this time?' I asked, echoing
Amberley's jest when she caught sight of the melta he was carrying on
Gravalax. He smiled sheepishly.

'Must have slipped my mind, sir.'

'No problem. We'll just have to find something else for you to toast,'
I said.

'I'm not sure that would be wise,' Logash said, hurrying to join us,
and looking somewhat askance at the heavy thermal weapon. 'That
would pretty much vaporise the creature.'

'Along with a fair sized chunk of the wall behind it,' I agreed. Meltas
are designed to punch through tank armour, and using one to eradicate
a single creature might seem like overkill to most people, but so far as
I was concerned there was no such thing. Especially when you were
dealing with something the size of the beast I'd glimpsed before.

'Then we might never know what it was,' Logash objected. I shrugged.

'That's a disappointment I could learn to live with,' I said, then took
pity on his crestfallen expression. 'But I'm sure it won't come to that.
Jurgen's choice of weapon is purely for worst-case contingencies.'

'I see,' he said, nodding, and clearly trying to imagine what those contingencies might be. Well, he was going to find out soon enough.

'We're here,' the pointman said, his voice tinny in my comm-bead.
The squad sergeant, a stocky young woman called Grifen, called a halt,

and Logash shut up, eager for a sight of our quarry. I would have preferred to be accompanied by Lustig and his team, as they'd been down here before, but Penlan was too stiff from her healing injuries to tackle any more ice faces and I didn't want to be backed up by an under-strength squad. Besides which, as veterans, they were needed at the front line, especially with the approaching menace of the gargant.

Grifen's squad had seen little combat so far, and the sergeant herself was newly promoted, so this little errand had seemed like an ideal chance to break her into command without too much pressure (ironic, as things turned out.) Her troopers seemed competent enough, and had got over their impulse to gawp at the ice formations and the sparkling reflections in the first few minutes, settling into the routine of a xeno hunt with reassuring efficiency.

I looked down the tunnel to where the beams of our luminators reflected back from the tumbled heap of ice shards which marked the boundary of the hole I'd fallen into before. It was as eerily beautiful as ever, and despite the grimness of our errand I found myself savouring the sight as I turned to speak to Grifen.

'This is it,' I said. 'The end of the map. Once we pass this point we're in unknown territory.'

'Understood, sir.' She saluted crisply, without betraying her nervousness to anyone less skilled than I was at reading body language. She began to issue orders to her squad. 'Vorhees, on point. Drere and Karta, cover him. Hail, Simla, watch our backs. We're moving as soon as the commissar gives the word, so look alive, people.' Despite her inexperience she was a good motivator, and I began to feel a little easier about our travelling companions – most of them, anyway...

'Are there any tracks?' Logash asked eagerly. Grifen looked at him with an air of vague surprise, as though it had slipped her mind for a moment that we were being accompanied by a civilian. She shrugged.

'You're the expert. You tell us.' Anyone else, I suppose, would have had the sense to realise he was being snubbed, but Logash, like most of the tech-priests I've come across, had the social skills of a bath mat.[1] Instead of subsiding like any normal person he nodded eagerly, and started waving an auspex around as though it were an incense burner.

'There are some interesting striations in the ice layer,' he said, 'which could be frozen-over claw marks. Still too vague to make a clear determination, though...'

---

1. *Probably something to do with all those augmetics. It must be difficult to interact with mere humans when you feel you've got more in common with a beverage dispenser.*

I caught the sergeant's eye, and raised my own brows in a pantomime of tolerant exasperation. She smiled back a little nervously, not quite sure how to respond to a commissar with a sense of humour, and no doubt in awe of my reputation.

'I think if your people are ready we might as well move on,' I said, already sure they would be, and she gave the order with alacrity.

'Vorhees, front and centre. Let's get ourselves a new trophy for the mess room wall.' Logash shot me an unhappy look, which I ignored, and the pointman dropped nimbly through the hole in the floor.

'I'm down,' he said, his voice still attenuated in the comm-bead. 'No sign of life.' The rest of his fireteam[1] followed him, rappelling into the darkness below. The glow of their luminators was visible now, diffusing through the ice floor like the first faint echo of the dawn breaking somewhere a klom or two over our heads,[2] rippling like an aurora borealis.

'Our turn,' I said, with a cheerfulness I hoped no one would realise was forced, and stepped confidently up to the gap, trying to suppress the memory of my vertiginous plunge into the unknown the previous day. I bounced down the slope, the support of the rope more of a comfort than I'd realised, and found my boot heels crunching against the hard-packed scattering of ice crystals on the floor before I even knew it. The chamber was just as I'd remembered it: featureless save for the tunnel mouth we'd come to investigate. But it was crowded with troopers this time. A moment later Jurgen slithered down next to me. The heavy melta slung across his shoulders pulled him over to one side, but he regained his balance and hefted it properly back into position. The small knot of troopers around us took a step or two away.

Logash came next, clinging too tightly to the rope so that he descended in a series of jerks and wild parabolas. The Guardsmen and women watched his progress with unconcealed amusement and the expectation of an ignominious tumble to come. To his credit he made it though, letting out his breath in a wild rush as he reached the floor of the cavern.

'Are you all right?' I asked, reaching out a hand to steady him. He nodded.

'Yes. Fine. I'm just not very good with heights, to be honest.' He caught sight of the splash of ichor from where I'd shot our quarry and

---

1. *The Valhallan 597th divided its squads into two fireteams of five troopers each, a common, though unofficial, practice in regiments experienced in urban warfare.*

2. *In fact, according to the schematics, the lowest level of the mines was almost three kilometres below the surface at this point.*

went scuttling off to examine it without another word. Soon I heard him muttering in disappointment at the way our boot prints had disturbed any tracks the thing might have left.

I looked up to check the progress of Grifen and the remaining four troopers, who were all descending without any problems. When I looked back the little tech-priest was arguing furiously with private Vorhees. I strode over to investigate, wondering once more whether bringing him was turning out to be more trouble than it was worth.

'What's going on?' I asked, trying to sound reasonable. Vorhees had the young tech-priest held firmly by the upper arm, evidently restraining him. The trooper jerked an irritable head at the mouth of the tunnel down which the creature had disappeared.

'He tried to get past me,' he said. I shone my luminator into the darkness, the beam catching a thousand glittering highlights from the irregular walls. Then I turned to glare at Logash.

'I thought I made it clear you were to stay close to Jurgen,' I said. My aide had accepted the ad hoc bodyguarding assignment as phlegmatically as he did every other order, and I suppose Logash could be forgiven for being less than enthusiastic about it. That wasn't his main concern at the moment though. He jerked his arm free of Vorhees's restraining grasp with a degree of petulance which reminded me of a sulky juve, and pointed at the tunnel floor in the pool of light from my luminator.

'I was looking for tracks,' he said, clearly wanting to say a great deal more. 'The ground in here's too trampled to tell anything from.'

'Right. Fine,' I said. I turned back to Vorhees. 'Keep him in sight. He goes no further than five metres.' I returned my gaze to Logash. 'That should be enough for you, right?'

'Oh yes, indeed.' He trotted a couple of paces into the tunnel, spot lit by the beam of the luminator Vorhees had taped to the barrel of his lasgun, and squatted down to wave the bloody auspex around. Sure he could still hear me, I turned to grin at Vorhees.

'Maybe we'll catch it quicker if we leave some bait out.'

'Worth a try,' he agreed, with a smile of his own. Logash ignored us, already wrapped up in his data-divining rituals. After a few moments he walked back to join us, still muttering under his breath as he studied the display of the little machine.

'Well?' Grifen demanded. 'Can you tell what it is yet?' Logash looked confused.

'Well, there are indications. If we were anywhere else I might take a guess. But the habitat's all wrong...'

'Then just give us what you can,' I encouraged gently. Grifen nodded, flicking her black hair out of her eyes as she tried to make out the runes

on the screen, but they were all tech-priest gibberish and none of the
rest of us could make head or tail of it. Logash shrugged.

'It definitely burrowed these tunnels,' he said. 'There are claw marks
on the walls and ceiling as well as the floor.' A flicker of apprehension
rippled around most of the troopers. The narrow passage was high
enough to stand up in without stooping, even for me,[1] and if not quite
wide enough for two abreast had at least enough room for us to be able
to see past the man in front (and shoot, too, which was more to the
point.) The creature must have a considerable reach – that much was
obvious.

'Well, we're not going to find it by standing here,' I pointed out, more to
steady the troops than anything else. 'And we still have to map these tunnels.' So we set off into the dark, our nerves taut with fearful anticipation.

I WAS MORE at ease down here than any of my companions with the
possible exception of Jurgen, who simply accepted the situation as he
did everything else, with taciturn stoicism. These tunnels were different
from the ones I was used to, however. They turned and meandered
apparently at random, with innumerable branching corridors which
came to a dead end or turned back on themselves to rejoin the one
we'd just left, or split into further radial passageways. I had several occasions to thank the Emperor for my sense of direction, without it I'd
have been disorientated within moments, but the subconscious
instinct which lets me know roughly where I am and how far I've come
in an underground environment proved as reliable as ever.

'It's a frakking maze down here,' one of the troopers, Drere I think,
muttered under her breath. Grifen silenced her with a few well-chosen
words, in the manner of sergeants the length and breadth of the galaxy.
Logash was travelling in the middle of the group next to me, as I hoped
to keep a respectable number of heavily-armed troopers between me
and the creature whichever direction it approached from. Logash
agreed, heedless of the sergeant's admonishment.

'Surprisingly extensive for so recent an excavation,' he added. Just
then the palms of my hands started tingling, in the way they do when
my subconscious warns me of something my forebrain has yet to grasp.

'How recent?' I asked. Logash pointed out something on the screen
of the auspex, which I couldn't see clearly.

'A few weeks,' he said. 'A couple of months at the most.' In other
words, about the same time the orks turned up, and that was just

---

1. *Cain was just under two metres in height, and was generally among the tallest in any
given group.*

too much of a coincidence. Not that I believed for a moment it was some kind of squig[1] we were after. The chances of that were extremely remote, as anything the greenskins had brought with them would have arrived at the same co-ordinates. But the space hulk which had brought them to the system (and, to my intense relief, dropped back into the warp again within hours) could have carried any number of other horrors in its bowels, and if that were so it wasn't unlikely that something else had seized the opportunity to make planetfall at the same time.

I made a mental note to ask Quintus to look through the sensor logs of the refinery's orbital traffic control system when we got back. The chances were the blaze of warp energy emitted by the hulk's emergence, a thousand times stronger than that of a starship, would have swamped them, but there might be a clue there we could disentangle given time.

Any further opportunity I might have had to muse on the matter was abruptly curtailed as I felt a faint tremor through the soles of my boots. My palms tingled again, foreboding flooding through me. The narrow passageway seemed even more claustrophobic than before, although that's not a sensation I'm normally familiar with either. The faint tremor intensified, and I stopped trying to identify it. I felt a yielding impact against my shoulder blades as Grifen walked into me, and halted in her turn.

'Commissar? What is it?' she asked.

'Quiet!' I looked back and forth down the tunnel, craning my neck to see as best I could past the troopers on either side of me. The light from our luminators receded in both directions, still striking dazzling highlights from the deep blue surface of the ice around us. 'Something's coming!'

'Nothing here,' Vorhees said, his voice crackling over the comm-net from a hundred metres or so up the tunnel.

'Nothing back here either,' Private Hail chipped in, her voice tense. I can't say I blame her for that, the rearguard is the second most vulnerable position in the column. Everyone stared at me, probably wondering whether the commissar had gone bonkers. Except for Jurgen of course, who had doubtlessly made up his mind on that score years

---

1. *A generic term for a bewildering variety of organisms apparently associated with orks. Opinion in the Ordo Xenos remains divided as to whether they represent true symbiosis, or are simply an entire genus of unpleasant creatures sufficiently close to the greenskins' peculiar metabolic processes to flourish in close proximity to them. It is undeniable that they do seem to accompany most orkish infestations, however. Where Cain picked up the word is conjectural, presumably from the same source as the rest of his smattering of orkish.*

before. But all my hiver's instincts insisted I was right, something was coming, even if we hadn't seen it yet...

Sudden understanding punched me in the gut. The creature we were hunting was a burrower! It didn't need to come at us along an existing passageway. No doubt it had detected our presence in some way, probably picking up the vibrations of our footfalls, and was heading straight towards us by the most direct route.

'Jurgen,' I shouted. 'Give us some elbow room!' Divining my intentions the troopers nearest to us scattered back along the passageway. Logash was hauled away protesting by Grifen, who couldn't be bothered trying to explain. His voice was drowned out abruptly by the hiss of the melta as Jurgen fired at the wall, instantly flashing a dozen cubic metres of ice into steam, which condensed almost instantly in the sub-zero temperatures, filling the narrow passageway with mist.

He was just in time, too. An instant later the newly frozen wall burst in on us in a hail of glittering ice shards, and the living nightmare I'd encountered before was among us.

By sheer foul luck I was the closest to it, and I barely had time to draw a weapon before it was upon me. This close up a gun would have been all but useless, so I drew my chainsword almost without thinking, and made a block with the instinctive lack of thought that comes from assiduous practice. It was lucky I had. An impossibly long arm, tipped with the talons I'd glimpsed before, swung at me as I thumbed the selector to maximum speed. It would probably have disembowelled me if I hadn't deflected the blow. The blade whined, cutting deep through plates of chitin which wouldn't have seemed out of place on a tyranid, and the thing howled with rage and pain.

I was vaguely aware of Jurgen standing aside to make room for some of the other troopers, whose barrel-mounted luminators spot-lit the confrontation. They were hoping they could get in a shot which wouldn't vaporise me along with the monster I fought, but the hope was a vain one. We were locked in too close, and circling too fast, for anyone to have a hope of getting a clear line of fire.

(It's moments like this, incidentally, which point up the wisdom of fostering the illusion that I cared about the common troopers. I have no doubt at all that, were I the type of commissar who relies on intimidation rather than respect to get the job done, and there are all too many of those around, most of the grunts would have taken the shot anyway and cheerfully reported that the creature got me first. It's a lesson I try to pass on to my cadets, in the hope that the less bone-headed among them might actually get to enjoy a reasonably lengthy career, but it's probably a wasted effort.)

I drove in under the thing's barrel chest, which barely came up to my chin, and tried to avoid the huge mandibles which snapped at my face as I ducked. Bizarrely the thing's unnaturally long arms were jointed about two-thirds of the way up its length, so the closer in to it I remained the harder it would be for it to reach me. Well that suited me fine. I swung the humming blade at its thorax, feeling the teeth bite home, and was rewarded with a spray of ichor and foul-smelling viscera. It screamed again, opening the mandibles impossibly widely, and bringing its head down to snap at me.

That was precisely what I'd been hoping for. The tactic worked well on some of the larger tyranid bio-forms, so I was ready and waiting, thrusting the tip of my trusty chainsword up through the open maw to chew its way contentedly through what passed for the creature's brain. I snatched my hand away quickly, fearing the reflex closing of those terrible jaws, and opening up a wide gash which split the side of its head open from the inside. A jet of blood and cerebral fluid sprayed the wall, which hardened to ice within seconds.

That was enough; the creature fell, making me scramble backwards in an undignified fashion to get out of the way, crashing into the ice at my feet. Thin flakes of powdered ice, condensed from the steam, rose into the air, and fluoresced like miniature galaxies in the light from our luminators.

'That was amazing,' Grifen said, clearly torn between protocol and the urge to pat me on the back. The murmur of voices among the troopers told me that she wasn't the only one to be impressed. Only Logash was looking at the creature rather than me, his face an almost comical mask of confusion.

'There's your specimen,' I told him, returning my trusty chainsword to its scabbard. 'Do you think you can identify it?'

'It's an ambull' he said, shaking his head in bafflement. 'But it can't be. They're native to Luther Macintyre IX...'

'Never heard of it,' I said. 'But it wouldn't be the first time a species jumped planets.'

'That's not the point. Ambull colonies are already known on dozens of worlds.' The young tech-priest looked completely bewildered. 'But they're all desert-dwellers, like their native stock. This creature shouldn't be on an iceworld at all.'

'Maybe it got lost,' one of the troopers suggested. His comment was accompanied by derisive laughter from his squad mates. I didn't join in. Something was badly wrong here, that much was evident, even without my tingling palms to underline the fact. And as I looked at the creature I'd slain, I noticed something else that wasn't quite right.

'Where are the lasgun wounds?' Jurgen asked, putting my thought into words an instant before I could. 'I definitely saw you hit it the last time...'

'It's a different one,' I said, looking to Logash for confirmation. 'That means there must be another one of these things down here with us.'

'More likely several,' he confirmed eagerly. 'Ambulls tend to form extended social groups.'

Better and better, I thought sourly. But if only I'd known, there was far worse still to come.

Editorial Note:

Thanks to the obsessive record-keeping of the Administratum it's possible to extricate practically any piece of information you may desire, however trivial, from the depths of the Imperial archives. That is, if you can actually find what you're looking for among the impenetrable thickets of worthless verbiage surrounding it. Suffice it to say that locating the minutes of the meeting between Kasteen and the officials in charge of the refinery complex was frustrating, to say the least, but on balance it was probably worth the effort, especially as the transcript provides some vital background information without which Cain's account of later events can seem a little confusing.

The minutes were taken by Scrivener Quintus, whose somewhat idiosyncratic recording style leads me to suspect that he never expected anyone to actually read them.

347

Minutes of the meeting of the Committee for the Defence and Preserva-
tion of Simia Orichalcae From the Orkish Incursion (by the Grace of
His Majesty), convened this day 648.932 M41 (just too early for a decent
breakfast.)

Those Present:
Colonel Regina Kasteen of the 597th Valhallan, a fair and gallant war-
rior, acting military governor of the Simia Orichalcae system.
Major Ruput Broklaw, her second in command, equally gallant but
not remotely as fair.
Artur Morel, professional hole-grubber.
Magos Vinkel Ernulph, senior tech-priest, with too much metal where
his brain should be.
Codicier Marum Pryke, the Emperor's gift to the Administratum, at
least in her own mind.
Me.
Assorted sycophants and hangers-on.

Order of Business:
Defence of the refinery (actually the only thing we discussed.)

Proceedings:
Colonel Kasteen called the meeting to order. Then she called it to
order again. Major Broklaw fired his bolt pistol into the ceiling, and the
meeting came to order.
Colonel Kasteen put forward a plan for disabling the gargant, and
hopefully eliminating a significant number of the besieging orks into the
bargain. This relied on the fact that the mining tunnels extended some
way beyond the perimeter of the refinery proper; given the immense
weight of the thing it should be possible to collapse the galleries underneath it with sufficient quantities of explosive.
Magos Ernulph wanted to know just how close to the refinery the
explosion would be, pointing out that the promethium tanks were
almost full, and that if things went wrong the entire refinery could be
reduced to a smoking crater.
Major Broklaw pointed out helpfully that in that case none of us
would be around to complain about it.
Codicier Pryke raised the point that a significant credit value was
attached to this installation, and that its destruction would result in a
0.017 per cent fluctuation in the mean commerce averages of the sector.

She went on to suggest that an alternative strategy should be found. Colonel Kasteen said she was welcome to go outside and ask the orks to go away if she thought that would help.

Morel offered the assistance of his miners in determining the optimum placement of the explosive charges, citing their expertise with the local geology, which the colonel appreciated (she has a very nice smile.)

As no one had any other suggestions for disabling the gargant, Ernulph conceded that we might as well blow the place up ourselves before the orks do it.

I raised the matter of Commissar Cain and his scouting party, asking how they were likely to fare if they were still underground when the mine was blown up. Kasteen and Broklaw evinced a degree of concern on this point, admitting that their chances of survival under those circumstances would be slim. Broklaw added that he was sure they'd be back by then, as the commissar had something of a knack for avoiding such difficulties. I suggested voxing them with a warning, but apparently they were too deep underground now to get a message through.

No doubt wherever he was, though, he'd be having a better time of it than we are.

SIX

I'M SURE I wasn't alone in brooding over Logash's off-hand announcement as we penetrated deeper into the maze of passages that made up the ambull den. The thought that we shared these tunnels with an indeterminate number of heavily-armoured predators wasn't exactly comforting, and we pressed on with renewed caution. The labyrinth was remarkably extensive, as the tech-priest had noted; if we'd had to walk every metre of it we'd still have been down there when the Emperor stepped off the throne,[1] but fortunately that wasn't going to be necessary. Between my hiver's instincts, Logash's knowledge of xenology, and the readings of his auspex we were beginning to get a pretty good idea of the layout of the place.

'Any idea how many more of those things there are down here?' I asked him, once I was sure we were out of earshot of any of the troopers (except Jurgen, of course, whose discretion I knew I could rely on absolutely). No point in spooking them any further if the answer was as bad as I feared. Logash looked pensive for a moment, as though

---

1. Such beliefs became remarkably widespread as the turn of the millennium approached. Cain wasn't superstitious enough to place any credence in such folk tales, of course, but like many others used the phrase metaphorically to mean the start of M42, which of course at that point was still sixty-eight standard years in the future.

communing with some inner voice. (Which he may well have been, I've known plenty of tech-priests with augmetic data stores plugged into what's left of their brains. But he may just have had indigestion.)

'Judging by the extent of the tunnel system, and assuming that your guess they arrived on the same space hulk as the orks is correct...' he began. (Which it wasn't, as we were shortly to find out, but the timing was the same so it didn't make any practical difference in the end.) He was interrupted by a fusillade of lasgun fire further down the tunnel, and a babble of shouting voices that overlapped into nothing but multitudinous echoes in the confined and twisting tunnels. I activated my comm-bead.

'Grifen. What's going on?' I asked.

'Contact. Another creature.' Her voice was crisp and steady, so the situation seemed under control. I hurried forward, not wanting to be too far from the bulk of our firepower if any more of the beasts were attracted to the sounds of combat.

'No more than half a dozen,' Logash finished, panting in my wake. No doubt he felt the same urge, only stronger than I did, as he was the only member of our party who was completely unarmed. Whether he still had enough meat on him to actually interest an ambull was a moot point, of course, but I declined to consider it at the time. 'Probably fewer by now,' he added, as the firing stopped.

Well, that was a relief. These creatures weren't all that tough, compared to some of the things I'd faced, and the news that we weren't likely to run into too many more of them was undeniably welcome.

The carcass of our latest victim was lying a few metres further on in a wider tunnel that opened out from the one we followed. It was surrounded by chattering troopers and riddled with the cauterised craters of las-bolt impacts. Vorhees was breathing heavily, trembling from the reaction, and shrugging off the attentions of the squad medic. The front of his flak armour was deeply scored, visible through the rents in his greatcoat. I gathered from the conversations around me that the ambull had just managed to get within arms' reach of him before he finally succeeded in dropping it.

'Well done,' I said, clapping him on the back; it never hurt to show the troopers I cared – even if I didn't. He grinned weakly at me.

'Persistent little frakkers, aren't they sir?' I nodded.

'Take a bit of putting down,' I agreed. Which of course indirectly reminded everyone I'd taken mine down hand-to-hand. I glanced at the carcass, wondering if it was the one I'd shot before, but Vorhees had made such a mess of it blazing away on full auto that there wasn't really enough left intact to tell.

'Fast, too,' Vorhees agreed. It seemed that the thing had come at him along the main tunnel almost as soon as he'd entered it. He'd just been able to bring his weapon up before it was on him.

'Interesting,' Logash said. He was looking at the walls of the tunnel, and messing around with his auspex again. After a moment he turned back to me. 'I think we've found one of the main runs.' Well it certainly seemed a lot wider than the tunnels we'd been following before.

'Which means?' I asked. The tech-priest shrugged, his white robe beginning to look distinctly grubby now, I noticed. Hardly the most practical garment for tunnel fighting, but evidently it hadn't occurred to him to get changed before setting out. Either that or he didn't have anything else to wear in any case.

'The main chamber should be at one end of this passageway.' He glanced uncertainly up and down it. I considered his words carefully.

'Main chamber meaning...?' I asked. Logash responded with the eagerness of the enthusiast.

'The central nesting site, or den. Ambulls are social creatures, with strong familial instincts, and tend to congregate when not out hunting or...'

'Vorhees,' I said. 'Which direction did the creature come from?' Logash looked a little hurt at being abruptly cut off (just as he felt he was getting to the interesting bit no doubt). The trooper jerked a thumb past the rapidly cooling chunk of meat, which was now surrounded by a garnet-coloured nimbus of frozen blood.

'That way,' he indicated. My sense of direction kicked in, and I absently noted that it was almost directly towards the ork siege lines. A sense of grim foreboding settled across my shoulders.

'If it was returning to the lair it would have been carrying prey of some kind to share with the others,' Logash chipped in helpfully.

The pool of light from our luminators revealed nothing apart from the dismembered ambull. There was the answer. We weren't going to be able to complete our reconnaissance mission without passing through a cavern full of these monstrosities. Wonderful. But bowel-clenching as the prospect appeared, I liked the idea of a horde of orks pouring through these tunnels to slaughter the lot of us even less.

'Close up,' I ordered. 'Be ready to concentrate your firepower.' Grifen nodded, and went to shout at Hail and Simla, who were blunting their combat knives by trying to hack the ambull's head off. Up to that point I thought she'd been kidding about taking a trophy back with us, but it seemed at least two of her troopers had taken her literally.

'Move out,' she ordered. 'By teams, covering the commissar and the cogboy[1].' Logash showed considerably more common sense than hitherto by pretending he hadn't heard her. I must confess to feeling a little better, though, knowing everyone else would be watching my back. (In case you were wondering why Grifen should care about my welfare, and Logash's – I was deemed to be the best judge of the value of any intelligence we might gather, and Logash... well, let's just say Kasteen didn't want to have any more dealings with the Adeptus Mechanicus than she already did.)

So we moved out cautiously, heading towards the centre of the maze, our senses alert for any sign of movement in the darkness. We'd debated dousing a few of our luminators in the hope that we'd make ourselves less obvious, but according to Logash it wouldn't make any difference as the creatures could see in the dark anyway. He started to explain how,[2] but it made no sense to me and I soon stopped listening.

Second team still had the lead position. Grifen was already showing a veteran commander's common sense when it came to hanging back enough to keep an objective eye on the whole squad, although Karta (the ASL[3] and corporal in charge of the fireteam) had rotated Vorhees back to where the medic could keep an eye on him, and had put Drere on point. It made a kind of sense, I suppose, as Vorhees was still pretty twitchy after his close encounter with the ambull, but I'd have been inclined to leave him where he was; if he was going to be trigger happy I'd rather have him where there was nothing but targets in front. I was behind him in any case though, so it was all one to me.

Jurgen, Logash and I trotted along in the middle, keeping a cautious distance between the leading team and the one covering our backs, because if either made contact I wanted to be well out of harm's way. Of course I was still uneasily aware of the ambulls' ability to carve their way straight through the ice to get at us, but I kept my ears open and

---

1. *A less than complimentary slang term for tech-priests, apparently derived from their symbol of office. It is common among Guard troopers, along with several others, most of which are considerably more offensive.*

2. *According to the Magos Biologos they can see heat rather than light. Rather an odd concept, I have to say, but having looked through a tau blacklight system recently I can attest from personal experience that such a phenomenon can be achieved by technosorcery, so I suppose it's not beyond the bounds of possibility that it might also occur in nature.*

3. *Assistant squad leader, a lower-ranking NCO trained to take command if the sergeant becomes a casualty. Where a squad has been divided into fireteams (which, as has already been noted, was standard practice in the 597th) the ASL will normally take command of the second team when it becomes detached from the first, and the direct control of the sergeant.*

my paranoia cranked up to maximum, and so far I hadn't noticed any of the telltale vibrations which might betray the approach of another of the beasts.

'So what do they taste like?' Jurgen asked. I stopped tuning out Logash's prattling to gather that his monologue on the subject of the ambulls' life cycle, social structure, and habitat had finally yielded some useful information. Apparently there had been a number of attempts to domesticate the things as a handy source of meat on desert worlds.[1]

'Rather like grox, I'm told.' Logash looked a little uncomfortable, and I clapped him on the shoulder.

'Excellent,' I said. 'We'll send a scavenging party back to recover the carcasses once we've cleaned out the nest.' All the refinery had to offer in the way of cuisine was a dozen different varieties of soylens viridians, which had already begun to pall, despite being fresh from their own vats. Of course, we'd brought our own supplies along, but a nice fresh steak would lift my spirits nicely, I thought. Besides, the creatures had been eating the miners, so it seemed fair enough to return the compliment.

'Good idea, sir,' Jurgen said with relish. Logash looked a little green for someone so heavily augmented. Maybe he was a vegetarian, if he still bothered eating at all.

'I can hear movement,' Drere said, her voice slightly flattened by the comm-bead in my ear.

'Close up. Prepare for contact.' Grifen issued the order with calm authority, and I found myself at the centre of a small knot of troopers as first team caught up with us. We picked up our pace, fell in with them, and began closing on the lights from the luminators of second team.

'There's a cavern here.' Drere's voice tightened a little, the tension she must have felt transmitting itself through the gently hissing comm-bead in my ear.

'Hold position,' Karta said, his own voice calm, but with audible effort. 'Wait for the rest of us.'

'Confirm that,' Drere said, a faint edge of relief entering her voice. The dancing lights ahead of us were closer together now, I thought, refracting more brightly through the crystal shards which rimed the irregular walls of the tunnel. 'I'm not about to stick my... Emperor's guts!'

A lasgun opened up, bright muzzle flashes strobing down the reflective tunnel, and the luminators ahead of us bobbed more wildly than

---

1. *With a conspicuous lack of success, if truth be told. Their burrowing abilities make them almost impossible to confine, with the inevitable result that the colonies which tried soon found themselves overrun with dangerous predators.*

before as their bearers broke into a run. We followed suit, our boot soles crunching on the ice crystals underfoot. Logash slipped from time to time as he lost traction. The Valhallans, of course, had no such difficulties, and I'd picked up enough expertise in running on ice from them over the years to avoid my own feet slithering out from under me. I drew my laspistol.

'Janny!' Vorhees shouted, and a second weapon opened up in support. A moment later there was a shriek which echoed through the tunnels, raising the hairs on my arms, and a howl of feedback through the comm-bead which made my teeth ache.

'Medic! Trooper down!' Karta yelled, and by that time the rest of us had reached the scene of the carnage. The tunnel had indeed opened out into a large central chamber, about thirty metres across, and with a handful of other passageways visibly piercing the walls at irregular intervals. Drere was down, steaming blood starting to freeze in a slick hard plate over a gaping wound in her torso. Her face was pinched and white from the shock. Vorhees stood over her, pouring lasfire into the monstrosity which had evidently inflicted the damage, driving it back, screaming in rage and frustration.[1]

The cavern was a positive maelstrom of whirling bodies and wild firing. Luminator beams and las-bolts strobed as the troopers swung the muzzles of their weapons to meet the nearest perceived threat. It was no place for me, I decided, standing aside to let Grifen's team join the mêlée. I held an arm across Logash's chest as though I intended to keep him from harm. (In actual fact, of course, if one of the beasts had come anywhere near us it could have had him and been welcome; and if I'd known just how much trouble he was shortly to cause us I'd probably have thrown him to the closest and bidden it *bon appetit*.)

The reinforcements pitched in with a will, targeting the seething mass of enraged monstrosities which were boiling out of the shadows at us. There were too many to count, or at least that's how it seemed at the time. When the ice chips finally settled it transpired that Logash's estimate hadn't been all that far out, with a mere five of the creatures stretched out on the floor. But if you had asked me to take a stab at the numbers amid all that confusion I'd probably have said dozens.

'Pick your targets! Fire for effect!' Grifen yelled, her actions matching her words. She squeezed the trigger methodically, placing single

---

1. *It's not entirely clear from this final subordinate clause whether Cain is referring to the ambull or the trooper; sometimes he lets his immersion in his memories run ahead of comprehensibility. After some reflection I've elected to let his wording stand, as under the circumstances either or both seem equally likely.*

shots on the head of the nearest ambull with commendable accuracy, aiming for the eyes and maw. A las bolt burst against the roof of the thing's mouth, blowing a large chunk of brain matter backwards which clung to the frozen wall, solidifying like an obscene outgrowth as the creature toppled backwards. It hit the floor with a concussion which I was certain I could hear even over the cacophony of combat.

'Omnissiah protect us!' Logash was shivering in shock, which surprised me with all that metal in him. Evidently looking at holos of exotic species in the comfort of his chambers was rather more fun than having the blood-soaked reality trying to tear his face off.

'Over there. Eight o'clock.' Jurgen swung his hand in a familiar gesture, lobbing a frag grenade over the heads of the nearest monsters to burst among the ones clustered at the back. (Juveniles just out of the nest, according to Logash when he had a chance to examine them, but they looked dangerous enough to me, pushing forward as maddened by bloodlust as any of the others we'd encountered.)

A scream to my right snapped my head round just in time to see a pair of hideous mandibles close around the arm of the medic with a loud crunching sound which spoke of broken bones or worse. As the creature lifted him off the ground I turned, chainsword shrieking, and leapt forward to lop through the distended jaw. He fell heavily, clutching his wounded arm, and scrabbled for a self-injector from his pouch with his uninjured hand. That should have been enough to establish my participation in the battle and allow me to go back to babysitting Logash, but of course the thing came at me. I swung the weapon again, cursing myself for my stupidity. Jurgen hefted the melta uncertainly, unable to get a shot without killing as many of us as the creatures, and I had a moment to wonder if I'd ever get the chance to suggest he settle for something a little more manageable like a hellgun or a flamer next time. Then a line of bloody craters stitched themselves across the ambull's chest.

'Thanks!' I called to Karta, and administered the *coup de grace* to my staggering foe, lopping the head from its shoulders as it fell to its knees. (Probably unnecessarily, but it was a suitably theatrical gesture for a hero of the Imperium to make, and the surrounding troopers seemed to appreciate it.)

Abruptly I became aware of the sudden silence around us, was broken only by the ticking of the re-freezing ice and the groans of the wounded.

'Casualties?' I asked, playing up to my caring image. Grifen made a rapid assessment.

'Two serious. A few cuts and bruises among the rest, but they'll live.' She turned her attention to the medic, who was treating Drere as best he could with his one good hand. He was assisted by a grim-faced Vorhees.

'How is she?' I asked, walking over to them.

'She'll be fine,' Vorhees said flatly, clearly in no mood to accept any other outcome; the memory of him calling her given name as the fight started came back to me, and I smelled trouble. The nature of their relationship, clearly more than purely professional, was pretty obvious. And if she died he'd no doubt blame himself for not having been on point instead of her. Or Karta for switching their positions. Either way, it was clear his mind was no longer on the mission objectives. 'Won't she, doc?'[1]

'Sure she will,' the medic said, the doubt in his voice obvious to everyone but Vorhees. 'Stick in an augmetic lung and a new liver, she'll be good as new.'

Provided we got her back in time. I hesitated. Our mission was far from over, but we'd seen no sign of any ork presence in these tunnels, and the greenskins weren't exactly subtle. Come to that, they wouldn't have left any ambulls alive down here either. Chances were the tunnel system was fully secure, and there was nothing more to be gained by completing the sweep.

On the other hand, I haven't made it through to my second century by being complacent. We needed to be certain the orks didn't know the tunnels were here, and even the slightest doubt could fatally undermine our plans for the defence of the refinery. But that certainty could only be bought with time; time Drere clearly didn't have if we were going to get her back in time to save her life.

I hate choices like that. There are no good outcomes, all you can do is pick what seems to be the least bad, and so I dithered. The certainty of safety, or the potential loss of my carefully nurtured image as a leader who cared about the troopers he serves with? The illusion that I was one of them had saved my life many times as they repaid the loyalty they believed I held for them.

It was Jurgen who broke the deadlock in my vacillating mind. As instructed, he'd stuck close to Logash, who, predictably, was ignoring the carnage around him. He was now pottering around the chamber waving his auspex about and digging chunks of ice out of the walls with his augmetic fingers for reasons entirely beyond me.

---

1. *A traditional nickname for the squad medic in most Guard units. Most aren't qualified doctors, of course, being trained simply in primary aid techniques designed to stabilise casualties long enough to get them back to a properly equipped aid station or chirugical facility.*

'Commissar. You'd better take a look at this.' As usual my aide's voice betrayed no excitement, but I knew him well enough to recognise the undercurrent of urgency in his tone. I walked over to the corner where the tech-priest was crouched, grubbing in the ice like a holidaying infant in the coastal sand.

'What have you found?' I asked, then got a good look over Logash's shoulder and wished I hadn't.

'It appears to be a midden,' he said, his voice curiously like a juve comparing scrumball statistics. He picked up a fragment of bone, which looked uncomfortably human in origin.

'A what?' Jurgen asked, his brow furrowing.

'A spoil heap,' Logash explained. 'Ambulls are quite organised, disposing of their waste in a specific part of the den...' I took a step backwards as it occurred to me just what the discolorations in the ice that he was so blithely digging through consisted of. The tech-priest prattled on. 'With proper analysis we should be able to determine what they were eating...'

'We know what they were eating. The miners.' Grifen came over to join us, and lowered her voice. 'Drere's in a bad way, commissar. Do we go on, or go back?' It was clear which alternative she preferred.

'I doubt that would have represented a sufficient food source,' Logash said, still digging, absently responding to the only part of her remark which interested him. He began to work something large out of the ice. 'What have we here?'

'It's a skull,' Jurgen responded helpfully, unable to identify a rhetorical question if one sat up and bit him. I glanced at it, idly wondering which of the luckless miners this was, then froze as something about the shape triggered warning bells in my mind. The cranium was low browed and heavy, the jaw prognathous, and as Logash brushed the obscuring ice away jutting tusks became visible protruding from the lower mandible.

'From an ork,' I added unnecessarily.

So I had my answer. Whether or not the greenskins were aware of it, there was a way down into this labyrinth somewhere beyond their lines, and any other choice I might have made was now moot. I turned back to Grifen.

'We go on,' I said.

SEVEN

THE NEXT DECISION I had to make was the all-important one of how best to maintain morale. I didn't think any of the troopers would actively defy a commissar, even Vorhees, whose concern for Drere looked like outweighing pretty much every other consideration, but simply abandoning our wounded wasn't going to be an option. It would leave everyone demoralised, wondering if they'd be the next to be left to die.

That's not a thought you want your troopers to start brooding on. It makes them jumpy and sloppy, and the next thing you know they're so concerned with preserving their own skins they're losing focus on the important stuff: fulfilling the mission objectives, and preserving mine.

I made a big show of consulting Logash where everyone could hear me.

'Are we likely to run into any more of these creatures?' I asked. He frowned uncertainly.

'Possibly,' he said at last. 'But I doubt it. We seem to have a breeding pair and their offspring here, and given the average size of a family group...'

'I'll take that as a no,' I said firmly, cutting him off before he could bog us all down in extraneous detail. 'Which means we can safely divide our forces.' As I'd expected, a flicker of interest passed around the faces surrounding me, except of course for Drere and the medic, who were too busy bleeding to take much notice. And Jurgen, who rarely showed much sign of interest in anything apart from porno slates.

'Divide how?' Grifen asked. I indicated the wounded, and Vorhees hovering anxiously over his recumbent girlfriend.

'Second team's down to three effectives, and it'll take two of those to carry Drere,' I said. Vorhees's head came up like a hound hearing a ration pack being opened, a spark of hope kindling in his eyes. 'That'll leave one to take point, and pick off any of the creatures we might have missed.' Grifen nodded, understanding and relief mingled in the gesture.

'You're sending them back,' she said, a statement rather than a question. I nodded.

'The sooner the better,' I added, before turning to Karta. 'Better get moving, corporal. We're counting on you.' Not that I gave a frak, you understand, but it sounded good, and it passed the buck nicely; if anyone died before making it to the medicae at least it was out of my hands now. Karta saluted.

'We'll make it,' he asserted, and peeled off to organise his people.

'Am I to understand we're moving on at half strength?' Logash asked, clearly wondering what in the warp I thought I was playing at. I indicated the skull he'd dug up.

'First team, Jurgen and I are,' I said. 'There's obviously a way down here from behind the ork lines, even if the greenskins haven't noticed it yet, and we're not going back until we've found it and plugged the hole in our defences.' Needless to say I wasn't expecting to actually encounter any of the brutes, or run into anything else down here capable of harming us now that we'd slaughtered the ambulls, or I'd never have dreamed of doing such a thing. At the time, though, I was just trying to find a reasonable excuse to linger down here for a while and avoid the gargant.

'I see.' Logash considered it carefully, taking on that half-lost look again. 'Then I assume I should continue to accompany you.'

I hadn't actually considered it, to be honest. I'd have welcomed the chance to get rid of him if the thought had occurred to me, but on reflection he would only slow the wounded down if he tagged along with them, and I supposed his auspex might come in handy. All in all it was marginally preferable to keep him with us, I decided.

'I suppose so,' I said, leaving Jurgen to keep an eye on him, and turning back to watch the wounded depart. I had a final word with Karta, making sure Kasteen would hear about the ork skull we'd found and reinforce the mine entrance until we got back. Then we wished them

the Emperor's speed and watched the bobbing lights from their luminators recede up the tunnel.

'Well,' Grifen said after a while, summing up what we all felt. 'Best get
to it then. No point waiting around, is there?'

Despite my confidence that we were alone down here, we moved out
in full combat order. Hail was on point, her lasgun held with the casual
readiness of the veteran, and I found the sight reassuring. Simla followed her. The two of them worked well together, sharing an intuitive
understanding which probably meant they had a personal association
going as well; only to be expected in a mixed unit, of course. Behind
him was Lunt, the squad heavy weapon specialist, who carried a flamer.
That was something else I was pleased to find ahead of me rather than
behind, although he had shown enough restraint to refrain from using
it during the fight in the ambull den, relying instead on the laspistol he
wore holstered at his belt.[1] (Just as well, really, as he'd probably have
barbecued his squad mates as easily as the animals.) Tall and heavy-set,
he carried the weight of his twin promethium tanks with ease, the liquid within them sloshing quietly as he walked.

I came next, along with Logash, Jurgen and Grifen, who kept a little
behind us and as far from my aide as possible, while Trooper Magot, a
small redheaded woman with disturbingly hard eyes, took up the rear.
Out of the entire squad she was the only one to address Grifen as 'sarge'
instead of 'sergeant,' and moved with the easy grace of an experienced
soldier. (I learned later that they'd served together for some time, and
she'd requested a transfer to Grifen's squad when her friend was promoted; beyond that I felt it prudent not to enquire.)

Despite everyone's unspoken apprehension we encountered no
more of the ambulls, which came as an immense relief believe you
me, and the only footfalls we heard were our own. Like everyone
else, I kept my ears open for the harsh guttural sounds of ork voices
and the crunch of iron-shod boots in the rime ahead of us, but the
only noises to be heard were the almost subliminal creaks and pops
of the slowly-shifting ice. We must have been moving for some time,
I recall, as the vox messages from second team had faded to inaudi-
bility by this point, when Logash stopped to examine the walls of
the tunnel.

'How very curious,' he said.

---

1. *Although not prescribed by regulations, many support weapon troopers and vehicle crews
carry a back up sidearm in case they have to abandon their heavy equipment or it malfunctions in the heat of the battle. (Of course if a flamer malfunctions there isn't likely to be all
that much left of the trooper carrying it, but Lunt was evidently an optimist.)*

'What is?' I asked, caution taking precedence over the surge of irritation I felt when his metallic elbow jabbed into my ribs as I stumbled into him. By way of reply he scraped a handful of ice from the wall. It crumbled, to reveal the dark grey surface of some kind of rock behind it, still grooved with the marks of the ambull's claws.

'We're below the ice layer. Actually down into the bedrock of the planet. Quite fascinating.'

'I'm glad you're finding the trip so entertaining,' I said, but the tech-priest was almost as impervious to sarcasm as Jurgen, and nodded in response.

'Not quite the word I'd choose, but it certainly beats recalibrating the interociters,' he said cheerfully. I had no idea what he meant, of course, so I smiled and suggested we get moving again. Unfortunately getting his legs going didn't slow down his mouth, and he prattled on about the underlying geology of the mountain range at inordinate length.

'Mountains are just there, aren't they?' Jurgen asked after some time had passed, blinking in befuddlement. Logash shook his head.

'To our limited perception of time, yes. But on a geological timescale, which is to say on the order of millions of years, a planet's crust is as fluid as a pan full of stew on the stove.' Well he understood which metaphors would appeal to Jurgen, I had to give him that. 'The lower strata rise to the surface, and are gradually worn down again by the processes of erosion.'

'So what you're saying,' Jurgen said slowly, 'is that these mountains are like a very large carrot?' I kept my face straight with an effort, although a strangulated snort escaped from Magot who was behind me.

'In a manner of speaking.' Logash was clearly unsure whether Jurgen was taking the frak or not. 'Floating on the surface of the pot. A few million years ago this whole area would have been an open plain, or the bottom of an ocean.'

'How can you have an ocean when everything's frozen?' Jurgen asked, all innocence. But Logash nodded as though pleased with a promising student.

'A good question.' He went on after a moment's thought, ignoring my aide's expression of pleased surprise. 'In its early history this would have been a far more hospitable world. But it's just too far from the sun, and it cooled down gradually. Where we are now is on a continental shelf, which is why we've penetrated as far as the bedrock. The ice goes down for tens of kilometres just out from the mountain range, which would have been an island chain in those days. Or perhaps this was a coastal plain which flooded as the oceans froze and increased in volume.'[1]

---

1. *Almost certainly the latter, given Cain's subsequent discovery.*

'There's something up ahead,' Hail reported a moment later, and I hurried forward to join her, grateful for the excuse to get away from the endless babbling. That may sound harsh, but believe me, after several hours of non-stop logorrhoea you'd have felt the same. As I did so I felt the palms of my hands begin to tingle.

'What is it?' I asked, joining her. She was halted next to the entrance to a side tunnel and peering round it. The luminator taped to the barrel of her lasgun skipped its cone of light around the walls and floor.

That was when it hit me. Unlike the irregular ambull tunnels we'd been following, this corridor was squared off, composed of regular lines and angles beneath its coating of ice. There was no telling who might have built it, of course, or anything else for that matter, as the frozen epidermis effectively obscured every detail.

'Lunt,' I ordered after a moment's thought. 'Get up here.' The hulking trooper ambled across to us, and aimed his flamer down the mysterious passageway, seeking a target. It stretched into the distance, swallowing our luminator beams as though they were the most tenuous of candle flames. After a moment he triggered the weapon, sending a gout of burning promethium down the corridor ahead of us, blasting the shadows from the corners and replacing them with flickering orange spectres. Steam hissed and water dripped from the walls as the pool of burning accelerant roared away on the floor, melting the ice around it.

The hairs on the back of my neck rose. It's an odd sensation, and one I've seldom felt. Grim memories from years before came flooding back as I recognised the obsidian architecture surrounding us, finely polished stone of absolute blackness seeming somehow to suck the light into itself, all the darker and more forbidding for the faint reflective sheen which coated it.

'Omnissiah preserve us,' Logash breathed at my elbow, and for a moment I thought he'd recognised it too. But the words that followed betrayed an ignorance that was almost blissful. 'We must make a full record of this at once. We had no idea that the planet was once inhabited...'

'Everyone out,' I commanded. 'Break out the demo charges and prepare to seal this now.'

'Commissar?' Grifen looked a little confused. I suppose she might have been forgiven for wondering if I'd gone a bit siggy[1], but by that

---

1. *A colloquial reference to the Guard medicae sanitorium in the Sigma Pavonis system where troopers suffering from mental illness and combat fatigue are sent for assessment and rehabilitation. The less chronic cases are returned to duty after treatment, while the more severe ones can receive long-term care, sometimes for years. Co-incidentally, the system's other claim to fame is as a manufactoria of combat servitors, many of which find their way into Inquisitorial service.*

point the last thing on my mind was how I appeared to the other ranks. 'Those are supposed to be used to seal the tunnels off from the orks.'

'There are worse things than greenskins,' I said. Grifen looked a little sceptical at this, what with the orks being the Valhallans' ancient blood enemy and all that (don't get me wrong, they'd happily pile into any of the Emperor's enemies who happened along, but give them a choice and they'd kill greenies every time), but took my word for it.

'Are you mad?' Logash raised his voice, clearly determined to challenge me. 'The knowledge contained in there could be priceless. We don't know why this structure was built, or by whom...'

'I do,' I said and pointed to one of the walls, where a curious arrangement of lines and circles was partially visible through a curtain of half-melted ice. It was illuminated by the dying flames of the promethium pool. 'The necrons built it.'

The name didn't mean anything to most of them, of course. Only Jurgen had encountered them before aside from myself, and that far less up close and personal than the terrors I'd escaped from on Interitus Prime. But the troopers seemed willing to take my word for it, at least. If only I could say the same for the tech-priest.

'But you can't just blow up a discovery of this magnitude!' Logash was practically beside himself. 'Think of the archeotech that must be down there! Destroying it would be a crime against the Omnissiah!'

'Frak the Omnissiah,' I said, finally shutting him up. 'I swore an oath to serve the Emperor, not a bucket of bolts, and that's exactly what I intend to do. Have you any idea what would happen if there are dormant necrons down there and we did something to disturb them?'

'I'm sure your soldiers could deal with them whatever they are,' Logash replied stiffly.

'Well I'm not,' I said without thinking. Then I remembered who else was there and carried on as though I'd meant to say more all along. 'I'd back this regiment against everything from eldar to daemons, but even the best soldiers in the Guard couldn't stand long against a full-scale necron incursion. These things aren't even alive as we understand the term. They can't be reasoned with, they can't be intimidated, and if they have the numbers on their side they simply can't be stopped. They'll just keep coming until every living thing on this planet is dead!' I was uncomfortably aware as I finished that my voice had risen in pitch. I fought it back to a semblance of calm.

'You're not being rational about this,' Logash said. 'If there were active necrons down here they would have killed the ambulls, surely?'

'Just for starters,' I said. My old nightmare of orks pouring through these narrow passageways bent on plunder and destruction seemed positively comforting now. I fought down memories of those blank metallic faces, fashioned in the semblance of skulls, advancing through a hail of hellgun fire as though it were a refreshing spring rain, and shuddered in horror. Logash might have a point, I supposed, the temple or whatever it was might well be abandoned, but then we'd thought that on Interitus Prime as well. And look how that had turned out. Entering so unhallowed a place was simply too dangerous to contemplate, and if Logash and his pals were that keen to take such an insane risk they could damn well do it once the orks were taken care of and we were long gone.

Not that I intended waiting around on this iceball until we'd got rid of the greenskins. Finding a necron artifact changed everything, and our best course of action was simply to evacuate our forces back to the *Pure of Heart*, turn the whole matter over to the Inquisition, and have done with it. I might even get to renew my acquaintance with Amberley, which would at least be one blessing in the affair – assuming she didn't drag me off on another suicidal escapade in the name of the Ordo Xenos of course.

Grifen didn't need telling twice, and was already breaking out the demo charges. Once again my undeserved reputation was working to my advantage, and she no doubt thought that anything bad enough to leave a hero of the Imperium in need of clean undergarments was something she didn't want to meet.

'You can't do this! I simply won't let you!' Logash practically screamed like a petulant child as Simla and Hail placed the charges. He stepped forward as if to interfere. Jurgen barred his way with the melta, and shook his head.

'Best to keep out of the way, sir,' he said. Logash raised a hand to the barrel, as though about to slap it out of the way. I was suddenly uneasily aware of how much strength he might have in his augmetic limbs, and Emperor alone knew what other little alterations the baggy robe might conceal. I stepped forward, ostentatiously loosening the laspistol in the holster at my belt.

'Might I remind you,' I said levelly, 'that this world is currently under martial law. That means you're as subject to my authority as any member of the Guard, and I'm fully within my rights to deal summarily with any attempt to interfere with the protection of this installation.' He took my meaning at once, but with ill grace, and subsided. He glared at me with an expression of malevolent disgust completely at odds with the demeanor of cheerful idiocy I'd come to expect. I suppose I might have found it intimidating if I hadn't been glared at by experts in my time (and trust me, until you've hacked off a daemon you've got no idea of what a real glare is), so I returned his gaze levelly until he broke eye contact.

'Typical meatbag[1] behaviour,' he sneered, failing miserably to regain any dignity. 'Just trample on anything you don't understand. You're no better than the orks.' Considering he was surrounded by heavily armed Valhallans it wasn't exactly the most tactful thing he might have said, but to their credit the troopers continued working with undiminished efficiency, merely breaking off for a second to stare sullenly at him. He must have realised he'd overstepped the mark, though, because he was quiet after that, apart from occasional barely audible mutterings about meatbag barbarians.

'If it's any consolation,' I reassured him, 'we're not destroying anything.' Not from choice, mind, but if the necron architecture I'd come across before was anything to go by the strange black stone would simply be too resilient to be seriously damaged by the meagre quantities of explosive we had at our disposal. 'We're merely sealing it off as a precaution. Once the refinery's safe you can grub around down here to your heart's content.' Just so long as I was at least a sector away by that point. Logash still looked sulky, but slightly mollified.

'Fire in the hole!' Magot bellowed, with rather too much relish for my liking, and we retreated to what I hoped would be a safe distance before she hit the detonator.

The explosion was satisfactorily loud, bringing down a chunk of the corridor ceiling, which proved to be composed of cubical blocks of the strange black stone roughly the length of my forearm. They tumbled down in disarray, followed by chunks of ice and bedrock that formed a solid-looking seal over the mouth of the corridor, reducing the ambull run we'd been following, to half its original width for a dozen paces or so.

'Shady!' Magot said, with evident satisfaction. 'I'd like to see anything get past that.'

'No you wouldn't,' I said. Solid as the blockage seemed, if there really were necrons beyond it they wouldn't take long to dig their way out. Those metal bodies were tireless and implacable, their weapons and equipment so powerful they made the most sophisticated toys of the Adeptus Mechanicus look like sharpened sticks. I forced the image of ancient horrors out of my mind again.

'Well if that was the way the ambulls got an ork down here it's pretty well sealed,' Grifen said. I nodded. It seemed likely, but I supposed we

---

1. *A derisive Adeptus Mechanicus slang term for the unaugmented, who they hold in noticeable contempt. Which, to be fair, is generally reciprocated.*

had to be sure. With an effort I dragged my mind back to the mission at hand.

'We'll make a final sweep and head back,' I decided, to everyone's relief. 'We have to report this. It takes priority over everything.'

'Commissar!' Simla called, from the other side of the spoil heap. 'Take a look at this!'

Cursing, I rounded the pile of rubble, homing in on the light from his luminator to find the sharp-featured trooper crouching over something metallic which had evidently been frozen into the floor of the tunnel and dislodged by the explosion. A crudely made bolter of some kind, the barrel sheared off by what looked like claw marks.

'An ork shoota,' I said unnecessarily. 'It must have been dropped by the one the ambulls killed while they were dragging it back to the den.' Simla nodded.

'So it must have come from further up the tunnel.'

Great. The hole in our defenses was still wide open. I dithered for a moment, but in the end there was really no other choice. The necron threat, though terrible, was only a potential one, and had been contained for the time being. But the orks remained a clear and present danger, and would do so until we'd completed our mission. Slowly and reluctantly I stood.

'Sergeant!' I called. 'Move them out. We're going on.'

Editorial Note:

Again I must apologise for inflicting another example of Sulla's overly purple prose on my patient readers (except for those of you who, quite understandably, may choose to skip it.) I do so because events were still moving along on the surface of the planet even as Cain made his disturbing discovery in the depths of the mine. And, as before I feel it important to present a little more background detail than Cain's typically self-centred narrative provides.

We pick up her account of events at a point where her platoon had been rotated back from the front lines for rest and recuperation, after taking a number of casualties while repelling a series of increasingly determined ork assaults.

Extracted from *Like a Phoenix From the Flames: The Founding of the 597th*, by General Jenit Sulla (retired), 097.M42

I'M PROUD TO say that despite the loss of so many gallant comrades in arms, whose sacrifice will ever be remembered,[1] our morale remained high and our determination resolute. Though the greenskins were

---

1. *Though not, apparently, their names, as she doesn't bother to record them.*

undeniably a nuisance, we had sent them packing on every occasion they troubled us, and it was almost with a sense of reluctance that we pulled back from our beleaguered redoubt and gave it into the care of Lieutenant Faril and the eager warriors under his command.

Wiser heads than ours had made the decision to relieve us, however, so there was no point in appealing it, and so we picked up our wounded and joined the trickle of tired but still resolute soldiery and headed back to the main refinery complex for a hot meal and a few hours of sleep. We were secure in the knowledge that the fray was far from over and that we would shortly once again have our chance to wreak the Emperor's vengeance on the greenskin barbarians who had had the effrontery to encroach on His sacred dominions.

As we trudged through the snow the sky above us was bright with the trails of the shuttles from our sturdy transport ship, and I reflected how beneficent fate, or the guidance of His Glorious Majesty, had so arranged matters that even now, as we faced and bested His bestial foes, His loyal subjects were being taken to the safety which our doughty vessel afforded. Indeed, the truth of the soldier's maxim, 'The Emperor Protects,' had seldom been made manifest to me with such crystal clarity.

It was while I was reflecting thus, and enjoying an unexpectedly lavish meal of the soylens viridians which the tech-priests who ran this palace of wonders had so generously provided from their own resources, that Colonel Kasteen summoned me to the command centre.

Upon my arrival my attention was immediately seized by the hololithic display, which the colonel was consulting along with Major Broklaw, Captain Federer of the engineering contingent, and a civilian I was given to understand had something to do with the mining operation here.[1]

As I listened to the plan which the colonel began to unfold, I was stunned by its boldness and elegance. For it was nothing less than to lure the loathsome greenskins into a trap which would surely annihilate both them and their awesome engine of war which, even as we spoke, was edging ever nearer. How fitting it seemed to use the creatures' impetuosity and overconfidence to lure them to their own destruction!

As I considered the plan in detail the keen intelligence behind the order to pull my platoon back became instantly apparent to me. By

---

1. *Undoubtedly Morel.*

replacing the weary units at the front with fewer numbers of fresh soldiers our forces could maintain the illusion of remaining at full strength, at least for the few hours necessary to prepare our trap, while we could continue to gradually reduce the number of defenders. When the time came we could easily pull the remainder back to lure our enemies in, covering our own forces' retreat from our positions on either side, and catching the orks in a withering crossfire which ought to distract them for long enough to detonate the mine.

From the sombreness of Colonel Kasteen's demeanour I had expected to be given the honour of acting as the lure in this most cunning of stratagems, but it seemed even greater glory was to be ours. The colonel explained that within the hour she had received a message from the gallant Commissar Cain, who even as she spoke was continuing his heroic reconnaissance of the lowest levels of the mine, to the disturbing effect that it was possible the greenskins had found a way into the tunnels. Though all were confident that a hero of his stature would easily repel any of the bestial foe incautious enough to venture there, it was felt necessary to provide an armed escort for the sappers and miners who were to prepare our trap; and since Second Squad of my own platoon had ventured into those very tunnels no more than a day before, with the commissar himself, we were the obvious choice for this vital assignment.

I must own up to it, my breast swelled with pride as I contemplated the honour of the task with which we had been entrusted, and assured the colonel that we would indeed prove worthy of her confidence.

EIGHT

NEEDLESS TO SAY the decision to continue our assignment was far from universally popular, although no one apart from Logash voiced any dissent. Grifen and her team were professional enough to understand the necessity of ensuring the safety of our comrades, not to mention ourselves, and so we pushed on in uneasy silence. The only sounds were the crunching of our boot soles in the thick frost that still coated the tunnel floor and the tech-priest's *sotto voce* imprecations. Besides which, no one in our party could have been more reluctant to proceed than me, you can depend on it. Every instinct of self-preservation I possessed urged me to flee the caverns at once, and find some excuse to board the first shuttle back to the relative safety of the *Pure of Heart*.

'Commissar?' Jurgen asked, and I suddenly became aware that I was murmuring one of the Catechisms of Command under my breath, something I swear I'd never done consciously since leaving the schola. Just goes to show how spooked I was.

'Nothing,' I said hastily, hawking a gob of rapidly cooling phlegm into the encircling darkness. 'Just clearing my throat.'

'Oh. Right.' He nodded, in his usual imperturbable fashion, and walked on, melta held ready across his body. Logash gave me a nasty look.

'"Fear is the mind killer," eh?' he asked, which at least told me his hearing was preternaturally augmented. 'I think you've already proved that today.' I could hardly believe it: here we were, caught between two of the nastiest foes you could ever hope not to meet, and he was still sulking about not being allowed to loot the bloody tomb.

'At least I've still got enough of a mind to know I ought to be scared,' I snapped back. We glared at each other like pre-schola juves whose vocabulary is too limited to prolong an exchange of verbal abuse, and for all I knew we'd have descended to shoving and finger-poking if Hail hadn't cut in on my comm-bead.

'I can see light up ahead.'

A shiver of apprehension shot through me. We were still deeply underground, and although the tunnel floor had been rising gently for the last couple of kilometres my natural affinity for these conditions told me we should be nowhere near the surface.

'Hold position,' I ordered, my irritation with the truculent tech-priest already forgotten, and hurried forward to join her. Jurgen's familiar odour followed, and we overtook Lunt and Simla. The big heavy weapons specialist watched as we passed, and began to ready his flamer, which now we were in front it was rather less comforting than his show of initiative might otherwise have been.

As we approached Hail's position I clicked off my luminator, and a moment later Jurgen did the same. As was my habit I closed my eyes as we did so, knowing my dark vision would adjust a little faster, for such things can mean life or death in these situations and all too often do. To my relief Hail had doused her own light, either from training or common sense, so there was nothing to impede my perceptions as I moved up to join her.

'Over here, sir.' The whisper came from one of the deeper shadows, into which the woman had blended almost invisibly. Her skin was very dark, almost the colour of recaf, and she used this natural advantage to the fullest.[1] As she moved her silhouette came into focus, backlit by a soft, greyish radiance from somewhere further down the tunnel. I sighed with relief. I'd been dreading the sight of the sick, greenish glow which had permeated the necron tomb I'd penetrated before, and the realisation that whatever we were coming to had nothing to do with them hit me with an intensity akin to euphoria.

---

1. *This was extremely unusual for a Valhallan; perhaps as a result of living underground they generally tend to the lightest of complexions. Hail's colouration is the norm on many other worlds in the sector, however, where the white skin typical of her homeworld would seem equally unusual, so it's probable that an ancestor or two of hers settled there after relocating for some reason.*

'Any sign of movement?' I asked, and Hail shook her head, a barely-visible motion in the darkness which I sensed as much as saw.

'Nothing yet,' she said.

'Good.' I stood still for a moment, letting my tunnel rat's senses attune to this change in our environment. As my eyes adjusted fully the pale glow seemed to strengthen, a faint, irregular disc about the size of my thumbnail throwing the darker stone around it into stark relief. And there was a faint current of air on my face too, sharp with the smell of cold and heavy with damp. Impossible as it seemed, it looked very much like a fissure to the surface. 'I think this is it,' I concluded.

'Surely we're far too far underground?' Logash queried at my elbow. Lost in my reverie I hadn't noticed him tagging along, and I started momentarily, to his unconcealed amusement.

'Could be the bottom of a crevasse,' Jurgen volunteered. It sounded plausible to me, and he had grown up on a world like this, so I nodded.

'That would explain our dead ork,' I said. 'It just fell down into the tunnels here.' Maybe the fall had killed it and the ambull who brought it home just got lucky, although in my experience it would take more than dropping a few hundred metres down a hole to finish off a green-skin for sure, especially if it landed on its head.

'So this whole expedition has been a colossal waste of time,' Logash concluded. I shook my head.

'Far from it. If one ork found the hole, others could, and they can climb down a rope just as easily as any other species.' That's not entirely true, of course, they're clumsy brutes at the best of times, but they're determined and resilient, and sometimes that's enough.

'Best go on and check it out then,' Hail said, more for the pleasure of contradicting the tech-priest than supporting me I suspected, but the display of solidarity was welcome nevertheless.

'I think so,' I said, and moved on, the others taking up their positions around me as we continued on towards the gradually intensifying glow. As we got closer the faint current of air grew stronger, and the almost tolerable low temperatures of the tunnels began to drop rapidly, so that I found myself shivering again even through the thick weave of my greatcoat.

'Smells like snow,' Grifen said cautiously. 'We must be getting close.' I was prepared to take her word for it, after all she knew snow and ice the way I did tunnels. I was mildly surprised to see even the stoic Val-hallan pulling her greatcoat just a little tighter. If I could trust her instincts as strongly as I believed, that didn't augar well.

In the event we were even closer than we realised. We turned a corner, skirting an outcrop of some deeply-veined rock I didn't bother listening to

Logash identify, and the full force of the blood-chilling cold I'd experienced after the shuttle crash hit me in the face along with a weak shaft of sunlight which seemed almost dazzling after the gloom of the tunnels.

'Emperor's bowels!' I said, pulling my scarf up over my mouth and nose, feeling sharp shards of pain skitter through my abused lungs. Somehow, incredibly, the ambull tunnel had broken the surface, hundreds of metres deeper than should have been possible. But we were undeniably outside again.

'Interesting,' Logash said, not even shivering, Emperor rot his augmented hide. Snow whirled in around us, stinging our eyes, and obscuring everything in front of us from sight. He pondered for a moment. 'Perhaps a small valley, cutting into the mountains...'

I considered it, overlaying a rough estimate of our position on the orbital images I'd seen in the *Pure of Heart's* hololithic bridge display. It was perfectly possible that we'd come right through the heart of the ridge forming one of the sides of the valley protecting the refinery complex, and found ourselves at the bottom of a defile of some kind that cut into it from the other side.

If so, that was both good and bad news. Bad in that there was indeed a way through the tunnels which breached our defences, but on the plus side we would be a long way from the main body of the besieging orks. The only ones this far down the other side of the ridge would be stragglers or scouting parties like the one we'd encountered before.

Even shivering as I already was, the thought was enough to send an additional chill through me. There was no telling how many such groups had struck out ahead of the main advance,[1] and if one had already discovered the tunnel entrance and reported back the entire army could be on its way to take advantage of it. Well, perhaps not that many, but a large enough force to cause us some real problems if they got loose behind our defensive line. (Not that it was going to hold for a second once the gargant arrived, of course, so I was just having to thumb my palm[2] that Kasteen had come up with some strategy to deal with it while we were running around in the tunnels.)

---

1. *Not that many, in all likelihood. 'Kommandos' as they're known (a loan word from some human culture according to the Ordo Diologus, as orks aren't able to conceptualise anything to do with subtlety for themselves) are quite rare among the greenskin forces. Most lack the patience or, to be blunt, intelligence for anything other than a brute force frontal attack. Which makes these occasional exceptions a danger out of all proportion to their limited numbers, as they generally succeed in taking their targets completely by surprise.*

2. *A good luck gesture Cain appeared to have retained from his early childhood, wherever that was actually spent.*

'Tracks.' Magot was kneeling on the ice a few metres back from the curtain of whirling snow, staring at it intensely. I couldn't see a thing myself, but once again I found myself putting my full confidence in the Valhallans' natural affinity for these dreadful conditions. Grifen moved to join her, squatting beside her friend.

'Looks like,' she agreed. 'Ork boots, I'd say.'

'How many?' I managed to ask, through the muffling scarf and my rapidly numbing facial muscles. Magot shrugged.

'One pair?' She didn't sound terribly sure. 'The floor's chewed up around here something awful.'

'One ork,' Logash confirmed, scanning the floor with his metal eyes, a hint of impatience entering his voice. 'And ambull tracks. The green-skin must have wandered in, disturbed it, and ended up as lunch.'

'Only one ork?' I asked. 'You're absolutely sure?'

'Of course,' Logash said. 'It's completely clear to anyone with the right eyes to see these things.' Normally I'd have found the hint of the typical tech-priest arrogance returning to his voice irritating, I admit, but at the time it almost came as a relief. I assumed it meant he was getting over his sulkiness. But I had more pressing concerns to consider.

'Then what happened to the others?' I wondered aloud. Orks were obnoxious and quarrelsome, but they were curiously sociable in their own brutal fashion, and our solitary ambull victim wouldn't have been out here alone. True, his friends wouldn't waste all that much time looking for him once they noticed he was missing, but they might still be in the vicinity. And that meant they could stumble in here just as easily as their erstwhile companion.

'A good question,' Logash conceded. 'I suppose you'll want to scout around and make sure there are no more of them outside?'

Well actually that was the last thing I wanted to do, but it was necessary, and I couldn't back down in front of the troopers now that someone had verbalised the thought, so I nodded.

'It's the only way to be sure,' I agreed, managing to conceal my reluctance tolerably well I believed. I was not quite sure whether I detected the ghost of a vindictive smile on the tech-priest's face.

Conditions outside were even worse than I could possibly have imagined. The snow continued to flurry all around us, driven by a wind keener than an eldar wych's flensing knife, and I found my eyes shutting reflexively before I was a handful of paces from the cave mouth. With a thrill of panic I realised I couldn't open them again: the wind-driven tears had frozen on my face and sealed them closed. I was just about to give way to the impulse to retrace my steps (a sure way of stumbling to my death down a crevasse or terminal hypothermia away from the vigilance of my companions), when a reassuring arm settled across my shoulders. I inhaled Jurgen's acrid odour gratefully, as though it were the bouquet of a fine vintage, mildly surprised to find that my nose was still working.

'Hold on, commissar.' Something settled across my face, and the stinging in my eyes abated a little. I blinked them clear, forcing them stickily apart, feeling the partially-melted ice crystals slither round the corners of my eye sockets. Jurgen's face came blearily into focus, the portion of it between his scarf and thick fur hat obscured by a pair of snow goggles identical to the ones I now realised were protecting my own sight. 'That should do it.'

'Thank you Jurgen,' I managed to force out through practically immobilised face muscles. His scarf twitched as though concealing a smile.

'Lucky I usually carry a spare.' That was the closest he would ever come to uttering a reproof, but he had every right to do so of course. The goggles were standard kit in a Valhallan regiment, and I had a pair of my own packed away somewhere in my quarters, but it had never occurred to me I might need them in the depths of the mine where whiteout conditions weren't exactly common. So once again I had cause to thank the Emperor for my aide's streak of thoroughness.

To my complete lack of surprise every trooper in first team had donned a pair as well, but, like Jurgen, these conditions were common to them. Warp it, judging by their body language, most of them were actually enjoying these hellish temperatures.

'Chill enough for you, sir?' Magot asked cheerfully, seemingly genuinely unaware of just how intolerable I was finding it.

'Wouldn't mind a pot of tanna about now,' I conceded, deciding the best approach was game but suffering a little more than I was willing to admit (rather than a hell of a lot more.) That way they'd keep a closer eye on me without resenting it.

'Wouldn't mind a brew myself,' she admitted, before trotting away to take her turn on point.

'This is all a complete waste of time you know,' Logash grumbled. I swear I would have missed him entirely if he hadn't spoken: his white robe was almost invisible in the swirling snow, and only his pale face and metallic eyes appeared wholly in focus. He appeared to hang in the air in front of me like an extreme version of Mazarin's levitation act. 'If there were any more orks around they'll be kilometres away by now. Or frozen to death.'

He was a fine one to talk, I thought, barely even seeming to notice the sub-zero temperatures. Once again I found myself wondering precisely what that robe concealed.

'They're a lot more resilient than you might think,' I pointed out, and Lunt nodded in passing.

'My grandfather found one frozen in a glacier once, back home, left over from the invasions. When they got it back to their camp and thawed it out it came back to life and tried to kill them. It's true, that's what he said.'

Him and every other Valhallan's grandfather, of course, 'The ork in the ice' is one of the most popular folktales on the planet, but I doubted that Logash would know that, so I nodded confirmation.[1]

'So I'd keep looking over my shoulder if I were you,' I added. I can't be sure, but I think Lunt winked at me, enjoying winding up the outsider and treating me as if I was Valhallan myself. Of course I've spent so much of my career serving with them I often find that I've picked up something of their speech patterns, dietary preferences, and so on. I suppose it's not all that surprising that they seem to have adopted me as one of their own in many ways.[2]

'We're in a defile, all right,' Grifen told me, glancing around at the barely visible topography. 'You can tell by the pattern of the snowflakes.' They just looked like a swirling wall of white to me, but I nodded as though I understood. I didn't actually need to know, of course: one of the most important principles of leadership is knowing when to rely on the judgement of your subordinates. But it's always a good idea to look interested.

'Can you tell which way the orks would have gone?' I asked. She nodded.

'They won't have left any tracks we can follow in this blizzard, but that way,' she gestured in what looked to me like a random direction, 'is closed off by the head of the valley. My best guess would be downslope.'

'Fair enough,' I decided. 'We'll check as far as the mouth of the defile. If there are any greenskins out here we'll find them. If not we can pull back and collapse the cave behind us.'

'That might be difficult,' she pointed out. 'We used most of our demo charges to seal the... whatever it was back down the passage.'

---

1. *And like many folk tales, there may be an element of truth to it. Although there's no way to be sure, there are still occasional reports of solitary orks being sighted in the Valhallan wilderness, sometimes even backed up by bodies. Chances are these are just corpses left over from the invasion preserved by the cold, but you can never take anything for granted where these creatures are concerned.*

2. *Actually, given the relationship between most commissars and the troops they serve with, this is pretty remarkable. As so often in his memoirs, Cain gives himself far too little credit for his own achievements.*

'We'll think of something,' I said, with more confidence than I felt. The constant swirling of the snow was making me feel vaguely nauseous, the cold was cramping my stomach muscles painfully, and my head felt as though someone was squeezing it in a vice. The sooner we got this over with the better. 'Jurgen's still got the melta, and I'm sure our cogboy friend will be able to point out a few weak spots in the ceiling.'

'I suppose you're right,' the sergeant said, and I glanced around, expecting some response from Logash, but the surly young tech-priest had vanished into the storm as thoroughly as though he'd never even existed.

I have to admit to feeling rather less sanguine on that point than she seemed to be. He was, after all, effectively invisible to us in the swirling snow, and I didn't think we stood a chance of finding him under these conditions in any way other than stumbling over him by accident. But if anyone could pick up his trail I supposed it would be the Valhallans, so I nodded in return.

'Better get moving then,' I said, echoing her words of a couple of hours before.

It wasn't that simple, of course. As I've already mentioned, the wind was sweeping up the defile, which was liberally strewn with grey, jagged rocks. These loomed up suddenly out of the swirling blanket of snow, promising a moment of respite from the razor-edged wind which, time and again, proved to be merely a delusion. The irregular topography simply broke the onrush of air into flurries and eddies which dashed handfuls of snow into these pockets of illusory shelter, adding a sudden unexpected lash of stinging ice crystals to an already miserable experience. The only consolation, if that was the right word, was that what little exposed skin I still had was completely numb by this time.

I slipped and slithered down the slope behind Grifen, grateful for the stolid presence of Jurgen behind me; several times he reached out a supporting hand just in time to prevent me from sprawling face down in the knee-deep snow. The Valhallans remained completely sure-footed, but any amusement they may have felt at my floundering progress was well concealed. Glancing back I could see that the furrows we'd left behind us were already beginning to fill with the ever-shifting drifts, and that without my companions' sure instinct for these ghastly conditions we would almost certainly never find the cave mouth again. That, at least, was something of a relief, as the chances of any green-skins stumbling across it were beginning to look reassuringly remote.

On the downside though, any tracks Logash had left would be obscured as completely as our own, so once again it seemed we weren't likely to stumble across him by any means other than sheer blind luck.

At least with all those augmetics I supposed he wasn't likely to freeze to death, in the short term at any rate, but right now I was beginning to think that was a very mixed blessing.

I had, by this time, lost sight of all my companions save for the reassuring presence of Jurgen, their camouflage greatcoats blending so perfectly into the snowstorm that they were effectively invisible. For that matter so was I; my dark commissar's uniform being so coated with the wind-driven flakes that I resembled one of those misshapen effigies children throughout the galaxy sculpt with the onset of winter. (On Valhalla, building snowmen is something of a cross between a serious art form and a competitive sport, with some quite astounding creations to marvel at, but that's beside the point.)

I was just on the verge of deciding that this was futile and ordering everyone to turn back, letting Logash take his chances with the elements as best he could, when Magot's voice crackled over my comm-bead.

'Contact, ninety metres down slope.' I could hardly see an arm's length in front of my own eyes, but she sounded confident enough. I was still trying to force my numb lips to form a reply when Grifen's voice cut into the net.

'Is it the cogboy?'

'Negative.' Magot's voice was tense. 'I can see a lot of movement down there.'

That could mean only one thing, of course, and I was already scrabbling for my laspistol with numb and nerveless fingers when she spoke again, confirming it.

'Greenies. Lots of them.'

'How many?' I asked, keeping hold of my weapon Emperor knows how, my fingers feeling thick and swollen in the cold. Luckily the augmetic ones were working as well as ever, at least enabling me to maintain my grip on the stock, but whether I'd be able to squeeze the trigger with my very real and probably frostbitten index finger would be problematic at best.[1]

'Hard to tell,' Magot replied. 'They're well spread out.' That was hardly surprising under the circumstances, the terrain being less than conducive to their normal habit of charging forward in a disorganized mob. 'But a dozen at least.'

'Contact.' Simla cut in too, and with a sudden thrill of horror I realised he was over to the left side of the defile, three hundred metres at least from Magot's position. No way he was seeing the same group. 'I've got seven. No, eight. Maybe more.'

'Me too,' Hail added, from our right flank. 'Looks like a full squad from here.'[2]

'Pull back,' I ordered. That made at least thirty, probably more, too many for us to take out here even with the Valhallans' ability to make use of the terrain and weather conditions to mount an effective

---

1. *Since Cain makes no subsequent mention of any medical treatment, we can infer that this is either exaggeration for effect or hypochondria rather than an accurate diagnosis.*

2. *Presumably meaning a group the size of an Imperial Guard squad, as ork mobs can vary greatly in size, and wouldn't recognise the concept of any formation as organised as this in any case.*

ambush. It also confirmed my worst fear (apart from the thought that the necrons were stirring down in the darkness beneath our feet.) The comrades of the dead ork we'd found had indeed made contact with the bulk of their army, and were on their way back with a full-scale raiding force intent on exploiting the gap they'd discovered in our defences. 'We have to secure the cave whatever happens.'

'Confirm that,' Grifen said, overriding whatever objections her subordinates might be on the verge of expressing. Not that I really expected any, but Valhallan antipathy to the greenskins ran deep, and the temptation to take a pot-shot at them before withdrawing must have been acute. To their credit no one gave way to it though, so I began to breathe a little more easily as we made our way back up the slope towards the welcome refuge of the cave. With any luck we'd be able to slip away before they even knew we were here.

I must confess that the thought of getting out of the bone-numbing wind was so strong, and so all-pervading, that I quite lost track of my surroundings. I stumbled through the snow like an automaton, following in the tracks ploughed by Jurgen, intent only on putting one leg in front of the other. The image of the tunnel mouth and the respite from the cold it represented loomed ever larger in my thoughts, driving out everything but the determination to keep my numbed and frozen limbs moving. So it was with a shock of genuine surprise that I heard the unmistakable report of a bolter round detonating against an outcrop of rock a few metres away.

Spurred by a sense of imminent danger I dropped out of my fugue state at once, bringing the laspistol in my hand around, seeking a target. A hulking shape loomed out of the snow, bounding forward with incredible speed, swinging a crudely-fashioned axe. So eager was it to spill my blood it seemed to have forgotten the primitive bolt pistol clutched in its other hand. I fired by reflex, finding that my panic-spurred finger was able to tighten on the trigger just fine now that the question was a practical one, blowing a hole through its torso. The creature staggered and came on, then dropped to the ground, already cooling, as a second las bolt took it from the side.

'Sergeant.' I acknowledged Grifen's assistance with a nod, and she gestured with her left hand, the right still holding her lasgun ready to fire.

'This way,' she said. I stumbled in her direction, sure that Jurgen would be with me as always, and in this I was soon proved correct. The unmistakable hiss of the melta opening up behind me made me turn, just in time to see my aide cut down a small group of the creatures that had evidently been following the first with a single ravening blast of thermal energy. After a moment spent scanning our surroundings he lowered the weapon and began slogging through the knee-high drifts towards us as implacably unconcerned as though he were out for an afternoon stroll. Maybe by the standards of his homeworld he was.

'Up here, commissar.' Lunt reached down from atop a tangle of rocks, grasping my outstretched hand, and lifting me bodily to the top without any apparent effort. Grifen scrambled up after us, barely slowing down, and a moment later Jurgen heaved himself over the rim, the bulky weapon now slung to facilitate climbing, and preceded as always by his unmistakable odour.

'I thought this would be a good spot to regroup,' Grifen said. I glanced around, feeling almost warm now that we were partially sheltered from the relentless wind, and nodded approvingly. She'd chosen an elevated position surrounded by tumbled boulders, from which we could look down on the tunnel entrance from an elevation of a couple of metres or so. That was good thinking: if the orks had made it there ahead of us after all there was no sense in walking up to the cave mouth wearing a big sign saying 'shoot me I'm here.' As I strained my eyes through the whirling snow I wasn't able to discern much, but as I've said before I'd trust her instincts where the greenskins were concerned.

Hail and Simla had made it to our refuge too, I was pleased to see, each raising a hand in greeting as Jurgen and I appeared before going back to scanning the horizon over the sights of their lasguns. I was just about to try contacting Magot and asking her position when a flurry of las-bolt detonations and a bellow of orkish pain somewhere off to our left answered that question quite satisfactorily. The diminutive redhead appeared in person a few moments later, grinning with malevolent amusement.

'There was this greenie over that way making a latrine stop,' she reported gleefully, 'so I shot him right up the...'

'Is it dead?' I interrupted. She nodded, still enjoying the approbation of her comrades, who seemed to think this was as hilarious as she did.

'Deader than Horus,' she confirmed. Good. Her tracks would have been all but obliterated by now, and with any luck the orks wouldn't have a clue where we were or how many of us they faced. Unless they found and interrogated Logash, of course, in which case it was credits to carrots they'd learn everything they needed to know in pretty short order. That left me with only one choice.

'We're pulling back to the cave as soon as we know it's clear,' I said. 'And prepare to collapse it behind us.'

'What about the tech-priest?' Grifen asked, clearly not terribly concerned, but sticking to the letter of her mission brief with admirable tenacity.

'He'll just have to fend for himself,' I said. Catching her look, I added 'I'll take the responsibility.' It went without saying, of course, that went with the scarlet sash.

'It's your call, commissar.' Well, she was right about that, but I could see abandoning a human to the mercy of the orks wasn't going to go down too well with the rank and file, even if he was an annoying little grox-fondler who'd brought it on himself, so I went all solemn.

'It goes against the grain I know,' I said. 'But our first duty is to the Emperor, the regiment, and our mission. The colonel has to know about the necron presence here. It changes everything, and until then the lives of all our comrades are at risk.'

Everyone nodded solemnly at that, apparently perfectly happy to hang the little tech-priest out to dry now I'd been able to make it seem like a noble sacrifice, and we prepared to move out.

As I glanced back down slope, straining my eyes through the swirling blanket of snow for some sign of another party of orks, I thought I caught a glimpse of something moving smoothly and silently through the frozen landscape. I inhaled, intending to call out, then dismissed the impulse as the blur of apparent motion vanished in the kaleidoscope of white. Chances were it was only wishful thinking on my part, I thought, and even if it was Logash he'd never hear me over the howling of the wind. Later, when I had the leisure to reflect on that moment, I was to shudder at how close I had probably come to dooming us all.

'It seems clear enough,' Grifen said, after a few more moments spent observing the cave entrance. So we moved cautiously towards it, putting our trust in the obscuring snow and what little concealment the rocks afforded. The troopers were well disciplined, I found, moving by stages as though we were already in combat, waiting until one of their comrades was in position to provide covering fire before moving to the next place of refuge. I did the same, falling into the rhythm with the instinct born of long practice.

At length we were ranged around the mouth of the cave. I stepped into it gratefully, feeling the barbed wind let go of my flesh, and gasping with the agony of returning circulation. For a moment or two my entire body felt as though I'd been hit by a flamer, then the pain subsided from unbearable to merely excruciating. Even so my survival instinct remained strong, and I was able to override the discomfort for long enough to sweep the tunnel before me with the beam of my luminator, keeping the barrel of my laspistol in line with it. (Under most circumstances, of course, there's no better way to make a target of yourself than that, but I was backlit by the tunnel mouth in any case so it wouldn't make any difference to an assailant lurking in the dark. If anything I might dazzle them for long enough to get a shot off.) As it happened there was nothing waiting to shoot me, and after a second or two I relaxed.

'All clear,' I called, and Jurgen joined me at once, his melta pointing away down the tunnel before us. Bearing in mind what we'd have to pass to get back to our comrades that eased my mind as much as was possible under the circumstances. I turned back to check on the rest of the troopers, who had all taken up positions behind what cover they could find in the immediate vicinity of the cave mouth. Grifen turned to wave at me, from behind a small boulder, and then froze at the unmistakable sound of bolter fire crackling towards us on the wind.

'What the hell?' she asked, seemingly forgetting for a moment that she was still broadcasting on the whole squad net rather than the command channel. Lunt grinned, readying his flamer.

'Sounds like a difference of opinion to me.' He could have been right, of course, greenskins have a definite propensity to settle disputes in the most basic of ways, but the sheer volume of fire I could hear argued against it. It sounded like a full-scale firefight to me. Well, good if it was, the more of each other they slaughtered the better. On the other hand... I strained my ears for the sound I most dreaded, the unmistakable ripping noise of a necron gauss weapon, but if it was there to be heard it was swallowed by the wind.

'Maybe they've found the cogboy,' Hail said slowly, clearly not relishing the idea. I nodded, sharing the same mental picture of the tech-priest fleeing blindly through the snow, howling greenskins in pursuit, firing their ramshackle weapons excitedly as they ran. That seemed unpleasantly plausible.

'Shouldn't we try to help him?' Simla asked. I shook my head, with as much reluctance as I could feign.

'I wish we could,' I lied. 'But we'll never get to him before they do. And unless we want his sacrifice to be in vain we have to report back what we've found.'

'The commissar's right,' Grifen said. 'Pull back, and prepare to blow the entrance.'

Before anyone could move, though, hulking silhouettes could be discerned through the swirling snow, charging towards us with the berserk fury of their kind. By some freak of the weather conditions the eddies of snow were lighter here, affording us an uncomfortably clear view of them as the visibility increased. Crude bolters barked, and chips of stone flew from the outcrops of stone surrounding the cave mouth. Grifen levelled her lasgun.

'Fire at will,' she said.

'Wait!' I ordered, an instant later, and thank the Emperor everyone had the presence of mind to obey. 'Just stay down and don't move!' It had suddenly struck me they weren't firing at us; the bulk of the bolter impacts were off to our left, and it seemed to me that they weren't charging the cave so much as fleeing towards it. And that, my tingling palms and a sudden spasm of the bowels told me, probably meant only one thing. The Valhallans froze, melting into the icy landscape in the way only they could, and even knowing where they were I found them hard to pick out.

A second later my worst suspicions were confirmed, as a vivid green beam, the colour of a festering wound, ripped through the air with the all too vividly remembered sound of tearing cloth, striking one of the orks full on. In less than a second he seemed to dissolve; skin, muscle, and skeleton whipping away to vapour, leaving only the echo of a howl of inhuman agony to mark his passing.

'Emperor on Earth!' Grifen breathed, horror suffusing her voice, and I have to admit to trembling with terror myself. The beam swept on, transfixing another victim, and was joined by another, then another.

The orks scattered, and began to fire back, a little more accurately now that their assailants had so considerately revealed their positions. The swirling snow parted, revealing the sight I had so dreaded, and yet had dared to hope I might be spared after collapsing the entrance to the tomb: eerie metallic warriors, striding silently forward, their carapace sculpted to resemble skeletons. These were surely death incarnate come to claim us all.

'So that's what they look like up close.' Jurgen, imperturbable as ever, his faith in the Emperor's protection still absolute despite taking a bolt to the head on Gravalax, raised the melta, sounding no more than mildly curious. Then again, given some of the horrors we'd faced together over the years, I suppose he just thought it was business as usual. One thing I can say for Jurgen, despite his unprepossessing appearance, he had reserves of courage greater than any man I've ever met. Either that, or he was just too stupid to understand the magnitude of the dangers threatening us.[1] I raised a hand to forestall him.

'Wait,' I breathed. 'Our only chance is to avoid being seen.' That I could attest to from personal experience, my natural propensity for running and hiding being the only thing that had saved me on Interitus Prime when everyone else had been slaughtered. To my relief Jurgen nodded, but kept the heavy weapon aimed, ready for use if it should prove necessary.

---

1. *I must confess to remaining undecided about that myself, despite having fought alongside him on a number of occasions.*

The orks had gone to ground by now, taking cover behind the nearest rocks, shooting back at the necron warriors with their usual lack of accuracy. Inevitably the sheer weight of firepower began to tell, however, a number of shells finding their targets regardless. As I'd seen before, the implacable metal warriors simply shrugged off the impacts, the detonations against their metal hides seeming to do no more than discolour whatever unholy alloy they were made of.

A few of the shots were more effective than the rest, though, more by luck than judgement. As we watched, one of the ork bolts detonated against the power pack attached to the weapon of the leading automaton, and an instant later an explosion ripped apart both the weapon and the necron carrying it.

At this the orks set up a great roar of triumph, and a few of the more incautious broke from cover to race forwards, apparently intent on tackling their gleaming metal assailants in hand to hand combat. Inevitably most died, ripped apart by the gauss flayers, but incredibly a couple closed the distance, swinging their crude, heavy axes as they did so.

One was unlucky, or too slow, his target turning with eerie precision to spit him on the combat blade mounted on the end of its weapon. Thick brackish blood poured from a gash which opened the creature from groin to shoulder blade, and the necron shook the eviscerated body from the end of its weapon with an air of weary disdain. The gutted ork fell heavily to the snow, where a slowly-spreading pool of blood began freezing into a thick, icy scab.

The other greenskin parried the blow aimed at it, and whirled around to strike at the necron's neck. Crudely-forged metal met aeon-old sorcery in a blinding flash of discharged energy, and the unliving warrior's head fell heavily to the snow. The ork's triumph was short-lived, however, as the concerted beams of the two surviving necrons ripped it to vapour in a heartbeat.

'Never thought I'd be rooting for the greenies,' Magot said quietly, sentiments I imagined we all shared. The surviving orks stood their ground with the brutish defiance of their kind, pouring inaccurate small arms fire into the area around the skeletal metallic figures, blowing gouts of snow and ice up around them for the most part, but still inflicting a number of hits which, for the first time, appeared to give the walking nightmares some pause for thought. More distant weapons fire could be heard over the wind now, speaking of other, equally desperate battles, and I allowed myself to feel a surge of hope.

'Everyone pull back,' I ordered quietly. 'Stay under cover. With any luck we can disengage while they're too busy to notice us.'

'Confirm that,' Grifen said, with heartfelt relief evident in her voice. The other troopers began to retreat deeper into the safety of the cave, crawling backwards for the most part, keeping their weapons trained on the unequal battle in front of us.

While the two necrons had concentrated their fire on the orks behind the boulders they'd maintained their position, a big mistake, as I would have been happy to point out if anyone had asked me. Orks are remarkably resilient creatures, driven purely by rage and aggression, so I was scarcely surprised when the one left sprawling in a sorbet of its own blood suddenly grabbed the ankle of its erstwhile assailant and yanked hard on it with all its feral strength. Mortally wounded as it was it clearly had no intention of dying with unfinished business left behind, and the necron fell heavily, its right shin now detached from its knee joint.

Bellowing in triumph the ork began belabouring the fallen warrior with the stump of its own leg, raising a clangour like a peal of cathedral bells (if they were horribly out of tune) and inflicting a remarkable array of dents on its torso and skull. I was under no illusion that this would be enough to incapacitate the hideous thing, though, so I was unsurprised when it swung its combat blade around with the same unhurried precision I'd seen before and sheared through the greenskin's neck. A brief flicker of bewilderment seemed to enter the creature's eyes as its head detached from its shoulders, with the concomitant geyser of gore, and it slumped across the battered metal torso of its murderer.

Abruptly the distant firing we'd heard since just before we first saw the orks ceased, to be followed at once by a howl of barbaric euphoria. It seemed that the main body of the greenskin force had won their battle, though no doubt at a terrible cost. (Not that it would bother them in the slightest, of course, they're not a particularly sentimental species by any stretch of the imagination.) The two necrons before us stopped moving abruptly, as though listening to something, and then simply vanished, along with the remains of their fallen comrades. No doubt their departure was marked by the same crack of air rushing in to fill the sudden vacuum I'd noticed when Amberley was teleported to safety by her displacer field, but if so I was unable to hear it over the howling of the wind.

'Emperor's bowels!' Grifen shook her head, clearly trying to comprehend what we'd just seen. 'Where did they go?'

'Straight back to hell, I hope,' Magot said.

'Close enough,' I confirmed. Even now they'd be reporting what they'd seen, and drawing up their plans for a major incursion, I knew that for a stone cold certainty.

The remaining orks were emerging from cover now, stamping about where the necrons had vanished, and looting the bodies of their fallen companions. Guttural expressions of surprise and confusion drifted towards us on the wind.

'What about the greenies?' Simla asked. I hesitated. They weren't our most urgent priority now, and with any luck would divert any necron attention from us as we scuttled back through the tunnels to warn Kasteen and the others. But then again they'd already found the mouth of the cave, and would be too close behind us for comfort if they felt the urge to do any exploring.

Abruptly the decision was taken out of my hands. The biggest ork in the group, who I took to be the leader,[1] pointed straight at the mouth of the tunnel and bellowed an order of some kind. With a last look back at the bodies of the fallen, half a dozen greenskins started moving towards us. I had no choice; the security of the mission, and more importantly myself, demanded it.

'Kill them all,' I ordered.

---

1. *Generally a safe assumption.*

TEN

THAT WAS AN order the Valhallans were eager to respond to, and they did so with alacrity, opening fire on the greenskins while they were still caught in the open. We took them by complete surprise, the first couple falling under a hail of lasfire before they even had a chance to react.

The others were quick, though, assessing the situation with remarkable acuity for such imbecilic creatures,[1] and scattering again to make themselves more difficult targets. A couple of them went to ground behind a tangle of rocks, and began to shoot back at us. Fortunately their marksmanship was no better than usual so they inflicted no casualties, but they managed to come close enough to make us take full advantage of our own cover, their bolts bursting uncomfortably close to our position. Something stung my cheek, and I wiped away a smear of blood where a chip of stone had caught me. That was too near for comfort and I retreated further into the darkness of the cave, bracing my laspistol against a convenient outcrop of rock to improve the accuracy of my retaliation.

Seeing that we were effectively suppressed the four remaining in the open ran forwards brandishing their blades and screaming at the top of

---

1. *Though brutal and primitive by the standards of other races, orks have an instinctive understanding of combat second to none.*

their voices in the way that they do. As they closed with us they fired their hand weapons sporadically, without even bothering to aim, which made a lot of noise but had little practical effect other than making even more sure that we kept our heads down.

'Lunt!' I yelled. 'Take the ones in the rocks!'

'Commissar.' His acknowledgement was crisp as he raised the barrel of his flamer cautiously over the outcrop he was sheltering behind. I directed a flurry of lasbolts at the snipers, if the perpetrators of such inaccurate shooting could be dignified with such a term, and to my relief Hail and Simla followed my lead. Grifen and Magot concentrated their fire on the charging orks in front of us, slowing them momentarily as the big ork in front with the horns on his helmet[1] took a las-bolt to the knee. He stumbled, falling face down in the snow, and a couple of his subordinates tripped over him. For a moment the hail of incoming fire dwindled as the fallen greenskins flailed at one another, exchanging guttural profanities and blows which would have stunned a grox, before floundering to their feet again.

The delay was enough for Lunt, however; he rose to his full height, and directed a searing jet of burning promethium at the tangle of rocks which concealed the shooters. With a roar which sounded more like rage than pain the two orks burst out into the open, like living torches, charging towards our position. Four lasguns spat as one, targeting them as they moved and the trailing one fell, but the one in front just kept coming, wreathed in steam from the snow which evaporated about him, charred bone becoming visible through the sizzling flesh.

'Emperor's guts!' Lunt swung the barrel, trying to line up another shot, then fell back, an expression of pained surprise on his face as a bloody crater exploded in his chest. I swung my gaze back to the main group of orks, who were now on their feet again, their crude weapons kicking up a flurry of snow and debris around the fallen heavy weapons trooper. Typically for their kind they concentrated only on the most visible threat, ignoring the rest of us for the moment; a fatal mistake.

'Jurgen!' I ordered, gesturing to the group which was now close enough to be a target for the melta. Smiling grimly, my aide took careful aim, sighting directly at the limping leader, who was still snarling in triumph at the death of our fellow trooper. (I'd seen enough bolter wounds in my time to know that such a hit would have been instantly fatal, smashing through the flak armour beneath his greatcoat to detonate inside his

---

1. *A common symbol of authority among the greenskins, apparently meant to prove that they've overcome something even bigger and nastier than they are.*

ribcage. There was nothing to be done for Lunt now other than avenge his demise.) The heavy weapon hissed once more, flashing the intervening curtain of snow into vapour, and reducing the ork leader and the two standing next to him to a rank pile of gently steaming offal. The sole survivor turned, blinking in what looked like stunned stupefaction, its left arm hanging limp and charred from flash burns, then turned and bolted (which just goes to show that at least a few of them aren't as stupid as they look).

I rose fully to my feet and took careful aim, bracing the laspistol in my hand across my left forearm as though I were on the firing range, and trying to still the trembling which seemed to have taken control of my body. Whether it was a delayed reaction to the terror the sight of the necrons had inspired in me, anger at Lunt's sudden and brutal death, or simply my abused body starting to respond to the relative rise in temperature I couldn't say, but I was grimly determined to slay the foul creature myself in spite of it. I squeezed the trigger, thankful for the steadiness my augmetic fingers imparted to my aim, and was rewarded with a gout of ichor from between the greenskin's shoulder blades. Grifen and Magot joined in as it stumbled, bellowing in pain, and between us we dispatched it like the beast it was.

It was only as I stood there, exhaling slowly as the tension eased from my aching body and the trembling gradually came under control, that I noticed the burning ork was still stumbling towards us, its steps faltering now as it staggered drunkenly to the left and the right, but still forging forward, fixated on reaching its tormentors. It was a ghastly sight to behold, I must admit, and I was on the verge of ordering the troopers to finish it off when it dropped abruptly to the ground in a gout of steam from the melting snow around it and at last lay still.

Silence descended, save for the relentless keening of the wind, and the rasping of my breath in my throat.

'Lunt?' Grifen asked, the flatness of her tone already answering her own question.

'Dead,' Hail confirmed, standing over his broken body, the spilled blood and viscera already glazed with ice. I forced myself to join her, looking down at the dead trooper, feeling I knew not what. (Other than my usual sense of profound relief that it wasn't me lying there, as it so easily could have been, of course.)

'He did his duty,' I said, the highest praise I could think of, and everyone nodded soberly. Grifen gestured to Hail and Simla.

'Bring him,' she said. 'We'll take turns.' I shook my head, conscious of how she must feel losing a trooper under her command for the first time. It never gets easy, I can tell you that, but after a while you learn to accept it. Despite what they say, the Emperor can't protect everyone, which is why I take such good care to do the job myself.

'I wish we could,' I said, as gently as I could manage. 'But we don't have the time. We have to get back as fast as possible.' I half expected her to argue, but she nodded, reluctantly.

'We'll come back for him later then,' she said. I shook my head again.

'I'm afraid we can't,' I said, explaining as tactfully as I could. I was suddenly aware of four pairs of eyes boring into me. (Jurgen, of course, would simply go along with whatever I said without argument, his dogged and unimaginative deference to authority being foremost among his well-hidden virtues.)

'Why not?' She wasn't challenging my decision, I was pleased to note, just asking for an explanation, which I supposed they were all entitled to.

'We can't leave any trace of our presence here,' I pointed out. 'Right now, the necrons are only aware of the greenskins.' At least I hoped they were. 'Our best hope of making it back to warn the others is by sneaking past while they concentrate on the threat they know about.'

'The orks.' Grifen nodded in reluctant understanding. 'But if they find Lunt's body they'll come after us too. I see.'

'I'm sorry,' I said again. 'But it's the only way.' I motioned Jurgen forwards, and he readied the melta. I briefly considered trying to salvage the flamer, but it would be more trouble than it was worth; the tanks were too bulky for anyone to add to their kit, and the firing mechanism looked damaged by bolter fire anyway. I checked Lunt's pockets for any personal effects which his family back on Valhalla might want (if he actually had any, I had no idea really, just taking comfort in the familiar routine), and collected his laspistol as an afterthought, giving it to Jurgen to carry. He might as well get the benefit of something less dangerous to the rest of us in case we found ourselves in close quarter combat again. Then I nodded to my aide, stepped back, and he pulled the trigger. Lunt's body boiled into vapour in a matter of seconds, helped by the volatile promethium left in the flamer tanks, and I led the others in a few ritual words commending his soul to the Emperor.

We were a sombre group as we turned away, you can be sure of that, the drifting snow already beginning to obscure the scar in the rock where the heat of the melta had sent our comrade to join His Majesty. Sometimes, when I sit in my study here at the schola and watch the flames in the grate through a glass of amasec, I can't help thinking of all the brave men and women I've seen fall on a battlefield somewhere without even a grave marker left behind to show they were ever there, and reflect that I'm probably the last man alive who even remembers they existed, and that when I'm gone the last trace of them will fade with me. Then I thank the Emperor that I've lasted as long as I have, and that I've seen my last war, and I might just defy the odds long enough to die in bed after all (someone else's, with any luck).[1]

We paused in the mouth of the cave, and Grifen started to take a quick inventory of our remaining stock of explosives.

'There's no time for that now,' I said, urging our party on without, I hoped, too obvious a show of impatience. 'Every minute counts.'

'Right.' She fell into step beside me. 'And there's no point in tipping off the tinheads, is there?'

'Exactly,' I said. Not only would collapsing the passage alert the next necron patrol to our presence, it would close them off from the orks, and the last thing I wanted to do was redirect their attention to the rest of the tunnel complex. Of course they could have found their way into the mines by now in any case, but I was betting that once they'd discovered an exit, and an enemy waiting beyond it, they'd ignore everything else until they'd exterminated the greenies; or at least as many of them as they could find in the vicinity. I explained this to Grifen, and she nodded.

'Makes sense to me,' she said.

'What I don't understand,' Jurgen said slowly, 'is how they got out of the tomb in the first place.' That had been worrying me too. I thought we'd brought down enough of the roof to keep them penned in for a great deal longer than this, but they had access to technosorceries which made the tau look like stone-age barbarians, so it never paid to underestimate them.

'We'll find out soon enough,' I said, apprehension settling across me like a shroud.

Normally I would have been profoundly relieved to have returned to the tunnels where I felt reasonably at home, but the knowledge that there were necrons abroad, possibly even sweeping the same narrow passageways we were so cautiously navigating, knotted my stomach with fear. I would have preferred to move on in the dark, relying on the eerie green glow given off by their gauss weapons to warn us of their presence, but none of the others had the advantage of my hiver's tunnel sense; they'd have been stumbling blindly in the darkness, and making more noise than a grox in a ceramics emporium to boot. So we moved at the double, the easy loping stride of the veteran trooper

---

1. *Ironically this part of the archive appears to have been composed only a matter of months before the thirteenth Black Crusade engulfed most of the segmentum, and Cain found himself dragged out of retirement despite his advancing years.*

which eats up the kilometres without dragging you down with exhaustion, our luminator beams reflecting just as brightly from the frozen walls as before.

'There's something up ahead,' Simla said, a couple of kilometres later, taking his turn on point. My palms tingled with dread anticipation as the formation slowed, weapons coming to bear down the tunnel.

'What is it?' I asked.

'I don't know.' His voice on the comm-bead sounded puzzled rather than alarmed. 'There's a lot of blood.'

Well that was something at least: if it bled it wasn't a necron. We closed up into a tighter formation, moving ahead a couple of hundred metres to join him as he walked cautiously forward, his luminator playing on what looked like a large pile of butchered meat. The ice around it was crimson, slick with frozen blood as he'd said. Absently, I realised there was too much there for the body to be human, then as we got closer the full size of it became apparent.

'It's an ambull,' Hail said, surprise suffusing her voice.

'Not any more,' Magot added helpfully.

'Where did it come from?' Jurgen asked, as ever displaying his talent for the obvious question. Grifen shrugged.

'Cogboy must have got his head count wrong.' That much was clear, of course. I was more concerned with how it had died. I moved closer to examine the cadaver, and almost immediately wished I hadn't. Beneath its glaze of ice, raw, bloody wounds slashed across its body. Whatever killed it had done so in close combat, wielding razor-sharp blades with surgical precision.

'Where's its hide?' Simla wondered aloud. Grifen shrugged.

'Do necrons use hearth rugs?'

'Not that I ever noticed,' I said, getting everyone moving again. Something about the dead animal spooked me, I don't mind admitting it. The necrons I'd seen before had killed efficiently and dispassionately, but this mutilated carcase spoke of a refined and gleeful sadism of the kind I associated with the eldar renegades who prey on their own kind with as much abandon as they do upon humanity.[1]

As we left the grisly trophy behind us, all trace of it soon swallowed by the suffocating darkness which closed in around the tiny refuge of light cast by our luminators, my apprehension grew even greater. Every

---

1. *If not more so. The eldar corsairs appear to be touched by the Dark Powers in some way, and the enmity between them and their untainted kin seems to run as deep as that between the loyal subjects of His Divine Majesty and the traitors who seek to subjugate humanity in the name of their blasphemous gods.*

step we took was taking us closer to that hidden tomb, and whatever horrors it might conceal. (I had a better idea than most, after my experiences in the depths of their catacombs, so you'll have to forgive me if I confess that taking those steps became progressively harder as I had to exert every iota of willpower I possessed not to turn and flee, screaming, towards the daylight.)

At length a fatalistic numbness settled over me. Retreat was clearly impossible in any case, as the orkish armies would kill us just as surely as the necrons if we tried to go back the way we'd come, and our only hope of safety lay in returning to the refinery complex and the protection it afforded. (Meagre as that looked right now, caught between a gargant and who knew what terrors from the dawn of time.)

My sense of direction, reliable as always, was telling me we should be almost on top of the entrance we'd found by now, and I urged my companions to even greater caution. To my relief they needed little urging, the oppressiveness of the tunnels and the knowledge of what awaited us no doubt weighing on their minds as heavily as it did upon my own. I'd kept my laspistol in my right hand ever since the firefight with the orks, and I reached across with my left to loosen my trusty chainsword in its scabbard. Like the pistol I'd carried it for more years than I cared to remember, so long that it had ceased to exist in my mind as a weapon, or even an object in its own right; now when I drew it the humming blade was simply an extension of my own body.[1] Knowing it was there was curiously reassuring, and I breathed a little easier as we rounded the last bend in the tunnel before the roof fall we'd caused.

We'd doused all the lights except Simla's, allowing our eyes to get a little more used to the gloom and covering him from the concealing darkness as he advanced, and at first all seemed well: the tumbled heap of rock, stone and ice lay across the tunnel, narrowing it to half its width as I remembered. The palms of my hands were tingling though, usually a reliable indicator that something my conscious mind hasn't picked up on yet isn't quite right, so I slowed my pace, scanning the pile of debris in the light from Simla's luminator, and waited for my tunnel rat's instincts to provide the missing clue.

---

1. *I can attest from my personal association with him that Cain was one of the most accomplished swordsmen in the sector. Even well into his retirement, and his second century, none of the combat instructors at the schola were able to match his skill, honed as it was by innumerable victories in the field. (Much to their chagrin, I might add.) Oddly, his memoirs give little detail about the actual techniques he employed in the mêlées he describes; probably because his fighting style was so instinctive he never bothered to analyse it.*

The rubble seemed undisturbed, however hard I stared at it, so it couldn't be that. My gaze flickered across a deep patch of shadow a few metres from it, and then on to the dimly-seen texture of the tunnel wall, where the light of our luminators bounced back in the sparkling reflections we'd grown so used to by now they scarcely registered...

'Simla. Tunnel wall, about five metres from the cave-in,' I directed, and waited for our point man to swing his luminator round.

'Emperor's bowels!' Grifen brought up her lasgun, her shocked exclamation putting all our reactions into words. The shadow was no such thing, of course, the texture of the tunnel wall should have been visible there too, as my subconscious had been trying to tell me. A fresh passageway was now gouged out of the rock, leading off Emperor knew where. The work, presumably, of our butchered ambull.

'Claw marks,' Simla confirmed, shining the beam of his luminator around the mouth, and then into the depths of the new tunnel. His posture altered suddenly, the lasgun the luminator was taped to coming up into the firing position. 'Golden Throne!'

We ran forward to join him, anticipating Emperor knew what, and clustered at the tunnel mouth. At first it seemed no different from the other ambull runs we'd been travelling through. Then I followed the beam of light, saw what was illuminated by it, and swallowed hard.

'Orks,' Jurgen said, as phlegmatically as if he were handing me a fresh bowl of tanna leaf tea.

'You think?' Magot chipped in, with grisly relish. 'Kind of hard to tell without their skins.'

There were six of them in total, all dead, all flayed the way the ambull had been. Beneath their thin glazing of ice they looked for all the world like anatomical models, laid out for the instruction of apprentice medicae (if the greenskins ever bothered with such niceties as chirurgery, of course).[1]

'What killed them?' Hail asked, paling as much as she was able to. At that point I was past caring, to be honest. Their presence here was a strong indication that at least one group had made it into the tunnels ahead of us, and that an indeterminate number of the brutes might even now be wreaking havoc behind our defensive lines. Not to mention standing between us and safety. All I knew was that the necrons must somehow be responsible, and that whatever tomb-spawned horror had killed them like this was something I didn't want to meet. With a premonitory tingle I realised that the new tunnel was running almost parallel to the necron one we'd blocked, and suddenly felt a violent urge to be somewhere else as quickly as possible.

---

1. *Actually they do, although not in any fashion we would recognise as good medical practice.*

'Look at this, sir.' Jurgen held up one of the crude bolters the orks had carried, an expression of mild curiosity on his face. It had been sheared clean through, the metal bright where a blade of unimaginable sharpness had sliced it in two, along with the hand that had held it if the amount of blood frozen to the stock was anything to go by. Automatically I scanned the scattered equipment around the bodies, looking for some kind of clue as to what their purpose had been. It was hard to be sure, but something about the weapons they carried and the few pieces of rag which hadn't been stained with blood reminded me of the scouts who'd shot down our shuttle.

That was a logical inference, of course, but quite disturbing in its way. It meant we could be up against orks who, untypically for their kind, were skilled at moving quietly and waiting in ambush rather than announcing their presence with loud voices and indiscriminate weapons fire.

'Shouldn't we see what's at the end of the tunnel?' Grifen asked, reluctance audible in her voice. I shook my head.

'No.' It took all the self-control I could muster to sound calm and collected, instead of screaming the word. 'Nothing's more important than reporting back what we've found.'

'Besides,' Magot chipped in, indicating the mutilated orks with a casual wave, 'that looks like a pretty definite Keep Out sign to me.'

'Then let's take the hint,' I said. Grifen nodded.

'You'll get no argument from me.'

'Hold it.' Hail had moved back to the main tunnel, and was now guarding our rear, standing next to the rockfall which had buried the entrance to the tomb. (And which, thanks to our stray ambull, had turned out to be a complete waste of time.) 'I think I can hear something.'

'Can you be a little more specific?' I asked, lowering my voice instinctively, even though no one else would hear it through the comm-bead in her ear.

'Movement. Beyond the rockslide.' Her voice was equally hushed. Simla scuttled forward to support her, dousing our last remaining luminator, and plunging us into darkness. I've never been prone to claustrophobia, a consequence of my upbringing I suppose, but at that moment the weight of the gloom around us seemed crushing. I found myself obscurely grateful for Jurgen's familiar odour, which reassured me that I had at least one ally down here I could trust, and drew my chainsword from its scabbard.

I strained my ears, listening for any change in the ambient noise around me, tuning out the sounds of my own breathing and my hammering heart. At first I heard nothing except the susurration of the lungs of my companions, and the faint rustling of their clothes as they moved into positions of readiness. Then it came to me, rising up out of the echoes: the sound of boots crunching on hoarfrost, and guttural voices whispering in orkish.

'Let them get close,' I sub-vocalised, hearing the reassuring murmur of response from the rest of the team, and hunkering down to present the smallest possible target. 'Take them when they come round the rockslide.'

It was a good strategy, and probably would have worked, except for my companions' inexperience of tunnel fighting and moving stealthily in the dark. I never knew if Hail or Simla was to blame, but as they settled into the shelter of the tumbled heap of rubble one of them dislodged a small piece of debris.

I held my breath as it skittered away across the ice, and the advancing footsteps halted. A loud sniffing sound echoed through the dark, followed by a muttered conversation in what, for greenskins, were hushed tones. I picked out the word, '*humiez*,'[1] which I'd heard often enough before to be sure of, and knew that our ambush had been discovered.

A glimmer of orange light was now visible behind the rockslide, flickering like fire, and a sick presentiment gripped me. One of the approaching greenskins apparently had a flamer, the pilot light providing illumination for the group as well as heavy support, and a vivid mental image of the immolated orks Lunt had killed rose up unbidden in my mind. I determined to make the bearer my highest priority target; of all the ways to die I'd seen on the battlefields of the galaxy, burning to death looked among the least pleasant.

'Stay back,' I sub-vocalised, probably unnecessarily, as I'm sure the others were all thinking the same. Then I levelled my laspistol at the constriction in the passageway where the greenskins must surely appear, and waited.

To my surprise, however, they didn't charge blindly forward into combat as I'd expected. A couple of small objects flew through the gap, bouncing on the frost-covered floor, and skittering wildly in random directions.

'Grenade!' Simla yelled, just before they detonated, and a storm of shrapnel ripped through the air. He fell backwards, ugly wounds peppering his body. Even the flak armour beneath his greatcoat couldn't stop all of the shards, and crimson stains began seeping across it as he

---

1. *The closest the orkish larynx can come to the Gothic word 'humans'.*

tried to get to his feet. Hail was luckier, her partner taking most of the blast, but I could see her left arm was bleeding heavily and hung limply at her side. She leapt forward into the gap, screaming in anger, and fired her lasgun one-handed on full auto at the no doubt surprised green-skins beyond. She must have hit at least one, too, judging by the howls of rage and pain which echoed round the confined space.

'Hail! Get back!' Grifen shouted, but she was too late; a volley of bolts tore Hail apart in a rain of blood and viscera, and then the orks were among us. Simla tried to raise his lasgun as the first bounded through the narrow opening, but before he could pull the trigger a massive cleaver swung down to bisect his skull. The greenskin bellowed in triumph, but it was short-lived as Magot and I shot it almost simul-taneously, and it dropped, most of its head blown away. Grifen kept up a steady suppressive fire against the opening through which they had to come, attempting to dissuade any more from following, but it was a futile hope. When the blood of an ork is up they have almost no sense of self-preservation, seeming happy to die if they can take a few of their enemies with them. Another greenskin dived through the choke point, spitting bolts from the crude pistol in its hand, and to my horror the flickering glow of the incendiary weapon was growing brighter, indi-cating that its operator would be the next to emerge.

'Jurgen!' I shouted, pointing, 'take out the flamer!' He nodded, and sighted the melta carefully. I had no more time to consider his actions after that, or anyone else's for that matter, because the greenskin was upon me, swinging its heavy blade at my head.

I ducked, bringing up the screaming chainsword to block it instinc-tively, and felt the sturdy mechanism shudder as adamantium teeth met crudely forged metal. Sparks flew, miniature orange suns melting tiny craters in the ice which coated the floor, before I turned my body, deflecting the brute's headlong charge into the wall. It roared as its head impacted with the unyielding ice-coated stone, and turned back towards me, thick ropes of drool hanging from its tusks. Now it was really hacked off.

Good. I cut at its leg, slashing a wound that would have disabled a human, but which seemed to affect it little more than a scratch. It brought its cumbersome blade down to block the strike, as I'd anticipated, and I slashed upwards, taking the loathsome creature in the neck. It looked star-tled for a moment, as if wondering where all the blood was suddenly coming from, and dropped heavily to its knees. With any other species this would have been a mortal blow, but I'd faced greenies too often before to underestimate their resilience. I swung the blade again, laterally this time, and took its head from its shoulders.

The whole fight could only have lasted a second or two. As I turned away my eyes were stabbed by the searing flash of the melta.

'Got him,' Jurgen confirmed, as I tried to blink my retina clear of the dancing after-images, and cursed myself for my carelessness. That degree of disorientation could cost me my life down here.

'Look out!' The breath was suddenly driven from my lungs as Magot dived forwards, catching me around the waist, and barging me out of the way of a large and unfriendly rock which had become detached from the ceiling. It crashed to the ground where I'd been standing less than a second before.

'Thanks,' I said, still trying to pick out the image of the redheaded trooper from the bright green haze which seemed to float between me and the rest of the world. I thought I could make out a grin, and realised she'd switched her luminator on again.

'Any time,' she said.

'The whole roof's coming down!' Grifen yelled, and I became aware of the creaks and rumblings which told me she was right. Apparently the explosion we'd touched off here earlier had left things even more unstable than we'd realised, something I suppose an old tunnel rat like me should have spotted if I hadn't been too busy being terrified of the necrons.

'Back!' I shouted, my childhood instincts kicking in at last; the worst of it sounded as if it was ahead of us. So we ran back to the shelter of the fresh ambull tunnel, and waited for the noise to stop.

'Emperor on Earth!' Grifen said, when the dust had finally settled. I can't say I blamed her. Of the nine troopers she'd set out with only Magot was now left, and she must have felt the loss of so many of her subordinates keenly. Scintillating ice motes danced in our luminator beams as we took in the full import of the sight ahead of us. Where half the passageway had once been blocked, an impenetrable wall of debris now barred our way. Of the orks, and our fallen comrades, there was no sign at all.

'We're frakked, aren't we?' Magot asked. I shook my head, afraid to speak. It looked to me as if she was right.

'I can try another shot,' Jurgen suggested. 'See if that might clear it.' More likely it would bring down even more rubble, and finish us off into the bargain. I shook my head again.

'Probably a bad idea,' I said, surprised at my restraint under the circumstances.

'We could go back,' Grifen suggested. 'Try to get to the refinery overland.' Over a mountain range, swarming with orks. In a blizzard. That would be suicide, and the dubious tone of her voice told me she realised that even as she spoke.

'We've got one chance,' I said, my mind skittering reluctantly away from the thought even as I voiced it. I tried to picture the map of the ambull tunnels Logash had been compiling on his auspex, and over-laid the mental image with the fresh one we'd just discovered. With a lot of luck it might intersect one of the others before too long, and allow us to bypass the blockage ahead of us.

On the other hand, it was also running more or less parallel with the passageway we'd been trying to block off in the first place, and it seemed pretty obvious that the necrons were already using it. If we went ahead we'd almost certainly die.

Well, almost certainly offers a bit more hope than definitely, which was what our other options amounted to, so in the end it was the only choice to make. It was a grim and silent group which started out, already half the size we had been when we passed this way before, and with the gravest peril we had to face still in front of us.

I averted my eyes from the mutilated orks as we filed past their silent and frozen bodies, and wondered if I'd doomed us all.

ELEVEN

By THAT POINT we'd given up any attempt at maintaining a proper skirmish formation, advancing instead as a single group, huddled together for protection like the natives of some feral world scared of the daemons beyond the circle of firelight. The difference, of course, was that we knew the daemons were real, and that we were walking straight into their infernal realm. (And speaking as someone who's met a daemon or two in his time, I can assure you that the sensation was not at all dissimilar.)

We had by some unspoken agreement left all the luminators apart from Magot's switched off, so that only a single beam of light preceded us down that narrow and forbidding passageway. As a result, the shadows closed in around us even more suffocatingly than before, despite the reflective qualities of the ice which still coated the walls, intensifying the sense of brooding menace surrounding us. Moreover, my tunnel rat's instincts told me we were descending slowly once again, ever deeper into the bowels of the planet, and the deeper we went, the closer the enshrouding gloom seemed to wrap itself around us, until the air against my face seemed thick and warm, almost choking in its closeness.

Abruptly I became aware that the two phenomena were real, not psychological. The ambient temperature was gradually rising, and our single beam was reflecting less and less from the walls around us as dark rock began to emerge from behind its coating of translucent ice. The resultant humidity was making the air seem damp and thick, a faint mist rising from the floor ahead of us. It was still pretty chilly by any normal measure, you understand, but compared to the temperatures we'd been exposed to on the surface it began to feel almost tropical. The Valhallans certainly seemed to notice it, both women loosening their greatcoats and Jurgen removing his thick fur hat, which he stuffed into one of the equipment pouches he was habitually festooned with.

'Wherever we're going, I think we're here,' Magot volunteered, after an indeterminate period of silence during which we heard nothing apart from our cautious footsteps which seemed to ring like thunder with every pace, echoing all the louder in our ears for every pain we took to muffle them. I nodded, my mouth dry. A faint humming was discernable in the air now, hovering just on the edge of audibility, and a faint acrid tang tickled the membranes of my nose. All things I remembered only too well, and had hoped never to experience again.

'Move carefully,' I warned everyone, completely superfluously no doubt. I gestured to Magot. 'Kill the light.'

She complied, and with a sense of mounting horror I realised that the darkness around us was no longer absolute. A faint luminescence was visible from up ahead, percolating into the tunnel; a sick, gangrenous hue which turned my stomach.

'Down that way.' There could be no doubt at all now: whatever secrets the necrons had buried down here were waiting for us, and there seemed no way to avoid confronting them.

'I'll go first,' Jurgen offered, swinging the bulk of the melta up into a firing position. 'This ought to clear a way for us if we need it.' Frankly I doubted it, where we were going no amount of firepower would make a difference, but the thought that he might at least buy us a little time was a comforting one, so I nodded.

'Good man,' I said, somehow finding the time to enjoy the expression of perplexity on Grifen and Magot's faces. Jurgen was an easy man to underestimate until you got to know him, and few people ever bothered. I tried to look calm, but I'd be surprised if I fooled them for a second; both women looked almost sick with apprehension, and knowing what awaited us I have no doubt my appearance was even worse. 'Ready?' I asked.

'Ready.' Grifen gave Magot's upper arm an encouraging squeeze, and the redheaded trooper nodded.

'As I'll ever be,' she confirmed, and snapped a fresh power cell into her lasgun, more for the comfort the familiar action afforded than because she needed to reload, I suspected.

We emerged into a vast shadowy cavern, full of machinery of strange design and incomprehensible function. Vast geometric slabs rose into the gloom about us, leaking that rancid illumination from vents and thick pipes of stuff which looked like glass but undoubtedly wasn't, suffusing the whole space with shadows and flat, directionless light. In the pale green glow we looked like corpses, long dead and rotting, and I found myself wondering how I had ever hoped to come through this unscathed.

We probed forward cautiously, scuttling from one deep shadow to the next like mice on a cathedral floor, our minds assailed almost to the point of physical nausea by the sense of wrongness everything exuded. This was no place for the living, that much was plain.

'Emperor protect us,' Grifen breathed. We had come through a doorway high enough to admit a titan, hugging the walls of that vast chamber whose roof rose up beyond sight, and stopped short, our breath stilled by the prospect which awaited us. For those walls were composed of niches, each the height and width of a man, and in each stood a necron warrior, the sickly light gleaming from its metal surface. As we moved the shadows seemed to ripple across those blank, inhuman features, imparting expressions of utter malevolence.

For a moment we stood, transfixed by horror, until I realised with a surge of relief that this apparent motion was an illusion, and that each warrior stood utterly immobile.

'They're in stasis,' I breathed, as though saying the words aloud might alone be enough to wake them.

'Then they're harmless?' Magot asked, clearly not expecting the answer she wanted to hear.

'No,' I confirmed. 'Just dormant. If they were to wake...' I swept my eyes up and along that dizzying vista, seeing nothing but metal bodies receding to infinity, and gave up trying to calculate how many there were. Hundreds of thousands, at the very least, in this one chamber alone. I tried to envisage the havoc which such an army would wreak if it were ever unleashed upon the galaxy, and cringed inwardly at the scale of the carnage that would ensue. 'They have to be destroyed.'

'I think we'll need bigger guns,' Grifen said dryly, wrenching her eyes away from that all but infinite legion, and hefting her lasgun as though ready to fire. Nerves taut, we flicked our gazes left and right, alert for any sign of movement which might betray a threat, but the vast tomb seemed utterly empty apart from us.

'Then we'll get bigger guns,' I reassured her. Nothing in our inventory would even come close to doing the job, but an astropathic message to the nearest naval unit would bring a task force here within weeks, and a flotilla of battleships ought to be enough to level the continent. A couple of barrages from their lance batteries would be enough to excise this cancer, however deeply it was buried.

Of course the planet would be rendered uninhabitable for genera-tions, but no one in their right mind would be willing to set foot here once the necron presence was known in any case, so the question was pretty moot. And if anyone were foolish enough to demur, I had no doubt that Amberley would bring the full force of the Inquisition to bear on the objectors the moment I appraised her of the situation.[1]

We pushed on cautiously, trying to keep the outer walls of the cavern in sight as much as we could; if there was indeed a way out of here I intended to find it. I simply refused to consider the alternative, that the ambull tunnel we'd come in by had been the only entrance left, as that way lay nothing but madness and despair.

'Movement!' Jurgen warned, melting into the shadows at the base of some vast mechanism which hummed away to itself oblivious of our presence. The rest of us went to ground too, finding what concealment we could. I crouched behind some metallic outgrowth which looked both regular and organic, and which felt warm to the touch. A moment later I saw it too, harsh angular shadows at first, presaging our initial sight of the necrons themselves as they rounded the corner of the metal canyon in the depths of which we lurked.

As the monsters themselves came into sight I could scarcely sup-press a gasp of pure horror. I'd seen terrors enough on Interitus Prime, but these monstrous creations exceeded even those. At first I took them for ordinary necron warriors, fearsome enough in themselves as I knew only too well, but these were something far worse. Their fin-gers ended in long, gleaming blades, smeared with a substance which looked black in this pestilential light but which I had no doubt was truly red. Most terrifying of all, their metal torsos were hidden from view. For a second, as my appalled mind refused to acknowledge the sight before it, I found myself wondering why in the name of the Emperor these unfeeling automata would have donned clothing against the cold; then the realisation hit me, along with a spasm of nausea. They were draped in the flayed hides of the dead orks we'd found. (If one of them was wearing the ambull I failed to notice it, which believe me was quite easy to have done under the circum-

---

1. *He was not wrong in this assumption.*

stances. If the Emperor Himself had tapped me on the shoulder at that moment it probably wouldn't have registered.)

'Golden Throne!' Grifen breathed, unable to contain her revulsion, and I froze, terrified that she might have been heard, but to my unutterable relief the hideous apparitions strode on oblivious,[1] with the inhumanly fluid motion I'd come to associate with all their forms, and after a moment they slipped away down a wide boulevard between arcane devices the size of a warehouse.'

'Should we follow them?' Jurgen asked, phlegmatic as always, as though he'd seen nothing more disturbing than my morning's messages, and I was instantly grateful for the sound of his voice in my comm-bead. It was a welcome touch of the ordinary which I seized on gratefully, and I felt my shattered sensibilities begin to stabilise. I glanced across at Grifen, who was breathing shallowly, her face pale in the ghastly light, and Magot, who was muttering prayers to the Emperor under her breath, all trace of her usual cockiness gone. If I didn't do something to snap them out of it fast they were likely to lose it completely, or go catatonic on me, and neither was an appealing prospect at the moment. And Jurgen's suggestion at least had the merit of keeping the monstrosities in front of us, so I nodded.

'Good a plan as any,' I conceded, then turned to Grifen. 'Sergeant. We're moving out.' To her credit she responded almost at once, turning slowly to face me with wide eyes into which I could see a measure of hard-fought self control begin to return.

'Right,' she confirmed, and reached across to take Magot by the arm again. The trooper failed to respond. Grifen increased the pressure a little, forcing her to take a single step to retain her balance, and after a moment she broke off her muttering to look at the sergeant. 'Mari. Mari, we're going now.'

'We shouldn't be here,' Magot said, an undercurrent of hysteria too close to the surface for my liking. 'We have to get out.'

'That's just what we're going to do,' I assured her, with more confidence than I felt. 'But we need your help to do it. We need you alert, all right?'

'Right. Yes.' She swallowed, incipient panic still bubbling under the surface, but fighting it now. She took a couple of deep breaths. 'I'm on it.'

---

1. *Despite decades of intensive study by both the Ordo Xenos and the Adeptus Mechanicus the sensory mechanisms of the necrons remain a mystery. Sometimes they seem almost preternaturally able to detect an enemy, while at others, as in this instance, they overlook targets almost literally under their noses. At this time the Inquisition has no explanation to offer for this paradox; and if the Adeptus Mechanicus has one they're not sharing it.*

'Good. Because we're relying on you,' I said, in my most sincere voice. 'If we stick together we'll make it, you have my word.'

'I won't let you down,' she said, a hair's breadth from hyperventilation, and Grifen patted her on the shoulder, a brief, supportive show of human contact.

'I know you won't,' she said kindly. 'So get your arse in gear and let's try to make it back before hell thaws out, OK?'

'OK, sarge.' Whatever the bond between them it seemed to outweigh the terror of the necrons, at least for the time being, so I signalled to Jurgen.

'Move out,' I said.

How long we followed those ghastly apparitions for I had no idea, but it seemed like an eternity, time shifting and blurring until it had no meaning, a phenomenon I'd also noticed in the catacombs of Interitus Prime. At times we passed through forests of glowing tubes, uncannily reminiscent of plague-ridden trees, and at others we scuttled along in the shadows of blank-sided metal slabs the size of a starship. At least twice we passed through more stasis chambers, as full of dormant horrors as the one we'd first encountered, but looking back I find my recollections hazy, as though my mind was simply refusing to accept what it was seeing (probably just as well for my sanity). Abruptly I became aware of a fluttering of motion in my peripheral vision, and dived for cover again, with a sibilant warning to my companions.

And just in time, too. A group of ordinary necron warriors appeared from a side passage, which, like the one we travelled, seemed more like a street than a gap between warehouse-sized machines, and, turning as one with a precision which would have left any Imperial Guard drill instructor worthy of the name seething with envy had they been there to witness it, followed their charnel brethren towards whatever destination awaited them.

As I looked closer I could see faint traces of combat damage on their shiny metal torsos, the dents and craters left by the weapons of the orks already fading as the metal seemed to flow together, healing their wounds by some sorcerous process I was at a loss to understand.[1]

From somewhere up ahead, at the end of that cyclopean thoroughfare, we could now discern a glow brighter than the rest but no less repellent in its hue, and something about the shape of the mechanisms surrounding us seemed vaguely familiar. I began to feel a formless

---

1. *An understanding which the Ordo Xenos would give a great deal to achieve, incidentally. It goes without saying that whatever inroads the Adeptus Mechanicus may have made into the problem, they're keeping to themselves.*

sense of recognition, which hardened into certainty as we approached that vivid corpse-light, and the source came into view in the centre of a broad open space the size of a starport landing pad.

'It's an active warp portal,' I breathed, making the sign of the aquila by reflex. Not that I expected to invoke any additional protection by doing that, of course, but believe me, under those circumstances every little helps.

'Are you sure?' Grifen asked, clearly awestruck at the prospect. Feeling this wasn't the time for lengthy explanations I simply nodded.

'Absolutely,' I said.[1] Ahead of us the flayed ones, as I later learned the Inquisition classified the trophy-takers, stepped into that eldritch glow and vanished, no doubt to some hell hole elsewhere in the galaxy. I must admit to wondering, for a panic-stricken instant, if they were merely teleporting to some starship in orbit, but a moment's reflection was enough to reassure me that no vessel could have emerged from the warp early enough to be here already without registering on the *Pure of Heart's* sensor array long before we set out on our ambull hunt, what seemed like a lifetime ago now. (But which my chronometer stubbornly insisted had been less than a day.)[2] A moment later the warriors followed suit, evaporating from our sight like the vestiges of a nightmare on waking, and the warp portal dimmed back to the level of the ambient illumination.

'Emperor on Earth!' Magot said, a faint trace of her old bravado beginning to return. 'How's that for an exit?'

'It'll do me,' Grifen said grimly. 'Especially if it's permanent.'

'Maybe the greenskins were too much for them,' the redhead said hopefully.

'I wouldn't count on it,' I said. 'This was just a scouting party. They'll be back.'

'How soon?' Jurgen asked, his tone, as usual, no more than mildly curious. I shrugged.

'Emperor alone knows,' I said. 'Long enough for us to get the frak out of here I hope.'

Magot muttered in agreement. I stole a glance at the portal, which, though dormant now, seemed to pulsate with malevolence, as though ready to vomit a tidal wave of metal warriors across the planet at any

---

1. *Cain is almost certainly the only human in the galaxy to have survived a transit through a necron warp portal, during the adventures on Interitus Prime to which he has previously referred. His account of the incident is elsewhere in the archive, and need not detain us further at this time.*

2. *Cain is generally imprecise about the passage of time in his memoirs; it's usually possible to infer roughly how much time has passed between the incidents he describes, but this is about as specific as he ever gets.*

moment. I thought briefly of trying to rig up something to destroy it from our remaining stock of explosives, but dismissed the idea at once. For one thing, if it was as robust as the equipment I'd seen on Interitus Prime we'd barely be able to scratch it with what little we still carried, and for another, the time it would take us to try would be far better spent looking for an exit. (If I'm honest, the thought of lingering for even a moment longer, certainly for the amount of time it would take to set the charges, was almost enough to start me running in panic; only the realisation that such a course would probably doom us prevented it.) And any attempt to interfere with the mechanisms here would most likely draw attention to us, which would be best avoided to say the least. Though many of the machines around us appeared to be powering down with the departure of the scouting party, which suggested we were alone down here now, there could be any number of alarms or sensors an explosion might trigger, and necron guards or their mechanical lackeys lurking in a corner somewhere prepared to deal with us if alerted to our presence.

'Which way, sir?' Jurgen asked, as though we were simply in the middle of a park somewhere looking for the quickest way back to the barracks. I hesitated. My instincts hadn't entirely deserted me, however arcane our surroundings, and after a moment's thought I pointed off to our left.

'The mines should be over that way, if I don't miss my guess.' Jurgen had been down enough holes with me to trust my sense of direction underground, and even if he didn't it was close enough to an instruction for him to follow without thinking about it, so he nodded, and began to move off in that direction. Grifen and Magot began to drift after him so I picked up my pace and fell in between my aide and the two women, feeling a little more secure (if that were even remotely possible considering where we were) now that I had armed troopers on either side of me.

Despite my growing conviction that we were unlikely to meet any more of the metallic monstrosities unless we did something to attract their attention I wasn't about to let my guard down, you can depend on that. In fact the closer we came to safety, or at least the promise of it, the more paranoid I became, starting at every minute sound, real or imagined. I scanned every shadow we passed, increasingly certain that every crevice concealed a swarm of scuttling metal insects or that a vast arachnoid construct lurked above our heads, but every time my apprehensions proved to be groundless.

'I can see the cavern wall,' Jurgen voxed, and we picked up the pace a little, an unspoken agreement sparking among us to quit this hellish place as quickly as we could. I began to see patches of smooth finished stonework ahead of us through the tangle of incomprehensible mechanisms and tried to estimate how far away we were, but my sense of perspective was confused by the strange geometries around us and I was still taken by surprise when we slipped through a grove of pipe-work the breadth of trees and found ourselves up against naked bedrock.

'It's completely smooth,' Magot said, running her hand along it, a tint of wonder entering her voice. She was right, the surface was sheer as glass, and I found myself trying to picture how the work had been done with such precision. The only explanation I could come up with was sorcery of some kind, which fitted right in with everything else I'd seen here since we arrived. I glanced to the left and right, hoping to find some sign of a tunnel, but in this I was predictably disappointed.

'Which way now?' Grifen asked. I didn't have a clue, to be honest, but I had a vague memory of the projected run of the ambull tunnels on Logash's auspex being more numerous off towards the right of where I estimated us to be, so I gestured in that direction with all the authority I could muster.

'That way,' I said. 'And pray to the Emperor for a miracle.'

'This whole place is a miracle, is it not?' a new voice asked. I whirled, bringing up my laspistol, and froze an instant away from pulling the trigger. The speaker sounded vaguely familiar, and a moment later I caught sight of a human figure in an emerald robe (which was actually white, of course, out of that ghastly illumination), whose eyes flashed dazzlingly green as they caught the light. 'All praise the Omnissiah, whose bounty has been revealed to the worthy despite the worst efforts of the unbeliever.'

'Logash,' I said, not quite sure if he'd gone barmy or not. 'We thought you were dead.' But he wasn't, worse luck; the treacherous little weasel had given us the slip in the snowstorm and come scuttling back here as fast as he could. Emperor alone knows what he was hoping to achieve with a couple of tonnes of rubble sealing the entrance to the tomb, but fanatics are like that, no common sense at all, and our stray ambull had solved the problem for him anyway. Of course he took that as a sign from His Divine Majesty, or the clockwork parody they worship, that he was intended to get in here all along, and didn't he just crow about that.

'The Omnissiah guided my steps,' he said, 'and the barriers were thrown down ahead of me. All praise the Omnissiah!' His voice rose, and I cringed inwardly, certain that he'd attract unholy attention. I hushed him with a gesture, and turned to find Magot's lasgun pointed straight at him.

'How come the tinheads didn't get you?' she asked, her finger a little too tight on the trigger for my peace of mind. Frankly, the way I felt now she could have shot him and welcome, but the sound of gunfire would echo around here like an Earthshaker barrage and I wasn't prepared to risk it. I deflected her aim gently with a hand on the weapon's barrel. Logash didn't seem to take offence, though, beaming broadly at the question.

'The holy guardians failed to notice me, as I would expect given my unworthiness. There are mysteries here far beyond my abilities to fathom, but no doubt those of greater wisdom can commune with the machine spirits of this wondrous place.'

'Assuming we ever manage to get out of here to tell them,' Grifen chipped in sourly.

'The Omnissiah will provide, you can depend on it,' Logash said, completely siggy beyond a doubt. (Even though with tech-priests it's often hard to tell.) I found it hard to credit that the necrons had simply ignored him, but I suppose it was a vast complex and it wasn't entirely unfeasible that they had simply failed to notice him as they had the rest of us, even though I had no doubt that he'd been wandering around in the open gawping like some hick up from the sump on his first trip to a guilder trade station instead of hiding like anyone with a micron of sense would have done.

'They certainly noticed the orks,' Magot pointed out. Logash nodded eagerly.

'Vile desecrators of these holy precincts. The guardians cut them down as they deserved.' There he went again, I thought, with a tingle of unease. Anyone who could use the word 'holy' to refer to this chamber of horrors had clearly become unhinged. I suppose the sight of all that technology lying around had overloaded his brain or something.

'Well that's good,' I said, a little too heartily, and prodded him experimentally in the back. To my relief he fell into step beside me. 'It'll still be safe when we tell the others all about it.'

'Oh yes, we must do that.' Logash nodded eagerly, and pulled out his auspex. It's probably a measure of how far gone I was that I was actually glad to see it. The rest of us clustered around anxiously as he called up the image of the ambull tunnels we'd mapped before, the ones in red extrapolated from the ones we'd actually walked.

'Is there another tunnel near here?' Magot asked, raising herself onto her toes to peer over the tech-priest's arm. He nodded, pointing off to the left.

'There should be another ambull run about two hundred metres in that direction.' Luckily no one said anything to me, although to be fair there did seem to be some other tunnels a bit further away in the direction I'd originally chosen. This wasn't the time to stand on my pride, however, so I nodded and patted the tech-priest on his shoulders (which were hard under the robe, and thudded dully under the blows).

'Good,' I said. 'Then let's find it.'

Editorial Note:

Despite my understandable reluctance to resort to this secondary source again I'm afraid it's necessary to fill a gap in Cain's narrative, which breaks off at this point only to resume after some time has passed. No doubt he felt nothing of significance had occurred in the interim, despite the passage of several hours.

As ever, my apologies for the style (or lack of it), and my assurance that readers with a refined appreciation for the Gothic language are perfectly at liberty to skip it.

It is, however, mercifully short.

Extracted from *Like a Phoenix From the Flames: The Founding of the 597th*, by General Jenit Sulla (retired), 097.M42

VITAL AS THE task with which we had been entrusted undeniably was, it could hardly be described as challenging. Once the miners had directed Captain Federer's sappers to the part of the workings where the flaws and stresses in the ice ensured our planned booby trap would work to best effect, there was little for us more practical soldiers to do other than fan out through the galleries to secure our perimeter against the remote possibility of infiltration by the orks. This we did, and although I have to admit that the task was a tedious one, to the credit of the women and men under my command they remained as alert after half the day had crawled by as they had at the commencement of our vigil.

This was disturbed at length by a vox message from deep in the lower galleries, so attenuated by the layers of intervening ice that I could scarcely discern it; and a moment's perusal of the tactical slate was enough to confirm what I'd already deduced. The source of the message was far deeper than the most far-flung of our patrols.

There could be only one explanation, and taking my command squad with me I made haste to respond, finding as we descended and the vox signal became clearer that my suspicions were correct; this was indeed a message from none other than Commissar Cain himself, returning with news of dire import, and demanding, as soon as communications became reliable enough, to be put through to Colonel Kasteen at once.

While my vox operator made haste to comply, his powerful backpack transmitter easily able to boost the tenuous signals of the commissar's comm-bead, I directed my troopers to his aid as rapidly as I could. Though the conversation had moved to a command frequency of a far higher level than those to which I, as a lowly lieutenant, had access, it was clear from the urgent tone of his voice that the tidings he brought were of such importance they must be disseminated as rapidly as possible.

The carrier wave was enough to lead us to the commissar's party, however, and I must confess to a moment of shock as I beheld the bedraggled survivors of what must surely have been a journey of epic endurance. Commissar Cain was, of course, the very picture of martial heroism he always presented, his bearing erect and eye steady, undaunted by whatever horrors he had faced, although his companions all too clearly showed the terrible ravages of the perils they'd fought their way through. The commissar's aide, in particular, looked as though he had come through hell, dishevelled in a way I had seldom seen in a trooper still living.[1] The other soldiers with him stumbled with exhaustion, horror written across their faces, and only the tech-priest at the rear of the party appeared to be in good spirits, doubtless because his augmentations had protected him from whatever had so afflicted the others.

'Help them,' I ordered, and my troopers made haste to obey, providing much-needed support for all.

---

1. *Sulla had clearly had little prior contact with Jurgen.*

It was only after I'd spoken that the commissar appeared to recognise me, looking in my direction for the first time, and I must confess to an overwhelming sensation of pride as he spoke my name, quite overcome at the confidence he so evidently had in my qualities as an officer.

'Sulla,' he said, in a voice clearly meant for no ears other than his own. 'Of course. Who else would it be?'

TWELVE

As you'll readily appreciate, all I wanted to do when we finally made it back to the refinery was eat, sleep, and grab a hot shower (preferably aboard the *Pure of Heart* while it was heading for deep space as fast as its engines would take it), but events were moving too fast to allow any such luxury. I managed to get rid of Sulla, who'd picked up my increasingly frantic attempts to contact the surface and been predictably unable to resist sticking her nose in, by asking her to make sure Grifen and Magot got to the medicae as fast as possible (which didn't hurt my reputation for taking care of the troops either, never a bad thing), and staggered off to meet Kasteen and Broklaw. At least I'd been able to get a tactical update from Sulla before she went, so I could concentrate on the immediate problem secure in the knowledge that the orks were still being held at our outer defensive line and the gargant was still too far away to open fire on us. For the time being at any rate.

'You look like hell,' the major said cheerfully as I entered the command post, but he held out a mug of tanna leaf tea as he said it, so I let him live.[1]

'You should see me from this side,' I told him, and dropped into a seat at the conference table. Now I was back in the warmth and relative safety of the refinery all the fear and accumulated fatigue of the last day

---

1. *Cain is, of course, joking here. Probably.*

or so bludgeoned me between the shoulder blades, and it was all I could do to keep my head from dropping onto the glossy wooden surface. As I tilted my head back to try and ease the tension in my neck something struck me as odd about the ceiling. 'Merciful Emperor! Did the greenskins get in here?' Broklaw followed the line of my gaze to the bolter holes filigreeing the plasterwork above his head.

'Just a small crowd control problem,' he said, smiling at some private joke. Well if he wasn't too bothered about it neither was I, and asking any more questions might complicate my life even further, so I returned my attention to the matter at hand.

'You should get some rest,' Kasteen said, looking at me with evident concern. I nodded.

'I should. Just as soon as we've dealt with the current situation.' I drank deeply, feeling the cobwebs lift a little from my mind as the tanna started to kick in. 'Did you get the old survey reports I asked for?'

'Right here.' She skimmed a data-slate across the surface of the table. I glanced at it, but the charts and technical data meant nothing to me. 'Scrivener Quintus has been remarkably helpful.' Broklaw grinned and winked at me, but in my dazed state I hadn't a clue what he was getting at.

'What does it all mean in plain Gothic?' I asked. Kasteen shrugged.

'I ran it by a couple of the engineseers in the transport pool.' That had been a calculated risk; they were cogboys, of course, so their first duty would be to the Adeptus Mechanicus, but they were our cogboys, and had fought alongside the rest of us for long enough to feel at least as loyal to the regiment as to their tech-priest colleagues. So long as we didn't force them to pick sides they'd tell us what we needed to know, or so I hoped. 'It's not really their field, but they seem to think you're right. There are other deposits of refinable ice on Simia Orichalcae much richer than this one.'

'Then why build the refinery here?' Broklaw asked. I shrugged.

'The magos would undoubtedly reel off a dozen different reasons why this particular deposit was easiest to process, or the topography of the valley made construction simpler, or why it was the will of this clockwork Emperor of theirs. He might even believe it himself. But if it smells like a sump rat and it squeaks like a sump rat...'

'Someone in the Adeptus Mechanicus knew that tomb was there,' Broklaw said. 'Someone placed highly enough to make sure the mine was put on top of it.'[1]

---

1. *The identification of those responsible for the decision wasn't difficult, but, as Cain surmised, hard evidence of conspiracy rather than an unfortunate coincidence continues to be elusive. Anyone with information which may prove helpful in resolving this matter will find an interested listener in Inquisitor Kuryakin of the Ordo Hereticus.*

'But why?' Kasteen was aghast. 'Surely they wouldn't be mad enough to think they could take on a planet full of necrons?'

I thought of Logash, who'd been driven all but insane by the desire to examine such a rich cache of archeotech, and tried to picture a cabal of high-ranking tech-priests pulling strings to set up the mine over so tempting a prize. It wasn't hard to do at all. If they even suspected such a thing existed they'd take any risk, however great, to get their sticky little mechadendrites on it. I'd learned that much at least from the Interitus Prime debacle.

'They probably assumed the tomb was abandoned,' I said. It wouldn't be the first time they'd made that mistake either, as I knew to my cost.

'The real point,' Broklaw said, 'is how many of the tech-priests here we can trust. Whether or not there was a conspiracy to start with, they all know what's down the bloody hole now.'

That much was true. If I'd had my wits about me I'd have got Sulla to detain Logash as soon as she brought us back up to the surface, but of course she ignored him (only a civilian, and a tech-priest to boot), so by the time I realised what was going on he'd already disappeared. No doubt filling Ernulph's head with visions of sorcerous bounty unseen in millennia even as we spoke.

'None of them,' I said. My head was hurting, the grim, relentless migraine that goes with utter fatigue, and I wasn't looking forward to the next few hours at all.

I GOT THROUGH them, of course, due in no small part to Jurgen's skill at fending off unwanted interruptions. By the time Kasteen called a full meeting to discuss the situation I'd managed to grab a little sleep, a lot of recaf, and a hot meal (just soylens viridians again, but for some reason I'd gone off the idea of retrieving an ambull steak), and was beginning to feel tolerably human once more. A bath would have topped things off nicely but sleep was even more urgent, and I just had to resign myself to the fact that I was probably beginning to smell as bad as my aide. Jurgen, naturally, looked no worse than usual, probably as a result of a catnap somewhere. He accompanied me, partly to underline my status, and partly to take the blame if my suspicions about my personal freshness were correct.

Of course I'd done a lot more than take care of my personal needs. Even before I staggered off to the mess hall and bed, in that order, I'd roused the refinery's resident astropath and sent the most urgently-worded communiqué I could to both the lord general's office and the rather more guarded channels Amberley had suggested I use if I ever came across something which merited

Inquisitorial attention. Well, a tomb full of necrons definitely qualified if anything did, but to my vague disappointment (though complete lack of surprise given the time lag inherent in even the most urgent interstellar communications) neither had responded by the time the briefing was scheduled to start.

The conference room was the most crowded I'd ever seen it as I entered the command post, the babble of conflicting voices almost loud enough to drown out the muffled explosions from the battlefield beyond the large picture window. My eye was drawn to it at once, searching for some sign of the gargant, and despite the ever-present snow whirling against the glass like a disconnected pict screen I was sure I could make out a dark, hulking shape against the mountains in the distance which hadn't been there before. Merciful Emperor, it was almost close enough to open fire on us, a handful of kilometres distant now. I thought of the havoc the massive belly gun would surely wreak, blowing apart buildings and storage tanks alike, and shuddered. Of course the greenskins would be trying to take the installation relatively intact, or at least the vast reserves of refined promethium it contained, so it couldn't really do its worst, but no one ever said orks were rational.[1] If the ork princeps, or whatever he called himself,[2] got over-excited this whole affair could end very loudly and suddenly.

'Commissar.' Colonel Kasteen looked up from her place at the head of the table, and indicated a vacant seat next to her. I dropped into it gratefully, while Jurgen went to find me some more tanna tea, and exchanged a nod of greeting with Broklaw who was seated on the other side of her. 'I'm pleased to see you looking so much better.'

'Thank you,' I said, as Jurgen materialised behind me with a large steaming bowl of the fragrant liquid. I glanced up and down the table, seeing all the faces I remembered from the previous meeting, and a lot more besides. 'Shall we get started?'

'By all means.' She nodded to Broklaw, who cleared his throat loudly, and to my astonishment everyone shut up and looked at him expectantly.

'Thank you for coming at such short notice,' he began, with barely a trace of sarcasm. 'As most of you are no doubt aware, the commissar's scouting trip has uncovered a much greater problem than the orks.' At

---

1. *Actually there have been a few xenologists who argued precisely this, claiming their actions make perfect sense in the context of their own barbarous society, but such views are generally considered eccentric at best.*

2. *Probably some variation of 'Nob' or 'Boss,' which appear to be the only major signifiers of rank and status their language possesses.*

this point he glanced meaningfully at the little knot of tech-priests clustered around Ernulph. Logash was sitting next to him, still wearing the
imbecilic grin he'd been sporting ever since we found him in the tomb
below our feet. I'd invoked my commissarial privileges to unlock some
highly classified files, so that everyone who needed to would know precisely what we were up against, but now the seed of suspicion had been
planted it was hard not to wonder if the magos had known most of it
already.

'How sure are we that it's a problem?' Ernulph asked, an edge of eager
acquisitiveness in his voice. 'If the necrons are in stasis we can surely
concentrate our efforts on repelling the immediate threat.' Meaning let
the poor bloody Guardsmen keep the orks off their backs while he and
his cronies pillaged the tomb, of course.

'They are the immediate threat,' I said, as mildly as I could. I sipped
my bowl of tea while the sudden flare of apprehension in my gut at the
very thought of those mechanical killers subsided. 'If we were up to our
armpits in orks, with a side order of kroot and eldar backing them up,
I'd turn my back on the lot of them to take out a single necron. I've
fought them before, and they're the biggest single menace in the entire
galaxy.'

'Surely you exaggerate,' Pryke said, looking at me sternly, as though I
was making the whole thing up. 'I've accessed the records of previous
encounters with these... whatever they are, and reports of them are
practically non-existent.'

'That's because they hardly ever leave any survivors to report anything,' I rejoined, feeling my hand begin to tremble as old memories
came rushing back. A small gobbet of tea escaped the bowl to pool on
the polished wooden tabletop, and Jurgen leant forward to mop up the
spillage with a handkerchief that left the surface even grubbier than
before. 'Everything else in the galaxy fights for a reason, whether it's for
territory, honour, or souls for the dark gods.' I heard a satisfying intake
of breath at that, having deliberately invoked the most shocking image
I could think of to wrong-foot any objectors. 'Necrons don't. They exist
purely to kill, and they know we're here now.'

'Are you sure about that?' Ernulph persisted. 'They certainly know
about the greenskins. But you escaped unscathed, I gather.' He glanced
at Logash for confirmation.

'The Omnissiah guided our steps,' the young tech-priest declared, 'so
that we might claim the bounty prepared for us.'

'The only preparation you'll get from the necrons is if one of them
fancies your skin as a waistcoat,' I said, having the slight satisfaction of
seeing him blench for a moment before his fanaticism kicked in again.

'The commissar is convinced that the party he encountered were simply scouts,' Kasteen said, determined to keep the business of the meeting moving. 'And while the warp portal remains active down there we can expect a full-scale incursion at any time.'

'What I don't understand,' Morel declared, cutting through the subsequent babble of consternation, 'is why now? They've been down there for Emperor knows how long. What got them so stirred up all of a sudden?'

'I think I can answer that.' As everyone turned to look at him, Quintus cleared his throat a little nervously.

'If you can make any sense of this mess I'd like to hear it,' Kasteen prompted after a moment. Quintus flushed even more, and stood, grinning nervously at the colonel. He produced a data-slate from the recesses of his robes, and projected a page onto the main hololith, which still jumped annoyingly as I tried to make sense of what I was looking at.

'These are the sensor logs from the traffic control system,' he began, before Ernulph interrupted.

'Those are technical documents which fall under the purview of the Adeptus Mechanicus. You have no business dabbling in theological matters!'

'I think you'll find,' Pryke rejoined, equally forcefully, 'that they are archive material, and therefore clearly the responsibility of the Administratum.'

'Their care and maintenance, possibly,' Ernulph persisted. 'But interpretation and consultation are the business of those appointed to commune with the numinous, not some jumped-up inky-fingered quill-pusher!' Pryke seemed on the verge of responding in equally trenchant tones, when Broklaw cleared his throat again. The room went suddenly quiet.

'Might I remind everyone,' Kasteen said mildly, 'that I'm in charge here and I decide who does what. And I want to hear what the scrivener has to say. Are there any objections?' Surprisingly there weren't, which might have had something to do with the way both officers had a hand resting casually on the butts of their bolt pistols; I began to suspect they'd been hanging around me a bit too much lately. She smiled at Quintus, who looked quite flustered for a moment, and nodded judiciously. 'Please continue.'

'Ah. Right. Yes.' Quintus cleared his throat again, and pointed to something in the middle of the display which looked like a stain of ackenberry juice. 'This is the flare of warp energy released when the greenskins' space hulk emerged into the materium.' Ernulph harrumphed disapprovingly at the young scrivener's use of the technical term, and a faint, fleeting grin appeared on Quintus' face just long enough for me to realise he'd done it on purpose to irritate the magos. 'And there was another one almost as strong when it dropped back into the warp.'

'We already knew this,' Ernulph said dismissively. 'Our instrumentation was practically overloaded. It's how we knew they were coming in the first place.'

'Precisely,' Quintus said. 'And because of the strength of the flare we missed that.' He pointed to something else with an air of triumph, undermined a little by the almost total inability of anyone else at the table to see what was hidden by his finger.

'Could you magnify it a little?' Kasteen asked. Quintus flushed, and complied, revealing another, almost imperceptible ackenberry stain. A murmur of voices rippled around the table, and Ernulph at least had the grace to look surprised.

'We missed that,' he admitted grudgingly.

'Quite understandably,' Kasteen assured him diplomatically. 'But can you tell us what it is?'

'I can guess,' the magos admitted reluctantly. Then he grimaced, as though biting into a bitterroot pasty someone had assured him was filled with sweetbriar,[1] and gestured to Quintus to continue. 'But I'm sure the young man has worked it out already. He seems quite bright for a bureaucrat, and we'd never have noticed this anomaly at all if it wasn't for his diligence.' I suppose for all his bluster he was a fair-minded man, but it must have pained him to swallow his pride like that. His colleagues looked positively dyspeptic, and Pryke was gazing at him in open-mouthed astonishment. Kasteen just nodded coolly.

'Thank you magos. I'm glad to see we all seem to be on the same side at last. Quintus?' For some reason the young scrivener became flustered all over again as she looked in his direction, and stuttered for a moment before resuming.

'Well it's outside my realm of expertise, as the magos pointed out, but it seems logical to assume that the flare of warp energy somehow activated the dormant portal in the tomb.' Ernulph was nodding in agreement.

'That would be my interpretation,' he conceded.

'Of course!' Logash butted in with the single-minded enthusiasm of the obsessive. 'That's how the ambulls got down there! They came

---

1. *Cain was evidently still hungry at this point, judging by the sudden flurry of culinary metaphors; hardly surprising given the amount of energy he had expended over the last couple of days.*

through the portal, and dug their way out of the tomb! That explains the anomalous habitat...' He trailed off, suddenly conscious of how very much nobody else in the meeting cared.

'And somehow the necrons noticed that it had reactivated.' Broklaw nodded. 'So they sent a scouting party through. That makes sense.'

'But where from, though?' Pryke asked, anxious to establish that her department was fully involved in things.

'Could be anywhere in the galaxy,' I said. 'Somewhere with ambulls, by the look of it, but that doesn't narrow it down much.'[1]

'That's not really the question at the moment,' Kasteen said, dragging everyone back to the point. 'What we need to decide now is what we do about them.'

'There's only one thing we can do,' I said, as calmly and decisively as I could. 'Evacuate the planet, while we still have enough time to get clear.'

'Evacuate?' Kasteen echoed, clearly stunned. I nodded, conscious that I was risking my whole fraudulent reputation, but that it was precisely that reputation for heroism which might just do the trick now. I adopted an expression of barely-contained frustration.

'I know how you feel. I've never run from a fight yet,' (which was not entirely true, of course, but no one needed to know that), 'and it goes against the grain to start now. But there are wider issues at stake here. The necrons in that tomb outnumber us by hundreds to one, and that's assuming we could disengage from the orks cleanly enough to take them on in a stand-up fight.'

'They'd still know they'd been in a scrap,' Kasteen said grimly. I nodded again.

'I don't doubt the fighting spirit of anyone in the regiment. But if we stand and fight now we will all die. That's a plain, simple fact. They'll overrun us in a matter of hours.' More like minutes, if the ones I'd seen before were anything to go by, but if I told her that she'd never believe me. 'And that's just the start.'

'The portal,' Kasteen said, the coin dropping. I nodded again.

'Hundreds of thousands of them would be let loose on the galaxy. We simply can't allow that to happen.' I paused for a moment, letting the implications sink in. 'We have to call in the Navy to sterilise the whole site from orbit. It's the only way to be sure.'

'You can't do that!' Pryke and Ernulph both shouted at the same time, then broke off to boggle at one another, completely taken aback to find themselves in agreement for once.

---

1. *Indeed not. As yet the world or worlds at the other end of the necron portal remain unidentified, despite the best efforts of the Ordo Xenos.*

'I can, and will,' I contradicted them. 'This facility is under martial law, which means the commissariat is the final arbiter of what can or cannot be done.'

'Have you any idea of the economic value of this installation?' Pryke asked, recovering first.

'None at all, and I care even less,' I said. 'So far as I'm concerned it's not worth the life of one soldier.' The soldier I had in mind being me, of course.

'But the archeotech!' Ernulph spluttered. 'Think of the knowledge, the spiritual advancement of mankind that you'd be sacrificing...'

'All we'd be sacrificing if we left that tomb intact is our lives,' I rejoined. 'Not to mention the millions of others who'd be slaughtered if the necrons down there revive and escape through the portal.'

'But they're in stasis,' the magos persisted. 'While they're dormant we can safely examine...'

'We don't know that,' Kasteen cut in. 'For all we know they're up and about by now. And even if they aren't, their friends could be flocking through the portal from somewhere else. We simply can't risk sending anyone back down there, and that's final.'

'On the contrary,' Ernulph replied. 'I don't think you can risk not sending anyone back.'

'Explain,' Kasteen said, although in a sudden agony of panic I realised what the magos was driving at. The worst of it was that he was right, damn it, and the spasming of my bowels told me who was by far the most likely candidate to get stuck with the job.

'You said it yourself,' he said triumphantly. 'The portal's still active. Even if you called in your naval strike it would be left intact and functioning for months before a flotilla could get here, possibly even years. The necrons would be long gone.'

'Emperor's bowels, he's right.' Broklaw looked more shaken than I'd ever seen him. 'We have to blow the portal before we pull out.'

I felt every pair of eyes at the table lock on to me like the targeting auspex of a hydra battery. The air grew tense with expectation, while my mind whirled frantically, trying to find some plausible reason why this was a truly terrible idea. But inspiration had, for once, deserted me. At length I nodded, my mouth dry.

'I can't see any alternative.'

'Neither can I.' Kasteen turned to me, solemnly pronouncing what I truly believed to be my death sentence. 'Can you lead a team back down to the tomb, commissar?'

THIRTEEN

OF COURSE I couldn't refuse, could I? Not in front of all those people. I'd been neatly impaled on my own rhetoric, and pulling out at this stage would have ruined the reputation I didn't deserve. More to the point it would have lost me the respect of the troops, which was probably the only thing I had left capable of preserving my miserable hide. So I made a few appropriately modest comments about appreciating everybody's confidence and hoping I wouldn't let them down before sinking into a torpor of absolute terror which, as luck would have it, was generally mistaken for fatigue.

As a result the rest of the meeting went by in a blur so far as I was concerned, and if anything else of consequence was discussed I must have missed it.[1] I did rouse myself for long enough to listen to a progress report into some suicidal scheme for disabling the gargant, which Broklaw assured everyone would be effective if the orks in command of it were spectacularly stupid enough to blunder into an obvious trap, but given the intelligence of the ones I'd encountered before in my chequered career this seemed like a safe enough bet.

---

1. *Quintus's minutes of the meeting are singularly unhelpful in filling in this gap, concerned as they are chiefly with the way the overhead lighting struck highlights from Kasteen's hair.*

Other than that I took no interest in anything apart from my bowl of tea, which Jurgen, attentive as ever, refilled at intervals.

So it came as something of a surprise when all the civilians stood up and filed out, the quill-pushers and cogboys predictably butting heads at the door over which of them had precedence while Morel and the miners guild delegation sailed serenely past them, and finally the room fell quiet.

'That went well,' Broklaw said, clearly not meaning it. Kasteen nodded.

'They've agreed to the evacuation, anyway. Not that they had a choice, but at least we won't have to waste any manpower herding them onto the shuttles at gunpoint.'

'Don't count on it,' I said. 'Once they've had time to think it over the tech-priests probably won't go without a fight.' At least most of the miners and Administratum staff had already gone, which only left a couple of hundred civilians still planetside. A couple of shuttle flights, no more than that, although lifting the regiment would be a lot more time consuming when the time came for us to pull out.

'Then they can stay and fight the necrons,' Kasteen said. 'I'm not putting any of our people at risk if they start playing silly frakkers.'

'Glad to hear it,' I said. Not that it would make any difference to me, with my molecules scrambled by a necron gauss gun. And that would be if I was lucky; I thought of the other monstrosities in their coats of ork hide, and hoped fervently never to meet them again. I turned my thoughts in more productive directions with an effort. I wasn't dead yet, and by the Emperor I didn't intend to be if I could find the slightest chance of weaselling out of the suicidal assignment I'd backed myself into. 'What's the tactical situation?' We hadn't discussed that in front of the civvies, of course, they were best being jollied along with vague generalities, and a resolute avoidance of phrases like 'we're frakked' which would only upset them.

By way of an answer Kasteen activated the hololith again and Mazarin appeared at her station on the bridge of the *Pure of Heart*, bobbing slightly in the current from a nearby air vent.

'None of this makes a lot of sense to me,' she admitted cheerfully. 'But you're the soldiers. What do you think?' Kasteen, Broklaw and I stared at the latest sensor downloads from the orbiting starship. The ork advance had unmistakably faltered, breaking against our battle line, and pulling back in places to cluster on their left flank. Broklaw frowned.

'The gargant's veered off,' he said. Well, thank the Emperor for that, I thought, at least I wouldn't have to worry about the booby trap they'd laid for it bringing the whole mine in on top of me while I was down there in the dark facing the necrons again... My hands began to tremble slightly as I thought about that, so I stuffed them into the pockets of my greatcoat and studied the hololith grimly. Something about the redistribution of the ork forces was nagging at my subconscious, and I felt my scalp prickling as I finally realised what it was.

'The tunnel entrance we found was about here,' I said, indicating a point on the opposite flank of the mountain from the valley we were so successfully defending. The bulk of the greenskin forces were moving in that direction, the gargant's unexpected diversion merely a part of the general ... re was only one obvious reason why the orks' attention ... distracted from the ongoing battle with us.

... Kasteen breathed, coming to the same conclusion. ... king the greenies!'

... dging by the number of reinforcements mov- ... ing the display in more detail. That wasn't ... orks will gravitate naturally to wherever ... be fiercest, but it was certainly suggestive. ... d, to my absolute astonishment. 'You know what

'Nope.' Mazarin shrugged in the corner of the hololith, her image shrunk to the size of my hand. 'Not my department.' But of course Kasteen hadn't been talking to her in any case.

'It means the bloody necrons are awake!' I said, a strange mixture of terror and relief dancing down my spine. 'We haven't a hope in hell of getting to the portal now.' I tried to feign disappointment, while wondering how best to ensure I was on the first shuttle up to the freighter.

'Not necessarily,' Mazarin chipped in, and the flare of hope in my chest withered and died. Luckily it was only her image in the room with us, or I'd probably have throttled her with my bare hands. (Not that it would have done me much good, I suppose, given the amount of metal she seemed to have in what was left of her body.) 'If I'm reading these energy spikes right the portal's being activated roughly every seventeen minutes.'

'Which means what, exactly?' Kasteen asked, taking far too much interest in what the bisected woman had to say for my liking. Mazarin shrugged, unless it was the air conditioning behind her kicking up another notch and bouncing her around.

'The necrons here are probably still in stasis. The ones fighting the orks are being shipped in from somewhere else.'

'Securing the tomb before they wake the others,' Broklaw said. Kasteen nodded.

'Sounds plausible.' She looked across at me. 'And they still have no idea we're behind them. You can be in and out before they even know you're there.'

'Lucky me,' I said, clenching my fists in my pockets until the nails drew blood.

'I'M NOT GOING to lie to you,' I said. I felt a vague sense of disconnectedness after that, the reason for which continued to elude me for a while, until I realised that contrary to the habit of a lifetime the subsequent statement was actually true. The harsh arc luminators of the main staging area just inside the mouth of the mine flattene͏͏ colours of the scattered equipment around us, including the lifter against which I leaned in what I hoped was a casual ṇ rather than revealing the weakness of my knees. 'Our chances ͏ ing back from this assignment are practically non-existent. But no exaggeration to say that the lives of everyone else on the pl͏ to mention uncountable others, hang on whether we succeed flicked my eyes along the impassive faces in front of me. N͏ them blinked. I ploughed on, feeling vaguely wrong-foote͏ you're the best team for the job, which is why I asked for y͏ only take willing volunteers. If anyone wants to pull out you have my word there won't be any disciplinary action taken or a word about it on any of your records.' Because I'd be too busy being dead to worry about it… I forced the thought away.

'We're up to it,' the storm trooper sergeant said, the unlit cheroot in the corner of his mouth waggling disconcertingly as he spoke. I gathered that it was some kind of tradition in his squad that he wouldn't light it until the mission was completed. The little knot of men behind him nodded in silent agreement. Not one of them broke ranks, which I would have found astonishing had I not spent a couple of hours combing the records for the most aggressive and disciplined squad in the entire regiment.

And Sergeant Welard and his squad were it: old school storm troopers (quite literally, they'd been together since the schola progenium assessors back on Valhalla had decided they were natural born cannon fodder). They were, accordingly, one of the few teams to have remained single-sex following the amalgamation of the two former regiments which now made up the 597th, since there was no point rotating in replacements for the casualties they'd taken on Corania[1] and wherever

---

1. *The system where a tyranid attack had decimated the imperial defenders, necessitating the amalgamation of the 296th and 301st to create the 597th in the first place.*

else they'd fought before. Schola-raised storm trooper squads generally fight better than most because they've been together so long and know each other so well that they share an instinctive rapport no outsider can ever fully share, but the downside of that is that once their numbers drop below a handful they become pretty much useless, and I've never understood why the Guard persists with the tradition.[1] Right now though, men who'd follow orders without thinking were precisely what I needed, and Welard and his team fit the bill nicely.

'I'm pleased to see my confidence wasn't misplaced,' I said. Apart from Welard there were five regular troopers left out of the original ten, so they were on the verge of falling below the critical threshold at which they would cease to be an effective fighting unit. Nevertheless, they would do. Numbers wouldn't help us on this mission, our only hope was to move fast and stealthily, and that, I knew, was something they were bound to be good at. (In the constant round of rivalries and practical joke playing between the different factions in my days at the schola the storm trooper cadets were by far the most adept at sneaking into the other dorms and common rooms to make mischief, and always set the most inventive booby traps, although I still maintain we had the edge over them on the scrumball pitch. In fact the only team that ever regularly beat the commissar cadets were the novitiates of the Adepta Sororitas, who seemed to think the point of the game was sending the greatest number of opponents they could to the sanitorium rather than scoring goals.)

'We'll get the job done,' Welard said, moving the cheroot to the opposite corner of his mouth, and the quintet behind him nodded in unison. Their silence was unnerving, but I suppose it was a natural consequence of the rapport they shared. Not a word or a gesture was wasted, to the point where, swathed in their greatcoats and hats, their faces partly obscured, they seemed almost as emotionless as servitors. Or the necrons themselves. An aura of almost palpable lethality played about them, which I began to feel almost comforted by, until I remembered the odds stacked against us.

'Any questions?' I asked. Answer came there none, so I drew myself up, straightened my cap, and tried to sound confident. 'Good. Then let's go.'

* * *

---

1. *Because the real reason for the practice is to provide properly indoctrinated foot soldiers for the Inquisition. Of course fewer than five per cent reach the exacting standards required, leaving the ones who don't make the grade to be palmed off on the Guard.*

THE EVACUATION WAS well under way as we set out for the lower levels, a steady flow of miners, Administratum drones and tech-priests walking towards the landing pads with the tense not-quite trot of barely-contained panic, lasgun-wielding troopers guarding the tunnels they thronged through. We strode against the tide, which parted almost miraculously in front of us, each step further from safety seeming like walking on knives to me. A babble of voices surrounded us like syrup, battering the eardrums but overlapping so much that individual words and phrases were indistinguishable.

'Comms check,' I said, more to distract myself than anything, and Welard and the other storm troopers sounded off one by one, although truth to tell, and I ought to be ashamed of it, I was so busy battling my own apprehension that none of their names registered with me. Everyone's comm-bead seemed to be working, though, so I nodded briskly. 'Very good.'

'General order.' Kasteen's voice cut in. 'Anyone in sight of Magos Ernulph report now.' There was an irritable pause, broken only by a faint hiss of static. 'Anyone with an idea of his whereabouts?' Another pause. 'Anyone seeing him, report at once.'

Great. It seemed the tech-priests weren't about to leave their prize behind after all, and were going into hiding until we'd left. Just so long as they stayed out of our way, though, it wasn't my problem.

The passageways we strode through were getting narrower now, the air cooler as we entered the mine workings themselves, and I told myself the shivering which seemed to be gripping my body was simply a result of the falling temperatures. Before long the walls around us were filmed with ice, and shortly after that there was nothing for the ice to coat; we were in the mine itself again.

Ahead of us a cavern opened out, harsh with the glare of luminators mounted on poles around its perimeter, the dark mouths of the main tunnels puncturing the walls at intervals. Equipment and storage crates littered the floor, and I recognised it as one of the main utility areas we'd passed through on our ambull hunt, little guessing the horrors we'd find in the depths below. Beyond this point our journey would truly begin.

'Movement.' One of the troopers raised his hellgun, and the others melted into the industrial detritus around us with breathtaking speed, leaving me feeling uncomfortably exposed. A lone figure was lurking at the mouth of the tunnel ahead of us, half hidden in the gloom beyond. After a moment to recover my composure, as the rational part of my mind kicked in to remind me that orks or necrons wouldn't be bothering with concealment, I strode forward unconcerned expecting to find some stray miner or tech-priest finishing off a last-minute job prior to joining the evacuation. As I got closer to the solitary figure I felt my spirits inexplicably lifting as I caught the faint whiff of a familiar odour.

'Jurgen,' I called out. 'What the frak are you doing here?' My aide stepped fully into view, and the storm troopers emerged from the cover they'd taken, looking mildly sheepish. 'I thought you were stowing our kit on the shuttle.'

'All taken care of, sir.' He produced a thermal flask. 'I thought you might like a bit of tea for later. And a sandwich.' He burrowed in one of his pockets for a moment. 'It's in here somewhere...'

'I see,' I said, silencing the barely audible snickering from a couple of the storm troopers behind me with a quick glance before turning back to Jurgen again. 'And the melta?' He shrugged, the heavy weapon slung across his back shifting as his shoulders moved.

'I couldn't let you carry your own provisions, sir. Wouldn't be fitting.'

'Quite,' I said, astonished yet again at the depth of his loyalty. For the first time I began to feel that I might actually get out of this ludicrous expedition in one piece after all. 'I suppose you'd better come with us, then.'

'Very good, sir.' He saluted as smartly as he ever did, which wasn't very to be honest, but more than made up for that in enthusiasm, and fell into step beside me. I motioned Welard and his men to the front and we set off into the darkness, towards the terrors which lay in wait for us in the frozen depths below.

Extracted from *Like a Phoenix From the Flames: The Founding of the 597th*, by General Jenit Sulla (retired), 097.M42

NOTWITHSTANDING THE FLOOD of rumours which had swept the regiment, most of them contradictory, but which all agreed in the main particular that Commissar Cain had discovered some new and potent threat in the bowels of the mine, I held fast to my duty and resumed my post at the front line. Whatever the truth of the matter I had my orders, and as a loyal officer that was enough for me. No doubt those better placed to evaluate the intelligence the commissar had so heroically gathered would inform us of whatever we needed to know to meet and overcome this latest vile stain on His Glorious Majesty's blessed dominions in the fullness of time, or so I told my subordinates, and until such information was furnished wild speculation about daemons, tyranids, or walking metal statues was merely a waste of time. This last flight of fantasy would, of course, turn out to have more than a grain of truth in it, but in the closing years of the forty-first millennium, with the true horror of the necron menace still unknown to all but a few, such talk seemed naught but the most febrile of fantasies.

My platoon had resumed its position in the forward line, with strict instructions to fall back at the specified time to draw the gargant into our carefully laid trap, and we had been engaging the main bulk of the greenskin army with a gratifying amount of success. So much so, in fact, that I began to fear that we were thinning them out too quickly, and that we would be forced to engage the towering war machine ourselves before the time came to disengage. The shadow of that grim colossus was falling across us as we gazed in awe at it, the shrieks of thousands of tonnes of unlubricated metal sliding across one another as it tottered forward on unfeasibly stubby-looking legs setting the teeth of every woman and man among us on edge, and I found myself comparing it most unfavourably to the swift darting elegance of the eldar walkers and the majestic nobility of our own blessed titans.[1]

I was on the verge of ordering those fortunate enough to be manning the forward trenches to engage those members of its crew who could quite clearly be discerned scurrying about on the main hull when the vast cannon nestled in the construct's belly spoke, the concussion sufficient to drive the breath from our lungs and cause cracks to appear in

---

1. *Most unlikely, as at this point in her career she had yet to see either. Unless you count holo-picts, of course.*

our stout fortifications even at this distance. I turned my head, expecting to see the most grievous havoc wreaked among the precious buildings of the refinery, only to see instead the distant gout of a vast explosion somewhere among the slopes of the mountains surrounding this vital outpost of the Imperium.

'It's veering off!' my communications specialist yelled, angling his head so I could read his lips, for the awesome sound of that titanic explosion had left my ears still ringing, and to my astonishment I beheld the truth of his words. It had clearly faltered, almost on the point of engaging our forward line, and was now turning ponderously towards the looming peaks it had so inexplicably attacked.

At that moment we received our orders to withdraw, so I cannot be sure of what I witnessed next, seeing it as I did at an ever-increasing distance in short, snatched glances over my shoulder as we ran, and through a curtain of falling snow. However, it seemed to me that the terrifying construct was surrounded by small structures, no higher than its knee, which had appeared by sorceries so arcane I was at a loss to explain them. Blank metal pyramids they were, dully reflective, and surrounded by a crackle of lightning which blurred their outline still further; sorcerous lightning without a doubt, for it lashed forth to scourge the hull of that mountain of metal, striking sparks so bright they hurt to look upon. Chunks of metal larger than Chimeras fell lazily to the snow, and the burning bodies of its luckless crew pattered down around them, so that I cannot for the life of me conceive how it could ever have prevailed. But whether it did or not I cannot truly answer, for the snow whirled in around that epic confrontation, and I saw no more.

FOURTEEN

ONE THING I have to say for Welard and his storm troopers, they were as fast and stealthy as I could have wished for. Jurgen and I had to work hard at keeping up with them even though they advanced as cautiously as though the enemy were already in plain sight. Two or three of them covered the tunnel ahead while the others darted forward to conceal themselves in crevices or patches of shadow before taking up the duties of guardians themselves to allow their comrades to move forward in their turn. They did all of this with an eerie precision apparently unhindered by the bulk of the melta bombs they carried, communicating only by hand signals and eschewing the use of the comm-beads, for which I was grateful, starting in dread at every superfluous sound which might call attention to us. But as we hurried on, following the route which had etched itself indelibly on the synapses responsible for my ability to navigate underground, we saw none of the signs I so dreaded. No gleam of metal in the darkness ahead, no green charnel glow forewarning us of the presence of death incarnate.

We advanced in semi-darkness, our luminators shrouded, so that the dazzling highlights which had been struck from the ice surrounding us on my previous trip into the depths were almost entirely absent. Now, instead of the refulgent background glow I'd grown used to, the walls threw back no more than a slick, almost organic-looking sheen, as though we were passing down the gullet of some warp-spawned leviathan. The thought was hardly a comforting one, and I shuddered from more than the cold.

At length we reached the dead-end passage where Penlan had fallen, revealing the existence of the ambull tunnels below the mine, and we paused to regroup.

'This is it,' I warned everyone. 'From now on our chances of meeting a necron are greatly increased.' What I meant was 'practically inevitable,' but I shied away from pronouncing those words. Not out of deference to the feelings of Welard and his men, who I had no doubt would have responded with the same lack of emotion that they had displayed thus far, but because I didn't want to face that thought myself. Welard waggled his cheroot, which had by now acquired a thin scum of frost over the tightly-packed tabac leaves it was composed of, and which crunched irritatingly between his teeth as he spoke.

'We'll be ready for them.' He gestured with his left hand. 'Hastur.' One of the troopers stepped forward to cover the hole with his hellgun while the rest rappelled down into the darkness with display team precision. I heard a couple of clicks in my comm-bead, almost as if it were picking up some stray interference from somewhere but which I knew was the signal from the advance party confirming that it was all clear down there, and the sergeant grinned at me. For the first time it struck me that he was actually enjoying this. 'Coming?' he asked, and disappeared down the hole after his men.

Why I simply didn't shake my head and run for the surface, intent only on making it to the next shuttle out, I'll never know. There was still my fraudulent reputation to consider, of course, double-edged weapon though that had become in the last few years, dragging me into these ghastly situations almost as readily as I was able to turn it to my advantage, but even now I found myself reluctant to surrender it. And it couldn't be denied that my chances of survival would be marginally better with a screen of storm troopers between me and the necrons instead of wandering around these catacombs alone. I glanced round the narrow chamber, steeling myself, and met Jurgen's eyes. The sight of him was instantly reassuring, despite his usual unprepossessing appearance, a visible (and olfactory) reminder of all the perils we'd faced and bested together. He grinned at me, and hefted the bulk of his melta.

'After you, sir,' he said. 'I'll watch your back.' A task, I have to say, which he performed admirably throughout our years of service together. I forced a smile to my face.

'I don't doubt it,' I said, then before I could change my mind I seized the line and slithered down into the bowels of hell.

I landed heavily, but retained my footing, and was able to step aside as Jurgen lurched down the rope behind me. The storm troopers looked mildly disdainful at our performance, the awkwardness of which was underlined a moment later by Hastur's descent, which he managed with the dexterity of an acrobat.

'Where to?' Welard asked.

'This way.' I indicated the right direction and waited while the storm troopers went through the gap first, falling into place behind them. With every step we took the knot in my stomach wound itself tighter, the memory of where we were going insinuating itself into my fore-brain, inextricably intertwined with images of the massacre I'd witnessed on Interitus Prime. This would be different, I kept telling myself. I wasn't fleeing in panic through an unknown labyrinth this time, I was heading for a known location, which, by the Emperor's grace, I had already entered before and escaped to tell the tale. Kasteen was right, the necrons would be concerned entirely with the greenskins, they didn't even know we were here...

'Found something,' the pointman said, snapping me out of my reverie and back to the claustrophobic confines of the ambull run. We closed up, the faint light from our shrouded luminators glinting from some detritus on the tunnel floor.

'What do you make of that, sir?' Jurgen asked, his feeble beam picking out something only he had noticed. Apart from myself, he was the only one of our party who had walked these narrow tunnels before, and would be able to notice any changes. The hairs on the back of my neck rose, something that happens in popular fiction far more often than it does in real life, and which I can assure you is a remarkably uncomfortable sensation. My aide was shining his luminator down a narrow cylinder punched into the ice lining the tunnel, about the width of my forearm and deep beyond the strength of the lamp he carried to pick out the end.

'They've been here,' I murmured. The only possible explanation was a stray gauss flayer shot striking the tunnel wall. I looked about us, finding several more of the sinister indentations.

'Then who were they shooting at?' Jurgen asked. That was a good question. If the orks had made it this far into the tunnels our job was about to get a great deal more complicated. I moved up to join Welard and the point man, who were staring in perplexity at a small mound of metal objects embedded in ice, ominously streaked with red.

'What do you think these are, sir?' he asked, the air of unassailable confidence taking a dent for the first time since I'd met him. I looked at the assemblage of tubes and wires for a moment, then the bile rose into my throat as I realised what I was looking at.

'They're augmetics,' I said, swallowing heavily. 'They've been ripped out of someone.' So that was where Ernulph had disappeared to. These might not be his remains, of course, but it was carrots to credits he'd led whatever foolhardy expedition this pathetic revenant had been a part of. I wondered vaguely if we'd find traces of any other victims, or if they'd all simply been vaporised.

One thing was certain, though. Thanks to these idiots the necrons would know there were humans on Simia Orichalcae now, and were most likely waiting in ambush ahead of us. This was just getting better and better.

Well, there was no point in standing around worrying about it, time was most definitely of the essence here, so I got everyone moving again and dropped back to walk beside Jurgen.

'Be ready,' I warned him, 'things could be about to get–'

I was interrupted by the dying shriek of our point man as he flared and dwindled to nothing in the necrotic glow of one of those hellish gauss weapons, and then the metallic warriors whose appearance I'd so dreaded were upon us.

'Place your shots,' Welard said calmly, and the surviving storm troopers unleashed a hail of hellgun fire against our attackers. The glare of the lasbolts impacting on the leading necron dazzled my eyes, then its chest gave way, seared and blasted by the precision volley, and it tumbled to the ice-slick floor revealing a fresh target behind it, already levelling another gauss flayer.

Credit where it's due, Welard and his men certainly knew their stuff. As I've mentioned before, the ambull tunnels were narrow, forcing the hideous automata to come at us almost in single file. But the storm troopers' discipline was excellent, and with the death of our first casualty they'd dropped into a practiced routine, the men at the front falling prone, those behind kneeling, and the ones at the rear standing up so that the whole squad was able to concentrate their fire as one. The second necron lost its head, quite literally, and fell heavily across the first with a sound not unlike someone kicking a bin full of scrap metal. As I watched it fall I realised, with a thrill of horror, that the first metallic warrior we'd all thought destroyed was rising slowly to its feet again.

'Jurgen,' I called, and my aide stepped forward levelling the melta. The storm troopers slipped easily out of his way, keeping up a barrage of hellgun fire to cover him while he aimed, and shielding their eyes as he squeezed the trigger.

The flare of actinic energy stabbed my retina, even through my closed eyelids, and the roar of ice flashing instantly into steam echoed all around us. The air against my face was suddenly warm and wet, as though I'd been teleported into a rain-forest somewhere. As I blinked my vision clear I could see nothing but puddles of molten metal surrounded by grotesque lumps of statuary, some of which still twitched, freezing almost at once into the rapidly-reforming ice. Then, in an instant, they faded away as though they'd never been, leaving behind nothing but drifting vapour and some oddly-shaped indentations in the tunnel floor.

'Clear,' Hastur called, taking the place of the disintegrated point man, and leading us on into the darkness. Welard nodded at Jurgen, an almost imperceptible tilt of the head as he passed my aide, the closest I suppose he could come to expressing thanks to an outsider, and jogged along in the wake of his men. I couldn't help contrasting the reaction of Grifen's team to the loss of Lunt with the storm troopers' matter-of-fact dismissal of the loss of one of their own, and mentioned as much to the sergeant.

'The mission comes first,' he said, his face hard, and that's all he would say on the subject. I wasn't exactly in the mood for idle conversation either, so I let it drop, and resumed straining my ears for the slightest sound which might indicate the approach of more of those monstrous guardians.

Luck or the Emperor must have been with us, though, as all too soon I beheld the baleful glow which forewarned us that we were about to reach our goal. We flattened ourselves against the ice-covered bedrock of the tunnel wall as we approached the entrance to that mighty cavern, through which I'd escaped only a few hours before, and strained our senses for any sign that we had been discovered.

All seemed quiet, except for that damnable humming and the artillery barrage pounding of my heart, so we crept out into the chamber I had so fervently hoped never to see again. My scalp crawled with apprehension, and I had to exert every micron of self-control I possessed to appear calm in front of Welard and his men. They kept their weapons trained on every patch of cover, every green-tinged shadow in the lee of those towering and incomprehensible mechanisms. If they were at all disconcerted by the sheer sense of wrongness surrounding them they gave no sign of it.

'Which way?' the sergeant asked, and I indicated the direction of the portal. He nodded. 'Move out.'

We scurried through that vast space as Jurgen and I had mere hours before, still sticking to the shadows of the towering machines, that ghastly charnel light bathing everything in a sheen of putrescence. Some of them were marked with the peculiar stick and circle hieroglyphics I'd seen on Interitus Prime, and you can be sure the memories the sight of them stirred up did little to calm my fears. By this time my nerves were stretched tighter than harp strings, and it was probably this sense of heightened paranoia which let me hear an almost inaudible sound, a faint scraping which reminded me of scuttling vermin. I signalled the sergeant.

'Five metres, two o'clock. Behind that... Whatever the hell it is.' Welard nodded, and gestured a couple of troopers to flank the gleaming tangle of green-glowing pipes. The rest of us closed up, ready to face whatever the threat was, and I drew my laspistol and chainsword. Not that I expected the latter to be much good against metal rather than flesh, but it had served me well on many occasions before now, and the weight of it felt comforting in my hand.

'Contact. No threat,' said one of the storm troopers, his voice slightly attenuated in my comm-bead, and fell silent again. I hurried forward to join them, cursing their taciturnity.

'Explain,' I said, equally terse, and afraid of transmitting for long enough to be triangulated on. If the trooper was surprised he gave no sign of it.

'It's a cogboy,' he explained flatly.

Not just any cogboy, of course, the Emperor has more of a sense of humour than that. Even before I joined them I had a sense of foreboding, which was amply justified as I looked down at the quivering bundle trying to wedge itself under the largest pipe.

'Logash,' I said. The young tech-priest must have recognised my voice, because he turned and looked up at me. Though his metal eyes made any expression hard to read, a sense of recognition began to surface through the expression of stark terror suffusing his face.

'Commissar Cain?' His voice trembled, wavering in pitch like a boy in early adolescence. If he wasn't bonkers before, I thought, he certainly was now. 'You were right, you were right. We were unworthy to trespass on the sacred mysteries of the Omnissiah–'

'Where are the others?' I interrupted, squatting down to his level, and keeping my voice calm. I haven't had that much experience with madmen, give or take the odd Chaos cultist, but I've seen enough cases of combat fatigue and his symptoms seemed similar; overwhelmed by the horrors he'd witnessed he'd simply retreated inside himself. 'Where's Magos Ernulph?'

'Dead,' he moaned, his blank eyes roving aimlessly, 'struck down by the guardians for our hubris. We should have listened to you, we should have listened...'

Resisting the temptation to say 'told you so,' albeit with some difficulty, I raised him to his feet as gently as I could manage. (Which wasn't very, to be honest, he was all but catatonic, but I succeeded in the end.)

'You're bringing him with us?' Welard asked, in tones which left me in no doubt what he thought of that idea. I nodded.

'We can't just leave him here,' I said. The sergeant looked dubious, and for a moment I wavered, thinking our mission here was hanging by a thread as it was, and adding a babbling lunatic to our number wasn't likely to help any. Then again, Logash had been down here longer than any of us, and might have information which could save our lives, or at least help us blow up the portal. As so often in my life it was an almost impossible decision to make, and one which no one else could, but that's why I get to wear the fancy cap. I pulled on the tech-priest's arm, reminded of Grifen's attempt to snap Magot out of her stupor not far from this very spot. 'We have to go,' I said. To my relief Logash nodded, and fell into step beside Jurgen and myself.

'I take it Ernulph asked you to guide him down here?' I asked, and the tech-priest nodded.

'I remembered the way. The Omnissiah guided–'

'Yes, quite,' I interrupted. 'Then what happened?' His face twisted.

'We entered the temple, and the guardians fell upon us. Some were cut down where they stood, in the very act of making obeisance to the machine god, while others fled. But the guardians pursued them without mercy.' That explained the remains we'd found in the tunnel anyway, a few of them must have made it that far out of here before they were cornered. Logash turned a pinched, anguished face to me. 'They were swift and terrible,' he whispered, 'and shrouded in horror.'

Well that sounded pretty much like every form of necron I'd ever encountered, and I dismissed his words as a figure of speech at the time, although I was soon to discover how right he was.

'Contact,' Hastur said, and opened fire. The other storm troopers followed suit, and I dived for cover, dragging Logash into the shadows with me. A moment later an acrid odour of unwashed socks indicated that Jurgen had joined us.

I levelled my laspistol, seeking a target, and was gratified to see that the storm troopers were doing sterling work in engaging the advancing party of metallic warriors. They were the skin-hunters we'd seen before, or identical copies of them, advancing with terrifying speed, their long blades whispering through the air as they swept back and forth. Instead of ork hides, though, the leading ranks were swathed in human skins, still wet and leaking, thin runnels of blood turned black by the corpse-light, which illuminated everything here, veining the metal torsos beneath. As I tracked the leading one, placing a las bolt squarely in the centre of its forehead, I realised with a shudder that the obscene covering it wore still had the vestige of a face; a face, moreover, which I recognised.

'Ernulph!' I whispered, revulsion twisting my stomach, as the creature inside his skin staggered backwards. I made sure of it with a flurry of follow-up shots, then turned my attention to the monstrosity behind it. The magos had been a pompous fool, it was true, but no one deserved a fate like that.

'They're behind us!' Hastur warned, before his voice rose in a throat-rending scream. I turned just in time to see him borne down by one of the razor-wielding automata, eviscerated in seconds, his blood left streaming down the sides of the bulky metal cabinet from behind which, a heartbeat before, he had been pouring hellgun fire into the main body of our vile assailants. A moment later the flayed one rose from a crouch, the still wet skin of the deceased storm trooper clinging to its metal torso by the stickiness of its own blood.

'Frak this!' I shouted. 'Jurgen!' On cue my aide unleashed another blast from his melta into the centre of the group, cutting a swathe through them as efficiently as before. Once again the necrons caught by the full force of the blast were simply annihilated, flashing into vapour as thoroughly as the victims of their own terrible weapons, while the ones at the fringe of that ravening burst of energy staggered, limbs and torsos seared and softened like candle wax. For a moment I expected them to rally, restoring themselves in that unnerving fashion I'd seen before, but the survivors simply vanished into thin air. For some reason Hastur's body went with them, but why they would want it was a mystery I was sure I would never want to know the answer to.[1]

'How far to the objective?' Welard asked, as the surviving storm troopers regrouped. Beyond a single glance at the coating of blood on the metal surfaces marking the spot where Hastur had died he seemed utterly unperturbed by the terrible fate which had befallen his comrade, and the rest seemed equally focussed on the outcome of our mission, scanning the halls around us for any sign of renewed necron activity. I was grateful for their vigilance, but I was beginning to find their complete lack of emotion somewhat unnerving.

'About three hundred metres,' I said, forcing my mind back to the issue at hand. Welard nodded, and waved to his remaining squad mates to move out. Jurgen and I fell in behind them as before, although

---

1. *Presumably for the same reason their harvester fleets abduct the populations of isolated colony worlds. Whatever that is.*

I was now acutely aware that an attack could come from any direction, and you can be sure that I scanned our surroundings with even more diligence than before. I got Logash moving again with a relatively light tug on the arm, and he trotted along with us, apparently perfectly happy to follow whatever orders I gave now I'd been proven to be right about the inadvisability of being here in the first place.

After a few moments I caught sight of a bright glow from beyond the concealing bulk of one of those vast machines, and indicated it to the sergeant.

'That's it,' I said, watching it pulse like the beating of a diseased heart, and fighting down the surge of dread which suddenly suffused me. 'The portal.' The glow intensified for a moment, with an accompanying thunder crack of displaced air which rumbled and echoed through that city-sized cavern as though presaging a tropical downpour. 'And it's active.' I tried not to think about how many reinforcements had suddenly arrived; rather too many, judging by the amount of air that had been elbowed out of their way as they materialised.

'Not for long,' Welard said, his confidence apparently undiminished by the loss of a third of his squad already.

'Movement,' one of the troopers cut in, as blandly unemotional as before. 'Eleven o'clock, thirty metres.' We turned to face this new threat, the quartet of storm troopers raising their hellguns, while Jurgen lifted the melta into a firing position. Logash was trembling violently.

'Omnissiah protect thy circuits,' he mumbled, 'let this unworthy relay speed the electrons of thy great computation, preserving us from burnout...' and other tech-priest gibberish. I glanced back at the storm troopers, and was astonished to see them quivering almost as badly.

'Emperor be with us,' the closest was muttering under his breath, 'protect us with the shield of thy will...'

Something was seriously wrong, I thought. After everything they'd already shrugged off it was hard to credit that they would be spooked so badly by a single group of warriors who barely outnumbered us. But Willard's jaw was clenched, bisecting the cheroot, most of which had fallen unnoticed to the floor. The hellgun jittered in his hands, wavering almost too wildly to aim, and he was muttering too, one of the catechisms of command which had evidently been drummed into him by the schola tutors, and rather more effectively than it had been with me judging by his demeanour up to this point.

He began firing wildly at the approaching warriors, and as if that were a signal the others opened up too, badly-aimed las-bolts detonating all round the necrons with barely a single hit scored, almost as inaccurate as orks. There was something about these warriors which was different from the others we'd seen, a more resolute, self-aware quality, which sent shudders down my spine as I took in more of the details of their appearance. Less skeletal than the others they seemed composed of ceramics as much as metal, and with writhing pipes and cables corded around their metallic bones which flexed like living muscles as they moved. Thin tendrils of despair seemed to wrap themselves around my very soul as they approached us, bringing not mere death but annihilation in their wake. Fear I was used to, could master and control at least to some extent, but this was different, a primal terror which rose up from somewhere deep within me, and threatened to swamp my very sense of self. Levelling the laspistol in my hand, and ironically grateful for the augmetics which steadied my grip in spite of the treachery of my own body, I fired at the leading one, gouging a neat crater in the centre of its forehead.

'The horror! The horror!' Logash was going foetal on me again, clinging to my ankles, and the storm troopers were breaking, fleeing in all directions with cries of terror. 'The horror returns!'

'Jurgen, get him off me!' I yelled, restrained from following only by the dead weight of the gibbering tech-priest. I fought against that rush of primal emotion, feeling my very sense of self under threat in a way I hadn't experienced since the Slaaneshi witch tried to sacrifice my soul to her perverted deity on Slawkenberg over a decade before, and shooting entirely by instinct now. The green lance of a gauss flayer beam missed me by a couple of centimetres, and punched a neat hole through the smooth-sided cabinet beside me. I shot back, taking my assailant in the chest, and making it stagger for a moment before resuming its unhurried advance.

'Come along, sir.' My aide was at my side now, prising Logash's fingers away from my boot, which wasn't easy given that they were closed by a rictus of terror and augmetic into the bargain. The pressure against my soul eased abruptly, as though cut off by the slamming of a door. I hustled Logash to his feet, and moved behind Jurgen as he aimed and fired the melta.

Once again the powerful weapon did its work, taking down our most immediate assailants, but this time there was to be no reprieve from them teleporting out to lick their wounds. The group had scattered to hunt down the fleeing storm troopers, and we only got a couple of them. As I looked around for some sign of our erstwhile companions I saw two of them taken down with gauss flayer shots, screaming into vapour even as I watched. Welard was backed into a corner between two blocky structures the size of Chimeras, eyes unfocussed, his mind clearly gone, hellgun hanging forgotten from his hand, babbling incoherently. He was still crying out to the Emperor for help which never came when the leading automaton swung the heavy blade of its polearm-like weapon and took his head off cleanly with a single sweep, spraying itself with a thick coating of his blood.

'Come on,' I said urgently. 'We have to get out of here!' Logash was beginning to recover whatever was left of his wits, and shook his head slowly.

'What happened?' he asked. I was beginning to understand, but there was no time now for lengthy explanations, and at our last meeting Amberley had impressed on both Jurgen and myself the paramount importance of not revealing his gift to anyone, so I just grabbed him by the arm to get him moving.

'Stay close to Jurgen,' I instructed, and we went to ground between a blank-faced metal cabinet about three storeys high and a loop of conduit which resembled a glowing green intestine. A faint shriek, abruptly cut off, confirmed the loss of the last storm trooper.

With pounding pulses we stayed put for some time, as Logash had undoubtedly done before, while those ghastly apparitions began what had every appearance of a methodical search for us. To my relief, however, they seemed to become mildly disorientated every time they approached our hiding place, veering off before they had come within a handful of metres of us, a deliverance I could only attribute to Jurgen's peculiar qualities.[1]

At length, when everything seemed quiet again, I decided it was time to move. The evacuation must be well under way by now, and I meant to be on a shuttle and safe aboard the *Pure of Heart* before anything else had a chance to go wrong.

'What about the portal, sir?' Jurgen wondered aloud. I shrugged.

'Nothing we can do about it now.' Which was actually true, as the storm troopers had been carrying the melta charges which were the only things which might have stood some chance of destroying it, and they'd been vaporised along with the soldiers. 'We'll just have to call in the Navy after all.' Tough luck on the galaxy, of course, but it's a big place, and even a necron army couldn't put that big a dent in it. I hoped. So we made our cautious way back to the tunnel we'd come in by, scurrying from cover to cover as we had done before, and freezing into immobility at every sign of movement.

---

1. *Perhaps correctly. The aura of terror projected by necron pariahs appears to be at least partly a psychic phenomenon, so it's quite reasonable to assume that a blank would repel them and mask the effect. However, since no other record exists of a blank coming into such close proximity to a group of pariahs, and they're far too rare and valuable to risk in deliberately testing this hypothesis, it must remain conjectural.*

To my immense relief we encountered no more of those terrible apparitions, catching sight of the more common warriors only at a distance. The aperture left by the ambulls was unguarded, to my delighted surprise, and I regained the sanctuary of the ice tunnels with a lightness of spirit which was almost intoxicating.

It was too good to last, of course, and inevitably it didn't.

Editorial Note:

As Cain began to make his way back to the surface, things were beginning to take an unfortunate turn there too. The tech-priests' incursion into the necron tomb had indeed, as he feared, drawn their attention to the existence of the human colony above their heads, while the orks, outmatched as they were, had begun to break, only to find the Valhallan defences weakened or abandoned altogether as they fell back. Not unnaturally many of the routing greenskins took advantage of the new line of retreat thus opened up, and began to threaten the refinery itself.

Under this renewed pressure the evacuation began to falter. Even though almost two full companies had thus far been ferried up to the orbiting starship the converted civilian shuttles aboard the Pure of Heart *simply weren't up to the challenge of embarking an entire regiment in a matter of hours. As the following extract from Captain Durant's log makes clear, the loss of well over half the men and women deployed just a few days before seemed almost inevitable.*

+++Vox-log record of Captain Durant,
Merchant fleet freighter Pure of Heart, 651.932 M41+++

STILL STUCK IN orbit around this miserable iceball. At the last count we
had most of the civilian staff and their families stowed away somewhere, only a couple of hundred still cluttering up the corridors with
their carcasses and personal effects, but Bosun Kleg has promised to
sort that out so I'm leaving him to it.

The Guardsmen have started arriving back up here too, although at
least they've got somewhere to bunk. The officers are having a hard
time keeping order, as most of them seem concerned about the majority still stranded planetside. Can't say I blame them, as Mazarin says
there's no way our shuttles can get many more runs in before the refinery's overrun by the greenskins or these metal creatures, or possibly
both. She keeps checking the sensor net and calling the surface with
updates, but so far she says the gropos[1] keep losing ground, and I can't
see any way of stopping that.

But then I'm only a starship captain, thank the Emperor, so what I
know about soldiering you could write on the back of a holocard. I
told Mazarin not to worry, that colonel looks as though she knows
what she's doing and their commissar's supposed to be some kind of
hero, but I can tell she wasn't convinced...

---

1. A contraction of 'ground pounders,' a Navy term for the Imperial Guard units sometimes billeted aboard their warships. Less common among merchant crews, Durant's use of it here implies
that this wasn't the first time the Pure of Heart had been pressed into service as a fleet auxiliary.

FIFTEEN

AFTER MAKING OUR way through the ambull tunnels without so much as a sniff of the necrons I began to think we might just be lucky enough to rejoin our comrades without further incident, and I must confess to a sensation akin to euphoria as we scrambled up the rope to emerge into the lower galleries of the mine itself. After the cramped ambull runs the high ceiling and the wide tunnels of the man-made workings seemed as broad and open as a city boulevard. We made good time back towards the surface, proceeding in line abreast at a rapid trot. Logash seemed to be a little more rational now we'd left that hive of the damned behind us at last, although being a tech-priest that was only relatively speaking of course, and he kept up with Jurgen and myself without any obvious difficulty.

Jurgen and I had set our luminators to full refulgence now we were back on what I fondly imagined was safer ground, and the beams were lighting our way some considerable distance in front of us. The surrounding ice was bouncing the light as it had before, throwing back the photons in the shimmering blues and star cluster sparkles I remembered so well, so it was a second or two before I realised that the gleam up ahead had come not from the walls but from a reflective metal surface.

'Kill the lights!' I shouted as the coin finally dropped, and twisted to the side as I did so, a reflex which undoubtedly saved my life. A bilious green beam cut through the space in which I'd been standing an instant before, illuminating for an instant the darkness which now enshrouded us, Jurgen having followed my lead, and throwing the three of us into sharp relief before it vanished again, evanescent as lightning. The situation was as grim as any I'd faced; to remain where we were would make us sitting targets as the necrons advanced, whereas the slightest glimmer of light would betray our position. A couple more dazzling green flares flickered past us to emphasize the point. Fleeing blindly down the tunnel would merely ensure we were shot in the back, if we didn't simply slip and fall on the icy surface. Our only option seemed to be to stand and fight, although judging by the positions of their weapon flashes the metal warriors were too spread out to make an obvious target for Jurgen's melta, negating the only advantage we had.

I had just drawn my laspistol, preparing for a bit of speculative fire myself in the no doubt vain hope that the necrons would think twice about rushing us (from what I'd seen of them before they didn't strike me as being easily intimidated), when I felt a light tap on my arm.

'This way,' Logash whispered, and I heard the faint scurrying sound of rapid crawling movement to my left. A moment later I heard the same murmur from somewhere in Jurgen's immediate vicinity (which wasn't hard to pinpoint, as my sense of smell was still unimpeded), and I realised with a thrill of hope that the young tech-priest's augmetic eyes were somehow able to function in the darkness which enveloped us.

Having nothing to lose I crawled rapidly in the direction of his voice, guided by occasional murmurs of 'straight ahead,' and 'left a bit... No, the other left, I meant mine...' until I found myself against the frozen surface of the wall. I was just about to ask what now when a gloved hand accompanied by Jurgen's unmistakable odour reached out to seize my arm.

'In here, commissar,' he whispered, giving me the full benefit of his halitosis, and I found myself squeezing through a narrow crevice in the ice. After a few metres it angled sharply, concealing us completely from the main shaft, and we held our collective breath as a clatter of metal feet echoed past our hiding place.

'Well spotted,' I said, when I was sure it was quiet out there, and adjusted my luminator to minimum refulgence. My companions' faces emerged out of the gloom, Logash's pale, and Jurgen's as impassive as ever. The tech-priest nodded.

'Praise the Omnissiah for our deliverance...' he began, and I hushed him quickly.

'Yes, good, thanks very much,' I said. 'Any idea where this goes?' It wasn't on the chart I'd seen before, but that was hardly surprising, showing as it did every sign of being a natural fault rather than having been dug.[1] Logash pondered a moment.

'It seems to be bearing towards the main processing area,' he said at last. 'Assuming it doesn't just peter out.' Well that was a risk I was willing to take, since the alternative was be facing Emperor knew how many necron patrols. I hoped they were simply scouting the mine rather than invading it in force, but I wasn't keen to hang around and find out one way or the other. At least this way we stood a better chance of avoiding them.

An hour or so later I was beginning to think we'd have done better taking our chances playing tag with the necrons. The fault was narrow and jagged, so we were climbing up slopes or slithering down them more often than we were walking, and chunks of ice kept catching at our feet or projecting from the walls at heights and angles calculated to bruise or worse. On several occasions we had to crawl, as the ceiling descended too low for us to walk, and once we were forced to worm our way forwards on our stomachs as the passage became too constricted even for that. Jurgen's bulky melta became wedged with monotonous regularity, requiring some laborious chipping away of the ice with our combat blades before we could free it. (My chainsword would have done the job in a tenth of the time, of course, but in that confined space one of us could all too readily have lost a limb by accident, so it remained in its scabbard.) Each time it happened I considered simply abandoning the cumbersome weapon, but it had proven its use too often to be lightly discarded, so I simply gritted my teeth at the delay and carried on.

My sense of direction was no less sure down here than in any other underground passageway, so at least I had the consolation of knowing that we'd come almost a kilometre from our encounter in the main gallery and were moving in the general direction of the centre of the complex, when Logash paused. He was continuing to lead us simply because the passageway was too narrow for any of us to change position, which had left me trailing in Jurgen's wake, uncomfortably aware that if the metal warriors found the entrance to the cleft and came after us I'd be the first one to know about it. The thought was an unpleasant one, producing an itching sensation between my shoulder blades, so I tried not to dwell on it.

'What's the matter?' I asked. The tech-priest shrugged.

---

1. *How Cain came to this conclusion he doesn't bother to explain; it was probably something to do with his affinity for underground environments.*

'Dead end,' he said. I could have throttled him, but fortunately Jurgen was in the way. I shook my head, unwilling to believe it.

'It can't be.' The words were a reflex denial, but as I said them I was sure that I was right, all of my tunnel rat's instincts told me so. I wondered for a moment why I was so sure, then realised I could feel a faint current of air on my face. 'There's a draft in here.'

'The passage seems to continue,' Logash agreed. 'But it won't do us any good unless you can get through a five centimetre gap.' That really was hard to believe. The passage had constricted before, of course, but that it could narrow so much, so fast, went against all my experience in such an environment. I said so, possibly a little more forcefully than necessary, and Logash squeezed against the ice wall to let me see for myself. Our way was indeed blocked, by a regular convex surface which curved down to just above the floor. Something about the shape struck me as familiar, and then I realised that it was the lower part of a vast cylinder some three or four metres in diameter.

'What the hell's that?' I asked. Logash thumped it with his hand, producing the unmistakable dull thud of thick metal.

'One of the main extraction pipes,' he said. 'Runs up to the processing plant on the surface.'

'And what's in it at the moment?' I asked, an idea so audacious I could barely acknowledge it beginning to form even as I spoke. Logash shrugged.

'Nothing now the plant's shutting down...' His voice trailed off as he evidently came to the same conclusion as I had. I reached an arm out towards him, past my aide.

'Can you get behind Jurgen?' I asked.

'I can try.' It wasn't easy, I can tell you that, but after what seemed to be an eternity of wriggling and swearing he and I were crouched behind what little cover we could find, and Jurgen was aiming the heavy weapon at the pipe. As before we were engulfed in a roar of steam as he fired, so it was a moment or two before our vision cleared enough to show us the metre-diameter hole he had successfully blasted in the wall of the conduit.

'That'll have to be logged for the repair crews,' Logash remarked conversationally, as if the place would ever be back in operation now the necrons were here, and after a moment to let the metal cool Jurgen hoisted himself through the hole and into the pipe.

I followed suit, the tech-priest bounding up ahead of me, to find myself in an echoing metal tube at least twice my own height floored with rapidly-refreezing slush where the metal had conducted the heat of the melta blast away. Stalactites of ice descended from the curved ceiling, where the uniform coating of rime had been disturbed by our blazing entry.

'This way,' I said, taking the lead again, and moving as rapidly up the gentle slope as I could manage on the treacherous surface. Jurgen had no trouble matching my pace, of course, having been born to conditions like these, and Logash apparently had some sort of augmetic balance enhancer, as he seemed as sure-footed as the Valhallan. Despite my tendency to slip unnervingly from time to time, and the faint curvature underfoot doing nothing to make the job any easier, I found the wide, unhindered passageway almost exhilarating after the cramped confines of the defile and set a good pace if I do say so myself.

After a while I became aware of a faint susurration in my ear, and realised that my comm-bead had come within range of the regimental vox net. We were closer to the surface than I'd realised, and a flood of relief almost knocked the breath from my lungs. If someone was still here I wasn't too late to get a shuttle out.

Not that they'd wait if they all thought I was dead, of course, so I lost no time in contacting Kasteen and passing on the status of our mission.

'Commissar!' She sounded surprised and pleased in almost equal measure. 'We were beginning to think you hadn't made it.'

'I nearly didn't,' I admitted. 'They were waiting for us. We never got close to the damn portal.'

'I see.' Resignation tinged her voice. 'How many survivors?'

'Just me and Jurgen.' No point in going into lengthy explanations now, so I glossed over Logash's presence. 'The necrons are moving through the mine. Have they broken out onto the surface yet?'

'No.' Her voice faded for a moment, as she presumably turned her head away from the voxcaster to talk to someone else, then returned with an edge of urgency. 'Wait one...' The link went dead.

Absorbed in my conversation with the colonel I'd hardly noticed that the pipe had come to an apparent dead end. As I craned my neck and shone my luminator upwards, I could see that it had made an abrupt turn to the vertical, soaring away out of sight.

'What now?' I asked. Logash grinned, and indicated a set of metal rungs protruding from the frost, slick with a coating of ice. 'You have got to be kidding.'

He wasn't, of course. He just grabbed a bar and started climbing, sure-footed as a Catachan up a tree, and after a moment I shrugged and went after him. Jurgen followed, as always.

'Why are these here?' he asked.

'The maintenance servitors use them when the pipes shut down,' Logash explained. 'There should be an access panel up here somewhere...'

Concentrating only on maintaining my grip on the treacherous, ice-slick rungs I was startled by the sound of Kasteen's voice suddenly in my ear again. I almost slipped, hanging on purely by the Emperor's grace and the strength of my augmetic fingers.

'We've lost contact with two of the pickets in the middle levels,' she said. 'We're reinforcing...'

'No!' I cut in, a little too loudly. 'Pull everyone back out of the tunnels! It's the only chance they have!' Bottled up in a confined space, unable to concentrate their fire, they'd be picked off easily. I'd seen that all too clearly before. 'Cover the entrances with everything you've got, and engage them as they emerge.' It probably wouldn't do us any good in the long run, but at least that way they'd be the ones held up by the bottleneck. I tried not to think about their ability to teleport, or move through walls...

'Acknowledged,' Kasteen said, clearly willing to defer to my greater experience with these hideous foes, and cut the link. I considered what she'd just told me, not liking the conclusions I was drawing. It was obvious the necrons were moving through the mines in considerable force if they'd been able to take out two of our squads before they even managed to get a vox message off. Maybe the ones in stasis were beginning to revive, and join the new arrivals...

'Found it,' Logash said above me, unnaturally cheerful under the circumstances, and began scraping the covering of frost from the wall, sprinkling me with a light dusting of powdered ice as he did so. He evidently knew what he was doing though, extending a thin metal probe from one of his fingers, and prodding hopefully at an indentation in the side of the pipe. 'Ah. That should do it...'

A section of the wall next to his hand withdrew suddenly, with a loud hum that set my teeth on edge, letting a blast of light and warm air into our frigid enclosure. The tech-priest vanished from sight, and after a moment of scrambling upwards I followed gratefully, heaving myself out onto a metal mesh floor illuminated by a dim electrosconce in the nearest wall. Despite its feebleness the yellow glow seemed incredibly welcoming as I turned to reach down and haul Jurgen up after me.

The chamber we stood in was small, barely large enough for the three of us, and glancing around I realised that it was merely a landing on a vast metal staircase which rose dizzyingly above us as well as descending to a vertiginous depth below. Logash glanced at some runes stencilled on the outside of the access panel we'd exited the pipe by, and nodded in satisfaction.

'Good,' he said.

'What is?' I asked suspiciously. Given his level of mental stability that could have meant just about anything by this stage. The young tech-priest indicated our surroundings with a casual wave.

'We're in one of the primary maintenance shafts. We should be able to get into the main control shrine a few levels up.'

'Best news I've had all day,' I said. 'Lead on.'

It was more than a few levels, of course, we must have been climbing for almost half an hour before Logash stopped at another access panel in the plain metal wall, and I'd lost count of how many flights of stairs we'd climbed. My knees hadn't though, and ached abominably, but it's surprising how motivated you can be with an army of murderous automata at your heels and I kept going. Jurgen, of course, showed no sign of strain or discomfort, even lugging the heavy weapon.

'This should be it.' Logash hesitated, and I noticed the door was larger and more elaborate than any of the ones we'd passed on the way up, decorated with the cogwheel symbol of the priesthood.

'Good,' I said. 'Then let's get out of here.'

'I'm not sure I should open it,' the tech-priest said slowly, eyeing Jurgen and myself with a speculative expression on his face. 'This is a holy place. Only ordained and sanctified personnel are permitted beyond this point...'

'Fine,' I said. 'We're on a mission for the Emperor. Can't get much holier than that, right?' Logash looked confused.

'That would be an ecumenical matter,' he said. 'I'm not sure I'm qualified to judge...'

'Don't worry,' I said. 'I am. Now are you going to open the frakking door or will Brother Jurgen do it?' My aide stepped forward, raising the melta, and Logash hit the activation rune with almost indecent haste.

I'm not sure what I expected to find inside, but my first impression was one of overwhelming technological sophistication. Unlike the necron tomb below us, though, whose incomprehensible sorceries pulsed with palpable malevolence, this was a shrine suffused with the benevolence of the machine spirit, harnessed for the good of humanity and blessed by the tech-priests who normally worked here. I made an automatic gesture of obeisance to the large stained glass window depicting the Emperor (in His aspect of the Omnissiah, of course, but the Emperor still for all that) which spilled patches of colour across the serried ranks of dark wood and polished brass lecterns, each one inlaid with a pict screen displaying some aspect of the plant's function.

'Try not to touch anything,' Logash warned, brushing past Jurgen, who was making the sign of the aquila, his jaw even slacker than usual.

No fear of that, I thought, shying away from the nearest lectern, when my eye was caught by the image on the pict screen. It showed a blurry, flickering image of what looked like one of the mine galleries, and to my horror the unmistakable shadow of a necron warrior passing swiftly out of sight. A moment later another of the metal monstrosities appeared, then a third.

'Logash,' I called. The tech-priest left off genuflecting to the alter in the corner with every sign of annoyance and ambled over to join me. I indicated the pict. 'Where's this?'

'Sector five, level fourteen,' he said after a moment spent consulting some runes on the lectern. He adjusted the controls, and the picture changed, showing another gallery. After a moment the leading necron appeared there. 'Moving towards sector three.'

'Can you see the whole mine from here?' I asked. He nodded.

'The rituals of focusing are very similar to those of your hololith. You may use this lectern if it will help.' After a few moments of instruction, the lighting of an incense stick, and muttering a few prayers over me he left me to it with an air of evident relief.

The picture I started to build up was grim, to say the least. It didn't take me long to establish that the lower levels were crawling with necrons, hundreds at least, and that they were systematically combing the tunnels, moving ever higher as they went. I voxed Kasteen.

'By my estimate we've got about half an hour before they reach the surface,' I said. 'If we're lucky.' At least the few troopers I'd found were already in the upper levels and pulling back, so she'd heeded my earlier advice. An external pictcaster had shown me the landing pad, already crowded with hundreds of our men and women, not to mention vehicles, waiting patiently for their turn to board one of the shuttles. With a sudden sinking feeling in my stomach I began to realise that the vast majority of them would still be there when the necrons emerged.

'We'll be ready,' Kasteen promised, but I already knew how hollow that promise was. They'd be massacred, no doubt about it, and more to the point I'd never make it to the safety of the starship either. There had to be something we could do to hold them off, if only I could think of it...

'Logash,' I called, but this time he ignored me, intent on some task at one of the other lecterns. I walked over and seized his arm. 'Logash, this is important.'

'So is this,' he said, a trace of irritation in his voice. 'The stabilisation rituals for the storage tanks have to be performed every six hours, and are already overdue. You must realise how volatile refined promethium is...'

'Oh yes,' I said, an idea so audacious I could hardly credit it myself beginning to form. I glanced past the glowing glass Emperor to the complex outside, where the huge storage tanks squatted, bulky as hab blocks. 'How much is in the tanks at the moment?'

'Roughly eight million litres,' he said. 'Since the tankers can't land with the orks about it's built up rather. But still within acceptable safety parameters, I can assure you.'

'I was rather hoping it was unsafe,' I said, and if he had any eyebrows I'm sure he would have raised them at that point. I pointed to the tangle of pipe work around the storage tanks. 'Do any of those pipes connect directly to the mine?'

'Not directly, no.' He looked at me quizzically. 'Why do you ask?'

'Because if we could dump all that liquid down the shaft it should really give the necrons something to worry about,' I said. A slow smile began to spread across the tech-priest's face.

'It would mean overriding a number of safety rituals,' he said, considering the idea. 'But it can be done.'

'Excellent,' I said, feeling a flare of optimism returning at last. 'Then you'd better get to it.'

'Indeed.' He huddled over the lectern, muttering gibberish, and what sounded suspiciously like an occasional high-pitched giggle, as he manipulated the controls. The chance to strike back at the creatures who had massacred his friends was obviously stirring up a lot of emotion, and I began to wonder if his fragile sanity would hold for long enough to implement our plan. Still, there was nothing to do but watch in silence while the minutes dragged by, and the automata in the pict screen moved ominously closer to the surface.

'Tanna tea, sir?' Jurgen materialised at my shoulder, proffering the flask he'd brought as a transparent excuse to join the expedition, and I took the fragrant liquid gratefully, suddenly aware of how tired and hungry I was. He still couldn't find the sandwich he'd stowed somewhere, to my barely-concealed relief, so we contented ourselves with the standard ration bars which tasted reassuringly of nothing particularly identifiable.

'Ready!' Logash said at last, another giggle rising to the surface. His face was preternaturally flushed, and his fingers trembled over the controls of the lectern, the first time I had ever seen augmetics do so. I nodded.

'In the name of the Emperor,' I said solemnly.

'In nominae Ernulph!' The tech-priest squeaked vindictively, and flicked a switch.

For a moment nothing seemed to happen, then I became aware of a low rumbling sound which seemed to suffuse the complex. Runes on several of the lecterns began to glow red, and a powdering of snow dislodged itself from the rim of the window outside. Then, for interminable moments, nothing seemed to happen at all.

'Look, sir!' Jurgen pointed to the pict screen, which I'd left tuned to one of the upper levels. A torrent of liquid became momentarily visible, filling the width of the gallery, sweeping all before it, tearing chunks of ice the size of Baneblades from the walls as it came and tumbling them casually ahead of itself. Then the pictcaster was ripped from its mounting, and the screen went dark. I switched to another just in time to see a party of necron warriors, far closer to the surface than I would have thought possible, trapped by the onrushing tsunami, picked up and thrown around like so many rag dolls. If I believed them capable of emotion I might have thought they stood dumbstruck before it before turning to flee, but it engulfed them all the same. I wondered if they'd fade away, smashed to pieces by that irresistible tide of pure promethium. Much good would it do them if they did; their tomb was at the lowest point of the tunnel complex and would surely flood in time, even though Logash had calculated that it would take the torrent around twenty minutes to seep down that far. Not that they needed to breathe, of course, but at the very least it should stop them using the portal until they found some way to pump the chamber out, by which time with any luck the Navy would be here to sterilise the planet.

All in all, I felt, a rather satisfying result.

I WAS STILL feeling pretty pleased with myself as I joined Kasteen and Broklaw on the landing pad a short while later, so buoyed with euphoria that for once I didn't even mind the bone-biting cold. The plain of ice was swarming with activity, Chimera engines rumbling as the engineseers marshalled them for embarkation and commenced the services of mothballing, and platoons marshalled by squads ready to take their place on the outgoing shuttles. A blur of motion in the corner of my eye resolved itself into a Sentinel, trotting eagerly round our flank, keeping an eye out for hostiles.

'Well done, commissar.' Broklaw shook me firmly by the hand. 'I don't think anyone else could have come close to achieving what you did today.'

'Well the next time we run across a necron tomb you're welcome to try,' I told him. He grinned, taking the remark for a joke, but any reply he made was drowned by the scream of a shuttle engine as one of the utility vessels from the *Pure of Heart* rose into the sullen air. Kasteen gestured at it as it howled over our heads and began to diminish into the leaden sky above.

SIXTEEN

So HORRIFYING WAS the sight of that gigantic war machine, battered, scarred, but still lurching forward almost unstoppably, that for a moment none of us noticed the ant-like scurryings around its feet. Only as the ear-splitting cry of 'WAAAAAARRRRRGGGHHHH!' forced itself through the echoes of the explosion still fuzzing up the inside of my skull did I become aware of the horde of greenskins racing across the frozen ground ahead of it. They were afoot mostly, with just a handful of bikes and trucks bouncing forwards to pull clear of the main pack, and I was pleased to see our Sentinels peeling off to engage the light vehicles. Their lascannons cracked repeatedly, punching holes in the crudely welded armour, and a gratifying number of the ramshackle vehicles slewed to a halt leaking smoke.

But my attention remained fixed on the gargant, which loomed over everything like a shadow of doom. Despite the great rents in its metre-thick armour plate and the fused wreckage of its primary armament it still looked unstoppable, lurching forward uncertainly with a shriek of tortured metal, the left leg dragging slightly as though limping from its wounds.

'Fire at will!' Kasteen roared, suiting the action to the word, and hundreds of lasguns crackled repeatedly, sending echoes booming like surf from the structures still standing. The orks replied enthusiastically, but, praise the Emperor, no more accurately than usual, so our casualties remained light in comparison to the scores who were falling and being trampled underfoot by their comrades.

'Target the gargant!' Broklaw ordered the Chimera crews, and dozens of heavy bolters began to hose down the looming tower of metal which continued to plod towards us, cracking the ice of the landing field under its weight with every tottering step. They didn't seem to be bothering it much, but at least they were keeping the crew's heads down, and the open galleries on its shoulders clear of the heavy weapon crews who would otherwise have been adding a hail of supporting fire to its own formidable armament.

'They're consistent at least,' Kasteen muttered at my elbow. True to their nature the orks were attacking us directly across the landing field, sweeping down the length of it parallel to the line of storage tanks, now shimmering behind a haze of promethium vapour from their rapidly-draining contents. At the sight of that wavering shroud my blood ran even colder than it already was. It would only take one stray round landing next to them for the entire complex to be engulfed in an explosion almost impossible to imagine. And us along with it, of course.

'Keep our fire directed away from the storage tanks,' I cautioned, and she nodded grimly, perceiving the danger too. Not that it would make a lot of difference in the long run, I thought. The gargant was swinging its remaining gun around to target the centre of our formation, which of course meant me along with the senior officers, and I began to think we only had moments left if that. The ork advance seemed almost unstoppable, for every greenskin that fell another dozen continuing to charge forward slavering with bloodlust.

'Shuttle three requesting landing co-ordinates.' A new voice cut into the comm-net, and I became aware of the roar of a powerful engine becoming audible even over the din of the ongoing battle. A flare of hope rose within me...

'Shuttle three, abort your approach.' Mazarin's voice cut in abruptly, shattering it, her tone calm and authoritative. 'The greenskins are all over the pad.'

'I can still make it,' the unseen pilot argued, and the blocky shape of the shuttle suddenly appeared over the refinery, banking sharply round to run in over the main bulk of the ork army. Something about his voice sounded familiar, and I wondered if it was the same one who'd got us down here in the first place. Sporadic small arms fire bounced off his hull, and I stilled my breath remembering our abrupt arrival here, but the orks didn't get lucky this time and he came in low over our heads, his landing thrusters screaming. A few of the troopers waved and yelled, but most kept firing grimly into the onrushing horde of blade-waving barbarity. Another couple of moments and they'd be on us. I drew my chainsword, preparing for the shock of impact, and continued spitting las-bolts into the wall of screaming ork flesh bearing down on us almost as fast as the tidal wave of promethium still scouring the mine beneath our feet.

The gargant lurched forward again, and impelled by panic or instinct I finally noticed the deep gash in its leg. It was a slim chance, but...

'Target its left leg!' I yelled, and the Chimera crews switched their aim, pouring a concentrated barrage of heavy bolter rounds against that single, vulnerable spot. For a moment I thought the desperate gamble would fail, but as the torrent of explosive fire chewed away at the torn and overstressed metal the towering leviathan began to sway alarmingly. The damaged limb seemed to seize up entirely, then failed altogether with a crack of rending metal which echoed like thunder between the encircling hills, audible even over the din of battle surrounding us.

Abruptly it lost its equilibrium entirely, toppling absurdly slowly at first, then faster and faster as more of that titanic bulk neared the ground. The orks around it scattered in panic, like ants beneath a descending boot, and a gratifying number of them failed to make it.

The impact shook the ground beneath us, cracking the ice for hundreds of metres around the huge wreck, swallowing almost a third of that vast bulk and opening chasms which engulfed the vast majority of the fleeing greenskins. From deep within that mountain of metal the dull thud of secondary explosions going off echoed like bronchitic coughs, and the lurid red glow of spreading flames began to join the smoke I'd seen earlier.

'Finish them off!' Kasteen ordered, and the Valhallans responded with a will, surging forward to engage the stunned survivors. After a short exchange of weapons fire it was all over, the few remaining orks fleeing beyond the effective range of our lasguns and Kasteen reining in the more enthusiastic platoon commanders who seemed on the verge of going after them with a display of profanity verging on the pyrotechnic. I'd expected Sulla to be leading the charge, but it turned out her company was the first to have been shuttled back up to the ship, so for once she didn't have the chance to do something stupid, which made a refreshing change.

'I think we should board as soon as we can,' I said, feeling our luck had already been stretched far thinner than we had any right to expect, and Kasteen nodded.

'I think you're right,' she said. 'Simia Orichalcae's rather lost its charm for me.'

'You and me both,' Broklaw agreed, and hurried off to organise the next stage of the embarkation as the incoming shuttle grounded at last.

I have to admit that the surge of relief I felt as I hurried up the cargo ramp and heard the comforting clang of metal beneath my boot soles once more left me almost giddy. Nevertheless I couldn't shake a strong sense of foreboding which intensified with every extra minute we remained on the pad, and continued to hover by the open hatch as a steady stream of Guardsmen and women made their way on board. Kasteen joined me there after a while, her face pensive.

'Looking for something?' she asked.

'Hoping I don't see it,' I admitted. 'It'll take more than a bath to see off the necrons if I'm any judge.' All the time we spoke I kept an amplivisor trained on the edge of the complex, dreading the sight of a flash of moving metal. Kasteen nodded ruefully.

'Shame you couldn't blow up the portal,' she said. I echoed the gesture.

'Shame you never got the chance to blow up the gargant,' I echoed. We looked at one another, the same thought occurring to us both simultaneously, and went to find Captain Federer.

'WE WERE GOING to detonate it by vox pulse,' Federer confirmed. He was a thin-faced, dark-haired man, whose enthusiasm for problem-solving was matched only by his lack of social skills. Rumour among the regiment had it that he'd once aspired to become a tech-priest but been expelled from the seminary for his morbid fascination with pyrotechnics, and he certainly seemed to have an almost instinctive understanding of the arcane technologies of the combat engineer. If the rumours were true, the Adeptus's loss was very definitely our gain.

WE FOUND HIM in the shuttle's main cargo bay fussing over the stowage of the small amount of equipment he'd been able to salvage; under the circumstances Kasteen had decided to abandon our vehicles and stores and use the space we saved to bring up another couple of platoons at a time. Riding back here would be hideously uncomfortable, but far better than still being around if the necrons stirred again.

'So you could still set the charges off from here?' I asked, raising my voice slightly to carry over the babble of voices from the troopers beginning to file in to the echoing hold. A few of them had evidently been in a similar situation before, unfurling their bedrolls into improvised acceleration couches as they settled. Federer nodded. 'Oh yes. You'd just need a sufficiently powerful transmitter. You could even do it from orbit if you wished.'

'That might be safer,' Kasteen suggested. 'After all, it's going to be a pretty big bang.'

'Oh yes.' Federer's face lit up with what I can only describe as unhealthy enthusiasm. 'Huge. Massive in fact. On the order of giga-tonnes.' His eyes took on something of a dreamy quality.

'We didn't place anything remotely that powerful,' Kasteen said, look-ing vaguely stunned. 'We'd have blown ourselves to pieces along with the gargant.' Federer nodded, his voice taking on something of the quality of Logash discussing ambulls.[1]

'That was before the commissar flooded the mine with promethium,' he explained. 'The liquid will have settled to the bottom levels by now. That means the upper galleries would be full of vapour. In effect you've created an FAE bomb several kilometres wide.'[2]

'Assuming the explosives you placed weren't washed away by the flood,' I said. Federer shook his head.

'We anchored them pretty firmly. We were expecting a gargant to tread on them, don't forget. We allowed for stresses in the region of...'

'Never mind,' I said, cutting him off before he could get properly started. Once enthused, as I knew from experience, he was hard to bring back to the point. 'If you say it'll work I'm sure it will.'

'Oh yes,' he said, nodding eagerly.

I MUST CONFESS that, despite the uneventful journey back to the orbit-ing starship, I didn't feel entirely safe until I heard the docking clamps engage at last and felt the reassuring solidity of the *Pure of Heart's* deck plating beneath my feet.

'You're back, then,' Durant greeted us as we arrived on the bridge. It was much as I remembered it from our last visit, except that the hololith was now showing a panoramic view of the snowscape outside the refinery. From the height and angle I judged that the pictcaster was mounted somewhere above the main hull of the last shuttle to leave that benighted place, the final few pickets withdrawing to the safety of its cargo hold even as I watched. The refinery complex still seemed as

---

1. *This is the last time Cain mentions the tech-priest in his account of these events. His subse-quent career in the Adeptus Mechanicus can best be described as unspectacular, rising to the rank of Magos without doing anything further to draw attention to himself. His last known assignment was at the Noctis Labyrinthus mine complex on Mars.*

2. *Fuel/Air Explosive, a type of bomb which releases a volatile gas before detonation to magnify its power and area of effect.*

deserted as ever, but I kept an apprehensive eye on the distant line of structures nevertheless.

'You seem pleasantly surprised,' I said. Durant made the almost-shrug I'd noticed before.

'Yes, well. The Munitorium might have argued about our charter fee if we'd left you behind,' he said, a little too gruffly to have meant it.

'Shuttle one preparing to lift, captain,' a junior officer called from a lectern somewhere to our left, and a palpable air of relief swept the whole chamber.

'Good,' the captain said. 'We've been sitting next to this damned planet so long I'm beginning to put down roots.' He gestured to Mazarin, who was huddled over her workstation with Federer, deep in discussion about something. 'Take us out of orbit as soon as they dock.'

'Aye aye, captain,' she responded, and hummed across to another console, where she busied herself with the rituals of engine activation.

'Better make it fast,' I said. As I'd feared, a glint of moving metal had appeared among the refinery buildings, moving rapidly towards the pictcaster. As it got closer I was able to discern a squadron of speeders, each one with what looked like the top half of a necron welded to it. All of them had a heavy weapon apparently incorporated into their right arm, and as I watched, dazzling green beams of malevolent energy lanced out to strike the hull of the slowly-rising shuttle.

'They're scratching the paintwork!' Durant roared, outraged. Truth to tell they were doing rather more than that, scoring visible channels in the metal. They were a long way from actually breaching it, shuttle hulls are sturdy to say the least, but the fact that they were able to inflict any damage at all spoke volumes for the power of the weapons they carried.

'They're going after the shuttle,' Kasteen said, her eyes on the skimmers which began to rise after it, wheeling about the slowly-climbing slab of metal like flies round a grox. They were growing in number too, I noticed with a quiver of unease, more and more of them rising to the join the swarm.

'They're not going to make it,' I said, alarmed. The pilot was making what evasive manoeuvres he could, but the craft was built for durability rather than agility, and several more of the deadly beams struck home. It could only be a matter of moments before something vital was hit...

'Don't be too sure,' Durant said. A moment later the main engines flared into life, vaporising any of the skimmers unfortunate enough to be behind the craft in a burst of superheated plasma, and lifting it cleanly away on an escape trajectory.

'They're falling behind,' Mazarin confirmed, and the projection obligingly rotated to show the remaining skimmers tumbling aimlessly in the wake of the shuttle's passage. A few moments later the image showed the reassuring refuge of our docking bay, and everyone breathed an audible sigh of relief. (Except for Mazarin, possibly, who may have had her lungs augmetically replaced.)

With our shuttle out of danger Durant had retuned the hololith to the aerial view of the refinery complex which he'd treated us to when we first made orbit.

As he magnified the tangle of buildings and storage tanks, now reassuringly far below us, my breath caught in my throat. A glittering tide of moving metal was emerging from the mouth of the mine, more warriors than I could count, blurring into a single amorphous entity which flowed between the buildings like flood water.

'They've woken!' I gasped, a spasm of fear gripping my bowels. They'd prevented the tide of promethium from flooding their temple, Emperor knew how, which meant their portal was probably still active...

'Broklaw!' I yelled, blessing the hurry that had left the comm-bead still in my ear. 'Stand to! Prepare to receive boarders!' Everyone looked at me as though I'd gone mad. 'They can teleport, remember?' I snapped, and Kasteen nodded grimly.

'They can swim, too, by the look of it.'[1]

'Federer!' I called. 'Now would be a good time!' The sapper grinned happily, exchanged a few more words with the hovering tech-priest, and prodded a rune with his finger. All eyes remained fixed on the cluster of buildings in the hololith. Nothing seemed to be happening.

'It didn't go off...' I began to say, then a gout of ice erupted from the plain at the mouth of the valley. Mazarin did something to enhance the clarity of the image, and in front of our eyes a vast, growing crater spread to engulf the nearby metal warriors. They tumbled into it like broken toys, more and more of them as the ground crumbled away faster than they could flee, and Federer punched the air as though he'd just scored the winning goal of a scrumball match.

'That would have seen off the gargant,' he said cheerfully.

'That it would,' I agreed, awestruck at the amount of devastation he'd wrought. But that had only been the prelude. Deep in the bowels of the pit a sudden flare of light erupted as the promethium vapour trapped in the caverns below ignited. A gout of flame fully a kilometre in height burst from the rupturing ground and raced across the snowscape at the

---

1. *More likely they simply waded through the flooded levels until they broke the surface.*

speed of thought, melting the fleeing warriors in an instant, throwing blazing fissures ahead of itself as it went.

There were other explosions now too, the entire surface of the valley erupting like pyroclasts, vaporised rock, ice, and necrons forming a low, looming cloud riven with thunderbolts as electrostatic discharges of incredible power jumped between the particles. The refinery disappeared, sliding into the hellish inferno below, and vanishing as though it had never been...

'Brace for impact!' Durant called out, as though this were just a minor inconvenience, and the *Pure of Heart* was suddenly picked up and shaken like a child's toy by the titanic shockwave as the very atmosphere of the planet bulged under the force of the energies released. Even the crew grabbed for handholds, and I found myself bracing Kasteen, who had fallen back against me (something I had no complaints about at all).

'Just a minute,' Mazarin called, playing the controls in front of her like the keyboard of a forte, and the shuddering gradually ceased. She grinned again, and I began to suspect she enjoyed the chance to push the limits of her engines. 'Lucky we were so high. If we'd been down where the atmosphere's thicker it would have been a bit trickier.'

'Is that it, then?' Kasteen asked, her eyes riveted on the scene of destruction below. Even from orbit the dust cloud could still be seen staining half the planet, and in spite of all the horrors I'd endured down there I couldn't help feeling a spark of regret at the scar across the face of the pristine world I'd first looked upon from this very spot a few short days before.

'I hope so,' I said, although the twist of apprehension in my gut didn't fade entirely until we'd dropped back into the warp and were well on our way back to the safety of the Imperium.

Although, of course, where the necrons are concerned nowhere is ever remotely safe, as we now know to our cost. At least that particular nest appears to have been dealt with, even if no one can ever go back to check; the first thing Amberley did when my message finally caught up with her was to place the whole system under Inquisitorial quarantine.[1]

If there was one bright spot in the whole affair it was that I got to spend a little free time with her, after the interminable debriefing sessions were finally over and she'd finished going round every trooper in

---

1. *Subsequent examination of the site showed no signs of an active necron presence, although if anything was left of their installation it would have been buried far too deeply to have left much trace of anything. I for one would not be at all keen to start digging holes to find out for sure.*

the regiment who'd seen or heard anything of what we'd found on that miserable iceball and threatened them with the wrath of the Emperor if they ever breathed a word of it again. Or the wrath of the Inquisition, which, trust me, is even scarier.

AMBERLEY WAS IN an uncharacteristically sombre mood on the last night we spent together, the occasional table in her hotel suite covered in data-slates as she collated all the witness reports, and looked up with a wan smile as I entered.

'You were damn lucky,' she said, the blue of her eyes clouded with fatigue. I nodded, and stood aside to let the room servitor trundle in with a tray of food. She saw it and raised an eyebrow.

'I took the liberty of ordering,' I said. 'You seemed busy.'

'Thank you,' she said, stretching, so I wandered across and massaged some of the tension from her shoulders as the servitor set out dishes and cutlery on the dining table. She smiled as the covers came off.

'Ackenberry sorbet. One of my favourites.' That hadn't been hard to remember, so I smiled in return.

'You did say you'd live on the stuff if you could the last time you ordered it.'

'So I did.' The smile widened as the main course came into view. 'What's that?'

'Ambull steak,' I said. 'I think they owe me that much.'

[Cain's narrative continues for several more paragraphs, but since it only covers personal matters of no interest to anyone else I've chosen to end this extract from the archive right here.]

THE BEGUILING

Night and the rain had both been falling for some time and I'd been getting steadily colder, wetter and more hacked off since the middle of the afternoon before we saw the light, glimmering faintly through the trees which bordered the road. The two gunners in the back of the Salamander with me hadn't helped my darkening mood either; they were fresh out from Valhalla, had never seen rain before, and found the 'liquid snow' a fascinating novelty which they discussed at inordinate length and with increasingly inanity.

To add insult to injury they had an ice-worlder's indifference to low temperatures, chattering about how warm it was, while I huddled into my greatcoat and shivered. The only upside to their presence was their transparent awe at being in the company of the famous Commissar Cain, whose heroism and concern for his men was fast becoming legendary.

Legendary, that is, in the literal sense of being both widely believed and completely without foundation. Since my attempt to save my own miserable skin by deserting in the face of a tyranid horde on Desolatia had backfired spectacularly, leaving me the inadvertent hero of the hour, my undeserved reputation had continued to grow like tanglevine. A couple of narrow scrapes during the subsequent campaign to cleanse

Keffia of genestealers, which aren't strictly relevant to this anecdote but were unpleasant enough at the time, had added to it; mostly I'd run for cover, kept my head down, and emerged to take the credit when the noise stopped.

So I should have had the sense to sit back and enjoy the relative peace the post I'd gone to some trouble to arrange for myself ought to have guaranteed; a rear-echelon artillery battery, a long way from the front line, with no disciplinary problems to speak of. But, true to form, I just couldn't leave well enough alone.

We'd been campaigning on Slawkenberg for about eight months standard, or about half the local year, putting down in the southern hemisphere of the main eastern continent just as the snows of winter began to give way to a clement, sweet-scented spring. Tough luck on the Valhallans, who bore the disappointment with the stoicism I'd come to expect, but just gravy so far as I was concerned. True to form we spent the spring, and the sort of balmy summer that vacation worlds build their entire economies on, flinging shells into the distance, secure in the knowledge that we were doing the Emperor's work without any of the unpleasantness you get when the enemy can shoot back at you.

I wasn't even sure who the enemy was, to be honest. As usual I'd given the briefing slates only the most perfunctory of glances before turning my attention to matters of more immediate concern, like grabbing the best billets for myself and a few favoured cronies. Since my instincts in this regard remained as finely honed as ever, I managed to install myself in a high class hotel in a nearby village along with the senior command staff, most of whom still cordially detested me but who weren't about to turn down a soft bed and a cellar full of cask-matured amasec. I had equally little time for them, but liked to be able to keep an eye on them without too much effort.

I made sure Colonel Mostrue got the best suite, of course, selecting a more modest one for myself which better fitted my undeserved reputation, and which had the added advantage of a pair of bay windows which afforded easy and unobserved access to the street through a small garden which was only overlooked by the apartment belonging to the hotel's owner. He wasn't about to challenge anything an Imperial commissar might do, and with the indispensible Jurgen, my faithful and malodorous aide, camped out in the anteroom, there was no chance of anyone wandering in to discover that I was entertaining company or had wandered off to amuse myself in the many houses of discreet entertainment the locality had to offer.

In short, I had it made. So, as the summer wore on, it was only a matter of time before I found myself getting bored.

'That's the trouble with you, Cai.' Toren Divas, the young lieutenant who was the closest thing I had to a friend among the battery, and was certainly the only member of it who would even dream of using the familiar form of my given name, tilted his glass and let the amber liquid slide down his throat, sighing with satisfaction. 'You're not suited to this rear-echelon soldiering. A man like you needs more of a challenge.' He fumbled for the bottle, found it was empty, and looked around hopefully for another.

'Right now I've got enough of a challenge with that winning streak of yours,' I said, hoping to bluff him into doubling his bet again. The best he could be holding was a pair of inquisitors, and I only needed one more Emperor to scoop the pot. But he wasn't biting.

'You're going stir crazy here,' he went on. 'You need a bit of excitement.'

Well, that was true, but not in the way he meant. He'd been there on Desolatia and seen me take on a swarm of tyranids with just a chainsword, hacking my way through to save Jurgen's miserable hide completely by accident, and bought the Cain the Hero legend wholesale. His idea of excitement was being in a place where people or aliens or warp-spawned monstrosities wanted to kill you as horribly as possible and doing it to them first. Mine was finding a gambling den without a house limit, or a well-endowed young lady with a thing for men in uniforms and access to her father's credit slip. And in the last few months I'd pretty much run out of both locally, not to mention other recreational facilities of a less salubrious nature. So I nodded, mindful of the need to play up to my public persona.

'Well, the enemy's leagues away,' I said, trying to sound rueful. 'What can you do?'

'Go out and look for them,' he said. Maybe it was the amasec, maybe it was the stage of the evening when you start to talk frak just for the hell of it, but for whatever reason I found myself pursuing the topic.

'I wish it was that easy,' I said insincerely. 'But then I'd have to shoot myself for desertion.' Divas laughed at the feeble joke.

'Not if you made it official,' he said. There was something about his voice which sounded quite serious, despite the amasec-induced preternatural care with which he formed the words. If I'd just laughed it off at that point, it would all have turned out differently: a couple of eager young troopers wouldn't have died, Slawkenberg might have fallen to the forces of Chaos, and I definitely wouldn't have ended up fleeing in terror from yet another bunch of psychopaths determined to kill me. But, as usual, my curiosity got the better of me.

'How do you mean?' I asked.

* * *

'LET ME GET this straight.' Colonel Mostrue looked at me narrowly, distrust clearly evident in his ice-blue eyes. He'd never fully bought my story on Desolatia, and although he generally gave me the benefit of the doubt he was never quite able to ignore the instinctive antipathy most Guard officers harboured towards members of the Commissariat. 'You want to lead a recon mission out towards the enemy lines.'

'Not lead, exactly,' I said. 'More like tag along. See how the forward observers are doing.'

'They seem to be doing fine,' Mostrue riposted, his breath puffing to vapour as he spoke. As usual he had the air conditioning in his office turned up high enough to preserve grox.

'As I'd expect,' I said smoothly. 'But I'm sure you've seen the latest intelligence reports.' Which was more than I had, until my conversation with Divas had drawn my attention to them. 'Something peculiar seems to be happening among the enemy forces.'

'Of course it does.' His voice held a faint tinge of asperity. 'They're Chaos worshippers.' I almost expected him to spit. 'Nothing they do makes sense.'

'Of course not,' I said. 'But I feel I'd be shirking my duties if I didn't take a look for myself.' Although I didn't have the slightest intention of going anywhere near the battlefront, I really was mildly intrigued by the reports I'd skimmed. The traitors seemed to be fighting each other in several places, even ignoring nearby Imperial forces altogether unless they intervened. I didn't know or care why, any more than Mostrue did; the more damage they inflicted on each other the better I liked it. But it did give me the perfect excuse to comandeer some transport and check out the recreational possibilites of some of the nearby towns. Mostrue shrugged.

'Well, please yourself,' he said. 'It's your funeral.'

So I FOUND myself later that morning in the vehicle park, watching a couple of young gunners called Grear and Mulenz stowing their kit in the back of a Salamander. Jurgen, who I'd co-opted as my driver, glanced up at the almost cloudless sky, his shirt sleeves rolled up as usual, a faint sheen of sweat trickling across his interesting collection of skin diseases. Even though we were in the open air, and he wasn't perspiring nearly as much as he had when we first met in the baking deserts of Desolatia, I kept upwind of him through long habit.

Jurgen's body odour was quite spectacular, and even though our time together had more or less immured me to it there was no point in taking any chances. Physically he was much less preposessing than he smelled, looking as though someone had started to mould a human figure out of clay but became bored before they finished.

Though I strongly suspected Mostrue had assigned him as my aide more as a practical joke than anything else, Jurgen had turned out to be ideally suited to the role. He wasn't the biggest bang in the armoury by any means, but made up for his lack of intellect with a literally minded approach to following orders and an unquestioning acceptance of even the mutually contradictory parts of Imperial doctrine which would have done credit to the most devout ecclesiarch. Now he looked at a faint wisp of cloud on the horizon, and shook his head.

'Weather'll be changing soon.'

'It seems fine to me,' I said. I suppose I should have listened, but I grew up in a hive and had never quite got the hang of living in an environment you couldn't adjust. And besides, it had been warm and dry for weeks now. Jurgen shrugged.

'As the Emperor wills,' he said, and started the engine.

WHAT THE EMPEROR willed on this particular morning was a steady increase in the cloud, which gradually began to attenuate the sunshine, and a slowly freshening breeze which stole the remaining warmth from it. The sky darkened by almost imperceptable degrees as we rattled along, making good time towards the nearest town, and I wasn't too surprised to feel the first drops of moisture on my skin while we were still some way short of our destination.

'How much further?' I asked Jurgen, wishing I'd comandeered a Chimera instead. The noise in the enclosed crew bay would have been deafening, but at least it would have kept the rain off.

'Ten or twelve leagues,' he said, apparently unperturbed by the change in the weather. 'Fifteen to the OP.'

I had no intention of accompanying Grear and Mulenz all the way to the forward observation post, but we were close enough to civilisation to make the quarter hour or so of mild discomfort I still had to look forward to seem bearable. 'Good,' I said, then turned to the gunners with an encouraging smile. 'You'll be there in no time.'

'What about you, sir?' Mulenz asked, looking up from his ranging scope. It was the first time I'd let them know I wasn't planning on checking in on the observation post; every artillery battery needs its forward observers, but it's a hard, thankless job, and a fire magnet for every enemy trooper in the area once they realise you're there. I smiled again, the warm, confident smile of the hero they expected me to be.

'I'll just be poking around to see what the enemy's up to,' I said. 'I'm sure you don't need me getting in the way.' That was always my style, making the troops feel as though they had my full confidence. A pat on the back generally works better than a gun to the head, in my experience; and if it doesn't you can just as easily shoot them later. Grear nodded, his chest swelling visibly.

'You can count on us, sir,' he said, positively radiating enthusiasm.

'I'm sure I can,' I said, then lifted myself up to look over the rim of the driver's compartment again. 'Jurgen. Why are we stopping?'

'Roadblock,' he said. The palms of my hands began to tingle, as they often do when something I can't quite put my finger on doesn't seem right. 'Catachans, by the look of it.'

'They can't be,' I said. I glanced ahead of us: a squad of troopers was fanning out across the road, lasguns at the ready. Jurgen was right, from this distance they did seem to have the heavily-muscled build which distinguishes the inhabitants of that greenhouse hell. But there was something about the way they moved which rang alarm bells in my mind. And besides... 'They're all assigned to the equatorial region.'

'Then who are they?' Jurgen asked.

'Good question. Let's not wait to find out.' No other instructions were necessary: he killed the drive to the left-hand tracks, and the Salamander slewed round to face the way we'd come. Grear and Mulenz sprawled across the floor of the crew compartment, taken by surprise by the violent manoeuvre; more used to Jurgen's robust driving style I'd grabbed the pintel mount to steady myself.

A few las-bolts shot past our heads as the ambushers realised we were getting away, followed by barely coherent curses.

'Emperor's blood!' I swung the heavy bolter around and loosed off a fusilade of badly-aimed shots at our pursuers. Grear and Mulenz gaped at me, obviously stunned at seeing the heroic legend come to life, until I grabbed Grear and got him to replace me at the weapon.

'Keep firing,' I snapped, pleased to see that I'd got a couple at least, and dropped back behind the safety of the armour plate. That required an excuse, so I seized the voxcaster. 'Cain to Command. We have hostiles on the forest road, co-ordinates...' I scrabbled for the map slate, which Mulenz helpfully thrust at me, and rattled them off. 'Estimate at no more than platoon strength...'

'There's more of them up ahead,' Jurgen cut in helpfully.

'Command. Wait one.' I peered cautiously over the rim of the crew compartment. Another squad had emerged from the trees lining the road, then another, and another... I could estimate at least fifty men, maybe more, straggling across the highway towards concealment on the other side. 'Make that company strength. Possibly a full advance.'

'Confirming that, commissar.' Mostrue's voice, calm and collected as usual. 'Targeting now. Firing in two.'

'What?' But the link had gone dead. We only had one chance. 'Jurgen! Get us off the road!'

'Yes, sir.' The Salamander swung violently again, lasbolts spanging from the armour on all sides now, throwing us around like peas in a bucket. The ride became a succession of sickening lurches, as the smooth rockcrete of the highway gave way to a rutted forest track. The flurry of bolts began to dwindle as we opened the distance from our pursuers. All except a few, which continued to pepper the front armour to little effect.

I risked another peek over the armour to see a small knot of men scattering in front of us: a couple of them weren't quite fast enough, and the Salamander lurched again with a sickening crack and a smell of putrescence which made Jurgen's odour seem like a flower garden.

'Who are these guys?' Mulenz asked, grabbing a lasgun and sending a few rounds after them for good measure.

'Care to guess?' I suggested, drawing my chainsword as one of the enemy troopers began clawing his way aboard. Despite everything I'd seen in my career up to that point, it was still a shock. The face was distended with infection, pus seeping from open sores, and his limbs were swollen and arthritic. But inhumanly strong, for all that. Even an ork would probably have thought twice about trying to board a vehicle moving at our pace...

With an incoherent scream, which the two gunners fortunately took for a heroic battle cry, I swung the humming weapon in a short arc that separated the head from his body. A fountain of filth jetted from it as it fell, fortunately away from the Salamander, making us gag and retch at the smell. By the time I was able to blink my eyes clear I could hear the first shrieks of the incoming shells.

The roar of the barrage detonating behind us was almost deafening, splinters of wood from shattered trees spattering the armour plate, and stinging my cheek as I ducked for cover. Jurgen kept us moving at a brisk pace, deeper into the cover of the woods, and the noise gradually receded. Grear and Mulenz were looking back at the flashes and smoke like juvies at a firework display, but I guess being forward observers they were used to being at the sharp end of one of our barrages. For me it was a novel experience, and one I wasn't keen to repeat.

'What do we do now, commissar?' Jurgen asked, slowing to a less life-threatening speed as the noise grew fainter behind us. I shrugged, considering our options.

'Well, we can't go back,' I said. 'The road will be impassable after that.' A quick conversation on the vox was enough to vindicate my guess; things had been chewed up so badly regimental headquarters was having to send patrols in on foot to confirm that the enemy had been neutralised.

I looked at the map slate again. The forest seemed awfully big now that we were inside it, and the rain was starting to fall in earnest, gathering on the over-hanging branches to drip in large, cold drops onto my exposed skin. I shivered.

'What I don't understand is what they were doing out here,' Grear said. 'There's nothing of any strategic importance in this area.'

'There's nothing in this area at all,' I said, mesmerised by the map. 'Except trees.' A faint line was probably the forest track we were on. I leaned forwards to show it to Jurgen. 'I reckon we're about here,' I concluded. He nodded.

'Looks about right, sir.' He switched on the headlights; the twisting track became a lot clearer, but the trees surrounding us suddenly loomed more dark and threatening. I traced the thin line with my thumbnail.

'If it is,' I said, 'it comes out on the north road. Eventually.' It was going to be a long, arduous trip, though. For a moment I even considered going back the way we'd come, and taking our chances on the shattered highway, but that was never really going to be an option; the Salamander's suspension would be wrecked in moments, and there were bound to be enemy survivors lurking in the woods. Pushing on was the only sensible choice.

FOUR HOURS LATER, cold, tired, hungry, and seriously hacked off, I was beginning to think fighting our way out through a bunch of walking pusbags wouldn't have been so bad after all. We'd probably have linked up with the first of our recon patrols by now, and be on our way back to the battery in a nice cosy Chimera...

'What's that?' Grear pointed off to the left, through the trees.

'What's what?' I brushed the fringe of raindrops from the peak of my cap, and followed the direction of his finger with my eyes.

'I thought I saw something.' Shadows and trees continued to crawl past the Salamander.

'What, exactly?' I asked, trying not to snap at him.

'I don't know.' A fine observer he was turning out to be. 'There!' He pointed again, and this time I saw it for myself. A glimmer of light flickering through the trees.

'Civilisation!' I said. 'Emperor be praised!' There could be no doubt that the light was artificial, a strong, warm glow.

'There's nothing on the map,' Jurgen said. He killed the headlights, and brought us to a stop. I glanced at the softly-glowing slate screen.

'We're almost at the highway,' I concluded. 'Maybe it's a farmhouse or something.'

'Not exactly agricultural land around here though, is it, sir?' Mulenz asked. I shrugged.

'Forestry workers, then.' I didn't really care. The light promised warmth, food, and a chance to get out of the rain. That was good enough for me. Except for the little voice of caution which scratched at the back of my mind...

'We'll go in on foot,' I decided. 'If they're hostile they can't have heard our engine yet. We'll reconnoitre before we proceed. Any questions?'

No one had, so we disembarked; the three gunners carrying lasguns, while I loosened my trusty chainsword in its scabbard.

The ground was ankle-deep in mud and mulch as we squelched our way forward. I ordered us into the trees to make for the light directly, cutting the corner off the curve of the track. The going was easier here, a carpet of rich loam and fallen leaves cushioning our footfalls, and the thick tracery of branches overhead keeping most of the rain off as we slipped between the shadowy trunks.

A line of thicker darkness began to resolve itself through the trees, backlit by the increasing glow behind it.

'It's a wall,' Mulenz said. No wonder they made him an observer, I thought, nothing gets past this one. I raised a cautious hand to it: old stonework, slick with moss, about twice my own height. I was about to mutter something sarcastic about his ability to state the obvious when we heard the scream. It was a woman's voice, harsh and shrill, cutting through the shrouding gloom around us.

'This way!' Mulenz took off like a startled sump rat, and the rest of us followed. I drew my laspistol, and tried to look as though I was hero-ically leading the charge while keeping the rest of the group between me and potential danger.

Something was crashing towards us through the undergrowth, and I drew a bead on it, finger tightening reflexively on the trigger.

'Frak!' I held my fire as the looming shape resolved itself into a young woman, her clothing torn and muddy, who I suddenly found clamped around my neck.

'Help me!' she cried, like the heroine of a cheesy holodrama. Easier said than done with a good fifty kilos of feminine pulchritude trying to throttle me. Despite the mud and grime and darkness I found her extra-ordinarily attractive, the scent of her hair dizzying; at the time, I put it down to oxygen starvation.

'With pleasure,' I croaked, finally managing to unwind her from around my throat. 'If you could just...'

'They're coming!' she shrieked, wriggling in my grip like a down-hive dancing girl. Under other circumstances I'd have enjoyed the experience, but there's a time and a place for everything, and this was neither.

'Who are you, miss?' At least Jurgen was paying attention; Grear and Mulenz were just staring at her, as though they'd never seen a pretty girl falling out of her dress before. Maybe they didn't get out much.

'Them!' She pointed back they way she'd come, where something else was thrashing its way through the undergrowth. The stench preceeding it was enough to confirm the presence of at least one of the Chaos troopers we'd encountered before. Shaking her off like an overeager puppy I raised my arm and fired.

The crack of the lasbolt broke the spell; Greer and Mulenz raised their lasguns and followed suit. Jurgen took slower, deliberate aim.

Something shrieked in the darkness, and burst through the surrounding undergrowth. A smoking crater had been gouged out of the left side of its body, a mortal wound to any normal man, but it just kept coming. Jurgen fired once, exploding its head, and it fell in a shower of putrescence.

'Sir! There's another!' Grear fired again, setting fire to a nearby shrub. In the sudden flare of light the enemy trooper stood out clearly, running towards us, a filthy combat blade in its hand. Jurgen and I fired simultaneously, blowing it to pieces before it could close.

'Is that the last of them?' I asked the girl. She nodded, shaking with reaction, and slumped against me. Once again I found the sensation curiously distracting; with a surge of willpower I detatched her again. 'Mulenz. Help her.'

He came forward grinning like an idiot, and I handed the girl across to him. As I did so a curious expression flickered across her face, almost like surprise, before she swooned decorously into his arms.

'Any movement out there?' I asked, crossing to Jurgen. He turned slowly, tracking the barrel of his lasgun, sweeping the perimeter of firelight. Welcome as it had been at the climax of the fight, now it was a hindrance, destroying our night vision and rendering everything outside it impenetrable.

'I think I can still hear movement,' he said. I strained my ears, picking up the faint scuff of feet moving through the forest detritus.

'Several of them,' I agreed. 'Back towards the road.' Almost the opposite direction to the one our guest and her pursuers had come from.

'Commissar, look.' Grear managed to tear his envious attention away from Mulenz long enough to point. Flickering lights were moving through the trees, heading towards us. He levelled his gun.

'Hold your fire,' I said. Whoever it was out there was moving far too openly to be trying to sneak up on us. I kept my pistol in my hand nevertheless. 'It might be...'

'Hello?' A warm, contralto voice floated out of the darkness, unmistakably feminine. A tension I hadn't even been aware of suddenly left me; even without seeing the speaker I felt as though here was someone to be trusted.

'Over here,' I found myself calling unnecessarily. The lights were now bobbing in our direction, attracted by the glow of the gradually diminishing fire, and quickly resolved themselves into hand-held luminators. Half a dozen girls, dressed like the one clamped firmly to Mulenz but without the mud and rents appeared; like her they all seemed to be in their late teens. All except one...

She stepped forward out of the group, almost a head taller, the hood falling back from her cape to reveal long, raven hair. Her eyes were a startling emerald colour, her lips full and rounded, pulling back to reveal perfect white teeth as she smiled. She extended a hand towards me. Even before she spoke I knew hers would be the voice I'd heard before.

'I'm Emeli Duboir. And you are?'

'Ciaphas Cain. Imperial Commissar, 12th Valhallan Field Artillery. At your service.' I bowed formally. She smiled again, and I felt warm and comfortable for the first time that night.

'Delighted to make your acquaintance, commissar.' Her voice tingled down my spine. Listening to it was like bathing in chocolate. 'It seems we owe you a great deal.' Her eyes moved on, taking in the corpses of the traitors, and the girl who still seemed welded to Mulenz. 'Is Krystabel all right?'

'Shocked a little, possibly,' I said. 'Maybe a few minor scrapes. Nothing a warm bath couldn't put right.' The words were accompanied by a sudden, extraordinarily vivid mental image of Krystabel luxuriating in a steaming bathtub; I fought it down, bringing my thoughts back to the necessities of the present. Emeli was looking at me with faint amusement, an eyebrow quirked, as though she could read my thoughts.

'We need to get her inside as soon as possible,' she said. 'I wonder if your man would mind helping to carry her.'

'Of course not,' I said. Judging by Mulenz's expression we'd need a crowbar to separate them.

So WE ACCOMPANIED the women home, which turned out to be a large, rambling manor house set securely in its own grounds. A plaque on the gates announced that this was the Saint Trynia Academy for the Daughters of Gentlefolk, which explained a lot. To my relief I saw that the forest track was paved from that point on, which would speed up our journey considerably when we set out again. But of course Emeli wouldn't hear of it.

'You must stay, at least until the morning,' she said. By this time we were in the main hall, which was warmed by a roaring fire; I'd expected the Valhallans to be severely uncomfortable, but they didn't seem to mind, crowding into the benches along the polished wooden dining table with the students.

We were certainly the centre of attention during dinner. Grear was surrounded by a small knot of giggling admirers, oohing and ahhing appreciatively as he enlarged on our day's adventures. Although he was making me out to be the main hero of the piece, he was painting himself a fairly creditable second. Mulenz had seemed remarkably subdued since Krystabel was detached from him and packed off to the infirmary, but he perked up as soon as she reappeared, chatty and animated now.

She perched on his knee as he ate, the two of them gazing into one another's eyes, and I found myself thinking I was going to have trouble getting him back aboard the Salamander in the morning. Even Jurgen was being flirted with outrageously, which struck me as truly bizarre. The only female I'd ever known to take a romantic interest in him before was an ogryn on R&R, and she'd been drunk at the time. He picked at his food nervously, responding as best he could, but it was clear he was out of his depth.

'Is the grox all right?' Emeli asked at my elbow. Protocol demanded I sat next to her at the top table.

'It's fine,' I responded. In truth it was excellent, the most tender I'd ever tasted, lightly poached in a samec sauce that was positively to die for. Which I nearly did, of course, but I'm getting a little ahead of myself. She smiled dazzlingly at my approval, and again I found my senses overwhelmed by her closeness. The sound of her voice was like the caress of silk, smooth and fine, like the fabric of her gown; it was the same shade of green as her bewitching eyes, clinging to the curves of her body in ways which inflamed my imagination. She knew it too, the minx. As she leaned over to pick up the condiments she brushed my arm lightly with her own, and a lightning strike of desire swept the breath from my lungs.

'I'm glad you like it,' she said, her voice bubbling with mischief. 'I think you'll find a lot here to enjoy.'

'I'm sure I will,' I said.

* * *

AFTER DINNER THE company separated. Emeli invited me up to her private apartments, and promised to arrange accomodation for the gunners, although by the look of things Greer and Mulenz had pretty much taken care of that for themselves. While Emeli went off to do whatever finishing school principals did in the evening I caught up with Jurgen in the hallway, and prised him away from his giggling escort.

'Jurgen,' I said. 'Get back to the Salamander. Vox the battery, and give them our co-ordinates. This is all very pleasant, but...'

'I know what you mean, sir.' He nodded, relief clearly visible in his eyes. 'The way the lads are acting...'

'They're acting pretty much like troopers always do when there are women around,' I said. He nodded.

'Only more so.' He hesitated. 'I was beginning to think they'd got to you too, sir.'

Well they had, nearly. But my innate paranoia hadn't let me down. If it's too good to be true then it probably is, as my old tutor used to say, and even though I wasn't sure exactly what was going on here I knew something wasn't right. I just hoped I could keep reminding myself of that when I was with Emeli.

Of course I should have been wondering why Jurgen wasn't affected like the rest of us, but that particular coin wouldn't drop for another decade or more; in those days although I'd read the manual, I'd never met a psyker, let alone a blank.

'Don't worry girls,' I reassured his hovering fan club. 'He'll be right back.' Jurgen shot me a grateful look, and disappeared.

'Ciaphas. There you are.' Emeli appeared at the top of the stairs. 'I was wondering what had happened to you.'

'Likewise.' I turned on the charm with practiced ease, and moved to join her; although I told myself I was climbing the stairs of my own volition, something drew me towards her, something which seemed to grow stronger and muffle my senses the closer I got. She moulded herself to the inside of my arm, and we drifted across a wide hallway towards her apartments.

I had no memory of entering, but found myself inside an elegant boudoir, smelling faintly of some heady perfume. Everywhere I looked were soft pastel colours, flimsy fabrics, and artworks of the most flagrant eroticism. I'd seen quite a bit in my time, I have to confess, but the atmosphere of sensual indulgence inside that room was something I couldn't have begun to imagine.

Emeli sank into the wide, yielding bed, drawing me down after her. Her breath was sweet as our lips touched, tasting faintly of that strange, sensual perfume.

Sandy Mitchell

'I knew you were one of us the moment I felt your presence in the woods,' she whispered. I tried to make sense of her words, but the sheer physical need for her was pounding in my blood.

'Felt?' I mumbled, drawing her closer. She nodded, kissing my throat. 'I could taste your soul,' she breathed. 'Like to like...'

The little voice in my head was screaming now, screaming that something was wrong. Screaming out questions that something kept trying to suppress, something which I now realised was outside myself, trying to worm its way in.

'Why were you out there?' I asked, and the answer suddenly flared in my mind. Hunting. Krystabel had been...

'Bait,' Emeli's voice rang silently inside my brain. 'Enticing those Nurglite scum. But then you came instead. Much better.'

'Better for what?' I mumbled. It felt like one of those dreams where you know you're asleep and try desperately to wake. Her voice danced through my mind like laughing windchimes.

'That which wakes. It comes tonight. But not for you.' Somewhere in the physical world our bodies moved together, caressing, enticing, casting a spell of physical pleasure I knew with a sudden burst of panic was ensnaring my very soul. Her disembodied voice laughed again. 'Give in, Ciaphas. Slaanesh has surely touched your soul before now. You live only for yourself. You're his, whether you know it or not.'

Holy Emperor! That was the first time I'd heard the names of any of the Chaos powers, long before my subsequent activities as the Inquisition's occasional and extremely reluctant errand boy made them all too familar, but even then I could tell that what I faced was monstrous beyond measure. Selfish and self-indulgent I may well have been, and still am if I'm honest about it, but if I have any qualities that outmatch that one it's my will to survive. The realisation of what I faced, and the consequences if I failed, doused me like a shock of cold water. I snapped back to myself like a drowning man gasping for air, to find Emeli staring at me in consternation.

'You broke free!' she said, like a petulant child denied a sweet. Now I knew she was a psyker I could feel the tendrils starting to wrap themselves around my mind again. I scrabbled for the laspistol at my belt, desperation making my fingers shake.

'Sorry,' I said. 'I prefer blondes.' Then I shot her. She glared at me for a moment in outraged astonishment, before the light faded from her eyes and she went to join whatever she worshipped in hell.

As my mind began to clear I became aware of a new sound, a rhythmical chanting which echoed through the building. I wasn't sure what it meant, but my tingling palms told me things were about to get a whole lot worse.

SURE ENOUGH, AS I staggered down the stairway to the entrance hall, the sound grew in intensity. I hefted the pistol in my sweat-sticky hand and cautiously pushed the door to the great hall ajar. I wished I hadn't. Every girl in the school was there, along with what was left of Grear and Mulenz. They were still alive, for whatever that was worth, rictus grins of insane ecstasy on their faces, as the priestesses of depravity conducted their obscene rituals. As I watched, Grear expired, and an ululating howl of joy rose from the assembled cultist's throats.

Then Krystabel stepped forward, her voice raised, chanting something new in counterpoint to the other acolytes. A faint wind blew through the room, thick with that damnable perfume, and the hairs on the back of my neck rose. Mulenz began to levitate, his body shifting and distorting in strange inhuman ways. Power began to crackle through the air.

'Merciful Emperor!' I made the warding sign of the eagle, more out of habit than because I expected it to do any good, and turned to leave. Whatever was beginning to possess my erstwhile trooper, I wanted to be long gone before it manifested itself properly. Not that that seemed likely without a miracle...

Lasbolts exploded over my head, raking the room, taking down some of the cultists. I turned, the sudden stench behind me warning me what I was about to see. Sure enough the entrance hall was full of the pusbag troopers, and for the first time I realised that Slawkenberg was under attack from two different Chaos powers. No wonder they were more interested in killing each other than us. Not that I was likely to reap the benefit, by the look of things.

The Slaaneshi cult was rallying by now, howling forward to meet their disease-ridden rivals in what looked like a suicidal charge; but it was only to buy Krystabel enough time to complete her ritual. The daemonhost which had formerly been Mulenz levitated forwards, spitting bolts of energy from its hands, and laughing insanely as it blasted pusbags and schoolgirls alike. I fled, ignored by the Nurglites, who grouped together to concentrate their lasgun fire on the hovering abomination. Much good it seemed to be doing them. I could hear screams and explosions behind me as I sprinted across the lawn, shoulderblades itching in expectation of feeling a lasbolt or something worse at any moment.

'Commissar! Over here!' Jurgen's familar voice rose above the roar of an engine, and the Salamander crashed through an ornamental shrubbery. I clambered aboard.

'Jurgen!' I shouted, dazed and delighted to see him. 'I thought they'd got you too!'

'No.' He looked puzzled for a moment. 'I ran into some of those enemy troopers in the woods. But they walked right past me. I can't understand it.' I caught a full-strength whiff of his body odour as he shrugged.

'The Emperor protects the righteous,' I suggested straight-faced. Jurgen nodded.

He crossed himself and gunned the engine.

'At least we know what they were doing in this sector now,' I said, as we raced down the paved track towards the road. 'They were trying to stop the summoning... Oh frak!' I grabbed the voxcaster. 'Did you vox in our co-ordinates?'

'Of course,' Jurgen nodded.

'Cain to command. Full barrage, danger close, immediate effect. Don't argue, just do it!' I hung up before Mostrue could start pestering me with questions, and waited for the first shells to arrive.

If being close to the first strike had been worrying, getting caught in a full barrage was serious change of undergarments time. For what seemed like eternity the world disappeared in fire and smoke, but I guess the Emperor was looking out for us after all or we'd never have made it to the road in one piece.

When we went back at first light the entire building had been obliterated, along with several hectares of woodland. I left out the bit about the daemonhost in my report; I'd been the only one to see it, after all, and I didn't want the Inquisition poking around in my affairs. Instead I made up some extravagant lies about the heroism of the dead troopers, which, as usual, were taken as a modest attempt to deflect attention from my own valour. And, so far as I knew at the time, that was the end of it.

Except that sometimes at night, even after more than a century, I find myself dreaming of green eyes and a voice like velvet, and I wonder if my soul is as safe as I'd like to think...

THE TRAITOR'S HAND

Editorial Note:

To my great surprise, not to mention personal satisfaction, the first two volumes of material from the Cain archive which I have prepared for circulation among those of my fellow inquisitors who may care to peruse them have been quite widely read; although it must be said that many of my colleagues appear to regard them as light entertainment rather than the more serious food for thought I originally intended, finding it hard to believe that an imperial commissar could fall so far short of the ideals he was meant to embody. Given his public reputation I find this incredulity easy to understand, but thanks to our personal association, I can assure my readers that he was indeed very much as he depicts himself in these memoirs. I would point out, though, that perhaps as a result of his own awareness of these shortcomings, he does have a tendency to judge himself a little more harshly than he might actually deserve.

Hitherto I've concentrated my efforts on some of Cain's encounters with alien enemies of the Imperium, although in the course of his long career he crossed swords with all manner of warp-spawned monstrosities as well, confounding the dark designs of the Ruinous Powers and their mortal minions on numerous occasions. It seemed fitting, therefore, especially given the interest in the previous volumes from inquisitors of ordos other than my own, to select one such incident to prepare for wider dissemination.

I was aided in this decision by the fact that it follows on chronologically from the previous two extracts, although Cain's tendency to record his memoirs piecemeal, as different anecdotes occurred to him, means that the original material forms a somewhat extended digression. This happened in his account of the famous incident during the 13th Black Crusade, when he was dragged out of retirement to defend an entire world with little more than a handful of his Schola Progenium cadets. That will have to wait for a subsequent volume, of course; in the meantime, I believe I have successfully filleted the material relevant to the Adumbria campaign and present it here as a reasonably coherent narrative in its own right.

Like the earlier extracts, these events took place during Cain's service with the 597th Valhallan and cover the fledgling regiment's first encounter with the forces of Chaos. A particular point of interest is Cain's description of the ordinary troopers' reaction to the Great Enemy and the form its machinations took, which I hope will sound a much-needed note of caution to those of my readers who might fall prey to the pernicious tenets of Radicalism.

Since, as usual, Cain is infuriatingly vague about most things which don't affect him personally, I have continued to insert extracts from other sources where necessary in order to present a more rounded account of events on Adumbria and in the system surrounding it. Unfortunately, as before, some of these are the logorrheic meanderings of Jenit Sulla, for which I can only apologise in advance; were any other alternatives available, you can be sure I would have used them.

In accordance with the previous volumes, I have broken Cain's largely unstructured narrative into chapters for ease of reading, and once again I have been unable to resist prefacing them with a selection from the collection of quotations he maintained for the instruction and amusement of his schola students. Other than this I have confined my interpolations to the occasional footnote, leaving Cain to tell his story in his own inimitable manner.

Amberley Vail, Ordo Xenos

ONE

'The wider he smiled and called us friend,
the tighter we clung to our purses.'
– Argun Slyter *'The Wastrel's Stratagem,'* Act 4 Scene 1

I'VE HAD MORE than my fair share of unpleasant surprises over the course of a century or so of fighting the Emperor's enemies, whenever running away and hiding from them wasn't an option, but the sudden appearance of Tomas Beije in the corridors of the *Emperor's Beneficence* is one I still can't recall without flinching. Not because the situation was particularly life-threatening, which I suppose made it unusual enough given the kind of surprises I usually got, but because of the associations the memory of it still triggers: a curious amalgam of anger at his subsequent pig-headed stupidity, which almost ended up handing an Imperial world to the Ruinous Powers neatly gift-wrapped with a pretty pink bow, and, more importantly, could have resulted in my ignominious execution had events not turned out as they did; and the flood of unpleasant memories his presence stirred up in me at the time. I hadn't liked him when we were commissar cadets together at the Schola Progenium and I suppose I would have disliked him still if I'd spared him so much as a single thought in the years since we were

501

judged fit to inflict ourselves on a regiment somewhere and sent off elsewhere in the galaxy. (Or in my case, I strongly suspect, handed a scarlet sash and politely shown the door because it seemed the easiest way of keeping my tutors from resigning *en masse*.)[1]

'Ciaphas.' He nodded a greeting, as though we'd always been on good terms, and a smile as sincere as an ecclesiarch distributing alms in front of the pictcasters smeared itself across his pudgy features. 'I heard you were on board.'

That didn't surprise me. By that point in my career, my reputation preceded me wherever I went, smoothing the way in a fashion which often made my life a great deal easier, and, as if to balance things out in some way, periodically dragging me into life-threatening situations of bowel-clenching terror. No doubt by now, three days out from Kastafore[2], the entire ship would be aware that Cain the Hero of the Imperium was aboard, and either pretending not to be impressed by that sort of thing or trying to find some way of scraping an acquaintance in order to further their own careers by coat-tailing on mine. Well good luck to anyone daft enough to try the latter, I thought.

'Beije.' I returned the nod curtly, irked by his use of my given name. We'd never been friends at the schola and I resented the presumption now. Come to think of it, I don't recall that he'd ever had any friends, just a small group of cronies as pious and self-righteous as he was, always whining on about the grace of the Emperor or running to the proctors with tales of the minor infractions of other students. The only time anyone was ever pleased to see him was on the scrumball pitch, where he got tackled enthusiastically at every opportunity whether he had the ball or not. 'I had no idea you were part of this little jaunt.'

The smile curdled a little as he registered the snub, but he was bright enough to realise that making an issue of it in public wouldn't be a good idea. The corridors were filling with senior Guard officers, the black coats and scarlet sashes of a handful of other commissars among them, all drifting towards one of the recreation halls where the lord general himself was expected to brief us in a few minutes' time. Not in

---

1. *In point of fact Cain's record as a schola student is best described as unremarkable. His academic results are, by and large, on the low end of average; the only areas in which he did better than this being sports and combat techniques. His disciplinary records are surprisingly free of infractions, which, given his character, probably means the one thing he truly excelled at, even in those days, was not getting caught.*

2. *An Imperial world recently cleansed of an ork incursion. For once Cain and the 597th had been out of the thick of the fighting, seeing relatively little action, and his brief anecdotes about the exceptions needn't concern us at this juncture.*

person, of course, as he'd be travelling in some style aboard the flotilla's flagship, but the tech-priests had apparently rigged up some method for him to pictcast all the vessels in the task force simultaneously before we made the transition to the warp.

'I'd hardly describe facing the enemies of humanity as a jaunt,' he said stiffly. 'It's our holy duty to preserve the Emperor's blessed domains from the merest taint of the unclean.'

'Of course it is,' I replied, just as unable to resist teasing the pious little prig now as I had been nearly thirty years before. 'But I'm sure he wouldn't mind if we had a bit of fun while we're doing it.' Of course, facing whatever horrors might be waiting for us wherever we were going was about as far from my idea of fun as it was possible to get, but it was the sort of thing a hero was supposed to say and it went down well with the crowd around us, most of whom were trying very hard to look as if they weren't listening to the conversation.

'I'm sorry to interrupt your socialising, commissar.' Colonel Kasteen cleared her throat and glanced at her chronograph with studied nonchalance. 'But I believe it would be impolite to keep the lord general waiting.'

'Thank you, colonel,' I responded, grateful for the intervention and conveying that fact with a glance no one else present other than Major Broklaw, her second-in-command, would have been able to pick up on. Our years of service together[1] had given us a rapport which came as close to friendship as our respective positions allowed and which helped no end in the smooth running of the regiment.

'This is your colonel?' Beije asked with undisguised incredulity. Kasteen's jaw knotted with the effort of reining in her instinctive response, which from long experience I expected to be short, pithy, and anatomically improbable.

Happy to return the favour she'd just done for me, I nodded. 'She is indeed,' I said. 'And a damn good one too.' Then I laughed and patted Beije on the back, which I remembered from our days at the schola was something he'd always detested. 'Surely you haven't forgotten how to read rank insignia?'

'I hadn't noticed them,' he muttered, his face slowly crimsoning. Well, maybe that was true. Kasteen had quite a spectacular figure, in a trim, well-muscled sort of way, and perhaps he hadn't bothered to look that high. 'She was standing behind you.'

---

1. *By this point, roughly five years after the adventures on Simia Orichalcae presented in the previous volume, Cain was almost a third of the way though his period of service with the 597th. His activities in the interim are recorded elsewhere in the archive, but are irrelevant to the present account.*

'Quite,' I said, unable to resist prolonging his discomfiture a little longer by making introductions. 'Colonel, may I present Commissar Tomas Beije, an old classmate of mine.' Kasteen nodded a formal greeting, which Beije echoed a little over-eagerly, trying to make up for his lapse in good manners. 'Beije, this is Colonel Regina Kasteen, commanding officer of the 597th Valhallan. And Major Ruput Broklaw, her executive officer.'

'Commissar.' Broklaw stuck out a hand for Beije to shake, which he did after a moment's hesitation, wincing as the major closed his grip. He'd tried the same thing on me the first time we'd met and I'd been grateful for the augmetic fingers on my right hand. 'Any friend of Commissar Cain is always welcome in our quarters.'

'Thank you.' Beije retrieved his hand, although whether he was astute enough to realise Broklaw's tone effectively ruled him out of that general invitation was unlikely. Trapped by social convention, he flapped it vaguely at the two men flanking him. 'Colonel Asmar of the Tallarn 229th, and Major Sipio, his second-in-command.'

I glanced back at Kasteen and Broklaw, amused at the contrast between the two groups. While the Tallarns were both short and dark-complexioned, swathed in the loose tunics of their desert home world, the Valhallans were about as physically different as it was possible to be. Kasteen was wearing her red hair drawn back in a pony tail, blue eyes as clear as the skies above the ice fields of her home world, while Broklaw's flint-grey gaze perfectly mirrored the night-dark hair which framed it. In deference to what they considered to be the stifling heat outside the areas assigned to us, which, as usual, they'd had refrigerated to temperatures which left the breath smoking, they were dressed in simple fatigues, only the rank pins on their collars denoting their status. So to be fair, I suppose Beije could have been forgiven for not realising who they were at first, but that wasn't going to stop me enjoying his embarrassment.

'A pleasure.' I nodded to the two officers. 'You have a formidable reputation as warriors. I look forward to hearing of the glorious victories of the Tallarn people.'

'We prevail by the grace of the Emperor,' Asmar said, his voice surprisingly mellifluous. Beije nodded, a little too eagerly.

'Yes, absolutely. Faith is the strongest weapon in our arsenal, after all.'

'Maybe so,' I said. 'But I'll still take a laspistol to back it up.' It wasn't the wittiest remark in the galaxy, I'll admit that, but I was expecting at least a smile. Instead, to my surprise, the Tallarns' expressions hardened imperceptibly.

'That would be your choice, of course.' Asmar bowed formally once and turned away, followed by his number two. Beije hesitated a moment, as if debating whether to go with them straight away, but just couldn't resist getting the last word in.

'I'm afraid not everyone shares my appreciation of your sense of humour,' he said. 'Our Tallarn friends take their faith very seriously.'

'Well good for them,' I said, beginning to understand why no one had shot him by accident yet. By luck or somebody's good judgment, he'd been assigned to a regiment of Emperor-botherers as humourless as he was. Of course, at that point, I didn't know the half of it; they had Chaplains like the rest of us had Chimera drivers, all of the kind that make Redemptionists look well-balanced by comparison[1]. Had I realised the consequences that were to flow from the impulse to irritate Beije and unwittingly offending his friends in the process, I suppose I'd have held my tongue, but at the time I remained in blissful ignorance and went into the briefing feeling rather pleased with myself.

Because of the delay in the corridor, Kasteen, Broklaw and I were among the last to arrive, but once again my reputation worked to our advantage and a trio of seats had somehow been kept clear for us despite there being not quite enough to go round. Beije and his Tallarns, I noticed in passing, were among those squeezed in at the back, standing uncomfortably and gazing resentfully at us as we made our way down to the front of the auditorium.

There were five regiments in all aboard the *Emperor's Beneficence*, an antedeluvian Galaxy-class troopship which seemed to be kept functioning entirely by the constant activity of her tech-priests and enginseers, and the senior command staff of all of them came to a tidy total; most had sent their entire complement to save the effort of repeating the exercise later on, and I was able to spot all of our own company commanders and their immediate subordinates scattered among the crowd before I sat down.

Apart from us and the Tallarns, the ship was carrying a Valhallan armoured regiment whose Leman Russes I had been delighted to see stowed in the hold next to ours (and who in turn seemed equally pleased to have found themselves travelling with another unit from their home world) and a couple of infantry regiments newly raised on Kastafore. The officers from there were easy to spot, thanks to the

---

1. *Cain is exaggerating a little on both counts. Tallarn regiments do tend to have an inordinate number of Chaplains compared to most others, often attached as low down the command structure as individual squads, but few of them are quite as fanatical as the members of the Redemptionist cult. It cannot be denied, though, that their entire culture is remarkably pious, and few natives of that world are prepared to take any significant decision without consulting a cleric for guidance as to the will of the Emperor in the matter.*

newness of their uniforms and the expressions of alert interest they directed at everything which caught their attention (most of which seemed to be the women from the 597th).

The cogboys[1] had been busy, there was no doubt about that. Wires and cables snaked across the floor of the chamber, being tended to by white-robed acolytes chanting the appropriate rituals of activation, terminating in what I recognised as a hololithic display unit of remarkable size and complexity. At the moment, it was projecting a rotating image of the Imperial eagle, which hazed and sputtered in the familiar fashion of all such devices, accompanied by jaunty music of staggering vacuity.

'Did anyone remember the caba nuts?' I asked, reminded of a public holotheatre, and a few of the nearby officers chuckled sycophantically. After a moment, the hum of conversation died away as the lights dimmed, the senior tech-priest ceremoniously kicked his control lectern and the familiar face of Lord General Zyvan replaced the aquila, looming down at us like an out-of-focus balloon. After a moment of heated discussion among the tech-priests, somebody yanked a couple of wires out of their sockets and the music stopped abruptly, enabling us to hear him.

'Thank you all for your kind attention,' the balloon said, its voice sizzling with static. It had been some time since I'd spoken to the lord general in person, our paths having crossed rarely since our first meeting on Gravalax about six years before, and most of those occasions had been fraught to say the least, occurring as they did in the middle of either a war zone or a diplomatic crisis. Nevertheless, we'd always got on tolerably well and I respected his concern for the welfare of the men under his command, which, since they included me, I thought was a decided asset in a military leader. 'No doubt you've been wondering why we've mobilised in such a hurry following the success of our campaign against the orks on Kastafore.' A few of the officers from there raised a cheer, which trailed off into embarrassed silence.

'Here it comes,' I murmured to Kasteen, who nodded grimly. Normally we would have expected to remain on the newly-cleansed world for some months at least, helping to rebuild the bits the greenskins had put a dent in, making sure the local PDF was back up to strength, and generally enjoying a bit of a breather before moving on to the next war. But instead we'd been hurried aboard the *Emperor's Benificence* almost as soon as we'd reached our staging area, the first shuttles already wait-

---

1. A slang term for tech-priests, common among the Imperial Guard, apparently derived from the cogwheel insignia of their calling.

ing to ferry our vehicles up to orbit as we'd arrived. One of the new
Kastaforean regiments had already preceeded us starside. Fortunately
they were too green to have staked out the most comfortable quarters
and accessible mess halls for themselves and were easily displaced by
the veterans of the 597th, so our troopers were as happy with the situation as it was possible to be. Which wasn't much: a mobilisation that
rapid had to mean trouble had blown up without warning in a relatively close system and we were being sent to deal with it. That meant
we'd be going in hot, with little idea of what we'd be facing, and
already caught on the back foot. Not a situation any warrior likes to be
in.

Zyvan wasn't too happy about things either, I could tell, although I
suppose being personally acquainted with him gave me an advantage
in that regard. He was hiding it well, though, his usual air of bluff competence barely impeded by the distortions of the hololith. Certainly
most of the people around me were buying it.

'Ten days ago we received an astropathic message from a naval task
force hunting a flotilla of Chaos raiders on the outer fringes of the subsector.' As I'd expected, Zyvan's face disappeared to be replaced by a
map of the local star group. Kastafore was off to the bottom left, almost
at the edge of the display, and a small cluster of contact icons overlapped it, marking the positions of our fleet.

I drew in a deep breath. If I'd read the runes correctly, we were the
only troopship on the move, accompanied by a handful of the warships. The rest were still sitting in orbit, twiddling their thumbs, no
doubt feeling mightily relieved that for one reason or another they
weren't quite ready to go. That meant we were the spearhead, first into
whatever might be waiting for us, which in turn meant we were likely
to soak up the bulk of the casualties. My stomach tightened at the
thought. I didn't have long to digest the implications, though, as the
display lurched suddenly, skipping a couple of parsecs to the right and
dumping Kastafore ignominiously into the void outside the projection
field. A couple of tech-priests started arguing in urgent undertones and
one of them disappeared under the lectern, his mechadendrites twitching.

'They've been tentatively identified as a group calling themselves the
Ravagers,' Zyvan's voice continued, blissfully unaware that the starfield
in the hololith was now bouncing like a joygirl on overtime. The image
steadied itself as a shower of sparks erupted from the control lectern
and the tech-priest emerged from beneath it, looking slightly singed.
After a final wobble, it zoomed in on a cluster of contact icons bearing
the runes of Chaos forces.

The hairs on the back of my neck prickled at the sight. Emperor knows I've faced a lot over the years, but the thought of the Great Enemy still disturbs me more than most. Perhaps it's because I've seen so much of what they can do, but I think it's their sheer unpredictability which makes them so worrying. Most enemies are rational, at least in their own terms: tyranids want to absorb your genetic material, orks want to kill you messily and loot your corpse, and necrons just want to kill every living thing in the galaxy.[1] But Chaos is random, by its very nature, and even if you can work out what it is the enemy's after, half the time only the Emperor knows why they want it in the first place.

'They've been hitting isolated systems and merchant convoys sporadically for the last few years,' Zyvan went on, while a red line considerately tracked the path of their depredations. 'Typical Chaos tactics, hit and run mostly, inflicting the maximum number of casualties, then withdrawing before the fleet arrives to give them what for.'

'Sounds like a Khornate cult,' I whispered to Kasteen and Broklaw, who looked a little puzzled, before remembering they hadn't encountered any minions of the Ruinous Powers yet and I was probably the only one in the room with much idea of the divisions within the ranks of the Great Enemy. That was some degree of comfort, anyway. In my experience they were the easiest type of renegade to deal with, having little ambition beyond getting into combat as quickly as possible and killing as many of our people as they could before being cut down themselves. That made them particularly susceptible to ambushes and flanking attacks, which would work to our advantage, particularly if we could stick the Kastaforeans out in front as bait.

'The Navy finally caught up with them on the fringes of the Salomine system, inflicting severe losses on their fleet,' Zyvan continued. I wasn't surprised, recognising the blue icon of a tau colony world, where the Ravagers were sure to have met far stronger resistance than they expected. That would have given the fleet time to catch up and join in slaughtering the heretics in the name of the greater good. The tau would have loved that, I was certain, until it dawned on them that they now had an Imperial fleet squatting on their doorstep instead, and the heretics had already weakened their defences. 'Several vessels did manage to flee into the warp, the exact number and type remain to be determined.'

'Which affects us how, exactly?' Broklaw murmured, with the groundpounder's typical distain for anything the Navy might be doing. A Guardsman to the core, his only interest in starships was how quickly

---

1. *Actually just the sentient ones. So far as we know.*

and comfortably they could move the regiment to the next planet we were supposed to kick nine shades of hell out of to maintain peace and stability in the galaxy.

As if to answer his question, Zyvan reappeared, pointing to an insignificant dot which looked to me pretty much like any other system.

'Our Navigators consider it highly probable that they'll end up here, in the Adumbria system, especially if their warp engines have been damaged. Apparently the warp currents are particularly strong and turbulent around Adumbria Prime and they're likely to be drawn there.' He shrugged. 'Unless they're setting course for the place on purpose, which the fleet Navigator thinks is quite possible, given their previous heading. What they might be after on a backwater like that is anybody's guess. It could just be the next convenient target on the list.' His voice hardened in the manner that I knew from experience meant he'd made up his mind about something and wouldn't be dissuaded by anything short of a direct command from the Emperor himself (or possibly a quiet word from the Inquisition). 'In any case, when they arrive, they're going to be in for a surprise. If the warp currents remain favourable, we'll be there ahead of them. If we're really lucky, the rest of the task force will have had time to catch up too.'

I don't mind admitting it, the last sentence sent a chill down my spine. What he meant was that barring a miracle, we'd be on our own, facing anything up to a full-scale invasion fleet with just five regiments and a handful of ships.

'And if we're not?' Kasteen asked quietly, clearly coming to the same conclusion I had.

'Then things are about to get very interesting,' I said, keeping my voice steady by a preternatural effort of will. As it turned out, that was to be one of the biggest understatements of my life, although even in my most pessimistic imaginings I never thought we'd find ourselves embroiled in a plot so diabolical as to threaten the very fabric of the Imperium itself.

Editorial Note:

Although Cain makes sufficient references to the peculiar conditions prevailing on Adumbria to enable an astute reader to deduce them, he never bothers to elucidate them explicitly. I've therefore appended the following extract, which I hope will make everything clear and help to explain much of what follows.

From *Interesting Places and Tedious People: a Wanderer's Waybook* by Jerval Sekara, 145 M39

ADUMBRIA IS ALMOST unique, even among an assemblage of worlds as vast as our beloved Imperium, being as it is rotationally locked to its sun. This in itself is not so unusual, of course: the point of interest being that, unlike most examples of such planets, Adumbria falls within the primary biosphere of the star around which it orbits. The net result of this is that one side, a howling wilderness of blizzards and ice, is condemned to perpetual night, while its bright twin is seared by the pitiless heat of the sun without respite.

Unsurprisingly, the vast majority of the population live in the so-called Shadow Belt, a narrow strip running from pole to pole where temperatures remain tolerable. Here you will find cities to rival those of most civilised worlds, boasting bars, restaurants and places of entertainment of a standard ranging from the positively opulent right the way down to 'Society for the Assistance of Travellers recommended'.

Away from the centres of population, you may find such scant agriculture as the planet supports and two inland seas, fed by the snowfields of the dark side and surrounded by pleasant resorts. The prices are, of course, higher the closer you get to the sunward side, since the temperature of the water is correspondingly greater, as are the ambient light levels. Discerning holidaymakers generally make for the so-called 'sunset strip,' where the sun is so close to the horizon as to leave the sky permanently reddened in an ever-changing display of breathtaking natural beauty...

[Several paragraphs of extraneous travelogue omitted]

The sunward and dark sides of Adumbria have little to offer the discriminating wanderer, consisting as they do of little more than life-threatening extremes of temperature. Nevertheless, a few hardy (or perhaps foolhardy!) individuals manage to scrape a living there, hunting the native wildlife, which has adapted to such extremes, scrabbling minerals from the rocks and generally pursuing such labours as occupy the time of the artisan classes.

TWO

'One thing you can say for enemies;
they make life more interesting.'

– Gilbran Quail, *Collected Essays*

AT FIRST, DESPITE the apprehension which continued to gnaw at me as the *Emperor's Benificence* ground its way through the warp, it looked as though things might actually be going our way after all. We made the transition back to the material universe without incident, to find the Adumbria system completely free from heretical marauders. The only vessels to greet us were a somewhat surprised patrol cutter and the merchantman they were pursuing, who just had time to offer to sell us a variety of recreational products of dubious provenenace before the cutter crew boarded them and confiscated the entire cargo.

In short, by the time we made orbit round Adumbria itself, I'd almost allowed myself to be lulled into that sense of false security my innate paranoia generally keeps firmly at bay.

'Interesting place,' Kasteen said, joining me at the observation window of the portside recreation deck. I nodded, still lost in the contemplation of the planet below. I'd seen a fair few worlds in my years of rattling around the galaxy and was to see a great many more before finally making it through to an honourable retirement, but not many of them stick in my memory the way Adumbria did. It wasn't that it was beautiful, not by a long way, but it had a kind of defiant grandeur about it, like a faded dowager refusing to acknowledge the passing of the years.

By this time our troopship had joined the cluster of merchant vessels which naturally accreted at the point where the equator crossed the shadow belt, hanging just a few kilometres above the planetary capital[1] which rejoiced in the uninspiring name of Skitterfall.[2] To my surprise, the eye was drawn naturally away from the glare of the bright face, which I'd expected to be the focus of attention, to the unexpectedly subtle attractions of the dark side. Far from being wrapped in impenetrable blackness, as I'd expected, this shone with the faint blue lustre of reflected starlight, bouncing back from the plains of ice and snow which covered the entire hemisphere. The more I stared, the more I became aware of a thousand subtle shades and stipplings in that apparently uniform glow, resulting from the light rebounding unevenly from mountains, canyons and who knew what other geographic irregularities.

'It'll be good to get down there,' Kasteen said, following the direction of my gaze. That was a matter of opinion, of course; I've always disliked the sort of intense cold my Valhallan colleagues seemed to thrive in and was already anticipating the bone-crushing temperatures awaiting us on our deployment with less enthusiasm than the approaching Chaos fleet. But to be fair, I'd never heard a Valhallan complain about the excessive heat they felt they encountered pretty much wherever they went and I wasn't going to undermine my reputation, not to mention my leadership, by seeming less stoic than they were.

'I'm sure the troopers would agree,' I said instead. We'd been through some winter seasons on temperate planets in the last few years, but hadn't visited an ice world since our brief and abruptly truncated sojourn on Simia Orichalcae. The dark side of Adumbria wasn't quite the same thing, but it would be cold enough to feel like home as far as they were concerned.

A faint vibration shook the deck plates beneath our feet, too familiar even to register consciously, and we watched one of the dropships slip-

---

1. *The equivalent point on the opposite side of the planet was occupied by one of the land-locked seas, making this one the obvious site for the largest starport on Adumbria.*

2. *A local dialect word describing the exact degree of twilight prevailing at that particular location. The Adumbrians have over thirty nouns for semi-darkness, each one more improbable-sounding than the last, and deliniating a subtlety of difference which could only matter to a people with far too much time on their hands.*

ping away towards the planet below. Its engines flared brightly for a second as it corrected its course, and then it disappeared among the countless number of other shuttles coming and going from the starport beneath us. Sharp, distinct pinpricks of light in the distance would be the larger vessels they tended, merchants for the most part, as Zyvan had left the bulk of our warships to form a picket line in the outer system. Apart from the *Emperor's Benificence*, the only vessel from our relief flotilla to have made it all the way to Adumbria itself was the *Indestructible II*, an Armageddon-class battle cruiser the lord general had chosen to carry him and his senior command staff.[1] When I'd first arrived on the observation deck I'd amused myself by trying to pick it out, but at this distance the effort was futile and I'd rapidly abandoned the game in favour of studying the world we were here to defend.

'It seems as though our Tallarn friends are equally eager to get down there,' Kasteen commented, watching the shuttle disappear. Her tone was studiously neutral, but the implication was clear; she was glad to see the back of them, and so was I. In the month or so we'd been transiting the warp, the regiment had passed the time in all the traditional ways, including challenging the others to a variety of sporting competitions. The 425th Armoured had thrown themselves into socialising with all the enthusiasm you might expect of a regiment which had discovered not only that they had the good fortune to be sharing a troopship with another unit from home, but that it consisted largely of women, while the Kastaforeans had done their best to hold their own against a regiment of battle-hardened veterans and acquitted themselves tolerably well, all things considered. The Tallarns, on the other hand, had remained aloof, their idea of a good time apparently consisting of innumerable prayer meetings of unimaginable tedium.

Relations hadn't turned really frosty, however, until they'd refused to take part in the inter-regimental unarmed combat competition because the 597th had included some of our women in the team. This, Colonel Asmar curtly informed us, was 'unseemly.' To no one's surprise except Asmar and probably Beije, their regimental champion was promptly and informally challenged to an impromptu bout the next time he wandered into the recreation deck. I have to report with a certain degree of satisfaction that he was subsequently pounded flat by Corporal Magot, a cheerfully sociopathic young woman who barely came up to his chin. (Which made little difference, as it only took her about a tenth of a second to bring it down to the level of her knee.)

---

1. *Presumably because none of the capital ships were ready to break orbit in time.*

Beije, of course, had been beside himself, and came storming into my office demanding to know what I intended to do about it.

'Nothing at all,' I said, smiling disarmingly and offering him the least comfortable chair. 'I've already dealt with the matter.' I turned to Jurgen, my odiferous and indispensable aide. 'Jurgen. Would you be so kind as to fetch Commissar Beije some tea? He seems a little agitated.'

'Please, don't bother on my account.' Beije paled quietly, having been exposed to the full effects of my aide's aroma while I left him to stew in the anteroom for as long as I thought I could leave it before he gave up and left. No doubt his appetite had been somewhat impaired by the experience.

'It's no bother,' I reassured him. 'I normally have a little break for some refreshment at about this time. Two bowls, please, Jurgen.'

'Commissar.' Jurgen saluted as awkwardly as ever and slouched out, somehow contriving to look as though his uniform never quite touched his body, which given his casual attitude to personal hygiene and perpetual eruptions of psoriasis, you could hardly blame it for. Beije watched him leave with an expression of stark incredulity.

'Why in the name of the Emperor,' (and damn me if he didn't make the sign of the aquila as he pronounced the Holy Name), 'do you tolerate such a slovenly lack of standards? That man should be flogged!'

'Jurgen's something of a special case,' I said. Quite how special I had no intention of disclosing, of course, as Amberley had impressed upon both of us the necessity of keeping his peculiar abilities as quiet as possible[1] and I had no wish to attract the attention of any inquisitors other than her. Beije looked sceptical, but commissarial etiquette demanded that he defer to me in all matters concerning the regiment whose morale I was entrusted with safeguarding, so he would just have to lump it. No doubt he'd assume some nefarious or discreditable reason, though, which he might be tempted to gossip about, so I decided to give him a little of the truth.

'Despite his appearance, he's a remarkably able and efficient aide, and his loyalty to the Emperor is as fervent as that of any man I've ever met.' More to the point, he was the only man in the galaxy I completely trusted to watch my back, and his vigilance had saved my life on more occasions than I could recall without effort. 'I think that matters rather more than the fact that his uniform's a bit untidy.'

---

1. *Jurgen, as I discovered shortly after my first meeting with Cain, was a blank; an incredibly rare ability which effectively nullifies any psychic or daemonic forces in the immediate vicinity.*

All right, calling Jurgen a bit untidy was rather like saying Abaddon the Despoiler gets a bit cranky in the morning, but I knew adopting a casual attitude would be the surest way to get under Beije's skin. I knew my man well (as you'd expect given the number of times I'd left unpleasant surprises in his bunk at the schola), and noted the faint tightening of his lips with well-concealed satisfaction.

'That would be for you to decide, of course,' he said, as though trying to ignore a bad smell. A moment later he actually was, as Jurgen returned with a tray containing a couple of tea bowls and a gently steaming pot. I waited while he poured, enjoying the way Beije flinched before taking the bowl my aide proffered, then took my own. 'Thank you, Jurgen. That will be all for now.'

'Very good, commissar.' He indicated the data-slate he'd brought in with the tea and placed on my desk. 'When you have a moment, there's a message there from the lord general.'

Beije nearly choked on his tea as Jurgen and his aroma left the room.

I nodded sympathetically. 'I'm sorry, I should have warned you. Tanna's a bit of an acquired taste.'

'Aren't you even going to look at it?' he asked.

I glanced at the screen. 'It's not urgent,' I assured him.

Beije looked at me censoriously. 'Everything the lord general decrees is urgent.'

I shrugged and spun it around where he could see it. 'He just wants to know if I'll be free for a bite to eat and a game of regicide after we land,' I said. 'I don't think it's very high on his list of priorities.'

The expressions which chased themselves across Beije's face were priceless: shock, disbelief, naked envy and finally carefully-composed neutrality. 'I wasn't aware you were personally acquainted.'

I shrugged again, as casually as I could contrive. 'We've bumped into one another a few times and we seem to hit it off. I think he just enjoys the chance to unwind with someone outside the chain of command, to be honest. Hardly fitting for him to socialise with Guard officers, after all.'

'I suppose not,' Beije muttered. In truth, I suspect that really was the main reason Zyvan took an interest in my career and made a point of inviting me to dinner now and again[1]. He took another cautious sip at

---

1. *Cain is probably being too modest here. Zyvan had a healthy respect for his tactical sense and Cain's position outside the chain of command meant he could express his opinions rather more freely than most of the lord general's subordinates would. His eventual appointment as the commissarial liaison to the lord general's office was at Zyvan's instigation and his role there was as much as an independent advisor as it was as a commissar.*

the tanna and regarded me through the steam. 'I have to say you surprise me, Ciaphas.'

'How so?' I asked, denying him the satisfaction of showing any irritation at his use of my given name, and savouring the bitter aftertaste of my own drink.

'I'd expected you to have changed more.' His chubby face took on a puzzled frown, making him look uncannily like a colicky infant. 'All those honours, the glorious deeds you've done in the Emperor's name...' Well actually they'd been done in the name of keeping my skin in one piece, but of course no one needed to know that, least of all Beije. 'I heard about them, of course, but I never quite understood how a wastrel like you used to be could have achieved half of them.'

'The Emperor protects,' I quoted with a straight face.

Beije nodded piously. 'Of course he does. But you seem especially blessed.' The frown deepened, as though he was about to bring up a posset of milk[1]. 'I know it isn't for us to question divine providence, but I don't understand...'

'Why me?' I finished for him, and Beije nodded.

'I wouldn't put it quite that way, but... well, yes.' He spread his hands, spilling tanna tea on his sleeve. 'You've seen so much divine grace, the hand of the Emperor has been extended to you so often, and yet you still have the same flippant attitude. I'd have expected more piety, to be frank.'

So that was it. He was morally outraged that his old enemy from the schola had achieved so much success and glory while he was stuck in a dead-end posting with a bunch of Emperor-botherers as humourless as he was. Green-eyed jealous, in other words. I shrugged.

'The Emperor doesn't seem to mind. I don't see why you should.' I sipped my tea and favoured him with my best open, friendly, frak off now smile. His mouth opened and closed a few times. 'Was there anything else?'

'Yes.' He produced a data-slate for me to have a look at. 'Copies of the disciplinary proceedings against Trooper Hunvik.' The name didn't mean much until I read the charges at the top of the sheet and realised that this must be the man Magot had pounced on.

'Assaulting a superior officer?' I asked mildly.

Beije scowled. 'The... the soldier from your regiment was a corporal.'

---

1. Cain's apparent familiarity with the habits of infants is not explained anywhere else in the archive. However, he was serving with a mixed-sex regiment at the time, so it's quite likely that the inevitable occurred on more than one occasion. If so, as the regimental commissar, he would have been responsible for ensuring the welfare of all concerned.

Funny how he couldn't bring himself to say 'woman,' I thought. Somehow that must have rankled even more than the simple fact that their regimental champion had been bested. I nodded. 'She still is.' His eyes narrowed as I continued to skim through the slate. 'I see you didn't apply the death penalty on that charge though.'

'There were extenuating circumstances,' Beije said, a hint of defensiveness entering his voice.

I nodded. 'Quite. Knowing Magot, she undoubtedly threw the first punch.' And probably the next couple too. Mari Magot was a woman for whom the word 'overkill' was inherently meaningless. 'I trust the infirmary is making him comfortable?'

'As much as they can,' Beije said tightly.

'Good. Can't flog a man for brawling while he can't stand up, can you? Wish him a speedy recovery from all of us.' I downloaded the file to my desk, as though I could be bothered to read it, and added another to Beije's slate before handing it back.

He glanced at it and his jaw knotted. 'That was how you dealt with it? Reprimanded and returned to duty?'

I nodded. 'Magot's the new ASL[1] in her squad. They're just getting used to her. Reorganising them now, just as we're entering a war zone, would undermine their efficiency to an unacceptable extent.'

'I see.' His eyes hardened. 'She's another special case.'

'She is,' I agreed. Again I had no intention of telling him just how special she was, since the official line on the Simia Orichalcae fiasco was that it was a glorious though somewhat pyrrhic victory over the nasty grubby greenskins, and Amberley had made it very clear that the wrath of the Inquisition would fall on anyone who so much as breathed a word of what else we'd found there. And I knew her well enough to know that she never made idle threats. But the fact remained that Magot, then just a trooper, had walked through a necron tomb beside me and emerged from it at least as well-balanced as when she went in (however much that might have been). The Guard needed soldiers of that calibre, and if I had to bend a few regulations to keep them standing between me and whatever the warp might be about to vomit up at us, I'd make origami out of the rulebook without a second thought.

'Then our business is concluded.' Beije stuffed the data-slate back inside his greatcoat, no doubt deducing a highly improper relationship between trooper and commissar which probably added to his evident

---

1. *Assistant Squad Leader, a junior non-commissioned officer trained to take over if the leader becomes a casualty. When, as was the case in the 597th, squads are routinely split into fireteams, the ASL takes command of the second team when they operate independently.*

jealously of me. (Completely erroneously, of course. For one thing, I've never been that stupid, for another, Magot's preferences ran in an entirely different direction, and most importantly of all I've only got room for one lethally dangerous woman in my life.)[1]

'I suppose so,' I said, dismissing him completely from my mind. If I'd realised at the time how much animosity I was stirring up in him and by extension the Tallarns, I'd have been a great deal more diplomatic, you can be sure. However, I didn't, and the consequences of that conversation were still lurking some weeks in the future, so all I felt watching that shuttle depart was a sense of relief at the fact that I'd managed to avoid Beije for the rest of the voyage and was unlikely to ever have to set eyes on him again.

But, as I've remarked on more than one occasion, the Emperor has a nasty sense of humour.

THE FIRST STAGE of our disembarkation went as smoothly as a mouthful of fifty year-old amasec. We were the second regiment to be ferried down, and the dropships began loading troopers and equipment as soon as the Tallarns had cleared their holds. Within moments the hangar bay took on a reassuring reek of burned promethium as our trucks and Chimeras began chugging up the loading ramps, and the high space echoed to the profanity of NCOs doubling their squads into the passenger compartments. Sure that, as always, Jurgen had packed our personal possessions with his usual matchless efficiency, I found myself able to relax and enjoy the spectacle.

And what a spectacle it was. For sheer impressiveness there's little to match the sight of a well-drilled Guard regiment on the move: almost a thousand people bustling around stowing gear, moving it, losing it, finding it again, and generally getting in each other's way in some arcane fashion which still lets things get done with almost superhuman efficiency. From the vantage point I'd adopted on a gallery overlooking the main hangar floor, I could see vehicles and troopers milling around on a vast plain of steel, receding almost a kilometre into the distance, where the dropships standing in a patient line were diminished by perspective so that the most distant were reduced to the scale of toys.[2]

---

1. *Which I choose to take as a compliment...*

2. *One of the reasons the Galaxy-class troopship remains so popular, even though none have been built since the Age of Apostasy and the means to do so are now thought lost, is that it has sufficient hangar space to embark an entire regiment under optimum conditions. Of course this assumes that it would have sufficient dropships aboard for the task, which few do, the slow-moving shuttles being easy targets in a war zone, and difficult to replace.*

'I've stowed our gear on the lead shuttle, commissar.' Jurgen's voice, preceded by his remarkable bouquet, broke in on my thoughts.

I nodded absently. 'Thank you, Jurgen. Are they ready to depart?'

'Whenever you are, sir.'

'Might as well get to it, then,' I said, trying to still the faint flutter of apprehension which rose in my stomach. Here, in the belly of a starship, it was possible to believe in the illusion of safety, and once we hit dirtside we'd be twiddling our thumbs waiting for the war to start (or so I thought at the time). But I'd had too many vessels shot out from under me not to be aware of how vulnerable they'd be once the heretics' war fleet arrived and I knew my chances would be a great deal better on the planet below. I activated my comm-bead. 'Colonel. I'm embarking now.'

'Emperor speed, commissar.' Kasteen sounded distracted, as she was bound to be by now, juggling a dozen minor crises at once. 'See you on the downside.'

'We'll be waiting,' I assured her.

She or Broklaw would be on the last shuttle down, making sure the departure went smoothly, while the other would take the first one possible once the pressure began to slacken. (Protocol forbade the colonel and her number two to fly on the same dropship unless something went hideously wrong; otherwise it would only take one lucky shot for the enemy to effectively decapitate the entire regiment.) By long custom I would be on the first shuttle to land: partly because it fitted my reputation to appear to be leading from the front, but mainly because that would give me a head start in procuring the best quarters wherever we were going to be billeted.

'Commissar.' Lieutenant Sulla, the most eager and irritating of the platoon commanders[1], saluted as Jurgen and I trotted up the boarding ramp. I returned it casually, threading my way between two rows of Chimeras which had been neatly parked and secured. Absently I noted in passing that they'd been turned to face the exit, ready for a rapid deployment, and nodded approval. If nothing else the woman was efficient.

'This is a pleasant surprise.'

'I might say the same,' I said, as diplomatically as possible. 'I thought fifth company was taking point this time.' Each of the four infantry

---

1. *Though she was later to rise to a position of great prominence in the Munitorium, being the first (and so far as I'm aware only) woman to gain the position of Lady General, Cain appears to have been blind to her potential; in fact he seems to have found her consistently annoying throughout their service together.*

companies would normally take it in turns to be first down, officially so that none of them would hog the glory of being first into combat every time, and rather more pragmatically so that none of them would suffer significantly higher attrition rates. That would be bad for morale and would degrade the unlucky company's overall efficiency as it absorbed a higher than average number of fresh recruits.[1] Third company, our logistical support arm, would normally wait until the landing zone was properly secured.

Sulla shrugged. 'Something's gone wrong with their lander. Tech-priests are still taking a look at it.' I craned my neck past the line of vehicles, catching a glimpse of white-robed figures scuttling around through the open cargo door. 'It'll take forever to offload everything, so they're sitting tight until it's fixed.'

'And this was the next shuttle due to go,' I finished.

Sulla nodded eagerly. 'Lucky for us, eh?'

'Quite,' I said, passing through the bulkhead and into the passenger compartment.

Contrary to what you may be thinking, the first thing which strikes you on boarding a fully-loaded dropship is the smell. Having Jurgen around for so long had given me an unusual degree of tolerance for such things, but two hundred and fifty troopers cooped up in a confined space can thicken the atmosphere nicely, let me tell you. Especially when they're Valhallans in what to most people would be a mildly warm environment, and nervous to boot. As I walked up the aisle between the rows of seats and crash webbing I had to fight to keep my face straight.

The second thing you notice is the noise, a murmur of conversation in which little or nothing can be distinguished, but which is loud enough to drown out anything being said to you unless you can see the lips of whoever you're trying to converse with. Nevertheless, I made a point of catching the eyes of a few random troopers as I passed and spouting off a few platitudes about honour and duty, and the mere fact that I seemed to be bothering started to spread little ripples of calm and

---

1. *Like most Guard units, the 597th returned to their home world every few decades to replenish their ranks; in the meantime a steady trickle of fresh troopers was provided by the Munitorum recruiting stations back on Valhalla. Thanks to the inertia of the Administratum and the fact that they were originally formed by the merger of two severely depleted regiments, they were fortunate enough to receive double the usual allocation of fresh soldiers, no one in the upper echelons of the munitorium having noticed that the 296th and 301st no longer existed. This bureaucratic quirk not only accounts for the regiment remaining at full strength throughout Cain's association with it, but also the fact that the numbers of male and female troopers stayed roughly equal.*

reassurance throughout the shuttle like small rocks dropped into a pond. Wherever I looked I saw men and women holding on to their kitbags, checking lasguns and dipping into their primers for inspiration or amusement. A few hardy souls were slumped in their restraints, getting a little extra sleep, or pretending to, which I suppose is one way of keeping the gribblies[1] at bay.

I managed to ditch Sulla as we passed her platoon and she dropped into her seat, and I settled into my own at the front of the passenger compartment, close to the door of the cockpit. I didn't anticipate having to go up there, but since our abrupt arrival on Simia Orichalcae I'd got into the habit of sitting close enough to the flight deck to be able to intervene in person if the pilot got jittery.

'Commissar.' Captain Detoi, the company commander, nodded a polite greeting and resumed discussing administrative trivia with his subaltern. I returned it and fastened my crash webbing. A moment later a faint vibration transmitted itself through the hull and the frame of my seat and I aimed a reassuring smile at Jurgen.

'We're on our way,' I said. He nodded, his knuckles white. There was very little in the galaxy which seemed to perturb him, but travelling by shuttle or atmospheric flyer most definitely qualified. I found it mildly ironic that a man who'd stared into the faces of necrons and daemons without flinching could be so thoroughly put out by something so mundane, but I guess everyone has their weak spot. Jurgen's was a tendency to motion sickness, which made itself manifest every time we hit atmosphere. Fortunately he generally breakfasted lightly before a drop, seeming to feel that throwing up in front of the rest of the troopers would undermine the dignity expected of a commissar's aide.

The familiar lurching sensation in the pit of my stomach told me that we'd dropped clear of the troopship at last, and a moment later the main engines ignited, nudging me gently in the small of the back.

With nothing better to do, I thought I might as well get whatever rest I could and closed my eyes, only to be roused a few moments later by what at first I took to be the usual buffeting which always shakes a shuttle entering an atmosphere.

'Commissar.' Detoi was shaking me gently by the arm. 'Sorry to disturb you, but I think you should hear this.'

'Hear what?' I asked, the palms of my hands beginning to tingle, as they often do when things are about to go horribly wrong. By way of an answer he tapped the comm-bead in his ear.

---

1. *Nerves, persistent worries. One of the many Valhallan colloquialisms Cain acquired during his long association with the natives of that world.*

'Open channel D,' he suggested. I raised an eyebrow. That was the Tal-larns' assigned command frequency and normally we'd have no business monitoring it.

'I wanted to know how their deployment was going, so they wouldn't be getting in our way once we got down.' Detoi seemed completely unabashed, clearly having formed as low an opinion of the desert fight-ers as the rest of us. At least they'd be stuck on the other side of the planet once we deployed, though, so that would be something.

'And?' I enquired, retuning my own unit as I spoke.

Detoi flipped a strand of lank blond hair out of his eyes. 'Most of them have cleared the starport. But the stragglers seem to have run into some kind of trouble.' By this time I was able to hear for myself and was forced to agree with his assessment. It sounded as though Asmar's com-mand team and a fair few others were in the middle of a firefight. Who with, though, was anybody's guess.

'Better prepare for a hot drop,' I said, and Detoi nodded. While he began issuing orders I retuned the comm-bead to the starport control frequency, which seemed to be choked with panicking voices.

'Say again?' Our pilot sounded incredulous, always a bad thing in a Navy veteran with Emperor knows how many combat drops to his credit.

A quavering voice, unsteady with stress, responded. 'I repeat, abort your landing. Remain circling until we know what we're dealing with.'

'Frak off.' My relief at the pilot's pithy response was profound. If we followed that instruction we might just as well be towing a sign saying 'shoot me down now.' Our best chance was to hit the ground fast, where we could deploy the troops and find something for them to shoot at.

'You will comply, or face charges.' The voice sounded on the edge of breaking; no doubt whoever it belonged to was having a very bad day. Well tough, I was about to make it worse. I cut into the channel, using my commissarial override.

'This is Commissar Cain of the 597th,' I said. 'Our pilot is acting with the full authority of the commissariat. We are landing, and any further attempt to prevent us from engaging the enemies of the Emperor will be regarded as treasonous. Is that clear?'

'Absolutely,' the pilot agreed cheerfully. Words apparently failed the traffic controller, as transmissions from the tower suddenly went dead. 'Better hang on back there, we're going in hard and fast.'

'Acknowledged,' I said, making sure my crash harness was fully fas-tened and cutting into the general comm-net to warn everyone else to take the same precaution. Jurgen was looking even less happy than usual, so I checked his too, just as the dropship lived up to its name and began a vertiginous plunge towards the planet below. 'Any idea what the problem is?'

'The Tallarn command team and one of their platoons is pinned down here,' Detoi said, producing a data-slate on which a plan of the starport was displayed. 'They seem to have been ambushed as they left the main cargo handling area.'

I studied the plan. It was a good site for an ambush, there was no denying that. The Tallarns were pinned between the perimeter wall and a complex of warehouses, which would split them up and force them into a series of freefire zones if they tried to break out. I tapped the line of the wall.

'Why don't they just blast through this and retreat across the landing pads?' I asked.

Detoi shrugged. 'It's thirty metres high and ten thick. It's supposed to contain the explosion of a shuttle crash. Nothing they've got could even dent it.'

'Great,' I said. That meant if we came down on a pad ourselves we couldn't go to their aid without being bottlenecked by the same gate they'd been ambushed at. We'd blunder straight into the same trap. But my high-handed dismissal of the starport drone had committed us. By now the news that the celebrated Commissar Cain was on his way to rescue the stranded troopers would most likely be halfway round the city, so leaving Asmar and his men flapping in the breeze wasn't an option. Not if I wanted to stay on the lord general's invitation list at any rate, and being permanently deprived of his chef's cuisine would be a severe blow, so I had to think of something else fast. I scanned the surrounding terrain. 'What's this?'

'It's a monastery,' Detoi said, looking puzzled. He pulled up some data on it. 'The Order of the Imperial Light.' A faint grin appeared on his face. 'Rather ironic, considering the local conditions.'

'Quite,' I said. 'What's this around it?'

Detoi shrugged. 'Vegetable gardens, according to the plan of the city in the briefing slate. Didn't you read it?'

I hadn't, having found better things to do with my time aboard the *Emperor's Benificence* (which generally involved a pack of cards and other people's currency).

'Open ground, in other words.' Well, relatively open. I relayed the co-ordinates to our pilot, who received them with undisguised enthusiasm. 'I think we've just found our drop zone.'

'Works for me,' Detoi said. He switched frequencies again, to our general command channel. 'Listen up everyone, we're hitting dirt in two.

It'll be hot, so look alive.' A flurry of activity broke out across the passenger compartment as troopers donned their helmets and snapped fresh power cells into their lasguns. In deference to the temperatures we expected to find when we landed, they'd left their greatcoats and fur hats in their kitbags, but most, I was relieved to see, had kept their flak armour on through force of habit. That was good. It showed they were still on the ball despite having expected a routine deployment. Whatever was waiting for us on the planet below was in for a big surprise, I reflected grimly.

Come to that, so were the monks. Our shuttle lurched a couple of times, making Jurgen swallow convulsively, then the sudden pressure of the landing thrusters kicking in hit me in the base of the spine. My aide's knuckles whitened even more, although being Jurgen it would probably be a little more accurate to say they became a paler shade of grey. Then the whole hull shook, a couple of deafening bangs and a metallic screech echoed through the passenger compartment, and we came to rest.

Loud metallic clangs and a rush of cool, sweet air told us the boarding ramps were down, and with a roar like surf crashing on a beach, second company rushed to meet the enemy.

THREE

'Incoming fire has the right of way.'

– Old artilleryman's maxim

MY FIRST IMPRESSION on leaving the shuttle was one of confusion, although to the credit of the troopers they all snapped into their immediate action drills as smoothly as if we were on exercise. Squads of them were fanning out, looking for trouble, ignoring a herd of squawking crimson-robed anchorites who were milling around as though the sky was falling (although, to be fair, I suppose from their perspective it just had). I could only hope they'd all had the presence of mind to run as soon as the shuttle appeared overhead instead of standing there waiting to be squashed like the rather unpleasant pulpy thing I'd just put my boot through.[1]

---

1. *Probably a local vegetable known for some reason as a 'squinch' which remains a popular crop on Adumbria, though more for the fact that it's one of the few edible plants capable of surviving in the perpetual twilight than that it's actually palatable. Medicae records for the district show no fatalities among the anchorites, although several were subsequently treated for minor injuries apparently related to treading on hastily-discarded gardening tools.*

'Third platoon mounted up and ready to go,' Sulla reported, as a roar of engines heralded the appearance of half a dozen Chimeras which bounced down the port aft loading ramp and made a terrible mess of what was left of the crop we'd just landed on. Her head and shoulders were visible protruding from the turret of her command vehicle, easily distinguishable from the others by the cluster of vox antennae on top of it, and she waved cheerfully as she caught sight of me and Detoi. I raised a hand in return, though more to forestall any precipitate action on her part than to be social, and glanced at the captain's data-slate again.

'The hostiles appear to be concentrated here and here,' he said, bringing up icons to indicate their positions, and I nodded. The Tallarns were still boxed in, but making a fight of it for all that, and the messages we were receiving on their tac frequency were a good indication of where the enemy, whoever the hell they were, had set up their firing positions. 'They've called for reinforcements, but the bulk of their forces left by the main gate, so...'

'They're still at least twenty minutes away,' I finished, and Detoi nodded. They could shave a good five minutes off that by cutting straight across the starport, of course, but they'd run straight into that damn gate and just make sitting ducks of themselves. I considered the layout of the streets, and could tell by the faint grunt of satisfaction he emitted that Detoi had come to the same conclusion as I had.

'We'll take them here and here,' I said, indicating the two main streets the heretics had effectively turned into shooting galleries. It was a fair bet that they'd set up their trap intending to butcher any Tallarns trying to break out, and that they'd be completely unprepared for a counter-attack in the opposite direction.

The captain nodded. 'We'll need to secure the flank too,' he pointed out. I concurred, having already seen the danger. If they became aware of our forces approaching from behind they might try to break away to the left, into the city, before being caught between us and the Tallarns. The other way was effectively blocked to them by the wall of the starport, which was actually working for us in this instance.

'Send Sulla,' I suggested. 'Her people are ready to go.' The flanking force would take a couple of minutes longer to reach their objective, so it made sense to send the platoon which was already mounted up and ready to roll. More to the point it would keep her sidelined, I hoped, where her tendency to reckless bravado would have less chance of getting somebody killed.

'Works for me.' Detoi nodded crisply and transmitted the data from his slate. 'Third platoon, secure the flank. First and fifth, you've got the main boulevards. Second, take the side streets by squads, sweep up anyone trying to get past our main thrust. Fourth, secure the perimeter, don't let anyone out who isn't one of ours until the noise stops. Hold anyone who looks like a civilian for questioning, shoot anyone bearing a weapon. Any questions?'

He was good, I had to give him that. The platoon commanders acknowledged, a faint note of disappointment just discernable in Sulla's voice, and Detoi turned to me.

'What about you, commissar?'

'I'll take the flank,' I said, having considered my options carefully, raising my voice above the howls of third platoon's Chimera engines as they ploughed their way out of the monastery garden. There was no sign of a gate, but then there wasn't much left of the wall either, the minor earthquake caused by a couple of kilotonnes of dropship impacting the ground having taken care of that quite nicely. Most of the shrine appeared to be intact, though, which I was pleased to see, as hacking off the ecclesiarchy tends to lead to more doleful sermonising than I care to sit through. The tracks of Sulla's command vehicle bit into the rubble and scattered it, and then she was gone, her quintet of squad transports bouncing in her wake.

Detoi looked doubtful. 'If you're sure that's wise?' he said.

'I am,' I assured him. 'Sulla's a good officer, but inclined to be impetuous.' He nodded, all too aware of this tendency. 'I'm not saying she might do something rash, but it's vital she holds position in case the enemy bolts. Knowing I'm around might prove to have a moderating influence.' More to the point, it was going to be a great deal safer sitting things out on the flank than it appeared, if our assessment of the enemy's state of preparedness was wrong. Charge headlong down a narrow fire lane? Not if I could avoid it.

'You'll need to move fast to catch up,' Detoi said, clearly conceding the point.

'Not a problem,' I said, tapping my comm-bead. 'Jurgen. We're moving out.'

By way of an answer the roar of a powerful engine echoed from inside the cargo hold and a Salamander bounced down the exit ramp, slewing between the Chimeras like a predator among grazers. Jurgen swung it to a halt beside me, raising a spray of mud and vegetable slime which caused the nearest monks to dive for cover just as they'd plucked up the courage to approach us and ask what the hell was going on, and crushing what remained of a small greenhouse to splinters under its tracks.

'Right here, commissar,' he said, phlegmatic as always, only a faint grimace that might have been the prototype of a smile betraying his relief at being back on terra firma.

'Good,' I said, clambering into the rear compartment and checking the pintle-mounted bolter I normally try to ensure is fitted to whatever vehicle is assigned to me. It might not seem like much, but the extra firepower has saved my neck on more than one occasion, and if nothing else it lets me look as though I'm doing something positive while getting away from trouble as fast as possible. 'We're attaching ourselves to third platoon.'

'We'll catch them,' Jurgen promised, gunning the powerful engine and sending the little scout vehicle hurtling in pursuit with all the alacrity of a startled pterasquirrel. Inured by years of experience to his unique and enthusiastic driving style I kept my feet, striking a heroic pose at the bolter for the benefit of the troopers who had still to mount up.

'I don't doubt it,' I said, clinging a little harder to the pintle mount as we bounced over the line of rubble which used to be a wall, and made the easier going of the street.

It was only then that I had time to take stock of our surroundings and got my first good look at the capital of Adumbria.

My first impression was one of gloom, which was hardly surprising given the perpetual twilight which held sway here. The buildings seemed to hang low over our heads, deep shadows falling between them, accentuated by the warm glow of light from a few of the windows. It was only as I got used to the conditions here that I came to realise that most of them were as elegant and well-proportioned as those of any other Imperial city, and that it was merely the endless evening which produced that illusion.

The streets seemed surprisingly empty until I checked my chronograph and realised that, despite the half-light which pervaded everything, it was the middle of the night according to the local custom.[1] That was something anyway; there would be fewer civilians around to be caught in the crossfire. Come to that, anyone still in the area after hearing the all-too-obvious sounds of battle in the distance was probably involved in the insurrection in any case, so we wouldn't have to worry much about collateral casualties. My spirits lifted at the thought; every innocent servant of the Emperor killed by mistake diminishes the whole Imperium, and, more to the point, would dump a pile of extra paperwork on my desk.

---

1. *Since ambient light levels were completely unchanging wherever you were on the surface, the Adumbrians had adopted a local convention of sleep and work periods which held true for the entire world, thus avoiding the shifting time zones common to most inhabited planets.*

'There they are.' Jurgen accelerated past a startled-looking local praetor on a motorcycle who seemed commendably, though foolishly in my opinion, eager to investigate the source of the disturbance, and I waved casually as we moved ahead of him. No doubt the sight of a clumsy-looking armoured vehicle overtaking him, let alone one with an Imperial commissar in the back, was something of a shock, but the scout Salamander wasn't my vehicle of choice for nothing. Its powerful engine gave it a respectable turn of speed which, allied with Jurgen's formidable driving abilities, could get me out of trouble almost as fast as my reputation could get me into it in its more inconvenient moments.

Fortunately, there seemed to be little other traffic and most was moving in the other direction at speeds which would no doubt have attracted the notice of our praetor friend under any other circumstances, but they'd be netted by fourth platoon's cordon before they got much further so I paid them no mind. In any case, I doubted that they'd prove to be anything other than what they seemed: local workers and cargo handlers on the late shift who'd noticed what was going on and were getting as far away from it as possible. A couple of groundcars were pulled over at the side of our carriageway, the dents in their bodywork and the angry expressions of their drivers mute testament to Sulla's single-minded determination to close with the enemy, and I began to think that I'd made the right decision to hold her leash in person.

Jurgen swung us into place at the rear of the convoy, slowing our pace to match that of the Chimeras, and a moment later the praetor howled past us, his siren going. For an awful moment I thought he was going to cut in ahead of Sulla's command vehicle and try to flag her down, which would only result in him becoming an unpleasant stain on the blacktop, but to my relief he kept going, no doubt sticking to his orders to report back on whatever was going on.

'Commissar.' Sulla's voice in my comm-bead sounded surprised and pleased. From this distance I couldn't make out her facial expression as she turned in the turret to look at me, her blonde pony tail fluttering in the wind like a battle standard, but I could picture the toothy grin quite well enough. 'I guess we're about to see some action after all, if you're here.'

'That remains to be seen,' I said levelly. 'But if the heretics break they'll only have one place to go. Making sure they don't get away has to be our highest priority.'

'You can count on us,' she assured me, that cocky tone I'd learned to dread colouring her voice, and I sighed inaudibly. She was going to need watching closely, I could tell.

As we neared our assigned deployment zone the troop transports began to peel off, heading down side streets and through courtyards to take up their positions, and before long our convoy had been reduced to three: Sulla, ourselves, and one squad of troopers.

'This is it,' I said at last, and Jurgen spun the little Salamander on its tracks, slewing us to a halt broadside on, effectively blocking the entire carriageway and swinging the autocannon to point in the vague direction of where the enemy ought to be. Sulla's command vehicle coasted to a halt rather more sedately, a few dozen metres ahead of us, and began to reverse, its engine little more than idling. The troop transport swung sideways to bump over the central reservation, blocking the road in the opposite direction and rotating its turret-mounted bolter to face any oncoming traffic (which fortunately seemed to be non-existent by this time). After a moment, Sulla's driver backed her Chimera neatly into the gap, plugging the entire thoroughfare.

'No one's getting past us,' she said with some satisfaction.

'They'd have to try pretty hard,' I agreed, glancing round at the position we occupied. We were on an elevated stretch of highway, the ground below was a broken wasteland of rubble and discarded refuse. A few fires glowed, betraying the existence of a scavvy[1] tribe or some local equivalent, but other than that there was no sign of life.

'Platoon one ready to go.' A new voice broke into the tactical net, the familiar one of Lieutenant Voss, as cheerful as if he were ordering a round of ales in a bar somewhere. A moment later it was echoed by the rather more restrained report of Lieutenant Faril, commander of fifth platoon, who confirmed that his troopers were ready as well.

'Good. Move in.' Detoi was as crisp as ever. 'The Emperor protects.' I waited tensely, swinging the bolter I still leaned against round to face the direction from which we expected the enemy to come.

'Better disembark the troops,' I suggested to Sulla, and even from here I could see the faint frown of puzzlement on her face.

'Wouldn't it be better to leave them in the Chimera?' she asked. 'In case we have to move in to support the others?' That was the whole point, of course; if they were on foot she couldn't order an impetuous charge on the spur of the moment, but I made a show of considering her words.

---

1. *Marginal members of most hive societies who live quite literally at the bottom of the social order, salvaging whatever they can from the debris which falls from the higher levels. Cain makes frequent allusions to having been a hiveworlder by birth, and certainly possessed an uncanny affinity for tunnels and similar underground habitats, but firm details about his origins remain a mystery.*

'That's true,' I said. 'But we'd only lose a few seconds embarking them again. And if the enemy does try to get past us I want everyone ready.'

'You're right, of course.' She nodded, almost masking her disappointment, and the squad began to deploy, taking up positions behind the vehicles and whatever other cover they could find. I made a point of nodding to Lustig, the sergeant leading them, whose professionalism I knew from long experience that I could rely on absolutely.

'Sergeant.'

'Commissar.' He returned the nod and went about the business of ensuring the readiness of his subordinates with the quiet efficiency I always found reassuring. 'Jinxie, get your people set up on the right. I want overlapping fire lanes with first team.'

'Sarge.' Corporal Penlan nodded and started dispersing her fireteam. Recently promoted in the same round of advancements that had elevated Magot, she was shaping up well as ASL despite the reputation for being accident prone which had led to her nickname. In fact, troopers being troopers, morale in her team was unusually high, her subordinates appearing to believe that she'd attract any bad luck in the vicinity and leave them unscathed.

With nothing else to be done we waited, while the crackle of weapons fire in the distance intensified and my nervousness increased. The signals traffic in my comm-bead told me things seemed to be going well, the first and fifth platoons taking the traitors completely by surprise and the Tallarns gaining fresh heart from our intervention. For a moment I thought things had gone as I'd hoped and they'd be annihilated without involving me at all, but of course I'd reckoned without the fickle workings of chance.

'Contact, moving fast,' Penlan called, and I swung the bolter round a few degrees to bring the rapidly-moving dot in the distance squarely into the sights.

Sulla raised an amplivisor, stared through it for a moment and shook her head as she lowered it again. 'It's just the praetor.'

'And he's got company,' I added, making out a line of equally fast-moving motes a short way behind him.

Sulla snapped the amplivisor back up and tensed. 'Hostiles, closing fast. Prepare to engage.'

Lovely. It was obvious what had happened, of course. The praetor had blundered into the firefight, been spotted, and a unit of the enemy had been dispatched to keep him from reporting back. And now they were swarming down on me.

'Try not to shoot the praetor,' I added. If he had any pertinent information he might as well share it.

By this time he'd drawn close enough to be clearly seen, and his pursuers were beginning to come into focus as well. There seemed to be about a dozen, a motley collection of groundcars and light cargo haulers for the most part, and I began to relax, sure of our ability to take them. Not only did we have them comfortably outnumbered, we had overwhelming superiority of firepower on our side to boot.

'Fire at will,' I ordered, and opened up with the bolter at the line of vehicles beyond the praetor. The others followed suit with enthusiasm and a fusillade of lasbolts arced off into the semi-darkness, glowing brightly as they went. A second later the full-throated roar of the autocannon joined them as Jurgen clambered up beside me to trigger it.

The results were most gratifying, the leading vehicles in the fast-moving convoy breaking and scattering, one of them leaking smoke. The range was still extreme, of course, so we were lucky to hit anything, but these were civilian vehicles rather than the armoured targets we usually shot at, so even a glancing blow would be enough to put them out of commission.

'That'll give them something to think about,' Sulla said with some satisfaction, as the praetor slid to a halt next to us, his face white. I looked down at him and introduced myself.

'I'm Commissar Cain, attached to the 597th Valhallan,' I said, trying to look as friendly as I could. 'If you have any information about what's going on I'd be pleased to hear it.'

'Kolbe, traffic division.' The praetor pulled himself together with a visible effort. 'There's a major disturbance going on down by the starport, some gang fight we think. Our riot squads are responding, but...'

'It's worse than that,' I told him. 'Heretic insurgents have attacked a Guard unit. But it's all under control.'

I hoped it was anyway. There seemed to be a lot more activity at the other end of the bridge than I'd anticipated, and with a shiver of apprehension I realised that each of the groundcars which had been pursuing Kolbe contained several people. It was hard to be sure at this distance, especially in the twilight, but they seemed to be dressed for some kind of carnival. I revised my initial estimate of their strength upwards, trebling it at least. Sporadic return fire began, wildly inaccurate for the most part, but a las-bolt struck the armour plate protecting our crew compartment. I ducked reflexively, dragging Kolbe into more solid cover. 'Jurgen, if you would...'

The autocannon roared again, to be joined by the heavy bolters of the two Chimeras. This gave the heretics facing us serious pause for thought and they scurried for cover with gratifying speed. Gratifying, but worrying. This wasn't the sort of behaviour I'd expected from confederates of the Ravagers, who if my guess about their patron power was right, should have been charging forward obligingly ready to be cut down by our massed firepower.

'We've got them,' Detoi reported suddenly, his voice loud in my comm-bead. 'Complete surprise on both streets. The Tallarns are mopping up the survivors.'

'Good.' That was something at any rate, even though I was aware of the irony; if I'd gone in with the main attack I'd have been safe by now. There was no time for regrets, though, as the heretics seemed to be recovering a bit of courage, and some rather more purposeful fire began to pepper our armour plate. Jurgen responded enthusiastically and it was a second or two before I could reply. 'We're meeting a little resistance out here on the flank.'

'No problem, commissar,' Sulla cut in. 'I'm bringing first and third squads round to flank them.' I was relieved to hear it, if we could keep our assailants pinned just a little while longer we'd have them bottled up nicely.

It was at that point that Kolbe spun round, a bloody crater opening in his chest, and I turned to see a bizarre figure aiming a laspistol into the open crew compartment of the Salamander. It was a young man, the cut of his clothes leaving very little doubt about that. He was swathed in silks of a vivid pink which did nothing for his colouring. He was flanked by a similarly armed young woman with dyed green hair, whose costume seemed to consist of little more than leather straps (and damn few of those), and an elderly gent in a crimson gown clutching a stubber, whose pomade verged on chemical warfare. Other shadowy figures were in the gloom beyond them, clambering up from below the bridge.

'We've been flanked ourselves!' I yelled, swinging the bolter around, but by now they were too close and I couldn't depress the barrel far enough. I dived to one side just as the trio opened fire, but fortunately they lacked any real idea of how to handle a weapon and their shots went wild. I hit the rockcrete of the roadway, rolled by instinct, and came to my feet drawing my trusty chainsword. That might seem a bad choice against guns, but under the circumstances I thought it best. From such a close range I'd have little chance of aiming my laspistol on the fly, and the more I closed the distance the less likely my opponents would be able to either.

By sheer chance I was close enough to bring the blade up, already thumbing the activator as I gained my feet, and took the girl's left leg off at the thigh. She fell, fountaining arterial blood, and giggled. No time to worry about that, people do strange things in extremis after all, and I already had another target – pink boy was aiming his pistol at Jurgen, who had given up on the autocannon and was beginning to bring his standard issue lasgun up to fire from the hip. He wasn't going to make it in time, so I gave him the extra second he needed by lopping his would-be killer's hand off at the wrist, letting the gun fall harmlessly to the ground.

'Oh, yes!' The man was clearly deranged, an expression of ecstasy spasming across his face. 'Again!' Then his head exploded as Jurgen found his aim.

'No! It's my turn!' Greenhair called, slipping in the pool of her own blood as she scrabbled towards me. She raised her laspistol, but before she could pull the trigger the pomade bomb stepped in between us, raising the stubber.

'Age before beauty, my love.'

'Frak this. You're all insane!' I kicked him in the stomach, sending him sprawling back over the girl, and drew my laspistol with my other hand. A quick burst of rapid fire saw to both of them, and I turned, expecting to see a full battle raging, but it had all gone quiet again. Roughly a score of bizarrely-dressed corpses lay on the rockcrete, most of them bearing the telltale cauterised craters of lasgun wounds. Sporadic firing from the other end of the bridge and the familiar growl of Chimera engines were enough to tell me that first and third squads had arrived and were enthusiastically engaged in mopping up the rest of our assailants.

'How's Kolbe?' I asked, after making sure none of our troopers were down.

The squad medic glanced up at me, her expression impatient, and went back to tending him. 'He'll live. His armour took most of it.'

'Good. We'll need to debrief him.' I glanced at the scattered corpses around us. 'I don't suppose there'll be many of these frakheads left to interrogate.' As if to underline the point, the firing at the other end of the bridge suddenly ceased, and Sulla gave me a cheerful thumbs up.

'All clear,' she reported. 'No casualties.'

'Good.' I was just beginning to relax again when I became aware of a faint rumbling in the rockcrete beneath my feet. I glanced up, back down the highway, and saw a dozen more Chimeras approaching at speed. 'Now what?'

The lead vehicle slowed as it approached and a familiar figure appeared at the top hatch, waving us imperiously out of the way.

'Clear the road.' Beije yelled. 'Our colonel's under attack.'

'Already taken care of,' I told him, stepping out of the shadow of the Salamander so he could get a good look at me and I could savour the expression of pop-eyed astonishment that spread across his face. 'Check your command channel.' He listened to his comm-bead for a moment, his jaw clenching. I smiled. 'No need to thank us,' I added.

Editorial Note:

Given Cain's usual disinterest in the intricacies of the political situation then prevailing on Adumbria, or indeed anything else which didn't concern him directly, I felt the following would prove helpful in placing much of what follows into some kind of context.

Unlike most popular histories of this kind, it's substantially accurate, the author having been given access to as many of the official records as were deemed fit for public consumption as part of the planet-wide commemoration of the twentieth anniversary of these events, and having taken the time and trouble to interview as many of the surviving participants as he reasonably could.

From *Sablist[1] in Skitterfall: a brief history of the Chaos incursion* by Dagblat Tincrowser, 957 M41

THE DEATH OF Governor Tarkus on 245 936 M41 could hardly have come at a worse time, expiring as he did little more than a year before the Great

---

1. *Another Adumbrian dialect word, meaning a state of almost total darkness with a barely perceptible glimmer of light still visible. Adumbrian readers would have found the title a witty play on words, the rest of us merely irritating.*

Enemy made their move against us. Indeed it has been suggested by many commentators that this was too fortuitous to have been entirely coinciden-tal, and much time and ink has been expended on fruitless speculation about whether a conspiracy actually existed to assassinate him, who the participants might have been and why no evidence of who to blame has been uncovered in the two decades since. This last fact, in particular, has been seized on by the more rabid of the conspiracy theorists as a kind of proof in itself of their wilder speculations, since they seem to believe that the complete absence of anything concrete to confirm their suspicions merely proves the efficiency of the ensuing cover-up.[1]

Confining ourselves to the incontrovertible, therefore, we should merely note that Governor Tarkus died of what at the time were recorded as natural causes entirely consistent with a man of his advanced years who had a wife and two known mistresses all over a century younger than he was, and move discreetly along.

In most cases of this nature, the succession of his heir would have been a mere formality. Unfortunately, Tarkus died without having provided one, provoking a discreet but ferocious free-for-all among the noble houses of Adumbria, a situation exacerbated by the fact that, thanks to almost two centuries of energetic fornication by the erstwhile incumbent, all were able to present candidates with some plausible claim to being related by blood.

In order to prevent the day-to-day business of running the world from grinding to a halt entirely, a compromise of sorts was eventually reached: the highest-ranking member of the Administratum on Adumbria was appointed Planetary Regent, with wide-ranging executive powers, pending the eventual resolution of the welter of claims and counterclaims to the vacant throne. Since the Administratum were doing most of the actual work, this left the situation pretty much as it had been, except that the Regent was expected to refer for approval all matters of policy to an ad-hoc committee made up of all the rival claimants before taking a final decision. Since few of them could be persuaded to agree on anything and most disliked each other intensely, it will be readily appreciated that achieving anything significant became virtually impossible.

And into this quagmire of inertia came the news that a Chaos raiding fleet was about to attack the planet, followed shortly be the arrival of five regiments of Imperial Guard and a squadron of warships.

It would hardly be an exaggeration to say that panic ensued.

---

1. *Or the agents of the Ordo Malleus, who would surely know the truth of this if anyone does.*

FOUR

'If you don't expect gratitude you'll seldom be disappointed.'
— Eyor Dedonki, *Memoirs of a Pessimist.* 479 M41

'THERE'S NO DOUBT about it,' Lord General Zyvan said, pausing for emphasis and sweeping his gaze around the council chamber. 'The threat to your world is even greater than we feared.' The assembled great and good of Adumbria, or to be more precise the rich and powerful, which in my experience is less often the same than it ought to be in a fair and just galaxy, reacted pretty much as I'd expected. Some looked as though they'd developed severe indigestion, some went pale and the majority just stared at him with the same expression of bovine incomprehension which I'd seen so often before in people so used to sycophancy that they simply lacked the intellectual capacity to take in bad news delivered in plain language. There were about a dozen·of them, all drawn from the local aristocracy so far as I could tell, although what qualification they had other than that to be there was beyond me; the lack of a chin, perhaps.[1]

---

1. *The summary of the local political situation was no doubt one of the things he'd neglected to read in his briefing slate.*

The only exception was the man chairing the meeting, who had been introduced as the planetary regent; that was a new one to me, but I heard enough to gather that he was in effect the acting governor of this Emperor-forsaken backwater, so I smiled affably at him when he caught my eye. He smiled back and nodded, so either he was a lot less stuck-up than the collection of aristocratic by-blows surrounding us or he was aware of my reputation. Surprisingly, he was wearing the gown of some high-ranking bureaucrat, but at least that meant he had some idea of how things actually worked, so I resolved to keep an eye on him. His name, I gathered, was Vinzand, and being handed the job had come as something of an unpleasant surprise to him, which I found comforting, as in my experience the last people who should be given any real power are the ones who actually want it.

'You're referring to the attack on your soldiers, of course.' He nodded, smoothing back the white hair which still hung thickly around his face and hitching up the arms of his crimson robe, which seemed to be a couple of sizes too big for him. I was incongruously reminded of Jurgen and suppressed a smile, which seemed wholly inappropriate under the circumstances. 'I trust the wounded are recovering well.'

'Fine, thank you,' Colonel Asmar said, scowling at me. I had no idea why he should be so sniffy about having his bacon saved, other than that he might have been embarrassed by feeling beholden to another regiment, but that was just stupid. Under the opposite circumstances we'd have welcomed the assistance, and if he'd rather have ended up as traitor bait, more fool him. It went deeper than that, of course, but at the time I didn't have a clue what was biting him.

'Commissar Cain's timely intervention undoubtedly turned the tide,' Zyvan said, to my great satisfaction, and Kasteen grinned at me. We were seated together with the other regimental colonels and their commissars at a long table along one side of the council chamber, leaving Zyvan and his staff to take the place of honour on a small stage in front of the delegates, who all sat behind data lecterns like a bunch of overgrown and overdressed schola students. The other Valhallans were next to us, of course, on our right, then the two Kastaforean regiments, with Asmar and Beije at the other end, as far away from Kasteen and I as they could possibly get. This suited me fine, as it happens.

Vinzand was sitting almost opposite us, where he could watch the lord general and his own aristocratic parasites with equal attention, surrounded by low-ranking Administratum drones who seemed to be taking copious notes of everything said and done. The only other person there who seemed to stand out was a lean looking fellow in military attire, a plain grey uniform unornamented by anything other than rank pins I was too far away to read, who watched everything with pale eyes of a similar hue to his clothing.

'There have been protests from the Order of the Imperial Light,' Vinzand said mildly, 'concerning damage to the fabric of their property and the loss of a great many squinches.'

Having tasted the things at almost every meal since our arrival, I felt that to be no great loss, but tried to look as if I cared. 'Please feel free to convey my strongest regrets to them,' I said. 'But under the circumstances I felt I had no other choice.'

'No other choice?' Beije bristled at me, his face purpling. 'You desecrated a holy shrine! What in the Emperor's name were you thinking?'

'I was thinking that your colonel and his men were about to be butchered by heretics,' I said. 'How could a loyal servant of his divine majesty stand back and let that happen?'

'We would rather have perished than have our survival bought at the price of blasphemy,' Asmar said, his voice censorious.

I fought down a flash of disbelieving anger. 'We'll know better next time,' I said as blandly as I could, and had the quiet satisfaction of seeing his jaw clench at the same time as Zyvan suppressed a grin.

'Our sappers are already over there repairing the damage,' Kasteen put in helpfully, not wanting to miss the chance of giving Asmar another poke in the ribs while she could. 'Perhaps you could spare a few of yours to help them?'

'We have little time for fortifications,' Asmar said, 'other than the citadel of our faith in the Emperor. We do not trifle ourselves with mere physical barriers.'

'Fair enough.' Kasteen shrugged. 'We'll get the priests to bless a few of the bricks in your name if you like.' Her face was so straight even I wasn't sure if she was joking for a moment, and after glaring suspiciously for a second or two Asmar nodded.

'That would be acceptable.'

'Good.' Zyvan nodded. 'Then if we could get back to the main point, it seems we could be facing a war on two fronts. As the raiding fleet approaches, we can expect more attacks from their confederates aimed at hindering our ability to respond.'

'How great a threat are these insurgents?' Vinzand asked.

By way of reply Zyvan gestured towards me. 'Commissar Cain is probably the best man to answer that. He's fought more of the agents of the Ruinous Powers at close quarters than anyone else in my command.'

I stood, shrugging laconically. 'I've had help,' I said, playing up to my reputation for modest heroism and enjoying the ripple of amusement which swept through the room. 'Usually from an army. Nevertheless, I suppose it's true I've seen heretics and their machinations more often than most.' I stepped out from behind the table so that the gormless aristos could see me properly. Most of them looked agog at the prospect of a briefing from a Hero of the Imperium.

'Then I'm sure your observations will prove most enlightening,' Vinzand said in a tone of voice which didn't need to add 'so stop playing to the back row and get on with it.' I began to suspect that there was more to the regent than just a fancy title.

'By all means.' I nodded. 'Chaos cults are insidious, and they can spring up practically anywhere, sucking in the basest and most degenerate specimens of humanity. Their greatest threat, however, is that as they grow they bring in more recruits who may remain unaware at first of precisely what it is they're joining; they may think it's a street gang, a political movement, or a social club for those with a particular kind of sexual deviancy. Only as they grow more corrupted by their patron power do they realise the full extent of what they're now a part of, and by that time the lies and illusions are too strong. They've become damned and they don't even care.'

'Then how do we know the difference?' the grey man in the corner asked. 'We can hardly bring in every social and criminal organisation in the city for questioning.'

'That's a good point, sir,' I said. Even though I still didn't have a clue who he was, he sounded like someone in authority, and he'd had the sense not to speak until he had a specific question. Under the circumstances, I felt it best to be polite. 'But believe me, the problem won't be confined to the city. Chances are the cults will be established in every major population centre by now. If they're showing their hand openly it's because they think they're strong enough not to fear retaliation.'

'Or they're panicking,' Beije interrupted. 'Knowing that the wrath of the Emperor's servants is about to fall upon them–'

'Ought to drive them even deeper underground,' I pointed out mildly. He glared at me and shut up.

The man in grey nodded. 'That much seems evident.' He turned to Vinzand, pointedly ignoring the rabble of aristos. 'I'll need to consult with the Arbites[1] and see if they've noticed anything out of the ordinary.'

'Of course, general,' Vinzand said, and I blessed the impulse to have been polite; this must be the commander of the local PDF. No doubt they'd be as undisciplined as most of their kind, but at least their leader looked as though he knew what he was doing.[2] Vinzand turned to

---

1. *Having ultimate authority over matters of law enforcement, the Arbites representatives on Adumbria would have access to the relevant records for the entire planet.*

2. *Like most Guard officers, Cain had a low opinion of the average Planetary Defence Force.*

Zyvan. 'Might I also suggest General Kolbe liaises with your people too? Your greater experience of these things might well prove helpful.'

'Indeed.' The lord general turned to me. 'Perhaps Commissar Cain could be prevailed upon to make the arrangements, since he and the general already have an acquaintance in common?'

Well you might think I'm pretty dense, but it was only at that point that the coin dropped, and the significance of the general's name became clear to me.

'How is your son?' I asked, hoping my guess was accurate. It was, as it turned out, gently enhancing my reputation for being on top of the little details.

Kolbe senior nodded. 'Recovering well, thank you.'

'I'm glad to hear it,' I said. 'He showed exemplary courage under extremely trying circumstances.'

General Kolbe swelled a little with paternal pride. I was to learn later that his youngest son's decision to join the praetors rather than the military had rankled for some time, and that the incident at the bridge had initiated a reconciliation that both would have been too stubborn to try for under other circumstances, so at least some good had come out of it. (Other than a pile of dead heretics, of course, which always brightens the day.) Out of the corner of my eye I could see Beije all but grinding his teeth at the sight of me hitting it off with yet another high ranker, which made the moment all the more enjoyable.

'Then that's settled,' Zyvan said. 'We'll arrange a joint intelligence committee to pool what information we have. The regent will be appraised of what we can determine at the appropriate time.'

'That's entirely unacceptable,' a new voice cut in as one of the over-dressed fops stood up to lean on his lectern. Up until that point I'd almost forgotten they were there, to be honest; it was as if one of the chairs had had the temerity to interrupt.

Zyvan frowned at him, like an eminent tragedian peering over the footlights to try and identify a drunken heckler. 'And who might you be?'

'Adrien de Floures van Harbieter Ventrious, of House Ventrious, rightful heir to the...' A sudden clamour of outrage from all the other parasites drowned the rest of his sentence and continued until Vinzand pointedly called the meeting to order.

'One of the members of the Council of Claimants,' he corrected, and Ventrious nodded tightly, conceding the point.

'For the moment, yes,' he said. 'And therefore entitled to be kept appraised of all that affects our world. Especially in the current dire circumstances. How else are we to reach a swift and effective consensus about what is to be done?'

'A point of order, if I may.' A pale, colourless youth in turquoise hose and a shirt trimmed with fur rose to his feet, his acne flaring with embarrassment. He caught Zyvan's eye and bowed awkwardly. 'Humbert de Truille of House de Truille. Um, I know I haven't been to many meetings and all, but, um, well, aren't there supposed to be, you know, emergency powers and stuff? So the regent can act without convening the council in, well, emergencies I suppose.'

'There are.' Vinzand nodded in confirmation. 'And your point is?'

Humbert flushed even more deeply. 'Well, it seems to me, um, this is sort of an emergency. Shouldn't you, you know, invoke them or whatever? So things don't get bogged down like they usually do?'

'Out of the question!' Ventrious thundered, striking his lectern, while several of the other drones nodded in approval. 'That would strike at the very heart of the reason for the council's existence. How am I...' he corrected himself hastily, 'is the eventual appointee supposed to govern effectively after being sidelined during the biggest crisis our world has ever faced?'

'A lot more effectively than he would after being slaughtered by heretics,' Zyvan said, his voice all the more resonant for not being raised. 'The lad's suggestion should be adopted.'

'Absolutely not,' another periwigged halfwit chimed in. 'House Kinkardi will not stand for it.'

'Nevertheless the proposal has been made,' Vinzand said mildly. 'All those in favour please indicate in the usual way.' The silken rabble prodded at runes on their lecterns, and an ancient hololith sparked into life over the stage, projecting three green dots and a rash of red ones into the air. Zyvan nodded slowly, taking in the result.

'Before you commit yourselves to your final vote, please bear in mind that the alternative is the imposition of martial law. Make no mistake, I have no desire to take so drastic a step, but I will do so if the alternative is to leave our forces hamstrung by a lack of clear leadership.' His voice had that 'damn the plasma bolts' quality again, making several of the councillors quail visibly in their seats. Gradually the red dots began to change to green, although a few remained glaring defiantly red. Looking at Ventrious's face I had no doubt that his was one of them.

'The motion is carried,' Vinzand said, tactfully refraining from gloating at the result. 'Supreme executive authority is hereby transferred to the regent for the duration of the emergency.'

'Good.' Zyvan permitted himself a wintry smile. 'Then if you would be so good as to clear the chamber we can get to work.' A howl of outrage rose from the assembled aristocracy as it suddenly dawned on them that they'd voted themselves out of the loop.

'Gentlemen, please!' Vinzand tried vainly to restore order. 'This is most unseemly. Will the delegate from House Tremaki please withdraw that remark.'

'Allow me.' Zyvan gestured to our table. 'Commissars, would you be so kind as to escort the councillors into the foyer? They seem to need some fresh air.'

'With pleasure,' I responded, and three black-coated figures rose to their feet to back me up. Beije, I noted, was noticeably slower, trailing after the rest of us as we shepherded the aristos out of the room and closed the door on them, abruptly attenuating the noise.

'Good.' Zyvan relaxed for the first time since we'd arrived and sat back in his chair with every sign of satisfaction. 'Now let's hunt some heretics.'

FIVE

'When the traitor's hand strikes, it strikes with the strength of a legion.'

– Warmaster Horus (attributed)

To MY GREAT delight, the extra duties Zyvan had so casually dropped in my lap kept me in Skitterfall for the better part of two weeks, making the most of the equitable temperatures, while Kasteen and Broklaw took the regiment off to our assigned staging area in the frozen wasteland of the dark side. As I'd expected, the troopers were in something of a holiday mood at the prospect of being back in sub-zero temperatures again, and this exuberance manifested itself in a steady stream of minor infractions which kept me busy enforcing discipline and placating a succession of bar owners, praetors, and aggrieved local citizens whose sons and daughters apparently found something irresistible about the contents of a Guard uniform. Fortunately, as always, the ever-reliable Jurgen proved to be an invaluable buffer between me and the more onerous aspects of my job, politely informing most of my callers that the commissar was unavailable and would be dealing with whatever they were upset about at the earliest opportunity.

The positive aspect of all this was that, in the interests of appearing to be both interested and conscientious, I was able to visit a wide selection of bars and gambling dens in the guise of investigating these complaints while my aide dealt with the paperwork, and was thus able to discover a few congenial places to while away my leisure time far more quickly than I might otherwise have done.

Fortunately, by the end of the first week the troops had all been deployed, which left me free to concentrate on the more important matters of filtering the reports from the joint intelligence committee and taking full advantage of my impromptu recon sweeps. There was no way a single regiment could be expected to hold down an entire hemisphere on their own, so they were being held in reserve at a mining complex close to the equator where the dropships from the *Emperor's Benificence* could, in theory, rush them to wherever the approaching raiders looked like touching down before the invaders got there. Assuming the Tallarns or Kastaforeans didn't ask for them first, of course; that was a real headache for Zyvan, who kept harrying the rest of our task force to get their act together and join us as quickly as possible in an increasingly terse series of astropathic messages. Five regiments with which to defend an entire planet[1] was beginning to seem like a bad joke, less and less funny as the punch line got closer.

The Tallarns naturally got the hot side to deal with, and I have to admit I was heartily pleased to see them go. I hadn't encountered either Beije or Asmar since the briefing in the council chamber, but the knowledge that they were the other side of the planet from our own regiment was a great relief. At least the sand-shufflers' abstemious habits meant that they were unlikely to turn up in the bars and bordellos frequented by our grunts, any more than a trooper from the 597th was likely to waste any of their R&R time going to church, so the brawls I'd been dreading never broke out. (At least not with the Tallarns. It went without saying that I was swapping datafiles with my opposite numbers at the 425th Armoured and the two Kastaforean regiments with monotonous regularity. Or I would have done if Jurgen hadn't been keeping on top of it for me, citing the pressing need to collate intelligence reports for the lord general to cover my absence.)

The 425th, to their evident disappointment, were stuck in Skitterfall for the foreseeable future instead of joining our people out on the glaciers, as Zyvan wanted the tanks to defend the capital when the raiders arrived. I couldn't fault his logic, as, at the time, it seemed to be the most likely target for the invaders to strike. The Kastaforeans, too, were

---

1. *He seems to completely discount the PDF, which outnumbered the entire expeditionary force by at least four to one, as an effective fighting force. As later events were to show, this does them a considerable disservice.*

deployed around the shadow zone, bolstering the PDF wherever they looked particularly weak (which to my apprehensive mind meant practically everywhere).

As things settled down, however, I began to find the assignment as congenial as could be expected. Whatever state of readiness his men might be in, and time alone would answer that, General Kolbe at least seemed competent enough. True, he'd never seen any actual combat, apart from a few occasions when the PDF had been mobilised by the Arbites to put down the sort of civil disorder that flares up from time to time pretty much anywhere in the Imperium, but he was methodical, incisive and bright enough to listen to advice. It was at his suggestion that we went back through the archives with the benefit of hindsight, trying to see if there was any possible link between some of those previous incidents and nascent cult activity.

'At least if we can find a connection, that'll give us some idea of how long they've been active on Adumbria,' he pointed out.

Zyvan nodded slowly. The three of us, Vinzand and Hekwyn, the senior arbitrator on the planet, were cloistered in a heavily-shielded conference suite in the high-class hotel Zyvan had commandeered as his headquarters. If nothing else the place was extremely comfortable, as befitted his status, and I'd lost no time in grabbing a room for myself there too. After all, I was supposed to be liaising closely with his staff, so it made perfect sense for me to hang around there now that my regiment was half a hemisphere away.

'Up to a point,' he agreed. 'Although it would be safest to assume they've been infiltrating here for a generation at least. Possibly several.' The three Adumbrians looked shocked at that, even more so as I concurred.

'It might be worth checking the starport records for the last century or two as well. Chances are that the local cult was founded by a handful of heretics arriving from offworld.'

Hekwyn, a stocky man with a shaven head and the pallid complexion of most Adumbrians, paled even further. 'That would be millions of names,' he said.

Vinzand nodded. 'Possibly as much as a billion,' he agreed drily, with the indifference to large numbers common to Administratum functionaries. He made a note on his datapad. 'I'll have my staff look into it. But frankly I'm not hopeful.'

'Neither am I,' I admitted. 'But right now we're critically short of hard data. Even a shred would help.'

'I'll have my people follow up from their end,' Hekwyn offered. 'We monitor the cargo areas closely, checking for contraband. It's possible we might have netted a heretic or two along with the smugglers.'

'Excellent.' Zyvan nodded. 'Any leads from your street sources?'

Hekwyn shrugged. 'Vague at best. There have been a few incidents, gang fights and the like, but if there's an agenda behind it the pattern's hard to read.'

'I'll take a look at it,' I said. My years of paranoia have given me the ability to sometimes see connections that others with a less finely honed survival instinct might miss. I turned to Kolbe. 'Any unusual incidents involving the PDF?'

'If you mean have we been infiltrated, nothing's come up so far to suggest that.' His voice was level. 'But given the amount of time these heretics may have been active we have to assume that cultists have penetrated the command structure.' My respect for the man rose even more. Most PDF commanders in my experience would have been outraged at the idea, vehemently denying the possibility and refusing to allow a proper investigation.

'I meant have any of your units come under attack?' I said. Since the strike against the Tallarns four days ago we'd been braced for more similar incidents, but the second boot resolutely refused to drop. Of course we'd tightened security since then, so the heretics wouldn't find so soft a target again, but somehow I thought that was unlikely to deter them. With the Guard regiments on a state of alert and the PDF providing a plentiful supply of easy targets spread out across the entire shadow zone, they ought to be next in the firing line by any reasonable logic. Of course reason and logic aren't exactly high on the entry requirements for a Chaos cult, so second-guessing them is never going to be easy, unless you're as bonkers as they are.

Kolbe shook his head.

'Since you've raised the matter,' Zyvan said mildly, 'what precautions are you taking against infiltration?'

'We're running thorough background checks on every officer, starting at the highest level and working back down the chain of command.' He essayed a wintery smile. 'I'm pleased to report that so far I appear uncompromised.'

'And who investigated the investigators?' I asked, the palms of my hands beginning to tingle as a bottomless spiral of mistrust and suspicion began to open up beneath my feet.

Kolbe nodded. 'A good question. So far they've been investigating each other, two teams independently verifying the loyalty of a third. It's not infallible, of course, but it should go some way towards preventing fellow cultists covering for one another. If there are any there in the first place, of course.'

'Of course. And in the meantime they've got us chasing our own tails, diverting Emperor knows how many resources and man hours...' I broke off, suddenly sure that this was the main reason for the cultists alerting us to their presence by attacking the Tallarns in the first place. But if that was their agenda, we had to go along with it; any other course of action would be impossible. I voiced my suspicion and Zyvan nodded.

'I'd come to the same conclusion.' He shrugged. 'But that's Chaos for you. A hidden agenda in even the most irrational-seeming action.' He sighed in irritation. 'Why is there never an inquisitor around when you actually need one?'[1]

I kept quiet at that remark, having discovered more about the Inquisition and its methods than I'd ever wanted to know, since becoming Amberley's occasional cat's-paw, but reflected that just because you can't see them it doesn't necessarily mean they're not there. A thought which brought little comfort, stoking as it did the sense of paranoia that had already got me in its grip.

'We'll just have to do the best we can with what we've got,' I said, unsure as ever just how much Zyvan knew about my tangential activities as a reluctant agent of the Inquisition. He must certainly have been aware of the personal relationship between Amberley and myself, and he was definitely astute enough to realise that it probably went further than the merely social, but had never asked and I wasn't about to volunteer the information.[2]

'Quite so.' Zyvan stood and stretched, walking around the conference table to the small one at the side of the room holding a pot of recaff, some tanna tea for me (which nobody else would touch, but he knew my fondness for the stuff and was considerate like that) and a selection of snack foods. It was a common enough thing for him to do, especially as the conference had already been going for over an hour, but this time it was to save his life. 'Can I get anything for anyone else while I'm up?'

Before I could ask for some fresh tanna, the sludge at the bottom of my cup having turned unpalatably tepid, the window erupted in a hail of bolter fire which shredded the seat the lord general had vacated a moment before. I dived for cover, heedless of the shower of glass splinters still falling all over the room, knowing the explosive projectiles would wreak havoc with any of the furnishings I might seek refuge

---

1. *Not entirely true, as our earlier encounter on Gravalax quite clearly demonstrates.*

2. *Zyvan was wise enough to know that there were things he didn't want to know, and to direct his gaze accordingly.*

behind. The only option was the wall itself, beside the shattered window, and I flattened myself against it, drawing my faithful old laspistol as I did so.

I didn't have to wait long for a target. A rising whine outside the building abruptly terminated in a *crump* of impact which left my ears ringing, and the nose of an aircar ploughed through the gap of the window frame, wedging itself fast. It was an open-topped model, I noted absently, the interior luxuriously appointed in furs and fine leather, the metal of its bodywork filigreed with gold decoration, mangled beyond recognition by the impact with the side of the hotel. The driver slumped over the brass handle of the grav regulator as I shot him through the head, making a real mess of his elaborate coiffure, and his front seat passenger bounded over the wreckage like a man possessed, brandishing the bolter.

I looked round for my companions, but only Zyvan and Kolbe were reacting, both drawing bolt pistols and seeking a target. Vinzand was huddled in a corner, his face a bloodless mask of shock, and Hekwyn was down, bleeding heavily from the stump of where his left arm used to be.

'Help him!' I shouted, and the paralysed regent moved forward to try and stem the flow of blood before the arbitrator expired from shock. I had no more attention to pay to either, though, as bolter boy brought up the cumbersome weapon as smoothly as if he were wearing Astartes armour. I fired, the las bolt blowing a bloody crater in his bare torso and obliterating a tattoo which had made my eyes hurt. I expected him to drop, but to my astonishment and horror he just kept coming, giggling insanely.

'Frak this!' I dropped and rolled as he aimed the bolter at me, staying ahead of the stream of explosive projectiles by a miracle as they gouged a line across the wall. The firing abruptly ceased with the bark of two bolt pistols almost simultaneously; the man with the bolter seemed to explode, spraying bloody offal around the room and doing the expensive wallpaper no favours at all. 'Thank you,' I added for the benefit of the two generals, and drew my chainsword to meet the charge of the rear seat passengers, who had spent the second or so it took to dispatch their comrade clambering over the driver's corpse. A space this confined was no place for firearms in a general melee, the chances of hitting a friend instead of a foe far too great.

Not a consideration for the heretics, of course, who all seemed completely out of their skulls to begin with, on 'slaught unless I missed my guess, the distended veins in their flushed faces being a dead giveaway. I sidestepped a rush by a woman naked except for a leather mask, gloves and thigh boots, and kicked her in the back of the knee, bringing her down just as she aimed the stubber in her hand at Zyvan. No time to worry about her after that, as a fellow built like a Catachan in voluminous pink silks swung a power maul at my head. I ducked it, blocked with the chainsword and took his hand off at the wrist. By luck or the Emperor's blessing the maul kept going, pulping the head of the stubber girl as she rose to her feet, and I spun round to take the third assailant in the midriff, a willowy youth of indeterminate gender in a flowing purple gown and far too much makeup.

He or she came apart in the middle, giggling gleefully and scrabbling forward on blood-slicked hands, trying to recover the laspistol that had fallen to the floor as they dropped. I kicked out, driving the sundered torso back, my boots slipping in the spreading lake of blood, but even enhanced with combat drugs, the human frame can't last too long in that state: the eyes rolled back in their sockets and after a few more twitches the hermaphrodite lay still.

Which left only one, the muscleman in pink. Catching a flicker of movement out of the corner of my eye I ducked, drove my elbow back into a midriff which felt like rockcrete, and reversed the humming blade in my hand to stab backwards under my own armpit. It spitted him nicely, opening up his entire ribcage as I withdrew the blade and turned, swinging the weapon to take his head off. This was a bit of a grandstanding gesture, to be honest, but probably necessary for all that. I'd seen before what 'slaught could do, and it was quite possible the fellow would have continued to fight until he bled to death in spite of his wounds.

'Commissar!' Zyvan called, from over by the door, and I looked up to see the other four on the verge of leaving the room. Gradually it dawned on me that the whole fight had been over in less than a minute. 'Are you all right?'

'Fine,' I said, as nonchalantly as I could, holstering my weapons. 'How's Hekwyn?' Not that I cared particularly, but it wouldn't hurt my reputation to seem more worried about someone else now that I was safe again.

'Vinzand's stemmed the bleeding.' Zyvan was looking at me oddly, and for a moment I wondered what I'd done. 'I'll be recommending you for a commendation for this.'

'Absolutely,' Kolbe chimed in, while I tried to mask my astonishment. All I'd done, as usual, was try to save my own neck. 'I can see your reputation for selflessness is richly merited. Holding them off single-handed like that, so we could attend to Hekwyn...' So that was it. My impulse to seek shelter by the wall had put me between the heretics and the others, and they thought I'd done it on purpose.

I shrugged as modestly as I could. 'The Imperium needs its generals,' I said. 'And you can always get another commissar.'

'Not like you, Ciaphas,' Zyvan said, using my given name for the first time. That was truer than he knew, of course, so I just looked embarrassed and asked after Hekwyn again. He was looking grey, even for an Adumbrian, and I was mildly relieved to see a medic among the squad of Zyvan's personal guard who were doubling along the corridor towards us, hellguns at the ready.

'You can stand down,' I told them. 'The lord general's safe.' No point in not gently underlining my supposed heroism while I had the chance.

The Guard commander looked a little embarrassed, having taken almost two minutes to respond to the first sound of gunfire, but the hotel was huge and Zyvan had insisted on seclusion for our conference, so I suppose it wasn't really his fault. In any event, he made up for it by dispatching Hekwyn to the medicae with commendable promptness and insisting that Vinzand went too: by now the regent was showing signs of shock, which I couldn't really blame him for, being a civilian and not really used to this sort of thing.

'How did they get past our security cordon?' Zyvan asked.

The Guard commander had a short, somewhat intense conversation with someone on the other end of his comm-bead. 'They were broadcasting the appropriate security codes,' he confirmed after a moment. Kolbe and Zyvan exchanged glances.

'I suppose that answers the question of whether the PDF has been compromised at any rate,' I put in.

The Guard commander frowned. 'I'm sorry, sir, perhaps I wasn't quite clear. The codes identified the vehicle as belonging to a member of the council of claimants.'

'Find out which one and have him arrested,' Zyvan ordered. The commander saluted and trotted away. The lord general turned back to Kolbe and me. 'This is just getting better and better.'

'It doesn't make sense, though,' I said, the palms of my hands tingling again. We were missing something, I was sure of it. 'If they have someone that highly placed it would be madness to expose them simply to carry out such a risky attack. They must have known their chances of success were minimal.' And that was putting it mildly. Five untrained civilians, however fanatical, could never have prevailed against a roomful of soldiers. True, the death of Zyvan would have crippled our command structure, but even so…

'Clear the building!' I shouted, the coin dropping. This was a diversion, it had to be. The main attack would be somewhere or something else, and the instinctive paranoia jabbering at the back of my skull told me what that was most likely to be. Despite the clear breach of protocol, I shoved the two generals heavily in the small of the back. 'Run like frak!'

'Evacuate the building,' Zyvan said levelly into his comm-bead and started running down the corridor.

After a moment Kolbe followed, with an astonished glance in my direction. I might have felt a moment of satisfaction at the sight, as there are precious few men alive who can say they've given orders to a lord general, let alone had them obeyed, but I suppose he was a bit more inclined to listen given my commissarial status.[1]

As I watched them go, every fibre of my being urged me to sprint after them, or ahead if I could barge my way past in that narrow corridor cluttered with expensive nick nacks on delicate tables, but I forced myself to remain where I was. If I was wrong about the threat I perceived and the whole idea had been to force us out into the open, I'd be running headlong into a trap, and I didn't dare take that chance; despite the risk, I had to be sure. I turned and ran back in to the conference suite.

The room was as big a mess as I remembered, the wreckage of the aircar filling my vision as I clambered over the splintered remains of the conference table, slipped in some spilled viscera and scrambled into the shattered vehicle. The dead driver was in the way, so I grabbed him by the scruff of the neck and pitched him backwards out into space, where he fell the thirty or so floors to the rockcrete below. Belatedly I remembered that Zyvan's entire headquarters staff would be milling around down there by now, and hoped he didn't hit anyone, least of all the lord general; that would have been the crowning irony. (As it turned out, he burst harmlessly on a porch roof, so that was all right.)

No point trying to pop any of the maintenance hatches, as the metalwork was buckled beyond all hope of repair, so I thumbed the selector of my chainsword to maximum and sliced through the thin sheeting with a fine display of sparks and a screeching sound that set my teeth on edge. Heedless of the raggedness of the tear and the concomitant risk to my fingers (the real ones anyway), I levered the makeshift flap aside, taking as much of the pressure on the augmetics as I could.

I stared into the engine compartment, my bowels spasming. My guess was right.

---

1. *Typically, it doesn't seem to have occurred to Cain that Zyvan was reacting out of the regard he held for him personally.*

'The powercells have been rigged to blow,' I said into my comm-bead. 'Get me a tech-priest – now!' There was no time to run, of that I was certain; I'd never make it out of the building in time. It was even debatable whether I could have made it if I'd fled with the others, who would barely have made it as far as the fire stairs by now.

'This is Cogitator Ikmenedies,' a voice said in my ear, with the flat unmodulated cadences of an implanted vox unit. 'How may I assist you?'

'I'm looking at a timer,' I told him, 'attached to what looks like the promethium flask of a flamer. They've both been taped to the powercells of the aircar which rammed the building. The timer has less than a minute to run.' The wire connecting it to the powercells had been jarred loose by the impact, I noticed with a sudden thrill of horror. If it hadn't been for that it would probably have detonated almost as soon as the heretics hit the building. As it was, the timer was running in intermittent jerks, counting off a few seconds then pausing for a couple before resuming its inexorable march towards zero. 'I need you to tell me how to deactivate it.' For an instant I found myself wondering if the fault would give me enough time to get clear after all, but logic overrode the impulse to flee with the stark truth that doing so would just get me far enough for my shredded corpse to be entombed under most of the building when it collapsed.

'The mysteries of the machine god cannot be lightly revealed to the unconsecrated,' Ikmenedies droned.

I gritted my teeth. 'Unless you want to explain that to him in person in less than a minute that's precisely what you're going to have to do,' I told him. 'Because if I can't defuse the bloody bomb I'm going to use the last few seconds of my life to organise a firing squad.'

'How is the timer powered?' Ikmenedies asked, as tonelessly as ever but with almost indecent haste.

'There's a wire to the powercells. It's already loose.' I reached out a hand towards it. 'I can pull it out quite easily.'

'Don't do that!' Somehow the tech-priest managed to inject a frisson of panic into his level mechanical drone. 'The power surge could trip the detonator. Are there wires leading to the promethium flask?'

'Yes, two,' I said, trying to still my hammering heart and giving thanks to the Emperor that at least I still had two fingers which failed to tremble in reaction to my near-fatal mistake.

'Then it should be simple,' Ikmenedies said. 'All you have to do is cut the red one.'

'They're both purple,' I said, after a moment's inspection.

I heard a muffled curse, then there was a short pause. 'You'll just have to use your best judgement.'

'I don't have any!' I practically shouted. 'I'm a commissar, not a cog-boy. This is supposed to be your department.'

'I'll pray to the Omnissiah to guide your hand,' Ikmenedies said help-fully. I glanced at the timer, seeing only a handful of seconds left. Well, a fifty-fifty chance of survival is a lot better than some of the odds I've faced over the years, so I picked a wire at random, wrapped my aug-metic fingers around it, took a deep breath, and closed my eyes. For a moment fear paralysed my arm, until the survival reflex kicked in and reminded me that if I didn't do this I was dead for sure, and I tugged spasmodically at it with a whimper of apprehension. It came free sur-prisingly easily.

'Commissar? Commissar, are you there?'

I became aware of the voice in my ear after a moment and let my breath out in a single gush of relief. 'When you see the Omnissiah, say thanks,' I said, sagging back into the overstuffed upholstery.

'Ciaphas?' Zyvan's voice cut in, concern and curiosity mingled in it. 'Where are you? We thought you were behind us.'

'I'm still in the conference suite,' I said, noticing for the first time that the refreshment table had somehow survived the melee. I clambered out of the aircar and staggered towards it, avoiding the larger pieces of heretic. The tanna pot was still warm so I poured myself a generous mug. 'After all that excitement I feel I could do with some tea.'

Editorial Note:

While Cain was keeping himself occupied in Skitterfall, the rest of his regiment had been successfully deployed in and around Glacier Peak, a mining town situated conveniently close to the geographical centre of the dark face, or 'coldside' as the Adumbrians succinctly termed it. Since this process had gone as smoothly as could reasonably be expected, the details of it need not concern us here: what is important is that they had seen action unexpectedly early, an encounter which would, with hindsight, prove to be a vital turning point in the campaign as a whole.

As we might have expected, Cain has virtually nothing to say about this, displaying his usual disregard for anything which didn't affect him personally, so I have felt it incumbent upon me to insert an account of the incident from the perspective of an eyewitness. Unfortunately, this comes from the second volume of the memoirs of Jenit Sulla, which, as you'll no doubt realise within a sentence or two, is no more readable than the first. As ever I feel I should apologise for including it, but offer the shred of consolation that it is at least mercifully brief.

From *Like a Phoenix on the Wing: The Early Campaigns and Glorious Victories of the Valhallan 597th* by General Jenit Sulla (retired), 101 M42

THOSE OF MY readers not fortunate enough to have been native to an iceworld, as we were, can scarce imagine the fashion in which our spirits rose to find ourselves once more treading the permafrost which, with every bootfall, would send our blood thrilling with the visceral memory of home. Not that nostalgia was our ruling passion of course; far from it. That, as always, was our duty to the Emperor, which every woman and man of us held so dear, even to the shedding of our own precious blood in his glorious name.

We had not been long in Glacier Peak, a picturesque spot surprisingly little blighted by the shaft heads and hab domes erected by the miners who worked so hard to scrabble a precarious living[1] from the veins of merconium[2] so far beneath our feet, when the chance we all longed for to fulfil that duty came at last.

I was summoned to the command post set up by Colonel Kasteen early one morning (although in the constant night in which we now found ourselves living, such distinctions were all but irrelevant), to find myself entrusted with a mission of the utmost importance. Our perimeter sensor net was being constantly disrupted by the seismic disturbances of the miners as they went about their work, and, as she gravely informed me, no junior officer seemed so suited to the task of ensuring our security from heretic infiltrators as myself. It is no exaggeration to say that my heart swelled within me to hear so fulsome a vote of confidence from my commanding officer, and I accepted the assignment eagerly.

As can be readily appreciated, this required the undertaking of periodic patrols to check the proper functioning of the sensors, for which the tech-priests assigned to our regiment as engineers thoughtfully provided us with the appropriate rituals. Despite my natural trepidation that such things were best left in the hands of the duly ordained, they declined to accompany us on our excursions, assuring me that the prayers and data downloads would prove equally efficacious if performed by the highest ranking trooper present, and indeed this proved

---

1. *In actual fact the work was well paid and highly sought after.*

2. *A naturally-occuring substance most notable for its ability to bond irremovably with almost anything.*

to be the case. In order to be even more certain of our success in this vital task I took to accompanying each patrol myself, reasoning that as the highest ranking member of the platoon I would thus ensure the greater favour of the Machine God.

And so it was that I found myself present with the women and men of fourth squad in what at the time I took to be a mere skirmish. Only hindsight and the tactical genius of Commissar Cain were to later reveal just how significant that minor incident would prove to be.

My first intimation of trouble appeared as our Chimera came to a halt some half a kilometre from the site of the sensor package we'd been sent to bless, and stood there, its engine idling, for some time. At length, Sergeant Grifen, an experienced trooper who had earned the respect of the commissar (which was no easy task as those of us who had done so could attest), approached me, raising her voice slightly to be heard over the rumble of our engine.

'I think you should take a look at this, L.T.'[1] she said. Knowing that she was unlikely to be perturbed without good reason I followed her, savouring the chill which struck through the weave of my greatcoat as I descended the boarding ramp.

It wasn't hard to see what had so excited her curiosity. A few metres ahead, cutting across our own course, was a twin line of tracks, clearly left by a vehicle of some kind. I commended the vigilance of our driver, for spotting them would have been no easy task in the constant darkness which enveloped us. I stooped to examine them.

'They're heading for the settlement,' Grifen concluded, and I was forced to agree; the constant wind was eroding the marks even as we watched, and over to our left they were all but obliterated already. Time was clearly of the essence: if we were to follow, and follow we surely must if only to assure ourselves of the innocence of these mysterious travellers, we had to set out quickly before their trail vanished before us like smoke in a gale.

A quick call to the command post confirmed that no other units were out here and no civilian traffic had been cleared through our perimeter, so as we commenced our pursuit I urged our women and men to be ready to face the enemies of the Emperor. True to form,

---

1. *A familiar form of address between a senior NCO and the lieutenant commanding them, in the same way that their own subordinates might abbreviate their title to 'sarge'. It seems that whatever Cain may have thought of Sulla she at least had the respect and confidence of the troops she led.*

they were enthused at the prospect and immediately fell to checking their lasguns and other equipment while our faithful Chimera closed the distance rapidly.

'There's a light ahead,' our driver reported, an instant before any doubts we may have had about the intentions of the vehicle we followed were answered by a pattering of stubber rounds against the armour of our hull. Our gunner swung the turret and unleashed a hail of retaliatory bolter fire.

Unable to resist seeing for myself what was going on, I clambered up to the top hatch and stuck my head out, shielding my eyes from the flurrying snow with the unconscious ease of reflexes ingrained since girlhood. A mining crawler stood crippled before us, great rents torn through its thin unarmoured body, its crew piling out to engage us with a variety of small-arms. They would no doubt have proved poor opponents for the doughty warriors under my command, but even as I opened my mouth to give the order to disembark and engage them the crawler exploded in a vivid orange fireball which reduced it to smouldering wreckage in an instant, immolating in the process the heretics who had dared oppose the Emperor's will.

SIX

*'Paranoia is a very comforting state of mind. If you think
they're out to get you, it means you think you matter.'*

– Gilbran Quail, *Collected Essays*

'THE QUESTION IS,' I said, 'what were they doing out there in the first
place?'

Kasteen nodded and handed me a steaming mug of tanna, which I
accepted gratefully. 'Carrying weapons, we think. I had Federer go over
what was left of the crawler, and he says he found traces of fyceline
among the wreckage.' I had no trouble believing that. Captain Federer,
the officer in command of our sappers, had an enthusiasm for all
things explosive which bordered on the unhealthy and if there were
traces of the stuff to be found he would undoubtedly be the man to
uncover them. 'He says it looks like the bolter shells penetrated the
cargo compartment and cooked off whatever was in there.'

'I suppose it would be too much to hope that just for once Sulla left
us some survivors we could interrogate?' I asked, sipping the fragrant
liquid and savouring the sensation of warmth it ignited on the way
down. I'd just arrived in Glacier Peak, our main staging area, and found
it even less inviting than it sounded. Not only was the coldside living

up to its name, as I'd steeled myself to expect, the perpetual night was beginning to get to me, and I'd only been there for an hour.

Well, technically at any rate, we'd left the shadow zone some six hours before that, the pervasive gloom I'd got used to in Skitterfall gradually deepening over the preceding two, and I'd grown sleepy as the monotonous snowscape crept past the window. To my thinly-disguised dismay there were no air transports available, and I'd had to make do with a compartment on one of the railway trains transporting miners and their supplies back to the outpost we'd no doubt overrun with our own people.[1]

Despite the three carriages coupled to the rear of the freight wagons being crowded in the extreme, with several passengers being forced to sit on their luggage in the corridor, Jurgen and I were left with an entire compartment to ourselves. At first I thought this was due to the respect our Guard uniforms commanded, but after observing the way the crowd parted whenever my aide left his seat to use the sanitary facilities I was forced to conclude that this had more to do with his distinctive aroma than it did with my charisma. Used as I was to this, and pleased as I might otherwise have been to have the extra legroom, after eight hours with him in a confined space I was beginning to think they had a point.

The upshot of all this was that by the time I'd arrived at our destination I was tired and irritable, and in no mood to hear that Sulla had taken it upon herself to bag a crawler-full of heretics without bothering to find out what in the warp they were doing out here in the first place.

'All blown to frak, along with the crawler,' Kasteen said. She shrugged. 'On the plus side, I suppose at least that's one batch of weapons the heretics won't be getting their hands on.'

'Assuming they don't have a whole lot more where they came from,' I said.

The palms of my hands were tingling again, but for once I couldn't tell if it was from apprehension or returning circulation. The cold outside was every bit as bone-chewing as I'd anticipated, and chill as it was here in Kasteen's command post, where I could still see our breath

---

1. *In actual fact, Glacier Peak was a fair-sized town, with a population of around thirty thousand. Only about a third of these were directly involved in the mining operation, the rest being made up of storekeepers, tavern owners, and other service sector workers, not to mention the families and dependants of the economically active local citizens. The abrupt arrival of a thousand or so Guard troopers would have had an impact on the community, no doubt, but not the overwhelming one Cain seems to imply. Then again, as the regimental commissar, his perceptions were almost certainly coloured by the inevitable exceptions he would be required to deal with.*

puffing visibly with every word or exhalation, it felt almost tropical by comparison. She and Broklaw had their sleeves rolled up to the elbows, and the vox operators and other specialists coming and going were similarly lightly clad.

All, I was pleased to note, still wore their flak armour though, the lord general's strictures on remaining alert still being in effect. (I still had the carapace armour I'd been given on Gravalax concealed beneath my greatcoat, as I generally did whenever things looked like they might get uncomfortable without warning; it was getting a bit battered by now, but as far as I was concerned that just reinforced the wisdom of forgetting to return it to the stores in the first place.)

'Quite.' Broklaw nodded, his eyes thoughtful, and kicked the portable hololith with all the assurance of a tech-priest. It hummed into life, projecting a topographic recreation of the surrounding countryside. (I use the word loosely, although no doubt the Valhallans could appreciate subtleties in it denied to me.) 'I think we can safely assume that whatever they had planned though, we were the target.'

'Almost certainly,' I agreed. The crawler had been heading for Glacier Peak, that much was certain, and we were the only significant military presence there, so it hardly needed an inquisitor to join the dots.

I gazed at the image, something nagging at the back of my mind. The ring of red icons around the town would be our sensor packages, of course, and the thin line snaking its way through the valleys was the railway which connected us to the civilised delights of the shadow zone. There were no roads, as the constant snow would have rendered them permanently impassable, so the ribbon of steel was the only way in or out apart from the occasional flyer. If you needed to go anywhere else, like an outlying settlement or mining claim, the only way to do it was by crawler.[1]

'The skirmish happened here,' Broklaw added helpfully, adding a contact icon more or less where I'd expected it to be. The heretics' intended course was clear enough, following a valley down towards the edge of Glacier Peak, at which point they'd simply have merged into the traffic on the streets and vanished.

'They must have had contacts somewhere in the town,' Kasteen said.

---

1. *Since these are alluded to repeatedly, but never described, in both the Cain archive and Sulla's scribblings this seems as good a place as any to elucidate. Crawlers were locally manufactured vehicles which came in a variety of forms, the main characteristic of which was the wide tracks which enabled them to move reasonably efficiently across snow and ice at a brisk pace and in as much safety as might be expected under the circumstances. Most were about the size of a Chimera, the vast majority with enclosed passenger or cargo bays.*

I nodded slowly. 'That seems likely. Even if they were planning to carry out the strike themselves, they'd need somewhere to hole up while they were preparing it. That means confederates.'

'We're liaising with the local praetors,' Broklaw said, forestalling the next inevitable question. 'But so far they don't have much to go on. Not even a missing person report.'

'Outsiders then, almost certainly,' I agreed. 'The question is, where did they come from?' There weren't that many outposts of civilisation on the coldside, and the others were all a long way from here; too far to make the trip by crawler anything other than insanely risky. Of course these were heretics we were talking about, so insanity was pretty much guaranteed, but even so I felt we were missing something.

I tried to trace the path of the crawler back from the point at which Sulla had encountered it, and felt a nagging sense of wrongness about the topography. The valley was broad and long, but surrounded by mountains and with no sign of a pass leading into it. I voiced my concern. 'That looks like a dead end to me.'

'You're right,' Kasteen said, dropping her head to examine the projection from eye level. She glanced at Broklaw for confirmation, seeing in his almost imperceptible nod that he'd reached the same conclusion. 'There must be a cache of weapons out there somewhere.'

'Sounds likely,' I said, unable to think of another explanation. 'Our heretics must have been on a supply run.' The thought wasn't comforting. For the crawler to have blown up like that implied that it was carrying a lot of ordnance, and that in turn probably meant there was a lot more of it out there. Certainly no one would bother taking a single crawler-load out to bury, then bring it all back again in one go. No one sane, in any case. Once again I reminded myself that we were dealing with the minions of Chaos here, and that nothing could be taken for granted.

'Where did it come from in the first place?' Broklaw asked.

I shrugged. 'The starport. Hekwyn said they had a problem with smugglers. The weapons must come in hidden among the cargoes and then cultists in the city distribute them. They probably arrived in Glacier Peak disguised as mining supplies.'

'Not that difficult if you think about it,' Kasteen agreed, pouring herself a fresh mug of tanna. 'There are legitimate shipments of explosives arriving on practically every train.'

'Then we have a place to start, at any rate,' I said, feeling a sudden flare of hope that we might just be getting one jump ahead after all. I turned to Broklaw. 'We need a list of everyone in the mines with access to explosive shipments. And who might have a chance to tamper with them while they're en route too.'

He nodded. 'I'll get on to the Administratum,' he said. 'They should have all the records we need.'

And a lot more besides, if I knew them. 'While you're doing that, I'll contact the Arbites in Skitterfall,' I said, the optimistic conviction beginning to grow in me that the key to all this lay in the planetary capital. With a bit of luck I could find an excuse to be on my way back there by the time the next train left. 'They must have some idea of how this stuff is getting through the starport.'

'IT'S AN ELEGANT theory, commissar.' Hekwyn's head floated in the hololith, nodding pleasantly, as if reluctant to batter my deductions with anything as crude as solid facts. He was looking a lot better than the last time I'd seen him, even allowing for the slight instability imparted to his virtual presence by the equipment. His image was partially overlaid with Zyvan's, since I felt the lord general should be kept informed of the latest developments, and the pair of them looked like some strange piece of two-headed warp spawn. I hit the projector the way I'd seen Broklaw do, and to my vague surprise the images from the two pictcasters separated, at least some of the time, flicking apart and back together at irregular intervals. 'But it's just not possible for large quantities of weapons to be coming through the starport.'

'You told me yourself that you have a smuggling problem,' I riposted, unwilling to let such a neat chain of reasoning go without a fight. The arbitrator nodded and scratched his chin with his new augmetic arm, not quite getting the distance right; I remembered similar problems adjusting to my new fingers back on the Reclaimers' battle barge[1] in the Interitus system all those years before.

'We do. With a port that size it's almost inevitable. But believe me, arms and explosives would almost certainly be detected. In the quantities you describe, they'd be found for sure.'

'I've known psykers pull some pretty slick disappearing acts,' I said, grasping at the last straw I could think of. 'And we are looking for Chaos worshippers. If they've got a witch or two in tow they could walk past your inspectors with a baneblade and no one would notice.'

'Except for our own sanctioned psykers,' Zyvan pointed out mildly. 'I've had a couple posted at the starport ever since we arrived. No one's used any witch talents there, you can be sure of that.'

---

1. *Cain was attached to this Astartes Chapter as the Imperial Guard liaison officer for a while during his previous assignment at brigade headquarters. His activities during this period are described elsewhere in the archive.*

Great. I watched the best lead I'd been able to construct crash into ruins in front of me, along with my ticket back to somewhere my blood wouldn't freeze. I sighed heavily.

'Ah well,' I said. 'My apologies for wasting your time then.'

'You've hardly done that,' Zyvan assured me, more from politeness than strict accuracy, I strongly suspected. 'It was an astute piece of deduction.' He smiled. 'But I'm afraid even you can't be right all the time.'

'But we're right back where we started,' I said, fighting the impulse to pinch the bridge of my nose. Now that the consuming sense of urgency to communicate my reasoning to the high command had been punctured, the weariness I felt from my journey was beginning to make itself felt again.

Hekwyn scratched his chin once more, a little more accurately this time.

'Not quite,' he pointed out, and Zyvan nodded in agreement. 'We know that your regiment seems to represent a particular threat to them.' I felt a shiver of apprehension running down my spine, already sure of the lord general's next words.

'Precisely. Of all the targets on the planet they could have struck at, they seem to be going to inordinate lengths to prepare an attack on you. Have you any idea why that might be?'

'None at all,' I said, hoping I hadn't answered too hastily. The only thing which made the 597th any different from a million other Guard regiments was the presence in it of Jurgen, whose peculiar gift of nullifying psychic or warp-derived sorceries had saved my life (and probably soul) on a number of occasions. If the heretic cult was aware that there was a blank somewhere on Adumbria, and had psykers among their number, they'd stop at nothing to eliminate so potent a threat, and the chances were that I'd be standing right beside him when they struck. After all, I could hardly start avoiding my own aide (however tempting the notion became when the temperature rose above the moderately warm). Then again, his strange ability was a secret known only to the two of us, Amberley, and presumably at least some in her retinue,[1] and I was damn sure no one on that select little list was in the habit of chatting with heretics.

'Perhaps there's something about the town which is significant to them,' I suggested, partly to deflect the conversation away from this

---

1. Only two, in point of fact: Mott, my savant, who would undoubtedly have deduced it for himself if I hadn't told him, and Rakel, who, being a psyker, had most decidedly noticed the fact. Indeed it was her hysterical reaction to Jurgen's presence at our first meeting which had initially piqued my interest in him.

sensitive area, and partly to try and allay my own fears, 'and our presence here is merely incidental.'

'Perhaps.' Zyvan looked unconvinced. 'But we're not going to know until you get some hard evidence.' I noted his use of 'you' with intense foreboding, but nodded as sagely as I could.

'We're following up all the leads we can,' I said. 'If there's a heretic cell anywhere in Glacier Falls, you can rest assured we'll find it.'

'I don't doubt that for a minute,' the lord general said. 'But it's just as possible that the answer lies elsewhere.'

'I can be back in Skitterfall by tomorrow,' I started to say, but choked myself off after the first syllable as a familiar topographic projection superimposed itself over the two men in front of me. As luck would have it, the wretched machine was keeping their images separate at the time, or the combined interference would probably have rendered the whole thing incomprehensible.

Zyvan gestured at the valley next to the mountain ridge his head and torso were protruding from like some strange geological wart. 'You say that this valley is a dead end.'

Already sure of what was coming next, I nodded numbly, my mind racing to find an excuse and failing miserably. That's what happens when you call senior and influential people without sufficient sleep or recaf, and why I strongly recommend against it.

'It certainly appears to be,' I conceded.

'Then by your own logic there must be some trace of the heretics' arms cache out there,' Zyvan went on cheerfully, while Hekwyn nodded in agreement. 'Possibly more weapons we can trace back to their source.' He shrugged. 'Who knows, maybe even some hard evidence we can use to identify the ringleaders.'

'We can lend you a forensics team,' Hekwyn offered. 'You'd be surprised how many traces people leave behind, even when they think they've covered their tracks completely.'

'Thank you,' Zyvan responded, as though he'd just been offered a cyna bun. 'That would be very helpful. And we can bring in one of our spooks[1] to give the site the once-over too.'

'Assuming we ever manage to find it,' I said, my eyes drawn again to the vast expanse of snowscape represented by the hololithic valley.

Zyvan turned his head to stare straight into the pictcaster. 'You're a remarkably resourceful fellow, Ciaphas. I'm sure you won't let us down.'

---

1. *An Imperial Guard slang term for sanctioned psykers, less pejorative than most, but still surprising coming from a man of Zyvan's rank.*

Well what else was I supposed to say after that? Frak off, you're out of your mind? Tempting as it was, and don't forget that technically as a member of the commissariat I could have done just that, it really wasn't an option. My fraudulent reputation left me with only one possible response, and I gave it, nodding gravely as I did so.

'I'll get right on it,' I said.

TO BE HONEST, the thing I really got right on as soon as I finished my far from satisfactory conversation with the lord general was my bunk, where I remained for the next several hours sleeping off the rigours of the day's journey. Technically by now, I suppose, it would have been the previous day's journey, but the unvarying darkness outside made it hard to keep track, and I really didn't care much in any case. Being an old hive boy I'd grown up believing that light levels (or lack of them) were pretty much constant in any given location, and had found the whole business of day and night something of a wonder the first time I'd found myself on the surface of a planet somewhere; not to mention thoroughly disconcerting until I'd got used to it. So all in all I suppose I found the curious conditions on Adumbria rather less of a strain to adjust to than most of my companions (with the probable exception of Jurgen, who accepted them as phlegmatically as he did everything else).

The result of all this was that by the time I awoke, feeling a great deal better about things and with my aide's distinctive odour wafting into the room laced with the rather more inviting one of fresh tanna, the problem I'd been handed last night seemed a lot less intractable. (Which I like to think proves the wisdom of my course of action. Rushing off to try and organise things while my mind was still clouded with fatigue wouldn't have got us anywhere, or at the very least would have got us to the same place with a great deal more stress and irritation to all concerned.)

'Good morning, sir.' Jurgen's voice joined his odour, and I cranked my eyes open in time to see him place the tray of tea things beside the narrow bed. The room he'd found for me was comfortable enough, as I'd have expected given his almost preternatural talent for scrounging things, but it was a far cry from the standard of luxury I'd grown used to while hanging around in Zyvan's headquarters. (On the other hand, it was a considerable improvement on some of the accommodation I've occupied over the years. Believe me, once you've experienced the hold of an eldar slavers' ship even the most spartan of conditions seem perfectly tolerable.)

'Good morning,' I responded, although the darkness beyond the window was as absolute as ever, relieved only by the faint gleam of arclights in the compound below. The reassuringly familiar sounds of Chimera engines and shouted orders drifted in, even through the double thickness of thermocrys, which at least kept the temperature in here at a reasonable level. 'Any news on the heretic hunt?'

Jurgen shook his head dolefully as he poured the tea. 'No progress to report, sir. Major Broklaw was quite definite on the point when I asked on your behalf.' I could well believe it. Broklaw was a man who'd never seen the point of internalising his frustrations.

'Well, let's see if we can improve his mood,' I said, savouring the first mouthful of tanna. 'The lord general has suggested a rather interesting approach.'

'I'M NOT SAYING it can't be done.' Broklaw stared at the hololithic image of the valley as though wishing he could somehow strangle it. It seemed Jurgen hadn't been exaggerating about his mood; but then, knowing his propensity for literal-mindedness, I'd hardly expected him to be. 'I'm just saying it'll take a long time. Searching an area that size could take weeks, even with an entire platoon on the job. Which we can't spare,' he added hastily, in case I thought that was reasonable.

To his visible relief I nodded. 'I quite agree,' I said. 'Even if we were desperate enough to try it, the chances are the enemy fleet would have arrived here long before we found anything.'

'Then what do you propose?' Kasteen asked levelly. She'd probably had no more sleep than her executive officer, but still managed to project an air of calm authority.

By way of an answer I pointed to the little red dot almost overlapping the contact icon which marked the spot where Sulla had terminated the renegades' journey with such lethal emphasis. 'Sulla was on her way to bless this sensor package, yes?'

Kasteen and Broklaw nodded, not seeing the connection. 'That's right. They've all been malfunctioning since the day we got here.' The colonel looked at me curiously, no doubt wondering if I still needed a few more hours of sleep to clear my brain. 'What with the mining charges going off all the time, and the vibrations from the railway every few hours, I'm amazed we're getting any usable data from them at all.'

'Exactly,' I said, and the two officers glanced at one another, clearly wondering what the procedure was for notifying the Commissariat that my elastic had finally snapped and could they have a sane replacement please. 'And both those things are known events. The mines have records of when their charges were set, and the trains run to a timetable. More or less.'

Expressions of dawning comprehension broke across their faces as they finally realised what had occurred to me in the curious state between sleep and full wakefulness, when the mind makes connections it might otherwise have missed.

'So if we filter out the known interference from the data we've recorded, we might pick up some sign of activity that'll point us in the right direction,' Broklaw said, looking happier than I'd seen him since I'd got up. I nodded.

'We just might,' I said.

Of course it was all far easier said than done, and it took most of our enginseers most of the day to carry out the appropriate rituals. Long before they were finished the drone of their chanting and the choking clouds of incense around their data lecterns had driven all but the hardiest of us from the command centre. Nevertheless, by the evening I was able to report to Zyvan that we'd tentatively identified about a dozen sites where anomalous readings might, just possibly, indicate human activity where no human was meant to be.

'Why did your people miss this in the first place?' he asked, not unreasonably.

I stifled a sneeze, my eyes still sore from the acrid smoke, and tried to look composed. 'They had no reason to look for it. The data was being swamped by other readings, and they were only looking for anomalies on or near the perimeter. Until Lieutenant Sulla ran into that crawler, no one even suspected there might be heretics lurking that far out in the wilderness.'

'Fair enough,' the lord general conceded. Then he smiled. 'I look forward to hearing what you find. I'm sure you're itching to get out there and get stuck in.'

At those words my blood ran as cold as if I was already being exposed to the biting winds that were sure to be howling through the mountain passes, and I suppressed a shiver. If I'd managed to cling to a vestige of hope that I'd be able to stay safe and warm in the command centre while I palmed the dirty work off on some deserving candidate (and I had the perfect one in mind, you can be sure), Zyvan's pleasantry torpedoed it as thoroughly as a battleship swatting a destroyer. If I didn't seem to be leading from the front now I'd lose his confidence, which meant no more bunking up in the lap of luxury the next time I was able to wrangle my way into his headquarters, and no more pleasant social evenings enjoying the genius of his personal chef. So I nodded soberly, like the stoic old warhorse he took me for, and tried not to cough.

'As eager as I always am,' I told him truthfully.

SEVEN

*'The most dangerous thing on the battlefield
is a junior officer with a compass and a map.'*

– General Sulla

GIVEN THE LORD general's personal interest in our little recon sweep and the number of potential sites we had to check, I found it easier than I'd expected to persuade Kasteen and Broklaw to assign a full platoon to carrying it out, along with our entire troop of sentinels. After all, we now had a definite mission to complete. It wasn't as if we'd be wasting our time out there for days on end, casting around searching for nothing in particular.

After some consideration (or at least the show of it) I'd picked Sulla's platoon for this assignment. After all, she'd got us into this mess, so she might as well clean it up too. Not that she saw it like that of course, prattling on about how much she was looking forward to gutting more heretics until I felt like strangling her. Feeling that, on the whole, it would be unwise to give in to the impulse, I decided to risk sticking my head out of the Chimera despite the cold – right then pneumonia seemed distinctly preferable to much more of her conversation.

It was my first real view of the coldside, and despite the sensation of having my face flayed by flying razor blades the moment my head cleared the rim of the top hatch I found it curiously captivating. Up until then all I'd seen of it had been from inside well-lit windows, which the all-pervading blackness turned into mirrors, or within the precincts of Glacier Peak. There, of course, the streets were permanently lined with luminators, supplemented by the light spilling from every building, and all that had done was intensify the darkness surrounding them until it seemed the entire town was enveloped in suffocating velvet.

Out here, though, there was nothing apart from the spotlights of our vehicles to get in the way, and I found myself staring at a night sky littered with stars in a profusion I had seldom seen from the surface of a civilised world. They burned, too, with a cold, hard brightness, which struck from the snows all around us, imparting a faint blue glow to our surroundings.[1] So uniform was this illumination that it cast no shadows except in the deepest of crevices, which appeared by contrast to be maws of the uttermost darkness, exuding a sinister fascination; after all, anything could be lurking inside them undetected. As I considered this I caught sight of a flicker of starlight reflecting from the metallic shell of one of our sentinels, keeping easy pace with us and shining its spotlight into each of the crevices we passed, and the knowledge that we were unlikely to be ambushed by unseen lurkers put my mind as much at ease as was possible under the circumstances. And even if we were, I suppose we wouldn't have had too much to worry about; the firepower of the three walkers and second squad's Chimera a score or so metres behind us, would be more than enough to even the odds.

After some consideration, Kasteen had decided to split our recon force into three, in order to minimise the amount of time it would take to check out all the possible sites we'd identified. That had seemed reasonable enough to me: two full squads and their Chimeras, with a squadron of sentinels for backup, ought to be more than enough to handle the handful of heretics we might expect to find out here. And if we were wrong about that, they'd certainly be strong enough to disengage without any problems and keep the traitors pinned for long enough to call in some backup.

Despite the obvious drawbacks, I'd decided to attach myself to Sulla's command squad for the duration of the mission. For one thing there were only five of them, which meant that even with all the extra vox and sensoria equipment cluttering up the passenger compartment there was still a

---

1. *Adumbria had no moon, which no doubt made them appear even brighter by contrast.*

lot more room for Jurgen and myself than if we'd been jammed in along-side half a score of troopers, and for another I thought we might actually acquire some useful intelligence if I was around to restrain her generally commendable impulse to slaughter everything in sight that was not wear-ing an Imperial uniform. I suppose we could have tagged along in the Salamander, which would probably have helped my mood, but only at the expense of frostbite. One look at the open-topped vehicle was enough to resign me to Sulla's company as by far the lesser of two evils.

'Rooster one to mother hen,' a voice crackled in my comm-bead. After a moment I recognised it as Sergeant Karta, whose recent elevation to the leadership of first squad had opened the way for Magot's problem-atic (and probably temporary, knowing her record) promotion. 'Objective two's a bust. Proceeding to three.'

'Acknowledged, rooster one.' Sulla sounded vaguely affronted, as though the heretics were somehow cheating by not coming out to play according to the plan. It was no surprise to me, though; conditions were hellish out here, the landscape unstable, and the first site on our list had turned out to be nothing more than an icefall of quite epic pro-portions. Our third group, squads four and five, had had no more luck than the rest of us, and the young lieutenant was visibly champing at the bit. (An analogy which occurred quite naturally to me, since her long narrow face bore a distinct resemblance to an irritable horse at the best of times.) I have to say, though, had I realised just how soon her craving for action would be satisfied I would have been considerably less casual about my next remark.

'Stay sharp,' I cut in, more to remind everyone that I was there than because I had anything useful to say. 'Every site we eliminate brings us closer to the real one.' As I spoke I narrowed my eyes against the swirling snow, sure I'd caught a glimpse of yellow light out here where none should be. It could have been nothing, of course, but I didn't get to my second century and an honourable retirement by ignoring the slightest presentiment of danger.

I switched frequencies to the local tacnet, bringing in Sulla, Sergeant Lustig in the other Chimera, and the three sentinel pilots. 'Kill the lights,' I ordered.

'Commissar?' Sulla sounded curious, but the spotlight of our own vehi-cle went out immediately, as did the one on second squad's transport and the sole sentinel I could still see. I peered through the obscuring flurry of whiteness, seeing nothing for a moment, and had almost convinced myself I'd imagined it when the momentary gleam came again.

'There's something out there,' I said, ducking back behind the armour plate, and regaining the blessed warmth of the passenger compartment.

(All right, the temperature had been adjusted by Valhallans, so it was still pretty cool by most objective standards, but after a moment or two outside it felt positively hot.) 'Two o'clock relative, moving slowly.'

'Got it,' the auspex operator confirmed after a moment. 'Big, metallic, heading for town. Doing about forty klom per hour.[1]'

'Captain, if you wouldn't mind?' I asked the comm-bead.

'My pleasure.' Captain Shambas, commander of our sentinel troop, ordered his squadron into the attack with the gusto I'd come to expect from him. 'You heard the man. Last one to bag a heretic buys the beers. And try to leave a couple alive for the commissar to interrogate.'

'Yes, sir.' His flankers acknowledged, and I watched the screen of the auspex tensely as the three dots of the fast-moving sentinels peeled away from us to intercept the contact.

'Tea, sir?' Jurgen appeared at my shoulder, pouring a cup of steaming tanna from the flask he'd produced from one of the equipment pouches he was habitually festooned with. I took it and sipped the warming liquid gratefully.

'Thank you, Jurgen,' I said. The auspex operator flinched away from him, momentarily blocking my view of the display, so I heard rather than saw the engagement begin.

'It's a crawler,' Shambas reported, to my total lack of surprise. 'Looks like an ore truck. Jek, take the tracks.' The distinctive crack of ionising air told me he'd triggered his own multi-lasers an instant ahead of his subordinate's lascannon.

'On it,' Jek acknowledged. A moment later his voice took on a smug note. 'Tracks frakked.'

'They're popping hatches,' a female voice added, an instant ahead of a confused babble of noise. A moment later she was back. 'Sorry commissar. They had a rocket launcher.'

'Can't be helped, Paola,' I said, pleased that the momentary hesitation before I recalled her name had been so slight. But then there were only nine sentinel pilots in the entire regiment, and, in the nature of things, their names tended to cross my desk rather more frequently than most of the other troopers.[2]

---

1. Kilometres per hour.

2. Sentinel pilots are recon specialists, used to acting away from the supervision of their superiors to a far greater extent than most Guard troopers. This tends to breed a casual attitude to correct procedure which, on occasion, can spill over into outright insubordination. A wise commander or commissar, which Kasteen and Cain most definitely were, will recognise their value and accordingly cut them a little more slack.

The third sentinel in the squadron carried a heavy flamer, so there was no point in asking if there'd been any survivors; the gout of burning promethium would have flooded the cab, incinerating anyone inside. 'Better them than one of you.'

'My sentiments exactly,' Shambas said, the bright dots of the sentinels peeling away across the auspex display to rejoin us. A moment later the stationary blip disappeared and a dull *whump* punched its way through the hull to reach our ears.

'Oops,' Paola said, with the flat tone of someone who doesn't really mean it.

I shrugged. 'Well I guess that answers the question of whether they had any more weapons back at the cache,' I said.

'And where it is.' Sulla had been busy at the chart table behind us, and directed my attention to the hololithic image displayed there.

My heart sank. Our position was on a line almost directly between Glacier Peak and the next objective on our list. There could be little doubt that we were heading directly for the heretics' outpost.

'I think you're right,' I said, doing my best to sound casual. I shrank the scale of the holomap to the point where the other two groups appeared, far too far away to have any hope of joining us until long after we'd reached the objective. Sulla watched curiously.

'Do you want me to bring the others up to join us?' she asked. I nodded as though I'd been thinking about it, which of course I hadn't. We knew for certain there were heretics where we were going, so waiting an hour or so to assault them with a full platoon instead of two squads, one of them half strength,[1] was the only sensible thing to do as far as I was concerned. Mildly embarrassing if the outpost turned out to be deserted, of course, but I thought that would be something I could live with.

'That might be prudent,' I said, as though her raising the point had been the thing to make up my mind. 'Normally I'd be inclined to push on and see what's there, just as we planned, but now that we know there's a heretic stronghold of some kind up ahead I'd like to be sure we've got them properly surrounded before we move in. No point in letting any of them slip away if we can avoid it.'

'Of course,' Sulla said, slouching over to the vox unit as though I'd just insisted she finish her homework before she could go out. She gave the orders as crisply and efficiently as any other officer, though, and I was relieved to see both icons respond by changing course to join us.

---

1. *Typically command squads in the Imperial Guard consist of an officer and four troopers, as Cain has already mentioned, instead of the ten soldiers of a line squad.*

Group three (fourth and fifth squads along with Sentinel squadron three) was the closer and had the advantage of clearer terrain to boot, with any luck they'd be with us in half an hour or so. Group one had a crevasse field to negotiate so would take at least twice as long.

As I listened to the brief exchange of messages, however, another thought struck me. Surely there hadn't been time to get another crawler out here, loaded, and halfway back to town in little more than a day? The shipment we'd intercepted was probably a replacement for the one Sulla had destroyed, which meant the heretics manning the outpost had somehow known that it had failed to reach its destination and had dispatched a replacement. And that meant…

'Scan all the frequencies,' I ordered the vox operator, rounding on him so suddenly he visibly started. He hastened to comply, while Sulla watched me curiously.

After a moment the man began to nod. 'I'm getting some traffic,' he said. 'Hard to pin down, but it's local. They're trying to contact someone called Andros.'

'The heretics,' I said. 'They must be trying to raise the crawler.' Which at least meant they hadn't got a call off before Paola toasted them. But since they were too busy being dead to reply, it wouldn't take their friends long to realise something had gone seriously ploin-shaped. Sulla looked at me, an expression of eager expectation on her face, and I nodded slowly. 'We've run out of time.'

'Move in,' she ordered, and the Chimera jerked violently as the driver floored the accelerator. I grabbed the chart table for support and enlarged the scale again to the point where we, the other Chimera, and the trio of sentinels appeared as separate runes. She started to hoist herself up into the cupola, then hesitated. 'Commissar. Would you care to…'

'Ladies first,' I said. 'And I wouldn't want to inhibit your ability to command in any way.' Not to mention stick my head out from inside a nice solid box of armour plate while we engaged Emperor knew how many heavily-armed heretics.

'Thank you.' She shot me a grin and scrambled up into the top hatch. I glanced at the tactical display again. The walkers were pulling ahead, splitting to flank the heretics' position and transmitting what data they could back to our command transport. Grainy images began to form on three pictscreens above our heads, snow and static mingling to render them almost incomprehensible.

'I'm picking up heat sources,' Shambas reported after a moment. 'Could be humans.' Or something like them, I found myself thinking. Not all followers of Chaos qualified any more, if they ever had to begin with. 'No sign of habitation though.'

'I'm guessing it's that.' Jek's pictcaster twisted to settle on a large snowdrift, far too regular to be a natural formation.

One of the Valhallans next to me snickered and hefted her lasgun. 'Shoot the camo party,' she said. I could understand her amusement. If even I thought the mound looked suspicious, to the natives of an ice-world the heretics might just as well have painted it orange and put up a neon sign saying 'We're over here!'.

'I'm sure somebody will,' I assured her, getting a wide grin in return.

'Could just be,' Shambas responded to his subordinate. 'Paola, find anything?'

'They've been busy.' She was over on the other flank, with Jek between her and the captain, which explained why he'd seen the mound first. 'Don't ask me why, but there's a cleared space here the size of a shuttlepad.' Her pictcaster showed me she hadn't been exaggerating – someone had gone to a lot of trouble to clear a large area of rock and level it off. Of course it was knee deep in drifting snow by now, which on a sentinel is roughly up to the chest, but even so it had obviously been prepared with great care. Determining why it had been done, though, would have to wait until we'd taken the place.

We struck with a gratifying amount of surprise, the two laser-armed sentinels striking the dome from the flanks while both Chimeras opened up with their heavy bolters. As the covering of snow boiled away, flashing instantly to steam from the laser hits, I could see the unmistakable outline of a prefabricated hab dome identical to Emperor alone knows how many others scattered across civilised space.[1] Jagged rents were appearing in the rockcrete surface as our bolter shells gouged and chipped away at it.

'Found the main entrance,' Paola voxed, the image from her pictcaster showing a swarm of thickly-bundled figures boiling from it like ants from a kicked-over nest. A bright orange flare of burning promethium gouted from somewhere below the imager, sending them scattering and plugging the gap. I found myself hoping that there was nothing too inflammable beyond it, like another ammo dump. That would be all we needed, another pile of smouldering wreckage in lieu of answers.

'It won't be the only one,' I cautioned, having seen enough of the structures facing us to be familiar with its layout. There would be four in all, equidistantly spaced around the circumference, access to the cargo area opposite the main personnel door Paola had just blocked and two auxiliary ones between them. All, I knew, would be heavily

---

1. *This, of course, is because they're one of the STC artifacts found pretty much anywhere there's a need for them.*

defended; a guess which was confirmed a moment later as our Chimera slewed to a halt, small-arms rounds pattering from the armour plate of its sides. Our turret-mounted bolter traversed to return the favour and the familiar dull roar echoed through the interior of the transport.

'We have to get inside,' Sulla voxed. 'Second squad, disembark and prepare to assault the side entrance.' She was right, unfortunately, the success of our mission depended on penetrating the building and recovering what intelligence we could, but the price was going to be high. Lustig's troopers were going to take some heavy casualties getting past the guards on the door. Worse still, I'd have to go in with them or lose the good opinion of the lord general. I debated internally for a moment whether to join them now and hope I could hang back enough to keep out of the way of the worst of it, or try to make some work for myself in the command Chimera until they'd cleared the way and risk giving the heretics a chance to regroup while I floundered through the snow once the noise had stopped.

Then my nose caught the familiar scent of Jurgen, approaching to retrieve his tanna flask, and a third alternative occurred to me. He was carrying a melta, as was his custom whenever we were expecting to run into trouble (which seemed to be most of the time these days).

I cut into the command circuit. 'Wait a moment,' I said. 'I've had an idea.' After a brief exchange of words with Sulla and the sentinel pilots, I steeled myself as best I could and piled out into the bitter cold, pausing barely long enough to adjust my snow goggles. (I'd been caught in the open without them once before, on Simia Orichalcae, and I wasn't about to make that mistake again.)

The shock of it punched the air from my lungs and left every exposed part of my face stinging like the aftershock of a neural whip, but I kept going by sheer force of will, slogging through the knee-deep snow as if my life depended on it (which of course it did). Jurgen waded after me, sure-footed as only an iceworlder could be in these conditions, and I found his presence as reassuring as always. I glanced around, seeing the looming bulk of second squad's Chimera a few metres away, which felt like kilometres to traverse, and plodded doggedly towards it. So focussed had I become on reaching my goal that I had almost forgotten the presence of the heretic defenders, until a gout of snow flashed into steam a few centimetres ahead of my foot.

I whirled, drawing my laspistol and seeking a target, grateful for once for the black uniform of my office, which would be nicely blurred in the all-pervading darkness. A flicker of motion caught my eye as a heavily-muffled heretic raised a lasgun and I shot him or her through the chest. The heretic fell back, wounded or dead, I couldn't tell and didn't care, and a moment later I gained the lee of the Chimera and the welcome cessation of that pestilential wind.

'We're ready when you are, commissar,' Lustig said, his voice attenuated by the perpetual howling of the gale and the crackle of small-arms fire which told me the sentinels were doing a bang-up job of keeping the defenders busy. I'd got them circling the dome, moving fast so they'd be difficult to hit, and laying down fire as they went. Chances were they wouldn't hit much (except possibly Paola), but that wasn't the point; they'd keep the heretics' heads down nicely, well dug in by the doors, sure they could keep us out indefinitely, which they probably could, under most circumstances. Unfortunately for them we didn't need a door to get inside.

'Whenever you're ready, Jurgen,' I said, after a short dash (for the Valhallans anyway, my progress was a bit slower and a lot less elegant) had brought us level with the gently curving wall.

'Commissar.' He levelled the melta and triggered it, while the rest of us flinched back and protected our eyes from the actinic flash of activation as best we could. The rockcrete burst into vapour, leaving a rapidly-cooling hole just wide enough for a trooper to get through.

'Pyk, Friza.' Lustig directed a couple of troopers through, and they took up position inside covering the corridor in each direction. Nobody shot them so I was next into the building, grateful for the sudden warmth despite the agonising cramps of returning circulation as my sluggish blood rushed back to my extremities. I began to take in our surroundings.

I wasn't sure what I was expecting to find inside, but this certainly wasn't it. Soft carpets covered the floor, growing soggy from the snow flurrying in through the gap, and the walls were covered with murals depicting acts of sensuous depravity which left my mouth momentarily hanging open in stunned surprise. Most of the troopers seemed hypnotised by them, with the single exception of Jurgen; which, given his fondness for porno slates, was quite an astonishing feat of self-control.

'I don't believe that's possible,' Penlan said, with a trace of envy.

'It's not,' I assured her, 'and even if it was it would be against regulations.' A thick, cloying scent was in the air, wrapping itself around my senses like the flimsiest of gossamer scarves, and a nagging sense of familiarity began trying to surface at the back of my mind. As my aide raised the melta and took up his accustomed place at my side, I found my head beginning to clear, although whether this was due to him masking the narcotic musk with his own earthier bouquet or his innate gifts blocking some insidious miasma of warpcraft I couldn't be sure.

In either case the priority now was to get the squad moving, and Jurgen was the key.

'Stay close,' I ordered, getting everyone organised around us, so that however Jurgen was doing it we all got the benefit. As a bonus, that put a fireteam on either side of me, so I wouldn't be the first in the firing line whether the heretics hit us from the front or behind. I got them moving fast enough after that, albeit with a few furtive glances back at the pictures as we left, and to my relief they began to focus on the mission again. 'And stay sharp. We could be facing warpcraft in a place like this, so be ready for anything.' As I'd expected, the prospect of facing sorcery had them so keyed up that I don't think they'd have been distracted by the living embodiment of the murals other than to chuck a frag grenade into the room.

'This reminds me of something,' Jurgen remarked as we advanced cautiously along a corridor decked with soft, colourful wall hangings. 'There's an odd smell in the air I think I recognise.' As always the irony of his words was lost on him. 'Can't quite place it, though.'

'Slawkenberg,' I said, with a sudden rush of realisation. The scent in the air was like the perfume Emeli the Slaaneshi sorceress had worn the night she tried to feed my soul to the monstrosity she worshipped, and a cold chill of dread squeezed my heart. Even after more than a decade (or now, after more than a century, if I'm honest) I still woke from my slumbers occasionally with images of that baleful seductress trying to lure me to my doom resonating in my head, as if the tendrils of Chaos were still reaching out to try to draw me in. I hadn't had that dream in months, though, and an irrational flash of petty resentment at the prospect of further nightmares rippled through my mind.

'Clear.' Penlan ducked back into the corridor after investigating a room full of cushions and pillows which had no discernable function that I could see,[1] and motioned us onwards. I'd been heading directly for the centre of the dome, on the assumption that whatever was going on here would be well protected, and the lack of resistance so far had me on edge. Of course that could just mean that our diversion was working far better than I'd expected it to, but in my experience battle plans seldom survived contact with the enemy.

'That's it. Nothing.' Penlan waved us forward into an empty storage area, bare save for a single luminator and the stained glass mobile beneath it which shifted with the air currents sending ripples of rainbow light around the room. It had clearly been used quite recently, though, as it was free of dust.

---

1. *For a man of the galaxy, as he undoubtedly was, I feel Cain is being a little disingenuous here.*

'Damn.' I hovered by the doorway, mildly irked to find my deduction proven hollow, and nagged by a vague sense of something being wrong about the shape of the room.

It was probably this moment of indecision which triggered what happened next, as I was in Penlan's way as she stepped back, still keeping the space covered like the good soldier she was. Lost in thought and trying to decide which new direction to try, I failed to move out of her way fast enough, nudging her elbow. Her finger tightened reflexively on the trigger of her lasgun, sending a hail of las bolts flying across the room and the rest of the squad diving for what cover they could.

'Sorry.' Her face flamed scarlet, bringing out the old flash burn scar she'd acquired on Gravalax, while her subordinates scrambled to their feet, grinning at the sight of her living up to her nickname.

'No need,' I said, seeing the need to restore her authority without delay. 'It was my fault entirely.'

From somewhere up the corridor I could hear the sound of running feet as someone came to investigate the noise. Great. So much for sneaking around and getting what we'd come for without anyone noticing. 'Everyone inside!'

I spoke not a moment too soon, as las bolts and stubber rounds began to pepper the rockcrete around the doorway and the troopers deployed to meet the new threat. A knot of armed cultists either extravagantly dressed or hardly dressed at all spilled out of the side corridors, getting in each other's way to a most satisfying extent and providing us with a target-rich environment of which my companions immediately took full advantage.

'Overlapping fire lanes. Keep their heads down and we can hold out here indefinitely,' Lustig said.

'That's a comfort,' I told him. 'But I don't think we're going to have to.'

Judging by the voices in my comm-bead, fourth and fifth squads, along with their escorting sentinels, had finally arrived to join the party outside. With the cultists drawn away from the doors to meet the unexpected threat within, Grifen and her troopers were already sweeping aside the sporadic resistance left around the main cargo bay and pouring into the dome.

I motioned to Jurgen. 'If you wouldn't mind clearing the corridor?'

'With pleasure, commissar.' My aide grinned at me as he levelled the melta. 'I'm afraid I forgot the marshmallows again, but heretics toast better anyway.' He squeezed the trigger and a gout of thermal energy ravened its way down the narrow passage, vaporising everything in its path in a most satisfying manner. The few surviving heretics shrieked and ran, and a moment later a crackle of lasguns told me they'd stumbled into fourth squad.

'Try to take a couple alive,' I reminded everyone again, and was reassured a moment later by Magot's cheery tone.

'Don't worry, sir. Got one here in one piece. She's leaking a bit, but she'll survive.'

'Good,' I said, feeling that things were finally beginning to go our way. Lustig and the troopers were already following up the opening Jurgen had made, running up the gently steaming passageway heedless of the damage the occasional greasy patch of heretic residue was doing to their boots, eager to fall on the defenders at the main door from behind. I was happy to leave them to it; I had no intention of putting myself in the way of any stray rounds at this stage of the game if I could help it.

I was just turning away to follow a little more sedately when I noticed something odd about the wall where Penlan's las bolts had hit. They'd penetrated it completely, whereas the las-bolts the heretics had been shooting at us had been stopped completely by the outer wall of the room. Suddenly the nagging sense of wrongness I'd felt about the shape of the space made sense to me; there was a false partition here, designed to conceal something.

Dismissing my first impulse to let Jurgen solve the problem with his melta, in case it took any crucial evidence directly to the Emperor along with the wall, I cast about carefully for some kind of panel or catch, feeling absurdly like the hero of a haunted house melodrama. I could find no trace of one, however, and at last I motioned him forwards, hoping that the weapon wouldn't do too much damage to whatever was behind the partition.

'Wait,' I said, just as he raised the melta and prepared to fire it. For some reason, perhaps the way his shadow fell across the wall, the outline of a panel had suddenly become visible.[1] I looked at it more closely, wondering how I could possibly have missed something so obvious, and within moments had determined the method of opening it.

'Emperor on Earth!' We both reeled back, gagging from the stench which poured out of the narrow space, and after a moment spent recovering our breath we leaned forward cautiously to peer inside. Jurgen produced a luminator from somewhere and shone it round the room thus revealed.

The first things we noticed were probably the bodies, how many we couldn't tell, flesh and bone seared and warped by sorceries I didn't want

---

[1]. *More likely he was masking some concealing sorcerous illusion. No doubt someone from the Ordo Malleus could explain the principles, if anyone cares.*

to imagine. Most disconcerting of all was that what remained of the faces bore expressions of what I can only describe as insane ecstasy. Jurgen, imperturbable as ever, swept the luminator beam around the walls, picking out arcane sigils which made my eyes hurt and compelled my gaze to skitter away like waterfowl bouncing from a frozen pond.

'Don't think much of the decor,' he said, with commendable understatement.

I nodded, swallowing hard. 'There have been foul sorceries done here,' I said. 'The question is, what and why?'

'I'm afraid I wouldn't know, sir,' my aide replied, taking the remark as literally as he did everything else.

'Neither would I, thank the Emperor,' I said. This was a job for Zyvan's tame psykers, and no business of honest men. Or me. I turned away with a sense of profound relief. 'Close it up and leave it for the experts.'

'With pleasure, sir,' Jurgen said, leaving the chamber of horrors as rapidly as he could and helping me manhandle the access panel back into place with almost indecent haste. Recalling the trouble I'd had finding it in the first place, I unwound the scarlet sash of my office from around my waist and wedged it into the gap before closing it, so that it hung from the wall like a jaunty flag.

'There,' I said. 'That should do it.' To my surprise the simple job had left me trembling with reaction, as though exhausted.[1] I had little time to muse on this, though, because Sulla was yelling in my comm-bead.

'Commissar! They're abandoning the dome.'

'Say again?' I asked, unable to credit what I'd been hearing. There was nowhere else for the surviving heretics to go out here, and insane as they undoubtedly were, choosing to freeze to death rather than surrender or die fighting didn't make any sense at all. Then the idea of a suicide bomb flashed into my mind, and I was running full tilt for the nearest exit. 'Everybody outside!' I yelled. 'They may have rigged the place to blow!'

In fact they hadn't, but the fear of it leant wings to my feet so that I was outside in time to be as startled as the rest of us.

'Incoming arial contact, closing fast!' the auspex operator cut in, his voice tense. I narrowed my eyes against the flurrying snow, fitting the goggles into place and wiping them clear with trembling fingers. A small knot of heretics was wading through the drifts towards the clear area, exchanging sporadic fire with fifth squad and trying to keep the swooping sentinels at bay with what looked to me like a couple of krak

---

1. More likely this was due to the psychic shock of being so close to the residues of sorcery.

missile launchers. They weren't having much luck, but they were managing to hold them back out of effective flamer and multi-laser range and I could see why Shambas hadn't ordered his pilots to close the distance. The traitors were obviously finished now, and they might as well wait for them to run out of rockets before moving in.

The shriek of powerful engines tore through the skies overhead, and a vast, dark shape blotted out the starlight as it passed.

'It's a cargo shuttle,' Jurgen pointed out unnecessarily. 'Where did they get one of those from?' It was a good question, but academic at the moment.

'Target their engines.' Sulla ordered, an instant before I could, but it would be a futile gesture at best. Even a civilian shuttle is ruggedly built, and a couple of lascannons and a handful of heavy bolters won't do much more than scratch the paintwork.

'Frak that,' Shambas retorted. 'Jek, Karis, go for the flight deck.' The two designated sentinels reared back on their haunches for maximum elevation and spat luminescent death at the approaching shuttle. It was a desperate gamble, and for a moment I thought they might just do it, but the armourcrys protecting the cockpit is tough enough to take the stresses of re-entry; even a couple of lascannon bolts wouldn't be enough to penetrate it. One struck home, however, leaving a vivid thermal bloom across the previously transparent surface, and the two sentinel pilots began a good-natured argument about which one of them had inflicted it.

It was enough to break the shuttle pilot's nerve, however, and the engine noise rose in pitch as the main boosters ignited, powering it back up towards wherever it had come from in the first place. A howl of disappointment rose from the little knot of heretics as they watched their expected deliverance disappear as suddenly as it had arrived, then, as the followers of Chaos so often do, they began to argue bitterly among themselves. One group threw down their weapons and began to trudge wearily back towards the dome, their hands in the air, while the others began firing at the encircling troopers with even greater desperation than before. And, inevitably, some of them began to gun down those of their fellows who were attempting to surrender.

I watched for a few moments, until the inevitable conclusion had played itself out, before trudging back to the command Chimera more troubled than I would have believed possible before setting out on this assignment. True, we'd found what we were looking for, but instead of giving us answers, it just seemed to have opened the way to even more questions.

Editorial Note:

As so often in his memoirs, Cain's tendency to elide the details of what he regards as uninteresting threatens to deprive what follows of some much-needed context. I have accordingly felt the need to insert some additional material at this point, which I hope will prove illuminating.

From *Sablist in Skitterfall: a brief history of the Chaos incursion* by Dagblat Tincrowser, 957 M41

DESPITE THE FEARS which understandably gripped most of the world in the weeks following the heretics' daring and unexpected attacks upon the newly-arrived expeditionary force, the traitors chose not to show their hand again for some time. With hindsight we can quite clearly see that this was simply because their short-term objectives had been met; the security forces were compelled to waste incalculable man hours and precious resources preparing for a campaign of guerilla warfare which never materialised, and the longer it failed to do so the more firmly convinced those in authority became that this was because the cults they were facing were small, weak and poorly organised.

This impression was abruptly dispelled by Commissar Cain's personal discovery of a hidden shuttle pad, cunningly concealed on the coldside within easy striking distance of Glacier Peak. It became instantly apparent that the conspiracy was far stronger and more organised than had previously been suspected, and that all they had done before was with the aim of diverting attention from this most insidious of threats. Who knew how many of their confederates had managed to infiltrate Adumbria undetected, and what manner of vileness they'd brought with them? Indeed, it would be no exaggeration to say that many within the Council of Claimants became convinced that the vanguard of the enemy fleet was already among us, awaiting their moment to strike.

Such a prognosis was, of course, needlessly alarmist, but there were few on Adumbria, and even fewer among the Imperial forces ranged in its defence, prepared to discount the possibility entirely.

To: The Office of the Lord General, by the grace of His Most Divine Majesty, protector of that part of the Holy Dominions known as the Damocles Gulf and Adjacent Sectors to Spinward.

From: Commissar Tomas Beije, charged by the Office of the Commissariat with the maintenance of True Fighting Spirit among his most loyal and fervent warriors of the Tallarn 229th.

My lord general,
I have received this day, 273 937 M41, your recent communiqué regarding the discoveries made by my colleague Ciaphas Cain and his rabble of a regiment, and perused it with interest. You may rest assured that in the opinion of both myself and Colonel Asmar, there is absolutely no likelihood of a similar rebel foothold being established on the so-called 'hotside' of Adumbria under the very noses of His Divine Majesty's most loyal and fervent warriors.

Nevertheless, as you are at pains to point out, additional caution is never a bad thing; I have accordingly given my approval to Colonel Asmar's proposal to widen the range of our perimeter patrols by up to five kilometres and have urged the priests of our company to say additional benedictions invoking the Emperor's guidance of their footsteps. In the unlikely event of such heretical deviants polluting that part of the divinely-appointed realm given over to our charge, our soldiers will undoubtedly be led straight to them by The Emperor's Grace as a result of this intercession.

I trust that this will prove sufficient to ensure the success of our Holy task.

Tomas Beije, Regimental Commissar.

Thought for the day: Faith is the strongest shield.

EIGHT

'Hope for the best, but prepare for the worst.'

– Imperial Guard tactical manual

It was a grim little group we made as we convened in a conference suite at the lord general's headquarters, virtually identical to the one we'd been using when our last meeting had been so rudely interrupted. Fortunately the hotel he'd commandeered possessed several, so the partial demolition of the other one during the heretics' botched attempt to assassinate Zyvan had turned out to be a minor inconvenience at best: in the manner of plush hotels across the galaxy it was almost impossible to tell the difference between the two rooms. Even the little side table of refreshments was in the same place I remembered it.

There were a number of significant details which had changed, though, the most noticeable one being the fact that we were now on the ground floor and a battery of Hydras were parked outside with orders to shoot anything that crossed the perimeter no matter how authentic its clearances seemed. The sight of the anti-aircraft guns reminded me of the earlier incident and I asked how the enquiries into that were progressing.

'Slowly,' Zyvan admitted, helping himself to a cyna bun from the table in the corner. Famished from the trip back from Glacier Peak, which had been undertaken with gratifying speed aboard a flyer dispatched to collect me by the lord general himself, I lost no time in following his example. 'We arrested the owner of the aircar, of course, but he maintains that it was stolen without his knowledge.'

'I suppose he would,' I said. 'Anyone we know?'

'Ventrious,' Zyvan said, to my complete surprise. The aristocrat had struck me as a pompous idiot, of course, and a damn sight too eager for power, but that pretty much summed up the entire breed in my experience, and try as I might I couldn't picture the red-faced buffoon I'd seen throwing a tantrum in the council chamber as a Slaaneshi cultist. He'd have looked ridiculous in pink, for a start.

'And you're satisfied with his story?' I asked.

Zyvan nodded. 'Our interrogators were very thorough. If he knew anything he would have told us.' I didn't doubt it, and said so. Zyvan smiled bleakly. 'Under any normal circumstances I would have agreed with you. But we were dealing with the possibility of warpcraft, remember. I had to be sure his memories were real ones.'

'I see,' I said, shuddering in spite of myself. I nodded cordially to the colourless young man in neatly-pressed fatigues devoid of insignia who Zyvan hadn't bothered to introduce. Hekwyn, Vinzand and Kolbe were all seated as far away from him as they reasonably could be, and I must say I didn't blame them. I'd met psykers before, and it had rarely ended well. Luckily I'd dispatched Jurgen to prepare my quarters immediately on our arrival, so there was no possibility of his secret being abruptly revealed by accident; I made a mental note to keep him as far away from the lord general's staff as possible, since there was no telling how many other mind-readers he had lurking about the premises.

'His mind was intact,' the young psyker assured me. 'At least to begin with.' He must have read something of what I was thinking on my face, because he smiled without humour. 'I was as careful as I could be. He'll recover, more or less.'

'Sieur Malden is one of the most capable sanctioned psykers on my staff,' Zyvan said.

I nodded again. 'I'm sure he is,' I agreed. Like I said, I've met several, albeit not exactly socially in most cases, and Malden (I noted the use of the civilian honorific as protocol demanded)[1] was clearly one of the sharpest

---

1. *Like commissars, enginseers, and other specialists attatched to Imperial Guard forces, sanctioned psykers are technically not part of the military command structure. This is probably because no sane officer would be willing to take responsibility for them.*

blades in the scabbard. Rakel, Amberley's tame telepath, for instance, was as barmy as a jokero and made about as much sense most of the time.[1]

Now you might think that someone with as much to hide as I have would have been terrified at the prospect of sharing a conference table with a telepath, but one thing I'd picked up about them over the years was that they're not going to be listening to your deepest, darkest secrets. Not without trying very hard, anyway.

Rakel once told me in one of her more lucid moments that catching stray thoughts from the people around her was like trying to pick a single voice out of a crowded ballroom, and even then it was just the surface thoughts she could detect. Going deeper takes a lot of effort and concentration, almost as dangerous to the psyker as the person they're trying to read, and for someone as practiced as I was at dissembling there was nothing on the surface for them to pick up on anyway.

'I've been to the installation you found,' Malden told me, his voice curiously toneless, which at least matched his appearance. The only word which fitted him was 'nondescript'. I must have been in the same room as him scores of times over the years, but I still can't recall his height, build, or the colour of his eyes and hair. 'I found the experience... interesting.'

I felt a faint tingling in the air, like the charge before a thunderstorm, and the hololith flickered into life without anyone touching the controls. Vinzand and Kolbe both flinched, no doubt muttering prayers to the Emperor under their breath, and I noticed the faint smile, genuine this time, which Malden almost succeeded in masking. Only Hekwyn failed to react, no doubt inured to unpleasant surprises as a result of his duties with the arbites.

'That's not quite the word I would have chosen,' I said casually, determined not to give him the satisfaction of seeming in any way disconcerted.

'Really?' The young psyker's eyes drifted towards me. 'What word would you have used?'

'Terrifying,' I admitted. 'It reminded me...' I glanced at the trio at the end of the table, and Zyvan nodded.

---

1. *In defence of my psyker I have to say that Cain exaggerates a little. Rakel isn't the easiest of people to get along with, and her conversation, not to mention her thought processes, do take some getting used to, but she's not completely insane. Besides, her medication is generally quite effective. As to the jokaero, whether they're actually sentient enough for the concept of sanity to be in any way meaningfully applied to them is still a subject of much debate in the Ordo Xenos.*

'Under the circumstances you can take it that everyone in this room is cleared for any information you may wish to contribute,' he said. 'Even that pertaining to the nature of Chaos.' I nodded soberly, conscious of the expressions on the three men's faces; a peculiar mixture of curiosity and apprehension. They all knew they were about to hear things that few citizens of the Imperium were ever made privy to, and were not exactly sure that they wanted to know them.

'Some years ago,' I began, 'I encountered a coven of Slaaneshi cultists, who were attempting to create a daemonhost.'[1] Kolbe almost choked on his recaff and Vinzand went pale, even for an Adumbrian. Hekwyn raised an eyebrow a millimetre or two and began to look marginally more interested. 'There was something about that hab dome which reminded me of them.'

'What happened to the daemonhost?' Hekwyn asked.

I shrugged. 'Destroyed, I assume. I called in an artillery barrage and levelled the place.' Almost killing myself in the process, I might add.

Malden nodded once. 'That might work,' he said with a casualness which only intensified my unease.

'Excuse me.' Vinzand coughed hesitantly. 'When you say create a daemonhost, you mean…' he waved his hands vaguely. 'I'm sorry, I'm rather new to all this.'

'They were summoning a daemon from the warp and confining it in a host body,' I explained, trying not to remember that the body in question had been one of the Guard troopers accompanying me. He still looked baffled, so after a sidelong glance at Zyvan for an almost imperceptible nod of approval I elaborated a little. 'Daemons are creatures of the warp, and draw their power from it. But dangerous as they are, they can't exist in the material universe for long without being drawn back to where they came from.' And a good thing too, if the ones I'd encountered before were anything to go by. 'Trapping it in a mortal body allows it to remain here, although its powers are diminished, and it's usually under the control of whoever summoned it in the first place.'

'Up to a point,' Malden agreed, and I deferred to his greater knowledge of warpcraft with relief. 'Any control over it is tenuous at best. You'd have to be insane to try it.'[2] He shrugged. 'But the commissar is substantially correct. The only other way for a daemon to interact with the materium for a prolonged period is to find a world or a region of

---

1. *Cain's account of the incident forms one of the shorter fragments of the archive, and need not concern us at this juncture.*

2. *Or a Radical member of the Ordo Malleus, which pretty much amounts to the same thing.*

space where the two realms intersect one another. Fortunately such places are rare.'

'The Eye of Terror,' I said, making the sign of the aquila as I spoke.

Malden nodded again. 'The vast majority are there,' he said. 'And the few exceptions are interdicted by the Inquisition.'[1]

'Who are far better qualified to worry about such things than we are,' Zyvan said, dragging the meeting back to the point at last. Knowing a little more about the Inquisition and its methods than he did I had my doubts about that, but if I voiced them it might have been bad for my health, so I said nothing and waited for Malden to turn back to the hololith. Just for once the image was still and crystal clear, and I found myself staring at a perfect miniature replica of the hideous chamber I'd discovered behind the wall.

'What are those symbols?' Kolbe asked, trying not to look too hard at them. I couldn't blame him for that as I was doing the same thing myself, although their hololithic representations were far less disconcerting than the real things had been.

'Some of them are wards,' Malden replied. 'If you wanted my best guess, I'd say that something had been confined in there. Something touched by the warp.' This time, I noticed, mine wasn't the only hand which moved reflexively to invoke the Emperor's protection.

'And the others?' I asked.

For the first time the young psyker seemed unsure of himself. 'I've never seen anything like them before,' he admitted reluctantly. 'My best guess would be to channel warp energy, perhaps to summon something.' He shrugged. 'The warp currents around here are strange enough at the best of times. You'd be better off asking a navigator or an astropath, to be honest. It's more their department than it is mine.'

'Perhaps they were trying to affect the flow of the currents,' Kolbe suggested. 'To speed up their invasion fleet or delay your reinforcements.'

'That would make sense,' Zyvan conceded, nodding slowly in a manner which told me just how much he didn't like that idea. 'I'll discuss it with the senior representative of the Navis Nobilitae.' It went without saying that the navigator of his flagship wouldn't lower himself to converse directly with the likes of us, and I have to say I was heartily glad of that fact. They're spooky little bastards at the best of times, and snobbier than a planetary governor with a

---

1. *Unfortunately it's generally impossible to pronounce Exterminatus on a so-called daemon-world, since, being outside time and space in the conventional sense, tried and tested methods such as virus bombing are at best ineffective and at worst counter-productive; the last thing you want to do in such a case is give them ideas.*

pedigree going back to before Horus. And on top of that they can kill you with a look. Literally.

'What about the bodies?' Vinzand asked, looking at them with a visible effort.

'Lunch?' I suggested. 'For whatever was stuck in there?'

Malden favoured me with a smile which actually contained a modicum of warmth. 'Possibly,' he conceded. 'Or something to pass the time. But my guess would be a sacrifice. Heretics are big on sacrifice, especially when they're summoning things.'

'Maybe one of the prisoners we took can tell us,' I said.

We'd ended up with half a dozen relatively intact specimens in the end, which wasn't a bad haul, and Hekwyn's promised experts from the Arbites were crawling over the entire dome looking for Emperor knows what, so at last it looked as though we were getting somewhere.

'Perhaps,' Zyvan said.

I raised an eyebrow. 'I thought your interrogators would have extracted everything they knew by now.'

'They appear to be unusually resilient. Some of them even seem to be enjoying themselves.'

'In the meantime,' Hekwyn said, with an audible sigh of relief as the hololith clicked off, 'we have at least been able to start rounding up the smuggling ring from the Glacier Peak end.' He favoured me with a smile and a nod of the head. 'Despite my scepticism, it seems Commissar Cain's assessment of the situation wasn't too wide of the mark after all. He just assumed the weapons were flowing into the town from Skitterfall instead of the other way round.'

'I'm pleased to hear your confidence in the security of the starport was justified,' I replied graciously.

'Up to a point.' The arbitrator frowned. 'The shuttle you scared off must have come from somewhere. My guess is it was one of the freighters in orbit.'

'We're already combing the traffic control records,' Vinzand chipped in. 'But with thousands of shuttle flights a day, it won't be easy to track. Let alone the previous landings.'

'If it's even one of those,' Kolbe suggested gloomily. 'Perhaps it came from one of the raiders, lurking in the outer system.'

'No.' Zyvan shook his head decisively. 'If there was a Chaos ship here already we would have detected it when we dropped out of warp. And our pickets would have intercepted anything emerging into realspace once we got here that wasn't in one of the shipping lanes.' I remembered the myriad of dancing lights I'd seen from the observation window of the *Emperor's Benificence*, and didn't envy whoever got the job of trying to identify which of them was our smuggler.

'Do we have any more of an idea when the raiders are due?' I asked.

The lord general shook his head again. 'Three to twelve days is the best estimate the navigators can give me. Assuming General Kolbe isn't right about their confederates on the coldside having found a way of speeding up the warp currents, of course.'

'Then we'd better assume they'll be here any time,' Kolbe said. He seemed surprisingly happy at the prospect, until it dawned on me that all this talk of daemons and warpcraft had him thoroughly spooked and he was grabbing the opportunity of returning the conversation to matters he understood with unconcealed alacrity. 'I'll put all our PDF units on full alert the moment I return to my headquarters.'

'A wise precaution,' Zyvan said, activating the hololith the traditional way by pressing the runes on the lectern and thumping it with his fist until it sputtered into life. This time the image was as fuzzy as usual, which I found vaguely reassuring, the almost preternatural clarity of the images Malden had shown us bringing back the sense of unease I'd felt in the habdome. A three-dimensional image of the planet appeared, with hundreds of green dots indicating the presence of the PDF forces arrayed in its defence. Most were in the shadow belt, of course, clustered most thickly around major population centres and sites of strategic importance, although a few were scattered across the hotside and coldside, where towns and other installations made convenient spots to place a garrison in the unforgiving landscapes.

After a moment of studying the coldside I was able to find Glacier Peak and the reassuring amber rune which marked the presence of my own regiment, although the handful of similar icons making up the rest of our expeditionary force were all but lost in the rash of PDF locations. The Valhallan tanks were easy to find of course, being overlaid on Skitterfall, and the Tallarns stood out reasonably clearly in the sparsely-garrisoned hotside, but I had to search for some time before I found either of the Kastaforean regiments. It was a sobering moment.

'How long before the reinforcements arrive?' I asked.

'Five to eighteen days, according to the last message we received.' Zyvan hesitated a moment before going on. 'And that was three days ago.'

'Three days?' Vinzand asked, the quiver of apprehension in his voice fortunately drawing everyone's attention and saving me the bother of controlling my own expression. The palms of my hands were tingling, which never augurs anything good. 'I was under the impression that you received updates on their deployment every twenty-four hours.'

'Normally that's true,' Zyvan admitted, with the expression of a man sucking a bitterroot. 'But our astropaths have been unable to get through to the rest of the fleet.'

'They say there seems to be some kind of disturbance in the warp,' Malden chipped in helpfully, which did absolutely nothing to calm my fears, I can assure you. Clearly whatever the cultists had been up to in Glacier Peak (apart from stockpiling Emperor alone knew how much lethal ordnance, which was bad enough) had succeeded. What that was I had no idea, but I knew enough about the Great Enemy to know that it would be nothing good, and just hoped I wouldn't be the one to find out the hard way. (A hope in which I was to be grievously disappointed, as things turned out.)

'So we're on our own until further notice,' Zyvan concluded.

Kolbe squared his shoulders. 'My men won't let you down, lord general. They might lack the experience of your Guardsmen, but they're fighting for their homes. That makes up for a lot.'

'I don't doubt it,' Zyvan said, although probably only I knew him well enough to see that he wasn't entirely convinced.

'What worries me is that we're spread so thinly,' I said without thinking, then realising what I'd said I carried on as smoothly as if I'd never meant to pause. 'If we're going to back up General Kolbe's troops effectively, we'll need to deploy as soon as we know where they're coming under pressure. By the time the dropships get down to us, loaded and away, we'll just turn up in time to join in with the victory parade.' Or bury the bodies, more likely, but saying that wouldn't be tactful. I didn't have to anyway – Zyvan knew the score well enough to know what I meant.

'I've been thinking about that,' he said. The image of the planet in the hololith shrank to make room for a couple of icons in orbit above the capital. His flagship and the *Emperor's Benificence*, I assumed. I was correct as it turned out, as his next act was to point out the troopship. 'Holding the dropships in reserve as I'd intended won't help, as the commissar has just pointed out. They'll be sitting waterfowl in orbit once the enemy fleet arrives anyway.'

'So what's the alternative?' Vinzand asked, probably only just realising that all those civilian starships above us would be giving the raiders some easy target practice on the way in as well.

Zyvan sighed. 'Five dropships, five regiments. I'm attaching one to each. That way at least one company can be ready to deploy in a matter of moments. With a bit of luck they can ferry Guard reinforcements in to wherever they're needed, and return to the staging area for another load.' He looked at me, thinking he could read my reaction in my face, and shrugged. 'I know, Ciaphas. It's a messy option, but it's the best we can do.'

'I suppose it is,' I said, trying to sound grave. It would leave the lucky company in question out on a limb, of course, but a formation that size ought to be able to take care of itself until the second or third run arrived. More to the point, all I had to do was find an excuse to stick close to the dropship and I'd have a way off the planet if things went sour, which they looked very like doing at that point. All in all things seemed to be getting a bit brighter so far as I was concerned.

I should have known better, of course.

NINE

'His loyalty couldn't be bought at any price;
but it could be rented remarkably cheaply.'

– Inquisitor Allendyne, after the execution of
Rogue Trader Parnis Vermode for trafficking
in interdicted xenos artifacts

JURGEN, EFFICIENT AS ever, had managed to get my personal effects
neatly stowed in the suite I'd occupied on my last sojourn in the lord
general's headquarters, so once the conference finally broke up I lost no
time in heading back there to avail myself of a hot bath, a good meal
and a large soft bed, in that order. About the only thing missing was
some feminine company, which would have rounded things off nicely,
and as I drifted into sleep I found myself wondering what Amberley
was doing at that moment.[1] That should have led to some very pleasant dreams, but seeing that damned hololith of the chamber I'd found
in the heretics' hab dome had apparently stirred up deeper, less pleasant memories, and my slumbers were to be far from restful.

---

1. *Shooting my way past a ridiculous number of inordinately persistent hrud, if I've worked
out the dates correctly.*

As I've mentioned before, I still had occasional nightmares about my earlier encounter with a nest of Slaaneshi cultists. Usually vague, formless things in which I felt my sense of self slipping once again under the psychic assault of the sorceress Emeli, who would appear as an insubstantial wraith as a rule, urging me on to damnation until I would wake with a shudder, entangled in sweat-soaked bedding. This time, however, the dreams were lucid, and vivid, and remained with me on waking, so that even now I can recall them in some detail.

It began in her chambers, where she'd lured me with her sorcerous wiles, my mind clouded by the air of sensuous luxury which had quite disarmed my companions.[1] In the manner of dreams, the room was exactly as I recalled it, small details I had barely noticed at the time standing out vividly, but with the perspective curiously distorted so that it seemed to be without physical boundaries. Emeli was reclining on the bed, half out of the green silk gown which so closely matched her eyes, smiling at me enticingly, drawing me towards her as she had before. Unlike the reality, however, the ugly crater of the laspistol wound was already clearly visible, punched through her torso, where I'd broken the spell she'd placed on my mind by the most desperate and direct method I could.

'You're dead,' I told her, aware as you sometimes are that you're dreaming, but somehow unable to reject the experience as entirely unreal.

Her smile widened. 'I'm coming back,' she replied, as though it were the most natural thing in the galaxy, and once again I felt drawn towards her, desire and revulsion mingling within me until I could barely tell them apart. 'Then I'll taste your soul as I promised.'

'I don't think so,' I said, reaching for my laspistol as I had in life, only to find that the holster had vanished, along with the rest of my clothing. Emeli laughed, the familiar enchanting trill of it drawing me in, and opened her arms to embrace me. I tried to pull away, panic flaring, and her face began to change, flowing into something I didn't dare to look upon but was powerless to turn aside from, more beautiful and terrifying than the mind was meant to perceive.

'Are you all right, sir?'

I woke abruptly, my heart hammering in my chest, to find Jurgen standing by the light switch, his lasgun in his hands. 'You were shouting something.'

'Just a dream,' I said, staggering to the decanter of amasec and downing a hefty slug, far more hastily than so fine a bottle deserved. I

---

1. *His account of the actual incident leads me to suspect that he wasn't quite as taken in as he says here.*

poured a second and drank it a little more carefully. 'About that witch on Slawkenberg.'

'Oh.' My aide nodded once, his own memories of the incident no doubt prompted by my words. 'Bad business, that.' And it would have been a great deal worse had it not been for his peculiar talent, which, at the time, we were both blissfully unaware of. He shrugged. 'Still. Dreams never hurt anyone, did they sir?'

'Of course not.'

I didn't feel like sleeping any more, though, and began to get dressed. 'Do you think you could find me some recaff?'

'Right away, sir.' He slung the lasgun over his shoulder and turned to leave the room, barely suppressing a yawn, and I realised for the first time that I must have woken him; he'd commandeered a sofa in the lounge of the suite, which I was using as an office and which was the other side of the bathroom. Some nightmare if he'd heard me from that far away, I thought.

'Better get some for yourself, too,' I added. 'You look as though you need it.'

'Very good, sir.' He nodded once. 'Will you be requiring breakfast?'

I wasn't sure, to be honest, still queasy from the nightmare and the amasec, which was beginning to look like rather a bad idea now that it had reached my head, but I nodded too. 'Something light,' I said, confident that he knew my tastes well enough and that I could trust his judgement better than my own at the moment. 'And whatever you feel like as well.' As he left and his distinctive aroma followed him from the room, I found myself trying to think of a reason to call him back.

This is ridiculous, I told myself firmly. I was an Imperial commissar, not a frightened juvie. I tied my sash tightly, placed my cap squarely on my head and tried not to feel quite so relieved when I'd buckled my weapon belt around my waist.

Nevertheless, as I walked through to the lounge area, fastidiously negotiating the litter of half empty plates around Jurgen's couch, I found myself wondering if what I'd experienced had been more than just a dream. Could some psychic residue of the cultists' ritual have crawled inside my head in the chamber I'd discovered?

The idea was so disconcerting I found myself on the verge of voxing Malden right then and there to ask if it was feasible. Then reason reasserted itself. For one thing, I'd had Jurgen with me the whole time, and I knew for a fact that nothing like that could possibly have happened in his presence, and for another raising the possibility was the surest way I could think of to have the young psyker rummaging around in my head before you could say 'The Emperor Protects.' And the thought of that, you can be sure, was enough to snap me out of my stupor post-haste. Apart from my own discreditable secrets, which I was keen enough not to have anyone else privy to, there was enough sensitive information about Inquisition resources and contacts cluttering up my mind to sign my death warrant ten times over[1] if they became known to anyone else.

Once I'd realised that it was quite enough to put a couple of bad dreams firmly into perspective, and by the time Jurgen returned pushing a trolley laden with comestibles (having taken my injunction to pick up anything he liked as literally as he did pretty much everything else), I was already at my desk wading through the routine paperwork. It might seem strange, given the momentous events I'd been discussing only a few hours before, but it continued to accumulate regardless. Troopers are troopers, after all, and if the enemy isn't obliging enough to keep them entertained they'll find their own amusements.

Now breakfast had arrived I found myself surprisingly hungry and managed to put a fair-sized dent in the stack of ackenberry waffles Jurgen had thoughtfully selected for me. Watching him eat was not an activity for the faint-hearted, so I returned to my desk where I could ignore everything but the sound effects, and was thus in a position to answer the vox myself almost as soon as the first chime sounded.

'Cain,' I said crisply, trying not to notice the choking sound as Jurgen attempted to mask his outrage at the breach of protocol. He took it as an Emperor-given right to filter my incoming messages, deflecting the vast majority with apparently inexhaustible patience and obstinacy, for which I was normally heartily grateful. This morning, however, I needed whatever distractions I could get, the echoes of the nightmare still leaving me on edge, and felt that for once he might as well finish his breakfast in peace.

'Commissar,' Hekwyn said, sounding surprised. 'I thought you'd still be sleeping.'

'I might say the same about you,' I said, wondering why he would be calling me this early in the day. Nothing good, I suspected.

'"The Imperium never sleeps"[2],' he quoted with a tinge of wry amusement in his voice. 'And something's come up I thought you might be interested in.' If I'd realised at the time just what this innocuous remark was going to lead to I would have cut him off with the first excuse I

---

1. *Once would have been sufficient.*

2. *The catchphrase of Arbitrator Foreboding, a popular holo character of the time, who battled criminals, heretics and mutants with relish and a very big gun.*

could think of and gone scuttling back to the relative safety of Glacier Peak, and to hell with the cold. At the time, though, I thought any distraction would do to lift my mood, and settled back in my chair to listen.

'Sounds intriguing,' I said. 'What have you been up to?'

'A bit of old-fashioned detective work,' Hekwyn said. 'Or at least watching the local praetors do some. They've picked up one of the middlemen in the smuggling operation you uncovered.'

'I'm impressed,' I said, meaning it for once.

Hekwyn's voice sounded quietly smug. 'It wasn't that hard. As you suggested, we took a look at people with access to the rail wagons going in and out of Glacier Peak. And frak me if there wasn't a freight dispatcher spending three times his annual income on obscura and joygirls.'

'And does this paragon of virtue have a name?' I asked.

'Kimeon Slablard. We've got him in a holding cell at the moment, thinking about all the terrible things that can happen to citizens who don't cooperate with the authorities in a properly public-spirited manner.' That made sense. If he was just a cat's-paw he'd probably spill his guts at the first opportunity, and making him sweat first would only help. If, on the other hand, he was part of the cult, he'd take as long to break as the ones we already had in custody and an hour or two's delay in getting started wouldn't make any perceptible difference. 'I thought you might like to sit in. Once he realises he's in the ordure with the Guard as well, he should snap like a twig.'

'It's worth a try,' I said. I risked a glance at Jurgen and decided he might as well finish his meal. It wasn't as if Slablard was going anywhere, after all. 'We'll be with you within the hour.'

IN ACTUALITY IT took slightly longer than that, the streets being choked by the citizens of Skitterfall setting off to work as though the day was perfectly normal and their entire world wasn't about to be ravaged by a fleet of Chaos marauders. But then I suppose that's a part of what makes the Imperium what it is: the indomitable spirit of even its most humble citizens. Or their incredible stupidity, which amounts to more or less the same thing half the time.[1]

At any event the carriageways were full of groundcars chugging along at a pace which left them being overtaken by the occasional energetic

1. *Cain is perhaps being overly cynical here. It's a common human reaction to cling to the familiar in times of uncertainty, and many of the Adumbrians no doubt found sticking to their regular routines a source of reassurance.*

pedestrian, and even Jurgen's remarkable driving skills weren't enough to manoeuvre the Salamander through the narrow gaps between the smaller, lighter civilian vehicles. I was just beginning to think we should have commandeered an aircar instead, despite my aide's reluctance to fly, when he accelerated abruptly up a flight of stone steps between two towering buildings.

'Short cut,' he said, heedless of the gaggle of Administratum drones scattering before us spewing an interesting assortment of profanity. He directed us across a wide plaza cluttered with statues of noble Adumbrian bureaucrats. A few vertiginous swerves later and an equally precipitate descent down another staircase apparently leading through a shopping district and a tram terminal, he drew up outside the Arbites building in a space reserved for official vehicles.

A couple of officers stared at us suspiciously, but a glance at my uniform and the heavy weapons aboard our sturdy little vehicle seemed to disincline them to challenge our right to be there.

'Thank you, Jurgen,' I said, clambering out, unexpectedly grateful for the amasec I'd drunk earlier after all. 'That was very resourceful.'

'Couldn't have you missing your appointment, sir,' he said cheerfully.

Further conversation seemed superfluous, so I left him to deal with the praetors who seemed to have plucked up the courage to approach by now, and went inside.

'Commissar.' For a moment I failed to recognise the young praetor who stood inside the cool marble atrium beyond the heavy wooden doors, clearly waiting for me, then the nagging sense of familiarity clicked. Young Kolbe. With his helmet off the resemblance to his father was quite striking, although his build was taller and slimmer. 'It's good to see you again.'

'I'm pleased to find you so well,' I said.

Kolbe inclined his head in the same manner as his father. 'Your medic did an excellent job. I'm supposed to be on light duties, but under the circumstances...' his gesture took in the bustle surrounding us. Uniformed praetors were hurrying in all directions, many of them leading prisoners who were either cursing loudly or protesting their innocence according to temperament, and I even caught a glimpse of a couple of black-bodygloved members of the Arbites itself.

'Things do seem a little hectic,' I said as he escorted me across the echoing space towards the bank of elevators under a vast and tasteless mural of the Emperor scourging the unrighteous.

'We've been rounding up every low-life in Skitterfall who might have a connection to the heretics,' he told me cheerfully. 'And then there's the usual unrest you get in a civil emergency.' We side-stepped a

redemptionist preacher and his congregation, still happily bawling his
lungs out about the apocalypse about to descend on the unworthy in
general and the riot squads who'd waded in to prevent them making an
early start on the vice district in particular, despite their escort's frequent and enthusiastic application of shock batons. 'So arbitrator
Hekwyn thought it might be a good idea to send me along to meet
you.'

'Good idea,' I said, as we gained the sanctuary of the elevators and the
relative shelter of the large stone eagles flanking them. Young Kolbe
punched a couple of runes on one, and the doors clanked open, the
brass filigree forming a pattern of interlocking eagles mirroring their
large stone cousins.

'Sub-basement seventeen,' Kolbe said, looking up and drawing his
own baton as the Redemptionist party collided noisily and violently
with a group of joygirls on their way to an adjacent holding pen. 'If
you'll excuse me?'

'By all means,' I assured him, grateful that here at least was a mess I
didn't have to worry about sorting out, and watching him wade into
the fracas with every sign of enjoyment. The doors creaked closed as I
pressed the icon he'd indicated, and I began my descent into the lowest level of the building.

After about thirty seconds of tedium, made even worse by a scratchy
recording of *Death to the Deviant* apparently performed by tone-deaf
ratlings with nose flutes, the doors rattled open to reveal a plain anteroom with a scuffed carpet and an arbitrator in full body armour
behind a desk pointing a riot gun in my direction.

'Commissar Cain,' I told her as casually as I could while staring down
a gun barrel I could have comfortably fitted my thumb inside. 'I'm
expected.'

'Commissar.' She put the clumsy weapon down and did something to
a keypad on the desk. She must have had a comm-bead inside her helmet, because she nodded at something I couldn't hear, and waved me
to a seat in the corner. 'The arbitrator senioris will be with you shortly.'
I'd heard that one before and was beginning to think I should have
brought something to read, but I'd barely had time to sit down before
a thick steel door behind her swung open and Hekwyn emerged.

'Glad you could make it,' he greeted me, holding out a data-slate in
his new augmetic hand. He seemed to be getting used to it now, judging distances as easily as he did with his original one. I took the slate,
skimming through Slablard's record as quickly as I could. It was similar enough to the military charge sheets I was intimately familiar with
for the job to take little time. By the time I reached the end we were

halfway along a plain corridor, finished in unpainted rockcrete, in which blank metal doors were set at intervals, identical save for the numbers stencilled on them. The air was close, smelling of old sweat, bodily fluids and the unmistakable tang of acute fear which no one familiar with an eldar reiver slave pit can ever forget. 'He's in here.'

The door looked no different from any of the others around us, but Hekwyn seemed positive enough, tapping a six digit code into the keypad too rapidly for me to follow. The door opened, releasing the smell of flatulence, and I motioned the arbitrator through ahead of me politely.

I was pretty sure our smuggler wouldn't have the wit or the determination to be waiting in ambush, in the hope of overpowering whoever next came through the door and making a run for it, but there was no point in taking any chances.[1] As it turned out, there wasn't much chance of that anyway, as he was quite firmly shackled to a chair in the middle of the chamber, and didn't strike me as the kind to chew his own arm off to escape. (Which I suppose pretty much ruled him out as Chaos cult material.)

I wasn't quite sure what I'd expected him to look like, but I knew I'd expected something a little more impressive. He was a small man with watery eyes which refused to make contact with whoever was talking to him and thinning brown hair; the net result was uncannily like a startled rodent.

'I want to see a legal representative,' he blustered as soon as we appeared. 'You can't just keep me here indefinitely.'

'What we want and what we get in life are seldom the same,' Hekwyn said regretfully.

Slablard squirmed. 'I want to talk to someone in authority.'

'That would be me,' Hekwyn said, stepping further into the room. Slablard's eyes widened at the sight of his uniform, then positively bulged when he saw mine. 'I have overall responsibility for the operation of the Arbites on Adumbria.' He paused a moment, giving this time to sink in, then indicated me. 'This is Commissar Cain, who you may also have heard of. I've invited him to sit in on our conversation as a matter of courtesy, since acts of treason also fall under military jurisdiction in a time of emergency.'

'Treason?' Slablard's voice rose an octave, sweat stains appearing under the arms of his coarse blue shirt as though someone had turned on a tap. 'I just moved a few crates!'

---

1. *From which we can conclude that Cain was now sufficiently past any residual trauma left by his nightmare to be fairly described as his old self again.*

'Containing weapons subsequently used to attack His Majesty's Guardsmen,' I said as sternly as I could. 'And that's treason in my book.' Slablard looked desperately from one of us to the other, finally fixing on Hekwyn as the slightly less intimidating of the two.

'I didn't know.' he whined. 'How could I?'

'Perhaps if you'd asked?' Hekwyn suggested mildly.

The little man wilted visibly. 'You don't know these people. They're dangerous. You don't want to cross them, you get what I'm saying?'

'These people are heretics,' I said. 'Worshippers of the Ruinous Powers, sent here ahead of the invasion fleet to undermine our defences against them.' I leaned forward, fixing him with my best commissarial glare, which had made generals turn pale before now. 'Have you any idea how much harm you've done?'

'They told me it was just black market ore!' Slablard was practically in tears. 'You have to believe me, I'd never have dealt with them if I'd known they were heretics.'

'It's not me you have to convince,' I told him. 'It's the Emperor himself. You'd better just pray that your soul hasn't been corrupted by your association with the agents of darkness, or you'll be damned for eternity.' All claptrap, of course, but I delivered it as fervently as Beije would have done and felt quite pleased with my acting ability.

'That's hardly our judgement to make,' Hekwyn reminded me, as if he actually cared. I began to suspect that after years of data shuffling in the upper echelons he was relishing the chance to indulge in some hands-on arbitration. 'Once the threat of Chaos has been neutralised it will be for the Inquisition to determine who is or isn't tainted by the Dark Powers.'

That did it, as I'd been pretty sure it would. At the mention of the Inquisition Slablard broke down in hysterics, which threatened to go on for so long I eventually sacrificed part of the contents of my hip flask just to get him to calm down enough to talk. It was a shocking waste of good amasec even if his palate was refined enough to tell the difference (which I doubted), but there was plenty more back in my suite, and I had no doubt that Jurgen could find another bottle once that was gone.

I stepped gingerly round the puddle of urine spreading across the rockcrete floor, finally divining the purpose of the drain in the corner, and resumed my casual-but-dangerous pose leaning against the door.

'These people,' I began. 'Who are they, and where do we find them?'

TEN

*'Competence on the battlefield is a myth. The side which
screws up next to last wins, it's as simple as that.'*

– Lord General Zyvan

THE ONLY REAL problem we had with Slablard in the end was shutting
him up. I downloaded the list of names, dates and locations he'd given
us to the hololith in the conference suite with the air of a conjurer at a
children's party producing an egg from an ear.

'If anything, we've got a little too much to go on now,' I said. Zyvan
and the senior Kolbe nodded, taking it all in as it scrolled up the display. Vinzand, I noticed, was absent, presumably because this was an
operational matter and nothing he needed to be concerned with. Well,
that suited me; the less debate there was before we took action the better, so far as I was concerned.

'My people should be able to pick up any of these individuals who
slip though the net,' Hekwyn said. 'But under the circumstances we're a
little stretched to be mounting simultaneous raids on half a dozen different addresses.'

'I see your point,' Zyvan replied, having evidently been keeping abreast of the situation in the city.[1] He turned to Kolbe. 'Perhaps the PDF could oblige us with the necessary manpower.'

He would rather have used Guardsmen I was sure, but we were so widely scattered it would have taken hours to bring sufficient troopers back to the city, and if the heretics noticed Slablard had disappeared in the meantime they'd be long gone by the time we were ready to deploy. The Valhallan tanks were already in place, of course, but I tried to picture a troop of Leman Russes moving stealthily through the crowded streets and had to suppress a smile; we might just as well vox ahead and let the cultists know we were coming.

'Of course.' Kolbe nodded, all calm efficiency, clearly confident in his troops' ability to deal with whatever awaited them. I hoped he was right. 'I can have a couple of companies at your disposal within minutes.'

'I'm sure that will be sufficient,' Zyvan said, straight-faced. That would give us practically two full platoons for each objective, which was as sure-fire a recipe for utter confusion as I could imagine; that number of troopers would be getting in each other's way more often than engaging the enemy. 'But perhaps we should assign personnel to the operations once we've determined conditions on the ground.'

That took a while, as you'd imagine, but at last we'd worked out the optimum troop deployment for each of the objectives and Kolbe had issued the orders. I stretched, glanced at my chronograph, and found to my surprise that it was still a few moments short of noon.

'Well, that appears to be that,' I said, as Hekwyn departed for the Arbites building and the two generals stood, preparing to walk down to Zyvan's command post.

The lord general nodded. 'I suppose you must be eager to return to your regiment,' he said.

I thought of the bone-chilling cold of Glacier Peak and the endless tedium of the train journey before I reached it, and nodded with every appearance of enthusiasm I could muster.

'My place is with them,' I agreed, unable to find a plausible reason to delay my departure. One crumb of consolation was that I should be able to hang around here long enough to grab a decent lunch before I went, though.

---

1. *Not to mention the rest of the planet. The praetors in every major population centre were tied up with heretic hunting and the suppression of civil disorder, just as they were in Skitterfall.*

Zyvan smiled, sure he could read my real thoughts. 'But you'd rather hang on here and see what the raids turn up, eh? After all, if it wasn't for you we wouldn't even have these leads.'

'I'm sure Arbitrator Hekwyn's people would have found them just as quickly,' I said, trying not to look too eager. If he meant what I thought he did, it looked as though I could hang around here in the warm, enjoying every comfort the place had to offer, for at least another day after all; maybe even longer if I drew out the process of appearing to evaluate the intelligence we gathered.

'I'm sure they would,' Zyvan said, sounding about as convinced of that as I had. 'If you don't mind delaying your departure for a while, it occurs to me things might go a little smoother this afternoon if we have a representative of the Commissariat along on the operation.' He shot a sidelong glance at Kolbe. 'No reflection on your people of course. It would just save us the necessity of forwarding a formal report to them afterwards.'

'By all means,' Kolbe said, no doubt happier at the prospect of his troopers' performance being scrutinised by me, rather than some rear-echelon data-pusher with the benefit of hindsight.

'It would be an honour to serve with your command,' I told him. 'Albeit briefly.'

If I'd known what I was about to get into, of course, my answer would have been very different, and I'd practically have run for the blasted train, but all I could see at the time was the prospect of another couple of days of good food and comfortable bedding.

So it was that, an hour or so later, I found myself rattling down a city boulevard in the back of the Salamander, half a dozen Chimeras behind me and my comm-bead full of excited chatter from PDF troopers all keyed up about their first taste of action.

'Vox discipline,' I reminded them, trying to make allowances, and the extraneous traffic died with gratifying speed. 'We're passing the outer marker.'

After some consideration, I'd attached myself to the group going after a house in the suburbs owned by one of the people Slablard had implicated, a woman called Kyria Sejwek, who Hekwyn claimed had tenuous links to a number of organised crime figures and probably ran a stable of high-rent joygirls. She also had a very good lawyer and connections to several members of the Council of Claimants, which meant that so far the Arbites had been unable to accumulate sufficient evidence for an arrest.

Taking on a handful of bodyguards and a house full of women seemed a lot safer than going in against the warehouse where the weapons had ended up, which was no doubt heavily guarded and stuffed with explosives to boot, although I hadn't shared those reasons for selecting this particular objective with the generals, of course.

'This is the obvious target,' I'd said, highlighting the warehouse on the holomap, and giving every appearance of being eager to storm the place single-handed. A few other icons glowed, picking out the secondary targets, and I pointed at the Sejwek house with just the right degree of a puzzled frown. 'But something about this place doesn't feel right.'

'How do you mean?' Kolbe asked obligingly, and I shrugged.

'I can't quite put my finger on it. But this woman's record – highly placed, intimations of vice – I'm probably reading too much into it, but...'

'It could be the centre of the Slaaneshi cult in the city,' Zyvan said, taking the bait.

I continued to look dubious. 'It's possible of course. But the warehouse is definitely our most promising lead.'

'Nevertheless,' the lord general said, the idea I'd planted clearly taking root in his mind, 'it's a possibility we can't afford to ignore. Perhaps you'd better accompany that platoon instead.'

'It might be wise,' Kolbe agreed. 'If there's evidence of sorcery there, the men would find your presence extremely reassuring.'

'Well,' I said, with every sign of reluctance. 'If you're both convinced of the need...'

By the time I'd finished protesting, of course, they were practically insisting I raided what I had no doubt was nothing more sinister than a high-class bordello, and I gave in with as much good grace as I could simulate.

'That must be it,' Jurgen said, indicating a high brick wall running along the edge of the pavement. It certainly seemed to be; the other houses, large rambling structures, their windows glowing warmly, were set back from the road behind lawns and shrubberies designed to emphasise the scale and ostentation of the buildings they contained. Only this one was sealed away behind what was beginning to look like a fortification, and my palms began to tingle with the intimation that perhaps this wasn't going to be the pushover I'd expected. Then again, given what we knew of her character and probable activities, Sejwek no doubt had a lot to hide in any case.

'It is,' I confirmed, after a surreptitious glance at the mapslate just to make sure. I activated the comm-bead. 'This is it,' I broadcast over the platoon tacnet, so everyone could hear me.[1] 'I don't have to tell you

---

1. *The PDF troopers wouldn't be equipped with personal comm-beads, like the Guardsmen Cain was used to fighting alongside (or more likely behind if he could contrive it), but each squad would have included a specialist carrying a portable vox unit.*

how important this is, for Adumbria and for the Imperium. I hope I also don't need to tell you that General Kolbe and I have complete confidence in you all, and know you won't let us or the Emperor down. Onward to victory!' It was one of the pre-battle speeches I'd been reciting by rote since the day I left the schola, but the PDF troopers had never heard it before and it did the job. Far better than I expected, as things turned out.

'You heard the commissar.' That was the platoon commander, an excitable young man called Nallion who looked barely old enough to shave, and who wore his officer's cap at what he no doubt thought was a rakish angle. 'Deploy to your positions!'

After a chorus of acknowledgements from the various squad leaders, the Chimeras split up, Nallion's command vehicle and first squad halting in front of the main gates (tasteless wrought-iron scrollwork with a hint of drooping lilies and far too much gilt) while the rest broke left and right, tearing up the lawns and flattening the shrubberies of the no-doubt outraged neighbours. Jurgen and I kept up with the left flank, which dropped a Chimera by the side wall before crashing through a boundary hedge to link up with another troop transport which had approached from the other side.

'Third and fifth squad in position,' I reported, more to remind everyone I was still there than because it was necessary. A ratling gardener was staring at us and the deep furrows across what had obviously once been a lovingly-tended lawn, with an expression of stupefied astonishment even more pronounced than was usual for his kind. As his eyes fell on Jurgen he started visibly and fled.

'Mister Spavin!' he cried as he went. 'Mister Spavin! The doom's come upon us at last!' He spoke truer than he knew, of course, but there was no time to worry about him or his employer now. I listened to a chorus of position reports in my comm-bead as the other squad leaders reported in, and Nallion gave the order to attack.

'All units move in!' he shouted in a voice which barely trembled from the tension, and with a roar of gunning engines the Chimeras moved forward, their heavy bolters opening up and blowing large sections of the wall to rubble. The Salamander jerked under my feet as we ploughed across it, but I kept my balance instinctively after nearly two decades of being driven by Jurgen, and I hoisted myself up behind the comforting bulk of the bolter. Gouts of dust and the rattle of heavy weapons fire in the distance were all the confirmation I needed that the other three elements of our assault were on the move, although to their credit the squad commanders kept their heads admirably and relayed a steady stream of status reports as crisply and concisely as a Guardsman would.

'Second squad disembarking,' their sergeant said, followed almost at once by similar messages from his counterparts in first and fourth. 'Resistance light.'

A crackle of small-arms fire could be heard from the direction of the house now, as the occupants responded to the unexpected attack. Absently I picked out the sounds of stubber fire from the sharper crack of the lasguns the PDF troopers bore, which confirmed that at the very least the occupants had access to illegal weaponry. Slugs began to rattle against the armour plate of the Salamander and I returned fire without thinking, hosing down the facade of the house as Jurgen continued to bear down on it across a lawn no less immaculate than the one we'd chewed to pieces next door.

Without warning, one of the Chimeras ahead of us lurched to a halt, the red flare of explosive detonation standing out starkly in the perpetual twilight, and panicked troopers began bailing out. A couple fell, caught by the blizzard of stubber fire.

'Third squad! Stay in cover, damn it!' I just had time to yell, before Jurgen swung the bucking Salamander hard to the left. Something shot past us no more than a metre away, leaving a trail of smoke, and detonated against what was left of the garden wall behind us.

'They've got missile launchers!' I voxed, trying to bring the bolter round to retaliate and reflecting that I could have been on a nice uncomfortable train by now instead of in mortal danger again. 'Leave the vehicles and move in on foot.'

'Acknowledged,' Nallion replied. 'All squads advance by fire and movement.'[1] He was on the ball all right, I had to give him that.

'Jurgen!' I called. 'Did you see where that rocket came from?'

'About one o'clock, commissar,' he responded, as calmly as if I'd just asked him to get some more tanna. I swung the pintel-mounted weapon around in that direction, and my bowels spasmed. There were at least two missile launchers being aimed at us from within a pair of tall glass windows, and what looked like a heavy stubber on a tripod. Most, to my vague surprise, were being wielded with considerable expertise by young women whose minimal state of dress left little doubt as to their day jobs.[2] Any second now we'd be joining the Chimera behind us, which was blazing away merrily by this time.

'Head for the nearest cover,' I yelled, squeezing the trigger and hoping to put their aim off just long enough for Jurgen to take us out of the

---

1. *A common infantry tactic, where half the squad lays down covering fire while the other half advances, then the first group of troopers provides covering fire for the rest to catch up.*

2. *Or night jobs, to be a little more accurate.*

line of fire. To my amazement he gunned the engine, accelerating even
more rapidly towards the house.

'Very good, sir.' He triggered the hull-mounted heavy bolter, reducing a
couple of the amazons to unpleasant stains, and before I had time to
realise what he was doing he had roared up the patio, scattering some
ornamental shrubs in the process, to ram us through the flimsy wood
and glass partition behind which our assailants had taken shelter. One of
the survivors disappeared under the tracks with an abruptly-curtailed
shriek, and the Salamander slammed to a halt against the far wall of an
opulent living room, reducing a marble fireplace to rubble in the process.

'Fifth squad! Follow the commissar!' The squad sergeant, Varant if
my memory serves, bawled in the comm-bead, and before I knew it
half a score of troopers had followed up our impromptu and precipi-
tous entry, finishing off the rest of the defenders in the process, which
at least saved us the bother. The survivors of third squad joined them a
moment later, and everyone looked at me expectantly.

'Very good,' I said, adjusting my cap and stepping down from the
Salamander as nonchalantly as I could. 'Let's get this done.'

'Yes sir,' Varant said, with an expression of awe on his face, and started
organising the men.

I looked at my aide. 'Jurgen...' I began, then decided there wasn't any
point remonstrating with him. He'd followed my orders after all, and
things had worked out as well as they ever did. 'That was...' Words, for
once, failed me.

'Resourceful?' he suggested, reaching back inside the driver's compartment for the melta, which, true to form, he'd brought with him.

'To say the least,' I said, drawing my laspistol.

'Second squad advancing,' their sergeant reported in my comm-bead,
his voice calm as ever. 'No resistance so far.'

'Copy that,' Nallion responded. 'First squad report.' There was a
pause, broken only by the hissing of static. 'First squad, respond.' My
palms were itching again, a sense of forboding I could almost taste fluttering in my gut. The lieutenant's voice took on an edge of asperity.
'First squad, where are you?'

'Fourth squad,' a new voice cut in, a note of suppressed panic quite
clearly detectable. 'We've found bodies. Could be them.'

'What do you mean, could be?' Nallion snapped.

'It's hard to tell, sir. There's not much left...' His voice choked off.

This wouldn't do at all. We'd clearly blundered into something very
dangerous, and if anyone panicked now it would spread like a spark in
a promethium tank. Which would cut my chances of getting out of here
in one piece more considerably than I found acceptable.

'This is Commissar Cain,' I cut in. 'Stay alert. Stay focussed. Fire on anything that moves which isn't one of ours. Is that understood?'

'Yes sir.' It seemed to have done the trick anyway, the man's voice was shaking a little less. 'Moving on to the next mark.'

'Good,' I told him, hoping to bolster the squad's sagging morale. 'Remember, the Emperor protects.'

I never finished the platitude, the vox channel suddenly becoming swamped with sounds which, in an eerie, overlapping echo, carried to our ears through the air a fraction of a second later. Screams, the chatter of lasguns on full auto and a sound which raised the hairs on the back of my neck: melodious, inhuman laughter. A moment later, the sounds of the evidently one-sided battle ended abruptly.

'Fourth squad, report,' Nallion bellowed, but no answer came, and if he honestly expected one he was the biggest optimist in the system.

'What do we do, sir?' Varant asked, and after a moment I realised he was looking at me, ignoring the lieutenant's voice completely. I assessed the situation rapidly. Retreat, always a good choice in my book, was impossible. Apart from the fact that it would undermine my reputation, it would expose us to Emperor alone knew how much fire from the house as we made our way back across that wide open lawn, and I didn't intend to become a bit of easy target practice for some civilian tart with a new toy. I shrugged, trying to look nonchalant and speak through a mouth which had suddenly gone as dry as the hotside.

'We complete the mission,' I said simply. 'There's something foul in this place, and we need to cleanse it.'

It seemed painfully obvious now that my carefully contrived excuse for being here was no more than the truth after all, which I suppose at least proves that the Emperor has a well-developed sense of irony, and I'd seen enough sorcery over the years to know that confronting it straight away is the only chance you've got of survival. Not a particularly good chance, I grant you, but trying to run from it only gives it more time to grow in power and come after you on its own terms rather than yours.

'I do hope that's not a criticism of the cleaning staff,' a mellifluous voice chimed in. 'They do their best, you know, but it's such a rambling old place it's hard to keep on top of.'

The woman who spoke smiled easily as she strolled into the room, as though finding a score[1] of armed men standing over the bodies of

---

1. *If Cain is being literal here we can infer that only two men from third squad were actually incapacitated after their Chimera was destroyed; however, it seems more likely from his other remarks that he's simply going for an approximate round number and that they suffered more casualties than this.*

her associates was the most natural thing in the world. I began to bring my laspistol up instinctively, my finger tightening on the trigger, then froze, my heart pounding. I'd come within a hair of shooting Amberley! For a moment I was so startled that I was literally paralysed with astonishment, something which up until then I'd always assumed was merely a figurative cliché in the more undemanding kind of popular fiction.

Her smile widened as she looked at me and the knot of troopers whose lasguns all hung slack in their hands.

'I know you must be surprised to see me here,' she purred, the words sounding impossibly sweet and seductive. Something tried to push itself towards the front of my mind, but the vision of her, lovely as the last time we'd parted, the flower I'd plucked impulsively from the hegantha bush on the veranda still tucked behind her ear, filled my senses.

'Margritta?' one of the troopers asked, as though he couldn't believe his own eyes, and the burgeoning thought became clearer. Something definitely wasn't right...

'Yes, my love.' Amberley reached out a hand, caressing him gently on the cheek, and a surge of white-hot jealously erupted through me. Before I could react in any way, however, the trooper screamed, his body contorting, seeming to wither like a dried ploin before dropping to the floor.

'Commissar?' Jurgen tugged at my sleeve, an expression of puzzlement on his face. 'Are you going to let her get away with that?'

'She's an inquisitor,' I started to say. 'She can do what she likes,' but when I looked up again Amberley had gone. (Well she hadn't, of course, because she was never there in the first place, but you know what I mean.) In her place, standing over the crumbling corpse of the fallen soldier, was a dumpy middle-aged woman in an unwise pink gown which would have looked fine on someone ten years younger and as many kilos lighter. She looked directly at me, an expression of surprise and outrage beginning to suffuse her vaguely porcine features.

'Madame Sejwek,' I said, savouring the flicker of uncertainty which rose in her eyes, almost losing my aim from the surge of anger which left my hand shaking from its force. Fortunately my augmetic fingers were immune to such an emotional reaction and kept the muzzle of my laspistol centred firmly on her forehead. 'Impersonating an inquisitor is a capital offence.'

She just had time to look even more startled before I pulled the trigger, and her warp-tainted brain erupted from the back of her skull to ruin a wall hanging which had evidently been chosen for its subject matter rather than its aesthetic qualities.

'What happened?' Varant asked, looking slightly stunned. The rest of the troopers were snapping out of it too now, muttering in low tones, making the sign of the aquila and generally looking sheepish.

'She was a witch,' I told him, keeping things as simple as I could. 'She did something to our minds. Made us see...' I made what I assumed at the time to be the obvious deductive leap, but which Malden later confirmed was a known power of Slaaneshi psykers. 'Someone we care about.'[1]

'I see,' he said, looking confused. 'Lucky she didn't fool you.'

'Commissars are trained to spot that kind of thing,' I lied smoothly, not wanting to draw any more attention than necessary to Jurgen. To tell the truth I was more than a little concerned that Sejwek had managed to get inside my head at all while he was so close. (To my relief, I learned later that he'd gone back to the Salamander for his lasgun while I was busy with the vox signals, taking me out of the range of his protective aura. It had belatedly occurred to him that his beloved melta might be a little counterproductive in such a potentially inflammable building; as always his pragmatism couldn't be faulted, although his timing left a lot to be desired.)

'Well, I suppose at least we know what happened to first and fourth squad,' the sergeant said, looking from the body of the witch to the desiccated husk of his erstwhile subordinate.

'Possibly,' I said. It didn't add up to me. Fourth squad had died quickly, in combat, not held by delusion to be picked off one by one. 'There's only one way to find out.'

And find out we did. The mortal remains of our comrades, and there were precious few of them left, were scattered around a ground-floor hallway at the foot of a huge wooden staircase, the banisters of which were carved in the semblance of fornicating couples in a bewildering variety of anatomically improbable positions. Blood and scorch marks spattered the walls, which were decorated with the kind of debauched murals that I'd seen before in the hab dome hidden away on the cold-side, and a nagging sense of familiarity fought its way to the surface of my thoughts.

'The rest of the house is clear,' Nallion reported, looking slightly green as he took in the carnage, but determined not to throw up in front of the commissar. 'No sign of anyone else on the premises.'

'False walls, hidden chambers?' I asked, the memory of the hab dome still fresh, that strange scent that had flooded the air there still faintly detectable through the more pervasive one of butchery.

---

1. *Which for Cain was positively effusive, and, I must admit, rather gratifying.*

Nallion shook his head. 'No sign of anything like that,' he said. 'We can bring in some tech-priests with specialised equipment…'

'Don't worry about it,' I told him, to his evident relief. 'The Guard will take care of that. You and your men have done enough, and done it well.'

'Thank you, sir.' He took the hint and frakked off, with a perfunctory salute and an air of undisguised relief.

'Jurgen,' I said, pointing to the staircase. It was large and apparently solid, but we could have parked the Salamander in the space it enclosed. 'If you wouldn't mind?'

'Of course not, sir,' he assured me, and a moment later the familiar roar of the melta and an actinic flash through my tightly-closed eyelids told me he'd done as requested. Despite his fears of accidental arson (which he confided to me later, a little too late to have been much help if they were founded, but with Jurgen following orders always came first) the surrounding wood failed to catch light. A large, smoking hole was punched through the treads, looking uncannily like the entrance to a cave. I borrowed a luminator from one of his ever-present equipment pouches and took a cautious look inside.

'Emperor on Earth!' I reeled back, choking from the smell. If anything, it was worse than the chamber we'd found in the hab dome, although the details were depressingly familiar. The pile of twisted corpses, still grinning in infernal rapture, the sanity-blasting sigils on the walls… I backed away until I was on the other side of the hallway and contacted the lord general directly.

'It seems we were right about this place,' I told him. 'It was being put to unholy use.' I hesitated. 'And if I'm right,' I added, the knotting of my guts telling me I was, 'we got here too late. Whatever they were doing, they've already done.'

Editorial Note:

Given the course of subsequent events, the following communication may prove some-what revealing.

To: The Office of the Commissariat, Departmento Munitorum, Coronus Prime

From: Tomas Beije, Regimental Commissar to the Tallarn 229th

Date: 285 937 M41

Astropathic Path: Blocked at this time. Delivery deferred.

Gentlemen and esteemed colleagues,
  It is with a heavy heart I feel I must call into question the competence of a fellow commissar, not least because the officer in question was a classmate of mine at the schola progenium, and as we all know such ties remain strong. However, I would be derelict in my duty not to bring this matter to your attention, and must set aside my personal

feelings for the sake of the Guard, the Imperium and the Emperor Himself. Truly our duty to Him must outweigh all else, and after much prayer and fasting I can see no alternative.

The individual in question is none other than Ciaphas Cain, the regimental commissar of the Valhallan 597th. I am aware that he has something of an inflated reputation, which may incline some of you to dismiss my concerns, but nonetheless I feel I have no alternative but to speak out. Indeed, it may be this very reputation which has led to his current sad decline as an effective commissar: how truly has it been said that the glory we gain blinds us first with its lustre.[1]

I have observed at first hand that discipline and proper order are practically non-existent in the regiment with which Commissar Cain has been charged, his own aide failing to reach the standards expected of a member of His Divine Majesty's blessed legions, while serious infractions and breaches of discipline are treated as minor matters barely worthy of his attention. Since arriving on Adumbria he has neglected his duties altogether, spending more time in the planetary capital than with the 597th, even going so far as to attach himself to a local PDF company rather than rejoin the Guard unit he should properly have been most concerned with.

It might be claimed that his discovery of not one but two concealed nests of heretic sorcerers vindicates his actions, but consider: in neither case was he in time to prevent their fell purpose, whatever that was, and his interference in a PDF operation in which he had no official interest may well have led to sufficient delay to have ensured such a failure on at least one occasion. I draw no inference from this, of course, but merely suggest the coincidence was fortuitous for our enemies.

May the divine light of His Glorious Majesty illuminate your deliberations.

Your Humble Servant,
Tomas Beije.

Thought for the day: The traitor's hand lies closer than you think.

---

1. A quotation from Caddaway's Paths to Damnation, a Redemptionist tract of dubious theology and even worse literacy.

ELEVEN

'I don't care how bloody sanctioned they are,
a psyker's a psyker, and anything to do with the warp
is more trouble than it's worth.'

– General Karis

I WAS BEGINNING to get heartily sick of the sight of that conference room by now. Every time I entered it, it seemed, my life became more complicated. Even the prospect of a hearty dinner and a comfortable bed, which had been sufficient to keep me in Skitterfall that morning, began to look like scant consolation, receding as they both were into an indefinite future. The damn place was getting steadily more crowded, too. Aside from Zyvan and myself, and a couple of his aides whose names hadn't stuck if anyone had actually bothered to introduce us, Kolbe, Hekwyn and Vinzand were present, and all had decided to mark the urgency of the situation by bringing a flunkey or two along themselves. Malden was there too, with the far end of the table pretty much to himself as usual, chatting to a woman whose sunken eye sockets would have marked her out as an astropath even without the distinctive robes she wore. The unease most of those present clearly felt at the sight of two spooks in the same room was palpable, although had I but known it the feeling was about to get a whole lot worse.

'Are you all right, Ciaphas?' Zyvan asked, and I nodded, trying to dismiss the image of the chamber we'd found from my mind. It wasn't easy, I can tell you that, and that struck me as slightly odd given the sheer number of horrors I'd faced in my career up to that point. It kept coming back to me, overlaid with the memory of the similar chamber we'd found in the hab dome and that damnable laughter I'd heard as the PDF soldiers died. That had a haunting sense of familiarity about it too, although how or why I couldn't put my finger on.

'I'm fine,' I said, picking up a mug of tanna from the refreshment table. As usual, I was the only one drinking it. I glanced around the conference room, which was filling up (except for the end where the spooks were), and tried to change the subject before he started asking any more questions. 'If that's everyone, I suppose we ought to get started.'

'Nearly everyone,' Zyvan said, helping himself to a smoked grox sandwich. Before I had a chance to ask what he meant by that, some kind of commotion erupted outside the door. Voices were raised, and I found myself reaching instinctively for my chainsword, but the lord general's relaxed demeanour forestalled the motion. (Not without an amused glance in my direction as he registered the movement, I might add.)

'Do I look as though I need to show your underlings my credentials?' The question was directed at Zyvan, as though there were no other people in the room, and to all intents and purposes there might as well not have been. A young woman, astonishingly petite but somehow managing to fill the entire doorframe with the force of her personality, strode past the quivering woodwork, the ashen faces of a couple of the lord general's personal bodyguards just visible in the corridor outside. Zyvan dismissed them with a gesture, and they hurried to close the door behind her with remarkable alacrity.

'Of course not.' Zyvan bowed formally. 'You honour us all with your presence.'

'Of course I do,' she snapped back irritably. 'And don't expect me to make a habit of it.' Her hair was dark and lustrous, the hue of open space, falling to the shoulders which her simply-cut gown left bare. The dress seemed to have been woven from fibres of pure gold, reflecting the light in a fashion I found almost dazzling, clinging to her pleasingly plump figure in a fashion which left very little of it to the imagination, and setting off the preternaturally pale skin of her décolletage to perfection.

The thing which held my eyes, and every other pair in the room, however, was the bandana around her forehead. It was woven from the same material as her dress, but in the exact centre of it the image of an eye had been embroidered in thread as dark as her hair. Without thinking I made the sign of the aquila, and believe me, I wasn't the only one.

'May I present the Lady Gianella Dimarco, navigatrix of the *Indestructible*,' Zyvan said, addressing the room in general, as though anyone present could possibly not have realised who she was (well, maybe the astropath, I suppose).

Dimarco sighed. 'Let's just get on with it, shall we?' She dropped into a vacant seat at the spooky end of the table, no doubt feeling she had slightly more in common with Malden and the blind woman than the rest of us.[1] Everyone else shuffled awkwardly into their chairs, leaving as wide a gap as possible between the psykers and themselves.

'By all means.' Zyvan inclined his head courteously. 'I'm sure we all appreciate you taking the time to join us in person.'

Well he might. I would have been just as happy with a written report and less of the superior attitude, assuming she had anything useful to contribute at all. (Which of course she had. And if I'd been thinking a little more clearly I would have realised she must have been scared witless to subject herself to the company of scruffy little proles like us in the first place.)

'Of course you do,' Dimarco said irritably. Her dark eyes swept the room, and despite knowing intellectually that they couldn't do me any harm, it was the one the bandana concealed which could kill in an instant, I shuddered, reluctant to meet them. 'But you're not going to like what I've got to say.'

That would have been true if we were discussing music or the weather, given what I'd seen of her personality (which, to be fair, was bordering on the amiable for a navigator), but even so I felt the familiar premonitory tingling in the palms of my hands.

'Nevertheless,' Zyvan said, inclining his head.

Dimarco sighed. 'I'll keep this as simple as I can, so even a bunch of blinders[2] should be able to grasp it.'

She leaned forward, her elbows on the polished wooden table, and supported her chin on her steepled fingers, revealing an impressive

---

1. *Perhaps, or she may simply not have registered the distinction. Members of the Navis Nobilitae seem to regard anyone who isn't another jumped-up little mutant with a warp eye as scarcely more than orks with table manners, and treat them accordingly.*

2. *A term used by navigators to describe those without their dubious gift of warpsight. As it's among the least offensive we can infer that Dimarco was making what she no doubt thought of as a considerable effort to be gracious.*

amount of cleavage in the process. 'The warp currents around Adumbria are strong, but predictable. Usually.'

'Usually?' Vinzand asked, a note of alarm evident in his voice.

Dimarco looked at him with the expression of an ecclesiarch who has just heard one of the congregation fart loudly in the middle of the benediction (something you get used to attending services accompanied by Jurgen[1]).

'I'm getting to that,' she snapped. 'Do I tell you how to count paperclips?' After a moment of embarrassing silence she continued. 'They normally form a complex but stable vortex, centred on the planet itself. This, in part, accounts for the system's position as a major trading port.'

The Adumbrians present nodded with more than a trace of smugness. Dimarco shrugged, with interesting effects on her dress and what I could see of its contents. 'I couldn't tell you why this is, though.' She glanced almost imperceptibly at her fellow psykers.

'It seems to be something to do with the orbital dynamics,' Malden said dryly. 'The fact that the world is rotationally locked sets up a resonance in the warp, which bends the currents.'

'Something of an oversimplification,' the astropath said, her voice surprisingly young. 'But unless you can feel them directly, it's the closest you're likely to get.'

'Wait a minute,' Kolbe said. 'You mean these currents are shifting?'

Dimarco sighed loudly. 'What have we just been saying? Of course they're frakking shifting!' As her voice rose in pitch I began to realise she wasn't just being a snotty pain in the arse, she was genuinely worried; probably more so than she'd been in a long time. (And when you consider she'd been serving on a battleship, which had undoubtedly been shot at a few times, that would be saying something.) 'Three times since we got here. Big, sudden shifts. Which, in case you haven't been paying attention, is something which definitely shouldn't be happening.'

'Three times?' I asked, before I could stop myself, and the woman's night-black eyes were on me again, spraying contempt like the barrel of a hellgun. Before she could say something trite and obvious, like asking if I was deaf, I nodded thoughtfully and continued to speak, overriding any sarcastic comment she might be about to make. 'Can you give us a precise time on that?' The effect was quite satisfying, I

---

1. *Which may seem surprising, given the cavalier attitude Cain usually expresses towards the pious and matters of faith. However, attendance at certain services would have been part of his commissarial duties, and therefore unavoidable; having his aide accompany him on these occasions would normally be a matter of protocol.*

have to say: a faint moue of puzzlement flickered across her features, and she bit back the words she'd been preparing to fling with a faint choking sound.

'Not precise, no,' she said. She turned to the astropath. 'Faciltiatrix Agnetha?'

The blind woman nodded. 'Since the first one was what cut us off from the rest of the fleet[1], I can tell you to the second. The others I'd need to check if you want more accuracy than within an hour or two.'

'That would be fine,' I said, a sudden sinking feeling telling me I'd just made an intuitive leap I really didn't want to be right about. Unfortunately I was: the most recent shift in the warp currents had happened earlier that day, shortly before our eventful raid on the Sejwek house. (The other attacks had all gone without a hitch, of course, including the one on the warehouse I'd been so keen to avoid: the heretics had already moved the weapons out, and the place was deserted when the PDF got there. The only consolation was that at least I'd survived the mess I'd got myself into, and had inadvertently boosted my reputation for sagacity and courage into the bargain.)

'So,' Zyvan said, looking as perturbed as I'd ever seen him, 'the heretics are doing something to affect the warp currents. The big question is why.'

'With respect, my lord,' Malden said, 'the big question is what. If they really are responsible for this, we're dealing with a level of power far greater than any mortal psyker could possibly wield.'

The growing sense of apprehension I felt curdled in my gut. There was an obvious answer to that, and I didn't want to be the one to state it. Nobody else seemed willing to verbalise the thought, though, despite the number of ashen faces around me who had presumably reached the same conclusion.

'When you examined the room we found in the hab dome,' I said at last, 'you said you thought some of the sigils there were part of a summoning ritual. Did you find any similar ones in the Sejwek house?'

'We did,' Malden said. 'Almost identical.' He permitted himself the ghost of a smile. 'It's hard to say if they were exactly the same, as your method of entry erased a few.' Along with the wall they'd been painted on, of course.

'In your opinion,' Zyvan said, clearly reluctant to hear the answer, 'could they have raised some kind of warp entity with sufficient power to affect the currents?'

---

1. *From which we can infer that Agnetha was the chief astropath from Zyvan's flagship, rather than a local civilian.*

'It's possible.' The young psyker nodded. 'There are daemons strong enough to do that.' An audible gasp of horror rippled around the room as he casually used the word everyone else had been so carefully trying to avoid. Dimarco looked as though she was about to be sick, and I could hear Hekwyn muttering one of the catechisms under his breath. 'I doubt you could hold on to one that powerful, though, at least for long.'

'Maybe they didn't have to,' Agnetha suggested. 'If it was cooperating with them voluntarily...' Her voice trailed away, leaving us all to contemplate the same uncomfortable thought. What possible bribe could tempt a daemon to work alongside human cultists, and what blasphemous goal could they conceivably have in common?

'Does that mean the thing's still at large somewhere?' Hekwyn asked, regaining his composure with a visible effort.

'They can't stay in the material world for very long,' I reminded him. 'It'll be back in the warp where it belongs by now.' I turned to Kolbe. 'Probably thanks to the heroic sacrifice of your troopers,' I added. 'From what I heard they were giving a good account of themselves.'

Actually it sounded like they were panicking and dying horribly, which was what you'd expect under the circumstances, but if we were really facing a threat that terrible the more I could do to boost morale the better.

'Until the next time they summon it,' Dimarco said limply, the arrogance well and truly knocked out of her by the realisation of what we were facing. (But not for long, of course – she was a navigator after all.)

'Assuming they do,' Zyvan said.

'Of course they will,' Dimarco rejoined, no doubt taking some comfort in being able to contradict someone. 'If they'd already succeeded in whatever they're trying to do we wouldn't be sitting around here discussing it, would we?' Which sounded like a fair point to me.

'Can any of you take a guess at what that might be?' I asked, trying to project an air of calm reassurance the way they'd taught me at the schola.

I certainly wasn't feeling either calm or reassured, you can depend on that, but the familiar routine of maintaining morale helped me at least look as though I was coping.

Agnetha narrowed her sightless eyes thoughtfully. 'Disrupting our communications, obviously,' she said. 'But they managed that the first time.'

'Cutting us off physically from the rest of the fleet,' Dimarco said, clearly fighting to keep her voice level. 'When I look at the currents directly, it's as if they're brewing up into a localised warp storm, centred on the planet. They're already getting too turbulent to navigate easily.'

'That doesn't make sense, though,' Kolbe objected. 'They'd be cutting us off from their own invasion fleet too.'

'Perhaps that's the idea,' I suggested. 'Let them in, and then close the door before our reinforcements get here.'

Malden looked dubious. 'That would require some pretty good timing,' he pointed out. 'And the warp isn't that cooperative.'

'Well, maybe they know something we don't,' Dimarco snapped, looking more like her old self with every passing minute.

'No doubt they do,' Zyvan said. 'But we know things that they don't, too.' He turned to Hekwyn and Kolbe. 'We need to track down every lead we can squeeze out of the sites you raided. The rest of the cult must have gone to ground somewhere.'

'We're already following up on that,' Hekwyn assured him. He exchanged a glance with Kolbe. 'We'll find them, don't worry.'

'I'm sure you will,' Zyvan said. 'But we're running out of time. If they really are trying to stir up a warp storm to bottle us in, we'll be sitting waterfowl for their invasion fleet.'

It was probably not the most tactful thing he could have said, under the circumstances. Vinzand and his civilian advisors started muttering among themselves, and Dimarco let out a strangulated squeak.

'Well let's make sure it doesn't come to that,' I said. Emperor help me, I was beginning to run out of soothing platitudes already, and the meeting looked like it was going to go on for hours yet. In reality, though, it was about to be abruptly terminated.

'Excuse me, sir.' One of Zyvan's aides approached him, a comm-bead visible in his ear and a data-slate clutched in his hand. 'I think you should see this.'

'Thank you.' Zyvan took it and studied the screen, his expression unreadable. My palms started tingling again. Whatever the news was, it had to be bad. After a moment he handed the slate to me.

'What is it?' I started to say, but the words choked themselves off as I glanced down the page, the breath freezing in my throat as surely as if I'd just stepped into a Valhallan shower.

'Ladies and gentlemen,' the lord general said gravely, 'I've just been informed that our picket ships are engaging the enemy in the outer system. As of this moment Adumbria is under martial law. All Guard and PDF units are to be placed on full invasion alert.'

Blast, I thought. After all I'd been through today, I wouldn't even get the dinner I'd been hoping for.

Editorial Note:

As usual, Cain takes little interest in anything which doesn't affect him directly, so his own narrative jumps rather abruptly at this point. Accordingly, I felt it best to insert some material from other sources in order to present a more balanced picture of the overall situation.

From *Sablist in Skitterfall: a brief history of the Chaos incursion* by Dagblat Tincrowser, 957 M41

If the first blood of the ground campaign had gone to the Valhallan 597th, the credit for the first victory of the conflict in space must surely be given to the crews of the picket ships patrolling the outer reaches of the shipping lanes. To fully appreciate their courage and that of their squadron commander Horatio Bugler, we must bear in mind that they were hopelessly outnumbered by the approaching invaders, and knew it; their job was simply to report as much as they could of the size and disposition of the enemy fleet and escape with their lives if they could. That they did so much more is a shining testament to the fighting spirit of the Imperial Navy and Captain Bugler's outstanding qualities as a tactician and leader of men.[1]

With only two frigates at his disposal, his own *Escapade* and the equally lightly-armed *Virago*, he somehow managed to cripple three of the enemy vessels before withdrawing, having sustained only minor damage to both ships.

From *Flashing Blades! The Falchion-class frigates in action* by Leander Kasmides, 126 M42

An interesting encounter occurred during the attempted invasion of Adumbria, a minor trading world on the fringes of the Damocles Gulf, by traitor forces in 937 M41. Two Falchions had been left on picket duty in the outer system when the main invasion fleet emerged from the warp. The *Escapade* under the command of Captain Bugler and the *Virago* under Captain Walenbruk were both all but untried at this time, having been attached to a task force sent to the Kastafore system a few months before directly from the shipyards at Voss. There they saw little action, having been relegated to extended patrol duties in lightly-contested regions; probably because, as a relatively new class of vessel, the fleet commanders had little idea of their capabilities, preferring to rely on the more familiar Sword-class ships at their disposal.

They were to prove their worth beyond any doubt in this engagement, however, being confronted by an armada of a dozen or so enemy vessels. Fortunately, the vast majority turned out to be armed merchantmen, carrying the ground forces intended to overwhelm the planet, but even so, the sheer weight of numbers would normally have been expected to overwhelm two lone frigates. By adroit manoeuvring, however, they were able to attack the enemy from behind, where none of the freighters could direct return fire, blowing two of them apart with torpedo volleys before concentrating their primary batteries against a third, gutting it completely. At this juncture, the escorting warships began to return fire, and the *Escapade* and *Virago* boosted away before they could close the range sufficiently to inflict any significant damage.

This might be considered unfortunate, as two of the enemy ships

---

1. *As most readers have no doubt guessed, this is an early incident in the long and glorious career of Fleet Admiral Bugler. Unlike General Sulla, however, he has yet to produce his own account of it, or anything else for that matter, for which we should probably be thankful.*

were positively identified as Infidel-class raiders; the very design which was stolen by traitors from the shipyards at Monsk, and the attempted reconstruction of which had resulted in the development of the incomparable Falchion class. A duel between these very different siblings would have been the first recorded clash of the two classes anywhere within the sector; as it was that epic confrontation would have to wait a little longer, until the Sabatine incident some seven months and over a hundred parsecs away...

TWELVE

'Hurry up and wait.'
– Guardsman's traditional summation
of the process of deployment

THE JOURNEY BACK to Glacier Peak was as tedious as I'd expected, despite being relatively short, the lord general having taken the trouble to put another flyer at my disposal. Within twenty minutes of us having become airborne, the rectangle of sky beyond the viewport had darkened to the perpetual night of the coldside, relieved only by the glimmering of the stars above, and I watched the blue-tinted landscape below us rippling away with a sense of ennui I could only put down to the dispiriting realisation that the crisis was finally upon us. Even the excellent amasec in my hip flask, which I'd taken the opportunity of replenishing from the lord general's private stock before we left, was insufficient to raise my mood. I found myself watching the skies for some sign of motion, despite knowing full well that the enemy fleet was still too far away for any of the vessels to be visible yet.

It was only as we began to descend towards the landing pad that I sat up and took notice of the scene below us, the vast familiar bulk of a dropship seeming to fill the entire field of compacted ice. Our pilot seemed competent enough, though, making a final approach and circling around the space-going behemoth in order to give us a better view of it. (Or so it seemed; no doubt he was merely trying to find somewhere to set down.) Under the constant glare of the luminators I could see a steady stream of vehicles the size of my thumbnail rumbling up the loading ramps, directed by arm-waving ants. At least Kasteen was on the ball. There was no point waiting until the traitors actually arrived before getting our rapid reaction force poised and waiting. I found myself nodding approval as our skids hit the permafrost at last and I went to rouse an ashen-faced Jurgen (who, true to form, had relished our short flight not at all).

'The dropship arrived about three hours ago,' Kasteen confirmed as I entered the relative warmth of the command centre, brushed a couple of centimetres of snow from the brim of my hat and sent Jurgen off to find me some tanna.

'As we didn't know how soon you'd be back, Ruput and I thought we should make the assignments without waiting for your input.' She was perfectly within her rights to do so, of course. Technically the regimental commissar is only supposed to scrutinise command decisions and suggest alternative courses of action if they have grounds to believe that the fighting abilities of the unit are being compromised. The habit we'd got into of including me in preliminary discussions and tactical meetings was a purely informal arrangement.[1]

'Quite right too,' I said cheerfully, masking a faint sense of being left out of things which vaguely surprised me. 'Which company did you pick?'

'Second,' Broklaw told me, looking up from the hololith, which was jumping just as badly as I remembered, presumably no one had bothered to get a tech-priest in to bless the thing in my absence. (Then again, our enginseers were probably too busy getting our vehicles into fighting trim to bother with trivia like that.) 'None of their platoons were assigned off-base when the dropship came in, and they've already had a bit of practice at rapid deployment here.'

He grinned at me, and after a moment I realised he was referring to our impromptu rescue of the Tallarns on the day of our arrival. So much seemed to have happened since, I found it hard to believe it had only been a couple of weeks ago.

'Good choice,' I said, turning as Jurgen's returning odour told me my tanna had arrived. I took the drink gratefully and let the mug warm a

---

1. And a striking testament to the rapport he'd built up with Kasteen and Broklaw. Most Guard officers in a similar position would consider the regimental commissar a nuisance at best and keep him as far removed from most command decisions as possible.

little feeling back into my non-augmetic fingers. (The pilot had had to set the flyer down some distance away, and it had been a long, cold walk back to the command centre.) 'I'm sure Sulla's got her platoon's Chimeras stowed already.'

'And is offering helpful advice to the other platoon commanders,' the major confirmed dryly.[1]

'So what's the news from HQ?' Kasteen asked.

'We're neck deep in it, as usual.' I sipped the tanna gratefully, feeling the fragrant liquid warming me gently from the inside out. 'You've seen the latest sitreps?'

The colonel nodded, her red hair bouncing gently against her shoulders. 'Enemy fleet inbound, ETA around three days from now. Heretic sorcerers playing frak with the warp and possibly a daemon on the loose. Oh yes, and Emperor knows how many smuggled weapons in the hands of an as-yet undetermined number of insurgents hiding among the civilian population. Have I left anything out?'

'Not really,' I said. 'Unless you count the fact that the Navy doesn't seem to have enough firepower to stop the enemy fleet before it gets here.'

I hadn't envied Zyvan the call on that one. I didn't really understand the problem, naval tactics not being the kind of thing I generally paid attention to, but the main thrust of it seemed to be that the traitors had split their forces. In the kind of warfare I was familiar with, which was all about taking or holding ground, that would have been a fatal mistake, but it seemed things were different on a system-wide scale. Apparently it takes spacecraft so long to get anywhere that once they're drawn out of position they'll never get back to it in any reasonable time frame, so the sort of mobile reserves we generally relied on to bolster a sagging line wouldn't be an option.

When I left, the lord general was still discussing things with his captains, wondering whether to try intercepting one group at a time and risk some of them getting through, or to keep his handful of warships in orbit where the enemy could strike at leisure and almost certainly break through somewhere by concentrating on a weak point.

'Neck deep sounds about right,' Broklaw agreed cheerfully. He turned back to the hololith, bringing it into focus with a practiced thump, I was beginning to think he might have missed his vocation. 'Any thoughts on our own dispositions here?'

---

1. *As a former quartermaster sergeant, Sulla would have had considerable expertise in logistical matters, which probably accounts for her skill in the stowage of vehicles which Cain has remarked upon before. How welcome her willingness to share this knowledge with her fellow officers may have been, we can only speculate.*

Well, I hadn't really, or at least none that he and Kasteen hadn't already had themselves, but the discussion was calming, and I eventually went off to bed feeling considerably happier than I'd expected to. Come what may, I thought, the 597th was as ready for action as it could possibly be, and everything else was in the hands of the Emperor.

AFTER THE RIGOURS of the day you'll no doubt appreciate I was pretty exhausted, and even my spartan quarters in Glacier Peak seemed pretty comfortable by the time I shed my clothes and collapsed into bed. I fell asleep almost at once, but my sleep was to be far from restful. I awoke some time later with a pounding headache, dazed and disoriented, my quarters suffused with a familiar odour.

'Are you all right, sir?' Jurgen asked from the door, and with a curious sensation of *déjà vu* I realised he was holding his lasgun ready for use. I blinked gummy eyes open, yawned loudly, and became suddenly aware that I was holding my laspistol (which, from long habit, I had carefully stowed where I could draw it without leaving the bed[1])

'Bad dreams,' I said, trying to chase the elusive fragments of imagery which were scuttling away from my conscious mind as I became progressively more wakeful.

Jurgen frowned. 'The same as last time, sir?' he asked. The casual question hit me like a jolt of electricity. I nodded slowly, the dim recollection of green eyes and mocking laughter beginning to surface through the throbbing fog in my skull.

'I think so,' I said, becoming steadily more convinced that I had indeed been dreaming of Emeli again. I supposed this was hardly surprising after encountering another of her kind, but even so I found the notion unsettling. I tried to recall the details, but the harder I tried the more elusive they became. 'It was the sorceress again.' I shrugged. Unsettling as it was, it had just been a dream after all. Nevertheless, I found the idea of going back to sleep distinctly unappealing. 'Could you get me some recaff?'

'Of course, commissar.' Jurgen slung the lasgun across his shoulder and left the room, leaving me to drag myself into the shower.

At length, feeling marginally refreshed, I wandered back to the command centre. There was nothing really for me to do there, but as always the sense of waiting for the enemy to make the first move was subtly unnerving, and I found the bustle of troopers going about their business and the constant clamour of messages coming in and out

---

1. *A practice he stuck to whatever the circumstances, even in the most apparently secure locations.*

reassuring; it meant that we were ready for whatever might be about to happen. (Or so I thought at the time; as it turned out no one sane could possibly have predicted the magnitude of the threat we were actually facing, and a good thing too. If I'd had even an inkling of it I'd have been catatonic with terror.)

I wasn't the only one reluctant to rest either: as I snagged a mug of tanna from the urn in the corner and turned to face the room, a flash of red hair caught my eye and I made my way over to Kasteen's desk. She was sprawled back in her chair, her feet on the desktop, snoring faintly. Unwilling to wake her, I turned away, intending to catch up on some of the routine disciplinary reports which were no doubt cluttering up my own desk by now, but she was too good a soldier not to be roused by a nearby footstep.

'What?' She sat up straight, brushing her hair from her eyes with her left hand, the right hovering just above the butt of her bolt pistol. 'Ciaphas?'[1]

'It's all right,' I said. 'Sorry to wake you.' I handed her the mug of tanna, feeling she needed it more than I did. 'Haven't you got a bunk for that sort of thing?'

'I suppose so.' She yawned widely. 'I was just resting my eyes for a moment. Must have dozed off.' She grinned. 'I suppose you'll have to shoot me for sleeping on duty now.'

'Technically,' I pointed out, 'you should have been off duty hours ago. So I suppose I can overlook it just this once.' I shrugged. 'Besides, can you imagine the sheer number of forms I'd have to fill out?'

'I'd hate to put you to that much inconvenience,' Kasteen agreed gravely. She stretched and stood up. 'So, did I miss anything?'

'Haven't a clue,' I admitted cheerfully. 'I've only just got here myself.'

Rather than get involved in a conversation I'd rather avoid, I resorted to a half-truth. 'I couldn't sleep.'

'I know how you feel,' Broklaw said, appearing round a partition with a half-eaten sandwich in his hand. 'It's the waiting that gets to you.' He seemed as edgy as the rest of us, in that curious adrenaline-fuelled state where you feel too tired to rest.

Despite myself I felt a smile beginning to spread across my face. 'Well, we're a fine example for the lower ranks,' I said. 'Jumpier than a bunch of juvies on Emperor's Day Eve.'

'Except it's the heretics who are going to get the presents,' Broklaw said, with undisguised relish. 'Death and damnation, gift-wrapped by

---

1. *It's extremely unusual for senior officers to be on first name terms with their commissars, another indication of Cain's remarkable rapport with the regiment he was attached to.*

the 597th.' I can only assume it was the lack of sleep we were feeling, because the remark struck us all as hilarious, and when the hololith flickered into life with the image of the lord general the first thing he saw was the three of us howling with laughter like a bunch of drunken idiots.

'I'm pleased to see morale in the 597th remains high,' he remarked dryly, as we sobered up and the two Guard officers tugged their uniforms back into shape. He raised a quizzical eyebrow. 'Although I'm surprised to see you all awake at this hour.' He wasn't, of course; he was an old enough campaigner to know exactly how we all felt.

'The feeling's mutual,' I said, being the only one of the three of us who could converse with him without being hamstrung by protocol. The palms of my hands were tingling again, whatever he wanted at this time of night, it wasn't a social call. 'What's happened?'

To my surprise, the image split, Colonel Asmar appearing on the opposite corner of the display. No doubt we had appeared in his at the same time, as his face betrayed a flicker of hastily-masked hostility before he could compose his features again.

'Commissar.' He nodded once, ignoring the others, which at least told me which one of us Zyvan wanted to talk to.

'The Tallarn 229th have discovered something perturbing in their sector,' the lord general explained. His own face took on an expression of barely-masked exasperation. 'A little late in the day, but I suppose we must be thankful for what we can get.'

'The Emperor provides what we need,' Asmar quoted from somewhere, 'not what we want.'[1]

Zyvan's jaw tightened, barely perceptibly. 'What I want are regimental commanders who undertake search and destroy missions when ordered to, instead of going through the motions and doing the least they think they can get away with, and commissars who aren't afraid to get their hands dirty.' My ears pricked up at that, you can be sure. I hadn't a clue what had riled him so much, but it was clear that Asmar, and probably Beije, had hacked him off in no small measure. Probably by spouting Emperor-bothering gobbledygook instead of following orders, if I was any judge. But if the Tallarn's skiving had been backed by his commissar there wasn't a whole lot the lord general could do about it, of course.

'We'll be pleased to help in any way we can,' I said, grabbing the opportunity to stir it as eagerly as you can imagine.

---

1. *From Nordwick's* Considerations of the Divine, *a chapbook of daily meditations (most of which are as platitudinous as that one).*

Zyvan nodded. 'I don't doubt it.' The implied rebuke to Asmar was about as subtle as an ork breaking wind, and the Tallarn colonel's face coloured slightly. 'I was hoping for your input on this, as you seem to have had the most experience of the enemy's sorcerous activities.' To my carefully concealed delight Asmar looked distinctly nervous at this point, and made the sign of the aquila.

'I've shot a few heretics and raided a couple of their hideouts,' I said, conscious of the unmerited reputation for modest heroism that Zyvan expected me to maintain. 'But I think any credit should go to the troopers with me. They did the bulk of the fighting, and not all of them were as lucky as I was.'

'Quite,' the lord general said, buying it wholesale. 'But you have the experience in intelligence assessment and you've fought the Great Enemy before.'

'True,' I said, nodding my head. 'So what's the information our gallant Tallarn comrades have uncovered?' Asmar looked a little suspicious at that, no doubt realising I was taking the frak, but prepared to take the question at face value. (No doubt he had some pious quotation to cover that as well.)

'One of our rough rider patrols encountered a nauga[1] hunter this morning,' he began. 'He mentioned seeing traces of activity near some caverns to the north of our position, so they went to take a look.' Zyvan's expression was hardening by the moment, I noticed. 'What they found there was…'

Words seemed to fail Asmar for a moment, and he made the sign of the aquila again. 'Unholy,' he concluded at last, his face paling.

'Let me guess,' I said. 'Bodies, twisted in some foul fashion, peculiar sigils painted on the walls?' Asmar nodded. 'Did your troopers encounter any resistance?'

'No,' Asmar said. 'The place was deserted.' If he made the sign of the aquila much more, I thought, his fingers were going to fly away. 'But the miasma of evil was palpable.'

'Lucky for them the daemon had already gone,' I said, unable to resist prodding him again. I was rewarded by an expression of unmistakable terror flickering in his eyes. I turned my attention to Zyvan. 'It sounds as though we've found the site of the third ritual.'

'That was my conclusion too,' the lord general agreed.

---

1. *A species of animal indigenous to the hotside of Adumbria. Its toughened hide is highly prized for certain hard-wearing applications, particularly the covering of sofas in waiting rooms.*

'This could be the break we've been looking for,' I went on. 'If Malden can examine a site uncontaminated by battle damage, he might be able to determine precisely what the heretics are up to.'

'He might,' Zyvan agreed. 'If Colonel Asmar and Commissar Beije hadn't taken it upon themselves to destroy the site before he had the chance.'

'It was the only thing to be done,' Asmar insisted. 'Is it not written in the *Meditations of the Saints* that the shrines of the unholy must be cleansed with the fires of the righteous?'

'And is it not written in the manual of common sense that trashing an enemy installation you've had the luck to capture intact before it can be properly examined for useful intelligence is the act of a cretin?' I responded, unable to credit that anyone, even Beije, could have been quite so stupid.

Asmar flushed angrily. 'I know my duty to the Emperor. When I stand before the Golden Throne to meet his judgement, my conscience will be clear.'

'Wonderful,' I said. 'I'm delighted for you.' I returned my attention to Zyvan. 'So in sum, all we know about the enemy's activities on the hotside is that they were definitely there.'

The lord general nodded. 'That's about it,' he agreed.

'Where is "there", exactly?' Kasteen asked.

By way of an answer, Zyvan leaned forward to manipulate some controls we couldn't see, and Asmar's face was replaced by a rotating view of the planet from orbit. A single contact rune marked the position of the heretic shrine, which, on this reduced scale, seemed to be on exactly the opposite side of the planet from Glacier Peak. She nodded. 'Hm. That's interesting.'

'What is?' Zyvan asked.

'It's probably just coincidence, but they form a triangle. Look.' She pointed out Skitterfall, where the other shrine had been. Sure enough, the planetary capital was equidistant between the two points.

'There's no such thing as coincidence where sorcery's concerned,' I said. 'It must be significant somehow.'

'Only if you draw the line from us to the Tallarns directly through the core of the planet,' Broklaw pointed out. 'Would that make a difference?'

'Emperor alone knows,' Zyvan said. 'We're dealing with warpcraft, so little details like a planet being in the way might not matter to them. I'll talk to Malden and the others, see what they think.' He nodded thoughtfully. 'Well spotted, colonel.'

He seemed on the verge of cutting the link, so I stepped in quickly.

'One other thing,' I said. 'Any word from the fleet yet?'

Zyvan shook his head. 'The warp's still too churned up for the astropaths to get a message through. When or if they arrive is in the lap of the Emperor.'

'About what I expected,' I said. He cut the link. Kasteen, Broklaw and I looked at each other in silence. After a moment, the major put what we were all thinking into words.

'I think it's just risen to our chins,' he said.

Since the battle in space played a decisive part in what was to follow, and Cain doesn't bother to mention it at all, another short extract from Tincrowser's account of the campaign seems to be called for at this point. He is somewhat imprecise on the details, as one might expect from a civilian, but he covers the main points well enough.

From *Sablist in Skitterfall: a brief history of the Chaos incursion* by Dagblat Tincrowser, 957 M41

As the enemy fleet continued to make its way towards Adumbria it fragmented, splitting into three groups, no doubt in an attempt to evade the gallant defenders. Two of these seemed relatively unthreatening, consisting as they did of lightly armed vessels[1] while the third contained the majority of the transports and their escorting warships.[2]

---

1. *Three each of the armed merchantmen so casually dispatched by the Falchions in the earlier engagement.*

2. *The two Infidel-class vessels mentioned by Kasmides, a Desolator-class battleship and between five and eight transport ships. The records are a little hazy on this point due to the high volume of legitimate merchant shipping in the system at the time.*

Having shown their mettle in the first engagement and being the only vessels in a position to intercept them before they made orbit, the *Escapade* and *Virago* were each given the task of harrying one of the smaller flotillas; this they did successfully enough, although neither was able to prevent all of their intended victims from reaching the planet. The *Escapade* fared the better of the two, managing to destroy all but one of its targets and suffering minimal damage in the process, while the *Virago* destroyed one completely. Unfortunately, in so doing it was caught in a crossfire by the remaining pair, doing sufficient damage to its engines that it soon fell behind, unable to continue the engagement.

The main body of the enemy fleet continued to drift inwards towards Adumbria, daring the remainder of the Imperial Navy forces to intercept it, but they refused to rise to the bait. The *Indestructible* remained in orbit above Skitterfall, where it was joined by the squadron of destroyers[1] which had until then been patrolling the inner shipping lanes.

So it was that three vessels of the enemy advance guard were able to enter orbit and deploy the troops they carried, the first to pollute the soil of our beloved home world. One at least was to regret its temerity, however, as the hotly-pursuing *Escapade* caught and overwhelmed it almost immediately, sending it plunging to a fiery doom in the upper atmosphere.

This would be scant comfort to the gallant defenders, however, as for the first time combat was joined on the surface. And, as before, the Valhallans were to find themselves in the forefront of the battle.

---

1. *Three Cobras: the* Gallant, Impetuous *and* Spiteful.

THIRTEEN

'If your battle plan's working, it's probably a trap.'
    – Kolton Phae, *On Military Matters*, 739 M41

IRKSOME AS IT had been waiting for the enemy to arrive, once they did
the monotony and tension which had suffused the last couple of days
began to seem positively welcome in retrospect. I was in the command
post with most of the senior staff at the time; Kasteen, Broklaw and all
the company commanders who weren't deployed elsewhere, watching
the contact icons lighting up in the hololith as the enemy troops made
planetfall. I'd been expecting a concerted assault on the capital, but
within moments it began to look as though the planet was suffering
from a case of the underhive pox, red spots appearing all over the place
apparently at random.

'What the hell are they up to?' Detoi muttered at my elbow, clearly
chafing at the lack of any obvious troop concentrations to deploy
rapidly against.

'Beats me,' I said, having fought the minions of Chaos too often
before to expect much of what they did to make sense. With hindsight,
it was explicable, but at the time we were still missing some vital pieces
of the puzzle.

'It looks to me as though they're just getting the troops down as quickly as they can,' Kasteen said. 'They can't expect the transports to last long unsupported.' As if to emphasise her words, one of the three contacts in orbit flared suddenly and began to descend, spewing debris and shuttles as it went.

'Well, that's something,' I said, indicating it. 'Looks like the Navy's saved us a bit of spadework there.'

From the patterns of the landings and the occasions when I'd been part of a force moved by a freighter rather than a specialised troop-ship, I knew that the civilian shuttles they carried would have to make several trips back and forth to disembark all the warriors aboard. Of course, I wouldn't expect Chaos fanatics to worry too much about safety margins and overcrowding, but even so the descending fireball above us would only have had time to disembark about a third of the cannon fodder they carried. Normally a ship that size would be expected to carry a full regiment of Imperial Guard, but again there was no telling if the enemy had packed in more than that.

'The Tallarns are going to take a battering,' Broklaw remarked, not seeming terribly concerned at the prospect.

It was true that there seemed to be a concentration of enemy forces building close to their position on the hotside, but that was their problem. Ours was defending the population of Glacier Peak. I glanced at the hololith again, seeing the final wave of shuttles from the doomed freighter screaming down through the atmosphere towards us.

We were ready for them, our troops deployed around the town in what should have been an impenetrable cordon. Second company remained in our compound, as their vehicles were still stowed aboard the dropship, which I was suddenly aware would make a very tempting target if the enemy had any aerospace units. (As it turned out, though, that was a needless worry. The freighters only carried civilian shuttles, which were unarmed, gratifyingly easy targets for the PDF fighter pilots, who made sure that damn few of them were able to make more than a couple of drop runs.)

I turned to Detoi. 'Better make sure your people are sharp,' I said. 'We might need them to defend this position if they're not called on for support somewhere else.' I was only trying to encourage him at the time, knowing he'd rather be ordering their embarkation for some distant battlefront, but I spoke truer than I knew. In theory, first company had a couple of platoons in reserve to do the job, but Glacier Peak was a big enough place to take care of, and it was perfectly feasible that they'd find themselves otherwise occupied at the time.

He nodded dutifully. 'Incoming,' one of the auspex operators said, her voice tense. 'Five contacts, airborne, closing fast. They're widely scattered.'

'All units prepare to engage,' Kasteen said, as calmly as if she were ordering another mug of tanna. She glanced up at me. 'Commissar?'

I made some encouraging remarks over the open vox link, invoked the protection of the Emperor and turned to Detoi.

'If you don't mind, captain,' I said, 'I think I'd rather join your company while this is going on.'

This might seem a little odd, given that I was in a warm, bullet-proof building at the time, but as usual my paranoid streak was thinking about a number of uncomfortable possibilities. For one thing, we knew the heretics had had plenty of time to infiltrate the local PDF, even though nobody senior had been netted by Kolbe's investigators yet, and they certainly had some ears among the Council of Claimants (or at least their households). It wasn't entirely unfeasible that they knew where our regimental headquarters was, and if that was true and any of those incoming shuttles were armed, I was currently sitting in the middle of the most tempting target for a bombing run on the entire coldside. Out in the open, on the other hand, unpleasant as it was, I'd have a much better chance of surviving an aerial attack.

'Have fun.' Kasteen grinned at me, no doubt believing I was just eager to be in with a better chance of facing the enemy.

I directed a carefully composed smile in her direction. 'We'll try to save a couple for you,' I promised, as though she was right, and fell into step beside Detoi as we left the bustling room behind us.

'Commissar.' Jurgen was waiting outside, and had been for some time judging by the aroma of old socks which suffused the corridor. He pulled himself to a semblance of attention, his usual collection of mismatched equipment pouches rattling slightly as he shouldered his precious melta, which clanked against his lasgun. Detoi returned his salute crisply and without a trace of a smile. She was one of the few officers in the regiment who at least pretended to consider him a proper soldier.

'Jurgen.' I nodded a greeting, relieved to see him, and surreptitiously adjusted the straps of the carapace concealed under my greatcoat. Clearly we were both expecting trouble. 'We were about to take a small constitutional around the compound.'

'I thought you might, sir.' My aide burrowed in one of the pouches. 'So I took the liberty of making a flask of tea. Knowing how you feel the cold a bit.'

'Very thoughtful,' I said, forestalling the motion. 'But perhaps later.' The faint sound of engines was audible now, and if they were about to attack the building we didn't have much longer to get outside. I turned to Detoi. 'Shall we go?'

'By all means.' He led the way outside into the perpetual cold and night. I glanced up, the sky even clearer than usual now that the lumi-nators had been doused in anticipation of an enemy attack, the stars burning down at us colder and harder than ever. A few of them seemed to be moving, the whine of their engines growing louder by the minute.

I tapped the comm-bead in my ear. 'Visual contact,' I said. 'I can see three of them, approaching from due east. High and fast.'

'That's odd,' Broklaw said. 'A couple of them are overshooting the town.'

'Heading for us, maybe,' Kasteen cut in.

'They're dispersing,' the auspex operator confirmed. 'They're in a landing pattern, but it seems uncontrolled.'

'Hardly surprising,' I said, taking the amplivisor Jurgen was holding out with a nod of thanks and raising it to my eyes. After a moment of searching, I found one of the shuttles and brought its magnified image into focus. 'With the amount of damage they've taken it's a miracle they're flying at all.' In the faint orange light of the early dawn I could make out jagged rents in the hull and a plume of smoke from its engines. It was juddering wildly and must have been hell to keep under control.

Well, good. If it crashed that would be one less bunch of lunatics left to deal with.

I lowered the lenses and handed the amplivisor back to Jurgen, who stowed it away somewhere. He was growing steadily more visible as the sun rose behind me, a faint shadow beginning to stretch from his feet. My own also became gradually visible on the hard-packed snow. Absently I found myself thinking it was the first time I'd seen it since we'd arrived on Adumbria…

'Emperor on Earth!' I said, the coin finally dropping, whirling round to stare at the fireball scorching its way across the sky above us. For the first and last time in Adumbrian history, the coldside was wanly illuminated by the death throes of the traitors' transport ves-sel, and the troopers around me raised a spontaneous cheer at the sight. Well, who could blame them? As it faded over the western horizon, setting as abruptly as it had risen, a scream of tortured air followed it, like the howling of daemons clawing free from the warp.

After that, an eerie silence seemed to settle across us, leeching the sound from the air as the light faded back to the constant faint blue of the endless starlight.

'That's going to make a dent when it hits,'[1] Detoi prophesied, and trotted away to find his command team. There was little time to waste on idle conversation after that, as the enemy were suddenly upon us.

'One contact down. No, three,' the auspex operator reported. 'One two kilometres to the south, another in the north-eastern suburbs.'

'We can see it,' a new voice I recognised as one of the platoon commanders from fourth company chimed in. 'First and third squads moving in to contain them.'

'Contact three down in the town centre,' the auspex operator continued.

'Fifth company, encircle and eliminate,' Kasteen ordered, while another platoon from fourth moved up to support their comrades in the suburbs. I was beginning to think about ducking back inside and following the action on the chart table, which would be a great deal preferable to freezing out here now the threat of an air attack was almost past.

'Contact four heading due west,' the auspex operator droned on. 'Looks like they're overshooting.'

'Engaging,' a lieutenant from first company cut in, her voice shrill with excitement. 'They're practically overhead.' Her words were almost drowned out by the roar of half a dozen Chimeras unloading both their heavy bolters at once, and I was hardly surprised to hear a faint cheer over the channel a moment later. With all that firepower they must have hit something, even by sheer blind luck. 'Got him! He's trailing smoke... Frak it, he's still airborne.'

I glanced up, seeing a dark mass scream overhead, vivid orange flames licking around its main engine before it disappeared into the distance in the vague direction of the hab dome we'd found. They wouldn't find any help there, I reflected grimly. Asmar had been right about one thing: a place that tainted couldn't be allowed to exist. The difference had been that we'd made damn sure we'd learned everything we could about it before we'd let Federer out to play. All the descending heretics were going to find (if they got down in one piece, which didn't seem all that likely at this point) was a scorched pile of rubble and third platoon, fourth company, who'd been camping out there for

---

1. *It eventually impacted on the hotside, about a hundred kilometres from the nominal boundary of the shadow zone, gouging a crater a little over three kilometres in diameter. A half-hearted attempt to promote the site as a tourist attraction after the war understandably failed, since few citizens could be bothered to put up with the time and discomfort required to look at what was really nothing more than a big hole in the ground. The caravansari established for their use eventually became a holiday lodge for affluent city dwellers who fancied the idea of a weekend nauga hunt.*

almost a week by this point and were just itching for something to kill to relieve the monotony.

'Recon one, two and three heading out to contact two,' Captain Shambas reported. 'Let's see what the frakheads are up to.' That made good sense: the three sentinel squadrons were designed for just such a task and would get to the shuttle which had grounded to the south far quicker than any other units we had.

'Good luck, captain,' Kasteen said, making it official, although the sentinel pilots would be hard to dissuade now the idea that they had a target-rich environment all to themselves had had time to sink in. Any other response would be far more trouble than it was worth. Calling them off would be difficult and time-consuming and probably involve an inordinate number of freak vox failures, so on the whole it was probably best to just let them get on with it. (Which they did, mopping up the entire group quite happily without needing to call for backup.)

That just left one of the incoming shuttles unaccounted for, and with a thrill of horror I realised that the engine noise which so far had been a loud, consistent sound in the background was rising in pitch alarmingly.

'Incoming!' I shouted, just as the auspex operator managed to find her arse with both hands and a map.

'Contact five inbound, closing fast,' she reported. 'Estimated LZ within half a kilometre.'

'It's a frak sight closer than that!' I shouted as the frozen air around us lit up with las bolts, the troopers spitting defiant small-arms fire at the descending ship. The heavy bolters mounted on the company Chimeras might have made a difference, of course, but they were still aboard the dropship, and I might just as well have wished for a battery of Hydras while I was about it. 'Prepare to engage!'

'Look out, commissar!' Jurgen grabbed my arm, urging me to duck as the ungainly shuttle swooped overhead, seeming close enough to touch, the wind of its passing grabbing the cap from my head and spinning it off into the darkness. A vice of cold clamped itself around my temples, driving needles of ice into my forebrain and the back of my eyes. I scrabbled instinctively after my tumbling headgear, which probably saved my life, as the snow around me began puffing into vapour under the impetus of multiple las bolt impacts.

'Frak this!' I drew my trusty laspistol, grabbing my elusive cap with the other hand and jamming it over my head. The migraine receded a little, and what felt like a couple of kilos of melting slush mashed itself into my hair and slithered down my neck. I turned in time to see the wounded shuttle hit the snow, skid and plough itself to a halt in a long groove of friction-melted ice, which began to freeze instantly around it. In the process, it shed the dimly-glimpsed figures which had been hanging out of the rear cargo doors firing wildly, coming so close to hitting me. They cart-wheeled through the air, striking the permafrost with an impact sufficient to shatter bone and liquefy flesh. And serve them right, I thought. None of them stirred again, merely acquiring makeshift shrouds of lightly-drifting snow as the battle raged about them.

For battle it was. There were plenty of their comrades left aboard, and they came boiling out of the steam-shrouded wreck like parasites fleeing a dying grox, firing wildly as they went. The Valhallans returned fire with all the disciplined professionalism I'd come to expect, dropping them by the dozen, but the survivors swept on, frenzied as an orkish war band.

'Something's not right about this,' I said, firing my pistol at the onrushing mob, then ducking for cover behind a snow-shrouded drum of some foul-smelling lubricant the enginseers had been using on a partially disassembled Chimera. The cultists we'd faced before had been fanatical, of course, but they'd shown a modicum of tactical sense.

'No kidding.' Corporal Magot jogged past, grinning happily, her fireteam in tow, lobbing frag grenades in the general direction of the enemy. 'It's almost too easy.' One of the troopers with her went down suddenly, a spray of fresh blood freezing almost instantly into a bright, hard scab across his chest.

'Medic,' I voxed, dragging the man under cover. It was a good excuse to keep my head down and it never hurt to seem concerned about the ordinary troopers. Magot shot me a grateful smile with an edge colder than the flensing wind.

'Thanks, boss.' Her voice rose. 'Are we going to let 'em get away with that?'

'Hell, no!' the rest of the team chorused in unison.

'Then let's frag one for Smitti!' With a roar that sounded almost like a mob of orks, they charged off into the snow looking for something to kill. I began to feel almost sorry for the enemy.

I busied myself looking after the wounded trooper until the medic arrived, then glanced back up over our makeshift barricade. The compound was in uproar by this time, small knots of traitors in flimsy crimson fatigues and black flak armour[1] engaging squads and fireteams

---

1. *Presumably by this time the luminators had been rekindled, as these colours would have been almost indistinguishable under the starlight, or Cain may simply be writing with the benefit of hindsight.*

almost at random. They fought with the fury of the possessed or the truly insane, heedless of their personal safety or anything resembling tactics, apparently intent on charging into close combat as quickly as they could.

'If they made it any easier they'd be on our side,' Jurgen said, triggering his melta for the third or fourth time and bringing down what seemed like most of a squad. The snow around them was littered with steaming chunks of meat where their predecessors had fared little better.

'Blood for the Blood God!' A red-uniformed trooper came screaming out of the endless night at me, his old-fashioned autogun held across his chest like a pole arm, apparently intent on using the wickedly-serrated bayonet clipped to its barrel. I assumed at the time that he was out of ammunition, but for all I know he was just carried away by bloodlust.

'Harriers for the cup!'[1] I riposted, shooting him in the face. His head liquefied under the impact of the las bolt and he fell heavily to the snow at my feet. I looked around, feeling that things were getting a little out of hand here.

'Captain Detoi, report.' Kasteen sounded calm enough, so at least none of the fanatics had made it as far as the command bunker yet. 'What's going on out there?'

'The captain's down,' Sulla reported. 'I've taken command.'

Wonderful, I thought, as if we weren't in enough trouble already. But she had the seniority, and interfering now would be seriously counter-productive, so I just cut in with some encouraging platitudes. 'We're containing them, but they're persistent little frakkers.'

'Well, we won't have to hold them much longer,' I pointed out, drawing my chainsword in time to bisect a persistent enemy trooper who was trying to interrupt me with a rusty-looking combat blade. His movements were slow and sluggish, the flesh of his face and hands pinched and blue. 'The cold's going to finish them off for us pretty soon.'

After that I shut up and let Sulla get on with it, just keeping an ear on the vox channel to make sure she didn't do anything too stupid, although to be fair she did a reasonable job of co-ordinating the different platoons and had the sense to put Lustig in charge of her own. By this time trooper Smitti had been carted off to the medicae receiving station, so I couldn't see any reason not to return to the command centre and let things play themselves out without me.

---

1. *A reference to a scrumball team in the subsector league (who were knocked out in the semi-finals that year, incidentally).*

I tapped Jurgen on the shoulder. 'We're heading back inside,' I told him. 'It's all over out here bar the clean-up.'

I should have known better, of course. Sometimes I think that the Emperor's listening to me just so he can spring a little surprise every time I say something like that.

'Second squad, say again,' a voice was shouting in my earpiece, one I recognised as Lieutenant Faril, the officer in charge of fifth platoon. It was one of a dozen routine exchanges I'd barely noticed in the course of the battle, but there was an edge of alarm in his tone which sounded new. 'Second squad, report.'

'It's unstoppable!' another voice replied. 'Heading for the perimeter...' The report choked off with a scream. I flicked my head around, certain I'd heard the sound overlapping in the way that means the source of a vox transmission is close enough for the noise to carry naturally through the air almost simultaneously, and sure enough, the intensity of lasgun fire in the immediate vicinity was growing.

'Get some backup to them,' Sulla ordered crisply, and Faril dispatched another couple of squads.

Well, that was enough to persuade me that I needed to be back in the command centre right away, where I could find out just what the hell was going on, and I hurried around the disassembled Chimera intent on nothing more than getting back inside as soon as I could. Abruptly, though, I found myself surrounded by running troopers, as by great bad luck my path intersected with the reinforcements Faril had just ordered in.

'Commissar!' One of the sergeants glanced over in my direction, his face a mask of delighted surprise. A ripple of resolve shivered almost visibly along the score of troopers double timing in his wake and I cursed under my breath. I couldn't duck out now without denting their morale and doing who knew what damage to my reputation. I nodded a genial greeting and dredged the man's name up from the depths of my memory.

'Dyzun.' I shrugged. 'I hope you don't mind me sticking my nose in, but it sounds as though something interesting's going on.'

'Glad to see you, sir,' he said, with every sign of sincerity, and Emperor strike me dead if I'm exaggerating, but the whole lot of them started chanting my name like a battlecry.

'Cain! Cain! Cain! Cain!'

Maybe it was that which took our opponent off-guard for a moment, mistaking it for the chant of the followers of his own blasphemous god, because he turned his head slowly to look at us, drawing his attention reluctantly from the corpses of second squad which lay all around him.

Only a few survivors still stirred, trying feebly to raise weapons or crawl to safety.

'Emperor on Earth!' I said, my bowels spasming. The man, if man he still was, was a giant, towering over us all. My months as the Guard liaison to the Reclaimers had left me familiar with the superhuman stature of the Astartes and with a healthy respect for the strength and durability of the armour they wore, but this was no paladin of the Emperor's will; quite the opposite. His armour was blood red and black, like the uniforms of the cultists still dying in droves around us, and chased with vile designs in burnished orichalcum. He carried a bolt pistol holstered at his belt, but apparently distained to use it. His hands, encased in massive gauntlets, gripped a curious weapon, like a battleaxe, but surrounded with whirling metal teeth like my own trusty chainsword.

'You swear by the corpse god?' The thing's voice was gutteral, from a throat constricted with rage, and so deeply resonant that I felt it reverberate through my very bones. 'Your skull will grace the throne of the true power!'

'Big red thing, five rounds rapid fire!' Dyzun ordered, remarkably calmly under the circumstances, and the troopers snapped out of their astonishment to comply. But the twisted parody of a Marine was fast, at least as agile as one of the true heroes he aped, and leapt aside, avoiding most of it. The few las bolts which struck his armour scored it, adding to the pockmarks already inflicted by the luckless second squad, and I felt vindictive laughter resonating through my bones.

As ill luck would have it, his leap carried him over the heads of most of the troopers, to land almost at my feet. I felt a bolt of sheer terror arc through me as the metal-clad giant tilted his head forward to look down at where I stood, and swung his chain axe with lightning speed. Which was his first mistake. Had he made any other attack he might well have killed me where I stood, still paralysed with fear, but the whining chain blades triggered my duellist's reflexes and I parried the blow with my own gently-humming chainsword without a second's hesitation. That snapped me out of it, you can be sure, and I began to fight for my life in deadly earnest.

'Is that the best you can do?' I taunted him, sure that in his arrogance he had expected an easy kill, and hoping to goad him into making a mistake. Not that I had any serious hope of besting him in a prolonged fight, of course; my unaugmented muscles would tire quickly, even without the strength-sapping cold, and his already superhuman endurance would be boosted by the power armour he wore. But if I could keep him pinned long enough for the troopers with me to line up a good shot and somehow disengage before they took it, I hoped I could wipe the smile off his face... if he still had one under that grotesque helmet.

I slashed at his chest, raising a shower of sparks from the abused ceramite. 'I thought the acolytes of Khorne were supposed to be warriors, not a bunch of pansies.'

'I'll feed you your own entrails!' the giant roared, slashing down again with his cumbersome weapon. This time I deflected it so that it struck his own leg, raising another shower of golden sparks and a cheer from the surrounding troopers.

'Like I've never heard that before,' I sneered, following through and getting right under his guard. I rolled in the snow, making as much distance as I could, seeing him turn out of the corner of my eye and raising the axe again.

He never completed the motion. The actinic light of Jurgen's melta stabbed the darkness, vaporising the middle of his chest, and he stumbled, dropping slowly to his knees. I scrambled hurriedly to my feet, having no desire to be crushed to death under all that falling metal, and holstered my weapons.

'Thank you, Jurgen,' I said, brushing the accumulated snow from my greatcoat.

'You're welcome, sir.' My aide lowered the cumbersome weapon as our defeated enemy slumped to the permafrost with a sound like an accident in a bell foundry. 'Will there be anything else?'

'Now you come to mention it,' I said, conscious of the rapt attention of the troopers surrounding us and straightening my cap with all the insouciance I could muster, 'I think now would be a good time for that tea.'

Editorial Note:

There were other engagements, equally hard-fought, across most of Adumbria, although naturally Cain doesn't think they're worth more than the most casual of references. Indeed, the attack on the regimental headquarters in which he was involved was arguably a minor sideshow to the main battle for Glacier Peak, in which the bulk of the regiment and the local PDF garrison acquitted themselves most creditably.

So once again we must rely on other sources to fill the gaps, and once again Tincrowser's populist account does a workmanlike job of sketching in the bigger picture.

From *Sablist in Skitterfall: a brief history of the Chaos incursion* by Dagblat Tincrowser, 957 M41

TO THE SURPRISE of many, Skitterfall itself saw relatively little action during this first incursion. In retrospect, this was almost certainly due to the presence of the warships in orbit above it, which would have made any direct approach almost suicidal. Indeed, the Cobra squadron and the triumphant *Escapade* made short work of the two remaining starships before either had the opportunity to flee back into deep space. But the damage had been done and several thousand enemy soldiers had landed by the time their transports had been repulsed.

The overall strategy of these raids, if there even was one, has been the subject of much speculation over the last twenty years. In very few cases did the enemy mass in sufficient numbers to pose a serious threat, and it seems most likely that they were there simply to allow their masters aboard the main fleet to gauge the strength of the resistance they were to expect when they arrived in force. Any damage they were able to inflict by these hit and run tactics would have been a welcome bonus, of course, and it cannot be denied that the psychological effect of their arrival was considerable; the panic and civil disorder in many of the major population centres certainly increased for a time, although this was followed by a period of relative calm, the populace no doubt reflecting that the worst of their fears had now come to pass.

As has previously been noted, relatively few of the enemy landed in Skitterfall itself, the defences around the starport proving a formidable deterrent for those few who tried. Indeed, so strong was the resistance here that the few shuttles which made it through were forced to land in the suburbs, far from the city centre, where the local PDF, ably assisted by the Valhallan tanks and Kastaforean infantry elements of the Imperial Guard, were able to repulse them in pretty short order. Rumours at the time of patriotic citizens forming ad hoc militia units to meet the threat can now, with the wisdom of hindsight, be seen for the wishful thinking they undoubtedly were, but such tales undoubtedly played a part in boosting the resolve of the civilian population to resist the invader.

The largest battles of the first incursion occurred in the most unlikely of places: the town of Glacier Peak on the coldside and an area of wilderness on the hotside of note only for the fact that the Tallarn element of the relieving task force had established their headquarters there in the remains of an old botanical testing station.[1] Given that Glacier Peak was the headquarters of the Valhallan 597th, it seems probable that part of the reason for the incursion was an attempt to inflict damage on the two Guard regiments most isolated from their fellows. If that was indeed the case, the traitors were to be sorely disappointed.

---

1. *A relic of an ambitious, and quite clearly doomed from the start, attempt to establish some kind of agricultural industry in the perpetual sunshine of the hotside in the early years of the third century M41.*

The Tallarn 229th were to prove their reputation for the mastery of desert warfare was richly merited, driving off and slaughtering their attackers with almost contemptuous ease. In this they were undoubtedly assisted by their familiarity with the harsh environment they found themselves in, as the heretics were to find the conditions there debilitating in the extreme. Indeed, one contemporary account suggests that almost as many were to die of dehydration and heatstroke as at the hands and weapons of the Guardsmen.

The same could be said of the contingent which attacked the coldside, many of them succumbing to the freezing temperatures as readily as to the martial zeal of the Valhallans, who, as natives of an ice world, found them no handicap. The town of Glacier Peak offered many refuges from the killing cold, however, and the struggle there became one of prolonged attrition, driving the invaders out street by street, building by building. And, despite the best efforts of the Guard troopers, many civilians were to suffer and die in the crossfire. Their sacrifice was not to be in vain, however, as at length the last of the heretic scum were hunted down as they attempted to flee the town on foot, braving the freezing temperatures of the wilderness. This, above all else, points to their sheer desperation, as there was undoubtedly no shelter to be found there.

FOURTEEN

'Things can always get worse.'

– Valhallan proverb

'WELL, THAT WAS unexpected.' Zyvan nodded gravely in the centre of the hololith. His head, about a quarter life size, was surrounded by others, orbiting around him like the moons of a gas giant: the commanders of the other Guard regiments, their commissars, Malden, Kolbe and a couple of other faces I didn't recognise but who probably had something to do with the PDF. To my vague relief there was no sign of Vinzand, so things would probably go a little more smoothly; no doubt Zyvan felt we were getting into things no civilian, however exalted, needed to know. I noted the absence of the lady Dimarco with slightly mixed feelings, she was decorative enough and her presence would have been a welcome distraction from the collection of military men, but her corrosive personality went a long way towards negating that.

And talking of corrosive personalities, Beije was there, along with Asmar of course, trying desperately to look as though he understood what was going on. Well, I supposed I could always amuse myself by needling him if things got too tedious.

'Are you absolutely positive about this?' True to form, Beije couldn't resist sticking his nose in, heedless of the opinions of anyone else in the conference link. 'Not that I doubt Commissar Cain's veracity for a moment,' his tone quite clearly implying the opposite, 'but I'm sure I'm not the only one here who finds this story a little hard to swallow.'

Asmar nodded in agreement, although most of the others remained stone-faced and a few visibly bristled, especially the CO of the Valhallan tankies and his commissar. 'I know he has something of a swashbuckling reputation,' Beije prattled on, cheerfully oblivious to the reception he was getting, 'but the idea of any man defeating a member of the Traitor Legions in single combat has to be difficult to credit.'

'Indeed it would be,' I responded, 'if that were the case. But I can hardly take the credit for the actions of others.' Not if there was a chance I wouldn't be able to get away with it, anyway. 'I simply exchanged a couple of blows with the fellow. The kill was made by my aide and a couple of squads of our troopers. Who, incidentally,' I added to Zyvan, 'I would like to recommend for commendations.'

I was rewarded by a projection field full of nodding heads and benign smiles. That was the trick which had always worked best for me: appearing to be modest about my supposed heroism. Now the legend would grow out of all proportion, until half the troopers on the planet would indeed be convinced that I'd bested a tainted superman in a contest of blades. The only exceptions, of course, were Asmar and Beije.

'Are we even convinced that it was one of the accursed traitors?' Beije asked, worrying at the argument like a kroot with a bone, completely unable to grasp that the more he tried to undermine my supposed achievement the more he consolidated the fact in everyone else's mind. 'It could just have been one of the cultists of unusual stature.'

'Pretty convinced,' Zyvan said dryly, the image in the hololith changing to show the corpse of the dead Chaos Marine. I didn't need to see the expressions on the assembled faces at that point, as the collective intake of breath was perfectly audible. There was absolutely no chance of mistaking that monstrous corpse for anything else. After a moment the image returned to the mass of heads. 'We've positively identified him as a member of the World Eaters Legion.'

'Are we to infer, then, that the next stage of the attack will be carried out by a Traitor Legion?' Kolbe asked, managing to keep his voice steady with an effort someone less adept than I was at reading people would have found hard to spot.

Zyvan shook his head. 'With Chaos, of course, nothing is certain, but I doubt it. Were that the case, we would be facing a far greater fleet and the World Eaters would be proclaiming themselves openly rather than hiding behind the banner of the Ravagers.'

'Not very big on subtlety, Khorne cultists,' I chipped in helpfully, underlining the fact that with the possible exception of Zyvan, I probably had more experience of facing the various factions of Chaos than anyone else on the planet.

Kasteen looked at me curiously. 'I thought you said they worshipped something called Slaynish?'

'The heretics we've been fighting so far seem to be Slaaneshi cultists,' I said, emphasising the correct pronunciation almost imperceptibly. 'Which is odd, to say the least.'

'What's the difference?' Beije asked impatiently. 'A heretic's a heretic. We should just kill the lot of them and let the Emperor sort them out.'

'I quite agree,' I said, enjoying the brief flicker of astonishment and uncertainty which crossed his face. 'But it may not be as simple as that.'

'Quite.' Zyvan nodded. 'What Commissar Cain is aware of, and some of you appear not to be, is that Chaos is not a single, unified enemy. Not very often, anyway, thank the Emperor.' The few in the conference circuit who knew what he was talking about looked visibly perturbed, no doubt visualising the Gothic War or the last Black Crusade. (Perhaps mercifully, none of us was even able to guess at the magnitude of the next one, lurking a mere sixty years or so in our collective futures.)

'Quite,' I said. I addressed Zyvan directly again. 'I assume everyone here has the necessary security clearance to be discussing this?' Of course they would, or he would never have raised the subject, but he enjoyed a bit of melodrama as much as I did and nodded gravely.

'You may continue,' he said.

Well, that was a bit of a shock, I'd been looking forward to dozing through the meeting, rousing myself just long enough to tease Beije if the opportunity arose, but I've never been averse to being the centre of attention, so I nodded as though I'd been expecting something of the kind.

'There are four principal Ruinous Powers,' I began, 'at least as far as we know. Heretics worship them as gods, and of all the warp entities so far discovered, only they are strong enough to challenge the Emperor Himself for dominion of the immaterium.'

'Challenge the Emperor?' Beije was outraged. 'The very idea is blasphemy!' He leaned forward, apparently reaching for the controls of his pictcaster. 'I'll listen to no more of this heretical twaddle.' His face vanished from the collection of disembodied heads floating in the hololith. Asmar's remained, but looked far from happy.

'The rest of you may care to note,' I said, concealing my amusement with some difficulty, 'that I said "challenge", not "defeat". That would indeed be heresy, and is, of course, utterly unthinkable.' Most of the heads nodded gravely. 'The precise nature of these powers is a subject to be studied and considered by those far wiser than I,[1] but the salient point is that all four are essentially rivals. They may make temporary alliances from time to time, but in the end they all seek complete dominion for themselves alone.' That I knew from personal experience; the sorceress Emeli, who for some reason kept invading my dreams of late, had been part of a Slaaneshi cult locked in a deadly struggle with a Nurglite faction for control of Slawkenberg. 'And none are more deadly rivals than Khorne and Slaanesh,' I concluded. 'If they're acting in concert here it would be almost unprecedented.'

'Completely so,' Zyvan confirmed. 'The only examples ever recorded are during events like a Black Crusade, when adherents of all four factions are somehow able to put their differences aside. Fortunately, they start stabbing each other in the back sooner or later, and the whole thing falls apart.'

'This is hardly on the scale of a Black Crusade,' one of the Kastaforean commissars pointed out mildly. I'd spent a bit of time in his company aboard the *Emperor's Benificence*, and felt the lad might have a reasonable future in front of him. He wasn't an overt Emperor-botherer, liked his ale and a hand of cards, and had a pretty good idea of when to be looking the other way instead of jumping on every minor infraction his troopers committed. 'More of a Black Skirmish.'

'Precisely,' I said, smiling at the witticism until a few of the others decided they'd better too. 'Which leaves us with two possibilities that I can see. One of which is that there's something on Adumbria both factions want to get their hands on.'

'What might that be?' Kolbe asked, looking understandably perturbed at the idea. It must be bad enough coming to terms with the fact that one of the Ruinous Powers is taking a special interest in your homeworld, never mind two.

'Who knows?' Zyvan said. 'Adumbria's been settled for millennia. That's a lot of time for someone to hide or lose a powerful artefact. Or it might be something that's been here even longer than the Imperium.' I suppressed a shudder at that thought, being reminded rather too forcibly of the necron tombs I'd stumbled across on Interitus and Simia Orichalcae. Still, I reminded myself forcibly, the metal monstrosities weren't the only source of archeotech, and it

---

1. *And the Ordo Malleus, of course. No wonder so many of them go off the deep end.*

was possible some long-lost hoard of the stuff remained buried away somewhere on this peculiar planet.

'What about the other possibility?' Kasteen asked.

'The Khornates are here to prevent the Slaaneshi from doing something that'll tilt the balance of power between them,' I said.

'Like raising daemons and frakking about with the warp currents,' the colonel concluded.

I nodded. 'Given what we already know about the activities of the Slaaneshi cult here, that would be my guess. Although I haven't a clue what they're hoping to achieve, or why the Khornates would be so desperate to prevent it.' Which was just as well. If I'd had even the remotest inkling I would have been gibbering quietly under the table by now rather than talking about it.

'Any further along on what's happening with the warp currents?' Zyvan asked Malden.

The young psyker shook his head. 'As we said before, they're turning in on themselves. It's as if whoever's behind it is trying to create a very small, very intense warp storm centred on the planet. How or why is still hard to pin down.'

'Thank you,' the lord general said dryly. He shrugged. 'So I'm open to suggestions.'

'How about the pattern of the attacks?' Kasteen asked. She brought up the display from the hololithic chart table. 'The first wave hit the Tallarns. Then they struck at Glacier Peak.'

'They struck pretty much everywhere,' Asmar pointed out, clearly relishing the chance to shoot down whatever theory she was developing.

But Kasteen merely nodded. 'They did. Which is hardly surprising, given the amount of ground fire their shuttles were taking and the fact that at least one of their transports was destroyed before it could offload most of its troop complement. Most of their forces didn't so much land as crash.'

'A good point,' Zyvan conceded. 'But I don't quite see what you're getting at.'

'I've been looking at the movements of the enemy here in Glacier Peak.' Kasteen magnified the map of the town and its surroundings. 'Five shuttles came down here. Two hit the town, one hit us and the other two deviated. One landed here, to the south, and the other crashed out here to the west, near the hab dome the commissar discovered.'

'I've read the AARs,'[1] Zyvan said, a tone of curiosity mingling with mild reproof.

---

1. *After Action Reports: a summary of an engagement, passed up the chain of command for subsequent assessment.*

Kasteen nodded. 'So have I. It was only while I was collating them that something struck me. Once the heretics were down, they only advanced in one direction. Due west. We assumed at the time they were hoping to take the town or reinforce the units attacking our compound, but I began to wonder if that wasn't the real objective.'

'If that's so, then what was?' the lord general asked.

Kasteen highlighted the hab dome. 'What if it was the site of the ritual? The shuttle that almost made it didn't overshoot the objective, as we thought at the time, the others all fell short.'

'What would be the point of that?' Asmar asked scornfully. 'The heretics had already completed their foul sorceries long before these renegades even entered the system.'

'But maybe they didn't know that,' I said, the pieces of Kasteen's chain of reasoning falling into place so neatly I was convinced she was right. And even if she hadn't been I wasn't about to let Asmar make her look stupid in front of the lord general. 'They attacked you too, didn't they? And you're practically sitting on the site of another heretic shrine.'

As I'd hoped, the reminder of that fact left him looking severely uncomfortable. 'Did any of them seem to be making for it?'

'It's possible,' the Tallarn colonel conceded after a moment, looking distinctly unhappy at the prospect. 'I'd have to check. Our traditional tactics rely heavily on hit and run strikes and rapid manoeuvre, so the heretics were scattering in all directions.'

'If you could let us know as soon as possible,' Zyvan said, making the simple request sound more like an order than if he'd visibly exerted his authority. Clearly the exchange I'd overheard before hadn't been the end of the matter.

Asmar nodded. 'By the grace of the Emperor, it will be done.'

'Good.' Zyvan's attention turned to Kolbe. 'Any hostiles approach the site in Skitterfall?'

'A few elements made it through,' Kolbe said. 'We assumed at the time they were hoping to find reinforcements there.'

'I see.' Zyvan nodded once. 'We'll have to improve our liaison channels with your people, obviously.'

'Which raises an intriguing possibility,' Malden said, in his usual drab monotone. 'The locations of the sites do indeed appear significant, as Colonel Kasteen suggested before, and this new enemy is as aware of their importance as the one we've been attempting to track.'

'Which helps us how, exactly?' Kolbe asked.

Malden spread his hands. 'The sorcerers clearly haven't been able to achieve their objective yet. This would imply that they need to perform their ritual at least once more, probably at a specific site or sites. If we analyse the pattern of the landings along the lines the colonel has pointed out, we might be able to locate it.'

'Excellent.' Zyvan nodded. 'I'll get our intelligence people on it right away.'

THE RESULTS WERE disappointing, however. After nearly two days of feverish activity by the analysts, during which time we twiddled our thumbs and reorganised ourselves to fill the gaps in our roster left by the recent engagements, Zyvan called us in person with the bad news.

'It looks like a dead end,' he told us gloomily. 'Colonel Kasteen was definitely right about the invaders aiming for the ritual sites, but that doesn't seem to help us locate the next one.'

'Why not?' I asked. By way of reply the image of his face in the hololith, which, thank the Emperor, one of our tech-priests had finally got around to doing something about, was replaced by the now familiar globe of Adumbria, which hardly juddered at all. As before, it was pocked with contact icons, the majority concentrated in the shadow zone.

'Most of the intruders don't seem to have moved with any real sense of purpose,' Zyvan explained, 'other than the groups she already pointed out.' The clusters around Glacier Peak, the Tallarns and Skitterfall glowed a little brighter to highlight them. 'The others just started attacking the nearest PDF, Guard unit, or civilian population.'

'Well that's Khornates for you,' I commented wryly, noting Kasteen's thinly veiled disappointment and hoping to lighten her mood. 'Show them something to kill and they just get distracted.'

'Quite,' Zyvan said, clearly as disappointed as the colonel; once again a promising lead had evanesced into nothingness before our eyes. 'Most inconsiderate of them.'

'Logically,' Broklaw put in, loyally backing up his CO, 'the next ritual site should complete a pattern. Surely your psykers can predict where it should be.'

Zyvan's face reappeared, looking pained. 'You haven't had much contact with psykers, have you, young man?' Broklaw shook his head, clearly quite satisfied with that state of affairs.

The lord general sighed. 'Then just take my word for it. Getting a sensible answer out of them isn't always as easy as you might think.'

I recalled my last few conversations with Rakel and nodded in sympathy. 'Malden seems relatively well-balanced for a spook,' I said.

Zyvan sighed again. 'A little too much so, if that's possible. He won't commit himself without more data, while the others on my staff are... more typical. The only other person with an opinion is the Lady

Dimarco, who seems to think the only prudent course of action is to leave the system while the currents are still marginally navigable, and tells me so incessantly.'

'Is that actually an option?' I asked as casually as I could, wondering how best to get myself aboard the flagship if it was.

Zyvan shook his head vehemently, taking the inquiry as a joke. 'Of course not. We're here to defend this place, and that's what we'll do whatever the warp throws at us.'

'Some of these units seemed to be moving,' Kasteen said, still studying the heretics' deployment in our chart table display. She highlighted a few, apparently skirting the shores of the larger of the landlocked seas. 'Perhaps we should be searching the shoreline.'

'All sixteen thousand kilometres of it?' Zyvan asked mildly. Kasteen coloured slightly, never a good sign in my experience, and I stepped in hastily.

'The sea is directly opposite Skitterfall,' I pointed out. 'A fourth site there would complete a geometrical figure.'

'We've already considered that,' Zyvan said, smiling wearily. 'I'm not completely dense, you know, Ciaphas.'

'I was beginning to wonder after that last regicide game,' I joked. For one of the greatest tacticians in the segmentum, he was surprisingly easy to beat, a fact about which I pulled his leg constantly. I suppose the abstract game was just too simple for him compared to moving entire armies around the void, but he was a gracious host and good company.

'According to Malden, anywhere along the coast would be too far out of alignment with the other sites. A couple of the others suggested that one of the poles would be a possibility, but none of the enemy units seemed to take a particular interest in either.' This was hardly surprising, really: one was occupied by a provincial town which seemed to subsist entirely on the cultivation of squinch, and the other by a PDF training facility which was stuffed to the gills with troopers and which annihilated the single shuttle-load of cultists that landed there in pretty short order.

'How about an island?' Broklaw suggested. Zyvan shrugged. 'There aren't any, at least far enough out from the coast to make a difference.'

'Well that's it then,' I said. 'We're right back where we started.'

'Not quite,' Kasteen said. I looked at her curiously and she smiled without mirth. 'All we have to do is wait for the invaders to attack again, and see where they're going.'

'If we don't get a break soon,' Zyvan said bleakly, 'it might just come to that.'

Editorial Note:

As so often, we find ourselves having to turn to another source at this juncture for a fuller picture of events. And, once again, Tincrowser's account covers the salient points as well as any other.

From *Sablist in Skitterfall: a brief history of the Chaos incursion* by Dagblat Tincrowser, 957 M41

The second onslaught began, as everyone had expected, with a clash in space between the two opposing fleets. By this point the invaders were committed, their course predictable, and the Imperial warfleet began to move out of orbit to engage them. The *Escapade* and *Virago*, the latter still limping from the wounds she had sustained earlier but eager for the fray nonetheless, boosted out to meet the enemy, accompanied by the squadron of destroyers.

Their orders were to avoid contact with the enemy warships as much as possible, concentrating their efforts on the transport ships, but this was to prove more difficult than hitherto. The enemy escorts had had time to deploy against the approaching defenders, and the destroyer squadron was soon caught up in a desperate struggle against a pair of raiders protecting the flanks of the flotilla.

They were ultimately successful, leaving one gutted and adrift in the void while the other turned and fled, grievously wounded, only to tear itself apart as its warp engines overloaded when it attempted to find refuge back in the foul domain from which it had sprung. This victory was bought at a high price, however, as all three sustained some damage, one being so severely mauled that it was reduced to a drifting hulk, its crew being forced to abandon it entirely.[1]

The victory of the others was to be short-lived, however. As they closed with the enemy fleet the vessel at the heart of it, no less than a battleship, moved ahead of the merchant vessels for the first time and opened up with the full awesome power of its forward batteries. Both surviving destroyers were crippled before they could even come within the range of their own guns, one[2] being reduced to little more than a cloud of drifting debris by the first salvo.

The two frigates were to fare little better, although they had succeeded in reducing the number of transports by three by this point.[2] The lance batteries aboard the terrifying behemoth licked out once, destroying the bridge of the *Virago* and crippling the engines of the *Escapade*, which was soon left too far behind to continue the fight.

All that stood between Adumbria and Armageddon now was the *Indestructible*, outnumbered and outgunned. Some expected her to go to the assistance of the stricken escort vessels, but she remained on station above Skitterfall highport, standing resolutely between the heavily-armed leviathan and the swarm of merchant ships.

Effectively unhindered, the remaining transport vessels in the invasion fleet slipped into orbit and began dropping their cargo of heretical vermin on the planet below.

---

1. *The* Spiteful *was salvaged the following year and returned to service in 948, eventually meeting its end in a rather more heroic manner: this was the vessel which rammed the battleship* Agonising Death *at the blockade of Garomar in 999 M41, destroying it completely along with itself, and saving the lives of an estimated eighty thousand civilians in the refugee fleet it was escorting.*

2. *The* Impetuous.

FIFTEEN

'You can never have too many enemies. The more you've got, the more likely they are to get in each other's way.'

– Jarvin Wallankot, *Idle Musings*, 605 M41

IN THE END, Zyvan wasn't so far wrong. We spent the remaining time until the enemy fleet arrived in a fever of preparation, knowing that the assault to come would make the one we'd beaten off before pale into insignificance. Fortunately, our casualties had been relatively light, at least compared to the Tallarns and the PDF, so the amount of reorganisation we had to undertake was less than I'd feared.

'Detoi's fit for duty,' Broklaw reported, helping himself to a refill from the pot of tanna Jurgen had brought into my office. It was a far cry from the opulent buffets in the conference rooms of the lord general's headquarters, but my aide had done his best to make the long meeting bearable for us, and given his almost preternatural talent for scrounging, he'd been able to keep us fed and watered well enough. I pushed the plate which had contained a trio of palovine pastries to one side of the desk to make room for the data-slate.

'I'm glad to hear it,' I said, skimming the medicae report.

Fit for duty was stretching it a bit, he'd taken a las bolt to the chest and was damn lucky the flak armour under his greatcoat had absorbed most of the impact, but there was nothing they could do for him now except wait for him to recover naturally and for the ribs to knit back together. Lying around in the infirmary wasn't going to make him heal any faster, and no doubt the thought that the longer he took to get up the longer Sulla would be in charge of his company was a hell of an incentive to discharge himself.

'Well, it simplifies the personnel reassignments,' Kasteen said, brushing a crumb of pastry from the corner of her mouth. My office was crowded with the three of us present, let alone Jurgen when he wandered through, but it was a lot easier to work in there than in the command centre. What we were doing was sensitive and a regrettable neccessity: reassigning personnel to fill the gaps in our organisation left by our dead and severely wounded.

In most cases, the best course of action was to do nothing, as a squad light by a trooper or two would still function reasonably well, and rotating people in or out of a smoothly-functioning team would be more disruptive to their efficiency and morale than just leaving well enough alone. In a few cases, though, where NCOs and officers were down, someone had to be brought in to fill the hole they'd left, or designated the new leader until they recovered. Which brought us to the delicate matter of first company.

'At least we're only looking for one new company commander,' I agreed. Captain Kelton had been unlucky enough to run straight into a group of heretics armed with rocket launchers, and a couple had penetrated the hull armour of her command Chimera with inevitable results. The platoon commanders had managed to hold things together reasonably well, but none of them had been clear about who had seniority and in the end Broklaw had had to take charge himself, directing them by vox from the command bunker. This was far from ideal and a striking example of why taking AFVs[1] into a cityfight against infantry is one hell of a risk.

'The question is, who do we appoint?' Broklaw said. 'After the last debacle, none of the lieutenants strike me as being up to the job.'

'I'm with you there,' Kasteen agreed. 'They're all good enough at platoon level, but someone should have taken charge on the ground as soon as Kelton was taken out. None of them had the confidence to step in, and that worries me.'

---

1. *Armoured Fighting Vehicles, a generic term used by the Guard to refer to anything from a Salamander to a Baneblade.*

'Right,' I concurred, making it unanimous. 'At least Sulla showed some initiative when Detoi went down. And she did a reasonable job too, under the circumstances.'

Which was perfectly true. She might have been the most irritating junior officer in the entire regiment and a damn sight too reckless for my liking, but she got things done and the troopers seemed to like her for some reason. So despite my personal reservations, I felt I should give credit where it was due.

'Sulla,' Kasteen said, a thoughtful tone entering her voice. Broklaw and I glanced warily at one another, already seeing where this chain of thought was taking us. But in all honesty I couldn't see a credible alternative.

Broklaw nodded slowly. 'She's been keeping second company together well enough,' he agreed cautiously. 'But she's been serving with them since the amalgamation and the other platoon commanders trust her instincts. Would a new company be quite so willing to work with her?'

'That's her problem,' I said bluntly. 'Either she's up to the job or she isn't. And there's only one way to find out.' I sighed. 'Besides, who else is there?'

'Quite,' Kasteen said. She looked thoughtful. 'A few of them are going to have trouble taking orders from another lieutenant, though. Especially as they match her in seniority.'

'Brevet[1] her up to captain,' I said. 'If she doesn't make the grade she can always have her old platoon back when we find someone else.'

'Fair enough.' Broklaw nodded his agreement. 'What do we do with third platoon in the meantime? Bump Lustig up to lieutenant?'

'He won't thank you for it,' I said, remembering some of the veteran sergeant's more trenchant comments about officers in general. 'Better just tell him he's confirmed as platoon sergeant for the time being, until he's had time to get used to being in charge, and make him up to lieutenant in the next round of promotions. That way if we have to put Sulla back in place no one loses face.'

'Good point.' Kasteen nodded decisively. 'Is his corporal up to running the squad on her own for the time being?'

'I'd say so,' I said. 'Penlan's a good soldier. She and Lustig should be able to pick a new ASL for themselves without any interference from us.'

---

1. *A form of battlefield promotion to be confirmed at a later date. Though entitled to wear a captain's insignia and be considered one in the chain of command, Sulla would remain a lieutenant for most administrative purposes until the change in her status was approved by the Munitorum. In theory, if she proved unable to do the job she could thus be returned to her original position and rank without the stigma of a demotion marring her service record.*

'Penlan?' Kasteen looked thoughtful for a moment. 'Isn't she the one they call Jinxie?'

'Yes.' I nodded. 'But she's not nearly as accident prone as she's supposed to be. I'll grant you she fell down an ambull tunnel once, and there was that incident with the frag grenade and the latrine trench, but things tend to work out for her. The orks on Kastafore were as surprised as she was when the floor in the factory collapsed, and we'd have walked right into that hrud ambush on Skweki if she hadn't triggered the mine by chucking an empty food tin away...' I trailed off, finally listening to what I was saying. 'You know how troopers tend to exaggerate these things,' I finished lamely.

'Quite,' Kasteen said, keeping a remarkably straight face. 'Is that about it?'

It was, more or less. We spent a few more minutes on personnel assignments and dealt with a few logistical matters, and were just about to separate to go about our other duties when Jurgen entered the office. I didn't take much notice, to be honest, as he'd been in and out several times over the course of the afternoon to deal with routine paperwork and keep us supplied with refreshments. Then he coughed stickily, his inevitable prelude to delivering a message when he thought my attention was elsewhere.

'Begging your pardon, commissar, ma'am, sir, but there's an urgent message from headquarters. The heretic fleet has engaged the warships and the lord general expects them to start landing troops as soon as they can.'

'Thank you, Jurgen,' I said as calmly as I could, reaching for my weapons. One way or another, the battle for the soul of Adumbria was about to be decided, although quite how literally I still had no idea.

DESPITE MY FEARS, the initial reports coming in from the battlefronts made no mention of giants in crimson power armour, so it looked as though we were to be spared an onslaught of Chaos Marines at least. This wasn't so unusual; according to some highly classified files Zyvan had made available to me, the World Eaters Chapter[1] quite often sent out a few of their number to advise the hordes of wannabe warmasters infesting the galaxy. (But what advice a follower of Khorne would listen to other than 'Kill them all!' is quite frankly beyond me.) It was quite probable that we weren't facing any more than a squad or two in the whole invasion force, which was still a disturbing enough prospect

---

1. *Technically Legion, as the traitors never underwent the reorganisation which followed the Horus Heresy.*

I grant you, but rather less intimidating than an army of psychopathic supermen would have been, especially if I didn't have to deal with any more of them myself.

'Eight shuttles inbound,' the auspex operator called. Kasteen and I exchanged glances. The palms of my hands were tingling again, and my mouth suddenly felt dry.

'We're taking a hell of a gamble,' I said.

The colonel nodded tensely. 'Well, it's too late to change our minds now.' We glanced at the dispositions of our forces in the chart table holo tank, and inevitably I felt a flutter of apprehension; if we'd made the wrong call things were about to get very ugly indeed.

After much deliberation, we'd decided to follow Kasteen's instinct and assume that the isolated hab dome would be their main target. Accordingly we'd deployed the whole of fourth and fifth companies in a wide ring around it, camouflaged as only Valhallans can be in a snowfield, hoping to close the noose around them once they were on the ground. Which, with second company still waiting to be deployed by dropship, left first to protect the town more or less unaided, unless you counted the handful of Hekwyn's people assigned there. Not for the first time I wondered if Sulla was really up to the job we'd handed her, and hoped I wouldn't get my answer in the form of a pile of civilian corpses.

This left the problem of ensuring the security of our compound. In theory, second company should be more than enough to do the job, as they had before, but this time they were already embarked aboard the dropship which stood, engines idling, awaiting the lord general's orders to deploy to Emperor knew where at a moment's notice.

We still had a couple of hundred warm bodies in third company, and being Guard troopers first and foremost they could shoot as well as anyone, but the thought of relying on a motley collection of cooks, medicae orderlies and the regimental band to protect our hides from a frothing swarm of homicidal lunatics wasn't exactly comforting. (Though it was marginally more so than the idea of the enginseers being issued with lasguns and shown which end to point forwards; being cogboys they could tell you every detail of how they worked, but couldn't hit the side of a starship if they were standing in one of the cargo holds. The sight of a group of white-robed tech-priests holding factory-fresh small-arms as though they were incredibly delicate works of art, being bawled at by Sergeant Lustig as he attempted to impart the rudiments of their use, will remain with me to the grave.)

'Contacts closing, fifty kilometres out,' the auspex operator droned, her voice as emotionless as a servitor. 'Descending rapidly. Forty-three kilometres and closing...'

The crimson blips crawled slowly across the hololith, heading straight for us and Glacier Peak. I tried to calculate the number of enemy soldiers that eight civilian shuttles might contain, then wished I hadn't. If they were packed out, each one could hold as much as a full company, which meant that in a worst-case scenario we could find ourselves outnumbered by two to one.

'On the plus side, they've probably forgotten their cold-weather gear like the last ones did,' Kasteen said, clearly doing the same piece of mental arithmetic I was.

'Let's hope so,' I said. It seemed likely; in my experience Chaotic troops tended to rush headlong into combat heedless of the suitability or otherwise of the equipment they had, or even if their weapons were adequate. And Khornate cultists were the most reckless of all. 'With any luck the cold will do most of the work for us.'

'It did before,' Broklaw said hopefully.

'Thirty-eight kilometres and closing,' the auspex operator chimed in. 'Maintaining descent vector…'

'Can you approximate an LZ yet?' Kasteen asked, her voice brittle with tension.

'It could still be any of the targets,' the operator responded. 'Thirty-two kilometres and closing…'

'Great.' Kasteen's hand closed on the butt of her bolt pistol, a reflexive response to stress I was long familiar with; indeed I tended to reach for my own weapons in moments of unease.

'Twenty-nine kilometres and closing,' the chant went on. 'Descent vector steady…'.

'Regina, look.' Broklaw pointed to the chart table, relief evident in his voice. The potential landing zone was projected into it, a steadily shrinking circle, diminishing as the approaching shuttles neared the ground. The majority of it was now well to the west of both Glacier Peak and our own position. 'You were right!'

'Emperor be praised,' Kasteen said fervently, relief evident in both her posture and voice. There could be little doubt now that the site of the hab dome was the heretics' main target. If they just kept going on the same course, they'd come down inside our noose neat as you please. Our trap was about to be sprung.

'Three contacts veering off,' the auspex operator said. 'The rest maintaining course and speed, eighteen kilometres and closing…'

'Veering where?' I asked, a tingle of apprehension beginning to run through me. It had all been going so neatly. By way of answer, subsidiary landing zone circles began to shrink in the chart table.

'Where do you think?' Broklaw asked grimly, and I bit down on a couple of choice underhive epithets. Two shuttles were heading for the town, and one was unquestionably targeting us. It seemed that the enemy had learned something from their first attack, probably from vox traffic, and wanted to pin us down while they took care of their primary target. Well they were in for an unpleasant surprise, of course, but that wasn't going to help us or the citizens of Glacier Peak.

'First company, stand by. You've got two shuttles inbound, ETA...' Kasteen glanced at the auspex operator for confirmation before continuing, 'three minutes. Engage on sight.'

'Understood.' Sulla's voice was crisp and confident, but then it always was with combat imminent. Well, there was no point worrying about it now, she'd just have to do the best she could. I just hoped to the Emperor we hadn't made a big mistake. 'We'll be ready for them.' She switched channels to her platoon command frequencies and began chivvying up her subordinates. I listened in for a moment, but she seemed to know what she was doing, so I returned my attention to the chart table.

'How long have we got?' I asked.

'Four minutes, give or take,' Broklaw said. I nodded tensely. It could have been worse, I supposed.

A single shuttle couldn't hold much more than a company's worth of enemy, I reminded myself, so even if it was packed we were in for a fairly even fight. Assuming our rear echelon troopers were up to the job, which they most certainly should be. And if push came to shove we still had a company of front-line combat troops in reserve.

'Should I disembark second company?' Broklaw asked, almost as if he could read my thoughts. 'Bolster our defences here?'

Kasteen shook her head. 'Leave them aboard the dropship.' She indicated the main hololith, where contact icons were springing up all over the planet. 'All hell's breaking loose. Emperor alone knows where they'll be needed before long.'

It was hard to disagree. From what I could see, bitter fighting was beginning to erupt in nearly every population centre and the PDF were being hard pressed throughout the shadow zone, even where they were being supported by the Kastaforeans. It was credits to carrots that Zyvan would be calling his mobile reserves into action any time now, and he wouldn't be at all thrilled to be told that they'd be with him as soon as they could but something else had come up.

'We should be able to handle them,' I agreed, hoping I was right.

'Contact at LZ one in one minute,' the auspex operator chimed in. 'Contact at LZ two in two.' That would be us, and I watched the descending blip in the chart table with a kind of weary resignation. 'Contact at LZ three in four minutes thirty.'

'Fourth and fifth companies, stand by,' Kasteen ordered. 'Five shuttles incoming, ETA four minutes. They've taken the bait.'

'They might be landing, but they won't be taking off again,' the commander of fifth company promised, and Kasteen nodded in satisfaction.

'I don't doubt it.' She looked across at Broklaw and me. 'Good luck, gentlemen.'

'Let's hope we don't need it,' I said.

What we really needed was some serious firepower, but the sentinels had all been deployed with the ambushers out at the hab dome, so the best we could muster was small-arms and a few man-portable heavy weapons. Unfortunately, the number of people on the base capable of using the heavy stuff, apart from the specialists in second company who had been strapped into their crash webbing aboard the dropship since the first alert, were few and far between. Not for the first time I began to think things might be a little healthier somewhere else.

Or not. A worrying thought was beginning to nag at me, all the more insistently the harder I tried to ignore it. I turned to the nearest vox operator.

'I need a channel to the lord general's office,' I said. 'Highest priority.' Just to make sure, I added my commissarial override code.

'Ciaphas.' Zyvan sounded harrassed, which I suppose was inevitable under the circumstances. 'This isn't really a good time.'

'I know,' I said. 'And I'm sorry. But this is important.'

'I don't doubt it.' Zyvan sighed. 'What's the problem?' Behind his voice I could hear the unmistakable rumble of heavy ordnance detonating in the background. It sounded like things were getting pretty rough in Skitterfall.

'Kasteen was right,' I told him. 'The heretics here are definitely targeting the ritual site.' The distant crackle of lasgun fire became audible in the distance, seeping through the walls around us. 'Mainly,' I added, in deference to the prevailing circumstances.

'Interesting.' Zyvan was no fool, of course, and could see the implications as clearly as I could. 'I'll check with the Tallarns and Kolbe's mob here in the city. Just to confirm. But that does seem significant.'

'It's still our best chance of finding out what the sorcerers are up to and stopping it,' I pointed out. 'If the invaders are concentrating anywhere we need to get in there fast. Preferably ahead of them.'

'I'll look into it,' Zyvan promised. I glanced at the gently rotating globe in the hololith, struck by the number of enemy icons clustering along the shoreline of the larger sea, in some areas it looked as though the entire coast was bordered in blood.

'I'd concentrate on the shoreline,' I said. 'There has to be something there whatever Malden thinks.'

'I'll take that under advisement,' Zyvan said diplomatically, which is general-speak for 'I'll make up my own mind, thank you very much.'

'We're missing something,' I said, turning to Kasteen. The sound of gunfire was a lot louder now.

'All the military intelligence we've got is on the hololith,' she pointed out. The coin dropped, and I turned to the vox operator so fast the man flinched.

'What about the civilian channels?' I asked.

'I'm sorry, commissar, I haven't been monitoring...'

'Of course you haven't,' I said patiently. 'It's not your job. But you can connect me to someone who has.'

'Hekwyn.' The arbitrator sounded as though he was out on the street somewhere, talking into a comm-bead. To my distinct lack of surprise there was gunfire in the background. 'What can I do for you, commissar?'

'I need to know if there have been any unusual incidents around the equatorial sea,' I told him.

He laughed briefly, without humour. 'One or two enemies of humanity wreaking havoc, I'm told.'

'Something more specific,' I said, filling him in rapidly on the situation. His tone changed. 'I'll get back to you,' he promised. 'But it might take a while.'

'Let's hope we've got long enough,' I said, cutting the link.

Becoming aware of a familiar odour at my elbow, I turned to find Jurgen standing there, the melta in his hands as always in times of trouble. It had been fired recently, the actinic tang of scorched metal hanging around the barrel. I raised an eyebrow in wordless enquiry.

'I thought you might be wanting to step outside again, sir,' he said. Well, not likely, with the compound being overrun with heretic foot soldiers and all, but I nodded anyway for the benefit of anyone who might be around to take notice.

'I'm afraid I'm needed here for the time being,' I told him, with the best air of frustrated martial zeal I could muster. It was at that point that I became aware that the gunfire outside had become very loud indeed, and that Jurgen's hat and greatcoat were covered in melting snow. 'What exactly is going on out there?' I asked.

Before my aide could reply, there was a loud explosion from the direction of the main door, which blew in, taking a couple of nearby troopers with it. Kasteen, Broklaw and I drew our side arms so fast it would have been all but impossible to tell who had been first, and turned to face this unexpected threat. A knot of red and black uni-formed fanatics stormed into the room, heedless of the hail of las and bolter fire which cut them down as they rushed at us.

'Blood for the Blood God!' one more fortunate than most screamed, charging forward as las rounds gouged chunks out of his flak armour and the flesh beneath, so carried away he barely seemed to register his wounds. I switched aim, shooting him in the leg, and he crashed to the floor in front of me, reaching out with a red-stained combat blade. 'Blood for the Blood God!'

'Fine, he can have yours,' I snapped, stamping down hard on his throat and crushing his larynx. It wasn't a particularly elegant kill, but at least it shut him up.

'They're all over the compound,' Jurgen said. I glanced around the room as Kasteen rallied her motley collection of vox and auspex oper-ators and began to beat back our assailants. It was clear the command centre wouldn't be much of a refuge now; even if we could clear it again it would remain wide open, and I didn't feel at all comfortable with the idea of remaining in an enclosed space under siege from a swarm of homicidal lunatics. I turned to Broklaw, who seemed more or less unharmed apart from a gash in his forehead.

'I'd better get outside,' I said, 'and try to rally our people.'

'Good idea,' he said, apparently unaware of the blood seeping down his face. 'If we lose vox contact with four and five now, our trap's pretty much frakked.'

'We'll keep 'em out,' I assured him, salving my conscience a little with the thought that at least someone would if I had anything to do with it. I turned to my aide. 'Come on, Jurgen. We've got work to do.'

'Right with you, sir,' he responded as phlegmatically as ever. I drew my chainsword and began hewing my way to the door, blessing what-ever it is about Khornate fanatics that makes them run at you with blades yelling their heads off instead of shooting their guns like any sensible opponent would, potting the odd one with the laspistol when-ever I got the opportunity. It wasn't often, to be honest. Kasteen was clearly revelling in the chance to get her hands dirty for a change instead of directing operations from a distance through a chain of sub-ordinates, banging away happily with her miniature bolter as though she was racking up the prize tickets at a fairground shooting booth. The explosive projectiles were making short work of both heretic troopers and their armour, leaving the walls decorated in abstract designs I didn't want to look at too closely.

'Not enough of them in here for you?' she asked as Jurgen and I swept past, my aide having switched to his standard-issue lasgun in deference to the confined space and the number of friendly soldiers in the vicinity. I plastered my best devil-may-care grin on my face.

'It seems churlish to take yours while you're having so much fun,' I said. 'Besides, you and Ruput are needed here.' I stepped aside to give Jurgen a clear shot at a red and black trooper running through the door and realised as the man dropped that there were no more behind him.

Kasteen re-holstered her weapon, looking vaguely disappointed. 'Which leaves me to keep any more from getting in here,' I finished.

'I guess so.' The colonel turned back to the bank of vox units, already assimilating reports from the other battlefronts. A few of our people were down, but damn few considering, and several of those were walking wounded. Broklaw was rallying the others and returning them to work.

As I hurried down the corridor with Jurgen trotting at my heels, a party of medicae passed us going in the other direction. I felt a strong sense of relief at the sight. They were carrying lasguns, true, but slung across their shoulders, and if they were able to respond so fast to a call for aid from the command centre they couldn't have been needed to help defend the place. My spirits began to rise.

'Commissar!' A young corporal greeted us as we broke through into the open air, and I pulled the scarf over my mouth and nose without breaking stride (bumping the side of my face with the butt of my laspistol as I did so, but I wasn't about to relinquish either of my weapons under the circumstances). His face seemed vaguely familiar, and after a moment I remembered having him flogged on Kastafore for starting a brawl with some civilians over the favours of a joygirl. I dredged his name out of the depths of my memory.

'Albrin,' I said, nodding, and the fellow looked absurdly pleased that I'd recognised him. 'Who's in charge here?'

'I think I am, sir.' He waved vaguely out into the darkness beyond the light leaking from the doorway behind us, where the scorched and blackened remains of the thick metal portal which used to protect it gave mute testimony to the fact that at least a few of the heretics hadn't been so far gone with bloodlust that they'd forgotten how to set a demo charge. 'My section saw a bunch of traitors heading this way, so we followed up and took them from behind.'

'Good work,' I said, picking out a number of mounds in the snow which had probably been enemy troopers a few moments ago. It made sense: Khornate fanatics would be so fixated on breaking into the building and massacring everyone inside, it probably hadn't even occurred to them to watch their own backs, even when Albrin's team opened fire on them.

The corporal flushed. 'After we cleared them out, we started fortifying the breach. It seemed the most sensible thing to do.'

I nodded again. For a quartermaster's clerk he had a pretty sound grasp of tactics. 'It was,' I said. They'd begun piling up cargo pods and other odds and ends into a makeshift barricade, which seemed reasonably defensible. I tried to find some more of the defenders on my comm-bead, but none of them had tactical communications kit, so it was a futile gesture; in the end I had to make do with voxing the command centre and letting them know what was going on.

'Are you staying with them?' Kasteen asked.

'No,' I replied, conscious that only my end of the conversation would be overheard by the ad hoc defenders. 'They seem competent enough.' As I'd expected, a ripple of pride and renewed resolve went round the little group of men and women. 'I'll head on out and try to find another squad or two to send back to reinforce them.' This was not only good tactical sense; I stood a much better chance of avoiding the enemy than I would if I stayed put at an obvious target point.

'Good hunting,' Kasteen said, completely misreading my motives, and after a couple of encouraging remarks to the defenders, Jurgen and I moved on into the darkness.

The truth was that by that time the battle for the compound was all but over, the superior training and skills of the defenders and the bone-chilling cold combining to cut the attackers down like grain before a harvester. But at the time, as you'll readily appreciate, I had no way of knowing that, and was as cautious as I might possibly be in my movements. I did have time to scan the tactical frequencies, discovering *inter alia* that our trap at the hab dome had worked as well as we could possibly have hoped, fourth and fifth companies having encircled their prey and now well advanced in the process of squeezing the life out of them, while Sulla's new command was still, to my mingled surprise and relief, doing a sterling job of defending the town from the depredations of the invaders. (Though not without some collateral damage, of course.)

'Commissar.' Jurgen was little more than a silhouette in the endless night, although my eyes had now adjusted enough to make him out without undue difficulty. Which was just as well, as the freezing temperatures and the scarf across my nose was depriving me of my usual method of keeping track of my faithful companion in the darkness. 'Movement.'

I followed the direction of his gesture, wondering for a moment what the whining sound in my ears was, until I remembered that the dropship engines were still running. Well, good, at least we'd still be able to respond when the lord general's call came. That was probably the main reason our base here had been attacked, I thought. If the first wave had reported the presence of the orbital transport to their masters in the invasion fleet, someone, probably one of the Traitor Marines, would have had the sense to realise why it was there.

There was no time for further thought on the matter though, as the movement Jurgen had spotted began to resolve itself into a mass of moving darkness, occulting the few low-lying stars I could see between the buildings. At first I took it for a squad of troopers, but as it moved out into more open ground I realised it was far too massive for that.

'Emperor on Earth!' I said, a faint vibration beginning to reach my feet and an all-too-familiar grinding and clanking sound beginning to build through the all-pervasive whine of the dropship engines. 'They've brought a bloody tank!'

'Say again?' Kasteen said, a tone of surprise in her voice.

'It's a Leman Russ,' I said. 'Or it used to be at least.' The familiar outline had been blurred with icons and trophies I was heartily glad not to be able to make out in the darkness surrounding us, and what looked like a strip of park railing stuck to it for no readily apparent reason. 'They must have taken a while to get it unloaded from the shuttle.'

'Confirm that.' Kasteen conferred with the captains of the other companies for a moment. 'They've got a couple of armoured units at the hab dome as well. None in town, thank the Emperor.'

'We can take it, commissar,' Jurgen said, unshipping his prized melta. We probably could too, it was what the weapon was designed for after all. The flaw in that plan, at least from my point of view, was that attempting to do so would probably attract the attention of its crew, and that in turn would undoubtedly be manifested in a hail of heavy bolter fire from the nearest sponson.

I was saved from having to find a plausible reason to keep our heads down by a sudden intervention from our left, where a squad of Valhallans broke from cover without warning to unleash a hail of ineffective lasgun fire against the metal hull. The engine growled and its turret turned, bringing its main cannon to bear.

'Oh, frak this!' I said, as heavy bolter rounds began chewing up the snow all around us, punching holes through flakboard buildings and generally making an unholy mess of everything in sight. 'Take the bloody shot.' In truth it was our best chance of survival, since there was no way we could get out now without being cut to pieces.

'Very good, sir.' Jurgen squeezed the trigger, aiming for the thinner armour of the flank, and the idiots who'd attacked it in the first place cheered wildly (at least, the ones who weren't thrashing around in the snow bleeding to death did). The blast of superheated plasma punched through the side skirts, shredding the tracks, and the metal leviathan slewed to a halt, its engine screaming.

'Come on, men! Do you want to live forever?' The noncom in charge of the squad must have been on something, I thought. Nobody spoke like that outside badly-written combat novels. It seemed to work, though: with a banshee howl the whole damn lot of them were up and running, scrambling all over the blasted thing, trying to lever the hatches off and drop frag grenades inside.

Good luck to them, I thought. The turret swung again, as though it were trying to shake them off, and then I realised it was trying to aim at something. I jerked my head around, my gaze meeting the vast metal slab of the side of the dropship.

'Frakking warp!' I yelled. 'They're going for the dropship!' I began waving at the troopers still swarming all over the crippled tank. 'Get out of the way!'

Jurgen couldn't fire again with those idiots blocking his shot, and if the traitors managed to get a shell off at this range they'd hit the orbital transport for sure. I tried to picture the size of the ensuing explosion if they managed to penetrate its hull armour, and failed; all I was sure of was that there'd be precious little of the compound left, and I'd be a small cloud of drifting vapour.

There was no help for it. Grabbing Jurgen by the collar, I started to run for the dropship, frantically retuning my comm-bead to find the pilot's frequency.[1]

'Get in the air now!' I shouted.

'Say again?' The pilot was on line, at least, but sounded bewildered. 'Who is this?'

'Commissar Cain,' I said, the breath beginning to rasp in my throat from the cold. 'You're in imminent danger. Lift now!'

It was even worse than I thought. The main cargo ramp was still down, warm yellow light spilling out of it, and if the traitor tank managed to get a shot off there wouldn't even be the hope of the hull armour stopping it. I redoubled my efforts, and after what felt like an eternity of slithering though the treacherous snow, but was in all probability no more than a handful of seconds, was rewarded by the clanging solidity of metal under-foot. Jurgen, of course, had no such difficulty and had outdistanced me

---

1. *Interestingly, it never seems to have occurred to him to order Jurgen to take the shot any-way, sacrificing the impetuous troopers for the good of the majority, a decision which most commissars would undoubtedly have taken without a qualm.*

easily. As I turned to look back he was already at the controls, stabbing at the closure rune with his fingers.

With a grinding hum the ramp began to rise, cutting off my view of that deadly battle cannon. My last sight of the tank was as the Valhallans who had assaulted it began scattering away, apparently having found a vulnerable point to chuck a grenade into. Whether it had any effect I don't know, as a sudden lurch underfoot knocked me to my knees.

For good or ill we were now airborne, and Jurgen and I were on our way to Emperor knew where. However, had I known our eventual destination and what we'd find there, I'd probably have charged the bloody tank myself and thought I was lucky.

Editorial Note:

At which point we find ourselves once again having to turn to other sources for a proper appreciation of the bigger picture. The first of which, at least, is readable.

The second is as painful as the rest of Sulla's assaults on the Gothic language, but I've included it for its summation of what was happening to the rest of the regiment while Cain was otherwise occupied. As Tincrowser summarises events adequately enough, readers of a refined sensibility may skip it if they wish, although it does provide a first-hand account of an aspect of the conflict which he, along with most Adumbrians, remains unaware of to this day.

From *Sablist in Skitterfall: a brief history of the Chaos incursion* by Dagblat Tincrowser, 957 M41

As THE ENEMY battleship continued to bear down on the flotilla of merchant vessels and the defiant *Indestructible*, which seemed all that stood between them and certain destruction, the surviving transport ships remained in orbit, pouring their cargo of traitors and heretics onto the planet below. Many of the beleaguered defenders still hoped for the mighty Imperial vessel to intervene, but it remained resolutely in place. In truth it could do little else by now, since to turn away in pursuit of a handful of scattered targets would achieve little beyond exposing itself to the guns of the enemy. Furthermore, there were the merchant ships to consider, a little over a thousand of them at this point, all helpless against the predator closing in on them.

Though no one wanted to admit it, the protection of the merchant vessels was the battleship's highest priority. These ships would be needed if the worst were to happen and an evacuation became necessary, so they had to be defended, while the now empty transport vessels, having succeeded in their fell design, presented little further threat.

Nevertheless, we can still appreciate the frustration felt by the crew of the *Indestructible* and the apprehension of the merchant crews as the Chaos Leviathan continued to coast towards them.

If the battle in space had become a waiting game, however, the battle for the planet below had reached fever pitch. The invaders had struck almost everywhere at once, concentrating, as one might expect, a considerable proportion of their force against the planetary capital. Skitterfall became a grim battleground, where PDF and Imperial Guard elements fought for control of the streets against apparently inexhaustible numbers of fanatical heretics, whose only imperative appeared to be to cause as much death and destruction as possible. Making no apparent distinction between defenders and civilians, they slaughtered their way into the city centre, while the gallant defenders withdrew to regroup in the northern suburbs. Here the fighting became even fiercer, as the invaders' confederates emerged from hiding to wreak further mischief of their own.

And this pattern continued all over Adumbria. On the coldside, hidden renegades appeared, intent on hampering the defence of Glacier Peak, although the Valhallans prevailed over them as easily as the invaders themselves. On the hotside, the Tallarns were hard pressed, as before, despite the lack of any obvious targets of strategic value, their rough riders galloping to the defence of the inhabitants of the scattered desert hamlets. And throughout the shadow zone the battle to cleanse the soil of our home world from the taint of the unclean continued unabated.

From *Like a Phoenix on the Wing: The Early Campaigns and Glorious Victories of the Valhallan 597th* by General Jenit Sulla (retired), 101 M42.

NOTWITHSTANDING THE IMPRESSION of imperturbability I took such pains to present to my subordinates, my readers will, I am sure, readily appreciate the apprehension I felt at the colonel's warning. I had scarcely had time to come to terms with my sudden and unexpected elevation, let alone come to know my new subordinates as anything other than the casual acquaintances of the officers' mess that they had until so recently been. Nevertheless, we were all soldiers of the Guard, the finest and most noble exemplars of humanity, so my confidence in their abilities was as high as it could be, and for my part I was quietly determined to provide them with the leadership such heroic women and men deserved.

With but a handful of minutes before the enemy onslaught was upon us, I checked the dispositions of the platoons under me in the tactical display of the company command Chimera, finding the routine comfortingly familiar. Indeed, were it not for the extra datafeeds and vox links surrounding me, I could almost have fancied myself back in command of my old platoon.

To my relief, our units were responding well to the alert, the platoon commanders as efficient as I could have wished, and glancing at the image in the hololith I was left in no doubt that our readiness to meet the heretic threat was as high as it was possible to be. All we could do now was wait for their shuttles to ground and move in as rapidly as we could to contain them.

And we weren't to be left waiting long. Within moments I heard the shriek of their engines, even through the thick armoured hull of the Chimera, a sound which was shortly to be terminated by the ice-shaking impact of their landing. One shuttle at least would not be returning to the vermin-laden vessel whence it came, as it had the misfortune to fly in directly over the heads of third platoon, who welcomed it as warmly as one might expect with the combined firepower of their heavy weapons and Chimera-mounted bolters.

'It's down and burning,' Lieutenant Roxwell reported, unable to keep a note of satisfaction from his voice, and under the circumstances I could scarcely reprove him for that. Even before I could give the order, he began moving his squads in to mop up the survivors, of which there were to prove far too many for comfort. Like the ones who had attacked us before, they fought like men possessed, heedless of their own safety or sound tactical doctrine. The fight became bloody, but their overconfidence was our strongest weapon, save for our faith in the Emperor of course, and it wasn't long before our superior competence and fighting spirit began to tell.

The second shuttle landed over two kilometres away, near the mine workings, but we had anticipated that, and first platoon were waiting for them, ready to give them the bloody nose all who dare to raise arms against the Emperor so richly deserve and invariably receive. Nonetheless, their charge was ferocious and our line buckled in places, allowing them to break through into the town itself before fourth platoon could move up to reinforce the gallant warriors of first.

Thus it was we found ourselves faced with two hordes of fanatics rampaging through Glacier Peak from opposite directions, firing indiscriminately at Guard troopers, praetor riot squads and unarmed civilians alike. Indeed, some even seemed to prefer the slaughter of innocent victims to facing our guns, cowards that they were.

The time was right for a bold initiative, and I ordered my unengaged units to consolidate around my command vehicle in the town square, where the twin thrusts of the enemy could be met simultaneously and held apart. For were they to meet and converge, the combined horde would undoubtedly have been able to wreak far more damage than either had managed alone. In this we were aided by two circumstances no one could have readily anticipated; the single-mindedness of the invaders, which allowed first and third platoons to wrap around their flanks and harass them all the way in, and the unexpected intervention of the underground cult we had spent so much time and effort attempting to expunge since our arrival on Adumbria.

It may be recalled that, as Commissar Cain was the first to point out, the invaders and the insurgents we had been engaging prior to their arrival appeared to owe their allegiance to rival Chaos Powers, and this was to be confirmed in the most unexpected fashion, as motley groups of armed civilians appeared in the streets to harass the invaders. I'm pleased to report that our women and men made no distinction between them, gunning down this breed of heretic whenever they appeared as eagerly as they did the crimson-uniformed foot soldiers of the traitor infantry, but the insurgents never retaliated in kind, concentrating all their efforts on killing the minions of their hated rivals even as they fell to the cleansing las bolts of the Guard. For my part, it must be said, I was considerably taken aback by their fixity of purpose, finding in it proof of the insanity which must surely be the state of mind of all who turn their gaze from the Emperor's light.

Nevertheless, they served a noble purpose, however base and corrupt their souls, for their intervention must surely have hastened the inevitable victory of the heroes I had the privilege to lead.

At the risk of appearing immodest, I have to say that my strategy worked: both arms of the invasion force met our solid centre and were successfully repulsed. Unable to break through, they were easily surrounded by the pursuing elements of first and third platoons, who used the superior mobility afforded by their Chimeras to good effect, and were utterly annihilated in gratifyingly short order.

It was, it must be admitted, our great good fortune that all the invaders who attacked Glacier Peak were on foot, since many of their other units were equipped with vehicles of their own. Indeed, the group which assaulted our base was supported by a battle tank, which Commissar Cain disabled single-handedly during his inspirational marshalling of our forces there, and the main force which landed west of the town, to be met by the bulk of our own troops, had a couple of tanks and a handful of armoured transports. These were disabled in pretty short order by fourth and fifth company, who had concealed their heavy weapons teams in ambush prior to the traitors' landing, and their victory, I'm gratified to report, was no less complete than ours, despite the greater numbers involved on both sides.

SIXTEEN

'Life's a journey. Shame about the destination.'
– Argun Slyter, *'Well What Did You Expect?'*,
Act 2 Scene 2

SUCH WAS MY relief at our deliverance from imminent destruction that for a moment or two I did little more than catch my breath, slumping to the cold metal floor of the cargo bay as the surge of skyward acceleration continued. I had precious little time to reflect on it, however, since my comm-bead was full of voices demanding to know what in the warp was going on.

'We're aboard the dropship,' I told Kasteen as quickly as I could, conscious that my short-range personal vox wouldn't be able to stay in contact with her for very long. 'It was the only way to keep it safe.' And myself, of course, which I must admit had been my main priority.

'Better stay airborne,' she advised. 'Things are still a bit hot around here.' As we were later to discover, the battle below us was almost over, but at the time no one had the benefit of hindsight, and discretion seemed the most prudent course of action. The dropship and the troopers it contained were a vital part of Zyvan's defensive strategy, and losing it now after it had escaped destruction so narrowly would have been embarrassing, to say the least.

That was advice I was happy to follow, you can be sure, the traitors having neglected to bring any aerospace support, so everything in the sky apart from their landing craft belonged to us; a fact which the PDF fighter pilots appreciated no end, enjoying themselves hugely at the expense of the lumbering shuttles. Predictably they ran out of targets before very long, and reverted to strafing the traitors on the ground with scarcely less enthusiasm.

'That might be best,' I conceded, with as much reluctance as I could feign. 'Although I must admit it rankles a bit to be sitting on the sidelines while you do all the work.'

Kasteen laughed. 'I'm sure the lord general will find something to keep you busy before long.'

The pleasantry punctured my happy mood, you can be sure of that; up until then I'd been too concerned with feeling relieved at having escaped the worst of the fighting to think any further ahead, but of course she was right. Any time now we'd be on our way to a war zone. Oh well, there was no point in fretting about it, I'd just have to take things as they came, just as I always did, and trust to my well-honed survival instinct once we got there.

The pilot was still yammering away on another channel, demanding to know precisely what was going on, so I responded to him next, if only to shut him up.

'Stay in a holding pattern for now,' I said. 'I'm on my way up to the flight deck to brief you.' Not that I needed to see him in person, of course, but it was damned uncomfortable in the cargo hold, and I had to retune my comm-bead to use the ship's vox as a relay instead of the rapidly-receding set in the regimental HQ. Besides, it made him feel important, which is always a good way to get what you want out of people.

As I might have predicted, my presence aboard made a considerable impression on the troopers we passed as Jurgen and I made our way through the passenger compartments. The news rippled ahead of us, so that by the time we arrived at Detoi's command group, seated next to the flight deck as they had been on our eventful descent from the *Emperor's Benificence*, the captain was smiling in our direction.

'I thought you might not be able to resist tagging along,' he said, jumping to the conclusion which my reputation tended to encourage. 'So I saved you a seat.' And indeed the ones Jurgen and I had occupied when we first arrived on Adumbria were still vacant. (Which isn't as surprising as it sounds. The dropships were designed to carry a full company, which in some regiments can mean six platoons instead of the five the 597th habitually fielded, at least during my time with them, and our platoons normally consisted of five squads instead of the six theoretically allowed for by the SO&E).[1]

'Very kind of you,' I responded with a carefully composed smile, and deposited Jurgen in one of the vacant chairs.

'So where are we going?' Detoi asked. He looked surprisingly fit, considering, but I suppose the prospect of action had perked him up. That, or the realisation that Sulla was out of his hair for good.

'Not entirely sure,' I admitted. 'I'm on my way to talk to the pilot now.'

The flight deck was cramped, of course, which was why I'd decided to leave Jurgen outside. Apart from the fact that I had no desire to be fending his elbow or the barrel of the melta away from my ribs every five minutes, being in a confined space with him was trying enough at the best of times, and I was used to it; for all I knew the pilot might be sufficiently distracted to plough us into a mountain or something.

'Commissar.' He glanced up from the polished wooden panel, inlaid with winking runes of inordinate complexity, and adjusted a large brass handle which I took to have something to do with our altitude as I felt the deck shift subtly under my feet as he did so. 'What's going on?'

I filled him in, while one of the tech-priests sitting at lateral panels of their own made the necessary adjustments to my comm-bead. (The other kept up the constant round of prayers and incantations apparently necessary to keep the engines functioning smoothly.) When I finished my account, resisting the urge to embroider it as I knew from long experience that a plain tale, plainly told, impresses people more than any amount of heroic posturing, the pilot nodded.

'Lucky you were there,' he said. 'A shell through the cargo hatch would have finished us all for sure.' He shrugged, dismissing the thought. 'I still need a destination, though.'

'Better maintain the holding pattern,' I said, playing for time. There were precious few significant targets on the coldside, which meant we were as far from combat as possible under the circumstances, and I wanted to prolong that happy state of affairs for as long as I could. 'I'd

---

1. *Slate of Organisation and Equipment, a slightly archaic term still in use by the 597th to refer to their personnel disposition. The so-called 'ghost squads' could be filled in by fresh recruits when the regiment returned to Valhalla to replenish its numbers, or, should sufficient inductees be found, an entire new company added to the roster. In practice, most commanders would prefer to have the new men dispersed among experienced platoons where they could learn from the veterans by example. It's by no means unusual for Imperial Guard companies to consist of fewer platoons, and the platoons of fewer squads, than their theoretical full complement; indeed, it was only the administrative error alluded to earlier which kept the 597th at a relatively steady number of soldiers despite their combat losses.*

hate to inconvenience the lord general by sending us off on a wild pterasquirrel chase.'

It was at that point, of course, that fate chose to intervene. I'd no sooner tucked my comm-bead back in my ear than a vaguely familiar voice began trying to raise me.

'Cain,' I responded, still trying to place it.

'Commissar. Glad to hear you're still in one piece.' The voice was drowned out for a moment by what sounded like an explosion. 'Sorry about that. They're trying to get across the bridge by the starport.' There was a short rattle of bolter fire. 'Of all the choke points in Skitterfall I have to end up back here. Ironic or what?'

'Kolbe,' I said, placing the young praetor at last. 'What can I do for you?'

'I thought it was the other way round. Excuse me a minute...' He was interrupted by a burst of incoherent screaming which sounded like the warcry of a Khornate fanatic and which terminated abruptly in a thud of a power maul on full charge and a gurgle which sounded distinctly unhealthy. 'Well he's not getting mine... Sorry commissar, where were we?'

'You seem to have some kind of message for me,' I prompted.

'Oh yes. Arbitrator Hekwyn said you wanted to be appraised of anything unusual around the equatorial sea. I had a quick skim through the reports, but there's nothing you wouldn't expect, given the current state of emergency. I was just starting on the maritime stuff when we were mobilised to back up the PDF here.'

'What maritime stuff?' I asked, a faint tingle of apprehension beginning to work its way up my spine. My palms were beginning to itch again too, always a bad sign.

'There's quite a lot of shipping on both seas,' Kolbe said, sounding surprised. 'Didn't you know?'

It hadn't occurred to me, being a hive boy born and bred; I'd just assumed the seas were large areas of open water, of no real use to anyone, and dismissed them as dead ground. But of course as they both stretched between the hotside and the coldside going around them, particularly the equatorial one just opposite Skitterfall would be more trouble than it was worth, and bulky cargoes wouldn't travel by air or suborbital. In short, the Adumbrians needed ships, and that meant the sorcerers could get to where they needed to be to complete their plans without any trouble at all.

'Can you transfer the maritime datafiles?' I asked, sprinting back into the passenger compartment and snatching a slate from a startled Detoi. Fortunately, young Kolbe wasn't too busy splatting heretics to transmit the information, and it began to scroll across the screen with startling rapidity.

'What are we looking for?' the captain asked.

'Anything anomalous.' I shot him a rueful smile. 'Not a lot of help, I know.'

'If it's there we'll find it,' Detoi promised, and started working through the list with the aid of his subaltern. I hurried back to the flight deck and tapped the shoulder of the cogboy who'd adjusted my commbead.

'I need a channel to the lord general's office,' I told him. To my pleased surprise he didn't argue, inputting the priority codes I'd given him as though it were a purely routine operation.

'Ciaphas.' Zyvan greeted me with the faintly abstracted air of a man who's really hoping that you haven't got bad news for him because he's got enough of that to deal with already. 'I hear you've hijacked one of my dropships.'

'It's a long story,' I told him. 'But I think we might need it. There are ships in the equatorial sea. The sorcerers could use one to get right where they needed to be in order to complete the ritual pattern.'

'Believe it or not that had occurred to us,' Zyvan said. 'But Malden said it wouldn't work. There needs to be some physical connection with the solid surface of the planet. It's a psyker thing.' His voice took on a tinge of amusement. 'I'm afraid you're whistling up the wrong fungal pod this time.'

'If you say so,' I said, far from convinced. The pattern was far too neat and I trusted my paranoia; it had kept me alive this long after all.

Zyvan's voice took on a harder edge. 'I do. Our immediate priority has to be the defence of the capital. I'm bringing in you, the Tallarn and the Kastaforean rapid reaction companies, and dispatching a tank squadron from the 425th Armoured. If you can deploy behind the invaders and cut them off we can put an end to this.'

'Until the Slaaneshi raise their daemon again and finish doing whatever the hell they're doing to the warp currents,' I said. I still had no idea what that might be, which was probably just as well, but I was pretty sure that would be the end for all of us in any case. 'I can't believe you're just going to ignore the possibility.'

'Of course I'm not going to ignore it.' An edge of frustration was entering the lord general's voice. 'But we've still got nothing to go on. Once we do, we'll take them down. But I'm a soldier, not a bloody inquisitor. I can only fight the enemies I can see!'

I couldn't really argue about that. After all, it was his army, and we were visibly up to our armpits in Khornate loonies. And after all those weeks of trying to uncover hidden enemies, he probably wasn't the only one to feel something of a sense of relief at finally having a target to shoot at.

'Transmit the coordinates,' I said. 'Our pilot will lay in the course.'

I returned to my seat surprisingly troubled. On the one hand, the assignment seemed easy enough, and I've never had any problem about shooting enemies in the back. In fact, I prefer it: it's safer. But I couldn't shake the nagging feeling that the real danger lay elsewhere and if we didn't seize the initiative soon we'd never get the chance.

'What's a mineral dredger?' Detoi asked, looking up from his data-slate, still ploughing through the reports I'd inflicted on him.

'Haven't a clue,' I told him. 'We don't get them in the hives, that's for sure.'

'Or on iceworlds,' the captain said. He busied himself for a moment, calling up the briefing files on local customs and culture I hadn't been able to summon any interest in reading aboard the troopship. 'Oh, that's interesting. They're floating manufactoria, which scoop up mineral deposits from the floor of the ocean and process them on the spot. Apparently they can do that here because the seas are so shallow.'

'Physical contact with the solid surface of the planet,' I said, a chill of nameless dread working its way unpleasantly up my spine.

Detoi nodded. 'I suppose so, technically speaking...' his voice trailed off as he noted my expression.

'What drew your attention to the dredgers?' I asked as evenly as I could.

'The Arbites logged a mayday from one, about the time the invasion started. Under the circumstances they didn't have time to follow it up.'

'Show me,' I said.

The transmission had been short and abruptly curtailed, but whoever had been on the other end of the vox had just had time to mention pirates before they'd been cut off. I pointed to the transcript. 'See that? Pirates. Not soldiers, not invaders. Someone either boarded them, or there was a mutiny among the crew.'

'I see.' Detoi nodded slowly. 'Sounds more like the cultists we were fighting before.' Then he shrugged. 'Unless it really was pirates, just out to loot the place.'

'Not the sort of thing that happens on Adumbria,' I pointed out. 'Where would they go to sell the ore? There's only one starport, and that's locked tight at the best of times.' I found the co-ordinates from which the mayday had been sent, and the palms of my hands tingled more strongly than ever. They were almost exactly on the opposite side of the planet from Skitterfall. Precisely where Malden had said the final ritual would have to take place if the sorcerers were to succeed in their heinous plans.

I tapped the comm-bead in my ear and contacted the pilot.

'We're changing course,' I said. 'Here are the new co-ordinates.' I'd expected him to argue, but he'd evidently been around Guard personnel for long enough to know that a commissar's authority outweighs even a lord general's.[1] After a brief acknowledgement I felt the subtle shift in my inner ear which told me the dropship was turning. Jurgen swallowed hard, his face white.

'Cheer up,' I told him. 'We'll be down before you know it.' And facing one of the most terrifying ordeals of my life to boot. But at the time, of course, I had no inkling of that.

---

1. *The Imperial Navy also has commissars attached to it, though in lesser numbers than the Guard. Even if he hadn't encountered one of them, the pilot would certainly have come into contact with a few of those travelling aboard the* Emperor's Benificence *with their regiments.*

SEVENTEEN

'If you go looking for trouble, you're sure to find it.'

– Gilbran Quail, *Collected Essays*

IF YOU'VE BEEN reading these memoirs with any degree of attention you're probably thinking that this apparent willingness of mine to rush headlong into danger is uncharacteristic to say the least. Well, perhaps it is. But the way I saw it, whatever the Slaaneshi were up to was the real threat, and seeing off a bunch of loony berserkers too carried away with bloodlust to use sensible tactics or even fire their guns half the time was little more than a sideshow. And, as I've said before, I knew from bitter experience that the only way to deal with warpcraft is to get in there straight away, before the witches or whatever's behind it have had time to finish what they've started.

So although I was as petrified as you might expect, I hid it with the ease of an experienced dissembler, and reflected that however alarming the prospect of facing sorcery might be, the consequences of not doing so were bound to be a damn sight worse. As so often in my life, it all came down to picking the course of action which offered the greatest chance of getting out with my hide intact, however great the immediate risk might be.

Besides, I had an entire company of Guard troopers to hide behind, and Jurgen's remarkable ability to chuck a spanner into whatever dark forces might be about to be unleashed, so all in all the odds seemed reasonably in my favour. And if they turned out not to be, at least I had a ship capable of making orbit.

On the whole I thought it might be polite to let Zyvan know his plan to disrupt the invasion was going to be short a company after all, but when I tried to raise him over the vox all I got was one of his aides.

'The lord general is unavailable,' he told me, with the unmistakable tone of a man who's making the most of the chance to be a pain in the arse. 'He's gone to inspect our forward positions.'

'Well, patch me through to his comm-bead,' I said.

The aide sighed audibly. 'Our orders are to maintain vox silence. If the enemy were to learn of his whereabouts–'

'Fine,' I said, making a mental note to find out exactly who I'd been talking to and make his life excessively unpleasant as soon as I got the opportunity. 'Then get me Malden.'

Fortunately, the young psyker was still at headquarters, and his familiar dry tone in my earpiece was surprisingly calming. If anyone on the lord general's staff could appreciate the danger we were facing it was sure to be him.

'Commissar.' He paused for a moment. 'I take it this isn't a social call.'

'I've found the fourth ritual site,' I said without preamble. 'It's a mineral dredger in the middle of the equatorial sea. I'm diverting a dropship full of troopers there now.'

'A dredger.' His voice was so flat that for a moment I thought he hadn't believed me, and was about to tell me not to waste my time. 'I wasn't aware that the Adumbrians use them. But then no one ever tells Adepta Astra Telepathica anything.' He sighed audibly. 'That does put a different complexion on things.'

'So the ritual could take place on one?' I asked.

'Without a doubt.' An unaccustomed edge of uneasiness entered his voice. 'I can only pray to the Emperor that you'll get there in time.'

Not the most comforting thing he might have said, I'm sure you'll agree.

'There's a time factor involved?' I asked.

'Probably.' The hint of emotion was draining away from his voice again as he became immersed in the problem at hand. 'My colleagues and I have been analysing the warp patterns and the timing of the previous shifts. It's very likely that the next and final one will take place within the next few hours.'

'Oh good,' I said, wondering if I should just tell the pilot to head for space now, commandeer a warp-capable merchant ship and have done with it. But then there was supposed to be an enemy battleship up there, or so I'd heard, so that didn't seem like a terribly healthy option either. Better to stick to the plan we already had, at least for now. 'No pressure then.'

'Not so you'd notice,' Malden said dryly.

'We need to inform the lord general at once,' I said.

'I quite agree. Unfortunately, I don't have any way of getting in touch with him.' A faint trace of amusement, almost imperceptible, seemed to enter his voice. 'However, I'll try to prevail on one of his aides to pass on a message. They can be surprisingly amenable if I talk to them in the right way.' Knowing how nervous most people were around spooks I could well believe it.

'I'll leave it with you then,' I said, and settled down for a long, tense wait.

THE SKY BEYOND the armourcrys viewport in the flight deck had lightened to twilight, the stars overhead fading to invisibility as the colour gradually brightened from the familiar blue-black through purple to a greyish blue which put me in mind of the pre-dawn quiet on some nice normal planet with a proper day-night cycle.

Only the brightest stars were still visible over our heads. Were we in the opposite hemisphere, we would have been able to see a great many more pinpoints of light, dancing like the sparks from a bonfire as the invisible sun reflected from the hulls of the hundreds of starships in orbit (at least away from the streetlights of Skitterfall), but here only a handful of genuine stars shone in the sky.

With difficulty I tore my mind away from the struggle taking place on the opposite side of the planet. Here, where the only things moving were the waves on the cold grey water below, it was hard to credit the scale of the carnage going on a few thousand kilometres beneath my bootsoles.

I'd listened in on some of the signal traffic, and it wouldn't be much of an exaggeration to say that things were looking grim. Zyvan's counter-attack had checked the main body of the invaders well enough, driving a wedge through their heart and scattering them even despite our absence, but incredibly the Khornates had rallied and were making a grim and desperate last stand which looked like becoming a long and bloody affair. Scattered reports spoke of a giant in power armour leading them, so at least one other Chaos Marine had made it down to the surface unscathed, and I didn't envy whoever it was who finally got to take him out.[1]

---

1. *The World Eater leading the assault on Skitterfall appears to have been killed with gratifying thoroughness by an anti-tank squad from one of the Kastaforean regiments. (Two krak missiles and a lascannon not having left an awful lot to identify for sure.)*

I'd also gathered in the course of my eavesdropping that Beije had tagged along with the Tallarn company who'd joined the assault, no doubt spouting pious platitudes and getting in the way of the fighting men, and couldn't help wondering how he'd react if he came face to face with the Tainted Marine, which after his snide comments about my own encounter would have been poetic justice at least. (It never happened, of course; although if it had things would undoubtedly have worked out with far less fuss and bother all round.)

'There it is.' The pilot pointed, and I was just able to make out a glint of metal and a hint of solidity in the moving mass of water below us. I'd been in the flight deck for some time, trying to get Zyvan on the vox (with a complete lack of success so far) and exchanging messages with Malden about what we might expect to find when we landed (which essentially boiled down to 'your guess is as good as mine'.)

If I'm honest, I was doing this mainly to keep my mind occupied in preference to sitting and brooding, but it also had the advantage of keeping me out of Jurgen's way. The prolonged flight wasn't agreeing with his stomach at all, and even though he'd managed to hang on to his last meal so far I'd rather not take the risk of being in the vicinity if his willpower gave out. 'Landing in five minutes.'

'Five minutes, everyone,' I voxed over the company command net, trying to think of a stock text to cover this and failing.

I moved to lean casually against the jamb of the cockpit door, where everyone in the forward compartment could see me, and looked into a row of tense, nervous faces. 'I can't honestly tell you what to expect when we get down there. But I do know that the fate of this world probably hangs on our actions when we do.' I paused, searching for the right words. 'All I can say is that I've faced warpcraft before, and I'm still here to brag about it.' A few nervous laughs rippled around the rows of seats as I played off my reputation for quiet heroism; Cain the Hero never boasted about his exploits, of course.

'Psykers and warpsmiths aren't to be taken lightly,' I went on, 'but in my experience they die just as easily as anyone else. I've yet to meet a witch who didn't find a las bolt in the head a severe inconvenience.' More laughter, a little louder and more confident this time. I shook off the mental image of Emeli, her green eyes filling with outraged astonishment as I shot her, and hesitated, my train of thought momentarily derailed. 'The Emperor protects,' I finished, finding refuge in a familiar platitude.

'We're on the final descent,' the pilot called. 'Better get strapped in, commissar.' I took a final glance back through the viewport and felt my breath still in my chest. The dredger was vast, filling the whole of the pane, and we were still some distance away from it.

In my ignorance I'd expected something not too different from a conventional ocean-going ship, maybe a little larger, because after all they had to process the ore they extracted somewhere, but my guess had been a long way wide of the mark. It loomed out of the sea ahead of us like a stranded hab block, fully a couple of kilometres from stem to stern, about half that wide and several hundred metres in height. And that, I suddenly realised, would just be the part above the waterline, there would be almost as much of the thing below the surface too. Even with a full company of troopers, searching a structure that size could take hours. Days even...

Well, in my experience, enemies were never hard to find once the shooting started, so I deferred that problem until we had to face it and staggered back to my seat to find Detoi engrossed in a set of schematics he'd managed to pull up from the files in his data-slate.[1] With a quick glance at my white-faced aide, who seemed no worse than before, I leaned across to look at them.

'Where do you think they'll be?' Detoi asked. I took in the bewildering array of compartments, ore processors and connecting passageways, trying to get a sense of the layout in my head.

'I'm not sure,' I admitted. In my experience, heretic cults tended to go underground, literally as well as metaphorically, so somewhere below the waterline, down by the keel, seemed like a good bet. On the other hand, there seemed to be a lot of machinery down there, which might get in the way, and I had a vague memory that water was supposed to disrupt sorcery somehow.[2] I tried to picture the chambers I'd found in the hab dome and the bawdy house, hoping to find some clue in their layout. 'They'll need somewhere large and open, with a high ceiling.'

'Doesn't narrow it down much,' Detoi said thoughtfully. 'We've got the hangars next to the shuttle pad on the upper decks, a few recreation rooms, a chapel for the tech-priests, docking facilities for the cargo boats down by the waterline, and some of these manufactoria are vast.'

'Eliminate those, and the hangars, and the boat docks,' I said. 'At least for now. The rooms I saw before were big, but not that big.'

Detoi nodded. 'Still leaves us with a lot of ground to cover,' he said.

I couldn't dispute that. 'Well we'll just have to trust in the Emperor to show us a sign,' I said, with rather less sarcasm than I usually would.

'Brace for landing,' the pilot said, and all around me men and women tensed for the impact, readying their weapons and preparing to release

---

1. Or, more likely, had had transmitted from somewhere. The plans of the dredgers would have been readily available to anyone with an appropriate security clearance.

2. A widely-believed piece of folklore, but quite baseless according to the psykers I've asked.

their crash webbing. Jurgen cradled the melta like a juvie with a favourite toy, looking happier than he had done in several hours. The retros kicked in suddenly, compressing my spine with the abrupt deceleration, and a loud metallic clang rang through the hull. 'We're down,' he added unnecessarily.

'Third platoon, deploy and secure,' Detoi said, picking the unit nearest the cargo ramp. Lustig's voice responded, calm and confident, and the captain shot me a sudden and unexpected grin. 'Jenit's going to be sick as an ice weasel about missing this,' he said.

'Sulla's got enough to worry about in Glacier Peak,' I assured him, having used the vox to keep abreast of the rest of the regiment while we were in the air. But his mind was already on the deployment of our own troopers and I doubt he even heard me.

'Come on, Jurgen,' I said, turning to my aide. 'Let's see if a little sea air can perk you up.'

'Very good, sir,' he responded, looking a little better already (which, with Jurgen, was something of a relative term, of course).

I turned to Detoi. 'See you outside,' I said, and hurried to the nearest debarkation point. Landers on the ground are horribly vulnerable if the enemy has sufficient firepower, and I wanted to be out in the open if we were going to be taking any incoming.

Not that that seemed particularly likely, of course, as we hadn't had a sniff of any anti-aircraft fire on the way in, but I found it hard to believe that the heretics we were hunting hadn't even noticed the arrival of a dropship; they're not exactly stealthy after all. Besides, if there were any abnatural forces at work here I wanted to get Jurgen where his peculiar gift would begin to disrupt them as quickly as possible; under the circumstances there was no way in the galaxy I was going to move far from his protective aura.

As we left the shelter of the dropship, I became aware of a keen wind whipping across the vast steel plain that surrounded us, bringing the unmistakable oceanic tang of ozone and salt. Next to the blood-freezing temperatures of the coldside, however, it felt positively balmy and I inhaled it gratefully, moving upwind of Jurgen as I did so.

If I hadn't seen the place from the air, I would probably have imagined we were in an industrial zone somewhere rather than aboard a floating construct. Structures the size of warehouses rose in the distance, looming threateningly in the perpetual twilight, and even the vast bulk of the dropship seemed shrunken to the size of an ordinary shuttle by the sheer scale of our surroundings. I'd seldom felt such a sense of insignificance, even in a titan maintenance bay (well, perhaps then).

Third platoon were moving out to secure the landing pad, the squads separating with practiced precision, advancing a team at a time to keep one another covered as they scurried from one piece of cover to the next. I saw Penlan jog past, shepherding her new squad with calm deliberation, and reflected that my confidence in her seemed to have been well placed. Lustig was standing at the base of the ramp, watching her go with an air of quiet pride.

'Good job all round, sergeant,' I said.

'She'll do.' He nodded. I indicated the rest of the troops, deploying with equal efficiency.

'I meant the whole platoon,' I said.

Lustig nodded again. 'We won't let you down, sir.'

'Fourth squad at the mark. No sign of hostiles.' I recognised the voice of Sergeant Grifen, and nodded.

'Stay put for the moment. And keep your eyes open.'

'No problem, commissar,' she assured me. I was pleased to have her squad on point. Grifen was a good leader who looked after her troopers but wasn't afraid to take the occasional chance when necessary. I'd been impressed by her qualities on Simia Orichalcae, when our routine recon mission had gone so spectacularly ploin-shaped, and in the years since she'd more than justified that confidence.

'Pad secured,' Lustig reported after a moment, and the other four platoons began doubling down the ramp to join us. As you'll appreciate, all those boots ringing on metal made a hell of a noise, and it took me a moment to realise that Detoi had joined us.

'Under the circumstances I don't think the vehicles will be much help,' he said.

'I think you're right.' There was undoubtedly enough open space to make use of them; indeed there were a few cargo haulers scattered around on the fringes of the pad, some of them still loaded with crates and bundles. But the noise they'd make on that metallic surface would be the Emperor's own row, and we'd soon have to venture into some tight spaces where they'd be far too vulnerable. Far better to advance on foot.

'Lustig', the captain went on. 'Detail a squad or two to cover the pad. I don't want us cut off from the dropship if we need to pull back in a hurry.' That was a sound precaution to my way of thinking too. Normally the lander would have pulled back, either returning to orbit (or in this case our staging area) to deploy another company of troopers, or remaining in a holding pattern overhead once we were satisfied there was no danger to it from ground fire, but under the circumstances neither option seemed terribly attractive. We were surrounded by water, with nowhere to go, and the dropship was our only lifeline.

'First and third squads, cover the pad. Second and fourth, stand by,' Lustig ordered at once.

Like it or not, I found myself thinking, he looked like getting a commission for sure if he kept this up.

Detoi briefed his platoon commanders quickly, giving each of them an area to reconnoitre, and I watched our troopers disperse with mixed feelings. True, we'd cover a lot more ground that way, but two hundred and fifty-odd soldiers seemed barely adequate to the task of searching an installation that size. I'd been counting on the idea of safety in numbers more than I'd realised, and as most of our complement disappeared into the shadows around us I began to feel uncomfortably exposed.

Well, standing around here wouldn't help much, so I began to jog forward, intent on attaching myself to the nearest squad (which, as it happened, was fourth, under Grifen). As I did so, I glanced across the landing pad, where Penlan was leading second squad from the front. She'd just reached the next mark, a light cargo hauler laden with something I took to be bins of processed ore, when she glanced back to wave her second team on, tripped on something at her feet and stumbled a pace before recovering her balance. Something about the way she and the troopers with her were looking down seemed vaguely disturbing.

'Second squad,' she reported a moment later. 'We've found a body. Civilian, shot in the back. Autogun by the look of the wounds.'

'Any sign of a weapon?' I asked.

'No sir.' Even at this distance I could see the angry set of her shoulders. 'This was murder, pure and simple.'

'It looks like he was running away,' one of the troopers chipped in helpfully. 'Rolled under here for cover, maybe.'

'Well it didn't help him,' Penlan said. Something about the tone of her voice promised bloody vengeance on behalf of whoever it had been. 'He must have been working up here when they landed.'

'If they landed,' I said.

Jurgen looked at me quizzically. 'There's nothing else on the pad,' I pointed out.

'Perhaps they took off again,' he suggested. It was possible, of course, but somehow I couldn't see our shadowy enemies leaving here until they'd done whatever they set out to do, and it all seemed far too normal for that to have been the case.

'First squad,' a new voice chimed in, on fifth platoon's channel.[1] 'We're in the boat dock. Looks like there's been a serious firefight down here. Lasgun and autogun damage mostly. Maybe a couple of stubbers.'

Well that answered that. The raiders had come in aboard one of the scheduled supply vessels, probably after hi-jacking it on the way, unless at least some of the crew had been cultists to begin with.

'Any survivors?' Lieutenant Faril asked, his habitual good humour absent for once, which was hardly surprising under the circumstances.

'No,' the sergeant replied. 'Just bodies. Security personnel mostly, judging by the uniforms. It looks like they were trying to hold the attackers off while the workers got out.'

They didn't seem to have got very far, judging by the complete lack of any signs of life we'd séen since our arrival. According to the data Detoi had pulled, there should have been nearly three thousand workers aboard. It was hard to believe that the attackers could have taken quite so many, but as the search continued and the body count rose, it became increasingly clear that this was precisely what had happened.

'In other words, we're wandering around looking for a frakking army,' Magot said, apparently none too perturbed at the prospect. I nodded, flattening myself into the shadow of a companionway, while Grifen and her team moved ahead to the next mark.

'It's beginning to look like that,' I said. An army would be something of an exaggeration, but it had taken a good few dozen raiders to fight their way out of the boat dock. Not all had made it either, I was pleased to learn, the outlandish clothing (or more often lack of it) of some of the corpses indicating that the dredger's crew hadn't gone down without taking a few of their assailants with them. After that, hunting down and murdering the panicked workforce in small groups would have been easy, especially if they already had confederates aboard who could point them at the most likely hiding places.

I had little time to muse on this bleak prospect, however, as my thoughts were interrupted by the distinctive crack of ionising air which accompanied a lasgun discharge. It was followed an instant later by

---

1. *Each platoon would have their own vox channel assigned, to which their troopers' personal comm-beads would be tuned. Their platoon commander would have access to this and the company channel, through which they would report to Detoi. In larger engagements the company commanders would have access to the regimental tactical net, through which they would report to Kasteen and Broklaw, and this arrangement would be repeated for higher levels of command right up to the lord general's staff. Cain, as a commissar, would have complete access to all the channels, enabling him to get an overall impression of the whole battlefield, albeit a somewhat confusing one on occasion. No doubt his training and years of experience would enable him to pick out any salient information from the rest of the traffic.*

others, the harsher bark of an autogun and what sounded like a couple of pistols.

'Contact,' a voice said in my comm-bead. 'Level twelve, sector two.' A moment later Lieutenant Luskom, the officer in charge of first platoon, chimed in on the company frequency.

'Third squad's in a firefight,' she reported. 'Sector two, level twelve. I'm moving first and fourth in to support.'

'Sector two,' I said, recalling the map Detoi had shown me and mentally comparing it with our own position. 'It must be down that way.' I pointed, although there was no need to really, the sound of gunfire intensifying in that direction as the fresh squads joined in the battle.

'Shall we go in to support them?' Grifen asked, and I shook my head. 'They seem to be handling it. I'm more interested in what the traitors are trying to defend.' And with any luck first platoon would be keeping them looking the other way while we went to find out.

Unfortunately, while the enemy might have been mad, they weren't stupid. As we rounded a row of storage tanks, finally moving out of the constant wind into some degree of shelter, a crackle of las fire sent us scurrying for cover. An itchy rain of dislodged rust pattered on my cap and greatcoat, leaving a stain on the sable fabric that would be the Emperor's own job to remove, and I inched forwards on my elbows to peer cautiously around the corner.

'Frak!' I said feelingly. The heretics had erected a makeshift barricade which looked solid enough for all that, crouching behind a rough assemblage of girders, packing crates, metal drums and other detritus. More to the point they'd set up a heavy stubber to cover the open space in front. Any attempt to get closer would simply get the whole lot of us killed. As if to emphasise the point it opened up, gouging a line of dents in the deck plating.

'Well we're not getting in that way,' Grifen said as I wormed my way back hastily to join her.

'We could work around and try to flank them,' Magot suggested. 'Lob a few frag grenades over the barrier. That'd give them something to think about.'

'It might,' I said. 'The problem's going to be getting close enough.' By luck or by judgement the heretics had chosen their position well, without much cover for a flanking attack. The storage tanks we'd taken refuge behind were the nearest piece of solid cover; I could only hope that whatever they contained wasn't volatile. Even Jurgen's melta couldn't help us this time, the range was too great. He got off a couple of shots, which at least kept the heretics' heads down, but the thermal energy dissipated too much for the metal of the fortification to be anything more than mildly scorched.

I sighed with frustration. 'We haven't got time for this. We'll have to go round another way.'

This was easier said than done and looked like getting harder. As we pulled back, the mocking catcalls of the cultists echoing in our ears, I was getting a steady stream of tactical reports through the comm-bead. By now practically every squad in the company had encountered resistance, and the few which hadn't (apart from the ones Lustig had guarding the dropship) were being rushed in to reinforce their fellows.

From training and habit I compared the positions of the firefights with the memory of the schematics I'd seen and nodded grimly. The heretics had sealed off sector twelve, reinforcing their perimeter to withstand a siege. Whatever they were up to was happening somewhere in that part of the dredger.

'Detoi,' I said. 'We have to find a weak spot. If we don't break through soon it'll be too late.'

'I know.' His voice was tight with frustration. 'But we don't have the numbers. The way they're dug in they can hold us off indefinitely.'

'We can call for reinforcements,' I said, without much hope. Even if Zyvan was reachable now it would take far too long for any other units to get here. 'But I doubt they'll arrive in time.'

'Maybe if we concentrate our forces,' Detoi said, his voice heavy. 'Pull everyone back and consolidate, try to force a breach in one spot.'

His lack of enthusiasm for the idea was evident in his tone, and I could appreciate why. Not only would we be bottlenecked trying to get to a single fortification, the enemy would have time to reinforce the point we attacked. The fighting would be vicious and bloody and we'd take massive casualties. Even then the chances of succeeding were low.

'There must be something else we can do,' I said, reluctant to commit us to so desperate an action unless we had to, but right then I couldn't think of an alternative.

'Then we'd better think of it fast,' Detoi said, the flatness of his tone revealing that he was under no illusions about our ability to do so.

'I've an auspex contact, inbound,' the dropship pilot cut in. 'Closing fast.'

'Any vox contact?' I asked, the sinking feeling in my gut already providing the answer.

'Not yet,' the pilot confirmed. 'But the IFF[1] says it's Imperial.'

---

1. *Identification, Friend or Foe: a beacon fitted to most military craft which transmits a code identifying it as a member of the Imperial forces. Generally reliable, but occasional malfunctions have led to unfortunate incidents of fratricide; it's not unknown for such devices to fall into the hands of enemies, deviants and heretics, enabling them to masquerade as servants of the Emperor for their own nefarious purposes.*

A sudden flare of hope lit within me. Malden must have been able to get through to the lord general at last, and with extra troops at our disposal we stood a chance of breaking through the heretics' defences and foiling their foul design. Whatever that might be.

'Lustig,' I voxed. 'Keep it covered anyway, just in case.' Things were dicey enough right now as they were and the last thing we needed was to fall for some heretic stratagem using a stolen shuttle.

'Acknowledged,' the stoic sergeant said, and I turned my attention back to Detoi. By this time the troopers, Jurgen and I were halfway back to the dropship, our boots ringing on the surface of the pad, and I could clearly see the captain and Lustig standing on the cargo ramp, shielding their eyes as they gazed to the west.[1]

'Better get everyone primed to disengage,' I said, 'just in case.'

'Already on it,' he responded. 'Their orders are to keep the enemy pinned, not expose themselves to fire, and be prepared to pull back.'

'Sounds good to me,' I said, with some relief. That kept our options open, at least for a little while longer.

I turned my head, looking in the same direction as the captain and the sergeant. The scream of an engine was audible now, closing fast, and ahead of it darted a sleek courier shuttle. I felt a sudden jab of disappointment. Another dropship with a full company would have been a bit much to hope for, but I'd been counting on a cargo shuttle with a platoon or two at least. The courier couldn't have held more than a squad.

I watched it touch down with a curious mixture of emotions I can only describe as inquisitive apprehension. Things were beginning to get out of hand again, and I didn't like the feeling. Its engines died down to an idle and I walked towards it, obscurely grateful for the familiar presence of Jurgen at my shoulder. Grifen and her troopers stayed at my back, a few paces behind, their hands on their weapons. As we got closer the ramp descended and a squad of Imperial troops disembarked at the double, lasguns held ready.

'Tallarns,' Griffen said, surprised. I have to admit I shared her emotion. Behind the desert warriors came a familiar figure in commissarial black who pushed his way through the knot of troopers to stand in front of me. He was fighting to keep his face impassive, and losing badly; something akin to a smirk kept writhing to the surface of his pudgy features.

'Beije,' I said flatly, sure that whatever he was here for was bound to be bad news. 'This isn't a very good time.'

---

1. *Quite why they would have bothered to do this in perpetual twilight I have no idea; perhaps it was just out of habit.*

'Ciaphas Cain,' he responded, bouncing on the soles of his feet with an excess of self-importance. 'You are hereby charged with desertion, cowardice in the face of the enemy and misappropriation of military resources.' He gestured to the squad of Tallarn warriors, beckoning them forward. 'Arrest him.'

Editorial Note:

Without more background information much of what follows will appear to make lit-tle sense. Accordingly I have inserted another extract from Tincrowser's account of the campaign as a whole, which ought to go some way towards explaining what would otherwise appear to be a coincidence so huge as to stretch the credulity of even the most open-minded of readers. Cain, of course, concentrates purely on his own experience, barely bothering to speculate about the wider causes and implications of what's going on around him.

From *Sablist in Skitterfall: a brief history of the Chaos incursion* by Dagblat Tincrowser, 957 M41

WITH THE INVASION force now apparently stalled, thanks to Lord General Zyvan's bold and incisive strategy, the tide at last began to turn in favour of the beleaguered defenders. Encircled by no fewer than four companies of Imperial Guard, landed by dropship to fall on their undefended rear, the invaders attacking Skitterfall faltered and began to consolidate to no avail; bolstered by units of the PDF the Guard began to tighten their cordon, slowly but surely winning back the streets of the capital step by step and corpse by corpse.

In space, however, things still appeared grim for the lone cruiser standing guard over Skitterfall highport, and the frightened huddle of merchant ships which looked like easy prey for the twisted leviathan bearing down on the besieged planet below. At ranges almost too great for the mind to grasp, combat was eventually joined, ravening energies of barely conceivable power reaching out to strike at the Imperial vessels in orbit.

The *Indestructible* was to live up to her glorious name, however, despite the grievous wounds she suffered from that first strike, retaliating with her dorsal lance battery which alone could match the range of the formidable firepower unleashed by the Chaotic vessel. It was a heroic gesture, but seemed to some observers to be futile, since it was far less powerful than the shots she'd received, but if nothing else it served to goad the battleship into reckless action, increasing its speed in an attempt to close and decide the matter. To the astonishment of all, however, the *Indestructible* reversed her engines, giving ground and retreating slowly in the face of the aggressor.

The despair which must have been felt by those merchant crews at such a sight is something we can only imagine, since it must surely have seemed that the Imperial cruiser was damaged beyond all reasonable effectiveness and hoping to withdraw. That was certainly the impression the marauder got, for rather than concentrating its fire on the limping *Indestructible*, its auxiliary weapons began striking out wantonly at the merchant shipping and it continued to accelerate towards the tempting array of targets laid out before it.

This was precisely the intention of the *Indestructible*'s heroic captain, Igor Yates, whose tactical brilliance finally began to become clear. Just at the moment her looming attacker was overcommitted, the *Indestructible* launched a volley of torpedoes, which impacted on the Chaos vessel with most gratifying results. Too badly damaged to launch torpedoes of its own, and with its dorsal armament now out of action, the cumbersome behemoth began burning retros in an attempt to bring its broadside to bear on the Imperial vessel. However the turn was too ponderous and the momentum it had built up too great; Captain Yates's trap was sprung.

Still trying to turn, the crippled leviathan drifted into the middle of the fleet of merchant ships which, until now, it had considered nothing more than easy prey to be picked off at leisure. The feeble armament of a cargo ship would normally be no threat at all to such a mighty engine of destruction, but now it was surrounded by nearly a thousand of them, which, instead of attempting to flee as the murderous cowards aboard the battleship would no doubt have expected, began to swarm towards them, bringing their puny defensive batteries to bear as they did so. Just as a lumbering grox can be stung to death by a nest of maddened firewasps, the mighty warship died by increments as the sheer number of its assailants began to take their toll. Though its powerful weapons lashed out again and again, swatting one or two at a time, it could never hope to make much difference to so mighty a host, and once the *Indestructible* had returned to the fray, crippling its engines, the end was inevitable.

For a moment, they say, a new sun blazed in the sky over Skitterfall, bright enough to dazzle the observers on the ground, and at that sight Guardsmen and PDF soldiers alike cheered in unison, knowing the back of the invasion had been comprehensively broken. All that remained was the scouring of the stain inflicted on our fair world, a task they set to with a will.

In the years since, that engagement has been studied and considered by many, and a few have wondered at the Chaos captain's apparent recklessness. Surely, they ask, he must have had some reason for acting as he did, some compelling reason to continue on so suicidal a course?[1] Such speculation is, however, as futile as it is fruitless. What this undoubtedly teaches us is that the Great Enemy's greatest weakness is overconfidence, nothing more.

---

1. *A question Cain's narrative answers beyond all doubt, but not in any fashion suitable for the good citizens of Adumbria to learn.*

EIGHTEEN

'Well, that was unexpected…'

– Last words of the Chaos Warmaster
Varan the Undefeatable

THE PHRASE 'UTTER astonishment' barely begins to convey my emotions at that moment. No doubt I would have stood there completely stupefied with Emperor alone knows what results, if it hadn't been for the troopers with me. But as the Tallarns stepped forward to obey Beije's order, Grifen and the rest of her squad brought up their lasguns to forestall them. The desert warriors hesitated, looking to their commissar for a lead.

'This is mutiny,' Beije said, completely lost in a world of his own by now. He drew his laspistol and began to aim at the Valhallan sergeant. 'You're hereby sentenced to death under section–'

'Oh be quiet you absurd little man,' I snapped, bringing my own weapon up to cover him. 'No one's executing any of my troopers unless it's me. And if you even so much as think about pulling that trigger you'll be dead before she hits the ground, I promise you.'

'Too right,' Magot agreed, stepping between Grifen and the outraged commissar. 'You want her, you'll have to go through me.'

'Shoot them all!' Beije waved a peremptory arm at the Tallarns, who began looking from one to the other with the unmistakable air of men who've suddenly realised that they've walked blithely up to the brink of a precipice.

'No one's shooting anybody,' I said calmly. 'Unless it's the heretics we came here to cleanse.' I gestured in the direction of the sounds of battle, still clearly audible, as the sergeant in charge of the Tallarns nodded almost imperceptibly to his squad. They lowered their weapons a fraction, and to my relief the Valhallans did the same.

'In case you hadn't noticed, there's a battle going on here, and if we don't win it pretty damn quick, all hell's about to break loose. Literally.'

'You can't hide behind posturing and rhetoric this time,' Beije snarled, taking a step forward and bringing his laspistol around to point at me. 'You ran away from the battle for Skitterfall and you took a whole company of soldiers out of the field with you. You've been obsessed with finding some excuse to hide out here as far from the fighting as you can get ever since that petticoat colonel of yours came up with her ridiculous theory–' He broke off, suddenly aware of the naked anger on the faces of the Valhallans facing him, and the lasguns in their hands.

'You can accuse me of anything you like,' I said, playing to the emotions of the troopers with me with the ease of long practice. 'But you will not disparage Colonel Kasteen in my presence. She's one of the finest soldiers I've ever had the privilege to serve with, and the regiment she leads is among the best in the galaxy.'

I holstered my pistol with what I considered to be a suitably theatrical gesture. 'No doubt this farcical situation has warped your judgement, along with your manners. When you calm down I'll expect an apology on her behalf. Failing that, I'm sure we can settle the matter quite amicably on the duelling field.'

If I'm honest, I didn't expect to be going so far as to call him out, but as so often happens in these situations my mouth gets ahead of my brain. The results were quite satisfying, in any event; he went several colours I had seldom seen in nature in rapid succession, and rallied as best he could. The troopers loved it, though, and I could tell it would be all round the regiment within minutes of our return that I'd challenged the pompous little squit to a duel over an insult to the colonel, and, by extension, the rest of us too.[1]

'Once this is over you'll have no time for duelling or anything else,' Beije snapped.

---

1. *As so often in the sections of the archive dealing with his service with the 597th, Cain appears to have been so close to the troops, particularly the senior officers with whom he had a personal friendship, that his technical status as an outsider becomes blurred not only in their minds but in his own as well.*

'Commissar.' Detoi's voice was a welcome distraction in my comm-bead. 'We need to decide what we're going to do. The heretics are still holding firm along the entire perimeter.'

'There must be a weak point somewhere,' I replied, noting with interest that Beije was surreptitiously retuning his own comm-bead to listen in. 'Try checking the schematics again. Maybe there's a cable shaft or an air duct we can infiltrate a kill team through.'

'I already thought of that,' the captain said. 'Everything's sealed tight.' He sighed. 'Barring a miracle it'll have to be a frontal assault. And it's going to be bloody.'

'I'm afraid you're right,' I said, my gut curdling at the thought. 'But we're out of alternatives.' I turned back to Beije and the Tallarns, my face as grim as I could make it. 'You heard that. We don't have any more time to waste on these ridiculous fantasies. If you're going to shoot us you'll have to do it in the back, and you'll be doing the work of the Emperor's enemies for them if you do.' It was a risk, I don't deny it, but I was pretty sure that taking that tack would disconcert a bunch of Emperor-botherers enough to shake their resolve. The sergeant, at least, looked as though he had enough sense to realise he was in way over his head.

I turned away, a little theatrically, the Valhallans at my heels. The Tallarns hovered uncertainly, looking to Beije for a lead and wincing visibly as Jurgen passed upwind of them. For a moment I tensed, anticipating a las bolt in the back and hoping the carapace armour under my greatcoat would hold, but they continued to hesitate just long enough for me to seize the initiative beyond all further doubt.

'If you want to face a real enemy and do His Majesty's work, you're welcome to join us,' I added over my shoulder. The Tallarns began to take a step forward, intent on following us, then hesitated, looking to Beije for a lead. The pudgy commissar looked after us, clearly at a loss and wondering how best to regain his authority.

'Go with them,' he snapped at last, petulantly. 'I'm not letting that posturing traitor out of my sight.'

'Good,' I said, wondering if I'd get the chance to nudge him into the line of fire before this was over. 'Let's get the job done before we convene the tribunal,[1] shall we?'

---

1. *Since Beije had no direct authority over Cain, or any other commissar for that matter, his accusations would have to be looked into by a tribunal of senior members of the commissariat. (Commissars not having a structure of rank in the conventional sense, seniority would be determined by length of service and number of commendations.) If found guilty, Cain would be executed or remanded to a penal legion by the authority of the tribunal as a whole rather than any one individual; in this manner the Commissariat is able to regulate itself reasonably effectively, despite its members being essentially autonomous in most regards.*

To my relief, Beije kept reasonably quiet while I consulted with Detoi, the two of us huddling over his data-slate while we tried to formulate a strategy for storming the heretics' makeshift stronghold.

'If we can breech the walls here,' I said, pointing out a workshop with a long expanse of steel hull plating in a patch of dead ground between two firing posts, 'we should be able to get inside before they respond.'

'Assuming they haven't thought of that and left us a surprise or two,' Detoi agreed. 'We'll concentrate our forces against their positions here and here. With any luck you'll be able to get your kill team into the dead ground while we're keeping their heads down.'

'How are you going to breech the walls?' Beije asked. 'Did you bring demo charges with you as well?' It was beginning to dawn on him that we were in deadly earnest and that we really were preparing to lay down our lives for the Emperor. Or quite a lot of other people's, anyway. I was going to stick close to Jurgen and hope that somehow we'd manage to escape the effects of whatever hellish sorcery the Slaaneshi were planning to unleash. That was why I was planning to go in with the assault team, despite the risk; that way seemed marginally less suicidal than charging a fixed position with Emperor alone knew how many fanatical heretics pouring fire into our ranks.

'Jurgen's melta,' I said. 'It'll do the job.' And provide the perfect excuse for him to be there, of course.

My aide nodded and hefted his favourite toy. 'That it will,' he agreed.

'Who are you taking?' Detoi asked.

I nodded at Grifen's squad, who were still eyeing the Tallarns with mutual distrust. 'Fourth squad, third platoon,' I said. 'I've done this sort of thing with them before.' Some of them, anyway. Only a few familiar faces were left from the group I'd led into the ice caverns of Simia Orichalcae, apart from Grifen and Magot. I caught the eye of Trooper Vorhees, who flashed me a grin, and returned to conversing in an undertone with Drere, his girlfriend, who had been badly chewed up by an ambull on that expedition but who'd survived (to my surprise, I have to admit) thanks to my decision to send back the wounded as quickly as possible. Since then Vorhees had considered me something of a hero, and I have to admit it hadn't hurt my standing with the regiment to seem so concerned with the welfare of the common troopers. (Which made the fact that so many of them were about to die uncomfortably ironic.)

'They're understrength,' Detoi said.

I nodded, conceding the point. 'Only by one.' Smitti was still in the infirmary in Glacier Peak, and I have to admit to feeling to a momentary stab of envy at the thought. 'And they're here. Besides, Jurgen will more than make up the numbers.'

'Will one squad be enough?' Detoi persisted.

'They'll have to be. We'll need everyone else for the diversionary assaults if we're to have even a hope of getting away with this.'

'We're coming too,' Beije announced, indicating the Tallarns. 'I don't trust you and I'm not letting you out of my sight.' He smiled maliciously, turning my own words of a few moments before back on myself. 'Until we can convene the tribunal, of course.'

'Of course,' I replied, determined to seem unruffled, and turned back to Detoi. 'Have you been able to narrow down the objective at all?'

The captain nodded. 'My guess would be here.' He pointed out a chamber deep in the heart of sector twelve. 'The chapel of the Omnissiah. It's about the size you specified, and it's about as far inside their perimeter as it's possible to get.'

'Makes sense.' I nodded. 'If anything, profaning a consecrated chamber would only increase the power of their ritual.'

'And how would you know that?' Beije asked, glaring at me suspiciously. 'You seem very familiar with the secrets of warpcraft.'

'I've faced it before,' I said shortly, not wanting to recall those occasions or waste time recounting them. 'If you haven't, count yourself lucky.'

'The Emperor protects,' Beije countered. 'The pure of heart have nothing to fear.' Which pretty much ruled me out, of course, but under the circumstances I thought a good strong dose of trepidation was the only sensible option in any case.

'Well bully for them,' I said, ostentatiously checking my weapons. I turned to Detoi, reluctantly about to give the order which would condemn so many brave souls to death.

'Better start pulling them back,' I began. 'We'll need about ten minutes to regroup, which should be long enough to get the assault team in position. After that you can start the attacks at your discretion...'

I was interrupted by a sudden tingling sensation which washed over my body like the moment before a thundercrack, and a feeling of almost intolerable pressure inside my head which left my ears ringing with tinnitus. Beije glanced around wildly, swinging his laspistol, looking desperately for something to shoot.

'Sorcery!' he gasped, his face draining of blood.

'Take cover!' I yelled to the troopers. The Valhallans did so with alacrity, long accustomed to trusting my paranoia in situations like these, and the Tallarns followed their lead after a moment's disorientation, recovering fast like the good soldiers they were. 'Enemy incoming!'

'Where?' Detoi asked calmly, with a disdainful glance at the other commissar.

'We'll see in a moment,' I said. I indicated an open area near the Slaaneshi defensive perimeter. 'Somewhere over there would be my guess.' I'd been close to teleportation fields a number of times over the years, and had even been through one on a couple of occasions during my time with the Reclaimers, so I'd had no difficulty identifying the unpleasant sensations which accompanied exposure to the fringes of one. It had to be an enemy making use of the arcane device; there was certainly no such thing in use anywhere in our makeshift battlefleet.

My guess was proven correct a moment or so later, as with a thunderclap of displaced air five crimson and black-armoured giants appeared more or less exactly where I'd anticipated.[1] My ears popped and cleared, the abnatural pressure created by the presence of so much naked warp energy dissipating as suddenly as it had come.

'Fire!' Beije screeched, waving his chainsword in the general direction of the Traitor Marines. 'Cleanse them in the name of the Emperor!'

'Don't waste the las bolts,' I said, and the crackle of lasgun fire from our lines (which had been almost entirely unleashed by the Tallarns in any case) dwindled to nothing. They were ineffective at this range, and the last thing we needed was to attract the attention of the Tainted Marines. 'We can use this.'

'Use it how?' Beije asked, narrowing his eyes suspiciously. I gestured at the World Eaters, who had unleashed a hail of bolter fire against the Slaaneshi barricade which had so frustrated our own efforts such a short time before. The cultists were falling, their return fire being shrugged off by the ceramite armour of the superhuman warriors who had so unexpectedly joined the fray.

'They're doing our work for us,' I pointed out, remarkably mildly under the circumstances. I turned to Detoi. 'Leave our people where they are, keep as many of the cultists as possible pinned at the other weak points. If any pull back to reinforce against the Traitor Marines, they can follow up and force a breech. Fourth squad with me, we'll follow these lunatics at a distance and get in through the gap they're making.'

I took a few cautious steps out of cover, prepared to dive back in an instant if any of the crimson giants so much as glanced in our direction,

---

1. *For the World Eaters to have mounted a successful deep strike by teleporter through the bulk of the entire planet would have been a remarkable feat to say the least; we can only speculate about how many attempts this would have taken, and how many would have ended up entombed in the core of Adumbria or drowned in the sea surrounding the dredger before this particular squad made it through. Or perhaps the distortion of the warp currents initiated by their enemies were what made it possible.*

but true to form they ignored us, intent only on charging home against the Slaaneshi. Sure I was safe, I turned a disdainful look on Beije. 'Coming?' I asked. 'Or would you prefer to wait for the noise to stop?'

Without a backward glance, sure he would be goaded into following, I led the Valhallans in the wake of the Chaotic killing machines. To my silent relief, Grifen and her team took point, leaving Jurgen and I between the two fireteams, theoretically a little more protected from both directions. To be honest, I'd have preferred to put the Tallarns in front, where they'd catch the first fire from the enemy, but it was even more essential than usual to appear to be leading from the fore as my unmerited reputation would have everyone expecting. Besides, I didn't trust Beije any further than I could throw a baneblade, and the further away from me the conniving little weasel stayed the better I liked it.

A quick glance back confirmed that the Tallarns were double-timing in our wake, Beije huffing a little as he scurried to keep up, and then my attention was entirely on the Traitor Marines ahead of us.

'Golden Throne preserve us,' the Tallarn sergeant muttered. I could see his point. The World Eaters had reached the barricade, tearing it apart in their eagerness to reach and slaughter the cultists sheltering behind the makeshift barrier. As before, they seemed to disdain the use of their bolters once they'd closed, striking out with the peculiar chain axes I'd seen all too closely when their colleague had led the attack on our compound; wherever they went blood fountained and Slaaneshi cultists screamed ecstatically as they threw themselves forward to be slaughtered, hoping no doubt to take their assailants with them.

'They're not invulnerable,' I assured him. 'I've fought them before.' He nodded dubiously, and I noticed with a flare of malicious amusement that Beije was visibly smarting at one of his own troopers having his morale boosted by me.

'And kicked 'em good,' Magot added. 'Hand to hand. You stick with the commissar here, you'll be fine.' For a moment I thought Beije was going to spontaneously combust, but the universe isn't that helpful, and I had to content myself with the strangulated gurgle he was unable to suppress.

'Wait one,' I said, flattening myself against the storage tanks we'd sheltered behind before. 'Let's make sure they're through before we commit.'

'I knew it.' Beije smirked triumphantly. 'Cowardice, pure and simple. A true servant of the Emperor never hangs back.'

'After you, then,' I suggested politely. 'Show us how it's done.' I gestured towards the vicious melee continuing by the devastated barricade. The crimson giants had almost run out of degenerates to slaughter, but their enthusiasm was undiminished so far as I could see.

Beije licked his lips. 'It's your mission,' he said at last. 'Do as you see fit. It's all extra rope to hang you with.'

'Then let's wait until we stand a chance of completing it,' I said, checking my comm-bead to see what was going on elsewhere along the perimeter. The rest of the company were following their orders, so far as I could tell, successfully keeping the majority of the cultists pinned down and occupied. That was good; the more of them they kept busy the fewer there would be to get in our way, and hinder the World Eaters in their drive for the centre of this poisonous place.

The Tainted Marines weren't getting things entirely their own way, though. As I watched, one of the Slaaneshi, a youth of indeterminate gender dressed in flowing silks, flung him or herself at the leading giant, laughing hysterically, to catch the twisted parody of humanity's finest in what seemed like a lascivious embrace. The sight was so grotesque it was almost a relief when the hermaphrodite exploded in a rain of offal, taking the Marine with it, and I realised he or she must have had a demo charge strapped somewhere under that voluminous garment. The stricken Marine tottered and collapsed to the deck, where the clang of ceramite against steel echoed almost as loudly as the explosion.

From my time with the Reclaimers, I had expected the remaining World Eaters to break off once the last of the defenders was dispatched to administer the last rites demanded by the traditions of their Chapter[1], but instead they ignored their fallen colleague, no doubt carried away on a tide of bloodlust, merely continuing their berserk charge into the depths of sector twelve.

'Time to move,' I said, suiting the action to the word, and we moved out at a brisk trot. As we reached the tumbled remnants of the barricade, I couldn't help breaking stride to check for some sign of life, but where the servants of Khorne had been there was no hope of that; I glanced at the shattered corpse of the dead Marine and shuddered. Even in death it gave off a powerful aura of malevolence and dread. Beije, I was amused to note, was staring at it as though it were Horus himself risen from the dead.

'Ugly frakkers, aren't they?' I said cheerfully, patting him on the back.

'Did you really kill one with a chainsword?' the Tallarn sergeant asked, a note of awe creeping into his voice. Behind him, I was gratified

---

1. *Cain presumably witnessed a Reclaimer or two recovering the geneseed from their fallen battle brothers after a skirmish, but appears not to have understood the significance of what he saw.*

to note, his squad mates were looking quietly agog and trying not to look as though they were listening.

'These stories get a little exaggerated,' I said, confirming it in their minds and consolidating my reputation for modesty at the same time. 'But they're not quite as tough as they look.'

'I'm glad to hear it,' he said dryly.

We pressed on, following in the wake of the World Eaters. Their trail wasn't hard to track, being blazed in the corpses of the cultists who'd resisted them. At every fork in the passageways, every junction in the service tunnels, the path to our ultimate destination was clear to see.

'It's definitely the chapel,' I reported to Detoi, who in turn informed me that resistance was weakening in several places as cultists withdrew to meet the new threat. 'They're heading straight for it.'

The interior of the dredger was as big a surprise to me as the outside had been. I'd been expecting a maze of corridors, like the interior of a starship, but the passageways were as wide as city boulevards, and the ceilings so high that the rooms leading off them were more like small buildings. Indeed, it was only the presence of the luminators overhead and the subtle sense of enclosure no hive boy could miss which reminded me that we weren't still outdoors. Many of the street-sized intersections had been hastily defended, the bodies of variously-armed cultists lying around in varying states of disassembly, and the marks of bullets and las bolts clear to see on the walls and floor.

It was also apparent that the Traitor Marines, for all their martial prowess, weren't getting things entirely their own way. Even conventional weapons would be a threat to them in sufficient numbers, and the heretics they faced were able to marshal a few heavier pieces in support. To the eyes of experienced warriors, like the Valhallans and myself, and the Tallarns too I suppose, it was obvious that they'd been finding the going harder as they went, a plethora of small, minor wounds slowing them down.

'Wait.' Vorhees was on point at this juncture, and gestured emphatically with his hand to reinforce the hissed instruction over the comm-bead. 'There's movement ahead.' We closed up, moving cautiously over the intervening distance, to peer round the next junction. As before, there was a barricade there, hastily thrown up to meet the advance of the tainted supermen, and just as casually thrown aside. But this time one of the defenders appeared to be moving.

'A survivor,' Beije said. 'We can interrogate him and find out exactly what's going on around here.'

'Be my guest,' I said dryly, knowing better than to expect any useful information; torturing a masochist is singularly unproductive, as

Zyvan's interrogators had already found out. But if he wanted to try, at least it would keep him out of my hair.

We moved forward again, hugging the edge of the thoroughfare from habit and sound common sense; just because the cultists we could see were in no fit state to fight it didn't mean that there weren't others, comparatively uninjured, lurking in ambush behind what remained of the barricade.

'Clear,' Magot reported at length, having lobbed a couple of frag grenades over the barrier to make sure. We rounded it, and I found myself looking down into the face of another of the cultists. As Vorhees had indicated, he was still alive, but only just, and I was sure the detonation of Magot's grenades hadn't exactly perked him up. He twitched feebly, bits of metal stuck through parts of his anatomy which looked extremely uncomfortable clinking against the deck plating, and reached out a hand to grab my ankle.

'She comes,' he said, an expression of imbecilic rapture on his face; by that point I don't suppose he had a clue who we were. 'The new world is at hand!'

'Who's coming?' Beije bustled up, kicked the hand away and squatted next to the fellow. 'What are you talking about?' He aimed his laspistol at the man's stomach, which was a bit of a waste of time given the fact that most of his intestines were already spread around the floor, then evidently realised the fact as he switched his aim to the man's hand at the last minute. The gun cracked, blowing a hole through the palm. 'Tell me!'

'Listen to you.' The cultist giggled, hoisting himself up Beije's chest with a sudden surge of strength which left the pudgy commissar gasping with surprise, and kissed him hard on the mouth. Beije leapt backwards, astonishment and outrage mingled on his face in a fashion which I have to admit struck me as extremely comical. Magot, Vorhees and a couple of the other Valhallans stifled audible snickers. 'You'll find out.'

'Vile degenerate!' Beije spluttered. 'How dare you... I'm not that sort.... Disgusting.' For a moment I thought he was going to shoot the man in a fit of pique, but the cultist saved him the bother, expiring before he could exact his petty revenge.

'When you've quite finished enjoying yourself,' I said sarcastically, 'do you think we might get on? Planet to save, daemon-summoning to stop, remember?'

'Do you think that's what he meant, sir?' Jurgen asked, hefting the melta as though it might actually be of some use against a hell-spawned abomination. 'When he said she's coming?'

'It's possible,' I said. My previous encounters with daemons had been mercifully brief, thanks to their inability to remain in the physical world for very long, and I'd had other things to worry about at the time than whether concepts such as gender had any real meaning for them. 'In which case he could have meant that the ritual has already started.'

'We've no time to waste then, have we?' Grifen began rounding her squad up. 'Move it people, clock's ticking here.'

'Better do the same,' I advised the Tallarn sergeant. 'What's your name, anyhow?'

'Mahat. Sir.' He saluted me, earning a black look from Beije, and turned away to follow Grifen's lead.

All at once the apprehension I felt, which had become a dull ache in the pit of my stomach so familiar that I'd almost been able to ignore it, redoubled, shaking me with its intensity. Jurgen looked at me curiously for a moment, then rummaged in one of his pouches for a flask of tanna tea.

'Bit of tanna, sir? You look like you could do with it.'

'I could indeed.' I swallowed a couple of mouthfuls of the fragrant liquid, feeling it warm its way slowly into my stomach. 'Thank you Jurgen.' There was no point putting it off any longer; for if I was right about the summoning being underway there was no hope at all of survival if we delayed here. And everyone it seemed was ready, except for me. (And probably Beije, who was so far out of his depth it was a miracle he hadn't drowned by now, which just went to prove the truth of the old adage that the Emperor takes care of the feeble-minded, I suppose.) I nodded to Grifen. 'Move out, sergeant.'

It wasn't even the thought of facing a daemon which had me so spooked, I realised, as we double-timed through the echoing passageways, heedless now of anything except the necessity of reaching our destination as quickly as possible. It was the dying cultist's other words. What was this new world he'd mentioned? Nothing good, I was sure.

So it was, torn between the growing fear of what we'd find at the heart of this lair of iniquity and the cast-iron conviction that not to face it meant death or worse (and I've seen enough over the years to know that there are plenty of things worse than dying), that we hurried on towards a confrontation which would shape the destiny of not only a world, but the entire sector.

NINETEEN

'The past is always with us.'

– Gilbran Quail, *Collected Essays*

THE DEEPER WE penetrated into that heart of darkness, the greater became the carnage we witnessed. The Slaaneshi cultists had obviously been intensifying their efforts to defend the site of their ritual, bringing in reinforcements from the perimeter in ever-increasing numbers, despite fatally weakening their defences there in the process. Detoi reported that all our squads were now making headway, and in a couple of places the barricades had fallen entirely.

'We can get reinforcements to you in a matter of minutes,' he said, and despite the flare of relief which accompanied his words, I found myself demurring.

'Better leave them to secure the perimeter for the moment,' I counselled.

Tempting as the prospect of more troopers to hide behind was, if I was right about what was waiting for us in the desecrated chapel, they wouldn't make any difference anyway; numbers had meant nothing to the PDF troopers in the bordello in Skitterfall, and I had no doubt that the daemon, if it was allowed to materialise again, would slaughter our people just as easily. Our only hope against it was Jurgen, and the fewer witnesses to that the better.

'If you say so,' Detoi replied, sounding vaguely disappointed, and I threw him a bone to cheer him up.

'We've still got the Traitor Marines to consider,' I reminded him. 'I'd feel a lot happier knowing they're bottled up tight if push comes to shove.'

It was at about that point we ran into one, almost literally. I'd noticed the scarring on the walls from weapons fire had grown more intense at the sites of the last couple of firefights we'd found the remains of, but quite how much firepower the heretics were able to bring to bear still hadn't consciously registered with me until I saw the wounded World Eater staggering along the corridor. His once-gleaming armour was pitted and stained by innumerable weapon impacts, and some had evidently taken their toll – his left leg dragged, the armour joint stiff, and he kept one massively-gauntleted hand on the wall for support, where it pressed dents into the steel every time he put his weight fully on it. His weapons had gone, Emperor knew where, and blood was leaking from several of the rents in his armour, forming sticky pools on the floor before hardening to the consistency of tar within seconds.

'Don't touch it,' I cautioned, as one of Mahat's men bent to examine the patch ahead of him. 'It might be toxic.'[1] He sprang upright at once, looking alarmed.

'Baseless superstition,' Beije scoffed, giving the patches a wide berth nevertheless.

'If you say so,' I said, quite happy to let him be the one to find out. At which point the Traitor Marine seemed to become aware of our presence for the first time, turning aside from his dogged progress towards the desecrated chapel.

'Blood for the Blood God!' he roared, lurching forwards, arms outstretched to grab and tear.

'I'm getting really sick of hearing that,' I said, bringing up my laspistol and cracking off a few rounds. The troopers with me, Valhallans and Tallarns alike, followed suit, and the front of the giant's armour rang like a foundry with the impact of scores of las bolts. Nevertheless, on

---

1. *Many Space Marine Chapters have the advantage of tainted blood, so that even in the act of wounding them the enemy harms themselves, and even if not actively toxic, the amount of alchemical and genetic enhancement in the modified blood which flows through their veins is unlikely to make it particularly healthy for the rest of us to be around for very long. Cain's caution is therefore quite understandable, particularly as a World Eater's bodily fluids are bound to have been even further altered by the mutating touch of Chaos.*

he came, swinging wild punches which caught a couple of unfortunate troopers, slamming them against the walls. I ducked a massive fist, shaking off a peculiar sense of *déjà vu* as I did so, and stepped inside his guard, hoping Jurgen could get off a shot with his melta as he had before. But this time there were too many of us in the way, and my aide hovered indecisively.

I had only one chance: my laspistol seemed useless against the giant, but by great good fortune my chainsword was in my other hand. Spying a rent in the ceremite armour, made by a krak grenade if I was any judge, I rammed the humming blade deep into the gouge, feeling to my intense relief the whirring teeth bite home on sinew and bone.

The giant roared in pain, shock and fury, and I ducked another wild swing of those sledgehammer fists, driving the blade deeper with all my strength. Abruptly he fell, shaking the deck, enabling my aide to run in close and dispatch him by vaporising his head.

'Two for two! Well done, commissar!' Magot shot me a wild grin and went to check on the wounded. Mahat stared at me, an expression I can only describe as awe on his face, as I retrieved the blade from the corpse (taking very good care to make sure none of the blood from it touched my skin). Beije simply stared, his jaw slack, as though unable to credit what he'd just witnessed.

'How are the wounded?' I asked, more to keep up appearances than anything else, but acutely aware that if I didn't find something else to concentrate on I'd end up undermining the moment with some snide and petty-seeming aside to the little weasel about his scepticism over my previous clash of arms with a World Eater.

Magot shook her head. 'Not going anywhere, that's for sure.'

The Chaos Marine's berserker charge had incapacitated three of the Valhallans (although they'd all be up and around again after the medicae had finished with them, a fact I could only attribute to the World Eater's astonishing degree of debilitation) and one of the Tallarns. There was only one thing for it; I detailed the squad medic to look after them and we proceeded as rapidly as we could towards the objective.

As we moved on, with a final glance back at the casualties and a call to Detoi to send someone in to collect them, I took in our diminished band with a sense of foreboding I tried very hard to hide. Apart from me and Jurgen, there were only five of us left now: Grifen, Magot, Vorhees, Drere, and Revik, a trooper from Magot's team I knew little about as he'd joined the regiment in the last batch of replacements and had so far committed no serious infractions. (Although with Magot as a role model, that happy state of affairs was unlikely to continue for long.) The Tallarns and Beije I more or less discounted, despite Mahat's obvious confidence in my leadership I couldn't bring myself to trust them, and the thought that we were now outnumbered should they stoop to some form of treachery was far from comforting.

So you'll understand my mind wasn't exactly easy as we hurried along in the wake of the World Eaters, afraid to get too close in case we attracted their murderous attention, but also acutely aware that time was of the essence if we were to stop the cultists at the heart of this web of corruption from completing their blasphemous task.

'Almost there,' I told Detoi, my knack for finding my way in enclosed spaces proving as reliable as ever, which the captain acknowledged with audible relief.

'We're still holding the perimeter,' he reported. 'All the defenders have withdrawn to meet the Traitor Marines. We could move in and mop up at any time.'

'Stay put for now,' I told him, not wanting his understandable eagerness to get in the way at this late stage. 'We'll vox you as soon as we know for sure what's going on down here. I'd hate to blow this by falling for a feint just when we're so close.'

'That would be a shame,' he agreed, almost managing to hide his disappointment.

'Listen.' Grifen held up a hand, and we paused, trying to distinguish the sound she'd heard. The dredger was full of background noise, of course, most of it barely noticeable – the hum and clangour of distant machinery, the moaning of the wind through the interstices of the vast structure, and, rather more obtrusively, the reverberations of weapons fire and dying screams as the Khornate Marines went about their butchery. I tried to filter them all out, along with the continual hiss of Drere's augmetic lungs, and after a moment I nodded.

'I think you're right,' I said grimly. It was a low, droning sound, which I felt as a vibration through the deck plates as much as I heard it directly. Chanting, which rose and fell in cadences no human throat should have been able to produce, and which raised the hairs on the back of my neck.

The troopers, Valhallan and Tallarn alike, looked uneasily at one another.

'What?' Beije asked, looking baffled.

'Come on.' I broke into a run, quickly, before my resolve could evaporate. 'We don't have much time.' How I knew this I couldn't tell you, not even after all these years, but my survival instinct had kicked in with a vengeance, and I trusted it. If we didn't face the enemy now we'd be too late, and death and damnation would follow. I knew that as unarguably as I knew that a dropped object would fall to the floor, or that Beije was an idiot. To my bemused surprise I found myself out in front as the Valhallans fell in behind me, and registered their presence with relief.

'Don't just stand there, get after him!' Beije shrilled. 'Can't you see he's trying to get away?' The Tallarns followed close on our heels, though more from the prospect of getting to grips with the enemy than because they believed a word of his idiotic accusations, I'm quite sure. The pudgy commissar huffed in their wake, his face crimson.

Up ahead the sounds of combat grew louder, and a confused melee was filling the street-sized passage ahead of us.

Detoi had been right, I could see; every cultist on the dredger had apparently converged on this one place with the evident aim of defending the chamber ahead of us. The cogwheel sigil of the Adeptus Mechanicus was embossed, taller than a man, on a pair of vast brazen doors beyond the mass of struggling bodies, and with a thrill of horror I realised that the sacred symbol of the priesthood of the machine had been profaned, lines added in a substance I didn't care to identify to warp and pervert it into the symbol of the unholy god of sensuous excess.[1] That was undoubtedly our goal, but reaching it would be more easily said than done: the full might of the Adumbrian cult of Slaanesh had been mobilised to defend the objective from the remaining World Eaters, and neither side expected or was capable of giving quarter.

For a moment, it seemed, even those superhuman warriors had met their match. The sheer weight of numbers ranged against them seemed to be telling; there must have been over a hundred of the cultists still on their feet, and at least half as many again already wallowing in their own blood. I've seldom witnessed carnage on such a scale, at least in a skirmish, and the sight affected even the veteran warriors with me.

'Emperor on Earth,' Grifen said. 'Where did they all come from?'

I presumed the question was rhetorical, as we'd already established that some at least had fought their way in from the boat dock, but it was plain that many had been part of the dredger's crew. Some were still in their work clothes, contrasting bizarrely with the outlandish costumes of their perverted confederates, and hard though it may seem to credit I even glimpsed the white robes of a tech-priest or two among their number.

Their victory over the tainted Marines should have been assured, their numbers telling against even so doughty a foe, and no doubt had they been Guardsmen or PDF troopers they would have prevailed

1. *Something Cain would be able to identify instantly, thanks to his previous encounters with the deluded minions of the Dark Powers.*

without taking a tenth of the casualties they had. However, these were civilians, not warriors, and barmy to boot. They threw themselves heedlessly at the armoured giants without the faintest hint of coordination or tactics that I could see, and consequently died in droves. Worse, they got in each other's way, so half the shots aimed at the Traitor Marines killed or wounded their own.

Not that the Khornates were getting it entirely their own way. Even as I watched, one was seized from behind by a cargo-handling servitor fully as large as he was,[1] its metal hands closing relentlessly on his helmet. For a moment, augmented muscle strained against ceremite, then the armour gave way under the pressure, bursting like a ripe molin. The thing's victory was short-lived, however, as the two surviving Marines turned on it as one, tearing it apart with their chain axes.

Incredibly, the remaining pair of World Eaters managed to break through the line of foes opposing them, so drenched in the blood they'd shed that it was impossible to tell now which parts of their armour had once been red and which originally black, to slam against the great bronze doors with an impact so great as to reverberate even over the screams and weapons fire. However strong and impressive that stout portal had seemed, though, it was no match for the accursed axes they bore; ceramite teeth squealed against metal, fountaining sparks like a firework display, and bronze tore and twisted like tissue paper as they ripped away at it with their gauntlets.

'What now?' Mahat asked, and with vague surprise, not to mention a certain degree of self-satisfaction, I realised he was addressing me directly, effectively ignoring his own commissar.

'We have to follow them,' I said. 'No matter what.' The Tallarn sergeant nodded grimly, reflecting the expression of the Valhallans, who seemed equally determined to see our errand through to the end (which looked uncomfortably close about now, let me tell you).

'That lot'll take some breaking through,' Grifen replied, hefting her lasgun and snapping a fresh power pack into it with practiced precision. Most of the others followed suit, no doubt reflecting that the middle of a glorious banzai charge was a pretty bad place to run out of ammunition.

'Maybe not,' I said, motioning Jurgen forward and acutely aware that the World Eaters had disappeared inside the chapel by now. Most of the surviving defenders attempted to pile in after them, choking the portal and getting in each others way, looking about as coordinated as a

---

1. *Presumably under the direction of one of the treacherous tech-priests whose presence Cain had noted before.*

bunch of drunken orks. 'They're all bunched up and looking the other way.'

'Traki[1] shoot,' Magot said happily. 'I love it when the enemy's on our side.'

With a suitably dramatic flourish of my chainsword I rushed forward, making sure a couple of the troopers outpaced me a little, and we fell on our unprepared foe like the wrath of the Emperor himself. Jurgen's melta ripped a ragged hole through their lines, vaporising flesh and bone, to leave a narrow corridor of flash-burned victims writhing and screaming on either side where the air around the superheated plasma burst had scorched and seared them, and the rest of us opened up on the survivors to widen it. The first wave fell, barely aware of our presence, and we had almost made it to the ravaged portal before they began to turn and regroup.

'Again!' I ordered Jurgen, and he happily complied, clearing the way entirely to the doors and widening the gap created by the Chaos Marines.

'Having fun yet?' Magot asked Mahat, hosing down a group of cultists with a burst of las-fire as they turned and began to raise their weapons.

'Doing the work of the Emperor is its own reward,' the Tallarn admonished. 'But this is quite satisfying.'

Inevitably, though, the heretics began to get their act together and return our fire, although with a gratifying lack of accuracy; if we'd tried the same tactic against even a moderately organised foe, even one of the calibre of an underhive gang, it would undoubtedly have been a different story, but most of their fire went as wild as it had done against the World Eaters. Some, however, hit; Revik went down, blood leaking from a jagged rent in his torso armour, and Vorhees and Drere picked him up by an arm each, barely breaking stride as they did so. They even kept firing, although aiming their lasguns one-handed didn't do a hell of a lot for their accuracy. A couple of the Tallarns went down too, being retrieved by their squad mates with similar dispatch and efficiency.

Abruptly I made it to the haven of the brazen doors, scuttling inside with a sense of relief I didn't even bother trying to hide, las bolts and slug rounds pinging off the metal behind me. A thick, cloying scent, like the one I'd noticed in the hab dome on the coldside, invaded my nostrils, and I was obscurely grateful for a full-strength whiff of Jurgen as he fell into place at my shoulder.

---

1. *A large, slow-moving creature native to Valhalla, much prized for its succulent meat and soft pelt. Most hunters find them too easy to kill to be much of a challenge, hence the local expression employed here by Magot.*

'Cover the others,' I said unnecessarily, as he was already turning to do so and they were only a couple of paces behind me.

I glanced around the antechamber we found ourselves in, looking for something we could use to our advantage. The bronze doors would afford us little protection now, having been forced by the World Eaters and thoroughly scorched by Jurgen's melta, but to my immense relief a polished steel side table stood nearby, covered in devotional candles and brightly coloured machine parts no doubt of great significance to the tech-priests who normally worshipped here.

I hurried over to it and tried to push it into the gap, my muscles cracking with the strain.

'Help me with this!' I called, beckoning to Beije and Mahat. They stood where they were, looking indecisive, while most of the troopers from both squads found what cover they could and poured fire through the gap. The only other exceptions were Magot, who was ripping Revik's body armour away in an attempt to find his wound and stem the bleeding, and a couple of Tallarns doing the same for their colleagues. Jurgen's melta belched its cleansing plume of white-hot air again, disrupting the incoming fire for a moment or two.

'That would profane these holy symbols,' Mahat said doubtfully, and Beije nodded smugly, like the most pedantic of schola tutors. (And until I became one myself I wouldn't have believed quite how petty some of them could be. But I digress...)

'We can hardly profane them any more than the heretics already have,' I pointed out, somewhat forcefully, and with a few extraneous adjectives which I needn't record at the moment. 'And in case you haven't noticed, this place isn't even dedicated to the frakking Emperor, it's a cogboy chapel to their clockwork one.'

'Well that's an interesting theological point,' Beije began. 'Some would argue that the omnissiah is simply another aspect of His Divine Majesty, which would mean–'

'Well you can ask him about it in person if you don't shift your arses and help me move this bloody thing,' I snapped, 'because the heretics outside will be all over us in another couple of minutes if you don't.' I'd be the first to admit I'm not the most likely man in the galaxy to win a theological debate, but I took this one hands down. After an uneasy look passed between them, Beije and the Tallarn sergeant hurried over to join me and between us we manhandled the cumbersome slab of metal into the gap, turning it over onto its side for good measure. (Which of course sent the candles and the ironmongery flying, to their evident consternation, but that couldn't be helped.) After that I set Drere and Vorhees to reinforcing the makeshift barrier with anything else readily portable they could lay their hands on, and took stock of our position.

'How's Revik?' I asked Magot, wondering if he was going to be in any fit state to hold a lasgun.

'Pretty bad. Seen worse,' she said, not bothering to lift her head and applying a pressure bandage. 'Lucky it was a las bolt.' As I've had occasion to be grateful for myself more than once, they tend to cauterise the wounds they make, cutting down the amount of bleeding considerably. A solid round will leave a hole you can bleed to death from frighteningly fast. Neither of the Tallarn wounded was getting up any time soon either.

'Grifen,' I said. 'You're in charge.' I glanced at Beije and Mahat, expecting some objection, but there was none from either of them; which, as you'll readily appreciate, I found all the more unnerving. 'Hold them off at all costs. If they manage to get in now and prevent us from stopping the ritual...' I had no need to complete the sentence.

'We'll keep 'em off your back,' the Valhallan sergeant assured me. 'You can count on us.'

I turned to Jurgen. 'Come on,' I said, overwhelmed by the sense of fatalistic detachment which often descends in those moments when you know your chances of survival are minimal, but still a damn sight better than if you do nothing at all. 'Let's get this over with.'

'Mahat.' Beije beckoned. 'You're with me. Bring Karim and Stoch.' The two troopers he'd indicated left their posts at the firing line at once, leaving Vorhees and Drere to plug the gap as best they could, and all the Valhallans to look collective murder at the overweight commissar.

'They're all needed here,' I said tightly.

Beije smiled without humour. 'I thought you had complete confidence in your people. After all, they're one of the finest regiments in the galaxy, aren't they?'

'We'll manage,' Grifen said, picking off a couple of heretics who were incautious enough to raise their heads as she spoke.

'We haven't got time to argue,' I said, turning on my heel and leading the way out of the antechamber. The route was obvious, the World Eaters having been as subtle as ever in their approach, a pair of ornately engraved brass doors buckled from their hinges in one corner. The chanting was louder in here too, the direction unmistakable, and as I listened it became overlaid with the unmistakable whine of chainblades and the gleeful roar of the Khornate Marines piling into more victims.

'Sounds like the big red buggers are saving us a job,' Jurgen said at my elbow as we ran towards the sound. I'd expected the chanting to falter

as the acolytes died, but if anything it seemed to swell, resonating in
my very bones. I wasn't sure what that meant, but I'd bet a year's tarot
winnings that it was nothing good.

'Golden throne!' Beije bleated as we burst through a ripped curtain
into the main chapel. For once I could sympathise with him. I'd had
some idea of what to expect, having seen the ruins of the ritual chambers in the hab dome and the bordello, but the full sanity-blasting
horror of the intact symbols on the walls surrounding us completely
was new to me, and sent my senses reeling. I'm sure it was only the
presence of Jurgen and his peculiar talent, which insulated my mind
from the worst of it.

'Don't look at them,' I cautioned, trying to focus on the carnelian
giants wading through the congregation of degenerates with single-
minded determination, slicing and hacking with their chainblade pole
arms. 'Stay focussed.'

My warning came too late for one of the Tallarn troopers, though,
Stoch I think – he curled up into a foetal position, bleeding from the
eyes and whimpering something which sounded like the first line of
the Emperor's benediction over and over again. Beije paled and threw
up, but rallied, to my surprise, reciting one of the catechisms of command in a faltering voice.

'What should we do, sir?' Jurgen asked, as phlegmatic as ever, his
voice as unconcerned as though he was asking if I wanted another cup
of tanna. 'Take them all out?'

In truth it looked as though that would be the only way. I nodded.

'Concentrate on the cultists,' I shouted, trying to make myself heard
over that hellish chanting. 'Leave the Chaos Marines for last.' There
must have been at least as many acolytes in the chamber as had been
defending it from the outside, and we were going to need all the help
we could get to be sure of killing the lot before their ritual reached its
climax.

But we never got the chance. Almost as soon as the words left my lips,
the chanting ended, a sudden silence pervading the chamber, broken
only by the sounds of slaughter as the World Eaters went about their
grisly work, and Stoch's ravings.

'She comes! She comes!' Five score throats abruptly yelled, a few of
them breaking off with a gurgle as the Khornate chain axes ripped
through them. Then even these suddenly ceased, their owners stopping
abruptly, like servitors with their power supplies cut. A sickly glow
began to suffuse the air, spreading through the crowd, and wherever I
looked, expressions of imbecilic ecstasy slithered across faces, distorting them in ways beyond the physically possible.

'Frak this,' I said, my eyes darting around the chamber for a target, any target, skittering away from the symbols daubed on the walls and ceiling before they had a chance to register on my forebrain. 'Let's kill something.'

'Oh, Ciaphas.' Mellifluous laughter rippled through the room. 'You haven't changed at all, I see.'

Several of the cultists close to us began to shiver, ululating in ecstasy, the flesh of their bodies flowing together like melting wax. The sight was more hideous than I can describe, and all I can say is if you think that's disappointing count yourself lucky you can't picture it.

'Emperor preserve us,' Beije gibbered, grabbing my elbow. 'This is sorcery, sorcery most foul…'

'It's worse than that,' I told him, a chill of pure dread rippling through me. The mound of flesh in front of us was changing by the second, smoothing out, taking on a clearly defined outline. Fully twice the height of a man, with limbs inhumanly lithe, a body curved and rounded in a manner indisputably feminine, yet for all that both hideous and attractive in a manner utterly inhuman. The face too was completely different from anything remotely familiar, but for a pair of eyes, emerald green, cool and disdainful, which regarded me with detached amusement.

'It's been quite a while,' the apparition said, addressing me directly. 'I hope you're well.' It reached down, picked up the stupefied Stoch, and bit his head off, chewing thoughtfully for a moment before discarding the body.

Mahat and Karim twitched, trying to raise their lasguns, but they seemed as paralysed as the World Eaters. 'That's better. So impolite to run off at the mouth while somebody's talking, don't you think?'

My nightmare came flooding back to me then, and with it a sense of recognition I couldn't ignore. It was impossible, I knew, but I couldn't prevent myself from blurting the name out.

'Emeli,' I said.

The daemon nodded. 'I told you I was coming back,' it said.

TWENTY

'Then the prophet spake: saying
"Frak this, for my faith is a shield proof against your blandishments".'

– Alem Mahat, *The Book of Cain*,
Chapter IV, Verse XXI[1]

WELL I MIGHT not be the biggest bang in the armoury, but I can put two and two together as well as the next man.

'Those dreams,' I said slowly. 'They weren't just dreams, were they?'

'What dreams?' Beije asked, gazing at the apparition in awestruck horror, as unable to tear his gaze from its repulsively fascinating visage as the rest of the congregation. The daemon and I ignored him, continuing our conversation as though we were completely alone. Only Jurgen showed any sign of animation, although his habitual expression of vague bafflement concealed it nicely, and I tried to keep the thing's

---

1. *This is the only quotation I've used which doesn't come from Cain's commonplace book. The thought that there's a fringe sect on Tallarn which reveres him as a prophet of the Emperor, and a physical conduit of His Divine Will, is a truly terrifying one. Nevertheless, in my more whimsical moments I must confess that I do find the idea somewhat appealing, if only for the fact that he would have been so utterly appalled at the idea if he'd ever found out about it.*

attention focussed on me. Once it realised what he was, and that there was still a chance of us derailing whatever plans it had, we'd have seconds at best to react before we became an unpleasant stain on the decking, or another impromptu snack.

'We have a connection,' the daemon said, its voice as low and seductive as I remembered from my encounter with the human it used to be. 'When the warp currents were favourable, or I was physically present on this drab little world, I was able to caress your mind from time to time.' It laughed again, a long, sinuous tongue moving about its lips like a grotesque parody of a flirting courtesan.

'I don't understand,' I said, playing for time. If Jurgen could edge a little closer and nullify whatever power the thing had to hold our companions in thrall, there was just a chance we could take it by surprise. I didn't expect a couple of lasguns to make much difference, to be honest, but Jurgen's melta might just be enough to hurt it, and if we could do enough damage to disrupt its physical presence here it would be drawn back into the warp. It wouldn't exactly be harmless there, but at least it would be out of our hair.

The daemon laughed again, and despite myself I felt a shiver of delight running through me, like the sensation you get on a crisp autumn morning when the sun is bright and the world seems full of simple pleasures. 'When we met before, I took you for human.'

'I was, silly.' The daemon glided away from us, just as I was about to signal Jurgen to act, and I stilled the gesture, biding my time. Emeli, and Emperor help me I still couldn't help thinking of the thing as the woman who had almost cost me my soul on Slawkenberg, moved between her acolytes, slinking around them, bestowing tender caresses with fingers, tongue and lithely twitching tail. And wherever she touched bodies fell, leeched of their souls, with cries of terminal ecstasy. 'But I served our prince well in life, and he received my soul gladly. I grew strong in the warp, and after a time I became able to affect things in the physical world too.'

'But not for long, thank the Emperor,' I said, and the daemon bristled, a naked and terrible anger marring the sensuous perfection of its hideous features for a moment.

'You dare to invoke the name of your corpse god in this holy place?' It tore one of the World Eaters in half in a fit of pique, which still seemed somehow coquettish and grotesquely endearing, his ceramite armour crumpling like paper. The other she picked up and threw against the wall, which deformed into a dent the depth of my forearm under the impact, leaving the corpse to bounce randomly and fall to the metal floor beneath with a sound like somebody dropping an armful of buckets (crushing a couple of her own cultists in the process, but I don't suppose she was too bothered about that).

'It was his first,' I pointed out. Well, technically I suppose it was the Omnissiah's first, but I'd had enough of that argument from Beije.

Emeli giggled, a grotesque echo of the flirt she used to be, and began moving back towards us, a smile on her face again. Provoking her was a risky gambit, but if I could only keep her mind focussed on me for long enough to lure her into range of Jurgen's strange abilities we might just be able to get out of this alive.

'Finders keepers,' she said, slithering around another group of deliriously expiring cultists. 'Now it's mine, and soon I'll be the queen of the whole world.' An expression of distaste flickered across her face. 'Dreary little place at the moment I know, but I can soon fix that. What do you think of violet for the sky? Or maybe pink.' A beatific smile spread across that terrible face. 'I love decorating.'

'Are you sure you'll have the time?' I asked, still trying to lure her in. 'As I recall, your kind doesn't stick around in the physical world for too long.'

A tidal wave of mellifluous laughter washed over me, leaving me tingling with joy, and despite the terrible danger we were in I felt a smile begin to play over my face at the sound.

'Poor Ciaphas. You really don't understand, do you?' Gleeful mischief danced in her eyes, as captivating as they'd been all those years before when she'd been the preternaturally seductive woman who'd almost lured me to my doom. 'I'm not going back to the warp this time. I'm staying, and my friends are coming out to play too. The energy I've absorbed from these playthings will be enough to break the barrier between the realms for good.'

The thrill of horror which shot through me at those words was enough to dispel the unnatural glamour the daemon had been able to exert on me, and I found the air curdling in my lungs. It was closer now than it had ever been, and the scent of her body washed over me, compelling and enticing, threatening to enthral me once again.

'You're opening a warp portal,' I choked out, and behind me I heard Beije moan in terror at the thought. Emeli's smile spread, that inhuman tongue flexing against her lips again.

'No, silly. I'm making the whole planet into a portal. Half in and half out of the warp, where my friends can come and go as they please and we can shape reality as we see fit. Won't that be fun?'

'For you, maybe,' I said, my head growing fuzzy with the nearness of her physical presence.

Despite the fear and revulsion still consuming me, the desire I'd once felt for her human form was stirring too, and the inhuman sensuality of her daemon body was somehow amplifying that. I fought against the impulse to open my arms to her, my skin tingling in anticipation of her touch. But still my survival instinct clung on, as it had in her bedroom the first time she tried to seduce me and claim my soul. To yield, I knew, meant extinction. 'Not so much for the rest of us.'

'You have no idea,' the daemon breathed, warm musk washing over my face and clouding my senses. 'The pleasures I can show you, the bliss we can share. I told you before, you could be one of us. Have powers no mortal can conceive, experience an eternity of rapture. All you have to do is take it. Take me...'

'Frak this!' I said, a sudden familiar smell displacing the one which had so bewitched me, and I thanked the Emperor for Jurgen's presence. He'd edged a little closer while Emeli was concentrating on seducing me, although why she should have been so concerned over claiming my little soul while there was a whole world stuffed with them up for grabs I've no idea. Perhaps she was just a sore loser and wanted to make some kind of point after our last ill-fated encounter. 'My soul's my own, and I'm keeping it!' Reflexively I brought up my laspistol and fired.

'You really are remarkably tiresome,' the daemon said petulantly, apparently unphased by the detonation of the las bolt, which did nothing beyond marring the pale flesh of her skin. 'Have it your own way, then.' The blemish disappeared, fading into invisibility in the space of a heartbeat. 'Let's see how you like being killed for a change, shall we?'

She charged forward, beautiful and terrible, scattering her few remaining acolytes as she came. I fired again, repeatedly, the las bolts just as ineffective as before, flinching as the daemon reached out for me...

And then reeled back, an expression of confusion and doubt clouding her strangely elongated eyes.

'What?' She glanced around in perplexity, and began to back away. 'What are you doing?' I fired again, and this time the las bolt left a real wound, a faint pockmark which leaked some ichorous fluid. I nudged Jurgen's arm, urging him forward. We had to stay close to her.

'Come on!' I yelled. 'It's now or never!' I swung my chainsword, eliciting a gout of ichor from one of the reaching hands, and a squeal of outrage which rang in my skull like an opera singer hitting and holding a perfect note. Mahat and Karim snapped out of their stupor and began firing, fortunately proving good enough marksmen to hit the huge target in front of them without endangering Jurgen or myself. More wounds began to open across that pale and sensuous skin.

'You can't do this, it's not fair!' the daemon howled, bounding forward again. I dodged frantically, opening a slash across its leg with the chainsword, and Jurgen leapt to one side, raising the melta but before he could fire, the thing's long, sinuous tail snapped round against the side of his head. He dropped to the ground, stunned, the precious heavy weapon falling with him. 'Stop it! Stop it, you horrible little man!'

It backhanded Karim, sending him flying backwards in a tangle of limbs and lasgun, but Mahat kept firing doggedly. Beije, I noticed, was still standing there, his mouth open, like a half-witted shop dummy.

'Shoot it, you moron,' I yelled, diving for the fallen melta, praying to the Emperor that they could keep the daemon occupied long enough for me to reach it, and that it would stay pinned within the radius of Jurgen's peculiar aura. My aide stirred, staggering to his feet, shaking his head groggily, and stumbled a step forward, trying to unsling his lasgun.

'What?' Beije seemed to become aware that he still held a laspistol, and cracked off a couple of badly-aimed shots, which at least attracted Emeli's attention. Her head snapped round towards him, that long, sinuous tongue lashing out to entangle his arm. Squealing in terror, Beije was pulled inexorably towards her gaping jaws.

'Good! Keep her busy!' I shouted encouragingly, while the pudgy commissar scrabbled frantically for his chainsword. I rolled to my feet, hefting the weight of the heavy weapon, marvelling for a moment at the ease with which Jurgen seemed able to lug the thing around, and pulled the trigger.

A bright, actinic flash seared through my closed eyelids, leaving dancing afterimages on my retina, I blinked my vision clear and found the daemon reeling, a hole punched clear through its torso. Any mortal creature would surely have found such a wound instantly fatal, but Emeli simply staggered, rallied and turned back to face me.

'Not this time,' she said, an expression of utter malevolence washing across her inhuman features, dropping Beije in the process. She bounded towards me with preternatural speed, failing to see Jurgen in her eagerness to close her hands around my neck.

'I'm coming, commissar,' my aide said, still dazed and entangled in the sling of his lasgun. He stumbled into the daemon's leg, and it screeched as though he was white hot, leaping away with an expression I can only describe as terror on its face.

That was all the opening I needed. I fired the melta again, blowing a chunk of its head away. The daemon howled, all pretence of civilisation gone, and rushed at me, intent on murder. I worked frantically to bring the heavy weapon round, cursing its weight and mass, sure I couldn't make it in time...

And it staggered, its entire body erupting in spatters of ichor. The crackle of lasguns echoed around the chamber, deafening me and drowning out even the shrieking of the doomed warp entity. For a moment it writhed, tormented, unable to decide where to go, then it vanished with a thunderclap of imploding air. Dazed, I stared around the room, finding it packed with Valhallan uniforms.

'You forgot to vox,' Detoi said laconically from near the door. 'So we came to see how you were getting on.'

'Not so well that we're not pleased to see you,' I said, sagging with relief. I indicated the handful of feebly-twitching acolytes still scattered around the chamber. 'Bring them, and let's get the frak out of here. And try not to look at the walls, they fry your brain.'

'No problem.' The captain beckoned a couple of troopers armed with flamers forward. 'Burn it all down.'

'Works for me,' I said, wondering for a moment what Malden would say, and deciding I didn't give a frak. I turned to Jurgen, who was looking as alert as he ever did, and handed him the melta, which he accepted with as close as he ever got to enthusiasm. 'You dropped this,' I said.

'Sorry about that, sir,' he responded.

'You think you've won, don't you?' One of the cultists turned to me, glaring defiantly for a moment before Magot jabbed him none too gently with the butt of her lasgun to get him moving again. There was something vaguely familiar about his face, and after a moment I recognised him as one of the aristocratic by-blows infesting the Council of Claimants, although if I ever knew his name I couldn't recall it.[1] 'But she'll be back. Slaanesh is eternal, and so are his servants.'

'Yes, but you're not,' I snapped, fighting the urge to put a las bolt through his head there and then. 'And you'll hang long before I do.' I turned to Beije, who was staring vacantly at the daemon slobber on his sleeve as though it might be about to sit up and bite him. 'See you at the tribunal,' I said.

---

1. *Umbart Segundo of House Yosmarle, the first of the conspiritors to be positively identified. The Ordo Hereticus spent several months cleaning house on Adumbria, and as so often in these affairs many of the prime movers in the cult turned out to be minor aristocracy in search of exotic thrills or hoping to gain some measure of power through the connections their membership of a secret society opened up for them. Only a few were sufficiently deluded to hope to gain more than this through currying the favour of their daemonic mistress, but as always those were the ones who did the real damage.*

TWENTY-ONE

'Revenge is a dish best served with mayonnaise
and those little cheesy things on sticks.'
– Osric the Loopy, planetary governor of Corania
(appointed 756 M41, removed from office
by the Officio Assassinorum 764 M41)

As IT TURNED out, I didn't have to wait long for my day in court. Under
the circumstances, Zyvan graciously allowed the Commissariat to convene the tribunal in his headquarters on Adumbria once the warp
currents had stabilised enough to put the astropaths back to work, and
a brisk exchange of signal traffic had established that no one could be
bothered making the trip out from the subsector office on Corania for
what everyone involved seemed to think was an open and shut case.

By that time the rest of our fleet had finally arrived, metaphorically
red-faced and panting, just in time to play a couple of quick rounds of
hunt the heretic. The last survivors of the Khornate invaders were
picked off in pretty short order once our reinforcements arrived, leaving the five regiments who'd borne the brunt of the fighting to grab
some much-deserved R&R, and Kasteen and Broklaw had found time
to meet me in Skitterfall and sit in on the proceedings.

'I appreciate this,' I said, making myself as comfortable as I could on the bench outside the conference suite where the two Kastaforean commissars and the Valhallan from the 425th were concluding their deliberations. Beije sat on the opposite side of the lobby, alone save for Asmar, still rubbing absently at his arm where the daemon had licked him; I suspected he'd acquired a lifelong nervous tic from the experience.

'It was the least we could do,' Broklaw assured me, cracking his knuckles and stifling a yawn. 'You've put yourself on the line for us any number of times.' This was true, albeit never from choice.

'Quite.' Kasteen shot a venomous glance at the other commissar. 'Is it true you challenged him to a duel for insulting me?'

'I thought of it more as an insult to the regiment,' I said, playing things down as usual.

Kasteen nodded, apparently not fooled for a moment. 'Thank you anyway,' she said.

'So how are things with the lord general?' Broklaw asked, breaking the awkward silence.

I shrugged. 'Pretty much as usual. Still not much of a regicide player.' Nevertheless, the social evening I'd spent with him the previous night had been a pleasant one, only slightly overshadowed by the possibility that it could have been our last. Neither of us expected Beije's ridiculous charges to stick, especially as Zyvan had quietly seen to it that the triumverate of commissars comprising the tribunal had been given access to some very highly classified files and been left in no doubt what would have happened if I hadn't acted as I did, but there was always the possibility that one or other of the Kastaforeans would apply the letter of the regulations rather than a dose of common sense. (Which, I've observed, is remarkably scarce in most cases.)

'I thought you might care for some refreshment,' Jurgen said, materialising a few paces behind his bouquet and passing round a tray full of tanna bowls.

I took one gratefully. 'Thank you, Jurgen,' I said, taking my first sip of the fragrant liquid.

'Commissars.' One of the lord general's personal guard appeared at the door to the conference suite. 'The tribunal is ready to announce its verdict.'

'Typical,' I said with heavy humour. 'Wait all afternoon for a decent brew, then...' I replaced the bowl on the tray.

'I'll keep the pot warm for you sir,' Jurgen said, which was as close as he would come to wishing me luck or expressing concern, and I nodded.

'I won't be long,' I said, stilling a sudden fluttering of nervousness which took me completely by surprise. Damn it all, I'd just faced down a daemon, and not for the first time either; a few minutes listening to my colleagues huffing with self-importance couldn't hold a sconce to that. So outwardly, at least, I was completely impassive as I walked into the conference room, Beije at my side, and stood at parade rest in front of the trio of black-clad commissars seated behind the polished wooden table.

Dravin, the commissar of the Valhallan tankies, was chairing the tribunal by virtue of his length of service (roughly twice that of either of his colleagues), and rested his elbows on it, cupping his chin on steepled hands.

'This has been an unusual case,' he began without preamble. 'And one which my colleagues and I have had to regard with the utmost seriousness. Fortunately, our verdict was unanimous in all particulars.' He paused for dramatic effect. Beije licked his lips nervously, and I remained impassive with the ease of the practiced dissembler; you don't play as much poker as I do without learning to mask your feelings. Dravin indicated the data-slate in front of him. 'We have no hesitation in finding all the charges made against Commissar Cain completely baseless and without foundation.'

I inclined my head, in what I calculated would be a sufficiently restrained response for a man of my reputation, and savoured the mew of disappointment which escaped from Beije's tightly clenched lips.

Dravin returned the nod. 'However,' he went on, 'we feel that under the circumstances we have had no option but to introduce new charges of our own. Charges I'm bound to say which disappoint us, and which reflect badly on the reputation for scrupulous conduct for which the Commissariat has always stood.' This was a surprise, I must admit, and a thoroughly unwelcome one at that. But I kept my feelings from my face just as easily as before, did my best to ignore the look of vindictive triumph on Beije's, and nodded gravely. No point in panicking just yet.

'I await your verdict with interest,' I said levelly.

'No doubt.' Dravin glanced down at his data-slate again. 'Tomas Beije, you are charged by this tribunal with conduct unbecoming to a commissar. Your unwarranted interference in Commissar Cain's pursuit of his duty could have had the most catastrophic of consequences not only for the world of Adumbria, but the entire sector.'

I glanced across at Beije. He seemed to be hyperventilating, incapable of making any sound other than 'Wha... Wha... Wha...'

'Under the circumstances we have no option but to recommend your immediate removal from field duties pending further enquiries. I'm sure you're aware that the most severe penalties may be deemed appropriate once properly formulated charges can be brought.'

So as you'll appreciate, it was with a light heart that I rejoined Kasteen, Broklaw and Jurgen in the corridor outside. Beije tottered out after me a moment later, looking as though he could already see the firing squad taking aim, and I took him gently by the arm.

'If it helps,' I said, with all the sincerity I could muster, 'I intend to testify that in my opinion you acted throughout from the best and most noble of motives. I'm sure you would have done the same for me.'

'Of course,' he said insincerely. He began to pull away. 'Now if you'll excuse me I really must break the news to Colonel Asmar…'

'Of course.' I nodded sympathetically. 'As to our other meeting, Jurgen will be acting as my second. When you've had time to appoint one, perhaps he would be so good as to convey a time and place convenient to you.'

'That, ah, won't be necessary.' Beije licked his lips, glancing at my chainsword, no doubt remembering I'd last used it on a Chaos Marine and a daemon. He turned to Kasteen. 'I may have passed certain remarks in the heat of the moment. If any offence was caused, I most sincerely apologise.'

'None taken, I can assure you,' Kasteen said graciously.

'Good. Well then…' Beije tottered away, and I smiled with satisfaction. I'd let him sweat for a couple of days before I pulled a few strings to get him off. I'm not really a vindictive man, for all my other faults, and there was no point in letting them shoot the man. He might just have learned something from the experience, and even if he hadn't, it was going to be far more fun watching him squirm every time he was reminded that he owed me his neck.

'Well then,' I echoed, turning back to my friends. Despite the damage the battling Chaos cults and our own forces had done, life in Skitterfall was returning to normal, and I felt I had something to celebrate. 'I seem to recall a rather pleasant little restaurant not far from here. Care to see if it's still standing?'

[At which somewhat self-satisfied juncture, Cain's account of the Adumbria incident comes to a natural end.]

YOUR NEXT READ

STRAKEN
by Toby Frost

Trapped in claustrophobic caverns with a massive horde of vicious orks, Colonel 'Iron Hand' Straken must deal with both the foe and tensions within his regiment.

An extract from

STRAKEN

by Toby Frost

The box was dented and battered. Shiny new metal winked through chips in the green paint. Across the lid some servitor a billion kilometres away had stencilled the words 'Departmento Munitorum XX Shotgun Shells'.

Straken held his gun in his left hand, and his steel right arm loaded the shotgun with a soft, hydraulic whirr. Each shell was only a few centimetres long. Strange how victory could come down to something so small, he thought. Like the twenty-two metres between this dugout and the last few tyranids on Signis VIII.

Captain Corris ran down into the dugout, stooping under the lintel. Like most Catachans, he was heavily muscled, and he only just fitted through the doorway. 'Colonel Straken?'

Straken looked up. From far away, artillery roared, a low rumble that ran through the dugout like a growl.

'Colonel, we've received a call from the Sixth Gordarian Artillery. They want to bombard the hill, sir. To wipe out the xenos once and for all.'

'To hell with that,' Straken growled. He got up and walked to the door. 'Tell them to hold fire. We can take care of this.'

'Yes, sir,' Corris replied. 'I'll let them know.' He followed Straken out the door.

The men waited in a loose half-circle. Their wargear was stripped down and modified, their uniforms torn, repaired and striped with dirt, but they still wore the red bandana of Catachan, the symbol that marked out the nine hundred remaining men as having the skill and toughness to survive one of the worst death worlds in the Imperium. In the centre, Corporal Thule hunched over the vox-rig, nodding as he relayed Corris's order. To the west, a Chimera rolled forwards, its tracks grumbling and squeaking as they turned. Tinny marching music blared out of speakers welded to its side. Behind it walked men with motion detectors, sensorium rigs, even the odd psi-tracker. The tyranids in this region might be dead, but they were quite capable of sowing the ground with dormant young.

It had taken three months to clear the planet out. Against an enemy like the tyranids, Straken thought, that was almost nothing. It had been tough going – it was never anything else, not against the tyranids – but the Navy had caught the infestation early. Then the Catachans had landed, among them the glorious Second, Straken's regiment, their mission firstly to scout, then to contain, and finally to eradicate. On the horizon, Straken could see the vast organic ruins of a bio-titan; they looked like dragon bones, slowly slipping into the mud. The job was almost done.

'Gentlemen,' Straken said, and nearly a thousand hard faces looked back at him. 'Over that ridge is one of the last psychic beacons holding the tyranids together. Kill it, and there'll be nothing more than animals left to fight – tough animals, but nothing meaner than you'd find back home. Whatever's over the ridge, it'll be big and angry.'

'So am I,' one of the men called, and there was a ripple of laughter.

Explosions rippled across the horizon, throwing black clouds into the air like soot across a painted landscape. Vendetta gunships swung in through the murk, lascannons slicing the sky. This might be the final great push against the tyranids, but the enemy would fight to the last.

'The Gordarian armour want to shell the hill. I've told them to belay that order. This started off as a Catachan job, and I mean to finish it that way.' Straken raised his shotgun. 'In a minute, I'm going to head out there and nail the last of these things. If anyone wants to stay here, they're welcome. You've done enough already, Emperor knows that. But if any of you layabouts want to give me a hand out there, and help take that tyranid's head for Catachan – well, sometimes I get tired of having to do all the hard work round here.'

It was about the mildest speech he had ever made, but his men deserved it. It would be wrong to order them to risk themselves when one allied barrage could finish things once and for all. But then, there was the honour of Catachan to consider.

His soldiers rose. Halda, the colour sergeant, grabbed the edge of the regimental standard and clenched his fist for a moment. Sergeant Pharranis cleaned the lens of his bionic eye on a rag, then folded it and screwed a fresh hydrogen flask into his plasma gun. Further down the line, a tough sergeant named Dhoi was testing the edge of his fang-knife, smiling grimly at the blade. Straken waited, hearing that familiar clatter of troops readying themselves to fight: fresh power packs clacking into lasguns; boots on mud; battered armour being checked; low voices murmuring prayers, praising weapons and cursing the danger to come. Corris caught Straken's eye and gave him a quick, curt nod. Straken felt at once at home and ready for war. He took a deep breath.

'Then let's move! Who's with me here? Are you going to

nail these alien scum, or do I have to do everything myself?' He turned to Halda. 'Colour sergeant, get that banner up. Now then!' Straken raised his metal fist. 'In the name of the Emperor – with me!'

Bellowing, he rushed into the open. A bugle blared and his men cried out behind him, as if their voices alone would speed them towards the enemy. They raced up the slope, boots pounding, roaring like beasts. As they reached the top, a lithe, blood-coloured alien leaped into view.

Straken saw it first: a mass of fangs, armour and spindly limbs ending in claws the size of scythe-blades. He glimpsed bestial eyes glaring with something more than just hunger – and then it sprang at them. 'Kill it!' he called, and half a dozen lasguns cracked. The tyranid fell backwards, ichor pouring from several wounds, and Straken suddenly saw the edge of the pit from which the xenos had emerged. The hole was almost ninety metres across, and deep: an ideal nesting place. A second tyranid loped from the bottom of the pit, hissing and snarling. It stood almost twice man-size, its uppermost pair of arms fused into a pulsing mass from which a bone tube protruded. *Deathspitter*, Straken thought. The beast's gun fired once, and a gobbet of whirling sludge shot over Straken's head. Then the rest of the enemy burst from their hiding places and attacked.

A monster with serrated blades instead of hands leaped onto Private Carne, one of the demolitions men. He fell down, flailing, and for a second Straken thought the man was finished. The next moment Carne was on top, stabbing down with his long knife as the alien thrashed beneath him.

Movement came from the left, and Straken whirled and fired. The shotgun kicked against his ribs, and a second leaper twisted in mid-air and fell dead. The tyranids poured out of the crater and were met with a vicious wall of lasgun fire. A Guardsman on

Straken's right took a direct hit from a deathspitter and stumbled aside, his screams drowned out by the terrible hissing sound of disintegrating flesh. In three seconds he had melted to nothing. A grenade flew overhead and hit a pack of slithering brutes as they rushed from their burrow. The explosion threw sinuous bodies into the air, then dropped them thrashing into the dirt.

Sergeant Pharranis unloaded his plasma gun into one of the monsters, and it collapsed in a sizzling, bubbling heap. On the right a corporal called Balt hacked at a wounded tyranid, sawing at its neck for a trophy-kill. He yanked the head away from the still-twitching body, a row of skulls already gleaming on his belt. Something exploded behind Straken – he couldn't tell whether it was a weapon or see the beast that fired it – and he glanced round. Where six men had stood, there was now carbon and reeking smoke.

Fire burst on the horizon. The crater rang with the crack of lasguns and the roars and yelps of the horde. Scythe-armed beasts leaped up from the ground as if hurled by catapults, sailing up to land among the Catachans. One trooper was eviscerated with a single swipe, beheaded by a second. Guardsmen drew long knives and swords, and waded in. Through the chaos, Straken heard a chainsword rev into life. Lieutenant Trask, always quick with a joke, staggered away, his right arm clutching his left.

A tyranid sprang down on Straken like a swooping hawk. He dropped to one knee and blew it in half, pumped the shotgun as he rose and finished it before it could crawl towards him. On his right, a hunter-slayer knocked a private to the ground and leaped on him, snarling like an attack dog. The man tried to push the alien's head back with his left hand and it bit off half his hand.

Straken cursed and raised his shotgun to blast the creature, but Corris grabbed the tyranid before he could fire, yanked its chin up and drove his knife through the side of its neck. He sliced down, cutting the beast's throat, and heaved it away. Straken blasted a second hunter-slayer as it aimed its bio-gun at him, and glanced back to see Corris dragging the wounded soldier to his feet.

'Nice work,' Straken said.

'One for the knife,' Corris replied, and Straken saw a dozen deep notches on the blade. 'Medic!'

The xenos fought wildly, but they were losing. The Guardsmen killed the aliens quickly, and now they had the advantage of numbers, there was nothing the tyranids could do except die. The last few hunter-slayers were shot down, or wrestled to the ground and stabbed. Men cheered – some cut trophies, others took the chance to reload.

Straken felt fierce pride, and then checked himself. Where was the node-creature, the big one they had come here to kill? The aliens that lay dead and dying around him were just the small tyranids, the foot soldiers. They were the things that the hive sent in to scout, or to use up the ammunition of its enemies. Something was wrong. Straken didn't know much about tyranids beyond how best to kill them, but every soldier in the Imperial Guard knew to shoot the big ones first.

He stopped and looked back. One man sat on the edge of the crater, his teeth gritted and his arm held across his chest. The unit medic crouched beside him, spraying the wound with anti-toxin. Tyranid creatures dripped with poisons worse even than those on the Catachan home world.

'That all of them, boss?' Halda called.

'Not yet,' Straken replied. 'Stay ready.'

They fanned out around him, instinctively forming a loose circle in the centre of the great crater. Straken felt exposed here, and knew his men would too. After fifteen years on Catachan, and nearly three more decades in the most vicious guerrilla wars that the Imperium could provide, he was as used to having cover as he was to the sound of lasgun fire.

Captain Corris said, 'It's a big one, right? Not like this.' He prodded one of the hunter-slayers with his gun barrel.

'That's what they said,' Straken replied.

The crater wall exploded in front of him. He turned aside and debris bounced off the metal side of his torso. A trooper shrieked and fell, clutching his face, and two men pulled him away.

Something huge burst through the cloud of dust. Multi-limbed, covered in armoured plates and over twice Straken's height, it opened a mouth crowded with fangs as long as fingers and roared at the sky.

'Bring it down!' Straken yelled, and he fired his shotgun, racked the slide and fired again.

The beast rushed forward on massive hooves, agile for its size, and Straken saw a pair of two-metre blades in its hands. Men yelled. Lasgun fire pattered off the monster's armoured hide.

Captain Corris leaped forward as he stabbed, but he was too slow. The alien's sabre swung down like a great pendulum, almost lazily, and buzzed as it sliced off Corris's arm and half his head.

The tyranid stood over the captain's body and bellowed at the Guardsmen. The adepts back in the rear echelon said that tyranids didn't have a language, that they didn't need to speak, but Straken knew what that roar was: a challenge.

He glanced over his shoulder. 'Demo!' he yelled, and a soldier sprinted over, shrugging his pack off as he ran. Straken snatched a thick, thirty centimetre-wide disc and clocked the dial to four seconds.

'Everyone clear!' he shouted, and as the Catachans drew back, still firing, he ran in and threw the charge as hard as his metal arm would allow, sending it skimming across the dirt.

It hit the tyranid's leg. The monster twisted round, saw it, and reared away. *It knows*, Straken realised. *The damned thing knows…* Then the charge went off.

The explosion threw him onto his back. For a moment he felt nothing, heard nothing and wanted just to lie there in the quiet. Then the world burst back into his senses, and Straken hauled himself to his feet.

'Get up!' he yelled at the men around him. 'Any wounded? No? Then follow me!'

They advanced, legs bent and guns ready. The smoke of the explosion was starting to clear. Within the crater, a fresh hole marked the place where the localised charge had gone off.

The beast lay on its side. Its two left arms were completely destroyed and both legs were twisted awkwardly. As Straken approached, he saw that his men had not missed either, for the massive body was pitted with las-burns.

Somehow, it raised its smoking, shattered head and snarled at him. Straken looked at it. *You're not so much*, he thought. *I've killed bigger things than you back on Catachan.*

He turned and looked back at his men. 'This is the smart one,' he called out, 'the one we've been looking for. Not looking so clever now, is he?'

'Can't be smart to mess with us!' someone shouted.

With its last strength, the tyranid lunged at him. 'Sir!' a voice cried. Straken whipped aside, and the creature's fangs slammed shut on the air in front of his chest. His hand shot out, caught the alien's smouldering neck, and his fingers closed.

Straken drew his long knife, the traditional weapon of a warrior of Catachan. Even with the added strength of his bionics, it took four hard blows to sever the alien's head.

'This is for Corris!' he cried, and he threw the smoking head onto the ground.

Tired as they were, the soldiers cheered. The crater was theirs, and now the war – this war at least – was over. The Catachan II had achieved their last objective, and Signis could be left to the local defence regiments and the cleanup teams.

Distantly, as if to applaud them, the artillery boomed. Under the sound of cheering, quiet at first, Straken heard the first thing to genuinely frighten him on this world: the high-pitched whine of a demolisher shell, reaching the peak of its firing arc above them – and then falling...

'Emperor,' he gasped. 'Incoming – everyone down!'

Men scattered to the edges of the crater, throwing themselves onto the ground. Beside Straken, a trooper stared at the sky, astonished. 'Those Gordarian morons are shelling us!' he cried.

'Then get down, stupid,' Straken snarled. A hundred metres beyond the crater, the first shell hit the ground, hurling dirt and scraps of tyranid twenty metres into the air. Straken strode over to the vox-operator, flexing the fingers of his metal fist. By the Emperor, he'd have the balls of whoever was responsible for this.

'Comms,' he called, 'get on that link and tell those morons–'

The second shell landed twenty metres away. The world spun. Straken heard and felt clods of earth battering down on him, a storm of dirt, and then the world went black.